RIDERS OF FIRE

1-3

EZAARA
DRAGON HERO
DRAGON RIFT

RIDERS OF FIRE COLLECTION 1

EILEEN MUELLER

Connect with the Author

EileenMuellerAuthor.com:

Website, newsletter and free books, including *Bronze Dragon* and *Silver Dragon*, Riders of Fire prequel novelettes: EileenMuellerAuthor.com/readers-free-books/

Join Eileen's Reader group: www.facebook.com/groups/RidersOfFire/

Ezaara, Dragon Hero and *Dragon Rift* and the *Riders of Fire* series are works of fiction. All characters, events and locations in this book are fictional. Any resemblance to persons or dragons, living or dead, is purely coincidental. No dragons were harmed in the making of this book, although there may have been a few injuries to tharuks.

This book is copyright. No part may be reproduced or transmitted in any form or by any electronic means, including photocopying, recording or by any information retrieval system without written permission from the author, except for short excerpts for reviews, in fair use, as permitted under the Copyright Act. Dragons' Realm, the Riders of Fire world, and its characters are copyright.

Ezaara, Dragon Hero, Dragon Rift, Riders of Fire © 2018-2019 Eileen Mueller
Typesetting © Phantom Feather Press, 2020, American English
Cover Art by Christian Bentulan © Eileen Mueller, 2019
Dragons' Realm Map by Ava Fairhall © Eileen Mueller, 2018
Phantom Feather Press Logo by Geoff Popham, © Phantom Feather Press, 2014
Paperback ISBN: 9798642891384

Phantom Feather Press
Wellington 6021, New Zealand
phantomfeatherpress@gmail.com
www.phantomfeatherpress.wordpress.com

Phantom Feather Press
Magic, every time you turn the page.

Dedication

For my readers all over the world.
You are the wind beneath my wings.

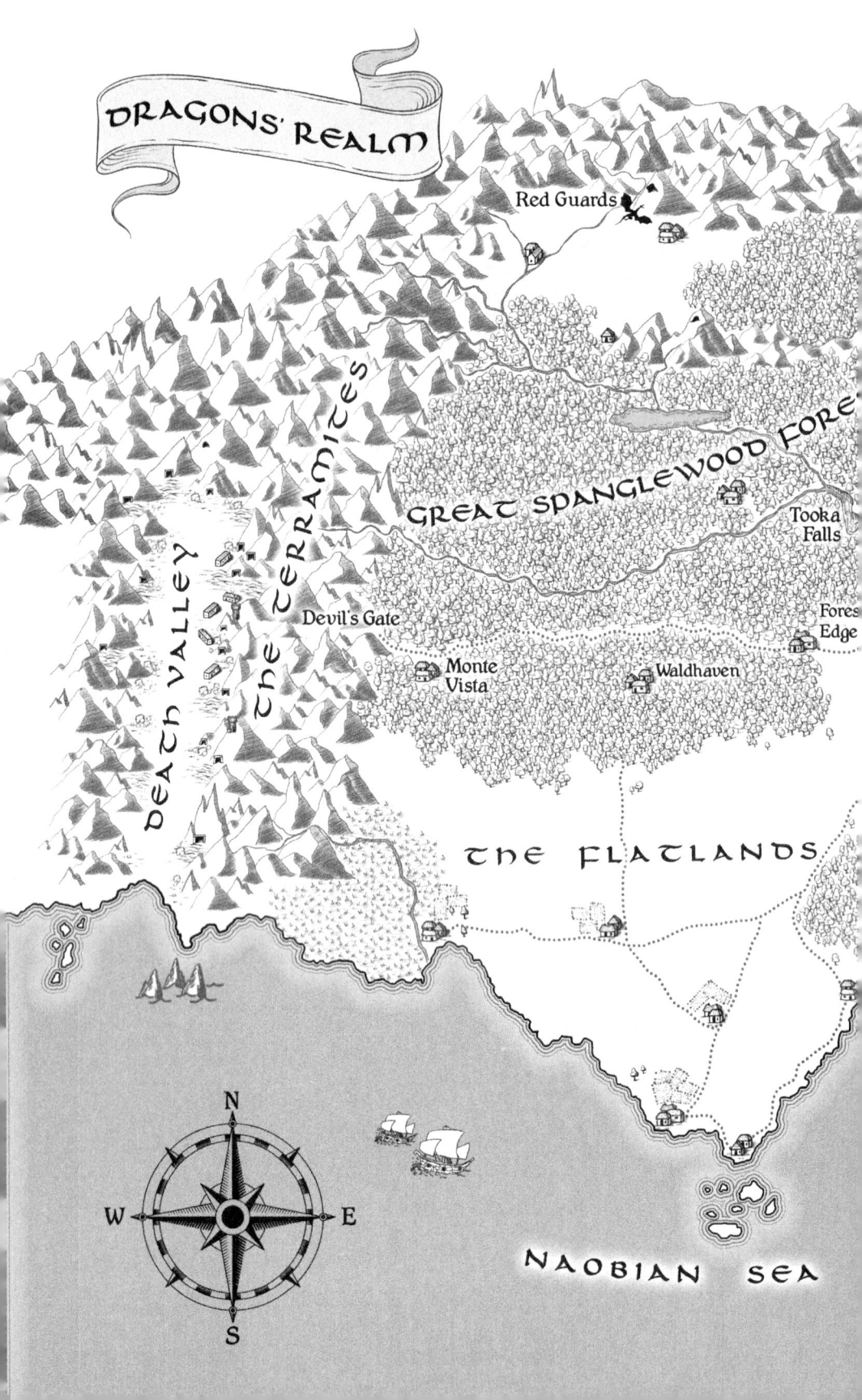

DRAGONS' REALM

Red Guards

GREAT SPANGLEWOOD FOREST

Tooka Falls

DEATH VALLEY

THE TERRAMITES

Devil's Gate

Forest Edge

Monte Vista

Waldhaven

THE FLATLANDS

N W E S

NAOBIAN SEA

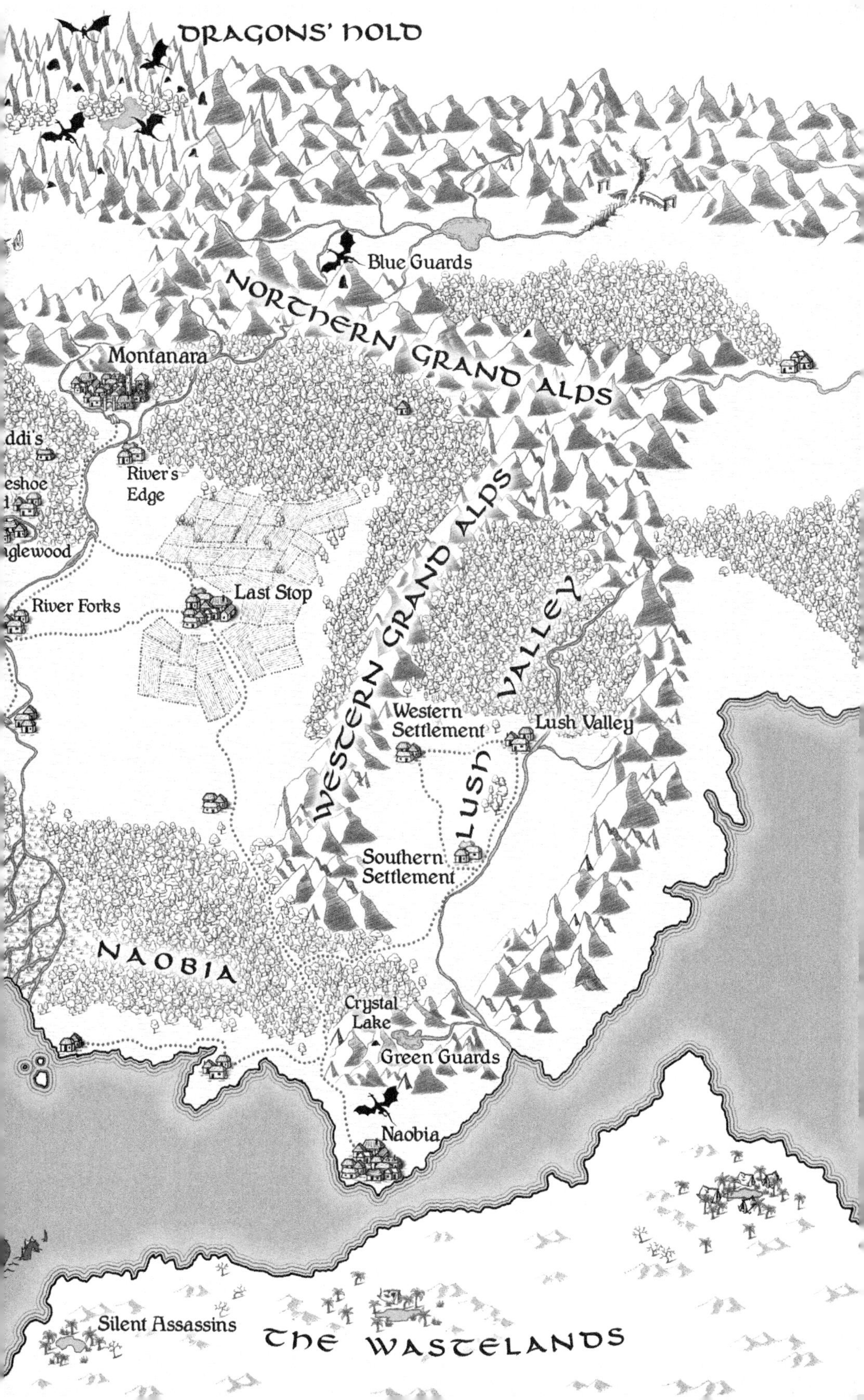

DRAGONS' HOLD
Blue Guards
NORTHERN GRAND ALPS
Montanara
River's Edge
Last Stop
River Forks
WESTERN GRAND ALPS
VALLEY
Western Settlement
Lush Valley
LUSH
Southern Settlement
NAOBIA
Crystal Lake
Green Guards
Naobia
Silent Assassins
THE WASTELANDS

Praise from reviewers for books in
the Riders of Fire series

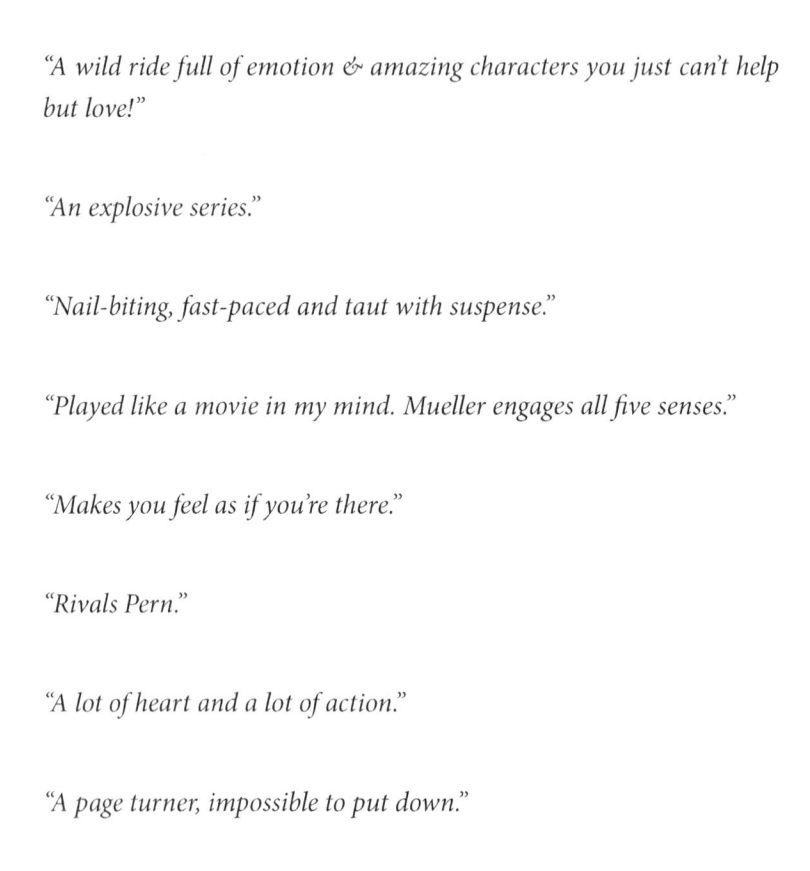

"A wild ride full of emotion & amazing characters you just can't help but love!"

"An explosive series."

"Nail-biting, fast-paced and taut with suspense."

"Played like a movie in my mind. Mueller engages all five senses."

"Makes you feel as if you're there."

"Rivals Pern."

"A lot of heart and a lot of action."

"A page turner, impossible to put down."

EILEEN MUELLER

EZAARA

RIDERS OF FIRE
BOOK ONE

Lush Valley

The scrape of a blade sliding from its scabbard cut through the hum of the market square. Ezaara dropped her herb basket. Spinning, she drew her sword.

Tomaaz. Wasn't it enough that he'd beaten her last time? And the time before? Of course not—today he had an audience. Sensing a fight, people backed toward stalls of plaited-onion wreaths, wood carvings and hats, clearing a ring around Tomaaz and Ezaara. On the far side of the marketplace, painted scarves fluttered in the breeze.

Tomaaz lunged.

Ezaara blocked his blow, then feinted. In a flurry of strokes, he drove her backward toward an apple cart. Typical. Quick to attack, he loved to corner his opponents.

"Take five to one for Tomaaz," Lofty yelled. The clink of coppers sealed bets. Folk always favored her brother.

Ezaara whirled as his blade whistled past her face, the whisper of its passage kissing her cheek. That was close, too close. She ducked as he lunged again, then she danced out of reach, saved by her footwork. They fought their way past brightly-patterned bolts of cloth. Tomaaz thrust to her right. Dodging, she bumped the table and the bolts went flying.

"Hey, my cloth," yelled Old Bill as Ezaara leaped over the bolts and Tomaaz gave chase.

Ezaara faced her brother. Perhaps she could distract him. "Seen any pretty girls today?" she taunted, thrusting under his guard. "Look, there's one behind you."

His blade answered for him. He was stronger. And faster. She blocked him, arm aching from the impact. Tomaaz's sword sliced dangerously near. He was so sure he could beat her. Slowing her steps as if she was tiring, Ezaara pretended to stumble, landing on one knee. "Ow!"

Tomaaz faltered. "Ezaara, are you all right?"

Driving her sword under his arm, Ezaara tapped his shirt. "I did it!" she cried, leaping to her feet. "I beat you."

A chorus of cheers erupted from the onlookers. Lofty called, "Go, Ezaara!"

A man yelled, "Lucky she's not a tharuk, Tomaaz, or you'd be dead meat."

A chill skittered down Ezaara's spine. Thankfully there were no tharuks in Lush Valley.

"Aagh, beaten," Tomaaz groaned. Sheathing his sword, he wiped the sweat from his brow.

Ezaara met his green eyes squarely. "You chose to fight me here."

Around them, coppers changed hands. Suddenly, Lofty was there. He pulled her close and kissed her, right on the mouth, mooshing his lips against hers. The crowd *oohed*. Ezaara shoved him away. Old Bill put a pile of grimy coppers into Lofty's hand. Lofty punched his fist in the air.

How dare he! Her first kiss—some shrotty smooch, for a bet? Ezaara's cheeks burned. Half the village had been gawking. She snatched up her basket. Market was only a few days each moon—a nice change from healing people with Ma—but Lofty had just ruined it.

A bellow rang out. "Is that those twins again?" Klaus strode through the scattering crowd. A head taller than most, and as wide as a draft horse, he was the settlement's arbitrator.

Lofty slipped away. The coward.

"Tomaaz. Ezaara." Klaus put his hands on his hips.

Some villagers, pretending to be busy, glanced their way. Others stared outright.

"It's my fault." Tomaaz squared his shoulders. "I challenged her."

"In the middle of the marketplace?" Klaus glared. "You could have taken out a littling's eye."

Whoops, she hadn't thought of littlings. Ezaara held up her sword. "Our tips were corked and the blades aren't sharpened."

Klaus examined Ezaara's sword with his thumb and finger. "In any case, you shouldn't have—"

"She tricked Tomaaz," Old Bill, the traveling merchant, called, "fighting sneaky, like a dragon rider."

As low as a dragon rider? Why was Bill mentioning dragons? Especially in front of Klaus. Was he trying to get her into trouble?

Klaus spun on Bill. "I only let you trade here if you keep our rules. If I hear you mention those filthy winged killers and their stinking riders again, you'll be acquainting yourself with our jail."

Old Bill glared at Ezaara. She shivered. He gave her the creeps.

Klaus pointed a blunt finger at Tomaaz. "No fighting in the marketplace."

"Sorry, sir, it won't happen again," Tomaaz replied.

Ezaara mumbled her apologies too.

"They knocked over my cloth," Old Bill protested.

"Help Bill to tidy up." Klaus threw a last glare at them and went back to his leatherwork.

Old Bill rubbed his hands together. "So, kissed by Lofty, eh?"

Ezaara wrinkled her nose at his fetid breath. The sooner they were finished, the better.

Tomaaz stared at Bill in disgust. "I can't believe you put Lofty up to that. I mean, he's liked her for ages, and now he's blown it. There's no way my sister's going to like him back now."

Ezaara rolled her eyes. "Would you two stop talking about me as if I'm not here?"

Tomaaz continued as if she hadn't spoken. "Come on, Bill, you should've bet Lofty a silver."

Men! Ezaara punched his arm. "Come on, let's get this cleaned up." She picked up a roll of green cloth and dumped it on Old Bill's trestle table. "Good morning, Lovina." Would she answer today?

No, as usual, Bill's daughter, Lovina, ignored her, staring at the ground, lank hair covering her face.

Tomaaz threw most of the bolts on the table, then wandered off.

Ezaara held the last bolt for a moment, rubbing the sea-blue cloth. She'd been admiring it earlier. She'd never seen the sea, but if it was anything like the rippling pattern of blues flowing across this fabric …. She sighed, placing it on the table. Maybe one day she'd see the real ocean.

Old Bill leaned over the stand, his gnarled hand plucking at Ezaara's sleeve like a roach clinging to a table cloth. "You'll like this." He opened his jerkin and pulled out a scrap of black cloth covered in vivid patterns. "Look." It was beautiful.

She didn't want anything to do with Old Bill, but she couldn't resist. Ezaara leaned in, staring. Dragons—the swirls of color were dragons. "That's forbidden," she whispered.

"Go on," he murmured, eyes glinting. "Touch it. I know you want to." He held the cloth out.

Someone would see. Ezaara snatched it. Holding it close, she opened her palm and stroked the wing of a golden dragon, then the tail of a bronze. Set against a dark sky dotted with silver pinpoints, the beasts were beautiful. Were dragons really gold, red and bronze? Or was it only the weaver's imagination?

"How much for this fabric with the wheat pattern?" A woman's voice startled Ezaara.

She crumpled the cloth and thrust it into Bill's waiting hand.

Bill tucked the scrap inside his pocket and elbowed his poor daughter, Lovina. She didn't respond, just kept staring at her feet. "Twenty-five coppers a measure, my lady," Bill crooned.

"Twenty-five," the woman exclaimed. "Why, that's preposterous! I'd only pay—"

Ezaara fled past the cobbler's stand, pushing her way through the crowded marketplace, toward Ana's stall. Old Bill was dangerous. If Klaus had caught her staring at dragons …. Swinging her basket to distract herself from her thumping heart, she strode past hawkers, bleating goats and littlings playing tag. The delicious scent of melted cheese wafted over her. If she could sell her last two healing remedies, she'd be done. And it was early, so she'd have the afternoon off. She headed toward Ana's hand-painted scarves. Ana had tried to teach her how to paint scarves, but instead of creating beautiful patterns, Ezaara's had been ugly and splotched.

"Morning, Ana," Ezaara called. "Need any herbs today?" She swallowed. Did Ana know her son had just kissed her?

Ana smiled, eyes crinkling. "What have you got for me today, Ezaara?"

So, Ana hadn't seen, thank the Egg. Ezaara passed a pot of healing salve and a bundle of clean herb across the trestle table. "You're lucky, these are my last."

Ana peered into Ezaara's basket. Her brow furrowed. "No owl-wort?"

"No." Strange question. Ezaara and Ma never usually picked owl-wort unless someone requested it. Most folk didn't need a herb that helped you see in the dark. Ezaara adjusted her basket on her arm. "It's still in season. I can bring some by later if you need it."

"Good, I'll expect you." Ana fumbled with her money pouch.

Was Ana planning on going out at night? Or was the herb for Lofty? He was always sneaking out with Tomaaz, getting into trouble.

Coppers clinked as they passed from Ana's well-worn hands into hers—three coppers. "You've given me too much."

"That last coin is for the owl-wort," Ana replied. "I want to make sure you bring it today."

So, *someone* was going out tonight. "I'll come by later."

Ezaara threaded her way through the villagers, past a weapons stand and Klaus' leather work. Near the cooper's stall, the clacking of sticks came from behind a stack of barrels.

Busy serving customers, the cooper's wife rolled her eyes. "Those naughty boys are fighting again," she grumbled.

"I'll check on them," Ezaara offered. She ducked down the side of the stall.

Behind the barrels, Paolo and Marco were going at it with sticks. Marco, a littling of only six summers, was blocking his older brother's strikes, even though Paolo had the stronger arm and longer reach. Then Paolo gave a mighty swing—too hard, too high.

"Watch out!" Ezaara leaped forward, too late.

Paolo's stick smacked Marco's face. Marco howled and clutched his nose, blood spurting between his fingers. Paolo's face froze in horror.

"Go fetch some water, Paolo," said Ezaara, striding between them. "Quick."

As Paolo dashed off, she sat Marco on a small barrel and checked his face. Luckily, his nose wasn't broken. "Bleeding noses hurt," she soothed him, "but you'll live to fight another day. Here, lean forward."

His blood dripping onto the ground, Marco was still crying.

Ezaara leaned in, whispering, "Even though Paolo's bigger, you almost had him."

"I did?" Marco's tears stopped.

"Definitely." She grinned.

Paolo returned, passing Ezaara a waterskin.

She pulled a cloth from the leather healer's pouch at her waist and sloshed water over it. "Now, be brave, like a warrior." She gently wiped Marco's face.

"Sorry," said Paolo. "We was trying to fight like you and Tomaaz."

Ezaara winced. She'd never thought of littlings copying them. "The first lesson Pa taught me was not to hit too hard," she said. "Remember, you're training with your brother, not slaying a dragon. You need to keep your sword nice and low, and aim at the body, not the head."

Paolo nodded wisely as if she was a great master.

She scooped some healing salve out of a tiny tub in her pouch and dabbed it on Marco's nose. "As good as new."

"You're lucky your folks taught you," Marco piped up, looking a lot better without blood leaking out of his nose. "Ours can't fight, but we're going to battle tharuks when we grow up."

Paolo nudged him. "Hey, I told you there are no tharuks in Lush Valley."

The boy had a good point. If there was no one to fight, why had Ma and Pa trained her and Tomaaz with the bow and sword since they were littlings?

Marco jumped down from the barrel, swinging his sword arm. "Don't care. Want to fight tharuks anyway."

She picked up their sticks. "I'll tell you what, I'll talk to Tomaaz. Maybe we can teach you to fight."

The boys' eyes lit up. "Really?"

She nodded. "We might have a couple of wooden practice swords you can use." The boys grinned. "But not now," she said. "Today, you two need to find something quiet to do."

Paolo put an arm around his brother's shoulder. "What about a game of scatter stones, Marco? You like those."

Ezaara laughed, leaving the boys clacking stones instead of sticks, and wandered back through the market.

"There you are." Tomaaz approached her. "I was looking for you."

"Marco got a bleeding nose from Paolo."

Tomaaz rolled his eyes. "Those two again."

"Now you sound like Klaus." Ezaara grinned. "They don't know the sharp end of a sword from a hilt, and Paolo swings way too hard. We should teach them."

"Good idea," Tomaaz said, tugging Ezaara toward their parents' produce stall. "Now, what was Bill showing you, on the quiet? You looked fascinated."

"Cloth—speckled with dragons of gold and bronze," Ezaara whispered. Her heart started thumping all over again.

"Contraband cloth?" Tomaaz's eyes flitted nervously. "Old Bill's bad news. And his daughter's strange too."

"You'd be strange too, if Old Bill was your pa." Ezaara nodded at a mother with littlings clutching at her skirts, waiting until they'd passed before replying. "Even if dragons are evil, the fabric was beautiful."

Ezaara and Tomaaz skirted a pen of piglets. "Lofty says dragons are honored beyond the Grande Alps," said Tomaaz. "One day, I'm going to look for myself."

She elbowed Tomaaz. "Someone will hear you."

"So what? I'm not going to live here forever, you know."

Turning to face him, Ezaara stopped. "You'd leave us?" Although they sometimes bickered, life without her twin would be like losing a part of herself.

His eyes slid away. "Don't know. Maybe."

Ezaara frowned. "That's why Lofty's ma wanted owl-wort—you and Lofty are planning to go tonight, aren't you?"

Tomaaz burst out laughing. "If only!"

So, he wasn't planning anything. "If you ever leave, take me with you," she insisted. There had to be more to life than Lush Valley.

"All right," Tomaaz said, "but no running off without me, either."

"Course not." They bumped knuckles.

At their family stall, Pa passed a sack of beets to a customer and pocketed the man's money. He faced Ezaara and Tomaaz, hands on his hips. "We didn't teach you fighting skills so you could create a ruckus on market days. What have I told you before?"

Tomaaz sighed. "To save our skills for battle."

"To practice in the meadows, not the market," Ezaara added.

Pa nodded. "Tomaaz, could you take this sack of carrots to the smithy?"

"Sure, Pa." Tomaaz shouldered the sack and left.

Ma glanced at Ezaara's basket. "So, you sold everything. I heard you beat Tomaaz."

"Only just, and through strategy, not skill."

"Strategy is also a skill." Ma put an arm around her shoulder. "Everyone's good at different things. Remember, you were climbing trees way before Tomaaz, because you weren't afraid of heights."

"I guess so." Tomaaz still couldn't climb a ladder without turning green. Who was ever going to be impressed by a head for heights? No one she knew. Ezaara handed Ma the money and basket. "Ana wants owl-wort, *today*."

"Owl-wort?" Her mother's eyes widened. "Collect some supplies for healing salve while you're at it." She gave Ezaara back a copper. "Get something to eat before you head back into the forest."

Pa winked. "Watch out for Lofty."

"I don't know what you're talking about." Heat rose in Ezaara's cheeks. Had Pa heard already? Worse, had he seen Lofty mashing his lips on hers?

"Soon everyone will be gossiping about something else." Ma patted her arm.

Ezaara groaned. This was worse than she'd thought. If only her first kiss had been private, special, not from her brother's best friend. From someone who meant more.

She hurried through the stalls, buying melted cheese on flatbread, then headed down the road to the riverbank, eating it. Water surged around the stepping stones as she crossed the river. Following familiar trails, she tucked peppermint and sage into the leather healer's pouch at her waist. Lifting fern fronds, Ezaara picked some feverweed. The gurgling of the river gradually faded.

Now, she needed arnica and owl-wort. Ezaara strolled deeper into the forest and came to the sacred clearing. Stepping into the sunlight, Ezaara stooped to pick arnica flowers. The ancient piaua, half as thick as a cottage, rose before her at the edge of the clearing, its bark pitted and gnarly. Blue berries peeked from its dark foliage. As a tree speaker, her mother often talked to the piaua whenever she collected its sacred healing juice. Placing her palm against the bark, Ezaara strained to feel a whisper. Nothing—again. She sighed. Not a tree speaker, then. What would her vocation be? Ma was happy as a healer and herbalist, and Ezaara didn't mind helping her, but she wanted something more. Excitement. Adventure. Maybe love.

The owl-wort vines grew among the knobby piaua roots. She parted the undergrowth and plucked a handful of leaves. Rising from a crouch, she opened her pouch.

A strange tingle ran through Ezaara, then a shadow fell over her. Something *swished*, a sudden breeze stirring her hair. She jerked her head up.

A dragon was circling the treetops. Ezaara recoiled in fear. With a snap of fangs or a swipe of talons, it could kill her. The owl-wort fell from her shaking hands. She tensed to flee.

But hesitated.

Sunlight played across the dragon's iridescent scales, making them shimmer. Its graceful wings swished ever closer, rippling with color. This beast was beautiful—beautiful, but deadly. She had to escape. But the tingling grew stronger. The amazing creature circled down toward her. Foliage rustled in the downdraught from the dragon's wingbeats.

A voice hummed in her mind. *"Ezaara,"* it crooned.

This creature could talk to her?

"We're mind-melding, sensing each other's thoughts and emotions."

She held her breath, drawn to the dragon. Rich colors cascaded through her mind. Sunshine poured into her soul. Ezaara wanted to soar. She glimpsed a vision—her riding the dragon, flying above the forest, over the Grande Alps and into the blue.

"This is your destiny, to ride with me."

Warning cries reached her—villagers. If only they knew *this dragon*, they wouldn't be afraid.

The dragon's hum built to a roar inside her. It dived.

Familiar faces shot into her mind. Her family! She couldn't leave them.

Ezaara's love for her family was swept aside as energy rushed through her. She was enveloped in a prism of rainbow-colored light, like reflections in a dewdrop. Music from the purest flute filled her heart. For the first time in her life, she felt whole. The energy coiled inside her and she sprang, lifted by the wind, hair streaming out behind her. In a flash of color, the dragon's scales were beneath her. Ezaara landed on a saddle in a hollow between its wings. She wrapped her arms around the dragon's spinal ridge, hugging it tight.

It felt so right.

The dragon regarded her with yellow eyes. Ezaara could've sworn it was smiling. *"I am Zaarusha. You were born to be my rider,"* it thrummed. The beast turned. Its belly rumbled and flames shot from its maw.

They flew off, leaving her home and loved ones behind.

Western Pass

Ezaara clung to the dragon's spinal ridge, wind tugging her hair. They soared above a carpet of bristling green. Her blood sang. Until today, she'd never lived.

Beyond the forest canopy, a patchwork of fields and cottages sprawled beneath the snow-tipped Western Grande Alps. Lazy twirls of smoke wound upward. They were nearly at Western Settlement, two days' ride by horse. They'd come so far, so fast.

Just today, she'd vowed she'd never leave Lush Valley without Tomaaz. Now, she was winging further away with each moment—leaving Tomaaz and her parents behind.

She glanced back, the village swallowed by endless forest. Her belly tightened. Could she ever go back?

"You have another destiny—with me. You chose when we imprinted."

She'd felt the connection, and still felt it now. Zaarusha was part of her. Their bond was like one of Ana's scarves—a thing of beauty, of glorious colors, protective and warm.

"Going back means facing the pitchforks of Lush Valley," the dragon mind-melded.

Ezaara swallowed. Everyone in Lush Valley was afraid of dragons—and their riders. She was now their enemy.

"Besides, your family is the reason you're here."

"What? No one in my family's ever seen a dragon."

"They know more than you imagine." A chuckle rumbled through the dragon's belly. *"Your mother and father are dragon riders."*

"No, they—" An image popped into her mind: Ma, much younger, astride a silver dragon; Pa was behind her, arms wrapped around her waist. The way the sun glanced off the dragon's silver scales looked real, but Ezaara wasn't fooled. Then, her mother's hair stirred in the breeze and she laughed. The truth hit her like a punch in the stomach. That was Ma's laugh. Pa's real smile.

"So …," Ezaara said, racking her brain for another answer. There was none. *"This is one of your memories, then."*

"Yes, and dragons can't lie."

"But—"

"I'm Queen of Dragons' Realm. Our families have been intertwined for years."

A dragon family intertwined with hers? And not just any dragon—the queen. *"I don't get it. Why didn't my parents tell me?"*

A wave of sorrow washed over Ezaara. *"Before you were born, your mother, Marlies, accidentally killed one of my royal dragonets."*

How awful. *"I'm sorry."*

"Marlies and Hans fled to Lush Valley to hide the truth, but perhaps that was fortunate, because now, I sense that dragonet's power, latent, in you."

So that's why. Ma was ashamed. Ezaara was here because of a mistake Ma had made, years ago. *"Me? Powerful?"* It was ridiculous.

"Not yet, but you will be." Zaarusha beat her wings, rising up the side of the mountain face.

Ezaara hunched over the queen's back, gripping her spinal ridge with white knuckles. *"But you're a queen and I'm … just me."*

They landed in the snow at the apex of an Alp. Fields lay like lazily-tossed rugs below. Settlements dotted plains that led to a barren range of snow-tipped hills, far to the west. Meandering ribbons of blue fed into lakes nestled among verdant green. A vast forest stretched northward, hemmed in by chains upon chains of mountains that seemed to go on forever.

"This is Dragons' Realm. We protect it. You, me and the dragons and riders that serve the realm."

And to think she'd been cloistered in a valley, afraid of dragons.

Zaarusha chuckled. *"Yes, you've outgrown Lush Valley, Ezaara. You're ready for this."*

It was true. She'd outgrown gathering herbs, and Tomaaz and Lofty's dumb tricks—and the superstitions of Lush Valley. With a surge of elation, Ezaara scanned the vista. It was her new duty to protect this. But how? She was so tiny compared to this vast rugged land of contrasts. The sweeping rivers, the jagged mountains, the homes scattered across the realm. The pristine snow, glinting in the sunlight, full of promise.

"This is what I want," Ezaara whispered. Gods, she already missed her family.

Roars cut the air. Then screams.

Ezaara spun in the saddle. *"That came from the south, Zaarusha."*

Zaarusha sprang. They were airborne, high above the Western Alps in moments.

"*There.*" In a pass, between two steep peaks, was a battle between men and beasts. "*Go, Zaarusha, go.*"

"*Tharuks, from the scent.*" Zaarusha's tone was grim. "*Probably a scouting party.*"

Ezaara hunkered over Zaarusha's spinal ridges. "*I thought tharuks were monster stories to keep littlings near home.*"

"*Only in Lush Valley,*" Zaarusha said, "*but not for long.*"

A chill snaked down Ezaara's spine. These beasts were making their way over the Western Grande Alps into Lush Valley. To her people, her family. "*Faster, Zaarusha, faster.*"

The queen sped through the sky. Ezaara leaned out, trying to see the fight far below, her eyes watering in the wind. Without warning, Zaarusha dived.

Ezaara lost her balance, sliding down the queen's side. She grasped at the saddle strap.

And missed. Her hands slipped over sleek scales. Then there was nothing—she was in midair. Wind tore at her. The ground charged upward. She was about to die.

A scream froze in her throat.

"*Relax and trust me.*"

The ground was rushing ever closer. What choice did she have? Ezaara let her body go loose.

Strong talons grasped her. Her breath whooshed out of her lungs. Ezaara gripped Zaarusha's legs. They flew to the closest peak and Zaarusha deposited Ezaara on a ledge. She climbed back into the saddle, her legs like Ma's egg pudding.

"*Now fasten the harness straps. Tight.*"

Ezaara gulped. "*I'm sorry.*"

"*No, it's my fault. It's been a long time since I had a rider.*" They took off, diving to meet the fight.

On an outpost, high on the ridge, blood from three dead men leached into the snow. A dozen tharuks were attacking two more men, who fought, back to back, trying to keep the beasts at bay. Other tharuks tossed wood down the mountainside.

Tharuks were awful, close up. With sharp tusks, the beasts were covered in thick matted fur and wore heavy boots and leather breastplates. They slashed long claws at the men. Zaarusha snatched up two tharuks, tossing them into the air. Their roars died as they thudded to the rocks, black blood splattering the snow. They stank of rotten meat.

Ezaara groped behind her for her bow. No, it was still at home. And her sword was blunted. She was useless, clinging to Zaarusha as the queen lunged again, flame shooting from her maw.

Tharuks shrieked, flailing on the ground, burning. More beasts ran at the men. Zaarusha flicked flame at them, forcing them back. *"I can't get too close or we'll burn our people,"* Zaarusha mind-melded.

One of the men screamed, clutching at his throat. Red pumped over his hands. He crumpled, dead.

A roar cut through the fighting. A huge beast thrust its fist into the air, bellowing, "Kill him!" More monsters surged over the ridge, joining their leader to surround the last man.

The warrior spun, jabbing with his sword, but he was outnumbered.

Zaarusha blasted a swathe of flame, cutting down a line of tharuks. Their snarls turned to shrieks that trailed off as their smoking bodies dropped, twitching in the snow. She dived, tossing more beasts down the mountainside.

"Zaarusha!" Ezaara's scream died as the last man fell to the earth.

Tharuks closed in, red eyes gleaming.

With a roar, Zaarusha wheeled in midair, her wingtip sweeping a tharuk off its feet. It tumbled down the slope in a flurry of gathering snow, limbs flying.

"Get to Lush Valley Settlement," the tharuk leader bellowed, spinning to face the queen, claws out.

Three beasts fled down the mountain toward Western Settlement and Lush Valley.

Five men dead. Ezaara pulsed with rage. *"Let me kill one."*

"No, that man needs your help."

Ezaara snapped her head around. Her healer's pouch. She *could* help.

Zaarusha threw another tharuk off the slope and swooped in for the leader.

A jolt of pain ripped through Ezaara. But it wasn't her—it was Zaarusha. *"Are you all right?"* Ezaara asked.

"Fine," Zaarusha snarled, ripping the tharuk's body in two. Black blood sprayed over the snow. His body thudded down the slope in the wake of the fleeing tharuk trio.

They landed, and Ezaara undid the straps, scrambling out of the saddle.

Rushing to the man's side, she knelt by him. She took his wrist, feeling his heartbeat, where the blood pulsed weakly over his bone. His chest was a bloody mess, making a wet sucking noise every time he breathed. The poor man. There was nothing she could do for him, except ease his passing. Ezaara raised his head and shoulders, resting them on her knees.

His eyelids fluttered and he groaned.

"Here, chew this." She placed some arnica flowers in his mouth. "They'll taste awful, but will help the pain."

He ground the flowers between gritted teeth. "My wife …" It was barely a moan. "My littlings …"

His jaw fell slack, shreds of arnica petals still on his tongue. His head lolled to the side.

Oh, gods. Ezaara folded the man's hands over his chest and laid his head to rest in the snow. Her eyes burned. She swiped at stray tears. *Zaarusha, I couldn't save him.*

Throat tight, she went to the other men, checking them. All dead. The snow was a mass of churned black and red, scattered with chunks of wood and bodies of men and beasts. *"We'd better clean up."* Only a few hours' flight from Lush Valley, and they were already burying people.

Ezaara gestured at the men. *"They were guarding the pass. This wood must've been for a beacon fire to warn Western Settlement of an attack. Some of those tharuks have slipped through. We have to go back and warn my people."*

"We can't go back," Zaarusha replied. *"I'll tell the blue guards—the riders and dragons who protect this part of the realm."*

"Dragons don't protect Lush Valley."

"Why do you think no tharuks have ever come over the Grande Alps before?"

Klaus was so wrong. Dragons didn't destroy at all. The very dragons he'd despised had kept them safe—unseen, beyond the chain of alps that encircled Lush Valley's wide basin—protecting the three villages cradled within: Southern Settlement, Lush Valley Settlement and Western Settlement.

"Let's light that beacon fire." Ezaara frowned. "Will people know what it means?"

Zaarusha replied, *"Your father, Hans, will."*

"First, we'll bury these men."

"We could give them a funeral pyre," Zaarusha suggested.

"No, their families need to be able to find them."

Zaarusha dug a grave and Ezaara buried the men, shoveling icy dirt into the hole with numb hands. She found stones for a cairn, and plucked a pine branch, wedging it between the stones as a marker. If only she could've done more.

Ezaara dragged a log back up to the pass, adding it to what was left of the warriors' wood pile. Zaarusha ripped out dead trees and flew them up. Ezaara could've left the queen to collect the wood, but the burn of her muscles and the ache in her limbs paid tribute to these men who'd tried to protect the pass.

Bit by bit, the pile grew.

"That's enough, Ezaara," Zaarusha said. "It'll be dark soon. Once I light this wood, the beacon will be seen for miles."

Ezaara wiped her brow, wrinkling her nose. The stench of tharuks made her gag, and the sight of them turned her stomach. "What are they? That black blood and rotten stench—they're unnatural."

"Years ago, a powerful mage opened a world gate and let Commander Zens into Dragons' Realm," Zaarusha said. A vicious face loomed in Ezaara's mind. She tried to block it out, but Zens' enormous yellow eyes followed her. "Zens created an army of tharuks, without breeding them—the way we take a cutting to grow a plant. They do whatever he commands. They catch and enslave our folk and use plant extracts to make slaves submit to Zens' will." Zaarusha shared memories of tharuks in mining pits, whipping slaves who were only half alive—thin shells with deadened faces.

Ezaara shuddered. "Throw the beasts on the fire, too. Erase every trace of them. This is not a funeral pyre to honor them—just their wretched bodies providing fuel to warn our people."

"My pleasure." A ripple of feral satisfaction radiated from Zaarusha.

When the fire was blazing, Ezaara clambered back into the saddle. Her back and arms ached and her feet were numb.

"Come, it's been a tough first day," Zaarusha melded. "I know a place where we can rest."

Gripping the saddle, Ezaara closed her eyes, but couldn't erase the images of the body-strewn snow. "We have to fight these beasts. Stop them slaughtering our people."

"I know, Ezaara," Zaarusha said, "that's why I need you." Flipping her wings, she flew along the ridge. "Eighteen years ago, my last rider, Anakisha, my mate Syan, and his rider were lost in battle."

Zaarusha shared a memory.

Zaarusha was wounded, roaring. Her rider slipped from her saddle and fell, dark hair flying and limbs sprawling, into a horde of tharuks. Claws out, the beasts swarmed over her. A massive black dragon dived into the midst of the monsters, his rider screaming, "Anakisha!" Syan thrashed his talons, sending monsters flying. Tharuks stabbed his belly and fired arrows into his wings, shredding them. His rider was dragged from the saddle and vanished under a pack of furry bodies. Bellowing, the dragon flamed tharuks, but for every beast he burned, three rushed forward. He lifted his tattered wings and flapped, rising, but a seething mass of tharuks grabbed onto his limbs, dragging him back to the ground.

Zaarusha fled, her bellows of rage and anguish ricocheting through Ezaara.

The queen's raw agony swept through Ezaara, making her chest ache and her eyes prick. She'd only left her family behind. Zaarusha had lost everyone she loved.

"*Without my clutch of eggs to protect at Dragons' Hold, I would've dived in and died too,*" Zaarusha said. "*I made the right choice. And now, I have you.*"

Ezaara reeled. "That could've been me, earlier, when I fell."

"*Luckily, we were high enough for me to catch you. Riders have broken bones by not trusting their dragons and being too tense.*"

"I'm glad I didn't know. That would've made it impossible to relax."

"*There's only one time when you shouldn't trust me—if tharuks give me sway-weed. This herb—*"

"—replaces love with hate, changing allegiance between men, or between man and beast," Ezaara recited.

"*So, Marlies taught you well.*" Zaarusha hesitated. "*Don't be scared by my past. We have a bright future together. I can sense it. Your name will be honored across Dragons' Realm.*"

Except in Lush Valley. They'd never honor her there.

Zaarusha dropped down a steep rocky face below the snow line, and landed on a broad scrubby plateau halfway down the mountainside. On the pass above them, the beacon was burning, barely visible in the gold and orange light of the setting sun.

"*Don't worry, soon that fire will be blazing against the dark,*" Zaarusha said. "*Come, I want to show you something before night falls.*" Zaarusha paced through scrub, entering a cave in the mountainside. She blew a small flame, lighting a torch in a wall sconce.

A shelf lined the wall, with waterskins and jars of preserves on it. Below, barrels were lined up like warriors. Someone obviously kept this place well stocked.

"A bed." Ezaara slid off Zaarusha and sank down onto the pallet. "This looks so good right now."

"Wait, there's something better." Zaarusha went outside and gestured with her snout toward a track winding through the scrub. "Go on. Take a look."

Ezaara hesitated.

"You're safe here. Tharuks can't climb down that sheer rock face or scale the cliff below."

Taking a deep breath, Ezaara leaned up and scratched Zaarusha's eye ridge.

The queen nudged her with her snout. "Enjoy yourself."

Ezaara followed the goat track through the tussock. The plateau was oddly fertile, given the granite cliff above. Thick grasses and scrub covered the area, with giant ferns towering over her. It was warmer here than up on the snow line, although in winter it would be decked in white. A hidden stream burbled nearby.

The track angled toward the cliff, edged in lush vegetation. The stream was growing louder. Maybe Zaarusha was sending her for a drink of fresh water. The setting sun cast a golden hue over everything. A strange scent hung in the air. The stream was louder now, the gurgle reminding her of Lush Valley and all she'd left behind. Ezaara's eyes burned. Not again. She'd cried enough today.

Stepping through ferns, Ezaara came to the end of the track—and gasped.

Misty tendrils rose off a narrow river flowing along the back of the plateau. But it wasn't mist—it was steam. Ezaara crouched and dipped her hand in the water. She groaned. It was *warm*. Further along the cliff, a waterfall gushed out of a hole in the rock, steam wafting from it as it cascaded into the thermal river. The water smelled like old eggs, but she didn't care. Shucking off her clothes, Ezaara climbed down the bank. She waded a few steps across the river and sat, leaning against the cliff, immersed to her shoulders.

"Aah, Zaarusha. This is better than food and a bed. It's wonderful."

"I knew you'd like it." Zaarusha chuckled. "You can bathe, but don't submerge your head or drink the water. It's good for aches and pains, but rough on your stomach."

Ezaara wanted nothing more than to duck under and scrub the grime from her face, but instead, she leaned against the bank, gazing upward. The water soothed her aching back and shoulders as, one by one, stars winked at her from the dark sky. She craned her neck, trying to spot the beacon. She couldn't see it, but hopefully Pa and Ma would.

"Actually, Marlies may see the beacon, but she won't be able to help anyone in Lush Valley. She's leaving to help me recover something I lost."

"Zaarusha, stop being so cryptic. What's going on?"

"My son is missing. Tharuks captured him. As Queen, I can't leave to look for him, so Marlies is searching for him."

So, Ma had a chance to redeem herself with Zaarusha. *"Can you let Ma or Pa know that I'm safe?"*

"Sorry, we're too far away to communicate with either of them." Zaarusha gave a grunt that blew the tired cobwebs from Ezaara's mind.

"Are you all right?"

"Just tired."

Something Zaarusha was saying didn't add up. Ezaara clambered out of the water and tugged on her clothes and boots, not stopping to dry herself. She hurried back along the trail, guided by moonlight. When she came to the cavern, she understood. *"Zaarusha, you're hurt!"* Ezaara rushed forward to examine a gash on Zaarusha's foreleg.

"It's nothing."

"It was that tharuk leader, wasn't it? I felt your pain when you grabbed him." She'd been so overwhelmed, she'd forgotten.

"That maggot-roach sunk its claws into me. But at least those tharuk scouts didn't have any poison-tipped arrows with them. This is simply a cut." Zaarusha flicked her tail, like an impatient cat.

"You should've told me before I bathed," Ezaara scolded out loud. It was strange to speak after mind-melding all day. "This is going to need stitches." She took her needle and squirrel gut twine from her healer's pouch and threaded it. "Hold still." The needle was too small, so in the end Ezaara had to pierce Zaarusha's hide with a knife from the cave and thread the twine through the holes to tug the edges of her wound tight.

Zaarusha was stoic, not uttering a sound, but an image of her ripping apart the tharuk leader's body repeatedly rushed through the queen's mind. *"Helps me manage pain,"* Zaarusha admitted with a dragonly grin.

When Ezaara was done, Zaarusha hooked a barrel toward her with her uninjured front limb. With a swipe of her talons, she pried the lid open. *"Help yourself."*

"Apples. How did they get here?"

"Marlies' dragon, Liesar, leaves supplies for our riders in hideouts across the realm."

So, Ma's dragon was still alive. How could they bear to be parted? Actually, Ma had had no choice. Ezaara's stomach grumbled. She took an apple and leaned against Zaarusha's side to eat it, tossing apples from the barrel to Zaarusha, who snapped them down.

Spiking an apple on a talon, Zaarusha toasted it with fire from her maw. *"Here."*

Juice ran down Ezaara's chin. "Oh, so sweet."

"Are you full?" The queen eyed the barrel. *"Mind if I finish these?"*

Ezaara took one more. "You can have the rest."

Zaarusha shoved her snout in the barrel, crunching and slurping until the apples were gone. Ezaara smothered a smile—sharing with a dragon wasn't exactly one for one. Zaarusha curled up on the ledge. Ezaara dragged the pallet and blanket over near Zaarusha and lay down, but her mind was too busy to relax.

"Sleep, Ezaara. We have a long journey ahead of us." The queen folded a wing over her. *"Let me tell you a legend to help you rest."*

Ezaara closed her eyes.

"In the beginning, there was the Egg. Not an ordinary egg, but the First Egg, which held the seed for all dragons. When the First Egg burst into a million shards, Dragons' Realm was born …"

Dragons' Hold

Roberto strode down the tunnel that connected the council chambers to his cavern, the thud of his boots echoing off the stone walls. As he rounded a corner, a familiar figure detached itself from the shadows.

Adelina's smiling face made the torchlight brighter—a welcome face after the council's bickering. "Are you all right?" She hugged him.

There were days, like today, when his sister was the only thing that kept him sane. "I'm fine. Just the usual—more arguing." They walked along the tunnel toward her cavern.

"I'm surprised you didn't enjoy it." She mock-punched his arm, grinning. "I thought you liked arguing. Well, you do with me."

Despite his mood, Roberto managed a weak chuckle.

She arched her eyebrows. "What was it this time?"

"Apparently, Handel has had word from Zaarusha that she's imprinted with the new Queen's Rider."

Her sharp intake of breath betrayed her. "Oh? Has she? I—"

Oh, shards! "Adelina." His voice softened. "We already knew it wasn't you."

She swallowed. "I know. But I still held hope." She gave him a too-bright smile. "It's great news. It's been eighteen years since Zaarusha had a rider. So, why were the council arguing?"

"Because her rider was found in Lush Valley, of all places."

Adelina rolled her eyes. "Really?"

Roberto rubbed the back of his neck, trying to dislodge the tension that had been building all night. "It'll be some ignorant, backward clod, terrified of dragons."

"From a superstitious backwater, dealing with the likes of Lars and Tonio." She shook her head. "And leading the council without knowing the politics here."

Exactly what he'd been thinking. "Tharuks haven't even made it to Lush Valley. How could someone with no fighting or combat experience lead us in war? What was Zaarusha thinking?"

"Maybe she was desperate for a rider after so many years alone." Again, hurt flashed on Adelina's face before she forced another smile. "It's not our problem. Everything will work out."

Typical. She was already looking on the good side again. No wonder she kept him balanced. Stopping outside Adelina's cavern, Roberto faced her. "It *is* my problem. I've been given the honor of training the new Queen's Rider." More of a burden than an honor.

Her eyebrows shot up. "Why?"

"Handel decided, for some unknown reason, and Lars and the council have ratified it, so the decision is binding. Zaarusha will be here tonight."

She grimaced.

The unspoken words hung between them. He'd have to use his talents. "I'll be fine." He had to be. Roberto squeezed her shoulder, then strode down the tunnel toward his quarters.

Huh! An ignorant settler from Lush Valley could be a traitor or a spy—someone Zens had turned without the queen or her rider knowing it. His job was to test this new rider, despite the memories that haunted him each time he had to perform his duty. He'd need to be thorough—for the realm, for Zaarusha. If there was the faintest hint that the Queen's Rider wasn't fit, Zaarusha would be seeking another.

§

Ezaara's chin drooped to her chest. She jerked awake and clutched Zaarusha's spinal ridge. The moon dragged fingertips across the tips of the forest below, not penetrating the dark mass. After three days and nights of flying with only short stops, her backside was sore and her shoulders ached. *"How's your leg doing?"*

"Much better. Thank you for stitching it," Zaarusha thrummed. "We'll be at Dragons' Hold soon. We're expected before dawn."

So, no chance of a decent sleep.

"Yes, I mind-melded and told the blue guards about tharuks entering Lush Valley, and advised them that we're coming."

"I didn't realize you could mind-meld with everyone."

"I can only meld with other riders when they touch me, but I can meld with their dragons if they're not too far away. They're keen to meet the new Queen's Rider."

Whoever 'they' were. *"In the middle of the night?"* Ezaara yawned. *"If they've waited eighteen years, surely they can wait a few more hours."*

Zaarusha snorted. *"Your imprinting bond and loyalty must be tested."*

"How?"

"You'll be fine. Just be yourself."

Fine? That was all right for Zaarusha to say—she wasn't about to face a horde of blue dragons for the first time.

They ascended a snowy mountainside, gliding above a summit. Moonlight caught on jagged peaks that formed a gaping maw around a dark basin.

"These mountains are Dragon's Teeth, the guardians of Dragons' Hold," Zaarusha said. *"Flying is the only way in."*

They swooped down, the basin swallowing them, and flew toward a mountain face, shooting through a tunnel into an enormous cavern.

Inside, the air was filled with dragons, their sinuous necks weaving to stare at her with wild eyes. They swooped and dived past Zaarusha, grim-faced riders upon their backs. Bill's scrap of cloth had been right—they were every color from emerald to blood red. Dragons snarled, flashing fangs. Their wings made torches sputter in their sconces, sending a chill down her spine.

Zaarusha roared, the air reverberating, setting Ezaara's teeth on edge. Her talons clattered on the granite floor. Twelve dragons landed, splayed in an arc on a rock platform that towered above Ezaara and the queen.

Ezaara gripped the saddle tighter. The whole of their farm would fit in this cavern, several times over.

The riders, women and men, dismounted, swords at their sides and dagger hilts peeking from their boots. They looked fierce. Intimidating. Wait, there were thirteen dragons. A bronze rider-less dragon was skulking in the shadows.

A man stalked down from the platform, boots striking the stone steps, moving like a lethal predator. Unlike the men in Lush Valley. Confident. Dangerous. He bowed to Zaarusha, dark hair brushing his shoulders. "Welcome home, Honored Queen." His hard, black eyes flicked over Ezaara. "I see you've brought your new rider for testing."

What a welcome. *"What happens if I fail this test?"* she fired at Zaarusha.

"You'll be banished to the Wastelands."

The Wastelands! *"Banished? But I'm—"*

"I told you, you'll be fine. Climb down, he's waiting."

Ezaara slid out of the saddle, stumbling as her feet hit the ground.

The man's lips twitched into a sneer.

She shrunk back, closer to Zaarusha, as all the stories she'd heard about killer dragons came flooding back to her. *"Zaarusha—"*

Zaarusha snorted. *"Ezaara, you have to do this on your own."* She broke mind-meld and flew to a high outcrop.

"Welcome to Dragons' Hold." His tone was cool, disinterested. Anything but welcoming. "I'm Roberto, Master of Mental Faculties." He was only a couple of years older than her, but his poise and arrogance made him so much older. Intimidating. "It's my responsibility to test you." He waved a hand at the dragons on the stage above them. "I present the Council of the Twelve Dragon Masters. Do you consent to be tested? If not, you'll forfeit your right to ride Zaarusha and be removed from Dragons' Hold immediately."

"Y-yes."

On the platform, the dragon masters bowed. Their dragons towered above her. Ferocious eyes fixed on her. A huge purple dragon roared, its wicked fangs glinting. They all joined in, rearing, clawing the air and shaking the ground.

Her stomach coiled. What had she done to deserve this? *"Zaarusha."* No answer.

Were they going to attack? Better to be impaled on the peaks of Dragon's Teeth than face these beasts. There was no way she'd pass their test. She'd be banished and die in the barren Wastelands across the Naobian Sea. Ezaara froze, rooted to the ground in terror.

Roberto raised his palm. The dragons quieted.

"Good evening, respected dragons and Council of the Twelve Dragon Masters," he said. "In keeping with tradition, Queen Zaarusha has brought her new rider to be tested. She has stood fast in the face of your wrath, passing the first phase of testing."

What? Being too scared to move had saved her from failure? If only her heart would stop bashing against her chest.

"She may have imprinted, with our queen, but how well?" Again, Master Roberto's eyes flicked over her. "We must determine whether she is fit to be trained as the true Queen's Rider."

He looked as if he was battling not to spit on her. Ezaara cringed.

The dragons bared their teeth, nostrils flaring. They roared, a low rumble building until the air vibrated and the stone floor pulsed beneath her.

Roberto flashed a cool smile and gestured at narrow stairs cut into the rock. "Masters, introduce her to your dragons." His voice echoed around the large cavern. "And dragons, be thorough."

Be thorough doing what? Her hands shook. Lofty and Tomaaz would hoot at her fear, call her ridiculous. Ezaara reached out for Zaarusha again. Still nothing.

"Ezaara, proceed to the stage. As you are tested, please remember the moment you imprinted with Queen Zaarusha."

Zaarusha had taken a gamble on her, and here she was, as scared as a littling hearing ghost stories. She couldn't let Zaarusha down. Despite the fear zinging along her veins, Ezaara forced herself to race up the steps toward a formidable purple beast with blue eyes.

The beast lowered its head. A master with a fair beard—and eyes the same shade as the purple dragon's—stepped forward and picked up Ezaara's hand, placing it on the dragon's brow, covering it with his own.

A jolt of energy flew along Ezaara's arm. Her memory exploded in her mind. She was in Lush Valley's sacred clearing, watching Zaarusha approach, her heart on fire as she mind-melded with the Queen of the Dragons for the first time.

The master spoke. "I'm Lars, Leader of the Council of the Twelve Dragon Masters. This is Singlar. Welcome to Dragons' Hold, Ezaara, Rider of Zaarusha, Queen of the Dragons."

Ezaara staggered. How had Lars known her name?

"From your imprinting memories." Singlar winked his purple eyelid. *"Besides, Zaarusha told us earlier."*

Lars motioned to his right. A female master took her hand and laid it upon a green dragon's head, covering it with hers. Ezaara relived her imprinting experience, emotions coursing through her again.

She repeated the experience with each of the dragons in the circle, until only two remained: a blue one and the lone bronze dragon, who regarded her with intense green eyes that reminded her of Pa's.

Roberto led her to the blue dragon. "This is Erob. I'm his rider."

"And the bronze?"

"He's not a member of the council." Roberto placed, not one, but both of Ezaara's hands on Erob's blue brow. "I need to test you more rigorously. Do you consent?"

She had no option. There was no way she was going to give up Zaarusha.

At her nod, Roberto put his hands on her temples.

Surprised, she flinched. Both Erob and Roberto gazed deep into Ezaara's eyes, Roberto's face a mask of concentration. Without a sneer—with his ebony eyes, high cheekbones and olive skin—his face was striking.

§

The girl had imprinted. Roberto was sure of it. Zaarusha had snorted at something, which showed they'd been mind-melding without touching—a sure sign of imprinting. But how solid was their bond? Ezaara had trembled at the sight of dragons, but she'd also stood her ground—so she had courage.

Courage or not, the Queen of Dragons' Realm deserved the best. If Zaarusha had made a mistake, he had to find out. The other masters and their dragons had confirmed the imprinting bond existed. Now he had to test the quality of that bond. And the Queen's Rider. If she wasn't good enough, it was his task to fail this backward girl from Lush Valley, and she'd be dispatched to the Wastelands before dawn.

Roberto took a deep breath, steeling himself. He hated using his talent, paid for with people's blood. He placed both of his hands on the girl's temples. It always came back to using his cursed gift.

He was in her mind.

Zaarusha spiraled down to meet Ezaara. Fear curled in the girl's stomach. Her limbs were paralyzed. She was petrified she'd be raked by talons, or die in the dragon's maw. But even as Roberto wanted to scoff at her naive fear, he was awed at the intensity of her emotions; the sharpness of her memories.

He'd tested many folk. Their experiences had been vivid, but compared to this, they were nothing: an overcast day compared to summer sun.

No, a few halting notes compared to an intricate harmony.

Ezaara's fear of the dragon queen melted into admiration, and her admiration to love. Zaarusha's scales were bright, her voice thrilling. The breeze of the dragon's wingbeats stirred Ezaara's hair. Her emotions soared. This girl's bond was the strongest he'd witnessed. Her jump onto the queen's back was incredible. She'd harnessed Zaarusha's power as if she'd trained for years at Dragons' Hold, not like an ignorant, terrified ….

He'd been wrong. Ezaara's love for the dragon queen was complete. Her imprinting bond was proven. The queen had a new rider.

He should break meld, and announce his conclusion to the council, but doubt nagged at him like a stone in his boot. Lars and Zaarusha were expecting him to be thorough. He didn't like using his gifts—having them was bad enough—but he knew how easily folk could be turned by Zens and his tharuks. So, he delved deeper, searching for treachery.

On their journey to Dragons' Hold, Zaarusha and Ezaara had fought tharuks, and buried warriors. That explained the soot and smears of black and red blood on her cheeks and tunic. He sifted through the experience. Anger pulsed through Ezaara—and grief. Only the queen's wisdom had stopped her from jumping into battle.

She was true to the realm and had bravery in pailfuls. All she needed was training.

Just as he'd been trained. A memory shot into Roberto's mind. *Ten years old, he was crouched behind the kitchen door, clutching Adelina's hand, listening to his parents.*

No! That's where the pain and betrayal had started. Roberto slammed the memory shut and yanked his hands away.

§

With Roberto's hands on her temples and his black eyes gazing at her, Ezaara re-lived her imprinting with Zaarusha: the warmth of Zaarusha's voice slid through her; the scent of the flowers in the clearing; the bright sun glinting off the dragon queen's smooth scales; the bubble of color that had swept her up onto the queen; the rumble of Zaarusha's roar; and the wind tugging at her hair.

Tears of joy slipped down Ezaara's cheeks.

She re-lived her journey to Dragons' Hold: the horror of tharuks killing those warriors; her sadness; the thermal pool and snuggling with Zaarusha; meadows and forests flying past beneath them; and then, the severe peaks of Dragon's Teeth.

A scene entered her head: crouched behind a heavy door, holding the hand of a little dark-haired girl. Voices yelling. Despair. What was this? Where had it come from?

Him. It was from him. A memory.

Roberto flinched, then pulled his hands away, and her mind was her own again. His gaze never left her, although its intensity softened. His voice was soft, too. "It's over." He breathed deeply. "You've been proven."

Proven? How? She didn't feel any different. And what had she seen? The door … the raging hurt was his. Who was the little girl he'd been protecting?

Exhausted and dizzy, she stumbled, her hands falling from Erob's head.

Roberto caught her. He smelled of sandalwood soap. She slumped against him, too tired to care what anyone thought.

His voice rang out, "Hail Ezaara, rider of Zaarusha, Queen of Dragons' Realm!"

The Council of the Twelve Dragon Masters cheered. Their dragons roared. The bronze rider-less dragon leaped into the air, circling the cavern before disappearing through a gap high in the cavern wall, its bellows echoing behind it.

§

Roberto shook his head, banishing the terrible memory that had struck out of nowhere. Burying the pain. Had she seen it? Hopefully not. Surely he'd broken mind-meld fast enough. Now the girl had passed out in his arms. So weak. No stamina at all. And this was the Queen's Rider.

"She's exhausted," Erob melded. *"Zaarusha traveled days to get here. You of all people should have compassion."*

"True," Roberto replied. He'd arrived here an outcast. *"You're right, I should know not to judge newcomers. She does look worn out."*

"Carry the Queen's Rider to her cavern," Lars called. "Shari, accompany him and see to her welfare."

That was odd. Why the master of livestock? Lars should have assigned Fleur, the master healer, to help Ezaara. Did Lars intend an insult to Fleur? Not that he'd blame him.

"She looks like a dragonet that's flown itself out," Shari murmured, her dark eyes on the girl's face. "She's pretty."

Pretty? Roberto took another look. Ezaara's eyes were striking green when open, but she was hardly pretty. He huffed. "Come on, Shari. Not even you can tell what she looks like under all that grime."

Shari laughed and slugged him.

They made their way along the tunnels to the cavern of the Queen's Rider. Shari opened the wooden door and Roberto carried Ezaara in. Asleep, she looked peaceful, vulnerable, and way too young to be training as the Queen's Rider. Ezaara had no idea what she was in for.

Roberto laid her on the bed. "Do you need any help?"

"Certainly not." Shari laughed again, making her braids swing. "Why don't you get back to bed? You look like you could use some sleep yourself."

"You know me, I never need much sleep."

"Still having nightmares?" She frowned, serious now. "Are you all right?"

Shari had been his champion when he'd arrived at Dragons' Hold and been treated like an outcast. She'd befriended him, encouraging him to leave his legacy behind and make a better man of himself. It hadn't been easy. There were days when he would've gone mad without her friendship.

"I'm fine." He shrugged, leaving as Shari tugged Ezaara's boots off.

His feet automatically took him along the tunnel. Ezaara was a conundrum. Young and terrified, but brave. Backward and ignorant, with a strong bond to her dragon—a deep bond. Untrained, inexperienced …. He sighed. This was going to be a challenge. War was so close and politics here at the hold could easily implode. He had his work cut out. He'd have to be relentless, tough, to ensure she was up to standard for their queen.

At the passage to his sister's cavern, he took the turn off into the shadows. There was no torchlight shining through the crack below Adelina's door, so she was probably fast asleep. He hesitated. Adelina often helped him order his thoughts. He valued her counsel. He had to tell her they'd underestimated this new Queen's Rider.

Footfalls came along the tunnel accompanied by hushed voices—a man and a woman.

"What are we going to do?" That was Fleur, master healer.

"She's getting old," Bruno, her husband and master of prophecy, whispered. "Hardly fit to rule."

"And now the queen's besotted with that girl," hissed Fleur. "That pathetic scrap of a rider."

Roberto moved deeper into shadow.

"Perhaps Zaarusha is going senile," Bruno said. "We'll have to see Lars."

Fleur's quiet reply was lost around a corner.

Roberto padded along the tunnel in the opposite direction and out of the caverns into the night. He ran along the mountainside on a goat track that led to Lars' cavern and his own. As surefooted as an ibex, he'd often taken bitter refuge on these wild tracks when he'd first arrived at Dragons' Hold.

He slipped past dragons' dens, their occupants opening a sleepy eye to see him pass. As long as Singlar, Lars' dragon, didn't see him, he'd be fine. Before he reached Lars' cavern, he climbed higher, above Singlar's den, and sat near the vent hole to Lars' main chamber.

Urgent voices drifted up. Bruno and Fleur had made good time. Guilt for eavesdropping twanged through Roberto, but, for Zaarusha's sake, he had to know what they were up to.

"She might have made a mistake," Fleur was saying. "It's been eighteen years since she had a rider."

"Are you insinuating that our dragon queen doesn't know what she's doing?" Lars' tone was disapproving.

"No, of course not," Fleur backtracked. "Our poor queen has suffered so much, being without a rider or a mate for so many years. Perhaps loneliness has impaired her judgment."

"We trust our queen," Bruno said, "but, you have to admit, it is odd that she chose a girl from Lush Valley. And one so young."

"Perhaps the girl has manipulated our queen. Or maybe Zaarusha's become a little unbalanced. Reckless." Fleur's voice was smooth, placating. "We don't want Zaarusha hurt."

Roberto clenched his fists. Surely Lars could see through their attempts to discredit the queen.

"You have a point there." Lars sounded weary. "But I won't act on suspicions. Bring me proof. And remember, Roberto has tested her and declared their bond fit."

"Exactly," Fleur purred. "He was a traitor. Maybe he's turned again."

"Enough." Lars' voice was icy. "Out, now! Don't come back unless you have evidence. I need at least an hour's sleep before dawn."

Roberto gazed down at the valley—still shrouded in shadow. It always came back to his past. His actions. Curse his rotten father's watery grave.

§

Ezaara awoke with a pounding head. She was tangled in a snowy quilt embroidered with gold dragons. Sunlight streamed through a hole in a stone ceiling, illuminating a hanging tapestry of more dragons flying across a battlefield beneath distant alps. Across the cavern, near an enormous archway, was a large bathtub with wood under it. The scent of relaxing herbs—bergamot, jasmine and lavender—hung in the air.

"Good morning," Zaarusha hummed. "Well done on your imprinting test."

Ezaara gazed around. Zaarusha was nowhere to be seen. *I hope there won't be any more tests.*

"Not like that one. Only tests of skill."

"Skill? I'm sure to fail, then. I'm not good at much, except herbs." Zaarusha should have taken Tomaaz as her rider instead.

"No, Tomaaz isn't the right rider for me. You are."

"Why me?"

Zaarusha appeared in the archway. "When my dragonet gave his life to bless your mother, some of his essence was passed to Marlies, for her progeny. I sense that you—and probably Tomaaz—have special talents, gifts from my baby."

"It's sad you lost your baby."

"Yes, I was devastated, but it was a long time ago."

Ezaara sat up. "So, what talents are you talking about?"

"These things take time to unfold. Be patient." Snaking her long neck into the room, Zaarusha winked and opened her jaws, shooting a jet of flame along the edges of the metal tub. Soon steam rose from the water. With one last burst of controlled flame, she ignited the timber under the tub. "Now, relax and enjoy your bath. I'll be next door in my den."

Ezaara smiled. That was much easier than fetching boiling water from a hearth.

The cavern floor was cool beneath Ezaara's feet. Clad only in her underthings, she shivered. Opening a drawer, she found clean underclothing. In another, dark jerkins and breeches like the masters had worn—dragon riders' garb. A majestic closet held beautiful robes, embroidered tunics and breeches—all made of luxurious fabrics in gorgeous hues. Were these all hers? She stroked a blue satin tunic, then ran her fingers down a soft green dress. She'd never had anything this fine in Lush Valley.

Her family's faces flashed to mind. She missed them: Tomaaz's pranks, Ma's understanding and Pa's teasing. She'd left Lush Valley on an impulse, without a thought for them or a goodbye. She'd broken her vow to Tomaaz. No! Now her eyes were stinging. She squeezed them shut. The Queen's Rider, crying? Surely Zaarusha deserved more.

Shoving her feelings aside, Ezaara strode to the steaming tub. On the wall above the bath were two crossed swords, ancient-looking things with ornately-carved hilts. One hilt was silver, the other, gold. Snarling metal-worked dragons—with tiny engraved scales—curled around the hilts. They were beautiful. She longed to hold one and test its weight, but she didn't dare. They were obviously ceremonial—much too pretty to fight with.

Ezaara dipped her hand in the tub, warm water trailing from her fingers. A bowl of herbs was perched on a ledge. She sprinkled some into the water, a summery scent filling the air. Stepping out of her underclothing, Ezaara sank into the bath. She had to become a good Queen's Rider. Develop her talents. She could do this. She had to. There was no place among these tough riders at Dragons' Hold for petty worries or loneliness. She had to be strong. But the bath's soothing warmth and herbal scent reminded her of home, washing away her resolve, and soon, her tears blended with the water.

§

Adelina hurried along the tunnel toward the Queen's Rider's cavern. Of all the favors Roberto could've asked! She had a million better things to do than babysitting an ignorant waif from Lush Valley. Why should she look after the girl who'd broken her heart and stolen Zaarusha?

Because Roberto had asked, that's why. She'd do it, but she didn't have to be gracious. Sighing, she knocked on the door.

No answer, but faint sounds came from within.

Adelina pushed the door open, turning on her charm, bowing low. "Good morning, Ezaara, Honored Rider of Queen Zaarusha."

A blonde girl was hunched on the bed, head bowed, half wearing a gorgeous blue satin robe. Seeing the simple ties on the dress, Adelina rolled her eyes. The new Queen's Rider hadn't even greeted her. Couldn't even dress herself. This girl was worse than she'd thought. If she'd been Queen's …. She wasn't. And Roberto had begged her help, insisting the girl was the true Queen's Rider. She had to try. If not for this girl, then for Zaarusha, for Dragons' Realm. The girl sniffed.

Adelina had expected incompetence or ignorance, not someone melting in self-pity. "Excuse me, are you all right?"

Ezaara's head shot up, cheeks flaming. "Um, yes. I'm fine." She smiled too brightly, her lower lip wobbling.

Familiarity knifed through Adelina—she had a whole arsenal of smiles that masked pain. What was this girl's hurt? At what cost had she come here? She smiled back. "I'm here to help you prepare for your first public flight."

"Thank you, that's kind of you."

She had green eyes, this girl. Brave eyes, despite her sadness. "Here." Reaching into the leather bag slung over her shoulder, Adelina passed Ezaara a bread roll and an orange. "You missed breakfast, but you'll feel better after eating."

"I'm fine, really."

Adelina arched an eyebrow. "Right, of course you are. Especially after a tough imprinting test with a bunch of strangers in the middle of the night, far from home. Absolutely fine."

Wiping her tears, Ezaara laughed.

Adelina had to grin. "I'm Adelina."

"Someone else should be Queen's Rider," Ezaara said. "I don't know how anything works around here. Not even this dress. I mean, I'd never seen a dragon before Zaarusha appeared. What if I fail?"

Obviously humble enough to learn, this girl wasn't so bad after all. "You'll be fine, with my help. Remember, you've already passed your first test."

Ezaara shuddered. "It was hideous."

Roberto had said Ezaara had the strongest bond he'd ever tested, and he'd know. "Master Roberto said you did well."

"I'm surprised he had anything to say about me at all."

"Tough, was he?" He did tough well. "I'll tell you what. He's sometimes tough on me too. Let's pay him back with a prank." She winked.

"But we'll get in trouble. He's a master. I—"

"It's only a bit of harmless fun. I promise."

This time Ezaara's smile was real. "I could use some fun."

Adelina laughed.

Dragon Flight

Roberto paced in the clearing under Zaarusha's den, stones crunching underfoot as he recited the words to the ceremony under his breath. It'd been two hours since Adelina had gone to fetch the girl. What was taking them so long? Over two hundred folk were gathered in the clearing and over a hundred dragons were perched on the mountainside, waiting. This was the biggest event they'd had at Dragons' Hold in years—probably in his lifetime.

Seated on a dais behind him with the other masters, Lars gave the signal. It was time. Ezaara had better show up. Roberto hesitated, remembering the mental ordeal he'd put her through in the middle of the night. Perhaps they should give her longer—last night she'd been so exhausted, she'd collapsed.

Far behind the crowd, Ezaara emerged from the main cavern. What was going on? They'd anticipated her appearance in this clearing, beneath Queen Zaarusha's den. Adelina should've known that.

Roberto raised the horn to his lips, blowing a haunting note that echoed off the granite mountainsides. He gestured toward the new Queen's Rider at the back of the crowd.

And stared.

§

That morning, Adelina had taught Ezaara how to saddle Zaarusha. She'd done her hair, helped her dress, then led her through the back tunnels and into the empty main cavern.

"No one will expect you to come this way." Adelina's brown eyes were warm. "You'll surprise them all."

Hopefully, not in a bad way. "Are you sure? I—"

Adelina hugged Ezaara. "Keep smiling and I'm sure you'll win everyone over. I'll be nearby, if you need me."

It was good to have a friend among these tough riders and fierce dragons.

When Ezaara stepped outside the cavern, a crowd was gathered. Her stomach fluttered. Luckily they were facing away from her, toward the dragon masters.

Roberto blew a horn and flung his arm toward Ezaara. Folk turned to stare.

§

Roberto inhaled. Ezaara was radiant. In place of the fearful travel-weary waif was a young woman worthy of a royal court. Her light-blue robe was threaded with green ribbons that fluttered in the breeze. The crown of her blonde hair was plaited and woven with more green ribbons, leaving long tresses loose over her shoulders and back.

Ezaara talked to those she passed, often touching someone's outstretched hand. Her laugh loosened something in his chest—something that had been tight for years.

Absently, he lowered the horn from his lips. *This* was the same girl he'd tested last night?

She'd passed that test brilliantly, and now she was passing the next hurdle—the folk loved her. They were smiling, shaking her hand. Excitement hummed through the crowd.

It had taken him a year to prove himself at Dragons' Hold. How had she done it in less than a day?

There was more to her than he'd suspected. He cringed at his harsh attitude before he'd known Ezaara was Zaarusha's *true* rider.

She passed through the crowd, murmuring a quiet word here and there, her slim figure coming ever closer to the Council of the Twelve Dragon Masters. Colors flitted through his head. Her, it was her. Ezaara's vibrancy tinged his soul.

Like the crowd of dragon folk, Roberto was awestruck.

But, unlike them, he couldn't afford to show it.

§

The crowd parted. Ezaara swallowed. It was now or never. She could do this. Maybe Zaarusha was right, perhaps she did belong here. Reaching out, she squeezed a little boy's hand. His face lit up and his mother murmured her thanks. Those nearby greeted her. Some smiled, others reached out to touch her. Ezaara made her way through the throng, the warmth of the dragon folk wrapping around her like a fluffy blanket.

Roberto was facing the crowd, his black hair curling where it touched his shoulders. A horn dangled from his fingertips. How had he created such soulful music with a single note?

Nearing the council, Ezaara stopped short of Roberto and inclined her head. She was determined not to give him reason to fault her. "Good day, Master Roberto."

Roberto stepped forward, his voice carrying across the clearing. "Beloved Council of the Twelve Dragon Masters, magnificent dragons, esteemed gentlefolk and riders of Dragons' Hold, I present to you Ezaara, verified Rider of Zaarusha, the Honored Queen of Dragons' Realm." He waved his hand toward her with a flourish.

So formal. What was she supposed to do now? Ezaara nodded in acknowledgment.

Roberto continued, "Before the Council of the Twelve Dragon Masters, she has proven her imprinting bond, her allegiance to the realm and …"

For a moment Roberto looked panicked. He'd obviously forgotten his words.

"This is boring," a little boy piped up.

Ezaara let out a giggle. The stares of the council members turned to ice. She quickly covered her mouth with her hand.

Roberto's cheek twitched, right by a tiny pale scar. He continued, "… her allegiance to the realm and her devotion to our queen. Do you accept her?"

People near them tittered. Others glared.

"Gentlefolk, do you accept her?" Roberto repeated, cheek still twitching.

"We do," the crowd called.

Roberto turned to Ezaara. "And do you, Ezaara, accept your obligation and vow to protect Dragons' Realm—rider, warrior, dragon, wizard, farmer, craftsperson, adult and littling alike—with your very life?"

"My life?" Ezaara squeaked.

Lars, council leader, nodded at her, face grave.

"Ezaara." Roberto's dark eyes bored into her. "Being Queen's Rider carries responsibility. Your decision today is binding and irreversible. You'll be revered and honored by folk in Dragons' Realm and despised by our foes. Your life will be in danger, and you may die fighting our enemies. Do you accept?"

Die? Like Anakisha? Was she ready to die fighting for folk she hardly knew? She remembered the man in the pass, dying in her arms. The weight of responsibility sank through her bones. This was her duty. "My life is Zaarusha's. I will fulfill my destiny as Queen's Rider."

The crowd cheered.

Roberto held his palm up, demanding silence.

"Every new Queen's Rider must undertake an evaluation flight before training begins." Roberto's eyes flicked to her dress. "Would you care to dress in your rider's garb while we wait, Ezaara, Honored Rider of Queen Zaarusha?" Scorn lurked in his gaze. Challenge. "How *long* will you need?"

Ezaara turned her back to him, facing the crowd, and pulled the ribbons on her gown. The front of her dress flew open, revealing her dragon rider's garb.

The crowd gasped.

Roberto opened his mouth then snapped his jaw shut.

Good, Adelina's trick with the dress had rattled Roberto—sweet revenge for his scorn last night. Twisting her hair into a tight coil on the back of her head, she tied it up with the ribbons. How Adelina had managed to find the exact green of her eyes, she had no idea. She took off the dress and handed it to Adelina, who was waiting at the edge of the crowd. Giving what she hoped was a demure smile, Ezaara said, "You see, Master Roberto, I didn't need *long* at all."

Whatever Roberto replied was lost amid the cheers of dragon folk as Zaarusha swooped down, scales blazing in the noonday sun.

Zaarusha's hum filled Ezaara's mind, *"Jump on. We'll make this flight memorable, so strap in tightly."*

Ezaara climbed up, fastened her harness and pulled the hood of her jerkin tight. Zaarusha sent her a mental picture of the maneuver they were about to perform. *"You're crazy! I'll never survive."* Naked fear sliced through her.

"Ezaara, we have no choice. We have to prove you're fit."

"But I'll slip, fall, I'll—"

"Trust me. I know how brave you are. We can do this." Zaarusha sprang into the sky and circled once, the breeze from her wingbeats stirring the spectators' hair.

"Zaarusha, I don't know if—"

"Trust me."

Her fear would cloud Zaarusha's focus. She had to overcome it. A memory flashed to mind. The first time she'd splinted a broken leg while an injured boy whimpered, she'd been terrified, but despite the boy's anguish, she'd done it with Ma's help. Maybe she could do this too. Ezaara steeled her nerves, patting Zaarusha's neck. *"I'm ready."*

A happy rumble coursed through the queen.

They gathered speed. Below, the upturned faces blurred. Ezaara threw her body forward, sliding her arms through leather loops on Zaarusha's neck, clinging to the hand grips. She locked her knees and dug her feet deep into the stirrups. Wind rushed past her. She was swept up in a whirl of color, and her heart soared with the sweetest music. Her mind was one with Zaarusha, sensing every wing beat, every movement of her dragon's muscles.

Zaarusha's exhilaration rushed through her. Fields whipped by beneath them. The dark forest was a blur. A granite cliff loomed, snow capping its upper reaches. Zaarusha flew straight at the mountainside. Within meters of the rocky face, she roared, folded her wings, and flicked her tail downward, propelling them up the sheer stone wall.

They sped up the mountainside, rock rushing past her dragon's belly. Suddenly, Zaarusha was upside-down. Gravity pulled at Ezaara, trying to claw her body out of the harness. She clung to the leather loops, arms aching. The world tilted and spun. Flashes of treetops. Rock. Snow. Sky. Her stomach dropped. Oh, she was dizzy.

"We're right side up again," Zaarusha announced, flipping over. "You can relax now."

Heart pounding, Ezaara released the grips and sat up. "We did it. That was incredible. Let's do it again!"

"We'll do many more loops, but not today. Now, take off your hood and unfasten the ribbons from your hair."

They flew toward fields of grain and vegetables.

"It's time for some fun." Zaarusha showed her another maneuver. "Hold your ribbons high."

Ezaara gripped Zaarusha with her knees, tensing her stomach. The dragon queen swooped up and down, leap-frogging across the grain fields, stalks rippling in their wake. Ezaara's blonde hair tugged her scalp as it whipped out behind her. The ribbons fluttered like banners in her hands.

The crowd clapped as they approached, chanting, "E—zaa—ra, Zaa—ru—sha."

The peal of the horn rang out over the basin.

"Give Roberto one of your ribbons."

"That cold, arrogant fish. Why would I give him anything?"

"Trust me. Give him one, but do it discreetly. I'll tell you when," Zaarusha commanded.

Ezaara didn't dare question the queen.

§

Erob's chuckle startled Roberto. *"No one's flown a loop since Anakisha. I dare you to challenge Zaarusha's rider now."*

Zaarusha landed in front of the applauding crowd, facing the council.

Shrugging off his dragon's quip, Roberto approached and helped Ezaara down. Last night, he hadn't noticed the sprinkling of tiny freckles, like precious flecks of gold, across the bridge of her nose. He shoved the thought away, turning to the crowd.

"Honored Queen's Rider." He projected his voice across the stony clearing. "You have been unanimously accepted by the Council of the Twelve Dragon Masters and riders of Dragons' Hold. Tonight, we'll feast to celebrate."

"Thank you." Ezaara's cheeks were flushed. Her windswept hair hung tangled down her back and she was winding a ribbon around her fingers.

Zaarusha roared, drowning out the crowd. She tossed her head high and spread her wings, blocking Ezaara and Roberto from the crowd's view.

Ezaara's small hand reached for his. "This is for you," she said.

Colors spiraled through his mind. There it was again—her.

She darted back to her dragon's side. No one had noticed their exchange.

Roberto opened his hand. Inside was one of Ezaara's green satin ribbons, still warm where she'd held it. He rubbed the satin with his thumb. Did she realize what this meant?

When Roberto looked up, Handel was watching him, bronze tail twitching ominously. Roberto snapped his hand shut and walked away.

Fishing

Roberto lifted the heavy saddlebags and carried them to Erob, who was waiting on the lip of his den. Far below, people were setting up trestle tables for Ezaara's feast. Tonight, fish would be roasted in honor of the new Queen's Rider, and Roberto, being Naobian, was the hold's chief fisherman. He checked Erob's saddle straps were tight, then touched the pocket holding Ezaara's ribbon. The gift confused him. According to tradition, accepting her ribbon made him her protector—unto death. Did Ezaara even know that?

He shrugged. Whether she knew or not, he'd accepted it—and he'd honor that commitment.

Ezaara's dizzying loop had been a spectacular feat. Impressive, along with her trick with her dress. He snorted. Adelina would've been behind that.

At Erob's rumble, Roberto clambered up and rubbed his dragon's neck. *"How did they do it, Erob? Could we fly a loop?"*

Erob huffed his breath out. *"I'd be too tempted to tip you off!"* He leaped off the ledge, soaring high above the folk. They flew north, over fields, toward the dark band of forest and the lake. *"Ezaara trusts her dragon completely—a rare gift."*

"It is," agreed Roberto.

Trust? Could the answer be that simple? And that terrifying. He hadn't trusted anyone for years—except Adelina and Erob. How could he?

After what he'd done, he could hardly trust himself.

The lake glinted silver. Erob spiraled down to the eastern shore and Roberto unpacked the fishing net.

"Work first?" he asked Erob. *"Or are you tired after your arduous flight?"*

Erob gave him a dragonly grin. He grasped each end of the fishing net with his talons and flew over the lake, his forelegs skimming the surface and the net trailing in the water. Erob was taut and focused, yet if there was a threat, he'd be beside Roberto in moments.

"If only humans could share the same bond."

"They can," Erob replied. *"I witnessed it once as an unborn dragonet. Some human mates have such a strong emotional bond, they can mind-meld the way you and I do."*

"What?" He'd never heard of that.

"Apparently Anakisha and Yanir could mind-meld." Erob rose above the lake, the dripping net full of flapping fish, and flew back to the shore. Roberto helped guide the net onto the grass, and opened it. Erob snaffled two large fish for himself, wolfing them down.

Roberto clapped his dragon on the foreleg. "Good fishing." He tossed Erob two more. Flipping and twisting, the fish scattered diamonds of water as they arced through the air into his jaws.

"I've finished my work. It's your turn, now." His dragon stretched in the sun. "I could roast one, if you like."

"I'm saving my appetite for the feast tonight." Roberto bent to sort the fish, killing the large ones and throwing the small ones back.

"Harrumph." Erob hooked a fish with his talon and roasted it with a moderate dragon flame.

"Erob, just because you're hungry, doesn't mean I am." The aroma of cooked fish making his mouth water, Roberto put their catch into sacks.

Erob shot another tendril of flame at the fish. Its juices sizzled. Shards, it smelled good.

"All right, if you insist." Roberto carried a flat stone to Erob, who placed the cooked fish on it to cool. He flopped on the grass and leaned against his dragon's sun-warmed side.

"A great invention of yours, that net," melded Erob.

He'd always been a good fisherman. It was part of his Naobian heritage. Before the net, he'd hunted for hours from Erob's back with a long-handled net or spear, but now they could catch fish quickly and then take time to relax.

"I bet it's just a rumor that humans can mind-meld." Roberto took a bite of fish.

"When I was an embryo, I met another couple who were mind-melding."

"And?"

"I don't know them, only the timbre of their minds," Erob replied. "I'd recognize her again, though."

"Her?"

"Yes, her. She was melding, so I sensed her mind. Through her, I felt his. Their love was like dragon and rider." Erob nudged Roberto with his snout.

Dragons didn't lie. It must be true, then. "I'm glad we imprinted. Life was grim until you turned up," Roberto mumbled. "Without you, I'd be dead. Or worse." He bolted the last of his fish.

"*Most relationships are not like your parents'.*" Erob flicked the tip of his tail at Roberto's ear.

Roberto batted his tail away.

"*Many humans are happily bonded.*"

Bitter memories rushed through Roberto. His throat tightened.

"*Your father's betrayal was—*"

"Not now, Erob," he barked.

"*You're not like him,*" insisted Erob.

His father's face loomed in his head, mocking him. Zens' bulbous eyes leered at him. The bodies of maimed slaves, piled high, stinking. Whips cracked. Screams. Muffled moaning. His forehead broke out in sweat. Roberto threw the sacks of fish into Erob's saddlebags and climbed on his back. It always came back to his father. "*Drop me at Fire Crag.*" He broke mind-meld.

Erob landed at their usual spot, an hour's run from the top of Fire Crag.

Roberto dismounted and slapped Erob's flank. He eased his mind open. "*I'm sorry, Erob.*" He could never stay mad at Erob for long. His dragon was right—his father had been a traitor.

Erob nudged his shoulder. "*I'll take the fish to the kitchens and be back in a couple of hours.*"

Roberto nodded. Letting his dragon's fire blaze through his veins, he set off on the punishing climb to the pinnacle, hoping the burn of his muscles could obliterate his searing memories.

§

Just before dusk, Ezaara and Zaarusha flew down to the feast.

"*Finally, you're a passenger fit for a queen,*" Zaarusha teased. "*Could you spare Adelina for a while so I could have my scales polished and talons clipped?*"

Ezaara swatted Zaarusha's neck. Although her fine clothes and fancy hair made her self-conscious, she knew she looked good.

Zaarusha spiraled upward, sending Ezaara images of a steep dive down to the feast. Heart pounding, Ezaara leaned forward, tightening her grip.

Zaarusha roared.

This was it.

The dragon queen chortled. "*I was only teasing. I wouldn't dive and mess up your hair.*"

Ezaara laughed as Zaarusha made a gentle descent.

§

Around Roberto, masters chatted quietly at the head table, which was laid with a creamy linen cloth edged in silver dragons. Murmurs from the crowd drifted on the evening air. Zaarusha roared, and everyone looked up, a hush falling over the crowd. Roberto squinted in the fading light. What were Zaarusha and Ezaara doing up so high? Showing off? Then he understood. Zaarusha was ensuring all eyes were upon Ezaara.

They landed and Ezaara sprang down, rubbing Zaarusha's eye ridge.

Roberto shook his head—the crowd was in awe again.

Ezaara's hair, tied in coils and loops, trailed fine silver and green threads that highlighted her eyes. A silver tunic and matching breeches hugged her curves, and she wore a healer's pouch at her waist. She glanced at him, cheeks flushed from flying.

A dizzying rush hit Roberto, as if he was standing on the edge of Fire Crag. Colors, like a blazing sunset, filled his mind, then they were gone.

Ezaara appeared not to notice. She smiled. "Good evening, Honored Dragon Masters. Thank you for calling this feast."

Roberto passed a glass of apple juice to Ezaara.

Lars raised his arms before the crowd. "We welcome Ezaara, Honored Rider." He turned to her, voice booming, "Enjoy tonight's feast as a token of our respect. On the morrow, you'll commence training for your duties as Queen's Rider. I propose a toast in your honor."

Everyone held their glasses high. "To the Queen's Rider." Their voices echoed off the mountainsides. The crowd drank, then whistled and cheered as Ezaara drained her glass. Roberto gestured for Ezaara to step forward.

"Me?" she replied, wide-eyed.

She obviously wasn't used to feast etiquette. "Of course. You need to reply to Lars' welcome."

She faced the folk. "Good people of Dragons' Hold, I'm honored at your trust. I hope to keep it, and to come to know each of you well. Thank you for preparing this feast in honor of Zaarusha, Queen of Dragons' Realm."

Zaarusha roared at the applause from the crowd.

Ezaara turned back to him. "Was that all right?" she whispered.

Her response? It was a bit short, not very formal, but straight from her heart, and gave honor to Zaarusha. Folk loved it, but that would only get her so far. Roberto nodded. "It was fine, much better than you giggling through your vows today. As Queen's Rider, you'll need more decorum."

"At least I didn't forget my words," she hissed.

It's not as if he had to swear in a new Queen's Rider every week. Anyone would've forgotten a word or two. He couldn't expect a girl from Lush Valley to understand that, but a Queen's Rider should. He guided her to a seat between him and Lars, and refilled her glass with apple juice.

"To a new era," Lars announced, "and Ezaara's successful training."

Everyone raised their glasses again, then helped themselves to food.

Erob's fish had ruined his appetite, so Roberto only put melon and sweet potato on his own plate.

Ezaara was staring at the laden platters, eyes as wide as a newborn dragonet's. Coming from Lush Valley, she'd probably never seen such a feast. She helped herself to some olives, sweet potato and fish and they made small talk.

Lars put a hand on Roberto's shoulder. "You did a good job this afternoon and last night, especially with only a short time to memorize the formal proceedings."

"Thank you, Lars. I'm happy to serve the council and my queen." Well, apart from serving with his mental gifts, but he wasn't about to admit that his strength was his biggest challenge.

"Zens' reach is growing, Roberto. You must train the Queen's Rider thoroughly, but quickly. We don't have the luxury of time."

"I'll do my best, Lars. We'll have to see what else she's capable of."

"I know you'll do a good job."

When Roberto turned back, Ezaara was leaving the dais.

He frowned. The Queen's Rider, abandoning the head table? Unheard of.

Queen's Rider

Ezaara popped a tiny purplish-black fruit in her mouth. So, Roberto hadn't liked her laughing that afternoon? He was so moody—he could go ride a dragon, for all she cared. She swallowed, but the fruit left a bitter aftertaste, like vinegar. Below the dais, hundreds of people were eating and chatting. She'd much rather sit down with them, than be up here on show.

"Do you like the olives?" Roberto asked, leaning toward her. "We grow them in Naobia."

So, he was being friendly again, was he? "I've never had this fruit before. What did you call it?"

"An olive. Fruit?" He laughed. "They do grow on trees, but we pickle them in vinegar, so they're savory, you see, not sweet."

"Oh." She felt so ignorant and stupid. Had he meant to sound like such a know-it-all?

He smirked. "Don't feel bad. Coming from Lush Valley, you've probably never seen them. You can't help being ignorant, having lived there."

Ezaara snapped her jaw shut. Conversation with him was as bitter as the olives. Everyone down below seemed to be having much more fun. The sooner she could get away, the better.

Ignoring Roberto and his arrogant comments, Ezaara examined the myriad of cutlery beside her plate. This place was dragon-crazy—even the dessert spoons had dragons on them. Luckily, Adelina had told her which cutlery to use for what. Picking up her two-pronged fork with a dragon's tail wound around the silver stem, she nibbled some sweet potato, careful not to drop any on her lovely silver tunic.

Roberto turned away to talk to Lars.

Now was her chance.

Ezaara took her plate and headed across the dais, down the stairs. She glanced back and caught Roberto's disapproving stare, then lost her footing. Her food went flying and she shrieked, landing in a heap, pain shooting through her ankle.

The babble of conversation ground to a stop.

Her cheeks burned. Great. That would impress everyone—the new Queen's Rider, smeared in sweet potato with a busted ankle. People were staring, some concerned, others smothering smiles.

"What do you expect?" a woman murmured. "She's from Lush Valley."

Someone snickered. A few more joined in.

Right, enough was enough. She may be from Lush Valley, but she wasn't deaf. "It's all right, everyone, I'm fine," Ezaara called. "Go back to your dinner and I'll collect mine." She plucked sweet potato and fish off her tunic, putting it back onto her plate.

Scattered laughter broke out. People resumed eating. At least they weren't staring anymore.

Zaarusha melded. *"You're injured. Do you need me to fly you home?"*

"No, my ankle's not that sore. I'll stay until the feast's over."

"Very well, but take it easy."

A blond man, about her age, rushed over. "Honored Queen's Rider, I'm the master healer's son, Simeon. My mother, Fleur, sent me to assist you."

No, not in front of everyone. "I'm fine, thanks. I'll be on my feet in a moment." Ezaara brushed the rest of the food off her tunic. The silver fabric was ruined, stained with dull spots of fish oil. As she clambered to her feet, another spike of pain lanced through her ankle. Oh gods, she couldn't put any weight on it.

Simeon gave her a lopsided smile, offering her his arm. "You need to sit down." Helping her to the nearest table, he asked people to move so she could have a seat. He put her plate of grass-speckled food on the table. "I'll be back in a moment with some salve."

He disappeared before Ezaara could tell him not to bother.

A girl passed a cup of apple juice to her. "Hi, I'm Gret. It's a shame you slipped. Reminds me of the time I fell in a puddle during my sword assessment." She flicked her long brown braids over her shoulders.

Ezaara pushed the food around on her plate with her fork, a plain one without dragons on it—so the special cutlery was only for those at the head table. "Did you fail your sword assessment, Gret?"

"My backside was soggy, but I passed, so it worked out in the end. How are you with a sword?"

Ezaara sighed. "Better than I am with stairs, fortunately, but nowhere near as good as my brother."

Another girl laughed, making her blonde curls bounce. "I'm Sofia. If you need the latest news, come see me."

"Gossip, more like," a blond boy said, taking a bite of bread.

Sofia elbowed him. "Just because I keep up with what's going on, doesn't mean it's gossip, Mathias."

Mathias raised an eyebrow at Sofia, then turned to Ezaara. "Welcome to Dragons' Hold."

Sofia leaned in. "Tell us, what's Lush Valley like?"

Ezaara shrugged. "I've never lived anywhere else."

"Is it true dragons are outlawed there?" Sofia practically held her breath.

How could she admit she'd never been sure if dragons existed?

"Come on, Sofia, you can't believe everything you hear. You also thought Naobia had never had rain. I'm never going to let you live that down." He laughed, dark eyes twinkling against his olive skin, black curls gleaming. From what Roberto had said, he was Naobian too. "I'm Rocco," he said. "You'll get used to Sofia's questions."

"We all had to," said another boy, spearing a piece of fish on his fork. "I'm Henry."

The last of the group moved like a lethal predator around the table toward her. Huge, he extended his well-muscled arm. "I'm Alban." His eyes were gray, flinty. "Welcome," he said, although his stance was anything but welcoming. "You'll be training with us."

Thankfully he'd be on her side in a battle, not fighting against her. Swallowing, Ezaara shook his hand. "Nice to meet you, Alban."

Simeon appeared at her shoulder. "Let's look at your ankle." His amber eyes were soft in the torchlight.

"I'm fine, thank you. Really. It's only a sprain."

"Fine is why you're limping, right?" He unlaced her boot and eased it off.

Ezaara had to grit her teeth to stop herself from groaning out loud. What a fantastic impression she must be making.

"I hope you don't mind me helping you." Flashing his lopsided smile again, Simeon gently propped her foot on an upturned pail. He uncorked a small pot of salve. An arid scent wafted from it.

No way was she having that stinking stuff on her ankle. Ma's salve smelled much better and worked wonders. She'd use that.

Before Ezaara could say anything, Roberto appeared behind Simeon, his voice slicing through the conversation. "I'll take care of the Queen's Rider. Go and enjoy your meal."

"It's no problem, *Master* Roberto." Simeon leveled a challenging gaze at him. "I'm happy to assist."

From the top table, Lars beckoned Roberto.

"Oh dear, duty calls," muttered Simeon.

"Watch your step, Simeon," Roberto threatened. He returned to the top table, boots thunking on the dais.

Irritable was an understatement. That man was downright hostile. "What was that about?" Ezaara asked Simeon.

"I don't know—he's always had a grudge against me." Simeon shrugged. "Don't worry, I'm used to it."

Sofia leaned over the table. "He can be very rude. They say Master Roberto was once—"

"Sofia." Gret gave an exasperated frown. "Ezaara can form her own opinions."

A ripple ran through the crowd as Roberto held his glass high and proposed a toast to Queen Zaarusha. Simeon passed Ezaara her glass, and she nodded as the crowd toasted her dragon's longevity and wisdom.

Glancing down, Gret said, "Wow, your ankle's the size of an apple."

"It looks tender," remarked Sofia.

"It's nothing." Ezaara managed a smile. "I'll be fine."

"Not without piaua juice, you won't," Sofia said, gesturing at Ezaara's healer's pouch. "But then you'd know that."

No decent healer would use *precious piaua* for a twisted ankle. "This is nothing, really."

Opening her healer's pouch, Ezaara extracted a strip of cloth and passed it to Simeon. "Could you please wet this for me?"

"Of course. Use plenty of my salve before you bind it. It will help." Simeon went off to get some water.

Wincing, she rubbed Ma's healing salve into her aching flesh, biting back another groan. She stowed it in her pouch and took the cork off Simeon's stinking salve, letting the harsh aroma mask the smell of Ma's.

Sofia's keen eyes missed nothing, so Ezaara held a finger to her lips and winked.

Grinning, Sofia murmured, "Wouldn't say a word."

Mathias rolled his eyes. "As if."

Simeon returned. "I'm glad you used my salve. That'll help."

Sofia giggled.

Simeon shot Sofia a puzzled glance as he bound the damp bandage around Ezaara's ankle. The coolness of the wet fabric was soothing. Moments later, he was proffering a heavily-laden plate. "You must be hungry, Ezaara. They say you arrived from Lush Valley late last night. That's a long way to travel."

In more ways than one. "That's so thoughtful, Simeon," Ezaara replied. "Thank you."

While she ate, everyone at the table chatted. They were courteous and witty, making her laugh, but although Ezaara thoroughly enjoyed Simeon's company, she felt hollow. No one here really knew her. They were only talking to her because she was Queen's Rider. If she'd failed the tests, it would've been a different story.

Ezaara turned to the top table. All of the other masters were there, but Roberto was gone. She scanned the crowd, but couldn't find him. She shrugged. Why should she care where he went?

Lars stepped down from the dais and perched on a stool before a giant harp. He plucked the strings, his gentle melody weaving its way through the crowd. As the music built, low-pitched notes rumbled through Ezaara like the roar of a dragon. Eyes closed in rapt concentration, Lars caressed the strings, increasing the intensity and pitch until a sweet harmony floated through the dark, making Ezaara yearn for dragon flight, the wild abandon, the sheer color, of winging through the skies.

Her heart soared. She *wanted* to be Zaarusha's rider, not a healer or a painter of scarves. This was her destiny.

The music came to an end, the last note vibrating through the night.

"Thrilling, isn't it?" Simeon whispered. "I've had a very pleasant evening, Honored Queen's Rider. Thank you for allowing me to keep you company."

It *had* been pleasant. "Thank you."

He laughed, touching her hand. "My pleasure, Ezaara." He smiled warmly. "Did you know my parents are masters on the council? As Queen's Rider, you'll soon be on the council too, so I'm sure we'll see much more of each other."

"That would be nice." It was good to be with someone friendly, instead of that arrogant …. Her gaze drifted to Master Roberto's chair. Where had he gone?

The soft note of a horn echoed from the shadows. People started clearing away the tables.

"Please take this and use it regularly." Simeon handed her the pot of his mother's smelly unguent, then helped Ezaara to stand, one arm around her shoulders. "Allow me to assist you home."

Roberto materialized from beyond the torchlight. "That won't be necessary," he snapped. "I'll take her home. Don't let me catch you hanging around the Queen's Rider again."

Ignoring Roberto, Simeon bowed. "Please, let me know if you need anything, my Queen's Rider." He stalked off into the dark.

Who was Roberto to say who could and couldn't walk her home? "Simeon was helping me. He only—"

Roberto stepped closer. "Are you all right?"

"Why wouldn't I be?"

"Simeon's not to be trusted."

She'd been on show since she'd arrived and she could do nothing right in his eyes. "At least *he's* friendly!" Ezaara hobbled away.

Roberto didn't get the hint. He fell into step and put his arm around her back to support her. "You need to be more careful."

"I'm nearly seventeen, and you're treating me like a littling," Ezaara snapped. She didn't dare admit that his support was easing the ache in her ankle.

Within moments, dragons' wings whooshed nearby. Zaarusha and Erob landed on the grass.

"Ezaara," Zaarusha crooned, *"are you all right?"*

"Yes, Zaarusha, I'm fine." Ezaara glared at Roberto. "Did you call them?"

"Erob can bring you home," said Zaarusha. *"You're in no condition to fly solo."*

"I don't want to fly with them."

"Roberto's going to be training you, so you should get to know him." The queen leaped into the sky, her wingbeats whispering through the dark.

Roberto scooped Ezaara up.

"Put me down. I can walk."

"It looks painful." Roberto replied, mint on his breath.

Not as painful as his comments about Lush Valley and her ignorance.

Carrying her over to Erob, he hoisted her onto the dragon's back. When he stepped back, there was sweet potato smeared on his shoulder.

"Oh, I'm sorry." Her cheeks flamed. "There must've been food on my tunic."

"As if that matters!" He laughed, swinging into the saddle.

"Gently," she sensed him think to his dragon, and they ascended skyward.

§

Lars raised his head. There it was again, a knock at the door. At this time of night? Careful not to wake Lydia, he nudged back the covers and pulled the heavy curtain across their sleeping quarters. He padded across the chilly stone in the dining cavern and opened the door.

"Tonio, come in."

The spymaster glanced back down the tunnel and shut the door, his sharp brown eyes flitting to their sleeping chamber. "Are we alone, Lars?"

Lars nodded and threw a log on the dying embers. "Lydia's fast asleep. Take a seat." They sat down. "What is it?"

"It's the Queen's Rider," Tonio said.

In the hearth, the log caught alight, and the fire spat.

So, this was about Ezaara. "Honestly? In the middle of the night?" Lars sighed. "It couldn't wait until morning?"

Tonio leaned forward, firelight flickering across the hard planes of his face. "I've been spymaster for thirty years. Something's off. I couldn't sleep."

Neither could he now. Lars sighed. "Look, I know it's been a long time since Zaarusha's last rider. Ezaara's young, inexperienced and needs training, but she can fly."

Tonio's eyes narrowed as he nodded in reply. "Yes, their stunt today was very impressive. But how do we know she's imprinted properly?"

"Well, Roberto says the bond is strong. That he's never seen one like it before."

"Convenient, isn't it?" There was nothing warm about Tonio's smile.

"What do you mean?"

"Come on, Lars. She's from Lush Valley, far from here. A superstitious place with no connection to dragons. We've never had riders from Lush Valley."

Where was this going? "Yes, we were all surprised."

"What if she's a fake? A traitor?"

Lars shook his head. "Impossible. Roberto has tested her. She's fine."

"Exactly." Tonio stabbed a finger in the air.

"Exactly what?"

"We only have Roberto's word."

"I trust him."

"I know. Others have made that mistake before, Lars."

"He's changed, Tonio, you should know that. As a council member, he's been impeccable." A memory popped to mind. Tonio had voted against Roberto becoming the master of mental faculties and imprinting. Lars gripped the arm of his chair.

RIDERS OF FIRE

Tonio was coiled, like a predator. "What if Roberto's been biding his time, waiting for an opportunity? What if she's a traitor too?" He leaped out of his seat, pacing. "What if Zaarusha's been given swayweed and Ezaara is a spy? It would be simple for Roberto to fake an imprinting test and give us a positive result. He's accomplished, good at what he does. I've never truly believed that he's turned his back on Zens."

"I trust Roberto. And Zaarusha." Lars stood. "With my life." Tonio had gone far enough. "You know if you come with a complaint, I need proof to take to the council, not hunches or gossip. And not at this hour."

The firelight cast shadows on the spymaster's clenched jaw. "Then I shall find you evidence. I'm sorry for interrupting your sleep." Tonio slipped out the door.

The log cracked and fell into the grate in a shower of sparks.

§

Roberto slid his knife under the wooden dragon's snout and smoothed the curve of the beast's neck. A few more shavings and he'd be done. He made small deft nicks in the wood, like scales, then held up his carving to examine it in the torchlight.

There, that was a good night's work. Better than tossing and turning.

He rubbed the loose shavings off his mother's cane, wincing as he remembered her using it in what should have been the prime of her life. Earlier tonight, the head of the cane had been broad and thick, before he'd shaped it into Zaarusha's likeness. He grunted. The dragon wasn't perfect, but it would do. Now it just needed oiling to bring out the hues of the wood.

Should he wait until morning? No, he was too restless to sleep, the colors of his brief mind-meld with Ezaara flashing into his head whenever he lay down. That, and the look on her face at Simeon's attention. He'd have to watch them. Roberto shook his head. Sometimes his talents were more trouble than they were worth. He longed for his littling days, swimming off the Naobian coast, fishing with his Pa, for life before—

No. He couldn't go there.

He laid the cane on his bed. He might as well oil it now. The walk to fetch oil would do him good. If he was quick, he could still catch a couple of hours' sleep.

The torches had burned low, casting more shadow than light, as Roberto walked along the tunnels to the craft halls. On a back shelf, among the woodworking tools, he found an earthen jar of walnut oil, and picked it up before heading back to his cavern.

Quiet footfalls echoed along the tunnel. It was nearly dawn. Who was sneaking around at this time of night? Roberto rounded a corner. A man was in the shadows of the corridor. Simeon? No, not Simeon. Someone with dark hair. Tonio, the spymaster, was emerging from Lars' cavern. Something dire must be going on for Tonio to be skulking around the halls at this time.

Tonio's eyes fell upon the jar Roberto was holding. He frowned as he passed, giving Roberto a curt nod.

"Morning," Roberto replied. Now was as good a time as any to tell Tonio what he suspected about Bruno and Fleur. "Tonio, do you have a moment?"

"Of course not," Tonio snapped. "It's the middle of the night. We should both be in bed." The spymaster strode off.

Prophecy

"Good morning, Ezaara."

Morning already? Groaning, Ezaara rolled over. Her ankle was throbbing.

"Sorry I woke you." Adelina set a breakfast tray on a table.

Ezaara struggled to sit up.

"Here, let me help you." Adelina raced over to the bed.

"I'm fine. Please. It's bad enough that I hurt myself and ruined my clothes last night. I don't want to be pitied or fussed over."

Adelina backed away. "I'd feel the same. Ready for breakfast? It's cinnamon and honey porridge, topped with fresh cream."

The aroma was incredible. Ezaara's mouth watered. "Soon." She flipped back her quilt and edged her injured leg off the bed. That hurt. She tried to stand, and grabbed the bedpost, wincing.

Understanding flashed across Adelina's face. "I need the latrine too. Shall we go together?"

"Great Queen's Rider I am. Can't even pee on my own."

Adelina smiled. "You've flown the first loop in years. You can't let a twisted ankle beat you."

"I'm just no good at any of this. In fact, I'm not good at much." Ezaara leaned on Adelina. "Back home, my brother was better than me at most things."

Adelina rolled her eyes. "I know the feeling. Mine's like that too."

"You have a brother?"

"Only one, thank a nest full of dragon's eggs! But he's not too bad."

"Mine's all right most of the time too." She'd broken her promise to him. What had Tomaaz made of her disappearing without a word?

Every step was agony, but Ezaara forced a smile and nodded at people in the tunnels. It took forever to get back to her den, and by then, she was starving.

Roberto was slumped in one of her chairs, dozing. Dark lashes swept his olive skin above pronounced cheek bones. Below his left eye was a tiny scar shaped like a crescent moon. Stubble edged his jaw. Last night, without him speaking, she'd heard him telling Erob to be gentle as they'd flown home—

strange—she must've heard his thoughts, or Erob's. Asleep, he looked peaceful. Younger.

Adelina helped Ezaara into bed, then slugged Roberto on the shoulder. "Hey, sleepyhead, wake up."

He rubbed his eyes. "I didn't realize I'd dropped off."

What? The master of mental faculties and imprinting hadn't frosted Adelina for punching him? Not like him at all.

Hands on hips, Adelina replied, "You've been up all night again, haven't you?"

Ezaara cringed. She was speaking like that to a master?

"I couldn't sleep." He ran a hand through his hair, then spotted Ezaara and stiffened, a cool mask slipping over his face. "Good morning, Ezaara, Honored Rider of Queen Zaarusha."

"I can't believe you're visiting before she's eaten," Adelina complained. "She's injured, exhausted and needs a break." She picked up the bowl of porridge and walked toward the bed.

"Look out," Roberto called.

Adelina tripped over a long stick leaning against his chair. The tray flew out of her hands. The bowl smashed, and porridge splattered over the floor. She glared at Roberto. "Who put that there? You?"

He jumped to his feet, picking up the largest pottery shards. "Sorry."

Adelina waved at the mess on the floor. "Now look what you've made me do!" Suddenly she laughed. "Between me and Ezaara, we're pretty good at throwing food. I'll grab a cloth and some more breakfast."

Roberto called, "No, I'll get—" but Adelina disappeared before he could finish. He picked up the tray, placing the shards on it, then turned and got the stick. Stepping over splatters of porridge and cream, he handed it to Ezaara. "Sorry about the mess," he said. "I came to bring you this."

It was a cane. The head was wrapped in soft leather. "For me?"

He nodded, onyx eyes scanning her face. "Go on, unwrap it."

Carved into the handle was a likeness of Zaarusha with a girl on her back. "Is this rider me?"

"It is." His voice softened. "Do you like it?"

"Like it? It's amazing. Look, Zaarusha has tiny scales." She didn't dare tell him the rider was much too pretty to be her. "Why did you make it?"

"I thought a cane would help you get around."

After her fiasco last night, she needed some dignity—a cane would help. Ezaara traced Zaarusha's snout and ran her finger down the spinal ridges.

Roberto shrugged. "Besides, I couldn't sleep, so I needed to do something." He took her hand and placed it over the girl's back. His palm was warm. "This is the smoothest place to hold, otherwise the spinal ridges will dig into your palm. If you use the cane on your good side, not the injured side, it'll take the weight off your sore ankle. Here, try it."

Ezaara got out of bed, leaned on the cane and took a couple of halting steps, careful not to go near the porridge. It was slow, but she could get around on her own. She sat back on her bed. The carving was exquisite, the detail so perfect. He'd made a masterpiece, to save her pride. "Thank you, this must've taken you ages."

He ducked his head, suddenly looking shy. It suited him. "I'm glad you like it."

"Here you go," called Adelina from the doorway. She had a new tray in her hands and a pail and some cloths slung over her arm.

Roberto took a cloth and started cleaning up the spilled food and broken pottery.

Adelina brought Ezaara's breakfast over. "I'm sorry, there wasn't any more porridge left, so I've brought you some fresh bread and fruit. That should—" She stopped, staring at the cane. Spinning, Adelina faced Roberto. "Is that Ma's walking stick?"

Roberto's boot crunched on a shard. His head snapped up.

Adelina stared at him, tension flickering in her gaze.

Ma's walking stick? Adelina's hair was dark, like Roberto's. They had the same dark eyes. His nose was long and straight, while she had a cute snub nose, but they both had that smooth olive skin—Roberto was Adelina's annoying elder brother.

She was the little girl in his memory, crouched, trembling, behind the door with him.

"Yes, it's Ma's old stick," he said. "Our Queen's Rider is in need, Adelina." He finished wiping up the floor, and put the last of the mess in the pail.

"I know *that*, dummy." She took the cane from Ezaara. "Wow, look at that handle." She grinned and slugged Roberto again. "I was right, you didn't sleep last night, did you?"

Ignoring Adelina, Roberto bowed. "Honored Queen's Rider, your training commences today. I'll see you in imprinting class after you've finished your breakfast. We'll be in the orchard. If you need assistance to get there, Zaarusha should let Erob know." He nodded tersely, picked up the pail of porridge and shards, and left.

Adelina laughed. "He's crazy. Imagine him carving all night."

"You don't mind me having your Ma's cane?"

Unease flashed across Adelina's face. "It's fine. She doesn't need it anymore."

Adelina didn't look fine. "Are you sure? I mean, I can always find another stick." Ezaara touched the handle. Not one as beautiful as this. "How did your Ma hurt her leg?"

Adelina's face shuttered. "It's complicated."

"Does she live here, at Dragons' Hold?"

Her features tightened. "No, Roberto and I came here alone, five years ago. I was ten and he was fourteen." Adelina stared off into the distance, frowning.

Ezaara ate in silence. She'd obviously touched a raw nerve. Adelina looked more like her brother with that dark expression on her face—not that he'd been brooding this morning.

Reaching for her cane, Ezaara made her way across the room.

Adelina passed her some riders' garb. "The jerkin should be fine, but it's going to be tough to get these breeches on over that ankle. What about a skirt?"

Ezaara shook her head. That'd make her stand out even more. "If you don't mind helping me, we could do battle with the breeches."

"Sure." Adelina smiled, looking more like her old self again.

When she was dressed, Ezaara hobbled out to Zaarusha, using her cane. Zaarusha's scales stretched high above her like a multi-faceted jewel glimmering in the sun. How was she ever going to get on her dragon with this rotten ankle?

I'm sure we can manage. Zaarusha crooned, crouching down.

Ezaara tried to climb, but pain shot through her ankle. She grimaced. The last thing she wanted to do was call Erob. She had to prove she could do something.

"Try this." Adelina boosted Ezaara onto the dragon's back. "You'll manage if you always get on this side so your injured leg gets dragged up behind you." Adelina passed up her cane.

"Thanks."

Zaarusha stood, jostling her ankle. *Sorry.* She leaped off the ledge, and they were airborne.

Relief whooshed out of Ezaara. She was riding on her own again—like a true Queen's Rider.

"What do you mean, 'like a true Queen's Rider'? You are *the* true Queen's Rider. Don't you forget it."

"I keep making so many mistakes."

"Don't be so hard on yourself. You can't learn everything in a day."

They spiraled down toward the orchard. Oh, shards! How was she going to dismount?

§

Roberto's students were clustered in the grass under the plum trees, heads bent as they discussed their parents' imprinting stories, trying to find common aspects. With students of all ages, it was a challenging class, often involving lively discussion.

At the swish of wings, Roberto turned from his students. Zaarusha and Ezaara were arriving. Ezaara's ankle mustn't be that bad if she'd managed to get onto her dragon alone. He was a fool for staying up all night, crafting a cane for that girl. And for risking strife with his sister. He shrugged. It wasn't as if Ma needed her cane anymore.

Zaarusha landed on the grass between the plum trees with a soft whump. Ezaara winced. So, her ankle was hurting. He *had* been a fool—fooled by her bravado.

The dragon queen strolled closer to the class.

The students' whispers were like leaves in the breeze.

"Quiet, please," Roberto said. "Show proper respect to the Queen's Rider." How was Ezaara going to dismount?

Zaarusha lay on the grass. Ezaara swung a leg over the dragon's back, then rolled onto her belly and held onto Zaarusha's spinal ridge with one hand, letting her body slide down the dragon's side until she was fully extended. Her cane was gripped in her other hand.

No, not with a swollen ankle. Roberto wanted to drop his history text, race over and catch her, but that wouldn't do, not with everyone watching. He set his book aside and strolled over. Of course, before he got there, Ezaara let go. She landed heavily on her good leg, letting out an agonized grunt. Facing away from them, Ezaara leaned against Zaarusha's side. She thrust her cane into the ground, her back rising and falling rapidly.

Ouch. He approached cautiously. "My Honored Queen's Rider, are you hurt?" he asked softly.

"I'm fine," she hissed, not turning around. "Continue with your class. I'll be there in a moment."

"As you wish." It was all he could do not to reach out and help her. If only the foolish girl had called for Erob. Smaller than Zaarusha, he was much easier to ride. Roberto strode back to the class. "I want the names of five of the realm's most important dragon riders and their dragons."

"Erob and Roberto," Kierion called.

"Enough flattery, Kierion," Roberto said. "I mean the important riders to the realm, not to you passing this class."

His students laughed.

"Lars and Singlar."

Roberto nodded. "That's more like it."

"Zaarusha and Anakisha, the last Queen's Rider."

"But now it's Ezaara and Zaarusha." The students' heads turned as they watched Ezaara hobble over. Behind her, Zaarusha flew off.

"Please welcome our Honored Queen's Rider," Roberto said.

Roberto observed Ezaara as his students greeted her. She was hurt, all right. Worse than this morning. So headstrong and stubborn. She was Queen's Rider, for the Egg's sake, and tharuks were attacking. War was coming soon. She had to be fit to lead them.

Unable to sit on the grass, Ezaara leaned her back against a tree, taking the weight off her injured leg. She wouldn't last long like that, and it was only early. He should have had Erob bring a stool for her.

"Come on," Roberto asked, distracting the class from staring at the new Queen's Rider, "two more examples of the realm's most important dragon riders and their dragons."

"King Syan and Yanir," Mathias called.

"Master Tonio and Antonika?" Sofia said.

"Yes, our spymaster is very important to the safety of Dragons' Realm," Roberto said. "Could someone explain the naming convention between dragons and riders?" Coming from Lush Valley, Ezaara had probably never heard of it.

Mathias answered. "The dragon's and rider's names share a common syllable. My sister's dragon took on a new name when they bonded."

"Ma renamed my brother after a dragon that was seeking a rider, then one day they imprinted."

Roberto frowned. Had Ezaara's parents deliberately named her so she had a syllable in common with Zaarusha? "It's not only names we share with our dragons, but some of their characteristics," he said. "Can you give me some examples, please?"

Kierion raised his hand. "You asked about characteristics, sir. Over years, the rider's eye color changes to match the eyes of their dragon."

"So, Kierion would lose his pretty eyes if he became a rider?" Sofia called.

Kierion rolled his ocean-gray eyes, flecked with blue, and mock-groaned. "Not much chance of me being a rider."

Always playing pranks and getting into trouble, Kierion hadn't been selected by the council as a trainee rider.

"Enough," said Roberto. "Any other characteristics that you know of?"

Leah raised her hand. Unusual. She was usually too shy to answer. "Sir, they say the spymaster has excellent hearing from his dragon."

"Too true." Roberto winked. "Be careful; he's listening right now. They say even these plum trees work for him."

Laughter rippled through the class.

"Anything else?"

"Prophecy?"

It was more a question than answer. Not surprising, given the lack of accurate prophecy at Dragons' Hold nowadays. Roberto had a theory on that, but he needed evidence. Keeping an eye on Ezaara, he continued. "Our dragons' mental or emotional talents are passed to us. This can happen at imprinting or over time as we bond more deeply. Strengths of the rider can also pass to the dragon."

A student stretched his hand high.

"Yes?"

"What strengths have you passed to Erob?" asked the tousled-haired lad.

There was no way he'd be telling them about his particular strengths. "Fishing."

"Perhaps you could teach us to fish, too, instead of this stuff," Kierion called.

The class laughed.

"Now, tell us what a rider of fire is."

"That's easy," Kierion blurted. "Riders of fire can harness dragon energy to use their talents."

"Exactly. We'll talk more about that next lesson." Roberto glanced at Ezaara. Her face was pale.

Erob, in the grass under some nearby trees, broke through his thoughts, *"Zaarusha is requesting the Queen's Rider."*

"We'll be there right away," Roberto melded back. Good—the perfect excuse to get Ezaara out of class.

§

"Ezaara, wake up."

"Zaarusha, is that you?"

No answer. The torch was low. It must be late. Leaning on her stick, Ezaara made her way out to Zaarusha's den, but the queen wasn't there.

"Ezaara." There it was again—deep, melodious and unfamiliar. "*Come outside.*"

She hobbled to the mouth of the den. The valley was peaceful, shrouded in darkness, moonlight catching on the tips of the Alps.

"*Look up.*"

A bronze dragon was circling down toward Zaarusha's den.

"*I saw you at my imprinting test,*" she melded. "*Who are you?*"

"*Handel is my name.*" His talons clattered on the rock, and he crouched, holding out his leg. "*Climb up.*"

Ezaara hesitated.

"*Your father, Hans, was my rider.*"

Pa's dragon. Wow. "Hans, Hand*el*! I should've guessed you were my father's dragon."

"*I am. Hans is still my rider—or will be when he returns. Climb on, there's someone you need to meet.*"

"Pa is returning?"

"*Some day.*" Handel supported Ezaara with his tail as she clambered up his leg and settled herself between his spinal ridges. Tensing his enormous haunches, he leaped into the air. The cool night nipped at Ezaara's bare legs as they climbed up the mountainside to a plateau.

Moonlight shimmered on the snowy mountain face. No, wait, what was that? The shimmer was coming closer. Ezaara sucked in her breath as a silvery shape materialized from the gloom. Moonlight played on silver scales, making them wink like stars.

"Did you know your father was the master of prophecy?" Handel asked.

"No."

"And your mother was master healer." The silver dragon's voice tinkled like a bell in a breeze. The beast stretched her neck out and nudged Ezaara's shoulder with her snout. "*I am Liesar.*"

The dragon closed her turquoise eyes—the same shade as her mother's—as Ezaara scratched her eye ridges. *Lies*ar, Marlies. "You're Ma's dragon."

"No, she's my rider. Dragons are never owned by humans."

"Of course." No one could ever own such wondrous creatures. The wind picked up, making Ezaara shiver.

"Tell her why she's here," Handel said.

"I must share a memory of your mother's."

A vision rushed through Ezaara's mind. She was astride Liesar in the middle of the night, Pa's arms around her middle. The vicious peaks of Dragon's Teeth rushed past beneath them, then they were swallowed by the night sky.

"Years ago, your mother accidentally killed one of Zaarusha's dragonets, so your parents fled from Dragons' Hold."

A transparent golden egg loomed before her, with a purple dragonet floating in it, limbs slack and wings drooping—so perfect, she could see its tiny scales and talons. A wave of sorrow washed through Ezaara, leaving her wrung out and hollow. Bitter wind sliced through her clothing. She trembled, tears stinging her cheeks.

"You feel your mother's sorrow at killing the dragonet, and at losing us."

The vision changed. Ma and Pa, years younger, were hugging Liesar's neck, faces pinched with anxiety as they parted. Ezaara's chest grew tight.

"You're feeling your mother's emotions," Liesar said. "That's the last time I saw them. It took Zaarusha years to understand that the dragonet gave its life willingly to bless your mother with fertility."

Handel melded. "Usually a rider can only meld with their dragon, but you can meld with other dragons. This was one of the dying royal dragonet's gifts to you."

"I never wanted a dragonet to die for me. Will Tomaaz, my twin brother, have this gift too?"

"You have a twin? Zaarusha hasn't mentioned him." Handel's tail twitched.

Liesar answered, "We'll have to seek him out. Perhaps he also has talents."

Handel turned his head, his green eyes, the same shade as Pa's, drilling through Ezaara. "You hold the key to the future of Dragons' Realm."

The key? She hadn't met a dragon until a week ago.

"Handel and I are leaving tonight to collect your father." Liesar tilted her head. "We'll collect your brother too."

"So, I'll see my family? Here?" Ezaara couldn't help grinning.

"Marlies is elsewhere," said Liesar.

"She has to find Zaarusha's son." Handel's voice was grave. "Once she's proven her loyalty, she may return."

Ezaara took a deep breath. "Is she in danger?"

"*Not yet,*" Liesar replied. That didn't sound promising. "*Handel, we must leave. I'll meet you near the hunting grounds.*" With a flip of her wings, Liesar soared away.

Handel was airborne in moments. Ezaara hugged his spinal ridge as dizzying visions flashed before her.

She saw herself in the main cavern the night she'd arrived, hair unkempt and face streaked with dirt. Roberto, lip curled in disdain, placed his hands at her temples. She collapsed, and he caught her, a rare softness flashing across his features.

A surge of energy flowed through Ezaara as more images from Handel flitted through her head: tharuks killing and maiming people; dragons blasting their enemies with fire; her falling and Zaarusha diving to save her; Tomaaz looking worn and sick; Ma unconscious, battered and bruised; Roberto, face twisted with hate, lunging at her, making her heart thud and breath catch in her throat.

"Handel. Stop!" she screamed.

The images subsided.

"What was that?"

"*I'm sorry, I didn't mean to scare you. Usually ancient dragon magic only lets me share prophecies with my rider, or with one whom it concerns. This rush of visions came, unbidden. Perhaps it's because you're the Queen's Rider and the fate of our nation hangs on your actions and Zaarusha's.*"

Hopefully these prophecies weren't fate. Tomaaz had looked gaunt and thin. Ma was obviously dying. And with the way Roberto had looked, who'd need enemies?

"*The future can change, depending on people's decisions. When I know more, I'll let you know. In the meantime, don't tell anyone that you can meld with any dragon.*" Handel clattered down on the mouth of Zaarusha's den. "*Be careful, my Queen's Rider.*"

Ezaara slid down his side. After seeing his visions, how could she know who to trust?

Knife's Edge

Ezaara leaned heavily on her cane. "How much further to the mess cavern?"

"Just around this corner." Adelina paused. "Wait, I've got something in my boot." She bent and undid her laces.

Ezaara suppressed a smile. "Adelina, I know there's nothing in your boot. They're laced too tightly for anything to get in. You're making excuses again to spare my ankle. Yesterday, when you said you needed the latrine, you forgot to go."

Adelina's cheeks flushed. "I— um." She grinned. "All right, I'm a lousy actor, but you need a rest. You have to impress the masters and the other riders."

Ezaara grimaced. "Too late for that, isn't it? Everyone saw me fall flat on my backside at the feast."

"They saw you fly a loop, too. Don't forget that."

"Come on, let's get my next blundering entrance over with."

Adelina giggled.

Ezaara smoothed her riding jerkin with her free hand, and they walked around the corner.

The mess cavern was a babbling hubbub of voices, more crowded than Lush Valley's square on market day. Ezaara recognized some of the masters, seated among riders at jam-packed tables. Her stomach grumbled as she helped herself to freshly-baked bread and spicy soup.

A woman rushed over, Simeon at her heels. Wisps of her blonde hair were haloed in light streaming from holes in the cavern walls. Simeon introduced her. "Ezaara, this is my mother, Master Healer, Fleur."

Ma's old role.

Fleur bowed. "My Queen's Rider, how's your ankle?"

"It's all right," Ezaara replied. The last thing she wanted was more fuss.

"I'm sure it's fine." Simeon winked behind his mother's back. At least he understood.

Fleur patted Ezaara's arm. "Simeon can pop by later to check you have everything you need. He often helps me in the infirmary and knows how to treat sprains."

Adelina gave Fleur an overly-effusive smile. "That won't be necessary. The Queen's Rider's ankle will be better in no time." She turned her back on Fleur and Simeon, gesturing to a nearby table. "Why don't you get a seat, Ezaara, and I'll bring your lunch."

"Please, let me help you." Simeon took Ezaara's arm.

It was a lovely gesture. "Thanks, but I can manage. This cane does the trick."

His eyes flicked over the carving. "Surely the help of a friend is better than an old stick?"

Her cane was hardly an old stick—it was a beautiful gift. Before she could respond, murmurs reached her over the clatter of cutlery.

"Twisted her ankle, silly thing …"

"She's too naive, too weak …"

Ezaara lifted her chin, pretending not to hear. So much for Adelina's theory—flying a loop hadn't impressed anyone for long. One fall, and it was forgotten.

As she sat, a tinkling peal cut through the din. Master Lars was shaking a bell. Everyone quieted, and Lars stood. "I'd like to welcome Ezaara, Honored Rider of Queen Zaarusha. She started classes today and will soon be engaged in full training. I trust you'll welcome and befriend her, and I wish everyone a pleasant meal."

Most of the riders applauded. A few snickered. Across the cavern, Roberto was scowling. She'd never impress him.

Simeon was attentive during lunch, but Adelina was as bristly as a boar, eating in silence. Soon Ezaara was laughing at Simeon's anecdotes about living among dragon riders.

"So, you're not a rider yet?" she asked.

"No, but I'll imprint soon enough. My parents are both riders, so it'll happen." He shredded a bread roll, scattering crumbs on the table. "Gives me more time to train before I have to fight tharuks face-to-face."

She shuddered, remembering the battle in the Western Pass. She'd never be good enough to lead an army of dragons and riders against tharuk troops.

Simeon's eyes met hers. "I'd love to fight tharuks beside you."

Ezaara's cheeks grew warm. She broke away from his gaze.

"Enough flirting for today, Ezaara," Zaarusha melded. *"I'm waiting."*

"Unfair!" she melded back. *"I'm not the one flirting. He is."*

"But you are enjoying it."

RIDERS OF FIRE

Adelina snatched up Ezaara's empty bowl. "You won't be fighting until you imprint, Simeon. Your dreams of glory will have to wait. My Honored Queen's Rider, I believe we need to get to knife throwing practice."

§

Ezaara was sitting with Simeon again, laughing at his smarmy jokes. Although she wasn't in immediate danger, Roberto had the irrational desire to wipe the smile off Simeon's face with his fist.

While Adelina was clearing the bowls, Roberto stepped into the space beside Ezaara's seat. "My Honored Queen's Rider." He felt stiff, stilted, as if he had a broomstick strapped to his back. "Please allow me to accompany you to knife throwing."

He led her away without offering her his arm. He wouldn't make her look weak in front of everyone, the way Simeon had. He swept out of the door, a little too fast, just to prove she could manage on her own. "Erob says Zaarusha is—"

"On the ledge," Ezaara interrupted. "She already told me."

"Of course." Shards, that was silly of him.

Soon they were airborne, Ezaara seated in front of him. The scent of her hair reminded him of dandelions; of summer days outdoors, running in the paddocks with his dog, Razo—before his father had changed. He shook his head to jolt his bad memories away as they descended to the knife-throwing range.

Roberto jumped down and helped Ezaara out of the saddle.

"I could've dismounted on my own," she snapped, eyes blazing.

"Of course," he replied, keeping his voice cool. "Good luck for your assessment. I'll wait here and fly you back to your quarters afterward."

"No, thank you." Her pretty green eyes were hostile. "I'll call Zaarusha when I'm done." She stalked away. With her sore ankle it wasn't impressive, but she was determined, he'd give her that.

Trying not to smile, Roberto placed his hand on Zaarusha's head.

I have to see Singlar and Lars. Stay, please, Roberto, the dragon queen said. *Watching her knife-throwing will help you assess her.*

"As you wish," he replied. Good. He was curious to see how Ezaara would do.

§

How dare Roberto manhandle her? And keep maneuvering her out of conversations with Simeon. He might be in charge of training her, but he had no right to control her friendships. Ezaara stalked away—although it was difficult to look indignant while negotiating uneven terrain with a cane. Soon she was near the other trainee riders. Gret, Sofia, Alban, Rocco and Mathias greeted her.

"Are you sure your ankle's up to this?" Derek, Master of Training, asked, shaking her free hand. Behind him, his dragon was shooting flame, blazing a line across the grass.

"I'm fine." Ezaara lied, dropping her cane in the grass. "See, no problem." Ankle throbbing, she tried not to grimace as she hobbled to the line of charred grass.

As the trainees lined up, knives in hand, Simeon rushed out of the trees, up to the line, out of breath. How had he gotten here so fast without a dragon? He winked at her and mouthed, "Good luck."

It was nice of him to support her.

"Have you done much knife throwing before?" Master Derek asked. When Ezaara shook her head, he passed Ezaara a knife and said, "Sofia, please demonstrate."

Sofia held up her blade.

Ezaara copied, but her fingers slipped, buttery with sweat. She wiped her hand on her breeches.

Sofia shot her a sidelong glance. "Hold your knife like you'd grip a hammer."

Adjusting her grip, Ezaara bent her elbow and raised the blade.

"That's better." Sofia flicked her forearm and her knife sailed across the field into a wooden target—a bullseye.

Other knives thunked into targets too, but Ezaara's knife glanced off at an angle, flying onto the grass. It wasn't even embedded in the earth. She stifled a groan. Everyone's eyes were on her.

"Keep your wrist in line with your arm or your knife will veer off. See, like this." Sofia hurled a knife into the target, blonde curls bouncing. Flashing a smile, she passed Ezaara another blade. "Here, try this one. It's my lucky blade."

"All right, wrist in line." Ezaara pulled her arm up and back, poised to throw Sofia's lucky blade.

"Kill the Queen's Rider," a dragon roared. As black as coal, with burning red embers for eyes, it flew straight at her. A wall of flame blasted out of its enormous maw, engulfing her, searing her skin.

Ezaara flung the knife at the dragon. Her ears filled with crackling fire, flames roaring at her. The scent of charred flesh stung her nostrils.

Dry retching, Ezaara lurched and collided with something solid.

The dragon disappeared. So did the heat and pain.

Her skin wasn't burned. She was sprawled on top of Sofia on the ground. The dragon had only been a vision, overpowering, but not real. But she'd smelled burning flesh ….

Sofia was screaming. A knife was sticking out of her thigh. Blood pulsed down her breeches.

She'd stabbed Sofia.

"No!" Ezaara yelled. Easing the blade from Sofia's leg, she ripped Sofia's breeches open and pressed her hands around the gash, applying pressure. "I—I'm sorry, Sofia." She reached for her healer's pouch, so she could stitch the wound. It wasn't there. She'd left it by her bed.

Roberto raced over. "What happened?" Others flocked around them.

"I—I was distracted." Ezaara's hands were covered in Sofia's blood.

Sofia grunted through gritted teeth. "It was an accident. I saw you stagger, like someone pushed you."

"But nobody did." Master Derek frowned. "And you retched. Are you sick?"

"I—uh ... don't know." Ezaara ripped a strip from Sofia's breeches. How could she explain where that fiery vision had come from? It had felt like a dragon, but Handel had warned her not to tell anyone she could mind-meld with other dragons. And there hadn't been a dragon in sight.

Above them, Erob was approaching.

Could it have been him? Had Roberto instructed Erob to put her off, to embarrass her in front of everyone? Did he want her to fail? Handel's vision flashed to mind: Roberto—lip curled, face full of hate.

"Sofia needs stitches. Roberto," Master Derek barked, "please fly her to the infirmary at once."

Ezaara bound Sofia's leg, then squeezed her hand, leaving blood on Sofia's fingers.

"Ezaara." Simeon's concerned amber eyes met hers. "You look unwell. Perhaps you should rest."

Master Derek nodded. "Good idea, Simeon. Ezaara, you're excused for the afternoon."

"But I—"

"Take a break," Master Derek snapped. "The rest of you, back to training."

Erob landed on the grass nearby. Roberto carried Sofia over and they flew off to the caverns.

On my way. Zaarusha was flying toward them.

Ezaara hobbled toward the queen, her ankle searing.

Simeon steadied her. "My Queen's Rider. Let me help."

"I'm fine, really." Ezaara leaned on him, tears welling in her eyes. "It was an accident, but it looked like I stabbed her intentionally, didn't it?" She tried to control the quiver in her voice.

"Well … um …" Simeon smiled brightly. "I know you didn't *mean* to hurt her. Come on, a cup of herbal tea will make you feel better."

He'd avoided her question. It was that bad.

Ezaara melded with Zaarusha. *"I've messed up."* She showed Zaarusha her memory of Sofia's wound. *"I've injured a new friend."*

"Stop being so hard on yourself. Riders get injured in training all the time. Sofia will be all right." Zaarusha landed, nudging Ezaara with her snout. *"Erob compared it to a tear in a wing muscle. It'll heal. I'm more worried about the rogue dragon that was imagining burning you. I've ordered all the dragons to search for the culprit."*

"There was a lot of blood."

"If Sofia had scales, she wouldn't have been hurt."

"But she was *hurt. And I did it."*

Simeon helped Ezaara into the saddle, then climbed up behind her and wrapped his arms around her waist. His warmth was comforting.

"My cane—" Where had she left it?

"Don't worry," Simeon said. "I've asked Mathias to bring it back."

"We should go straight to the infirmary to see Sofia."

"No, you've had a shock. You need to rest. There'll be time to see her after my mother has stitched her wound."

"But it's my fault. I should—"

"Ezaara, do you really think Sofia wants to see the woman who just stabbed her?"

"No," she whispered, slumping.

"Sorry if I sounded harsh." Simeon's voice was soft, near her ear. "I'm only trying to protect you."

Zaarusha landed on the ledge outside her den, lying flat so she could dismount. Ezaara's legs were shaking so badly, Simeon had to steady her.

He helped her sit on her bed and pulled off her boots, then took a cup of water out to Zaarusha, who heated it. Pulling a small pouch of herbs from his pocket, he sprinkled some in the cup, then left it to steep. He tugged the covers over Ezaara.

"Thank you." She lay back on her pillows, exhausted. "I keep messing up, Simeon. Now Sofia's hurt. I'm a terrible Queen's Rider."

"I believe in you." He hesitated.

"What is it?"

"Well … no, I shouldn't say disparaging things about Master Roberto." He bit his lip.

"Go on, tell me."

"Roberto has angry outbursts … dark secrets. Watch yourself around him, Ezaara. He's like a rogue dragon, unpredictable and dangerous."

Had Erob given her the burning vision? Did Roberto want her to fail?

"And his sister isn't always as sweet as she seems."

Ezaara frowned. Had Adelina befriended her to work against her?

Simeon smoothed her hair. "Now I've made you worried. Sorry, ignore me, it's probably nothing." He held out the cup. "Here, drink your tea. It'll help you relax."

Ezaara reached for the cup. The tea was bitter and gray; not woozy weed, then. She took a sip and wrinkled her nose. "What is this?"

"Restorative tea." He pulled a comical grimace. "You know, the worse it tastes, the better it works."

"This must be really good for me, then."

He chuckled, watching her drink.

The tea seeped through Ezaara, making her muscles warm and her eyelids droop.

§

Ezaara groaned and dragged her eyelids open. The den was swimming before her. Head pounding and muscles aching, she grabbed a basin and vomited. What on earth had she eaten?

The shrill notes of the dawn chorus pierced her skull. She'd slept from the afternoon, right through the night, until morning. Not a good look for the Queen's Rider. Especially after stabbing someone.

She had to check on Sofia. She should have gone last night. She swung her legs over the side of the bed, but the cavern spun.

After a few moments, everything stilled. Where was her cane? She groaned again. Mathias had forgotten to bring it back. *"Zaarusha."*

"Sorry, Ezaara, I'm in a council meeting. Tharuks are on the move, marching across the Flatlands, destroying settlements and taking slaves."

Great, while the Queen's Rider was in bed, monsters were attacking the realm. Maybe the realm would be better off if she was banished to the Wastelands. Stupid thought. She had to be less of a burden to the queen. Ezaara washed her face, then hobbled along the stone tunnels toward the infirmary.

Her ankle throbbed. She leaned on the rough walls for support, scraping her hands. She passed the mess cavern, but it was early, so few people were about. Torches flickered as she made her way west along the tunnel network. Around the corner, footfalls tromped on stone.

Alban appeared. "Where have you been?" he sneered. "You lowlife, disappearing after stabbing Sofia."

"I've been sick."

"You haven't visited her, haven't asked about her. Haven't even shown your face." His body was taut. His gray eyes, flinty. "You look as guilty as a vulture caught stealing dragonets."

"But I—"

"Stinking ignorant peasant from Lush Valley." He spat on the floor. "Great Queen's Rider you are. All you care about is yourself!" He strode off, his words echoing off the walls.

Heart hammering, she rushed along the corridor, ignoring her aching ankle. She shouldn't have listened to Simeon, although he'd had her best interests at heart. Alban was right. She was selfish for sleeping so long. Selfish for not visiting Sofia immediately. Too selfish to be Queen's Rider.

Ezaara entered the infirmary. Their backs to Ezaara, Fleur and Simeon were bending over Sofia while Fleur swabbed her leg. Sofia was asleep, curls splayed over her pillow. A blood-encrusted bandage lay on the bedside table. The stitches on her thigh were crooked and tight, making the wound pucker over an ugly bump. Ezaara cringed. It was worse than she'd thought. The gash was so awful, it wouldn't stay flat when stitched.

Taking a tub of yellow unguent, Simeon smoothed it onto Sofia's wound. The salve's acrid smell stung Ezaara's nostrils—that same smelly salve Simeon had given her.

When he was finished, Simeon turned, starting. "Oh, Ezaara. I didn't hear you come in." He shoved his medicinal supplies into a drawer in Sofia's bedside table. "How are you feeling?"

Fleur smiled as she bandaged Sofia's wound. "Good morning, Ezaara. Nice of you to visit."

"How's Sofia?"

"We gave her a pain draught so she could sleep, the poor thing," Fleur spoke softly. "Perhaps you should visit another time. You look tired; maybe you should rest."

Alban's accusations bounced around Ezaara's head. The last thing she needed was rest. She had to do something to help. Anything. "Perhaps you two would like an early breakfast while I sit with her? I mean, the accident was my fault."

Fleur cleared the dirty bandage away. "That's not really your role as Queen's Rider, Ezaara. Simeon will tend to Sofia. I must go soon. I've been summoned to a council meeting."

Fleur bustled about while Simeon sat by Sofia. Ezaara hovered, feeling useless.

"We don't use that yellow salve in Lush Valley. What's in it?" Ezaara asked.

"It's my own healing salve containing expensive herbs brought to me by green guards," Fleur replied.

"Green guards?"

"Dragon riders from Naobia, my dear. They ride green dragons. Being from Lush Valley, you wouldn't have heard of them, or their herbs." Fleur smiled. "I suppose you use old-fashioned remedies like arnica and peppermint?"

Ezaara nodded.

"Never mind, they do in a pinch." Fleur bustled out the door.

Ezaara had thought Ma was a great healer, but then, what did she know? Alban was right. She was an ignorant peasant from Lush Valley.

Moaning, Sofia opened her eyes. She scowled at Ezaara. "You! What are you doing here? Come to stab me again?"

Gasping, Ezaara took a step back. "I didn't mean—"

"Get away from me," Sofia shrieked. "Go away!"

Ezaara fled.

She staggered out into the tunnels. Sofia hated her. Blamed her. She'd been so understanding yesterday—a shock reaction? Supporting herself against the tunnel walls, Ezaara stumbled along, her ankle screaming. She welcomed the pain. She deserved it. It was nothing compared to how she'd hurt Sofia.

Deadline

Roberto traipsed into the council chambers, Erob's solid footfalls behind him. Council meetings weren't usually at the crack of dawn with the sky tinged honey-gold like the highlights in Ezaara's hair. He forced himself to focus. Zaarusha must have important news for them.

Curling his tail around his body and tucking his snout on his forelegs, Erob took his place behind Roberto's seat, near the back of the cavern, among the other dragons. *"I'll catch a few winks while you humans solve the realm's problems,"* Erob melded. Although he never actually napped during council meetings, he always threatened to.

Not that Roberto blamed him—their meetings could be boring. *"Don't snore, or Zaarusha might nip you."*

Zaarusha blinked a greeting to Roberto, her scales reflecting a myriad of colors in the torchlight.

He inclined his head, enjoying that familiar surge of pride at being on her council. There was no higher honor than serving their queen. She'd believed in him when he'd first arrived here. He'd never disappoint her.

Lars was already seated, drumming his fingers on the granite horseshoe-shaped table, talking with Tonio and Bruno, the master of prophecy.

Roberto slid into his chair beside Bruno. He nodded at Hendrik, a burly blacksmith and their master of craft. On the opposite side of the horseshoe, Aidan, Jerrick and Jaevin were seated, waiting.

Master of Horticulture and Livestock, Shari, leaned around Hendrik. "Morning, Roberto. Early, isn't it?"

Shari's dragon wasn't here. "How's Ariana doing?"

"Much better," Shari whispered, glancing at Bruno, Fleur's husband, the beads on her tiny braids clicking. "Fleur's tonic didn't work, so I tried the herbs I use on sheep. Ariana's sleeping, but I think they've done the trick."

"Good thinking."

"It's a relief." Shari smiled, white teeth flashing against her cinnamon skin. "A dragon with belly gripe is not a pretty sight—or sound."

Or smell. Roberto chuckled.

On the ledge outside, thumps and the skitter of talons on rock heralded the arrival of more dragons. A blue guard, in riders' grab with a blue armband, opened the chamber doors. Deep in conversation, Alyssa and Derek strode into the room followed by their dragons, who took their spots behind their masters. There were only two seats remaining: Fleur's; and the Queen's Rider's seat, which had been empty for years. Hopefully, Ezaara would soon be qualified to sit in it—although yesterday's abysmal knife incident made prickles of doubt play along Roberto's spine.

Lars cleared his throat. "We need to start. Bruno, can your dragon let us know when your wife will arrive?"

The quiet rumble of conversation made Roberto drowsy. He stifled a yawn. His all-nighter, carving Ezaara's cane, was catching up on him.

"They're almost here," Bruno announced.

Fleur and Ajeuria thudded onto the ledge and entered the council chamber. Ajeuria sat by the other dragons, preening her green scales. Fleur took her seat next to Roberto. Simeon's mother was the closest thing to a healer they had, but a far cry from the Naobian healers he'd known. Roberto had expected Dragons' Hold to have the best.

"Ajeuria is radiating discontent," Erob melded, *"like she has a tick under her scales."*

"If we de-lice her, Simeon would probably come crawling out," Roberto replied.

Behind him, Erob snorted. Luckily, Erob was excellent at shielding his thoughts from other dragons.

Lars called the meeting to order, and the murmurs died down. "Before we discuss the situation in the Flatlands, I'd like Fleur to report on Sofia's condition."

Fleur stood, her face as tired as unlaundered linen. "I stitched Sofia's gash, but it'll leave a nasty scar. She's stable now, sleeping off the pain draught."

Sofia's wound hadn't looked that bad yesterday. Fleur had probably botched it.

"Thank you, Fleur." Lars nodded. "You may sit."

Fleur remained standing. "It's terrible she was hurt here, at the hold, where she should be safe."

Zaarusha shifted, her talons scratching the stone floor.

Lars frowned. "Thank you, Fleur."

"Will there be steps taken to—"

A low rumble issued from Zaarusha's throat.

Roberto gripped the table so hard his knuckles ached. This was a barely-veiled attack on the Queen's Rider.

"I said, thank you." The tension in Lars' frame carried a threat.

Roberto relaxed his grip.

"Tharuks are harassing our people in the Flatlands," Lars announced. "Our blue guards are currently holding them at bay, but it won't be long until Zens starts all-out war." His voice was gravelly. "We must prepare. Tonio, please report."

The spymaster's gaze flicked over each of the masters. Roberto could've sworn it rested a moment longer on him. Tonio had never trusted him. Sure, they'd grudgingly worked together, but Tonio knew the full extent of his father's treachery, so he'd never given Roberto a chance.

"There's not a lot to say," Tonio barked. "These tharuks seem to be searching for something, but we're not quite sure what, or who, it is. They've burned one village so far. Luckily, only three people lost their lives, but they've taken slaves and until they find what they're looking for, there'll be more deaths. We must prepare our people for war." He sat, muttering under his breath, "How we're going to fight a war with a Queen's Rider who can't carry a dinner plate without spraining her ankle is beyond me."

Zaarusha thrust her head at Tonio, snarling.

Erob piped up, *Zaarusha's saying Tonio should shut up if he wants to keep his insides on the inside.*

"A shame Tonio doesn't understand dragon snarl." Roberto kept his lips from twitching into a smile.

Tonio leaped to his feet. "With all due respect to the queen, the new Queen's Rider is inexperienced. It was a metaphor, nothing more."

Roberto shifted in his seat. Not a metaphor, and directly aimed at him. Despite flying a loop, Ezaara's track record at the hold wasn't good, and he was responsible for training her. It was his fault she'd left the dais. And he'd been present when she'd had that strange accident and injured Sofia.

Tonio addressed him. "How is the Queen's Rider's evaluation going, Roberto? When will she be fit to lead us into battle?"

Roberto hesitated. They hadn't finished assessing Ezaara. They'd only tested her imprinting bond, flying and knife-throwing. What if her arrows all flew wide and she didn't know how to hold a sword?

"Roberto?" Lars raised an eyebrow.

Derek, master of instruction, cut in, "It's hardly fair, Tonio. We haven't seen her combat skills yet."

"She flies well," Alyssa, master of flight, commented. "Their loop was incredible for such a young imprinting bond. Zaarusha has chosen well."

A few nods rippled around the table. Not enough.

"A battle isn't won by flying a loop," Aidan, master of battle, bellowed.

Unease flickered through Roberto. "Thank you for your solicitous enquiry, Tonio." He deliberately kept his voice cool. "Ezaara's ankle is recovering, and her training is improving. I believe—"

"Improving enough to do what?" Tonio snapped. "Stab her fellow combatants?"

"I'm sure Ezaara—"

"Sure?" Tonio barked. "Be careful what you say, Master of Mental Faculties. I always base my claims on evidence."

"It was an accident. I was there. I saw how upset she was—"

"Upset?" Fleur snarled. "She didn't visit the infirmary last night to check on Sofia. That's how upset she was."

Roberto snapped his jaw shut.

A meaty palm slapped the granite table. Hendrik bellowed, "What sort of Queen's Rider doesn't visit the injured? Especially when it's her fault!"

"Well, she visited earlier this morning," Fleur said hurriedly, "but only briefly, and she fled as soon as Sofia awoke. Not at all what I'd expect of a Queen's Rider."

"I hate to be a harbinger of doom," Bruno muttered.

Everyone turned to him.

"Please go on," Lars asked the master of prophecy.

"Well, I …" Bruno glanced at Zaarusha with a wan smile. "With all due respect to our Honored Queen Zaarusha, I had a vision last night. Things don't bode well."

"Go on, Bruno." Lars' voice was clipped.

"I agree, it appears that tharuks are mounting a war, but my vision showed me that when they find what they're searching for, they'll retreat back over the Terramite ranges, leaving us in peace."

"And how does that bode ill?" Lars asked.

"It doesn't," Bruno answered. "It's good news. Our need to prepare for war isn't as urgent as our spymaster suggests. However, another vision showed me troubling news regarding the Queen's Rider."

Zaarusha shifted her weight, making the torches sputter. Then the room was silent, except for the hiss of the queen exhaling.

"The gift of prophecy is an onerous one." Bruno sighed, melodramatically. "I fear you may not like my news."

He was milking this, as usual.

"Spit it out, man." Hendrik slapped his enormous hand on the stone table again. On either side of him, Shari and Fleur flinched.

Bruno met Lars' gaze. "The Queen's Rider will betray us."

Zaarusha stood. Her roar juddered through Roberto's bones.

"My dear Queen," Bruno placated, "I cannot help what my gift shows me. To protect you and the realm, it's my duty to report what I see."

Roberto bristled. That whole family was rotten to the core. How dare Bruno accuse the Queen's Rider of treachery? It insulted Zaarusha's fitness to rule. It also insulted him—he'd tested her. Ezaara didn't have a disloyal scale on her hide.

"No chance of sleeping through this," Erob muttered. *"Almost makes me yearn for boring meetings again."*

"Our queen is a great dragon," Fleur added, "but she was lonely and desperate for a new rider. Maybe her judgment was flawed."

Bruno shook his head. "The queen is getting older …"

Zaarusha snarled. Yelling broke out. For the queen. Against her rider. Dragons raised their hackles. Masters leaped to their feet. Roberto ducked as Ajeuria's tail whipped through the air. Erob rose, beside Zaarusha, yellow eyes glowering at Ajeuria.

"Silence," Lars bellowed, cutting through the cacophony.

Lars placed his hand on Zaarusha's head. "Our queen commands no more slights on Ezaara. She has chosen her rider. Now, sit down. Everyone. I'm pleased Bruno advises us that war will not come, but however pleasing his prophecy is, we must prepare the Queen's Rider for battle. Roberto, please answer Tonio's original question. How long until she's ready?"

Roberto had to save face, for himself, for Ezaara, but mostly for Queen Zaarusha. They needed a trained Queen's Rider—and he'd give them one, if it meant slogging day and night. "She'll be ready by next moon," he announced.

Annoyance flashed across Tonio's face. "A moon? Ready to fight against tharuks? How? She's only been here a few days, and she's had one disaster after another. She's injured one of our most promising trainees, and you want to turn her loose in battle?"

"Maybe she'll injure some tharuks too," Roberto snapped.

Lars rapped the table with his gavel. "Roberto, are you sure you can do this?"

Of course not, but he had to try. "Yes, sir."

"Good. If you're that confident, I'll give you two weeks, at which time we shall reconvene and evaluate her worthiness as Queen's Rider."

"Yes sir." Roberto nodded. Dragon's fangs! How was she ever going to be ready in time?

§

"Ezaara! What are you doing here?" Gret crouched, her voice sharp.

Slumped against the wall halfway between the infirmary and the mess cavern, Ezaara shrugged. "Uh, resting …"

Gret's face softened. "It's your ankle, isn't it? Where's your cane?"

"Simeon said Mathias would bring it back from the field."

"Good," Gret said. "Mathias bunks in the boy's cavern, along here. I'll hunt him down."

"Thanks." Ezaara struggled to her feet. She couldn't put weight on her foot.

Soon Gret returned, out of breath. "Mathias didn't have your cane. Says Simeon never asked him to bring it back."

"But Simeon—"

"Forget Simeon," said Gret. "He has a reputation, you know."

Everyone was tough on Simeon. Were they all judging him, the way they were judging her? "Simeon's been nothing but friendly."

"Of course he has." There was an edge to Gret's voice. "Your ankle looks worse. What were you doing? Running on it?"

"I'll be fine. Just give me a hand, please."

Gret supported her along the tunnel, their footsteps echoing off the stone walls. "How are you going to train if you can't walk?"

Exactly what she'd been wondering. "Things will work out."

"They're saying you stabbed Sofia on purpose."

"It was an accident."

"I know that!" Throwing her hands in the air, Gret took a step back, leaving Ezaara unsteady. "I'm loyal to the realm and to you, but not everybody is. We have to combat these vicious rumors or you'll be put on trial and Zaarusha will lose her rider."

"Combat rumors? I'm struggling to walk. I can't even get back to my den."

Gret laughed.

"What?"

"Only dragons have *dens*. Riders have *caverns*."

"I have so much to learn, haven't I?"

Voices echoed beyond a bend in the tunnel. "Someone's coming," said Gret. "By the Egg, Ezaara, put a smile on your face, or everyone will think you're guilty."

Alban strolled around the corner, deep in discussion with another boy. "I was there." Alban stabbed a finger in the air. "The blood was horrendous. Poor Sofia."

"Ssh, she's coming," the boy replied. "She'll knife you next, if you don't watch it."

"Like to see her try." Alban's gaze was steely as he stalked past Ezaara.

Although she felt like screaming, Ezaara forced a smile as more footsteps sounded around the corner.

Roberto and Adelina approached.

"Ezaara!" Adelina hugged her.

"You're coming from the infirmary, I take it? Good." Roberto's eyes narrowed. "Where's your cane?"

"Simeon said Mathias would bring it from the knife-throwing range, but it's missing."

"Simeon?" Roberto's face tightened. "Leave it to me, I'll find it." He strode down the corridor, his boots striking the rock.

Shards, she'd lost the beautiful cane Roberto had carved for her—his mother's cane. Ezaara bit her lip, glancing at Adelina guiltily.

§

Roberto was astounded. He'd seen it again. When Ezaara had answered him, brilliant color had flashed through him. It was her. The brightness of her intellect, her mental resilience, whatever it was, they had a connection without touching.

He rushed down the corridor. The tunnels were too stifling, too narrow and confined for emotions this big. He needed to fly. He melded with Erob, *"Meet me on the ledge outside the mess cavern."*

"On my way."

Roberto broke into a run. The sooner he had space to think, the better. He took a bolt hole out onto the trails and ran along the goat track on the mountainside. Anakisha and Yanir had been able to mind-meld, so it was possible. But why Ezaara? Did she have a propensity for mind-melding like him?

He shuddered. He'd paid a terrible price for his skills.

Above the mess cavern, Roberto vaulted onto Erob's back. Two steps later, Erob was airborne. Roberto let out a gusty sigh. *"Sometimes I think the politics in this place are going to do my head in."*

"You're used to the Naobian Sea, the wide open coasts and endless blue. Living in this basin is hard on you."

"Not as hard as life in Naobia."

Erob coasted over fields of crops. *"Those memories will fade soon enough. You have your whole life in front of you. Where to?"*

"The knife-throwing range. That shrotty louse Simeon has hidden Ezaara's cane."

Erob roared, a tremor running through his body.

Roberto grinned. He felt exactly the same.

They descended toward the field. In the distance, a green dragon was returning to the caverns.

"It's Ajeuria," said Erob. *"The master healer must've been foraging for herbs."*

Roberto dismounted by the targets, scanning the grass. He'd felt Ezaara's anguish in the corridor; he knew Sofia's stabbing was an accident, but those keen to discredit the Queen's Rider were using this to their advantage. His boots tapped something in the grass—Sofia's lucky blade, crusted with blood. He stuck it in his belt and checked behind the targets. The cane wasn't there. Where had Simeon put it?

Erob melded, *"They flew off from over there, so perhaps it's nearby?"*

Roberto searched the bushes, the long grass at the edge of the field, and then scoured the surrounding trees. *"What a waste of a morning, and all before breakfast."*

Erob shot him a mental image of himself: face dirt-smeared, a twig in his hair and grass seed stuck to his jerkin. *"All in service to your Queen's Rider."*

"All in service to that slimy cockroach who's furthering his political interests and worming his way into the Queen's Rider's trust. Huh!"

But when Erob shot him the image again, Roberto had to chuckle. He looked a sight.

"Jealous?"

"What? Of that creep? Of course not."

§

Roberto found Kierion sharpening his blade against a grindstone. "Kierion."

The boy looked up. "Yes, Master Roberto?"

"I have a challenge for you."

Kierion's face shone as he sheathed his sword. "I'm your man."

"The Queen's Rider's cane has gone missing." How could he phrase this delicately? "I believe one of the trainees has played a prank on her."

"It wasn't me, sir." Kierion's voice was earnest. "I'd own up if I'd done it. Promise."

Roberto chuckled. A true prankster, Kierion was the most inventive of his students. "I'm not here to blame you, but to ask for your help."

"So, you want me to find it?"

"It was last seen at the knife-throwing grounds."

Kierion hissed through his teeth. "They're saying Ezaara knifed Sofia on purpose. I don't believe it, but I bet that's why someone hid her stick."

Roberto corrected him. "Her cane is ornately carved, much more than a stick, but speculation leads to gossip, Kierion. It's probably just a joke." If only. "Let's go. Erob's waiting."

"Erob!" Kierion grinned. "Wow, I'm definitely in. I've never been on a royal dragon before."

Roberto had to smile. Kierion's enthusiasm was catchy.

As they jumped off the ledge, Kierion let out a whoop. Roberto sighed—so much for searching without anyone noticing. They descended to the grass at the edge of the trees.

Kierion slid down from Erob, all business. "Where have you already searched?"

"Throughout the grass, among these trees and in those bushes. It could be anywhere. It might not even be here anymore."

Kierion bit his lip. "That's possible, but there are a few great hiding places around here. Follow me."

Traipsing through the trees, they came to a rotting log in the grass. Kierion knelt at one end and peered inside. "Empty. We'll try the next spot." They headed toward a cluster of bushes and tangled vines. Kierion and Roberto lifted up the edges of the vines and poked their swords into the bushes. Still nothing.

"There's one more spot, before we search the whole area," Kierion said. "Have you looked high in branches in case someone tied it in the top of a tree?"

"I had a cursory look, but nothing that thorough. Erob will scout from above."

"If your search wasn't that thorough, why did you end up with leaves in your hair?" Erob asked.

"Cheeky dragon," Roberto melded. *"If I admit it, Kierion will show me up."*

Erob chuckled and, within moments, was airborne, surveying the treetops.

Kierion took Roberto back toward the field. "We should've checked this spot first, but I thought it was too obvious." He stopped in front of a lightning-struck strongwood tree. "Give me a leg up?"

Roberto hoisted him up and Kierion's head and shoulders disappeared into a hole in the trunk.

"Found something." His voice was muffled. He pulled his head out. Burnt bits of bark were stuck in his hair and his face was soot-smudged. He yanked Ezaara's cane from the hollow, grinning. "We did it."

Roberto's breath caught in his throat—the cane was jagged, the shaft broken in half.

"Shards! Let me have another look." Kierion reached back into the hollow and fished out the other piece of the cane. He whistled. "That'll take some fixing."

Roberto's gut was hollow. A whole night's work, viciously broken. He took the pieces from Kierion, swallowing. "Thanks for finding it."

"Wow, look at that handle. Is that Ezaara on Zaarusha?"

Roberto nodded.

"Who made it?"

"I did, when she first hurt herself." Roberto coughed. "To show respect for the Queen's Rider." Warmth crept up his neck. Kierion was bright, but hopefully he wouldn't notice.

"Shards! What a way to frost Ezaara. Someone wants to delay her recovery, I'm guessing."

Too bright—he'd hit the nail on the head—but at least Kierion was gazing at the cane, not his face.

"That's only speculation," Roberto replied. "It was probably a prank." He attempted a laugh. "You know all about those."

Kierion turned beet red.

§

Roberto cornered Simeon near the infirmary. "It was you, wasn't it?"

Simeon grinned that same slow self-satisfied smile he'd grinned when Trixia had fled Dragons' Hold. No one had been able to pin anything on him then, either, but watching him now, Roberto was sure it was Simeon who'd fathered Trixia's littling. And, if the rumors were true and he'd taken the young woman by force, he was dangerous.

"What are you talking about?" Simeon's eyes widened in innocence, acting again.

"This." Roberto brandished the pieces of Ezaara's cane.

"What a *terrible* loss." Simeon's sarcasm made Roberto's skin writhe. "I'll have to escort Ezaara places, now, won't I?"

Roberto's hands clenched around the walking stick. "Don't you go near her."

"I'll do what I want," Simeon snapped. "You can't be everywhere."

"You lay so much as a talon on her and I'll make you pay."

"Is that a threat?" Simeon asked. "I wonder what Lars would say about a master threatening a subordinate? Did you inherit that talent from your father?"

Roberto forced himself to ignore Simeon's jibe. "Lars would have something to say about your antics."

"Oh no, he won't." Simeon smiled. "I've heard Lars likes proof, and plenty of it. And apart from some dumb broken stick, you're empty-handed."

Roberto wanted to smack the insidious smile off Simeon's face. "You can't hide behind your parents forever, Simeon."

"At least I have parents." Simeon smirked. "I bet your father used to beat your mother with that stick before he—"

"You've. Gone. Too. Far." Sword drawn, Roberto was icy with fury.

Although Simeon fled, Roberto stood seething, knowing he hadn't won at all.

A Testing Time

Adelina bustled into the Queen's Rider's cavern. Ezaara was already up and gone. Dragon's eggs, something stank. There, by the bed—a basin of vomit. Ew. She didn't mind helping the Queen's Rider, but she'd never thought her duties would involve *that*.

Putting down the breakfast tray, she picked up the basin and trotted off to the latrines. There was something odd about the smell. A strange, but familiar, tang. It was only when she arrived back in Ezaara's cavern that she realized what it was. Skarkrak, a herb used by the Robandi assassins from the Wastelands. How had it got to Dragons' Hold?

Snatching up a cup by Ezaara's bedside, Adelina sniffed it. It was skarkrak all right. Who'd given it to Ezaara, and had they realized that, while a mild dose helped with sleep, too much could cause vomiting or death?

Simeon worked in the infirmary. A shiver snaked down Adelina's spine.

She couldn't really tell Lars without proof, but she'd definitely mention her suspicions to Roberto.

§

"There's something I need to show you." Erob flipped his wings and glided across the lake.

"What is it?" Roberto shaded his eyes against the glint of the water.

"Brace yourself."

A vision shot into Roberto's mind. A wall of dragon flame seared his skin, stinking of singed hair and burned flesh. Blinding pain fried his nerve endings.

"That's a powerful illusion." He shook his head, focusing on the water lapping at the lake's shore. "Why are you showing me this?"

"Sorry, I should have told you earlier." A wave of Erob's guilt hit Roberto. Then Erob sent another image: Ezaara, screaming, her knife flying into Sophia's leg. Doubled over, she retched.

So that's why she'd been sick—from the stench of her own burning flesh.

"*Someone forced that vision on Ezaara?*" Someone with special mental talents. Who? Wait a moment. "*Why have you withheld this? Did someone suspect me?*"

Erob's guilty silence spoke for itself.

"*Erob, answer me. You can trust me.*"

An indignant rumble came from Erob's throat. "*Of course I trust you. I just showed you the vision, didn't I?*"

"*Come on. For the Egg's sake, Erob.*"

"*It would be better if you asked me questions.*"

"*You want me to guess, so you can say you didn't tell me?*" Roberto slapped Erob's scaly hide. "*Who's told you not to mention this?*"

Erob spiraled down to the grassy lakeside. "*Ezaara was so distressed, she tried to push the vision out of her head, inadvertently relaying it to all the dragons on the council. We all agreed not to mention it to our masters until we knew who'd tortured her with it.*"

Roberto dismounted, approaching Erob's head. "*She can send a vision to multiple dragons? That's crazy. No one's done that since Anakisha.*"

"*She has talents ...*"

"*Did she send it via Zaarusha?*"

"*No.*"

"*Ezaara can meld with dragons other than Zaarusha?*"

The silence hung heavy between them. Erob sprung, his wings flashing above the water. Within moments, he'd gulped a maw full of fish and thudded down beside Roberto again.

"*Maybe a dragon sent her the vision, then. Or it could've come from a rider with hidden mental talents.*" Roberto let out a gust of breath. His past was still shadowing him. "*Did* you *think it was me?*"

"*No. I've told Zaarusha it wasn't.*"

Roberto scratched Erob's eye ridges. "*But not every dragon believes you, right?*"

"*I'm sorry.*" Erob butted his snout against the flat of Roberto's stomach. "*You were so against having a Queen's Rider from Lush Valley. You keep everything so close to your heart. Can you blame them for not realizing you've changed? That you're loyal to the Queen's Rider?*"

"*Ezaara's in danger.*" Roberto's hand gave an involuntary twitch above his sword. "*We must protect her.*"

§

Ezaara gripped her knife and raised her arm. Again.

"Not like that." Simeon stepped closer, his warmth playing along her back as he adjusted her grip. "There, that's better. Remember how to hold your thumb?" His breath tickled her earlobe.

Heat flooded her cheeks. "Thank you, Simeon." It was bad enough being back here after what she'd done to Sofia, without blushing like a strawberry whenever he touched her. This was instruction, not a romantic interlude. She had to stop behaving like a besotted turkey.

"I know this is hard after yesterday, but take it easy. Throw when you're ready." His voice was gentle.

She'd known all the boys in Lush Valley since she was small. Here, the men her age seemed older, more confident. More experienced. She had to focus, throw the knife, not think about him. Ezaara flicked her arm forward, and the blade sailed through the air, hitting the bottom of the target.

"You're improving," Simeon said over-enthusiastically. "Well done. If you throw with more force, and aim a little higher, we'll have you hitting the bullseye in no time." He dashed toward the target to retrieve her knife.

It sounded so easy, but sweat coated her hands whenever she lifted the knife. She'd hurt Sofia. Another tremor ran through her. Remembering her skin bubbling and blistering made her feel like vomiting all over again.

"Have another try." Simeon was back, urging her on. "You can only get better." His cinnamon eyes were warm and encouraging. At least she had one true friend here.

She could do this, for him. Ignoring the flash of fire in her head, the twisting of her gut, her damp fingers, she threw the knife.

"That's better. I'll retrieve it for you."

If only she had her cane. Her ankle was aching, but she didn't want to admit it to Simeon when he was trying so hard to help.

Simeon grinned as he handed her the knife again. "Go on, one more."

As Ezaara raised her arm, a shadow fell over her.

"Here comes trouble," Simeon muttered.

He was right. Erob was here—and Roberto's expression was as dark as a storm cloud.

Ezaara sighed.

"Hard to please, isn't he?" Simeon murmured, squeezing her hand. He got it. He understood her so well, and he obviously knew Roberto. "Come on, Ezaara," Simeon urged. "Let's show him what you've learned."

She raised her arm. Simeon reached around her body, adjusting her grip again. "A little higher," he whispered. He stepped back as her knife sailed straight into the target.

Erob thudded to the ground, and Roberto swung out of the saddle, face thunderous. Striding toward them, he nodded at the target. "Much better," he said. His gaze flicked over Simeon. "What are *you* doing here?"

Simeon's lip curled. "Training the Queen's Rider."

"Training Ezaara is my job," Roberto snapped. "Not yours."

"Well, it's a shame you were too busy, isn't it? Anyone would think you want her to fail."

Roberto flinched. "Get back to the infirmary and your assigned duties."

"Yes, *Master* Roberto," Simeon spat. "Farewell, Ezaara. It was a pleasure being with you this morning." He flashed a sparkling smile and strode off.

"Let's get back to training," Roberto said.

"Until you two start treating each other civilly, I have no inclination to train with either of you." Ezaara stalked toward the target, masking her aching ankle.

Roberto caught up with her. "Ezaara." His deep voice shimmied through her. "I need to talk to you."

She was about to ignore him, when Erob mind-melded, *"Ezaara, listen to him. He has your best interests at heart."*

"His rudeness is a strange way of showing it," she melded back.

Erob chuckled as Ezaara pulled her knife out of the target and sheathed it in her belt.

Roberto put his fingers in his mouth and whistled. With a flap of wings, Erob leaped over to them. Roberto reached up and untied her cane from his saddle, holding it out toward her. His expression softened.

His mother's beautiful cane. "Where did you find it?" Her irritation evaporated.

He waved an arm at the nearby trees. "Hidden near here." His fingers traced a hairline break in the wood. "It was snapped in two. I used a dowel and some tree sap to fix it. It's not as good as it was, but it should do the trick."

"Broken in two?" That was hard to swallow. "That's pretty low."

Roberto's eyes flitted toward Simeon's departing back.

Of course, he suspected Simeon—her friend. Ridiculous. It was more likely to have been Alban.

"Thank you for mending it." Ezaara put her weight on the cane. "It's as good as new."

Roberto leaned against Erob's side, crossing his long legs. "Today, Ezaara, you and I are going to get to know each other a little better. And then we'll start training in earnest. You need to be ready for battle."

What if she didn't want to get to know him? And how could she train in earnest when her ankle was throbbing?

"Come on." He extended his hand and helped her onto Erob. He climbed up in front of her and slid her cane into a saddlebag. "Hold on tight."

Ezaara put her arms around his waist, inhaling his sandalwood scent. They took off, heading toward a lake that glinted silver among a dark carpet of trees.

"Is this where you go fishing?" Ezaara asked. It was a tranquil refuge from the gossip in the mess hall and tunnels.

Erob settled on the grassy shore.

He smiled. "Yes, and I swim here in summer."

Erob shot Ezaara an image of Roberto, muscular and sun-bronzed, cutting through the water.

Her cheeks grew warm. *"Honestly, Erob!"*

"What is it?" asked Roberto, sliding down, then helping her off Erob. "Don't you like swimming?"

"I love it." He'd noticed her blush, which made her blush even more—a vicious circle. "Um, what did you want to talk about?"

Roberto sat by the lake and patted the grass. "Please, sit down." He took a package wrapped in waxed cloth out of his pocket, then took his jerkin off and rolled it up. "Rest your ankle on this, it might help."

Simeon hadn't paid any attention to how her ankle was today. Maybe there was more to Roberto than she'd thought. "You seem to have practice in looking after invalids," she joked.

His face grew grave. "My mother was badly injured. I nursed her for three moons." He unwrapped the waxed cloth, revealing bread, a jar of relish and a wedge of cheese.

"What happened to her?"

His fingers were motionless for a moment. "She died."

The hollow ache in his voice made Ezaara's eyes prick. "I'm sorry."

"It was a while ago." He cut some bread off the loaf with his knife.

"How was she hurt?"

Roberto's face darkened. "Another time, all right?" He passed her the slab of bread, and sat with his blade poised. "Cheese?"

When they'd finished their makeshift sandwiches, Roberto asked, "Why didn't you tell me about the vision you saw when Sofia was hurt?"

"I, uh …" Handel had told her not to tell anyone she could meld with other dragons. Handel's prophecy of Roberto's face twisted with hate flashed before her. He didn't look hateful now. Concerned, maybe curious, but not hateful. "I haven't told anyone."

"Erob showed me. Is that what caused your accident with Sofia?" He looked at her as if he was really seeing her.

Something loosened in Ezaara's chest. Words tumbled out of her in a torrent. "My skin was searing, blistering. It was agony. My whole body was on fire. Made my stomach turn. When my mind cleared, Sofia was …" She shuddered. "Sofia was …" Tears stung her eyes.

She. Would. Not. Cry.

"Her blood was everywhere …. Everyone thought I'd done it on purpose."

"I didn't think that." Roberto's gaze was gentle. "I've tested you. I know you." Again, his gaze, *seeing* her. "And last night?"

"I meant to visit Sofia, but Simeon gave me a cup of tea and I fell asleep. The shock made me sick. Or maybe I ate something bad."

"Maybe."

Alban's words popped into her head. Incompetent, that's what he'd called her. Ezaara's shoulders slumped. "Zaarusha should send me home."

Roberto put an arm around her. Again, mint and sandalwood.

Her master was hugging her? She pulled away. "I, um …"

He dropped his arm, scratching his neck awkwardly. "Ah, how's your ankle now?"

"Still throbbing. It'll be a few more days until it's healed. I should stay off it."

"Ezaara, we don't have time. The council want you battle-ready. They're not prepared to wait." His eyes slid to the healer's pouch at her waist. "Is there something you could take?"

Piaua, but no, it was too precious. "It only needs rest."

He leaped to his feet, pacing. "Tell that to the council when they demand that you go to battle unprepared. I told them you need time. They wouldn't listen. We have two weeks to give you a lifetime's training."

"Two weeks!"

"Only if tharuks don't attack before then." Roberto's face was tight. "We have to heal you, Ezaara. Is there anything that could help?"

She couldn't fail Zaarusha or the realm. "Piaua," she whispered, gazing down at the grass. "But we can't …"

"Why not?" He crouched before her.

"I took a healer's oath. We only use piaua for grievous injuries."

"Ezaara," he breathed, raven eyes pleading. "It's urgent. You're the Queen's Rider. You have to be ready for anything."

As Queen's Rider, she needed to be fit—but she wouldn't waste such a scarce resource on a stupid ankle. Ezaara thrust his jerkin to one side and scrambled up. "Look, I'm fine."

In a flash, Roberto drew his sword and lunged.

She leaped back, pulling her sword from its scabbard and parried his blow. Her ankle twinged as she sidestepped his next move. Whirling, she ignored the throbbing, thrusting and counter-thrusting. Metal scraped on metal. Sweat stung her eyes. He swept his sword along the ground, making her jump and land on her ankle awkwardly.

"Aagh!" In a fit of anger, she lunged for his chest and struck home.

Flinging his sword aside, Roberto raised his arms. "You win."

"No," Ezaara moaned, "you do! Now I've ruined my ankle, so I have to use piaua." She sheathed her sword and slumped onto the ground.

§

Roberto crouched beside Ezaara, untying her boot. He sucked in his breath. He'd thought she'd give up and concede. But no, she was a fighter.

She glared at him. "You're a—"

He didn't wait to find out what she thought. "Shards! I'm sorry, Ezaara, I never expected you to fight back."

A glint of triumph shone in her eyes. She was breathing hard. "I should have stabbed you there and then."

Wincing, she let him roll up the leg of her breeches to check her ankle. It was swollen and red, almost as angry as her. "Sorry, I—"

"Curse it. Stop apologizing. You win. I have to use piaua juice so I can get on with training." Ezaara glared at him again with those startling green eyes. Wisps of blonde hair blew across her face. She jammed them behind her ears.

"I really didn't think you'd fight me with a sore ankle."

"So you said." She reached into her healer's pouch and passed him a slim vial of transparent green liquid. "Piaua juice is precious. The trees are rare, and draining their juice can kill them, so we only use it in dire circumstances." She frowned, lips pursed. "Not for a swollen ankle."

He'd forced her into this. "It's for the best."

Her eyes met his. "I know. Knifing Sofia and falling off the dais hasn't helped. I have to be ready for tharuks, and I have to prove to these tough old riders that I'm Zaarusha's rightful rider."

She understood. Roberto's breath whooshed out as he pulled the tiny cork stopper out of the vial.

"Wait. Don't spill any. Only use a drop or two." Her face showed her apprehension.

"Is it really as effective as they say?" he asked.

"Better. We play down its effects so people aren't tempted to drain the trees."

"I'd heard only tree speakers could collect the juice."

"True, and I'm not one, so this is doubly precious."

He held the vial over her ankle, tipped two droplets onto her swollen flesh, then passed it back to her. Ezaara capped the vial, and rubbed the oily residue over her bruised skin.

"Are you all right?"

"It burns a little. It's nothing." She bit her lip, and her brow furrowed as she worked the oil into her skin.

The swelling was receding before his eyes. The blotchy purple bruise was fading, growing lighter. Within moments, her ankle was normal. Incredible.

"This stuff's amazing." She had pretty ankles and feet, not that he'd ever noticed a woman's ankles before. Roberto coughed, glancing away.

Ezaara flexed her ankle and leaped up, dancing across the grass. She snatched up his sword and tossed it to him.

Dragon's eggs! She was beautiful, full of life.

There was no way he could ever act on how he felt—as if he'd be that stupid. Masters weren't allowed relationships with trainees. He'd never risk banishment after all he'd done to earn his position as master at Dragons' Hold.

"Now we can duel," she called.

"You'd better get your boots on," Roberto growled. "I'm going to put you through your paces."

Trickery & Stunts

Erob flapped his wings. Exhausted, Ezaara clung tighter to Roberto. Except for that first time, no matter how hard she'd tried, Roberto had beaten her every time they'd dueled today. He'd been remorseless, goading her with jibes as they'd clashed swords. Her beating him earlier had been a fluke, like when she'd beaten Tomaaz in the marketplace.

Erob descended to the edge of the forest and Roberto jumped off, making no move to help her. He strode toward a strongwood tree and hung a leaf on the rough bark of its trunk.

Ezaara slid off Erob. Although she was tired from dueling, it was great to walk and run properly again. She shrugged off her guilt about using piaua. It was too late now.

"Let's test your archery skills," called Roberto. "The leaf is your target."

Stifling a smile, Ezaara called, "It looks awfully small." This would be a cinch. She and Tomaaz had grown up shooting as soon as they were old enough to fetch arrows.

Roberto took two bows out of Erob's saddlebag. "Which one do you want to use?" He held a longbow in one hand, and a recurve in the other.

The elegant longbow needed more strength, but was taller and more cumbersome. The recurve was her favorite, the type her family used. The ends of the bow curved forward, creating more tension on the string so arrows could travel faster and further.

"This one, thanks." She took the recurve. It was similar in feel and size to her one in Lush Valley. Ezaara rubbed her fingers along the string, then sniffed them. Good, it had recently been treated with beeswax.

Roberto observed her, narrowing his eyes. "Do you need any tips?"

He was assuming she couldn't do anything—why not humor him? Ezaara sighed dramatically. "I'm fine, really." This could get interesting.

He passed her a quiver of arrows and she slung them across her back. Ezaara wiped her palms on her breeches, nocked her arrow, and raised it to sight the center of the leaf. It took a seasoned archer to evaluate a new bow with only one test shot. As she loosed the arrow, she twitched her bow to the side. The arrow whistled through the air and went wide, hitting a bush.

"Hmm," Roberto pursed his lips. "Although you sighted well, the bow jerked as you fired. Try again." He crossed an arm and rested his elbow on it, rubbing his chin.

This time, she let the bow jump to the opposite side.

"Same problem. Let me show you." He strode toward her.

"No, thanks, I'm fine. I'm just warming up." Ezaara bit her cheeks to stop herself from grinning. Her next shot was wide, and the one after, too high. All of her arrows had missed the trunk.

"Ezaara, allow me to help you." Roberto's jaw was tense.

She'd probably pushed him far enough. "One more shot, please?"

A terse nod.

She loosed an arrow, hitting the center of the leaf. Bullseye. Then she loosed another and another, until the leaf was shredded, prickling with arrows.

If Roberto's eyebrows rose any higher, they'd meet his hairline.

"What did you think of that?" She ran to the trunk and pulled out the arrows, tucking them back into her quiver.

"We have two weeks to train you, and you think we have time to play games?" He shook his head, then snapped, "Double your distance."

So, he'd lost his sense of humor? Fine. Two could play that game. Ezaara paced back from the tree to where she'd been standing, then paced that far again. Roberto replaced the leaf with a fresh one. Raising her bow, she loosed an arrow. Another bullseye.

"That far again," he called.

Pacing off, she turned and fired another shot. Her arrow hit the edge of the leaf.

"Center, this time," he barked.

"I'd like to see you try," Ezaara muttered under her breath as she nocked an arrow and let it fly. The arrow hit the leaf, knocking her earlier arrow off the bullseye.

Roberto gave a short nod. "A spinning shot, this time."

Ezaara faced away from the trunk, nocked her arrow and spun, slamming her front foot down, aiming and loosing the arrow in one fluid motion. It hit the leaf.

Roberto nodded and called her over.

He should be pleased, but no, he was frowning again.

He took her bow and quiver. "Since you're so proficient at archery, draw your sword."

Groaning, Ezaara obliged, and they clashed blades again.

§

At the crack of dawn, Ezaara and Zaarusha flew down to the archery range.

"*I could've easily slept longer.*" Ezaara yawned, muscles aching from yesterday's sword bouts with Roberto. She had bruises too.

"*He's a good trainer,*" Zaarusha melded. "*And not bad company, once you get to know him.*"

"*I'd rather befriend a wolf.*"

Zaarusha just chuckled.

Roberto was already there, oiling a dry patch on Erob's neck. He swung back into the saddle as Zaarusha landed. "Good morning, Ezaara. Don't get down. Today we're going to be shooting arrows from dragonback." He nodded at her bow and quiver.

He seemed pleased she'd brought them with her—as if she was a littling that would forget her weapons. Well, his weapons. He'd promised to take her to Master Archer Jerrick to get her own bow today. A shame she'd left hers in Lush Valley.

"*I didn't exactly give you time to pack,*" Zaarusha rumbled.

Or say goodbye. Her eyes pricked. Tired, she was just tired.

Roberto's charcoal gaze focused on her, then flicked across her face. He always seemed to know when she was melding with Zaarusha. Could he hear them?

"*No, he can't,*" Zaarusha answered. "*He can only access your mind when he touches your temples. That's his gift. I haven't seen another like him. Well, there is one, but …*" A dark shiver flitted across Zaarusha's mind.

Ezaara suddenly felt cold. "*Who?*"

"*Later. He's been patient enough.*"

Roberto, patient? Yesterday he'd goaded, commanded and prodded her until she'd nearly dropped from exhaustion. She raised her eyebrows at him.

"Have you ever shot arrows from horseback?" he asked.

"A few times." More than a few. Pa had drilled them until they could hit a target galloping. It had been a while, though.

"Good. It's different from dragonback, but you'll soon get the hang of it."

That was it? No hints or tips? "How is it different?"

His smile was wry. "You'll see. Hit the red targets. Erob and I will fly behind Zaarusha, so I can evaluate you."

So helpful.

Erob took to the skies, and Zaarusha followed, skimming along the tree tops at the edge of the meadows. Her bow and arrow at the ready, Ezaara scanned the trees. There, a red scrap of cloth was tied to a high branch. Ezaara sighted, aimed, fired. And missed. This was harder than it looked. She nocked another arrow, and aimed at the next target, fluttering in the breeze among the foliage.

Another miss.

Ezaara snatched another arrow out of her quiver. Zaarusha was flying a steady slow course and these targets were all at a similar level. If she was in battle, she'd be dead from a tharuk arrow by now. She aimed at another scrap of red, missing. And another, missing again. And again.

And again.

Erob popped up beside Zaarusha. "Want a few hints?" Roberto called.

Now he asked? "Not yet," Ezaara replied, then melded with Zaarusha. *"Could you slow down a bit and fly closer to the targets?"* There, that should be easier. Her arrow speared a branch. Closer, but not a hit. Pitiful. Absolutely pitiful. *"Why is it so hard?"* she asked Zaarusha.

"It's the air currents from my wingbeats."

"Well, that's great. If you stop flying in battle, I'll be too dead to shoot anything." Ezaara sighed. *"Unless you glide each time we pass a target."*

"That often works."

"So, if you knew, why didn't you tell me?" Ezaara sighted, aimed. Slightly closer.

"Sometimes, experience is the best teacher."

She snorted, still feeling the bruises on her ribs from Roberto's sword, and nocked yet another arrow. *"Gentle,"* she commanded Zaarusha.

A memory popped into her head: Pa teaching her to shoot from horseback. "It's all about the balance and the rhythm," he'd said, demonstrating how to rise up in the stirrups as he fired, to counteract the movement of the horse's gait.

As the queen steadied her wings, gliding past a strongwood, Ezaara rose in the stirrups and aimed. Her arrow snagged the edge of the red cloth. A hit, her first hit. Only a ragged corner, but better than a miss. She reached into her quiver, but it was empty.

Behind her, Roberto laughed. "Retrieving them is part of your stamina training." Zaarusha and Erob landed in the nearest clearing and Roberto dismounted. "Get down," he said. "We haven't got all day."

Ezaara dropped to the ground.

"Now, run." He gestured behind Zaarusha. "Back the way we came. Go and get your arrows."

She'd fired her first arrow ages back, but there was no way she was going to groan in front of Master Roberto. Ezaara set off at a run. She'd loved running through the forest back in Lush Valley and had done far too little of it at Dragons' Hold, thanks to her ankle and having Zaarusha to take her everywhere.

"I heard that," quipped the queen.

Roberto drew level, running beside Ezaara. His feet fell into time with hers. The steady cadence of their breathing contrasted with the rustling foliage and twitter of birds in the trees above. Ezaara was scanning the trees, trying to figure out which one she'd fired at, when he motioned toward a tree with a rope hanging from one of its branches.

"This one." He held the rope out toward her. "Start climbing, it's good for fitness."

Great—tree climbing, running and dragonback archery all in one.

It took Ezaara the rest of the morning to retrieve most of her arrows. When she was done, there were still four missing. Roberto motioned her to sit on a rock at the edge of the clearing. Moments later, Erob and Zaarusha dropped to the grass.

Striding to Erob's saddlebags, Roberto took out a small cloth bundle. "How are you feeling?"

Hungry and tired, but she wasn't about to tell him that. "As perky as a dragonet." If dragonets were even perky—she had no idea.

Opening the bundle, he passed her some bread, cheese, an apple, and a waterskin. He motioned at the skin. "Drink that first, it'll revive you."

It was sweet, delicious and vaguely familiar. "This is great. What is it?" Ezaara took another swig.

He grinned. "Watermelon juice, a Naobian treat."

So that was it. "I tasted watermelon once, when I was young. A trader brought some over the Grande Alps. He sold them straight from the river, where he'd submerged them in a huge sack, cooling. It was delicious. Such a strange, foreign delicacy." A pang of loss for Lush Valley shot through Ezaara. He was far from home too. "Do you miss Naobia?"

A wince shot across Roberto's face, so fast she almost missed it. "It's a beautiful place, but no, I don't miss it." His face shuttered. "What strategies could you use to find your lost arrows? They're a valuable resource. You won't find them, unless you're smart about it. Think, Ezaara. Think."

She'd hunted around the ground underneath the targets and searched the foliage to see if they were hidden there. She chewed her breakfast in silence.

"A Queen's Rider has to use strategy," Roberto said.

"Well, you're master of mental faculties. You should be an expert at that."

His face darkened. "This is an essential part of your training."

"I could ask the littlings from Dragons' Hold to find them."

"Now you're thinking. Delegation. What else could you do?"

"Get Zaarusha to shake the trees, and see if any of them fall out."

"How would you know which trees to shake?"

"All the ones with the ropes hanging from them."

"All of them? But you only lost four arrows."

Ezaara sighed. "I guess I should've marked the trees where we lost the arrows."

"Yes," Roberto answered, "you should have. But don't worry, today I did."

Biting into her apple, Ezaara said, "So now I have to search around four trees. Those arrows could be anywhere."

"Strategy, Ezaara, strategy."

The best strategy would be to walk away from his insufferable questions, but he was her master, so she didn't dare. "All right, I give in. What's your brilliant idea?"

Roberto gestured at the vast forest around them. "There was no way I could explain to you the effects of wingbeats on arrow flight, before you'd tried. Just as there's no way I can explain to you how to develop good strategies that will save you time in battle. Some things have to be done through trial and error. Sometimes experience—"

"—is the best teacher. I know. Long ago, someone wise once told me that."

"Not that long ago." Zaarusha chortled. *"And very wise."*

"I know, perhaps Zaarusha could help."

His eyebrows shot up. "How?"

"Maybe she saw where the arrows went."

"Of course I did. I always look." Zaarusha gave a small triumphant roar. *"I told him you were good, and now you've proven it."*

He just raised another stupid eyebrow. "Did you cheat and ask our Honored Queen?"

Ezaara threw her apple core at a tree trunk with more force than necessary. It splattered against the rough bark. "No. I. Did. Not." She got up and climbed on Zaarusha. "Now, let's find those arrows."

§

Ezaara was a fast learner, he'd give her that. And resourceful. No one else he'd trained had ever thought of using the dragons to shake trees, let alone asking them to mark where their arrows had fallen. Although dragons, with their superior intellect and excellent sight, often noticed details that riders missed, most novices were unaware of it. Formidable in battle, dragons were deadly enemies. Roberto was glad he wasn't fighting against them.

Within a short while, they'd found three arrows and were thrashing around in the bush, searching for the fourth. "Come on," Roberto said. "It's not worth spending any longer on this."

"I thought they were precious?" Ezaara snapped, her face streaked with dirt, and her hair fraying from her braid.

"When you're done questioning your master's ability to teach you," he said, "we'll do more shooting from dragonback."

"Sorry," she mumbled, her eyes the same shade as the foliage.

He grunted. "When you're back in the saddle, focus on Zaarusha's every movement: the flip of each wing and how she rises and falls on the breeze. Rising in the stirrups to make your shots was a good technique, but you have to perfect it. In battle, your targets won't be static. So far today, you've been shooting within close range, alongside a target. I'll know you're truly proficient when you can shoot at targets ahead, alongside, and behind you. Are you ready?"

She raised her chin, determination flashing in her eyes.

§

Ezaara ached all over. The last few days' training from dawn until dusk had been grueling, but at least she could now hit most targets from her saddle. Sitting on the edge of her bed, her stomach muscles groaned in protest as she bent to unlace her boots. Dragon's sit-ups, Roberto called them, but they were more like torture. He'd made Zaarusha run along the edge of the orchard, and every time a low branch hurtled toward Ezaara, she'd had to lie back to avoid being hit, then pull herself up using her core muscles. She snorted. And that was the least of it. Her days had been filled with sword fighting, tree climbing, running, balancing on ropes above a churning river, scaling rock faces, and eternal target practice. He'd even had her kneeling on the saddle to shoot. Of course she'd missed, how could she not miss when she wasn't balanced properly?

And through it all, he'd goaded her to be better, try harder, think more like a Queen's Rider and less like a girl from Lush Valley. She missed her family. Where were they? What was happening to them? Did Tomaaz miss her too?

Sometimes, she glimpsed another side of Roberto, the gentle side that gave her watermelon juice, or a special green apple from the tree his parents had planted. He never talked about them, nor his littling days. No matter how often she asked, he'd always change the subject.

Ezaara threw her boots near the bed so she could easily find them when Roberto came back for her tonight. So tired—and now he wanted her to do flight training. Why in the night, when she was exhausted? Ezaara collapsed on her bed, in her riders' garb, and drifted to sleep.

She awoke to a thud in Zaarusha's den.

"Erob's here," Zaarusha warned.

Moments later, Roberto appeared. "You skipped dinner."

"I was tired." She'd been asleep before her stomach had rumbled, but now she was ravenous.

"As Queen's Rider you need to take care of yourself."

"That's why I was sleeping." Ezaara rolled her eyes. "I'm exhausted. Is that any surprise after the last few days?"

"Not really," Roberto admitted, a flash of sympathy in his eyes. "Here." He reached into his pocket and passed her a small cloth bundle.

"Mm, smells divine." Like lemon and something. She unwrapped it. A lemon poppy seed cake. Ezaara moaned in pleasure as she bit into the warm gooey center and crunched the delicate seeds. "Thanks." It was just right. Not too sweet, not too sour.

He smiled, watching her eat. "I'm glad you like it." His voice was soft.

When she was finished, he strode out to the queen's den. Ezaara threw a heavy cloak around her shoulders and joined him.

"Sometimes riders lose their seat in battle, or half slip out of the saddle," Roberto said. "Tonight, we're going to practice stunt riding, so you have the skills to right yourself again if you get into trouble. You have to trust your dragon. Zaarusha knows what's best, so follow her commands, even if you can't see why she asks you to do something. Obedience is key."

"The cheek of him, after you and I flew a loop." Zaarusha's voice was more playful than indignant. *"Let's have some fun, shall we?"*

"Anything you say, My Queen. Obedience is key." Ezaara smothered a smile as she climbed into the saddle.

§

Ezaara's hair shone in the moonlight as she tied it back with her slender fingers. She was suppressing a smile. Her emotions were always so bright, so colorful, so close to the surface, like a bubble welling up in a spring.

He was falling for her, a little more each day he worked with her. He'd pushed her hard, demanding only her best, driving her to her limits. She hadn't cracked, rising to each challenge, her competitive spirit taking the bit and thundering for the finish line. Even her knife throwing had improved. Today she'd hit every target. But he didn't dare let her know how much he admired her. He had to maintain a hard exterior. She was his student. A slight whiff of indiscretion and he'd be banished, and everything he'd worked toward since his father's betrayal would crumble. His whole world would be lost if he revealed he loved her.

Lars and the council would soon test her to gauge whether her skills were up to scratch. He had to make sure she was ready.

They rose above the basin, the forest a shadowy cloak around the lake—glinting silver in the moonlight.

"Ezaara," he called across the air between them. "Take your feet out of the stirrups for a start."

Grinning, Ezaara did as he asked.

"Now you need to—" He gaped as she knelt on the saddle, then crouched and straightened to stand. "Ezaara!" He couldn't help the strident warning that crept into his voice. "Be careful."

"Why? You said we were going to do stunts." Ezaara grinned, full of life and mischief. She stepped—onto nothing. Arms wheeling, shock flew across her face. She plummeted into the darkness.

Zaarusha flipped her tail, plunging after her.

"Dive, Erob! Dive." Fangs! They were going to lose her.

Like a hawk after prey, Zaarusha sped down.

"Faster, Erob, faster." Roberto leaned forward on Erob's neck, willing him more speed. If she died …

Roberto glimpsed a bright thread of color, stretched taut between him and Ezaara. A thread that brought him joy and hope. That had given him hope since the day he'd tested her. A strong thread that could help him be a better person, if he could cling onto it. If she survived.

Still she fell.

No, not Ezaara, so vibrant and full of life. She couldn't die, not now. Not when he'd just realized how he felt about her. She was special, the first Queen's Rider in years. He'd always admired her: her bravery in facing the council after imprinting; her courage to try anything; her horror at injuring Sofia; her healing skills; and her joy of life. She hadn't had her littling life ripped away by someone she loved. She hadn't had her innocence destroyed, or been used as a pawn. She was wholesome, a backwater girl from Lush Valley, who loved life and trusted her dragon implicitly.

With a slap, like a whale's tail on the ocean, Zaarusha snatched Ezaara in her talons.

The Queen's Rider laughed.

Erob chuckled too.

And that's when Roberto realized it was a stunt.

§

The plunge through the night sky was exhilarating, making every fiber of Ezaara's being jump to life. To trust so completely, love so completely, to place her life in Zaarusha's hands—well, talons—*that* was living. This is what she'd yearned for in Lush Valley. She'd risk her life for the queen, give her life for her realm. She was Ezaara, Queen's Rider.

"*I told you back in Lush Valley, you were born to be my rider.*"

"If only I'd believed it."

"*Get ready.*"

With a whump, Zaarusha caught her, cradling her in her talons. "*I think we've frightened the scales off Roberto.*"

Ezaara laughed. "I didn't know he had scales; he must keep them well hidden. Maybe we've scared him into being nicer. Maybe he won't be so tough on me now. Not that I'd intended to scare him."

"*Really?*"

"Well, maybe a little."

"*He's not being tough. He's challenging you, so you can better serve the realm.*"

"Not tough? I'd hate to see him when he's trying to be."

"*Roberto has faced things that would break most men.*" Zaarusha flipped her wings, spiraling down toward a field. "*Stretch your legs, and tell me when to let you go. It'd be a shame to squash you when I land.*" The queen chuckled.

Ezaara's feet brushed the tall grass. *"Now, let go."*

She rolled as she hit the meadow. Luckily it was soft, not stony. Zaarusha thudded to the grass nearby, and moments later Erob landed.

Roberto dismounted and strode over, sword hilt glinting in the moonlight. He took her by the shoulders, onyx eyes stormy. "Ezaara." His breath was ragged.

She was about to mumble her apologies when he pulled her against his chest, murmuring into her hair. "Dragon's bleeding fangs! I thought I'd lost you." The scent of mint and sandalwood enveloped her.

For once, Ezaara had nothing to say.

Tharuk Attack

Last night he'd failed. He'd slipped up, taken her in his arms out of sheer relief that she was all right. And once she'd been there, it had been hard to let her go. The smell of her hair reminded him of the days before his father had turned. Happy days playing in the sun, fishing and tending the animals. Running through meadows, swimming in lakes and laughing.

His last few years with his family had seldom given him reason to laugh. And many reasons to cry. Until he'd hardened himself, locked away his tears and moved on. Only Adelina remained. His father had destroyed everything else in his life. Roberto kicked at an old shoe lying on his cavern floor.

Ezaara reminded him of everything good in the world. Of innocence. Of loving family bonds. Of fun, dare he think it. Of warmth and friendship. Everything he'd denied himself for years. He sighed and tugged his jerkin shut. And he would deny himself her, for her own sake, and his.

"I'm ready. Will you stop mooching around?"

Roberto snorted. *"Mooching?"*

"Now you're snorting almost as well as me." Erob gave a dragonly snort that echoed off his den walls outside.

Roberto chuckled. Where would his life be without Erob?

A shiver ran down his spine as he remembered his life among tharuks.

§

Whatever Roberto had demonstrated last night was gone. The tenderness she'd felt as he'd held her. The vibration of his deep voice through his chest. The warmth and firmness of his torso. The peace she'd felt, the sense of one-ness at being in his arms—it was gone.

All gone.

He struck her shoulder with the flat of his sword. "Faster." A tap on the hip. "Block, Ezaara."

She lunged, sweat trickling into her eye, and missed him. Their swords clashed again.

"A sleeping tharuk could do better. Try."

Whirling, she advanced, gaining ground. He beat her back.

They'd been training for hours. She was dying of thirst. "Water," she gasped.

He nodded. "Only a sip. There's no time to stop in battle."

No sooner had she taken a swig, he bellowed, "Run. Race you to the knife-throwing range."

Groaning, she ran after him. So unfair, he had a head start. She couldn't let him win. Sprinting, she chewed up the ground between them. Where in the Egg's name did he get his energy from?

Panting, Ezaara reached the range on his heels, spurted past him and threw her knife without stopping.

He whistled. "Good shot, but it may be a fluke. Another.

"And another.

"And another."

Roberto drew his sword and they were fighting again. His blade smacked her knuckles. This would never end. Dragonback archery was bound to be next. Ezaara's life was one endless, merciless round of sweat and pain.

§

Roberto woke to a battle horn.

"Wake up," Erob melded. *"River's Edge is under attack."*

Throwing on his clothes and boots, Roberto grabbed his weapons and jumped on Erob. *"To the council chambers,"* he melded. *"Tell Zaarusha that Ezaara should prepare for battle."*

"Already done."

Roberto and Erob reached the council chambers at the same time as Shari and Jerrick. Behind them Tonio, Bruno and Fleur were arriving. They dismounted and strode inside. Aidan and Lars were deep in discussion over a weathered map. Within moments, the council was gathered.

"River's Edge, a village near Montanara, is under attack by tharuks." Lars announced. "The village only has a small fighting force. Unless we engage, they'll be slaughtered. We're sending dragons and fighters. Our battle master will instruct us."

Aidan pushed the map along the table. He pointed his stubby finger at a village a few river bends south of Montanara. "The villagers are outnumbered. The fighting is so thick, dragons can't use flame for fear of hurting our people. Jerrick, we need a squad of forty archers on dragonback to circle the area and prevent tharuk reinforcements from reaching the village. Jaevin, ready your sword fighters. Alyssa's squad will drop them close by, for hand-to-hand combat. Alyssa, only three people per dragon, we don't want to tire them. The archers will form two squads to pick off beasts from the air—one led by Tonio, one by me. Bruno, any foresight about this fight?"

Roberto repressed a snort. They were asking *Bruno's* opinion.

Bruno's voice was assured. "This is nothing but a minor skirmish. My prophecy tells me you'll be successful."

"Tonio, any other intelligence?" Aidan demanded.

"Nothing," said Tonio. "We don't have any dragon corps spies near River's Edge, but blue guards from Montanara are on their way."

Aidan nodded. "Good. We'll leave as soon as everyone has formed up. Lars, the time is now yours."

Lars stood. "Fleur, prepare the infirmary for wounded, and take supplies and healers there." Lars stabbed the map, indicating the next village over. "We may have to ferry patients to you. Roberto."

Roberto's head whipped up.

"I want you to—"

The doors burst open. Ezaara rushed in.

Lars' surprise was painted across his face. "My Honored Queen's Rider, you haven't finished your training. This isn't a drill. We need capable archers, not novices."

Ezaara's chin lifted and her eyes flashed. "Master Roberto." She turned to face him.

Great, she was going to drag him into this.

"Am I a capable archer?"

A ripple of tension ran around the room. Roberto nodded. "Yes, of course. More than capable." Apart from Shari, all the masters looked incredulous. "Ezaara is one of the best archers at Dragons' Hold."

Jerrick's head snapped up. "Best archer? I don't believe it!"

"What's not to believe? I'm the Queen's Rider," Ezaara retorted, "not an ornament to be left on a shelf."

Erob melded with him. *"Zaarusha has warned me that Ezaara won't be fobbed off."*

Time to stick his neck out. Roberto stood. All heads swiveled to face him. "Our Honored Queen's Rider has a point," he said quietly. Was that relief that flashed across Ezaara's face? "We've waited long for a Queen's Rider. Now that we have one, she should fight."

The room erupted.

RIDERS OF FIRE

Zaarusha swooped through the doors, her roar bouncing off the chamber walls. The queen of the dragons stalked to Lars.

Lips pursed, Lars placed his hand above Zaarusha's eye ridges, so they could mind-meld. Turning to the council, Lars announced, "Zaarusha wishes to take Ezaara to battle. She says they've fought tharuks together before. I concur: she may go."

Excitement radiated from Ezaara. Colors cascaded through Roberto, then they were gone.

Lars stabbed a finger in the air toward Ezaara. "Honored Queen's Rider, you must stay on dragonback. You may engage as an archer, but only from the air. You are not, under any circumstances, allowed to fight on foot at close range with tharuks."

"Certainly," Ezaara replied, lashes lowered.

Her manner reminded Roberto of their first archery session and her flight stunt, putting him on edge. Was her concurrence a ruse? Would she put herself in danger? He touched the pocket holding her ribbon. He'd vouched for her, and whatever she did, he was sworn as her protector.

§

Zaarusha landed in the clearing below her den, Erob next to her. Ezaara could hardly sit still in the saddle, she was so jittery. The clearing was filled with dragons, gravel crunching underfoot as they landed. Roberto dismounted, pulled a bundle out of his saddlebags and came over, motioning her to get down. She slid down Zaarusha's side.

He passed her some rolled-up fabric. "Here's an archer's cloak to keep out the cold."

"Thank you." Ezaara wrapped the thick cloak around her shoulders and fastened it down the front, slipping her arms out the arm holes. Roberto adjusted her quiver so her arrows poked through the tailor-made hole.

Roberto took a deep breath. "Please, heed Lars' warning. Fight from dragonback only. You're too valuable for us to lose." Without waiting for an answer, he strode to Erob and jumped astride him.

Valuable—what was that about? Another way of pressuring her to keep Lars' rules?

A figure hurtled out of the main cavern, running through the dragons to Erob. Adelina reached up to squeeze Roberto's hands and murmured something to him. He smiled, a gentleness coming over his face that Ezaara seldom saw.

Adelina came over to Ezaara and squeezed her hands too. "Good luck, My Queen's Rider, may you fly swiftly and come home unharmed." A moment later she was gone.

Ezaara climbed into her saddle and cinched herself in.

Clatter filled the air like stones bouncing down a mountainside. Ezaara spun. It wasn't an avalanche, but the rustle of a hundred wings as more dragons swooped down from the mountainside.

All these dragons for a fight in a village? What would all-out war be like? Weapons clanked and leather creaked around her as riders adjusted the girths on their dragons' saddles.

A few dragons over, Gret was perched behind two others, sword at her side. She waved to Ezaara, grinning. So Gret would be fighting on the ground. Ezaara waved back. Hopefully, she'd be safe, facing those monsters up close.

Master Jerrick thrust an extra quiver of arrows into Zaarusha's saddlebag. "Make these count," he said. "If you're as good as Master Roberto says, every arrow should find a tharuk."

Ezaara nodded. "Yes, Master Jerrick."

Roberto raised his eyebrows. "Ready?"

Ezaara swallowed. "Of course." Around them, riders were watching. She forced herself to smile and sit straighter in the saddle.

Zaarusha melded, *"Whatever happens, hold on tight. I don't want to lose you in midair."* In the moonlight, her scales were glorious.

Aidan stood before the assembled warriors. "We've sworn to protect the realm, to preserve the peace, and not to let Zens' tharuks enslave our people. Get in fast, strike hard and save the settlers of River's Edge." He pumped his fist in the air.

Amid dragon roars, riders cheered. Zaarusha and Erob took to the sky. Tugging Roberto's cloak around her against the chill, Ezaara marveled as the undulating mass of dragons broke into four squadrons, North, South, East and West, each with a master at the front.

She and Roberto were at the center of the compass, protected on all sides.

"And from below," Zaarusha rumbled in Ezaara's mind. *"I'll blast anyone who attacks you, and Erob will protect you from above."*

"Above?"

"If necessary."

Ezaara gazed up at the dark sky, the stars like a littling's shiny scatter stones on a dark blanket. Could her family see the same stars tonight? Hopefully Ma was safe. And Tomaaz and Pa. Her chest tightened. If anything happened to her tonight, she'd never see them again.

Soon, the long fingers of dawn were stretching across the horizon, smearing yellow paint above the flatlands, glancing off the mountains to their left. The golden light cast Roberto's face a beautiful shade of bronze.

"*Focus,*" Zaarusha rumbled. "*We're nearly there. Ready your bow.*"

Alongside, Erob snorted and Roberto fastened his waist harness and nocked an arrow in his bow.

Ezaara leaned low, her bow nocked, as Zaarusha descended toward a plume of smoke. River's Edge was nestled in the sweeping bend of a broad river. Houses were on fire. Tharuks swarmed through the streets, attacking men, women and littlings. Screams and roars rent the air. More tharuks were flooding into the village from the forest. Isolated pockets of beasts were chasing villagers across fields.

Fleur broke formation first, flying further along the river with a few riders to set up her healing outpost. Aidan and Tonio's squads swooped over the town, shooting tharuks. Alyssa's squad flew to the far side of the village, depositing sword fighters where the battle was thickest. Dragons from Jerrick's squad defended the perimeter, blasting flame at monsters as they swarmed from the forest. Dragon riders' arrows were thick in the air.

A tharuk broke from the forest, zigzagging past arrows and sword fighters. Standing in her stirrups, Ezaara shot at its head and missed. She loosed another arrow, hitting the beast in the chest.

"*Nice kill,*" Zaarusha purred. "*Let's get some more.*"

A tharuk had a man cornered against a barn. Roberto released his arrow, shooting the monster through the back of the neck. Whipping another arrow from his quiver, he spun and shot another brute through the gut.

A desperate scream rang out. There, beneath her, a young girl was running away, a toddler on her hip. The girl tripped, regained her footing, and kept running. A tharuk pursued her across a meadow, grass trampled in its wake. Two more appeared from the trees.

Zaarusha swooped and blasted the rear tharuk with fire, incinerating him. "*The next is yours.*"

Heart pounding, Ezaara pulled back her bowstring and fired. Black blood sprayed from the beast's chest. It collapsed to the ground. She whipped out another arrow and nocked it. More monsters were coming.

With a roar, Zaarusha sped toward a gangly tharuk. It glanced skyward, giving Ezaara the perfect shot. The arrow flew true, piercing the brute's forehead.

The girl kept her head down, running. The littling on her hip screamed as the girl stumbled, then kept going. The monster chasing her mowed through the tall grass, intent on his prey.

Ezaara tried to line up a shot. It was impossible. She'd hit the girl. *"Zaarusha, let's try from the side. I can't get a clear shot."*

The dragon queen swerved, changing her angle, but the tharuk changed his position too.

"It's no use, Zaarusha," Ezaara cried. *"I'll hit the girl or the babe."*

The monster leaped, tackling the girl and slamming her to the ground. Her scream rang out above the sound of the distant battle.

"Zaarusha, let me down. Now." Ezaara unfastened her waist harness and pulled her feet out of the stirrups. *"I'm not having the lives of littlings on my conscience."*

Zaarusha swooped low. Ezaara swung her legs over one side of the saddle and eased herself down. A meter or two above the ground, she let go and dropped to the earth. Rolling to stand, she unsheathed her sword and ran at the monster.

The beast was holding the girl up by the neck, crushing her throat. Her fingers scrabbled at his furry hands. She was gasping for breath. The toddler ran at the beast, beating at its leg. The tharuk kicked it, and the littling went flying into a tree trunk, then dropped to the ground, motionless.

Ezaara's pulse sped. Racing up behind the monster, she plunged her sword through its back. The tharuk dropped the girl, swinging its arms wildly. Her arms aching from the impact, Ezaara ducked to avoid its savage claws. She held tight, pushing the sword with her full body weight. The beast groaned, dropping to its knees, black blood pumping onto the grass.

A roar split the air in the meadow. Ezaara yanked her sword out of the beast and turned.

Brilliant blue, Erob blew a gust of flame over three tharuks until they were smoking heaps of debris.

"Send the girl to me," Zaarusha melded. There she was, near a grove of trees.

The girl was kneeling by the littling, weeping and stroking its hair. More tharuks were pounding toward them.

Ezaara ran to the girl, shaking her arm. The littling was a boy. A wee boy, unconscious but breathing. "Quick, take the boy and go." She pointed to Zaarusha. "Flee."

The girl scooped the littling to her chest and ran.

"Ezaara, behind you."

Ezaara spun. A tharuk as wide as three men swiped at her with its claws. She ducked. Sliding forward on one knee, she drove her sword up into its belly. The beast's agonized roar nearly split her head in two, before it crumpled, knocking her flat. Sharp pain ran up her sword arm. She was trapped under its shoulder, its matted fur mashed into her face. The tharuk jerked. Her body twitched in response. She gagged on its stench.

"Ezaara," Roberto bellowed. "Incoming tharuks."

Pushing up, she tried to force the dead beast off her. Its enormous torso pinned her legs, preventing her from rolling. She was wet with its blood. The pommel of the sword, still lodged in its gut, was digging into her side and her hand was throbbing.

The ground thudded with footfalls. Something was getting closer. Ezaara frantically shoved and grunted, but she was trapped.

There were roars, grunts and cries, the wet thump of bodies hitting the ground.

"Ezaara!" It was Roberto. On his knees, he lifted up the tharuk's hip. "Dragon's eggs, this thing is heavy."

It gave her enough space to force one knee and her arms up. Together, they pushed. As the tharuk's weight slid off her, fresh air rushed back into her chest, making her gasp.

"Are you all right?" His face was tight with concern.

"Look out," she gasped. A tharuk was charging him. She scrambled to her feet.

He spun to fight the beast. Easily two heads taller than Roberto, its claws shredded his cloak as he danced out of reach.

"I've got the girl and littling," Zaarusha melded, now airborne above them. *"I'm taking them back to the healing post."*

Erob swept above the far side of the meadow, blasting any tharuks who dared approach.

Gripping the pommel of her sword with two hands, Ezaara placed her foot on the dead beast's gut and yanked. With a squelching suck, the sword slid free and she stumbled backward. Regaining her footing, she faced the monster attacking Roberto. After this one, there were two more to deal with.

Standing just beyond their swords' reach, the three monsters formed a wall, cutting off their retreat to Erob. A scar-faced tharuk crouched, ready to pounce.

The largest brute waved his sword menacingly, advancing on Roberto. The third rushed at Ezaara.

She feinted to the left, then thrust her sword to the right, gashing the tharuk's arm. Snarling, the beast swiped at her and she spun out of reach, standing at Roberto's back. This tharuk was smaller. With her sword, she had the longer reach. She leaped, attacking the beast.

Behind her, grunts and groans ripped the air before a high-pitched scream rang out.

"Scar-face is down," Roberto yelled amid snarls.

Ezaara's tharuk tried to knock the weapon from her grip. She chopped at its clawed furry hands. Her sword found its mark, piercing the monster's palm. It howled, then wrapped its other hand round the sword blade. Not caring about slicing its fingers further, the beast pulled, yanking Ezaara closer.

For an instant she resisted, then let her bodyweight fly, slamming the beast to the ground. Pulling a dagger from her boot, she thrust the blade through its throat, then stood, chest heaving, to retrieve her weapons.

The tharuks were dead. The meadow was silent, save for the crackle of Erob's flames as he kept further tharuks at bay.

Ezaara spun. Roberto was hunched over near the large brute, his body curled in pain.

She ran. Crouching next to Roberto, she examined him. Three gashes across his jerkin were stained red with his blood. Ezaara reached for her healing pouch at her waist, but cursed. In her haste to get ready, she'd left it behind. "Come," she said, "let's get you to Fleur's healing post."

His breathing was shallow, eyes wide with pain. "No, not Fleur. You can heal me back at Dragons' Hold."

He could bleed out before they got there. "No, Roberto. Fleur's closer."

"Never." He winced.

"Roberto, this is no time for prejudice. I know you don't like Simeon's family, but this is your life we're talking about."

"That's why I don't want Fleur," he spat through gritted teeth. Roberto gripped her hand, hurting it. "Promise you'll take me straight home."

Erob was still busy battling tharuks, but beyond the trees, she saw the glint of Zaarusha's wings. She nodded. *Zaarusha! Hurry! Roberto's hurt.*

Healing

Zaarusha thudded onto the ledge. Slumped over Zaarusha's saddle, Roberto twitched. Ezaara shook him. He groaned. A trail of his blood ran down Zaarusha's side.

"Roberto," she urged. "We're home. I can't lift you down."

"Get help," Zaarusha commanded. *"I'll let you know if his breathing changes."*

Leaving Roberto tied to Zaarusha's saddle, Ezaara dashed through her cavern into the main tunnels. Adelina wasn't in the mess. Nor the training cavern. She stopped a girl. "Do you know where Adelina is?"

"Try the infirmary. Lars asked her to relieve Simeon for his meal break."

Good, she'd need a few supplies to treat Roberto. Ezaara raced along the tunnel. The infirmary was empty except for Adelina.

"Hi, Ezaara, why are you back so early? Is the fight finished?"

Ezaara deliberately kept her voice low. "It's Roberto, he's injured."

Dismay shot over Adelina's face.

"A tharuk gashed his chest," Ezaara said. "I need your help to lift him off Zaarusha. At my den, um, cavern." She yanked open a drawer. "First, clean herb and bear's bane." She opened another drawer. Where was the vigor weed, clear-mind or heat herb? Not to mention basic supplies such as arnica or slippery elm powder.

"There's nothing in those drawers," Adelina said. "The only things I've found are endless tubs of smelly yellow salve, some green paste and grayish leaves."

Ezaara yanked open a cupboard, but only found more of the ghastly yellow stuff. "Fleur says it's made of special ingredients brought by the green guards."

"Green guards come from Naobia, like me, and I've never seen that stuff there." Adelina leaned closer. "Roberto doesn't trust Fleur's remedies, and I don't either."

Of course, Adelina shared her brother's ridiculous prejudice. Ezaara picked up a small pot of yellow salve. "I'd better try this, in case Fleur's right."

"Not on my brother, you don't."

"What's behind that old curtain?" Ezaara asked. While Adelina was distracted, Ezaara tucked the tiny pot in her jerkin pocket.

"I don't know," said Adelina. "Let's check."

Ezaara flung the curtain back to reveal an alcove of shelves crammed full of pots and jars all filled with the yellow salve or a sticky green paste. A few pouches contained gray leaves.

As she was turning away, Ezaara spied some earthenware jars at the back of the bottom shelf. "What's in those?"

Dropping to their knees, she and Adelina pulled pots of yellow salve off the shelf to get at the earthenware jars. They uncorked a few.

An oniony scent filled the air. "That's bear's bane," Ezaara said, pointing at Adelina's jar of clear salve. "This one's freshweed." She put the cork back and opened another jar of dried pale-green leaves with a familiar tang. "Clean herb! I've got what I need. Let's go."

"This stuff has obviously been hidden," Adelina said. "I knew they were up to no good."

"Hurry, Ezaara," melded Zaarusha. *"Roberto's breathing is getting more labored."*

"Quick," Ezaara said. "Roberto's getting worse."

While Ezaara hurriedly replaced the pots at the back of the shelf, Adelina took off her jerkin and bundled the clean herb and bear's bane pots inside it.

"So no one sees," Adelina whispered, her face tight.

They'd just stepped out of the alcove and pulled the curtain shut when footsteps echoed outside the infirmary. Ezaara jerked her head toward the doorway and she and Adelina rushed across the room, slowing as Simeon entered.

Ezaara smiled, stepping in front of Adelina so Simeon wouldn't see her bundle.

"My Honored Queen's Rider." He smiled warmly. "Are you hurt?" He took her in, head to foot.

She was splattered in black tharuk blood and red smears from Roberto. She had to think fast so Simeon didn't suspect anything. Not that she'd ever hold anything back from him, but Roberto's business was his own. "Zaarusha sent me to check on any injured riders, but none have arrived yet."

"You look a little nervous. Would you like a restorative tea to help calm you?"

"Hurry," Zaarusha melded.

"No, thanks. I'd better get back to the queen," Ezaara called. She and Adelina walked swiftly to the door.

"Adelina, aren't you staying to help?" Simeon asked.

RIDERS OF FIRE

Adelina smiled sweetly. "I've been asked to help in the kitchens, but I'll send someone right along."

Moments later, they were running along the corridor.

"He's losing more blood."

"Come on, Adelina." Ezaara rushed through her cavern to Zaarusha's den. Adelina dumped the remedies on a table and ran after her. Climbing onto Zaarusha, Ezaara fumbled with the ropes around Roberto's waist, untying him from the saddle. He groaned as she and Adelina lifted him down.

He was as heavy as a horse, but they managed to carry him to her bed. Blood soaked into the white quilt. Grabbing half a palm of clean herb, Ezaara threw it into a cup and thrust it at Adelina. "Fill it halfway with water and ask Zaarusha to warm it."

Roberto's eyes slid open. His gaze was unfocused, bleary. He gripped her arm. "Thank you … no Fleur." He slumped back on the bed, eyelids fluttering.

Slashing his tunic open, Ezaara examined the wounds. Three claw marks, not deep enough to puncture any internal organs, but deep enough to make him bleed like a stuck goat. "You're going to be all right, Roberto," she murmured as Adelina returned with the infusion and some cloths.

After cleaning Roberto's wounds, Ezaara smeared bear's bane over the edges, the pungent onion scent making her eyes water. Surely it was the onion—not his pale pain-laced face—that made her want to cry. This was her tough master, impossible to please, cool and detached.

"That stuff stinks like leek soup," said Adelina. "What's it for?"

Blinking back her tears, Ezaara answered steadily, "Numbs the wound, so it won't hurt when I stitch it." Hands trembling, she drew her needle out of her healer's pouch and started stitching his gashes.

Adelina clenched and unclenched her hands, then started pacing back and forth, her footsteps gnawing a hole in Ezaara's patience.

"Would you like something to do to keep your mind off things?"

"Please." Adelina's voice shook almost as much as Ezaara's hands.

"Fetch him some clean clothes."

"Good. I'll be back soon." Adelina rushed out the door.

Hands coated red, Ezaara pushed the needle through Roberto's skin, pulling the edges together. She hated stitching. Although she knew it helped, it always felt strange to put holes in people's bodies to make them better.

"Colors, so many colors," Roberto murmured, the trace of a smile on his face.

Great. Here she was, fretting over him, while he was having a pleasant dream. She shook her head. This was worse than she'd thought—he was delusional.

§

She was near—so close, but so far. Deep sea-greens and marine blues danced through Roberto's mind as Ezaara smeared onion salve over him, numbing his skin, making the stabbing in his chest ease to a blunt ache. He could feel her tugging at his wounds, but the sensations were disembodied, like they belonged to someone else.

And through it all was the bright thread that joined them together.

"Roberto." Ezaara sounded like she was calling through water.

He forced his eyelids open, but they kept sliding shut as his body dragged him back under.

"Roberto," she called, sharper this time.

Bolts of pink shot across his vision, behind his eyelids. She could do that? Just with her voice? He was riding a sea of sensation, like a raft on the ocean, drifting away from her again.

The tugging stopped.

Her hands rubbed across his chest, leaving trails of blazing fire in their wake. His wounds seared, the burn biting deep inside him, aching through his chest. His eyes flicked open to glimpse a slim vial in her hand, then thudded shut again. Piaua. This was piaua—the reason she'd winced as he'd applied it to her ankle. It burned its way through his flesh, knitting his chest together, the deep healing fire purging his damaged tissue.

By the Egg, it hurt.

"At least it won't leave scars." Warmth washed through him. It was her, speaking in his mind.

Roberto forced his eyes open. The fog lifted, his vision clearing. There she was: green eyes wide, leaning over him, rubbing his chest, her golden hair shining in a shaft of sunlight.

She smiled. "How are you feeling?"

Dragon's claws, she was beautiful. "Uh, all right. I didn't know piaua burned." He glanced down. His wounds were gone. Thin pink lines ran from below his collar bone, down across the right side of his chest. "That's incredible. I thought I felt you stitching me …"

"I used bear's bane so you wouldn't feel much. By stitching you before I used piaua, we avoided ugly scars. I could have just used piaua, but it seemed a shame …"

She hadn't wanted to mar his chest.

His gaze dropped to her fingers absently tracing the lines of his new scars.

Her cheeks tinged pink under his scrutiny and she snatched her hand away. He wanted to tease her and make her laugh. Nothing would please him more than flying through the skies on Erob with her in his arms. But he was her master.

Attachments led to betrayal. He'd learned that the hard way.

"Thank you for healing me, Ezaara." He sat up, flexing his arms and chest. "I feel as good as new." His shirt and jerkin were shredded. He pulled them off and cast around for something else to wear.

Ezaara corked the piaua vial and tucked it in her healer's pouch.

There was a knock at the door, and Adelina came inside, carrying a bundle of clothes. "Roberto." She raced over, throwing the clothes on the bed and hugging him. "You look amazing. I can't believe it!" She pointed at his new scars. "This is incredible."

He stood up, flexing and bending. "As good as new."

"You mustn't tell anyone," Ezaara warned. "I'm only supposed to use piaua in dire circumstances."

"Those gashes were dire enough." Adelina flung her arms around Ezaara. "Thank you. I won't breathe a word." She headed for the door. "I'll catch up with you two later. Benji wants me in the kitchens to help prepare food for our hungry warriors. Come and grab something to eat when you're done." She shut the door behind her.

Ezaara passed Roberto an open tub of pungent ointment. "I used some of this healing ointment on the cut on your arm." She gestured at a bandage on his left forearm.

This yellow stuff didn't look like any healing salve he'd ever seen.

"Use it sparingly," Ezaara corked the tub. "Fleur said the ingredients are expensive, only brought in by the green guards."

Green guards? They patrolled Naobia, yet Roberto had never seen such a strange salve in use in his homelands. "This is from Fleur? I told you I didn't want to be healed by her."

"She told me it was better than anything I had. I thought—"

"Well, next time don't. That family's worse than a scorpion's nest. They—" A knock at the door silenced him.

Shooting him a scathing glance, Ezaara strode to the door. "Why, Simeon," she said. "Come in."

That shrotty leech was here.

Simeon stepped over the threshold, his gaze sweeping over Roberto's naked torso and the bloodstained clothes on the floor. His eyebrows rose. "Oh? Am I interrupting something?"

"Not at all," said Ezaara, folding her arms. "Roberto was just leaving."

"No, no, don't leave on my account," that sycophantic leech said. "I was only wondering where Adelina is. Wounded riders have arrived, and I need her help in the infirmary."

"She's in the kitchens, on duty," Roberto snapped, tugging his clean shirt and jerkin on. "You'll have to find someone else."

"No problem." Throwing a greasy smile at Ezaara, Simeon left.

Ezaara shot Roberto daggers. "You didn't have to be so rude to my guest."

Perhaps he should tell her. "I've warned you about Simeon."

She folded her arms, fuming.

"Look, Ezaara, the council let you fight today because you promised not to get off Zaarusha."

Her jaw tensed. "So, you expected me to let that girl and her littling brother die?"

This was not a battle he was going to win. "No, you did the right thing. We had to help them, and you fought well, but if the council hears about this, we'll be flamed. Get changed so no one sees the blood all over you. Although it might be too late, because Simeon already has."

The look she shot him could have curdled blood. Even covered in tharuk gore and angry at him, she was stunning. She must never, ever get an inkling of how he felt. Roberto tamped his feelings down tight. "It's your job to heed the rules, Ezaara, not break them." He strode out the door.

§

Roberto was so sharding stubborn, so pigheaded. Ezaara scrubbed her face and arms and changed into clean clothes. They'd fought so well together. She'd saved a girl and her brother, but all he could do was lecture her. No kind word of praise. Not even a smile.

She flexed her torso, aching all over where the monster had pinned her. No doubt there were others more badly wounded. She'd forgotten to go to the infirmary when Sofia was injured, but she wouldn't make the same mistake twice. A Queen's Rider needed to serve her people. Making her way as quickly as possible down the tunnels, Ezaara came to the infirmary.

Fleur was back. She, Simeon, and two assistants were tending wounded riders and sword fighters whose moans echoed off the stone walls.

Ezaara went straight to Fleur. "Who should I first attend?"

"Oh, um … him." She pointed. "He's loudest."

She frowned. Her mother had always triaged patients, knowing the loudest often wasn't in the worst condition. Ezaara hesitated. She really should obey Fleur—it was her infirmary. She went to the man Fleur had indicated, and sure enough, his injuries didn't appear as bad as the lad next to his, who was lying silently on a spreading stain of red.

"How were you hurt?" she asked the boy.

"Arrow in my back," he answered through gritted teeth, staring at her with pain-filled eyes.

The man's moaning in the next bed was driving her to distraction, so Ezaara gave the man a stick to bite on and rolled the boy from his back onto his front. The arrow had gone deep, but from what she could see, the wound had been enlarged by whoever had removed it so clumsily, ripping the flesh further. Her blood boiled. This poor boy couldn't be more than thirteen. "Who removed this arrow?" she muttered.

Suddenly standing at her shoulder, Simeon smiled. "I did," he said.

Simeon was the son of a healer. He should know better. She bit back a scathing comment, only saying, "Please, fetch me warm water."

When Simeon returned, she was about to ask for clean herb, but remembered it was hidden in the alcove, so she muttered, "Thank you," and waited until he was gone to slip clean herb out of her healer's pouch and crumble it into the water. She cleansed the boy's wound, threaded her needle with rabbit gut twine from Lush Valley and stitched the ragged edges of his flesh together. The boy's body was tight with tension. Even when she gave him a stick to bite on, he whimpered.

"Simeon, do you have anything to numb the wound?" she called.

Tending a man nearby, Simeon shook his head. "Supplies were dreadfully low when my mother took over here. Sorry."

Hang on, there was bear's bane in the alcove. What were Fleur and Simeon playing at? Perhaps Simeon didn't know. Maybe his mother had kept supplies in reserve for an emergency. Surely this boy constituted such an emergency?

"Great job, Ezaara," Simeon called as he passed to fetch more bandages. He dropped some off at the boy's bedside. "Those are nice even stitches."

Ezaara's chest swelled with pride. It was true, her stitches had always been neat and tidy. Despite her not wanting to be a healer, her mother had taught her well. Thinking of Ma made her throat constrict. She blinked, hard. She had to focus on this boy and other patients. There'd be time enough later to dwell on family.

Hours later, when they'd finished treating the wounded, Simeon thanked her profusely and kissed her hand. Grateful at least someone had appreciated her today, Ezaara stumbled from the infirmary to the empty mess cavern.

Adelina greeted her. "You look exhausted. Here, take a seat. I saved you dinner."

"Infirmary," Ezaara grunted, ripping a bread roll, too tired to talk. She bit into the crust, groaning in pleasure.

Adelina bustled off, returning with a bowl of dark meaty stew, and sat beside her. "It's been a long day."

Nodding, Ezaara spooned stew into her mouth, occasionally pausing to dip bread into her bowl. When she was finished, she sat back and sighed. "Now, that was good, the best part of today."

"Thank you for healing Roberto." Adelina kept her voice low. "He said you fought valiantly, saving a girl and a littling."

Roberto? Ezaara bit back a bitter retort. During training, he was so tough, never giving a scrap of praise. "You know the strangest thing?"

Adelina shook her head.

"Simeon said they didn't have anything to numb wounds, but there's bear's bane in the alcove. Maybe Simeon doesn't know about the supplies in the alcove, but Fleur must do. I should have asked her. I …" Ezaara hung her head.

"What is it?"

"I did my patients a great disservice by not challenging Fleur."

"I don't trust Fleur," Adelina replied. "Neither does Roberto."

Despite her cynicism about her master, a prickle of mistrust ran down her spine. She'd have to watch Fleur.

§

Sitting on the edge of his bed, Roberto circled his arms again. He could still use his injured arm, but the gash was puffy and red. He rolled his eyes. That was probably due to Fleur's rotten salve. What had Ezaara been thinking? Well, at least his chest was as good as new, thanks to her.

He'd heard two healers in Naobia whispering about piaua when he'd taken his mother to them for her back … no, he mustn't think about that.

Now he'd seen piaua in action—and Ezaara using her healing arts. Queen's Rider, compassionate healer, competent archer, with a fierce loyalty and a wild beauty that nearly made his heart stop each time he glimpsed it. As her master, he had to know everything about her—talents, strengths, weaknesses, so he could truly prepare her to lead their army against Zens.

It was no good, he couldn't sleep. *"How about a flight?"*

Erob's snores were his only answer. Fair enough. His dragon had only returned a few hours ago, after ensuring every tharuk was either dead or gone from River's Edge. A walk would have to do instead.

Roberto pulled up the hood of his jerkin and strolled along the tunnels. Lost in thought, he realized he was near the Queen's Rider's cavern when Simeon appeared, sneaking along the tunnel. Roberto froze in the shadows. Simeon, furtively glancing back, stole down the short tunnel to Ezaara's cavern.

Roberto slipped after him.

Hand on the Queen's Rider's door handle, Simeon paused, listening.

"What are you doing here?" Roberto hissed. Grabbing Simeon's free arm, he twisted it behind his back. Simeon went limp, but Roberto knew that trick, keeping his grip tight as he marched him down the tunnels.

Simeon blathered. "I couldn't sleep for worrying about Ezaara. I just had to check she was safe."

"I'm not listening to your sniveling dragon dung," Roberto snapped. He'd tried his best to keep Ezaara busy, away from Simeon, Alban and Sofia, but he couldn't be everywhere.

When they reached the infirmary, and Simeon's family's living quarters, Roberto released him. "Stay there. All night. Every night. Or you'll see the sharp end of my sword." He gave a cutthroat grin.

Glowering, Simeon slipped into the infirmary.

Roberto exhaled. That had been lucky. He could've been asleep. If he hadn't been there, who knew what could've happened to their new Queen's Rider—to Ezaara. Dragons' Hold would be a lot colder without her smile.

Rider of Fire

A few days later, as her bruises from their fight at River's Edge were fading, Ezaara opened her door at Roberto's knock.

In usual terse form, he nodded. "Good morning, Ezaara. I have news. Lars has scheduled the Grand Race for today. All trainees must participate, including you." He passed her a pair of light shoes with flexible leather soles. "I thought you'd like these. They'll be easier to run in than your boots."

The shoes were made of supple leather, and hand-painted with a likeness of Zaarusha soaring over a lake, her shining scales reflecting all the colors of the rainbow in the water. These shoes were as beautiful as Ana's scarves. More so, because someone had made them for her. She scarcely dared breathe. "Did you make these?"

His smile warmed his eyes. "No, but I did ask our master craftsman, Hendrik, if he could make you some pliable shoes, suitable for running."

"When did you get time to do that?" Over the past week, they'd been together every waking moment, training.

"Right after the imprinting test." He shrugged. "I saw that you'd arrived in only what you were wearing, with a sword at your side. Once I knew you were Zaarusha's true rider, it was logical you'd need something to run in."

He was a man of such contrasts—a harsh taskmaster, but thoughtful. His mother's cane, these shoes, the treats and tiny things he was constantly doing for her. The way they'd fought together at River's Edge. There was hidden gentleness inside him.

"Thank you."

"Please, try them on. If they don't fit, you'll be running in your boots." He laughed, his face open and free.

She put them on and pulled the leather laces. "They fit perfectly." Ezaara took a few steps. They were light enough to dance in.

§

Hundreds of dragons settled on the ridges above the clearing, their rustling wings and restless feet sending stones skittering down the mountainside. Although riders were scattered among them, perched on outcrops or ledges, most of the crowd were gathered at the edge of the clearing and along a track leading through the meadows to the forest.

The race was due to start at any moment. Stretching her calves, Ezaara evaluated her competitors, all in cut-off breeches, stones crunching as they limbered up. Sofia was flexing her thighs, her vivid pink scar puckered over the awful bump on her leg, as if she was deliberately reminding everyone of Ezaara's blunder. Although Ezaara had several remedies that would help that scar tissue, she doubted Fleur or Sofia would want to know.

Sofia ignored her, but Alban scowled enough for both of them, shooting her dirty looks. Due to Roberto's rigorous training schedule, she hadn't seen much of Sofia or Alban—almost as if Roberto had intentionally kept her away. But whenever she had seen them, they'd snapped or muttered insults. So much for the Queen's Rider being respected. Alban was deliberately frosting her.

If she did well in the race today .... No, she'd scarred Sofia's leg. Nothing would help. She swallowed, missing the easy banter she'd enjoyed when she'd first met Sofia.

Rocco gave her a wave. He jogged on the spot, the breeze ruffling his dark curls. They looked fit, all of them. Henry had a much smaller stride than hers, so she should be able to beat him, but the others .... She'd messed up so many times, she had to prove herself today.

Bright laughter echoed around the clearing—Kierion was here. Lucky he wasn't running, or everyone would've found lizards in their shoes, or their boots nailed to the floor. Ezaara rotated her ankles. Shards, her new shoes were light.

Gret was the only one who approached her. Shaking her hand, she said, "Good morning, My Honored Queen's Rider. It's a privilege to be running beside you." Her voice carried across the clearing. Standing tall, Gret met the gaze of every competitor, including Alban and Sofia.

Ezaara clasped Gret's hand. "Thank you, Gret. Run well."

"Good luck. Here, at Dragons' Hold, it's tradition that a master also runs in the Grand Race." Gret flashed a grin. "They draw straws."

Beyond Gret, lanky Mathias gestured. "Here they come now."

Lars was talking with the masters as they approached. When they were alongside the competitors, Roberto sounded the horn. The crowd quieted.

"Good morning, riders, trainees, and gentle people of Dragons' Hold," Lars boomed. "Our trainee riders are participating in the Grand Race as part of their evaluation. There is only one rule: if there's any foul play, the perpetrator will be disqualified and banished." Ezaara could have sworn his gaze lingered on Alban. "Now," Lars said, pausing theatrically, and waving a bunch of straws in his fist as he scanned the competitors. "One lucky master will be racing with you. Masters, choose—the shortest straw runs."

Ezaara's stomach knotted. Who would it be? Tonio, always skulking on the edge of every crowd observing everyone? Or Lars himself? Hopefully, not Roberto—he beat her every time they ran. In Lush Valley she'd won a few races, but here, everyone was tougher, fitter, older. She wasn't racing the village littlings or Tomaaz and Lofty.

A hush enveloped the crowd. The masters drew straws. One by one, they held them up. Not Lars. Nor Tonio. Not Hendrik, who'd made these wonderful shoes. Ezaara flexed her feet. Alyssa held up a long straw, then Fleur and Bruno. Roberto had the short one.

Racing against him? She'd never win. So much for proving herself.

She'd have to get out in front early, or she'd be chewed up and spat out. Using the old techniques Pa had taught her, ignoring the tightening in her throat at the thought of her family, she visualized herself speeding ahead of everyone. *Good thoughts speed us*, he'd always said. A shame he wasn't here. *"Zaarusha, Handel and Liesar left ages ago to get Pa and Tomaaz. When will they be back?"*

"I don't know, Ezaara. Now, focus."

Lars stepped up to the mark, motioning the racers forward. Roberto gave her his usual nod of acknowledgment and joined them. Ezaara placed her hands on the ground and bent her front leg, ready.

"We'll start at Queen Zaarusha's roar," Lars announced. "May your feet be like wings of air."

Zaarusha melded, *"Good luck, Ezaara. Win by a decent margin!"*

Win?

Zaarusha was already roaring. The other runners were off, gravel hissing as they sped across the clearing toward the fields.

She'd missed the cue. Startled, Ezaara stumbled. Gaining her footing, she leaped forward.

Adelina cheered her on. "Go, Ezaara. Catch up!"

Ezaara pounded after her competitors.

Henry was clutching his side. "Cramps." His face was a tight grimace. Ezaara shot him a sympathetic look as she passed. As a healer, it didn't seem right to leave him, but she had to catch up to Roberto and the others. They were already through the first wheat field, and she was only halfway across.

Ahead, Roberto broke away from the main group. Someone followed—Alban. Sofia's mass of wild curls, the same hue as the golden wheat, bounced as she loped with the group, favoring her leg. Thankfully, she could still run. Ezaara swallowed the thought. She had to focus.

She caught the main group of runners as they ran between vegetable fields, dust flying under the warm sun. The scent of kohlrabi hung in the air. Her vest was already sticky.

Rocco spurted ahead, trying to catch Alban and Roberto. Shoulders tight, he was straining too hard. He'd never last the distance.

Ezaara forced herself to relax, her legs flowing across the ground. She moved along the outside of the group.

Sofia veered and stumbled, jabbing Ezaara in the ribs with her elbow.

"Ow!"

"Sorry." Sofia smirked, dripping sarcasm.

"Hey," Gret yelled at Sofia, "that's not on."

"A *mistake*, just like when that cow hurt me."

A flash of anger spurred Ezaara on. Pumping her arms and legs, she dashed forward, leaving the group behind.

She deserved every hit and blow and slur. If someone had hurt Tomaaz like that, she would've been livid. She couldn't blame Sofia for being angry, especially when Alban kept poisoning her with his nasty barbs. If she was ever to be a just Queen's Rider, she couldn't let peer politics get her down. But doubt and fear ate away at her as she ran on.

Rocco was closer, now. With steady paces, Ezaara chewed up the ground between them and overtook him as she crossed the last meadow. Glancing back with a sneer, Alban entered the forest. Roberto was long gone, somewhere among the trees.

Gradually, Ezaara increased her pace. She hit the tree line, welcoming the cool shade of the forest canopy. She blinked, helping her eyes adjust. This part of the forest was dense, branches woven together in a lattice of foliage. Vines with broad shiny leaves hung from boughs, occasionally twining their way across the path. As a tree-speaker, Ma would love this place. A pang of loss hit Ezaara. Alone. She was so alone here. Her family couldn't celebrate any of her successes. Or support her through her failures.

§

Roberto pressed ahead, Erob's power singing through his veins. Last time he'd glanced back, Ezaara had pulled away from the group and Alban was entering the forest. The muted thud of Alban's feet was back along the trail.

Leaping over a mass of vines, Roberto headed around a corner. A master running against trainees seemed unfair, but it spurred the trainees to push their limits. Masters, with the advantage of accessing their dragons' power, would always win. He, Lars and Tonio were the fastest at Dragons' Hold, although rumor had it that Lars had once been beaten by a master who was no longer here.

Roberto grinned. He'd beaten Lars the last few times they'd raced. His success was as much due to the strong bond between him and Erob and his mental aptitude, as it was to his fitness. Although he enjoyed training hard, exorcising the demons of his past.

Behind him, Alban's footfalls stopped. Roberto cocked his head as he ran. The winding path must be masking Alban's tread. He slowed, pacing himself for the descent into the stream and the grueling climb once he left the trees.

§

Ezaara skirted a patch of sludge and raced over some gnarly roots. This part of the track was tricky. Up ahead a mass of vines lay across the path, with no way around them. A leap should do it. She sped up and took a huge stride, launching herself into the air. The vines whipped up, smashing into her legs. She crashed to the forest floor, smacking her ribs on a root and whacking her shoulder. Rolling, Ezaara came to her feet. A wall of muscle was before her. Alban.

She ducked. Too late. His fist connected with her stomach. She dropped and rolled, staggering up as he pounced after her. With her back to a tree trunk, she feinted to the left, then jumped, aiming a flying kick at him. He sidestepped, but not fast enough. The full weight of her body hit his groin. They crashed to the ground and she rolled away.

Alban sprawled on the ground, grasping his groin. Ezaara whipped a knife from her waistband and held it near Alban's neck, breathing hard.

"So, you're going to slash me too," he spat, "the way you butchered Sofia? Do it. I'll report you, and you'll be banished."

The panting and footfalls of other runners were audible further along the track. A few more corners, and they'd be here.

Despite the anger sparking through her, Ezaara spoke softly, "You'll be banished too, Alban, for attacking the Queen's Rider."

"No one will know," he said staunchly. "No one will believe you." But his eyes were panicked. She had him.

"Nor you," she said. "Vow to keep your mouth shut and not breathe a word to anyone, even Sofia, and I'll do the same."

Nodding, he tried to sit up.

"Don't move yet." She pressed her knife more firmly against his throat. "Swear it, upon your life."

Alban made the vow, then, in the same breath, swore at her.

"What a shame you've fallen over these vines. I guess you'll be too sore to move until someone can help you up." Aiming a foot at his chest, Ezaara pushed Alban back to the ground and took off along the trail, tucking her knife into the back of her waistband.

She'd deliberately worn a vest that hung to her backside, disguising her weapon. Her hands shook as she ran. She'd never expected to use it.

She was the outsider. No one would believe her if she testified against Alban. Her gut ached, and her ribs and shoulder were sore. Heart pounding, she raced down the track, toward burbling coming through the trees. Good, a stream. Her mouth was dry. She could grab a drink.

§

Stooped in the calf-deep water, Roberto was taking a drink when he glimpsed Ezaara racing through the trees. So, she was faster than Alban—impressive. Mind you, she'd given him a run for his money when they were training, although he'd never let on, constantly pushing her to be better. He waited. He had nothing to lose. He'd pull away again as soon as they sped up the mountainside.

Face flushed and frowning, she looked worried.

Her expression cleared when she saw him and her green eyes widened. She splashed through the stream, then bent, scooping water into her hands. As she raised them to her lips to drink, sun slanted through the trees, and their eyes met.

She was beautiful. Something ached deep inside him. So beautiful.

Parting her lips, she drank, water droplets catching like crystals in the sunlight as they fell from her hands.

Vibrant colors flitted through his mind, swirling and eddying, stronger than ever before. A whoosh rushed through his chest, as if it was too small to hold his emotions.

Shards, she was gorgeous.

§

So beautiful. The words flashed through her in a deep male timbre.

It was him, Roberto, thinking about her. They were mind-melding. She saw an image of her, drinking from the stream. The way he saw her took her breath away.

Roberto grinned, the sun striking his dark eyes, turning them to burnished gold.

Water dribbled through her fingers as she stared at him, seeing him as she never had before. Every part of his face was painted with tenderness and wonder.

Something fluttered in her chest.

He was beautiful too. More than beautiful.

She reached up and stroked his cheek. A surge of strange energy hit Ezaara, rushing through her. Anything felt possible.

His eyes sparked as he spoke in her mind, *"Harness it. Run, run like the wind."* He tugged her hand. Sliding on the stones, they scrambled onto the bank and ran through a meadow of wild flowers toward the mountain.

Roberto laughed and his eyes met hers.

Ezaara's stomach jolted. *He liked her.* Her tough arrogant master, *more than liked* her. Every fiber of her being sang. He cared about her deeply.

Letting go of her hand, he smiled. *"Go, Ezaara, go! You're a rider of fire."*

Energy flooded her, pushing her on. She raced across the meadow, heading for the mountainside, Roberto keeping pace.

"Follow the flags." He pointed at a narrow trail dotted with red flags, leading up the granite mountain face and back down to the basin floor.

"I know."

They took off toward the thin trail. Ezaara's blood was on fire, the familiar heat of imprinting burning in her veins as she raced to the top of the track. Somehow, she was harnessing Zaarusha's energy to run.

Roberto melded. *"That's what we're called when we harness our dragons' energy—riders of fire."*

"I can see why." Her soul was ablaze, feet speeding along the mountainside. *"Can every rider do this?"*

"Most masters can harness their dragons' energy, but only a few are able to use it for running. You, Tonio, Lars and I can. Tonio also has dragon sight—he can see much further when he uses Antonika's energy."

"We're melding. How is that possible?"

"I don't know. I have certain mental abilities, and Erob told me that you can meld with other dragons, so you probably do too."

"Did Erob really say that?" she blurted out loud.

Roberto laughed.

They raced down the stony incline, Ezaara barely feeling her feet touch the ground.

She'd always loved running, but this was something else—so effortless and powerful. The sprint they'd maintained up the mountain and back down the path to the valley floor was phenomenal. Her body seared with dragon fire, driving her into a rapid dash, faster than Roberto, across the fields to the finish line.

§

Dragons were wheeling in the sky near the caverns. Heart pounding, Roberto crossed the finish line behind Ezaara. He'd expected her to run well, but this was incredible. Zaarusha's bellow shook the ground underfoot, signaling Ezaara's win. Ezaara leaped upon Zaarusha and rode her in a circle over the crowd's upturned faces. They erupted into a roar. Everyone was going wild, hollering, whistling and clapping.

Zaarusha landed, and Ezaara slipped off her back. Roberto was about to greet her, but Simeon dashed forward and snatched Ezaara in his arms. Spinning her around, he planted a kiss on her mouth. Ezaara turned tomato-red. Her surge of anger flared in Roberto's mind.

Simeon was taking liberties. Roberto's blood boiled. His hand automatically went for his sword, but it wasn't there.

"*Easy,*" Erob melded. "*You still have fire in your veins. Don't do anything rash.*"

Shards! What was he thinking? He was a master, not some lovesick youngling.

Simeon grinned and blew Ezaara another kiss. Someone in the crowd whistled. Others cheered. People surrounded Ezaara, pounding her back and congratulating her. Simeon hovered nearby—as if he'd trained her. As if he meant something to her.

Roberto was so enraged, he could barely think straight. He slipped his impassive mask into place, the one he'd learned to wear in Death Valley, and strode through the crowd.

"Roberto." Adelina reached out to him.

He shoved his way past her, ignoring the hurt that flashed across her face.

Ezaara had seen how he felt about her. If she revealed his feelings to anyone, he'd lose everything he'd worked for. He'd be banished, no better than his father. He couldn't afford to love her.

§

It was tradition for Lars to wait for all of the racers. He shaded his eyes. The last two runners would be here soon. The crowd had gone inside to feast Ezaara's victory. Knowing Lydia, she'd save him a bowl of stew and a good spot in the mess cavern. Behind Lars there was the thump of a dragon landing. Probably Tonio's.

Someone tapped his shoulder. Not Tonio. "Ezaara, what are you doing here? I thought you'd be enjoying your glory inside."

She shrugged. "It's too noisy. I'm not used to so many people."

"That was a fine performance. I've only seen a few run like that," said Lars. "Lately, Roberto's been first home, but years ago, your father beat me with an unprecedented burst of energy."

"Pa can run like that too? He's a rider of fire?"

"Hans was one of the best. It's a great feeling, isn't it?"

Ezaara rubbed Zaarusha's neck. "It took me by surprise."

Lars chuckled. "It always does, the first time. Different masters have different talents, not always running. It's all part of being a rider of fire."

"Master Roberto mentioned that."

"We've decided your sword evaluation will be tomorrow."

Her eyes widened. "Tomorrow?"

"Get a good night's sleep and stay warm." He pointed to the distant sky, voice grim. "There'll be snow in the far ranges tonight."

"I will." Ezaara got on Zaarusha, and they flew back up to the mess cavern.

The last two runners were nearly here. Sofia's leg seemed to have healed nicely. She was running with Alban, at a steady careful pace. Good, he didn't want her injured leg playing up. The scar was ugly. Fleur's half-botched attempts at healing didn't come near Marlies' skill, all those years ago, but she'd fled after that terrible incident with Zaarusha's dragonet. He shook his head. What a waste of a dragonet and a healer.

His dragon, Singlar, had told him Ezaara was Marlies' daughter. Poles apart, Ezaara had looked unpromising when she'd arrived. Knifing Sofia hadn't made things any better, but hopefully that was all behind them.

"Well done," he called from the finish line. "Your leg's holding up well, Sofia."

Flushed, Sofia gave a tired smile. "Thanks, Master Lars."

"And thank you for supporting her, Alban."

Alban stopped and bent, putting hands on his knees and taking a few deep breaths.

"Are you all right?" Lars asked.

"Fine," he said.

Sofia grinned. "He tripped over some vines. I slowed down to keep pace with him."

Alban glowered. "I said I'm fine."

"Come on, it's all in good fun." Lars clapped him on the back.

"Just like knife training," Alban shot as he stalked off.

Face clouding, Sofia rushed after him.

So, it wasn't behind them. Grudges were brewing—and grudges were not healthy for morale.

Lars lingered to watch a pair of dragons shoot across the basin. Now, there was competition at its finest—no grudges, no malice, just pure fun. The dragons reached the western mountain faces, then spun back toward him. He frowned. Over the ranges, in the far west, ominous storm clouds were brewing.

Test of the Sword

Ezaara was cold. There was fresh snow dusting Dragon's Teeth and a chill in the air. She pulled her cloak tight around her, blocking the draft from Zaarusha's wingbeats.

"*There's an unseasonal blizzard raging in the west and to the south,*" Zaarusha said. "*We got off lightly, but it'll be cold there for a few more days. Don't worry, your sword evaluation will soon warm you up.*" The dragon queen flew along the eastern side of the valley. "*There's the sword fighting arena.*"

Below them, two stone outcrops jutted out of the mountainside, forming a natural arena between them, walled on three sides by granite. Dragons were perched on the higher outcrop and people were sitting on the other, on heavy blankets, legs dangling over the rocks. More onlookers were gathered on the ground around the arena, Roberto, Adelina and Simeon among them. Blue guards, in their striking uniforms, were stationed around the edge of the crowd.

"*You told me I had a sword evaluation,*" Ezaara shot at Zaarusha. "*Not a ceremony with hundreds watching.*"

"*It's traditional to have a crowd,*" the dragon queen replied.

"*Of course, I should have realized. In Lush Valley we're well-versed in the traditions of Dragons' Hold.*"

Her sarcasm wasn't lost on Zaarusha—the queen was still chuckling as she landed.

The arena was strewn with rocks and tussock, a challenging surface for dueling. Luckily, the sun had melted the frost. Ezaara dismounted. "*Thanks, Zaarusha.*"

The queen flipped her wings and shot up to the outcrops, perching between a blood-red dragon and Erob. "*Good luck. Show Jaevin what you're made of.*" Head high, she surveyed the arena with a regal air.

Zaarusha was right. She had to prove herself. Winning the race had been a good start yesterday, but running would never win a war. She had to show these riders she was worthy of Zaarusha. She had to honor her queen.

Swordmaster Jaevin inclined his head. "Good morning, Ezaara, Honored Rider of Queen Zaarusha." He gestured toward the red dragon. "May I reintroduce you to Vino, my loyal companion. You met him at your imprinting test."

Thanks to her new feelings for Roberto, she could finally think of her imprinting test without cringing. *"The pleasure is mine,"* Ezaara melded, nodding at Vino.

He dipped his head in response.

Master Jaevin continued, "Today, I'll put you through your paces, testing your skills to determine what further training you require."

As if Roberto hadn't been putting her through her paces already. She ached from their training sessions. "Thank you, I look forward to it."

"Every time you strike me, you gain an advantage," he said. "Your time is up once you strike me twice, or I strike you five times. Vino will keep count, roaring for each strike."

On a wooden rack near the rock face were two ornate swords with engraved hilts—one gold and one silver. Both were sheathed in decorative scabbards. Familiar swords. They'd been on her wall above the bathtub until yesterday.

The swordmaster followed her gaze. "I see you recognize these. They're the ceremonial swords for the Queen's Rider's evaluation, passed down through generations. You may have heard of them?"

Of course, she hadn't, but she smiled and nodded anyway.

Master Jaevin turned to the assembled crowd, his voice booming. "The official swordsmanship evaluation for Ezaara, Rider of our Honored Queen Zaarusha, is about to commence." He flourished a hand at the swords. "Through the ages, every Queen's Rider has been evaluated with these ceremonial swords, blunted to ensure no one suffers grievous injury. Please present the Queen's Rider with her gold-hilted sword."

Roberto took the golden-hilted sword from the stand and pulled it from its scabbard. He strode over to Ezaara. Bending on one knee, he offered it to her. The blade had a strange sheen. The hilt was engraved with dragons—talons out and fangs bared.

"Nervous?" Roberto waited, gazing up at her.

A soft gasp escaped her. It was there again, that unnerving but thrilling power surging through her. *"So many people, just to see me."* Wiping her palms on her jerkin, she accepted the sword. "Thank you, Master Roberto."

"Relax. If you impressed me, you can impress Jaevin."

Impressed? From his attitude, she'd never have guessed. *"You never let on. I thought I was hopeless."* Her breathing eased. Despite the crowd—despite making a fool of herself so many times since she'd arrived—she could do this. After all, she'd beaten Tomaaz in the market. And she'd scored quite a few hits on Roberto over the last week. She only had to get two strikes. If she got in fast, she might catch Jaevin off guard.

"You're right. I never let on how good you were ... or how beautiful you are ..." Roberto's words shimmied through her mind, lighting every corner within her, taking her breath away. He was still on bended knee before her, in front of the crowd.

"Please stand, Master Roberto," she said, voice strong enough to carry.

Roberto's onyx eyes scanned her face as he rose.

"I thank you for training me so well." Her success would be his.

He bowed his head again. "Good luck, My Honored Queen's Rider." Her face was reflected in his midnight eyes—as if her likeness was seared into his soul. Roberto walked back to the crowd.

Master Tonio presented Master Jaevin with the silver-hilted ceremonial sword, then stepped back.

Jaevin towered above her. Broad and well-muscled, he twirled the sword absent-mindedly. He was good. To strike him, she'd have to use every strategy and trick she knew.

Upon the outcrop, a purple dragon flexed its wings—Singlar. Astride him, Lars lifted a horn to his lips and blew it.

The crowd cheered.

Master Jaevin lunged. Ezaara parried a flurry of thrusts. As quick as an asp, he struck her arm. Vino roared. Strike one.

If this were a real fight, she had no doubt Jaevin could kill her in an instant. Thank the Egg, it was only an evaluation. She parried a downward strike, the force reverberating through her arm. Jaevin feinted and she deflected it, blocking his next blow.

"Good," Jaevin called. "Nice block."

"Graceful move," Roberto melded, and an image flashed through her mind—her braid swinging and arm muscles flexing.

She looked like that? *"What? Oh, thanks."* Ezaara missed blocking Jaevin's next blow and had to duck sideways to avoid being hit.

"Timing is everything," Master Jaevin called.

"Yes sir," Ezaara replied.

"Your braid looks like spun gold in the sunlight." Warmth flowed through her at Roberto's words.

"At a time like this, you're admiring my hair?" Ezaara sidestepped as Jaevin swung again.

"Everything."

Her arm shuddered, blocking another strike.

"*You're a powerful melody thrumming through me, setting my bones on fire.*"

Bones on fire. She got that. Hers melted every time they melded.

Faster and faster, Jaevin whipped his sword at her, keeping her on the defensive. His style was similar to Tomaaz, driving her backward, giving her no chance to attack.

"Lift your guard a little," Master Jaevin called.

Ezaara did and their swords clanged.

"*Nice move.*" This time Roberto sent her legs, bronzed from the sun, thighs flexing to parry Jaevin's last blow.

Jaevin's sword shot past her guard, the tip tapping her shoulder. Vino roared.

"Your left side was open," Jaevin called. Strike two.

"Noted." She parried his next thrust. "*You cost me a strike, Roberto. How can I concentrate when you keep leaking emotions?*"

A rush of sweetness engulfed her.

"*It's wonderful, but not now.*" Ezaara danced out of Jaevin's reach.

"*Sorry.*" Just like that, Roberto was gone and her head was her own again.

§

A dam had broken. For years, Roberto had kept his feelings on a leash. He'd escaped a crucible of pain and never wanted to revisit it, so he'd barricaded his emotions behind a thick wall.

Ezaara had destroyed all that. From the first glimpse of her imprinting, she'd created a chink in his defense. He'd plugged the hole with cold indifference, austere instruction and dogged determination.

But her loyalty to the queen had created another rift in his wall. Her courage, another. By stealth, the chinks had widened. And during the race yesterday, at the river, the fire of dragon power had swept away his last flimsy pretense of indifference.

It had sneaked up on him like a wildcat and sunk its claws deep into him, and no matter how he tried to shake it loose, it clung to him, worming its way deep inside him.

He loved her.

And she knew it.

And if he acted on it, he'd be banished.

§

Jaevin's sword thudded against Ezaara's leather breastplate. Vino roared. No! Strike three, and she hadn't landed a blow yet.

She had to bide her time. She was used to holding out against larger opponents. Tomaaz was a head and shoulders taller than her. Lofty, even bigger. Dragging their bulk around, they often tired before her. But Jaevin wasn't showing any sign of tiring. It was a joke—she hadn't come near to landing a blow. At this rate, she'd only be proving her incompetence.

Ezaara dodged another strike and swung around so Jaevin couldn't back her up against the rock face. Sweat pricked her eyes. She darted back, out of range. Jaevin lunged again, intense thrusts driving her across the arena. Get in fast and attack him? How naive she'd been.

The clash of steel on steel rang among the rock faces as Jaevin launched another flurry of attacks. Her arms were tiring. Her breath rasped in her throat. Everyone's eyes were on her. She couldn't back down. She had to prove herself. Had to strike him, if only once.

She stumbled over a rock, and Jaevin tapped her leg. Vino roared, his scales shining blood red in the sun. Four strikes. None to her. One more from him and they'd be done.

"A short break," Master Jaevin called. "Water, please."

Ezaara slumped onto a rock.

"Well done, Ezaara," Adelina called out. "He's already beaten all of us, so you're in excellent company." A ripple of laughter floated across the arena.

Even though they weren't laughing at her, Ezaara wanted more. They had to take her seriously. Everyone had to see that she could fight, lead them, think strategically. If she were to lead them, they needed to feel confident in her abilities. She had to land a blow on Jaevin—and soon.

Roberto brought Ezaara a waterskin. She drank deeply, wiping her mouth while he held her sword. "Thank you," she gasped. "I needed that."

"Think strategically," Roberto mind-melded.

She nodded, too tired to reply.

"Come on, Ezaara. What's his biggest weakness?"

"Jaevin's fast, but he sometimes keeps his left side open. I'll try to use that move you used on me the other day." Roberto had repeatedly slipped his blade past her guard, tapping her forearm. She took another swig of water.

"It'll impress him if you can carry it off." Roberto's eyes rested on her face a moment longer than necessary before he passed her sword to her, took the waterskin, and went back to the sidelines.

Impressing Jaevin was no small order. She was up against the most practiced swordsman in the realm.

"Go, Ezaara!" Adelina and Gret pumped their fists in the air. Cheers broke out. Lofty was the only one who'd ever cheered for her at home. These riders wanted her to do well. She had to try. Mustering her determination, Ezaara stood to face Jaevin.

A deep note rang out from Lars' horn.

Ezaara leaped forward, but Jaevin was already there, aiming a blow at her chest. She parried, sword ringing, and lunged. He deflected her blade. She ducked low, feinting to Jaevin's left and leaped to his right. His side was open. She thrust up, hard. He twisted, sword flashing, but he was too late. Her blade hit his forearm.

Caught by the sun, red droplets sprayed through the air as he drove his sword across her blade, flicking the sword out of Ezaara's hand. Her blade clattered to the stone.

Dragon's fangs! She'd swung so hard, the blunted blade had cut him.

Vino roared, counting her first strike. But the crowd was silent—she'd injured a master.

Belly hollow, Ezaara gasped. "Sorry, Master Jaevin."

He grimaced. "Good hit. A little too much force for training, but it's only a scratch. I'll survive."

It was more than a scratch—although not a deep gash—but was bleeding impressively. Perhaps he was a bleeder, whose blood didn't clot properly.

"When unevenly matched, use more leverage," Master Jaevin said. "Strike with the strong part of your sword against my tip. Now, pick up your sword, Ezaara, and keep fighting. A tharuk wouldn't show you any mercy."

She snatched up her blade.

Blood running down his arm, Jaevin fought with a ferocity that made her knees tremble. Again and again, he struck and she blocked.

Blood ran down his hilt, drops flying—so much blood for such a small cut.

Her arms ached. Her legs were tired. If she faltered now, he'd strike her again—the last strike.

"*Steady,*" Roberto murmured.

She rallied, blocking the master's blows.

Gradually, Jaevin slowed. A sheen of sweat coated his face. His strikes weren't as strong as before. Face pale, Jaevin leaped onto a rock, deftly flinging his sword from his right hand to his left, then jumped back down to engage her.

Even using his left hand, he was good, but definitely weaker than before and tiring too fast. Ezaara parried him easily. She drove him back. He stumbled.

Lips tinged blue, Jaevin's breathing rasped as he lifted his blade to strike her—and dropped it, clutching at his chest.

"Master Jaevin, are you all right?" Ezaara sheathed her sword and leaped forward to support him.

Pale. Blue-tinged lips. Rasping breath. The edges of his gash were puckered and he was bleeding way too much. Dread filled her. Dragon's bane—it had to be.

But who had poisoned him? Amid murmurs from the crowd, Ezaara lowered Jaevin to the ground, positioning him against a rock.

She picked up her ceremonial blade, examining the tip. Despite the bloody end, the blade glistened with a clear substance. She sniffed it. Yes, it *was* Dragon's bane. Deadly if not treated. She had the remedy in her healer's pouch, back in her cavern.

"Unhand him!" A shrill voice yelled. Fleur.

"It's dragon's bane. He needs—"

Sofia yelled, "Another victim. She wants us all dead!"

"She's Zens' spy!" Alban joined in.

"Get away from him." Rushing over, Fleur knelt beside Jaevin. "Poison!" She pointed at Ezaara. "Seize her. She's poisoned the master of the sword."

If they didn't listen to her, Jaevin would die. "No, you don't underst—"

The blue guards grabbed Ezaara's arms.

In a flash, Roberto's sword tip was at a guard's throat. "Unhand the Queen's Rider," he demanded.

Within a heartbeat, Tonio leveled his dagger at Roberto. "You're threatening the blue guards?" he asked in a deadly-soft voice.

"They're threatening the Queen's Rider," Roberto snapped.

"Who has poisoned the swordmaster," Fleur barked, bent over Jaevin.

This was crazy. They were all at each other's throats. "Stop," Ezaara called. "There's been a misunderstanding. Jaevin needs—"

Zaarusha roared and swept down from the outcrop, thudding to the arena. *Don't worry, Ezaara, this is preposterous. I'll sort it out.*

Lars blew the horn as Singlar landed. "Order," Lars yelled. "Order, now!"

Everyone froze.

Shards, these riders had discipline.

"Stand down, Tonio and Roberto," Lars barked. They sheathed their weapons, glowering at each other. "Fleur, take Jaevin to the infirmary at once and purge this poison from him."

"Yes, Master Lars. I won't rest until I identify it."

"Master Lars," Ezaara said, "it's dragon's bane." The antidote was in her healer's pouch, tucked under her mattress for safekeeping, but it was common enough. Fleur probably had it by the jarful—or maybe not. "I have the remedy."

Fleur's gaze was glacial. "It's probably a ruse to feed him further poison and finish him off." She and Bruno bundled Jaevin onto Ajeuria, between them.

Ezaara watched, helpless. No one trusted her.

"Don't let anyone get their hands on the remedy," Roberto melded. *"Except you. Keep its whereabouts secret."*

"Why?" No answer.

Lars addressed the crowd. "No one will be apprehended without proof. However, there are suspicious circumstances, so we'll need the standard precautions. Everyone except the council members and blue guards are to go straight back to their assigned duties, now. If you know anything about Master Jaevin's poisoning, report to the council this afternoon."

The air was a flurry of murmurs and flapping wings as riders left for the caverns.

Lars addressed the masters and guards. "We'll meet as a council to discuss who may have poisoned Master Jaevin. Tonio, you will be disciplined for raising a weapon against another master."

Tonio's face flashed annoyance, but he nodded.

"Ezaara, as prime suspect, and I mean suspect only, you and Zaarusha will be kept under guard until we've sorted this out." Lars nodded at a hefty blue guard nearby. "Jacinda, your troop are assigned to guard the Queen's Rider and the queen in their quarters until the trial."

"We'll go quietly," Zaarusha said.

"Of course." Ezaara kept her head high.

Jacinda and her blue guards surrounded Ezaara and the queen at swordpoint, removing Ezaara's weapons.

"Roberto, for raising your sword against a blue guard, and as Ezaara's training master, you and Erob will also be confined to your quarters. Seppi, your troop will look after Erob and the master of mental faculties and imprinting." At Lars' words, guards manhandled Roberto onto a blue dragon.

Ezaara mind-melded one last time. *"Roberto, it wasn't me."*

There was nothing from Roberto, not even a backward glance or a mind-melded thought. It was as if she wasn't there.

Lars' gaze was fierce. "Jacinda, Seppi, you're tasked with everyone's safety as much as their containment. Check their food and water aren't poisoned. Make sure no one reaches their quarters to harm them. I intend to get to the bottom of this with everyone intact."

Suspicions

Guards hustled Roberto through the onlookers, the air a soup of murmured rumors and fetid body odor. He swiped a trickle of sweat from his forehead. It wasn't the first trial he'd attended—although at every one, memories of his father's banishment loomed. That old bitterness flooded his mouth. He swallowed it down.

The council chamber was packed with people, crammed into a makeshift gallery of chairs. More were standing, six-deep, around the walls. The other masters were seated, the granite horseshoe a giant shield around them. Ezaara should be sitting behind that table, not facing it on trial. The realm's ruling dragons were lined up along the rear wall like warriors ready for battle. Zaarusha's eyes were golden slits, focusing on a point in front of the crowd—Ezaara.

There she was. White-faced, on a chair facing the council, stiff-backed guards on either side of her. Even under duress, she was beautiful. Her smattering of freckles stood out like scattered stardust. Her head was high, gaze directly on the council. Facing them head on—like she'd faced every other challenge since arriving here.

Beyond her, Fleur, Bruno and Simeon were seated in the accusers' chairs. Fleur should be healing Jaevin, not here on a witch hunt. Roberto shrugged off the guards and strode forward, stopping before the council table.

"Nice of you to finally show up," Erob said from his spot among the other dragons.

Roberto sent him a mental snort.

Lars rapped a gavel on the table. The crowd hushed.

"We're here to establish who poisoned Master Jaevin." Lars scanned the room. "As spymaster, Master Tonio has been appointed as spokesperson for the accusers. Master Roberto, as Ezaara's official trainer, you are responsible for defending her."

Keeping his face a mask of disinterest, Roberto replied. "You're right, Master Lars, it is my duty—unless someone else volunteers."

He melded with Ezaara, *"Do you trust me?"*

"I do."

"Then, please, no matter what I say, don't protest." Tonio was Fleur's spokesperson. Tonio, who mistrusted Roberto and hated his father. Tonio, who was brilliant at slanting evidence to suit his case.

"I promise ... but—"

"Ezaara, they'll banish you if they believe you're guilty. Do you want to lose Zaarusha? Life here at the hold?"

"Are you going to lie?"

"I may have to. We can't afford to have you banished."

"You mean innocents can be banished?"

Roberto shifted his weight. "I've seen it happen."

The air was sticky with anticipation.

Lars shuffled some parchment and dipped a quill in his inkwell. "Master Tonio, I turn the time to you. Please outline the accusation and question the accused."

It was dehumanizing, hearing Ezaara referred to as *the accused*, but Roberto held his tongue, and steeled himself for Tonio's questions.

Tonio stalked around the table to stand near Fleur. Eyes fixed on Ezaara, Tonio addressed him. "Master Roberto, permission to question the accused directly."

A demand, not a request. And one he didn't want to submit to, but he couldn't refuse without making Ezaara look guilty, and Tonio knew it. "If you must." Roberto stepped back.

"The accused—*Honored* Queen's Rider." Tonio's tone was derisive. "Do you recognize these ceremonial swords?" He gestured at the swords Ezaara and Jaevin had dueled with that morning, now lying on the council table.

"Yes."

"Where have you seen them?"

"They've been hanging on the wall in my cavern since I came to Dragons' Hold," she replied.

Already things looked bad. She'd had access to the blades every day.

Tonio addressed the council. "When Zaarusha melded to let us know she was bringing a new Queen's Rider, Swordmaster Jaevin checked the ceremonial blades were blunted in preparation for her sword evaluation. He then hung them back in the Queen's Rider's cavern." His face darkened. "No one thought to check them again until after Jaevin was injured." He turned to Ezaara, his voice hard-edged. "*Your* blade was not only coated in poison, it had also been sharpened."

Ezaara met Tonio's dark gaze. "I didn't know what those blades were for. I thought they were decorative. It would make no sense for me to poison a decorative sword, or any sword. Besides, I've been training day and night, so anyone could've tampered with them."

"*Good point.*"

"No, Ezaara. Not anyone." Tonio's smile was feral. What did he have up his sleeve? "I call Fleur, Master of Healing, as my first witness."

Fleur rose, her chair grating against the stone, setting Roberto's teeth on edge.

"Master Healer, Fleur, what was the poison on the defendant's blade?" Tonio was charming—now he wasn't questioning Ezaara.

"I've never seen it before," Fleur said. "Neither have any of my assistants. It's something foreign to Dragons' Hold."

"It's dragon's bane," Ezaara announced, before Roberto could stop her, "as common as clover in Lush Valley. Any healer worth her salt knows that."

No! He'd been too slow. Now Tonio had rope to hang her with.

Tonio pounced. "What did you call it? Dragon's bane? Sounds dangerous." He flashed his teeth. "So, you brought the poison here, then?"

"I object," Roberto called. "He's planting a connection in everyone's minds, where there is none."

"Agreed." Lars rapped his gavel. "Continue questioning along a different line, please, Tonio."

"Did you bring this poison, this dragon's bane, to Dragons' Hold? Answer, please," Tonio snapped.

"No, I didn't. I'd never poison anyone. I've learned the healing arts, so I recognize some poisons."

"A healer must know many poisons."

"Well, that's true, my mother taught me to—"

"Your mother? Now, who was that?" Tonio purred dangerously.

Why was Tonio aiming at Ezaara's family? Was there dirt in their past?

"This isn't relevant," Roberto interjected. "We're investigating Jaevin's poisoning, not Ezaara's upbringing."

"Upbringing can have an effect on behavior, Master Lars," Tonio countered.

Lars scratched his beard. "You may proceed, Master Tonio, but please keep your questions relevant."

"Who was your mother?"

"Marlies."

Gasps rippled around the room. Those a generation older than Roberto looked shocked. Who was Marlies?

Tonio could barely conceal his triumph. "You mean the infamous healer who killed a royal dragonet, then fled before she could be convicted?" His face hardened. "Perhaps her blood flows too strongly in your veins. Perhaps you, too, had the desire to kill."

Lars rapped his gavel. "Order, Tonio. Keep your questions relevant."

But it was too late. The atmosphere was poisoned, as if Tonio had leaked dragon's bane into the air. Council masters' faces were tight, their posture rigid. Onlookers were pointing and whispering, hostile gazes on Ezaara.

"Don't answer any more of Tonio's questions," Roberto melded.

Ezaara's face was paler than before. *"I've messed up, haven't I?"* She was biting her lip, the picture of guilt. *"If only I hadn't struck Master Jaevin."*

"It was a duel. You were supposed to strike him. Someone has set you up. I know you're innocent. We need to convince the council. Try to relax." Shards! If she didn't change her expression, she'd be convicted on that alone.

Zaarusha roared.

Lars approached her and laid his hand on her snout. "The queen would like to give evidence." He nodded at Tonio. Both men placed their hands on Zaarusha's forehead. It was customary for two people to listen to a dragon's evidence, so no one could falsify it.

Lars spoke. "Zaarusha says to judge her rider upon her merits, not the mistakes of her mother. It's been years since she's had a rider, and she doesn't want to lose Ezaara."

Good, the queen was vouching for Ezaara.

As Lars and Tonio sat down, murmurs broke out. Lars rapped his gavel, then had to rap it again to get the crowd to settle.

"Tonio," Roberto said quietly. All heads swiveled to him. "This has all been coincidental. Do you actually have *any real* evidence?"

With a scathing glance, Tonio snapped his fingers.

A blue guard approached, passing Tonio a package.

"We searched her quarters." Tonio unwrapped the package and uncorked a terracotta pot. "My spy found this in the top drawer of Ezaara's nightstand. Fleur, would you please identify it?"

Fleur dipped a fingertip in the pot and sniffed it. "The same poison that's been used on Jaevin." She pointed at Ezaara. "Dragon's bane, she called it."

Dragon's bane in Ezaara's room. Roberto hadn't expected that.

"It's not mine," Ezaara blurted, panic etched on her face. "I've never seen it." "Roberto, it isn't mine, honest."

"Sit tight. Don't say another thing."

"But I have the antidote in my healer's pouch, hidden under my mattress. I could help Jaevin."

"Don't mention it."

"But—"

"Not a word. It's vital." Someone was plotting something far larger than ousting Ezaara. Her antidote could be their only chance of saving Jaevin. If Fleur got her talons on it, she'd destroy it and Jaevin wouldn't stand a chance.

Tonio slammed the pot of poison on the table, his voice as hard as granite. "What other lies are you going to tell us, Ezaara?"

Now—when Tonio had the whole crowd against her—he used her name. Intimately, as if he knew her. But if he knew her, he'd never accuse Ezaara of treason. She didn't have a treasonous bone in her body.

A guard burst into the council chamber and pushed through the crowd, rushing up to Lars.

The weary lines in Lars' face deepened. "Master Fleur," he said, "Jaevin is rapidly declining."

"I don't think I can save him." Fleur shot Ezaara venomous daggers, snapping, "I hope you're happy."

"Roberto, the antidote. I have to tell them."

"No!"

Fleur drew herself up. "Before I leave this chamber to attend to Jaevin, I would like to say one more thing."

Lars nodded. "Permission granted."

"The Queen's Rider is talented, that's undisputed," Fleur said. "My own son is quite enamored of her, and I'd considered her an asset to the realm."

Simeon's eyes roamed over Ezaara as if he'd devour her.

Clenching his fists, Roberto stuffed them in his pockets.

"After Jaevin was wounded, other incidents came to mind," Fleur continued. "When Ezaara was in the infirmary helping me, she questioned my judgment, often suggesting alternative remedies. Was she trying to poison my patients? And why did Ezaara knife Sofia? That incident has never been explained."

Roberto stood. "Master Lars, this is nothing but personal opinion and has no bearing on this morning's case."

Alban jumped to his feet. "If I may, Master Lars?" At Lars' nod, he continued, "Ezaara did not only knife Sofia. She also attacked me during the race, threatening me if I spoke up. You saw me yourself, sir, limping over the finish line."

"He attacked me and I defended myself!" Ezaara melded.

Alban had had it in for Ezaara since the knife accident. This had to stop. "Do you have any witnesses, not just people bearing grudges?" Roberto snapped.

Alban glowered, not answering.

Roberto nodded. "I thought so. No proof. This is another attempt to malign the Queen's Rider. I—"

"Sit down, Master Roberto."

Roberto sat, fuming. This was nothing but slander. Ezaara would never betray Zaarusha.

Or could she? Perhaps he was letting his heart get the better of him. He'd been betrayed before by someone he loved.

Fleur tucked a strand of hair behind her ear. "I must attend Master Jaevin and make his last hours more comfortable. Thank you for the opportunity to express my concerns." She exited the chamber, escorted by the guard who'd brought the news.

Tonio swept his hand toward Ezaara. "I present to the Council of the Twelve Dragon Masters, Ezaara of Lush Valley—daughter of Marlies, the dragonet slayer—who wheedled her way into our dragon queen's trust, only to smuggle poison into the hold and strike down Master Jaevin in an attempt to weaken our council. She planned to make this look like an accident, using a public event to disguise her murder attempt. No one suspected she'd poisoned the blade, except our intuitive healer, Fleur. I warn you, we have a traitor in our midst and would do well to be rid of her."

"They don't believe it was an accident!" Ezaara's anguish sliced through Roberto's mind, making him wince.

These coincidences were stacked against her. He had to find a sliver of proof that showed Ezaara's innocence.

"Master Roberto, please present your defense."

"Master Lars, council members, and esteemed folk of Dragons' Hold, with all due respect, we have no concrete proof and no witnesses against our Queen's Rider. It's all supposition. No one saw Ezaara poison the sword, because she didn't. The dragon's bane found in her cavern could have been put there by someone else. That she recognizes a poison from her home is unremarkable, especially when she's been trained to ease afflictions and promote health. She's an ignorant Lush Valley girl, who has imprinted with Zaarusha—not an assassin." He paused, letting the weight of his words settle. "I tested her imprinting bond. It's strong. I admit, she's been clumsy—dropping her dinner, twisting her ankle and then harming Sofia in an accident—but she's been training hard to be the best Queen's Rider she can be. And she adores our queen. Why would she throw all that away? It makes no sense. Master Lars, with your permission, may I perform a mental test on Ezaara to see whether she poisoned the ceremonial blade?"

Lars nodded. "It's within your role as Master of Imprinting and Mental Faculties. I trust you to be impartial."

It was ironic. Life had taught Roberto to be careful, to mistrust, to always question—and that was why Lars trusted him. "Ezaara, may I?"

"Of course, I have nothing to hide."

Roberto locked down his own thoughts, so Ezaara couldn't read them, and placed his hands upon her temples. There it was again, a bouquet of vibrant color swirling through him, as if he'd stepped into a summer garden. He flitted through her memories, accidentally stumbling upon their first mind-meld at the river. He tried to control the warmth spreading up his face. How did she do that? Make him feel so much, when he hadn't for years? He dug further. Despite how he felt about her, he had to prove the Queen's Rider hadn't fooled him.

Wait, what was that? Ezaara and Adelina, smuggling pots out of the infirmary. His gut hollowed. Was she guilty? Had she tricked Adelina into helping her? He chased the memory to its end. No, those were the medicinal herbs smuggled out to heal him after his chest was gashed. A breath of relief slipped out of him. He tracked further through her memories—her loyalty blazed like a beacon fire in the dark.

What a fool for doubting her.

Roberto released his hands and stepped away from Ezaara. "I'm satisfied, Lars. Ezaara did not poison the Master of the Sword. Someone is trying to blame her. They hid the dragon's bane in her room. We have a traitor among us."

Gasps rippled around the chamber.

"Excuse me, Master Lars," Simeon interrupted. "If I may … I mean, I don't want to interrupt, but I fear there may be more to Roberto and Ezaara's relationship than trainee and master."

What was Simeon inferring? *"He's bluffing,"* Roberto warned. *"Look surprised."*

The crowd tensed.

"I once stumbled upon Master Roberto half naked on Ezaara's bed. She was with him."

"What? When?" Then he remembered. "I was injured, and Ezaara was healing me." The words burst out of him before he could think.

Simeon screwed up his face. "I work in the infirmary. I don't recall you being injured."

"I took a tharuk gash to the chest when we fought at River's Edge. Ezaara treated it."

"That must've left a nasty scar."

"Of course it did," he barked.

"No, it didn't, Roberto," Ezaara melded. *"It's faded—I used piaua."*

Simeon had them backed into a corner.

"I don't suppose you'd be happy to show this scar to us, would you?" Simeon asked, all reasonableness. That leech.

"I'm not disrobing in front of half the hold, just to please you," Roberto snapped. "Master Lars, please call this man to order."

"To the contrary," Lars said. "A romantic relationship with Ezaara would prevent you from being impartial, invalidating your mental testing as well as being cause for banishment. Please show us the scar as proof of your injury. Or otherwise explain what you were doing half-naked in the Queen's Rider's quarters."

Roberto was silent. There was nothing he could do. *"Sorry, Ezaara."*

Guards stepped up to hold Roberto's arms and Tonio pulled his jerkin and shirt open.

There was an audible hiss as Tonio sucked in his breath. "No new scar," Tonio announced. "Only old ones."

At the front of the crowd, Adelina's face was stark, eyes wide with shock.

Tonio's voice sliced through the silence. "Son of a traitor! The apple doesn't fall far from the tree. You're the lowest of the low, consorting with your trainee, who's the daughter of a dragonet slayer and plotting to poison the council—of which you're an honored member." Tonio spat at Roberto's boots. "Honored no more."

"Steady, Tonio," Lars cautioned. "The council haven't cast their votes yet." He motioned to the guards, who circled Roberto, Ezaara and Tonio.

Ballot papers were handed to the council masters. The scratch of their quills made Roberto's scalp crawl. Masters passed their papers to Lars.

He opened and read the votes, his brow furrowing. His mouth grew tighter as he separated them into two piles. Only two papers were on Lars' right. The rest were piled up on his left.

"Ezaara, please stand," Lars called.

Chairs creaked as people craned past others to look at her. Roberto wished he could send them all away. Her legs were trembling. Hands shaking. But her shocked green eyes were the worst.

He'd failed her.

"Honored Rider of Queen Zaarusha," Lars said. "We find you guilty of attempted murder and treason. If Master Jaevin dies as the result of this incident, you will be guilty of murder."

Zaarusha bellowed, talons raking stone, shards of rock skittering across the floor.

They were convicting Ezaara. They'd throw her in the dungeons. Then banish her. There was no way she'd survive the Wastelands—the harsh red desert full of scorpions, rust vipers and Robandi, the tent-dwelling assassins who scoured the hot sands. If she didn't get caught in one of their cut-throat feuds, then the heat or a sandstorm would finish her.

Banishment was a death sentence.

He had to save Ezaara. He'd do anything to help her. Anything to secure the queen's rightful rider. Thoughts spiraled through Roberto's head with dizzying speed. Flee. Make a stand. Fight. Burn their way out and escape on Erob.

But all of those options led to Zaarusha losing her rider.

Steady, Roberto. You're only one man. You can't change the world. For once, Erob wasn't teasing.

His mind cleared, settling on one irrevocable course of action. Straightening his shoulders, he faced Lars. Roberto's thoughts slid over Dragons' Hold: the snow-capped peaks of Dragon's Teeth soaring high against the blue sky, fertile fields and forest sprawling at their feet. All he'd ever wanted was here. Especially now that he'd met Ezaara.

Roberto held his hand up. "Stop. I have more evidence, upon my word as a dragon master." Guards gripping his arms, he moved to the council table and met each master's gaze. "I poisoned Jaevin. I planted the poison in Ezaara's cavern. I'm part of Zens' plot to overthrow Dragons' Realm."

Lars gaped at him.

"No!" Shari gasped. "That can't be true. I know you, Roberto. You'd never do that."

Erob roared.

Tonio nodded, eyes narrowed. "I saw you with that pot after the feast. Is that when you did it?"

Adelina paled, mouthing, "No."

Shari's hand flew to her mouth.

What? Ezaara's shock seared him, burning through his bones. He'd saved her, but he'd lost her. She'd never trust him again. He tightened his resolve, slamming his mind shut. He pulled his mask down and turned to face her, sneering. "You were fools for trusting me," he said. "All of you."

Ezaara's face paled further, her freckles standing out like blood stains on snow.

Betrayal

Ezaara gasped. What about them mind-melding? What about their feelings for one another? *"So, it all meant nothing to you?"* Ezaara reached out to mind-meld with Roberto, but she came up against a wall of granite. She tried again. And again.

And again.

Nothing. Not a sniff of Roberto's thoughts. He'd blocked her out. Withdrawn.

Tonio's eyes were sharp, tone cutting. "Did you administer the poison? Or did your accomplice, Ezaara?"

"Ezaara!" Roberto snorted. "Hardly. That silly fool had no idea I'd poisoned the weapon. You heard her, she didn't even know what the blades were for."

Ezaara's stomach jolted, her breath knocked from her. She'd been a fool, all right. He'd deceived her and gained her trust—and she'd believed he loved her.

"When did you poison the blade?" Tonio asked.

"Yesterday, during the after-race celebrations."

The race had only been yesterday. A lifetime ago, when the world had been full of possibility. And love.

"Where did you source the poison?" Tonio asked. "If dragon's bane only grows in Lush Valley, did Ezaara give it to you?"

He rolled his eyes. "It's common in many places, including Naobia. Any *proper healer* would know that."

Master Bruno yelled, "I'll not have you speak about my wife like that!"

Roberto laughed, a hard, arrogant bark that made Ezaara's skin break out in cold prickles.

How could she have believed him? Their love had felt so real. So beautiful. Just what she'd dreamed of. His icy arrogance fit him like a natural skin. This was reality. The man she loved was a traitor, a liar, plotting against her queen.

Lars sighed. "Roberto." His voice was tender, as if he was speaking to a son, but grim lines furrowed his brow. "You saw the damage your father did. You vowed never to be like him. Your talents are valued here. Why would you do this?"

What had Roberto's father done?

Roberto stared at Lars, eyes cold, refusing to speak.

Lars tried again. "And your relationship with the Queen's Rider?"

Roberto's upper lip curled. "Relationship? What relationship?" He regarded her the way a buyer at a market would gaze upon rotten fish entrails.

Her cheeks burned with shame. She met his eyes. There was nothing warm there now. *"Roberto, this can't be true. Tell me it isn't. Please."* It was a desperate plea sent into a cold hard void.

"She's not the real Queen's Rider, is she?" Tonio's words struck Ezaara like a whip. "You only *pretended* to test her."

"Yes, I am," Ezaara cried.

Zaarusha roared.

"She is the Queen's Rider," Roberto said. "Their bond is strong. But banish me, and you won't have anyone to test your imprinting bonds again."

"Or feed that information to Zens," Tonio snapped.

Lars looked sick, his face tinged gray, sweat on his forehead. "Master of Mental Faculties and Imprinting, Roberto, son of Amato, is now stripped of his title and is no longer a part of this council," he announced. "He'll be banished to the Wastelands within the hour. Take him to the dungeons. His sister may farewell him before he goes. Ezaara, our Honored Queen's Rider, has been cleared of all charges. This trial is adjourned." The crack of Lars' gavel nearly split Ezaara's heart in two.

At the rear of the chamber, Erob bellowed, lashing out with his talons. Blue Guards restrained him with javelins and ropes as more guards marched Roberto out of the chamber through a side tunnel.

"Adelina," Ezaara called out, but Adelina ignored her, striding after Roberto, chin high and eyes shiny with unshed tears.

"Clear the room," Lars commanded. "The masters and dragons have urgent matters to attend to."

"Zaarusha!"

"It's all right, Ezaara. It was a mistake to trust him. It was lucky he confessed before you were cast out."

Gods, it *was* lucky. Because of his confession, her name had been cleared. *"What if he's lying?"*

"Erob said the same. But I doubt it. Roberto has obviously inherited his father's disposition, like Tonio always feared."

Ezaara was swept out the main doors amid the crowd. Although she was surrounded by people, everyone avoided eye contact and no one came near.

RIDERS OF FIRE

Fleur's and Tonio's accusations had created a granite wall between Ezaara and her people.

§

Adelina stumbled along the tunnel. Roberto. No, not Roberto. Ma, dead. Roberto, banished.

She had no one left. No one.

Not that her father had been a loss. They'd all been glad to see the back of him. Life had been peaceful after his death. After he'd paralyzed Ma. She choked back tears, cursing his watery grave. She hadn't swum in Crystal Lake again since he'd died there.

It hadn't been easy, growing up with an older brother who was fighting inner demons, but Roberto had always been gentle with her. More gentle than with anyone else. As if he'd understood her need to be protected, after what they'd been through. He'd become her mother and father. And fought tooth and talon to keep her, refused to foster her out, although that's what most thirteen-year-olds would've done if their parents were dead.

And now he was imprisoned, headed for the Wastelands.

He had no chance. Although Roberto had survived other forms of hell—everyone had said he'd never come back from Death Valley—he wouldn't be coming back this time. If cats had nine lives, Roberto had used all of his twice over.

There was something about the whole trial that was off. Roberto loved being a dragon master, loved the realm. There was no way he would've hurt anyone or risked being half naked in—

That must have been the day Ezaara had healed him and Simeon had walked in.

Why hadn't Roberto told Lars about piaua? Why hadn't he asked Ezaara to testify? Questions swirling in her mind, Adelina traipsed down the dingy tunnel to the dungeons, following her brother, the only other surviving member of her family.

§

"Adelina." Roberto's face was haggard. They clasped hands through the cold bars of the dungeon. "They'll banish me, they have to." He slipped something between them, into her pocket. His eyes were fiery with some insistent message that she couldn't grasp.

"Over my dead body!" Adelina snapped. By the Egg, they'd been through so much. It couldn't end like this.

"No," he insisted. "They have to, can't you see?"

He *wanted* to be banished. "After all you've worked for." Her throat tightened.

"And undone." His eyes flicked to the guards behind her. Those eyes were pleading with her to understand something important—but what?

"Time's up," a guard called.

"Yes," said Adelina. "Of course."

Eyes burning, she made her way back up the tunnels, determined not to cry. She'd had years of practice at hiding her emotions.

Slipping her hand into her pocket, Adelina drew out the Queen's Rider's green ribbon, warm where Roberto had held it. Oh, shards! He'd taken the blame to protect Ezaara. She blinked back tears, but it was useless. Warm rivulets coursed down her cheeks.

This was harder than Pa's treachery. His abuse. His death.

Harder than Ma's death. Because Roberto had been there.

And now, she had no one.

§

Ezaara raced to her cavern. She lifted her mattress, and snatched up her healer's pouch.

Roberto had been lying. He'd melded and shown her his true self, only it wasn't his true self. The man she'd glimpsed and loved had been a traitor. The admiration in his eyes, the way he'd lit every corner of her being with light, shone a torch on her darkest fears and given her strength to race with fire in her veins—it had all been a ruse. Some sort of mental trick to get her onside. The first step in destroying her.

A sham, nothing but a sham. Lofty's clumsy kiss had been more genuine than her mind-meld with Roberto.

But Gods, how she loved him. How she wanted him back.

Master of mental faculties, well, he'd proven that. He'd mastered melding and fooling her, easily. By the Egg, she was so ignorant. So trusting, so easy to dupe into love.

Only it wasn't love. It was *a lie*.

His lie. The master of lies, deceit and murder.

She ran, her feet pounding a tattoo into the stone floors to Jaevin's door. Hopefully, the dragon's bane hadn't finished Roberto's work. Hopefully, they had a chance …

Ezaara knocked.

A woman opened the door, wisps of sweat-drenched hair clinging to her worry-creased brow. She started. "What do *you* want?" she snapped. "Have you come to gloat?"

"Who is it?" a feeble male voice called.

"The one who poisoned you," the woman spat, pushing the door to shut it.

Ezaara jammed her foot in the gap, so the woman couldn't shut her door. "They've banished someone else. It wasn't me," she shot, her chest squeezing as she pictured Roberto's face. Shards, no! It was him. "I have the antidote. I can save Master Jaevin."

"I'm not letting you near my husband. You'll probably give him more dragon's bane." Jaevin's wife shoved on the door, but Ezaara held it fast.

"Threcia, let her in," Jaevin called. "I'm dying. If she finishes me off, at least I'll be out of my misery. But you never know, she might just save me. Any remedy is worth trying."

"Master Jaevin," Ezaara called. "I've been trained as a healer. I don't kill people—I save them, if I can."

"Go on, Threcia, please." Jaevin sounded exhausted.

His wife looked dubious. "Come in, then." Threcia barely held the door open wide enough for Ezaara to squeeze through.

Jaevin lay in a makeshift bed, in their living area, near a stoked fire. His face was pale and his breathing raspy. Ezaara felt his forehead—cool, but beaded in sweat.

"He's cold, always cold," said Threcia, tugging his blanket up. "And his breathing's shallow."

"What did Fleur give you?"

"This tea." Threcia thrust a cup at her.

Ezaara sniffed it. Woozy weed—a sleeping draft. No use against dragon's bane. "Did she give you any other remedies?"

"This, against the pain in his chest." Threcia passed her a tonic. Again, to ease a symptom, not the cause.

Dragon's bane made the airways, throat and lungs tighten and slowly close down. If the dose was strong enough, the victim would die within a day. Without an antidote, there was no chance of survival.

Roberto had done this.

It didn't make sense. His kind gifts, his tenderness, love and wonder when they'd melded …

But he'd looked every bit a hardened killer as he'd confessed, spurning her and the realm. He'd taken advantage of her ignorance. A slow burning anger spread through her, each thud of her heart a count of the ways he'd fooled her.

"Jaevin, can you swallow?"

He nodded, face pale, lips tinged blue. Threcia's eyes were locked on his face, shiny with tears. This was true love, tested over years, not the flashy show of emotion Ezaara had felt for her master.

"Threcia, get Vino to warm a third of a cup of water."

Threcia rushed off and was back within moments. Ezaara mixed eight pinches of antidote—a pale green powder made of finely crushed rubaka leaves—stirring until it had dissolved, then propped Jaevin up and helped him drink.

Once he'd swallowed the last drop, she sat, holding his wrist where the veins ran across the bone, feeling his heartbeat. Now that she'd administered the antidote, Ezaara fought her urge to rush out the door. She had to make sure this worked. Jaevin's life was more important than what was happening to Roberto.

Deep in the bowels of the caverns, a drum boomed. Then another. The stone under Ezaara's chair pulsed like a dragon's heartbeat, the floor resonating with a deep cadence that throbbed through her boot soles. Waves of sound kept rolling around them. The mournful keening of a dragon was a sad counterpoint to the drums' rhythm.

"The banishment drums." Threcia's gaze softened. "I'm glad it wasn't you."

"Who poisoned me?" Jaevin wheezed.

"Master Roberto." Ezaara's voice cracked.

"No," Jaevin whispered, face lined with shock. "No, not Roberto, I trusted him."

Exactly. Ezaara hardened her heart. She couldn't allow space for traitors. She mixed another draft and put it on the table. "Drink this in two hours."

Jaevin drifted to sleep, his breathing not completely right, but improved. Threcia walked her to the door and clasped Ezaara's hands. "Thank you."

"Please don't mention I've been here. If anyone else comes by, tell them he's sleeping."

Threcia narrowed her eyes. "Why? Master Roberto will be gone."

Gone. He flashed to mind, standing calf-deep in the water, eyes golden in the sunlight. Laughing and carefree as they'd raced together as riders of fire, his love washing over her. She'd never see him again. A pang shot through Ezaara, as strong as Alban's stomach punch. No! She fought it. He was a traitor. It was good riddance. "Keep Master Jaevin safe until he's fully recovered. He'll be weak for a few days, and it may be a while before he's himself again. Until then, it's best he doesn't have visitors." Especially Fleur, who was as good as useless. "I'll be back in a couple of hours to check on him, after you've given him the draft."

Threcia kissed Ezaara, her tears spilling onto Ezaara's cheek. "Thank you for saving his life."

It was a healer's duty to save lives, not take them. "I'm glad I could help."

"The Egg bless your mother for teaching you. I don't care what Tonio says, my family will serve you and yours." She bowed. "My Honored Queen's Rider."

Ezaara's eyes pricked. "Remember, not a word to anyone."

"Of course," Threcia said. "Master Roberto may have accomplices."

Adelina? She hadn't thought of her. Ezaara left, and ran, drums pulsing beneath her feet, Erob's howls filling the tunnels. She had to find Adelina. And, despite him being a killer, she yearned to see Roberto, one last time.

§

Heart thudding, Ezaara tried one passage after another. Strange—most of the corridors were empty. Finally, she found a tunnel with stairs winding down into the bowels of the mountain. It was cold down here, so cold. She pulled her jerkin tighter.

Feet pounding stone, she came to another tunnel with a locked door. Guards blocked it, swords drawn. "No admittance to the dungeons. Only the traitor's sister may see him."

Ezaara mustered her haughtiest tone. "Please move aside for the Queen's Rider."

"Sorry. Master Lars said you weren't to see him. It's for your own protection."

Nothing would sway them.

Ezaara tried to meld with Roberto. Nothing.

She'd have to wait for Adelina. She retreated along the tunnel, ducking into a deserted chamber, ricocheting drumbeats throbbing through her head, and her boots gnawing a hole in the stone.

Time seemed to last forever.

The drums stopped. Erob's keening died. The sudden silence stifled Ezaara like an overly-thick cloak.

Finally, along the tunnel, the door thudded. A small cloaked figure bolted past the chamber.

"Adelina," Ezaara called out.

Adelina sped up. She mustn't have heard.

"Adelina," Ezaara yelled.

Adelina raced up the winding stairs. She was deliberately ignoring her. No one could've missed that.

Ezaara quickened her pace, following Adelina along the deserted tunnels. When they'd walked so long that Ezaara was in a passage she'd never seen before, Adelina stopped outside a door.

She whirled to face Ezaara, eyes red-rimmed. Her usually cheerful face was closed. Hard. "I know you're following me, but don't."

"I need to talk to you."

"No, you don't. You're the last person I want to talk to."

It was a knife to her gut. "I want to check you're all right." And Roberto … she wanted to see him.

Adelina rolled her bloodshot eyes.

"What have I done?"

"What. Have. You. Done?" With each word, Adelina stabbed a finger in Ezaara's face. Eyes fiery, she snapped, "You've sentenced my brother to death."

"No!" What? Ezaara reeled, gut-punched. "No, Adelina, he poisoned Jaevin." The pot of dragon's bane, his confession, had sealed his fate, not her. "Tonio saw him with the pot …" The scathing hatred on Adelina's face stopped her.

"You're as dumb as Fleur." Adelina thrust open the door, strode through it and slammed it in Ezaara's face. "Go away!" she yelled through the wood.

That hurt. But not as much as Adelina was hurting. Hang on, this wasn't Adelina's cavern. Whose was it?

Ezaara pushed the door open. It was Roberto's. Erob's ornate saddlebags were leaning against a wall. Adelina was slumped on Roberto's bed, one of his jerkins in her hands. The cavern smelt like him—mint and sandalwood and male. A memory of flying with him came flooding back. Of him holding her, safely cocooned, after her stunt. She tried to swallow it down, but couldn't.

"You don't get it, do you?" Adelina wrung his garment in her hands. "I asked Roberto to tell the truth, but he refused."

"But he did tell the truth. At the trial, he said—"

"How could you be Queen's Rider and be so dumb?" Adelina's face was frankly incredulous. "My brother sacrificed his life to save yours. He's innocent."

"Oh!" Ezaara's stomach was a hollow yawning chasm. She was spinning, dropping into an endless void. "I—I—" She'd been too angry, too blind, too stupid to see …

"Why didn't you vouch for him?" Adelina demanded.

"He made me promise not to argue with him …. What about that pot Tonio saw?"

Adelina bit her lip. "The night you arrived. Oil for *your* cane."

Adelina's mother's cane. Roberto had freshly carved and oiled it, after only just meeting her. He'd cared for her, right from the start. And how had she repaid him?

"My brother would never poison Jaevin. How could you believe that?"

"When I told him I had the antidote, he said to keep it secret. Not to heal Jaevin … it seemed off. Why would he keep the remedy secret?"

"Well, think about it." Adelina tapped her foot against the bed like a mad woodpecker. "Do you trust Fleur?" Adelina's glance stabbed Ezaara. "Oh, figure it out yourself!"

Oh shards. He'd been preventing Fleur from destroying the remedy. She'd been a double fool. Now they'd lose him. But it wasn't too late. Surely she could do something. "I have to talk to him. Have to vouch for him, tell Lars."

"It's too late. He's gone." Her voice hollow, Adelina slumped on the bed. "Didn't you hear the banishment drums?"

"Yes, but—"

"When the drums sounded, everyone went to the main cavern to jeer at the *traitor* before the blue guards loaded him into saddlebags. I couldn't bear to go." She wrung his jerkin, twisting it into a tight coil. "He'll never survive the Wastelands. Never."

Oh shards, her *brother*. Her only living family member. This was so much worse for Adelina. Ezaara reached out to hug her, but Adelina shoved her away.

"My brother's life is worth more than a cheap apology. Just go."

It stung like tharuk claws raking flesh. This was her fault. She should have realized. Believed in him. Spoken up. Now it was too late.

Secret Plans

Ezaara ran to Zaarusha's den and threw herself against her dragon's side. Zaarusha's scales were warm, but nothing could ease the dark icy hollow inside.

"It's been a grueling day. How are you faring?" Zaarusha snuffled her hair, her breath tickling Ezaara's neck.

"Terrible. Adelina blames Roberto's banishment on me. Says he did it to save me. That it's my fault he's gone." It was. There was no other explanation. He loved her, she'd known that, but she'd taken his lies to save her too literally. She'd been too shocked to see the sacrifice behind his actions.

"I was surprised he'd betrayed us. I trusted him too." Zaarusha nudged her shoulder with her snout. "He even fooled Erob—and it's difficult to maintain a facade around a dragon. Erob bellowed at the council, trumpeting on about going to save Roberto until I pulled rank on him. Not pleasant at all."

"If you trusted Roberto, what changed your mind?"

"One traitor at Dragons' Hold puts the whole realm in danger," Zaarusha replied. "Roberto is clever. His mental abilities make him a dangerous foe."

His mind. Shards, his mind was beautiful. But dangerous? "But Adelina knows him better than anyone else, and she says he's innocent. What if we're banishing him wrongly?"

"Roberto's past holds dark secrets. Secrets that would make your stomach turn and send you running. I know you've developed a fondness for him, but it must stop. He's not what he seems."

Fondness? That's what Zaarusha thought these powerful feelings were?

Their love was an avalanche, hurtling headlong down a mountainside. Unstoppable. And she'd let this man go to his death.

"I disagree. We should save him, go tonight. We could try melding with the blue guard's dragon on the way. Perhaps we'll catch them before they abandon him in the Wastelands."

"Abandon him? Ezaara, he's been tried and banished. He poisoned Jaevin. You're probably his next victim."

RIDERS OF FIRE

Zaarusha might never understand. *"Adelina says the pot Tonio saw was oil for my cane, not poison."*

"Her sisterly affection is blinding her. He's been banished. And if you try to rescue him, you'll forfeit your right to be Queen's Rider and be banished, too."

Lose Zaarusha? *"But Zaarusha, I—"*

"You're as bad as Erob. We've had to put him under guard until he quiets down. My own son, imagine!" Zaarusha's voice was steely. *"I'll do the same to you, if I have to. I won't lose you, Ezaara. I won't have you assassinated."*

Ezaara clamped her thoughts down tight, so Zaarusha couldn't sense them.

Zaarusha was making her choose: Zaarusha, whom she'd imprinted with in a burning flash of color; or Roberto, whose love seared a fiery pathway through her soul.

A current of bitterness ran through her. She didn't want to choose. She loved them both.

"Thank you, Zaarusha. It's been a long day, and you're giving me good advice," Ezaara replied.

"You've been under a lot of stress. It must've been a big shock, being charged with murder, then released, only to have your master banished."

"Yes, it has been. I'm exhausted."

"Why don't you have a meal before bed? That might restore your energy."

Did dragons think food fixed everything? Ezaara didn't feel like eating, but she was hungry for action. *"Good idea. I'll be back soon."*

She ducked into the mess cavern and grabbed a bowl of stew. By keeping her ears open, she soon learned where Erob was being kept.

§

Ezaara hefted the lump of meat. Convincing Benji, the head of the kitchens, to give it to her so she could console poor grieving Erob had been easy. The hard part was going to be persuading the guards to let her feed him.

Low snarls rippled down the tunnel. Erob had stopped roaring a while ago, but he hadn't given up protesting.

"Erob," she melded.

"You!" he snarled back.

Ezaara swallowed. One word—so much venom.

"Erob, we have to rescue Roberto." She rounded a corner, the flickering torchlight making her shadow skitter along the wall.

"As if Zaarusha would condone that," Erob spat. "I've been shackled by my own mother—for loyalty to my rider."

"Zaarusha threatened to strip me of my role, but I'm going anyway."

"So, you saw through his subterfuge to save you?" Erob sounded surprised.

Ezaara swallowed, keeping her thoughts masked. Thank the Egg for Adelina.

"How could everyone believe him? How could they not see his innocence?" Erob's questions stabbed her.

Shards, she'd been so dumb. Guilt wormed its way through Ezaara. She had to phrase this right. *"We could go together."* Her heart thumped twice before she dared continue. *"But we'll have to convince them we're being obedient or we won't stand a chance."*

Ezaara rushed along the tunnel, bloody meat dripping on stone. There, on the right, was a barred cavern, in the shadows. Behind the bars, Erob sat on his haunches, yellow eyes slitted, still snarling.

"Halt. No one has permission to be down here." A blue guard stepped out, blocking her way. He was massive with a thick scar running down his neck. Two more were behind him.

"I've brought food for the dragon," she said. "It might soothe him."

The scarred guard grunted. "Orders are orders."

A smaller guard spoke up, "He's quite upset. Perhaps food would calm him."

"What if she doesn't touch him?" the third guard muttered.

The scarred guard grunted. "All right." They stepped aside.

"They think we can only meld when you touch me," Erob whispered in her mind, the perfect picture of a brooding dragon. *"If only they knew."*

Ezaara held up the meat, advancing slowly, letting her arms shake as if she were nervous. *"We have to be quick,"* she melded.

Erob's snarls ceased as he sniffed the meat. *"What's your plan?"*

"You need to calm down. We have to convince them that you don't need guards."

"Got it. As soon as they let me free, I'll meld and let you know." She passed the meat through the bars. His lips curled back and he took it in his fangs, retreating to the back of the cave. *"We can't leave until after dark."* Erob chomped on his meat, tail curled around himself protectively, as if he wanted to hide in a corner and lick his wounds.

"I can't believe the change in him," said the scarred guard.

Ezaara nodded. "In times of crisis, dragons need a source of comfort." She wasn't lying—their plan to rescue Roberto would comfort Erob more than any chunk of meat.

"Maybe that's why she's Queen's Rider," the third guard whispered, nudging the small one.

"Mm," murmured the small guard. "That and the way she can fly. Remember that?"

Ezaara retreated down the tunnels. Great, they'd believed her. Now for phase two of her plan.

§

After checking on Jaevin again, Ezaara returned to the mess cavern and pocketed some food. When she reached Roberto's cavern, Adelina was nowhere to be seen. She glanced about for somewhere to hide her supplies.

"Ezaara," Zaarusha's voice nearly made Ezaara drop the food. Dashing to Roberto's wardrobe, she stashed apples, smoked meat and bread among his clothes and slammed the door. The scent of his clothes conjured up his face, raven eyes tinged with sunlight, regarding her at the river. *Loving* her.

"Ezaara!" Zaarusha again.

Ezaara jolted the image away. *"Yes, Zaarusha?"*

"You've been gone a while. I wanted to check you're all right."

"I've been stretching my legs." Well, that was true, she had traipsed back and forth between the mess, Jaevin's, Erob's holding pen and Roberto's quarters.

"Come back soon. I'd like to see you settled before I go hunting."

"On my way."

When Ezaara returned to their quarters, Zaarusha was pacing in the den, hungry.

"*You seem more energized,*" the queen said.

"*Eating helped.*" It *had* helped Erob.

"*Stay right here,*" Zaarusha warned. "*I know you were keen on going after Roberto earlier.*"

Had the queen seen through her?

"*But I'm glad you've seen sense,*" Zaarusha continued. "*Colluding with a traitor would strip you of your privileges. The last thing I want is to lose another Queen's Rider.*" A potent wave of sorrow enveloped Ezaara with that same memory of Anakisha falling into a seething mass of tharuks.

"*What an awful way to die.*" Ezaara squeezed her hands tight, her nails biting her palms. She didn't want to lose Zaarusha.

"*Not as bad as at the hands of a traitor.*" Zaarusha glided off the ledge toward the hunting grounds.

Whichever path she chose, Ezaara would hurt someone she loved—the queen she'd pledged her life to, or the man she'd given her heart to. She sighed, walking with heavy feet through the archway to her cavern.

"*Ezaara, the guards have let me go.*" It was Erob. "*I'll meet you at midnight in my den.*"

It was happening. In a few short hours, she was walking out on her life as Zaarusha's rider. Walking out on everything she could ever dream of—except Roberto. She couldn't stay here and let him die in the Wastelands. Life without Roberto would be like living in a dead and empty shell, walking on knife-sharp shards every day.

"*I'll be there.*" Ezaara checked the supplies in her healer's pouch and added more of the clean herb and bear's bane she'd retrieved from the infirmary when she'd healed Roberto.

From what she'd gleaned in the mess caverns, the Wastelands were vast fierce deserts, inhabited by feuding tribes and rust vipers, four days' flight from Dragons' Hold. Roberto would be dropped off with a few mouthfuls of water, but no weapons or food. If she and Erob could leave tonight, they'd only be a few hours behind him—although it might take days to find him.

"*Ezaara, I need your help!*" a dragon's voice called faintly, as if it was far away.

"*Who are you?*" Ezaara mind-melded.

"*Septimor, a dragon with the blue guards. I have a young girl, attacked by tharuks, who needs healing.*"

She had to leave. She had no time. "*Master Fleur is in the infirmary.*" Guilt rippled through her. Sending patients to Fleur went against her grain. Fleur's healing was clumsy at best, her salves seemed useless, and Adelina was worried that Fleur would destroy the antidote to dragon's bane. She couldn't trust her with a master or a rider, but surely Fleur would heal a girl with a few cuts or scrapes.

"*I can't send her to Fleur,*" Septimor answered. "*I want her to survive.*"

Ezaara didn't miss the cynical edge to the dragon's reply. Or the urgency. "*What's wrong with her?*"

"Her arm's been mutilated and infected with limplock, a tharuk poison. She's dying."

Dragon's fangs and bones! *"Bring her to me. When will you be here?"*

"Soon. Master Roberto knows the remedy."

Septimor obviously didn't know Master Roberto had been banished.

Ezaara ran down the tunnels toward Adelina's quarters. Being Roberto's sister, maybe she knew the antidote too. *"Erob, something urgent has come up. Someone's dying and needs my help."*

"Yes," his answer came, *"Roberto in the Wastelands."*

"Come on, Erob. It's four days' flight, he won't even be there yet."

"True, but most die within two days of arriving. We can't delay forever."

"I have to help this girl. I can't let her die."

Erob melded again. *"If you can't come soon, I'll have to leave without you."*

"Erob, please, I'm a healer. This is my duty."

"And what of your duty to my rider?" Erob snorted. *"I'll give you one day. If you're not done by midnight tomorrow, I'm going without you."*

§

Gret sheathed her sword and left the practice cavern. Adelina was leaning against the tunnel wall, her eyes red. "Hi, Adelina."

"Erob wants to talk to you," Adelina said, pushing off the wall.

"I've never melded with any dragons in the royal bloodline," Gret replied. "Why would Erob want to talk to me?"

Adelina shrugged. "There's only one way to find out. He's on the ledge outside the mess cavern."

Gret put an arm around Adelina's shoulders. "Anything I can do for you?"

"I'm all right." Adelina's voice was brittle. "It's not the worst thing that's happened to me." She strode off.

That was true, but having your brother banished and sentenced to die must be tough.

The mess cavern was deserted, and Erob was the only dragon on the ledge. His large yellow eyes gleamed at Gret as she touched his head.

"Gret, thank you for coming." His voice rumbled through her mind. *"With Roberto gone, someone must protect the Queen's Rider. Are you up for this task?"*

"Of course, but why me?"

"I can trust you. Ezaara trusts you. You're fast with a sword and nimble on your feet, and you're young—you can keep vigil overnight without dozing off."

He showed her a vision of a secret alcove near Ezaara's cavern. *"Hide here. Be vigilant. There are some at Dragons' Hold who would do Ezaara harm."*

"I'll be vigilant. I owe it to my queen and Ezaara." Gret's heart swelled with pride. A royal dragon, no less, respected her swordsmanship.

"Thank you." Erob flapped his wings, sending the stray hair on Gret's forehead wafting in the breeze, then he was airborne.

Gret flicked her braid over her shoulder. Should she trust Erob? If Roberto was really a traitor, couldn't his dragon be traitorous too? She shook her head. No, Erob would never betray his mother, Zaarusha, and the realm. And despite what everyone was saying, neither would Roberto. Something strange was going on.

After careful inspection, she found the hidden alcove in the corridor opposite the door to Ezaara's cavern. Deep in shadow, a lip of rock obscured the entrance. She hid inside, starting her vigil.

Hours later, after midnight but still a while before dawn—the worst part of night watch—Gret stretched wearily, easing a kink in her neck. It was cramped in here. She didn't dare stamp, and there wasn't room to walk. She blinked and shifted her weight from foot to foot. So much for Erob's vigilance of the young.

A faint scrape on rock jerked Gret awake. There it was again. Moving her weight forward, she placed her eye against a spy hole. Someone was around the corner. Gret eased her knife from its sheath. Heart pounding, she waited.

A shadow flickered. Simeon crept down the tunnel, glancing furtively over his shoulder.

She should have known. That shrotty weasel had forced himself upon her best friend, Trixia, but no one had believed her—not with Simeon's parents, the highly-esteemed council masters, accounting for his whereabouts. Everybody had assumed Trixia's betrothed, Donal, had fathered the littling. Fleur and Bruno had insisted that Trixia be banished for tainting their son's name, but Lars had sent Trixia and Donal both back to Montanara. Trixia had lost her lifelong dream of becoming a dragon rider.

That rat—no, that tick on the backside of a rat—was nearly at Ezaara's door. Simeon peered through Ezaara's keyhole.

Now was her chance. Gret slipped out of the alcove. Approaching Simeon from behind, she grabbed his hair in her fist, and held her knife to his neck. "This stops right here, rat."

Simeon froze.

"Stand up. Slowly." She gripped his hair, keeping her knife at his throat, and marched him toward Lars' chamber.

§

Lydia had been asleep for hours, but Lars hadn't touched his pillow. Pacing in front of the fire, he rubbed his shoulder, trying to ease a stubborn knot. It was crazy, he'd trusted Roberto, but now he'd admitted he was a traitor. It felt wrong. Everything was off. But he was already gone to the Wastelands.

And Tonio was like a dog, yapping at his heels, determined to believe Roberto was evil. What if Tonio was wrong? There wasn't anyone else with Roberto's skills. Who would now test their imprinting bonds? Who would now ensure dragon riders were trained to withstand tharuk mind-benders?

There was scuffling outside his door. Lars strode over and flung it open.

Gret was outside, her knife at Simeon's throat. Eyes shining in the torchlight, she announced, "I've brought you a traitor."

Another one?

A trickle of blood rolled down Simeon's neck.

"Gret, stop! What are you doing?"

"I caught Simeon sneaking up to the Queen's Rider's cavern." Gret kept her knife at Simeon's throat.

"Come in, both of you." Lars waved his hand. "Down with the knife, Gret." He turned to Simeon. "It's the middle of the night. What were you doing near the Queen's Rider's cavern?"

Simeon's voice was smooth. "Master Lars, I was concerned for the Queen's Rider's health. There's talk that a rogue dragon wanted to burn her. I had a nightmare that she'd died, so I wanted to reassure myself that she was all right."

Gret snorted.

Lars had heard too many rumors to believe everything Simeon said. He turned to Gret. "Your opinion?"

"Like I said, he was sneaking around. It's not the first time he's wanted to harm—"

"I was only looking through the keyhole," Simeon interrupted, "to make sure she wasn't harmed."

"Liar. You were figuring out how to sneak in," Gret snapped, eyes fiery.

Simeon rubbed the scratch on his neck.

"Gret," asked Lars, "what did you actually see?"

"Ah, I—" She scuffed her boot on the stone floor. "He was acting sneaky, skulking along the corridors and peering through the keyhole—"

"And you?" barked Simeon. "Hiding in the shadows of the Queen's Rider's corridor, late at night? What were you doing?"

"Waiting for you," Gret snapped. "You're more trouble than a rat's nest."

Lars' instincts aligned with Gret's, but he had to have proof. "Simeon," Lars said, thinking fast, "turn out your pockets." Hopefully they could pin something on him this time.

Only healing salve. Not a weapon on him. That made sense, he was a healer's son. But something about this was wrong. If his parents weren't dragon masters, he wouldn't have believed him—about Trixia, or tonight.

Lars ran a hand through his hair. "Simeon, this is a warning. If you're caught near the Queen's Rider's cavern alone again at night, you will face trial and possible banishment. This is not your first warning."

That business with Trixia had never been resolved to Lars' satisfaction, but with two council members vouching for Simeon, there hadn't been much he could do. "Simeon, go straight to your quarters. Gret, please stay a moment."

Lars waited until Simeon left, and shut the door. He turned to Gret, whose fists were balled tightly against her sides. "Gret, I know your intentions are good, but you can't hold people at knife point. You can be aware and alert. You can keep an eye out. But you cannot draw weapons because someone is looking through a keyhole. No matter how much you dislike him. No matter how angry you are at him. Understood?" He sighed. "Tomorrow, report to the kitchens for duty. I can't have you injuring Simeon and going unpunished—no matter how slight his injury was."

Gret's shoulders slumped. The skin under her eyes was dark with weariness. "Yes, Master Lars."

"Now," he said, placing a hand on her shoulder, "go back to bed. You look like you need some sleep."

Healing Calls

It was late and Septimor still hadn't arrived. Ezaara paced between her cavern and the queen's den—waiting, doing nothing, while the blue guards were taking Roberto closer to the Wastelands. She couldn't even prepare for the trip with Adelina sitting on her bed. "Are you sure that's the right remedy?" Ezaara asked.

"Absolutely sure. I'm glad you remembered seeing these in Fleur's alcove." Adelina placed a vial of yellow granules back into the fleece-lined box. "Will you relax?" she said. "All that pacing is wearing me out."

Ezaara slumped in a chair, jiggling her leg.

"Quit that wiggling too." Adelina sighed. "All right, I'm sorry for snapping at you. It was Roberto's decision to banish himself, not yours. Did you realize what you were doing when you gave him this?" She fished a green satin ribbon out of her pocket.

Ezaara gasped. "That's mine. I gave it to Roberto the day Zaarusha flew a loop."

"I know. I put them in your hair, although I wouldn't have, if I'd known this would happen."

"What?"

"You still don't get it!" Fists on her knees, Adelina leaned forward in her seat. "By accepting your ribbon, Roberto vowed to become your protector until he dies."

"What?"

"You already said that." She rolled her eyes. "Ribbon gifting is tradition. Look, I don't want to be angry with you. I've been thinking about it. Roberto would've done the same for me. In fact, he probably would've done the same for you without this." She tossed the length of green satin at Ezaara.

The ribbon unfurled in the air, falling in a tangle in Ezaara's lap. "I didn't ask anything of Roberto. Zaarusha told me to give it to him."

"You should never underestimate a dragon, especially our queen."

Zaarusha had engineered Roberto to be her protector and had then allowed him to be shipped off? He'd been too convincing for his own good. Ezaara wound the ribbon around her finger, the smooth satin soothing her skin. She wound it onto the fingers of her other hand, and then jumped out of her chair and paced to the den and back. "*When* are they going to get here?"

"Why are you so uptight?" Adelina frowned, then her eyes flew wide. "Oh. This is about my brother, isn't it?"

Ezaara opened her mouth, but before she could protest, there was a whump in Zaarusha's den.

"Septimor's finally here!" Ezaara ran to the den, Adelina on her heels.

Septimor's wings were limp by his sides. *"I think she's unconscious from limplock and blood loss."* He craned his neck toward the girl slumped in one of his saddlebags.

"You look exhausted," Ezaara said.

"I'll hunt soon." Septimor glanced around. *"Where's Master Roberto?"*

"Banished." Ezaara was careful to mind-meld, so Adelina wouldn't get upset.

Septimor's eye ridges flew up. *"Whatever for? He's one of our best."* He lowered himself so they could lift the girl out of the saddlebag.

She was about thirteen and as pale as goat's cheese, with a deep bloody gash on her forearm and one of her little fingers hanging off by a scrap of flesh. Her hands were cold, fingers stiff and curled, but her forehead was burning.

"Her name is Leah. Take care of her, Ezaara. I have to get back to Seppi—he's still fighting tharuks." The blue dragon flapped his wings and left.

They carried Leah to Ezaara's bed.

"What's wrong with her hands?" Ezaara asked, trying to pry her fingers open. "I've never seen anything like it. And her breathing's shallow too."

"That's limplock. It sticks to your nerves, slowly paralyzing you." Adelina unlaced the girl's boots. "Roberto taught me about tharuk poisons when I was small. Look." She pointed to the girl's toes. Leah's feet were curled in and her legs were spasming. "I hope we're not too late."

"She needs a full vial of the remedy, sprinkled on her tongue, a little at a time." Adelina grimaced. "It'll be tricky because she's unconscious."

"No problem." Ezaara pushed Leah's lip against her tooth, making Leah automatically drop her jaw. "You give her that, while I staunch the bleeding."

"Good trick." Adelina sprinkled a few grains onto Leah's tongue.

Ezaara made a tourniquet on Leah's upper arm, out of a shirt and her knife, to slow the blood supply to her forearm. The bleeding eased. She examined the gash. Deep, but it could be stitched, and with the help of piaua … She dribbled the pale green juice into the ripped flesh, to heal the deepest layers. The girl twitched and groaned. The flesh slowly knitted together, but it could use some help. Ezaara threaded her needle with squirrel gut, then stitched the wound while Adelina held the edges together. Then she rubbed more piaua along the scar.

"Now we've got to deal with her finger." Ezaara exhaled forcefully. Although this wasn't a job she relished, she had no choice. The finger was already pale and bloodless. She had no way of stitching bones and nerves back together.

Ezaara went out to the den and called, *"Zaarusha?"*

"Coming. Septimor told me you have a limplocked girl here." The queen flew down to the ledge. *"How's she doing?"*

"Not good. I have to amputate her finger. Could you please heat my knife?"

"Hold it out." Zaarusha's grim tone reflected how Ezaara felt. The queen heated the blade until it glowed.

Ezaara dashed back into her cavern. She swallowed. "Adelina, c-could you help me with this?"

Adelina's eyes were grave as she held Leah's hand still upon a clean cloth on the bedside table. "We're ready."

It wasn't *physically* hard to cut off the flimsy flap of skin holding the girl's finger in place—yet it was the hardest job Ezaara had ever done. It felt like slicing off hope. Damning someone to a bleak future.

It felt like losing Roberto all over again.

As she held the hot knife against the stump of Leah's finger to cauterize it, Leah, still unconscious, whimpered. Ezaara tried not to breathe in the stench of heated flesh. Hot tears ran down her face. Adelina was crying too.

Ezaara dribbled piaua juice onto the cauterized stump, and then bandaged Leah's finger. With Adelina's help, she slowly released the tourniquet.

"She'll need feverweed tea," Adelina whispered, sloshing water into a mug and crumbling feverweed into it. She passed the mug to Ezaara and sprinkled more anti-limplock granules on Leah's tongue. "We're not over the pass yet."

Exhaling violently, Ezaara paced to the den, holding out the cup to Zaarusha. *"Not too hot."*

Zaarusha leaned in and shot a tiny flame at the cup. *"There, that should be warm now. You're doing a good job, Ezaara."*

Then why did she feel so hollow?

When Ezaara came back into her cavern, Adelina was sponging Leah's forehead. "She's burning up."

"This should help."

They propped Leah's head up and took turns dribbling tea into her mouth. She swallowed reflexively. After half an hour, her fever had cooled a little. Ezaara gave her more antidote, while Adelina and Zaarusha made more tea.

"Tell me more about limplock and numlock," Ezaara asked while they waited.

Adelina settled in a chair. "Numlock stops your emotions and reasoning and makes people seem slow and dull."

"How does it feel? Do you know anyone who has had it?"

"Like you're dead inside." Adelina's eyes slid away. "Anyway, limplock is different. It gradually paralyzes you, starting with your hands and feet and working its way through your body until you stop breathing." She dribbled tea into Leah's mouth. "If the dose had been stronger, she would've been dead already. We're lucky Fleur had the antidote in her alcove."

§

Ezaara awoke to whimpering. Leah was having another nightmare. Only it wasn't yet night—the sun was setting outside. They'd been up tending her all of last night and only dropped off this afternoon, when her fever had broken.

Adelina raised her head from the pallet next to Ezaara's.

"I'll go," Ezaara croaked. "Get some more sleep." She scrambled from her makeshift bed into a chair at the bedside.

Leah was shivering again. Ezaara pulled the quilt up and grabbed some sleeping furs from a chest, piling them on top of her. Adelina had said that the antidote could make Leah tremble and vomit. So far, they'd only had trembling, but Ezaara had a supply of pails near the bed, just in case. She held Leah's hand and stroked her forehead. Touch seemed to soothe her.

Erob melded. *"How's the girl?"*

"Not conscious yet. I can't leave her with Adelina until she wakes."

"I'm going hunting. It may be days before I can eat again." Erob hesitated. *"Ezaara, whether you can come or not, I'm leaving in a few hours."*

Ezaara twisted a button on her jerkin. *"Erob, please …"*

"I can't keep delaying. Neither of us want to find Roberto dead."

"But if he's injured, I can help heal him."

"Not if you're here, you can't."

All the people she loved were slipping, like salt, through her fingers: Roberto was gone; she had no idea where Ma, Tomaaz or Pa were; and when Leah was well enough, she'd be running out on Zaarusha. How had it come to this? A tear slipped down Ezaara's cheek. Why was life full of choices that hurt?

"I know he cares about you."

Ezaara froze.

Adelina was awake, watching her.

"I—"

"I know you care about him too," Adelina said, "but I don't think I can look after Leah properly if she's unconscious. I mean, what do I do if she never wakes up?"

"No one's asking you to."

"I know. I also know Erob well. I'm guessing he'll be leaving soon. You've been stretched as tight as a bowstring since yesterday. You want to go with him, don't you?"

Ezaara nodded. Leah was peaceful now, sleeping with a trace of a smile.

Adelina gestured toward her. "Let's hope she rouses. In the meantime, I'll visit the mess room and get some food. Where have you been keeping your supplies?"

Ezaara's cheeks burned. "In Roberto's cavern, so I can load them into Erob's saddlebags."

"Logical. I'll strap his saddlebags on him and start loading." Adelina hugged her. "I'm so glad you're going. I've been crazy with worry about him."

"How do you hide your anxiety so well?"

"You mean like this?" Adelina flashed her a sparkling smile. "I've had years of practice." Face grim, she strode out the door.

§

A scream woke Ezaara. Leah, again. Her neck hurt—she'd dozed off in her chair.

Sitting up in bed, Leah was wide-eyed. "Who are you? Where am I?"

"It's all right." Adelina put an arm around her. "You're with friends, safe at Dragons' Hold."

Ezaara patted Leah's hand. "You've been sick, but we're helping you." The torches had burned low. How late was it? Had she already missed Erob?

"Ezaara, I'll take care of Leah. Zens and his tharuks ruined my family, and I swore I'd always help any victim." Adelina gestured to the door, her eyes full of meaning. "Go. Give him my love."

A jolt ran through Ezaara.

She hugged Adelina. "Thank you." She fastened her sword at her hip. Snatching up her healer's pouch and the archer's cloak Roberto had given her, Ezaara ran out the door.

"Erob, I'm ready!" she cried.

"Good, I'll be back at my den shortly."

A surge of energy ran through her. They were finally leaving.

The tunnels were dim, torches low, as Ezaara raced toward Roberto's cavern, glad to be burning off some energy after caring for Leah for a night and a day. Jaevin's poisoning, her being accused and Roberto's banishment made no sense, but they were all connected. If only she could fit the pieces together, she'd be able—

A figure stepped out of the shadows. Simeon's teeth flashed in a grin. "You seem to be in a hurry, My *Honored* Queen's Rider. Going somewhere?" His eyes slid over her body, stopping on her face.

"Not really, I've just been busy and need exercise."

"So late? With such a warm cloak?" He approached her.

The blizzard in the south-west was still raging. She'd need the cloak as she traveled. Ezaara stepped back. "It's cold out."

He moved closer. Ezaara backed away. Her foot hit the wall behind her. Simeon crowded her, his body only a hand's breadth from hers. "I can keep you warm." He ripped her cloak off, tossing it aside.

Ezaara snatched her sword. Before she could raise it, Simeon grabbed her wrist, squeezing. Gods, his grip was an iron vice. Her bones crunched and she let go, sword clattering onto the rock floor.

Simeon slammed her hands above her and thrust his knee against her groin, his body pinning her against the wall.

Ezaara bucked and twisted. It was no use.

His eyes slid to her breasts. Trapping both her hands with one of his, he ripped a button off her jerkin, yanking the fabric open.

His breath was hot, harsh in her ears. "You're mine," he growled. "No running off to rescue him. He won't want you once I've had you."

Ezaara opened her mouth to scream, but Simeon slammed his hand against it, knocking her head on the rock wall. She bit down, hard. Grabbing his flesh between her teeth, she ripped.

His hand slid out of her teeth, smacking into her head as he lurched backwards. Ezaara shoved him, and Simeon sprawled on the rock. Snatching up her sword, she held the tip at his chest.

Gret ran around the corner. In a flash, Gret had Simeon on his feet, her blade at his throat and his arm twisted up behind his back. "Caught in the act, you filthy rat!"

Simeon hung his head. "I'm sorry, Ezaara. I truly am. I shouldn't have—"

"Shut up!" Gret snapped, then addressed Ezaara. "Let's get him to Lars. With two witnesses …" Her eyes took in Ezaara, picking up her cloak, sheathing her sword. "You're going, aren't you?"

"Ezaara! Where are you?" Erob. It was time.

Ezaara nodded.

"But Lars won't believe me without you to back me up. He's always asking for proof. Please," Gret pleaded.

Questions would turn into a trial, and a trial wouldn't happen now, in the middle of the night. She didn't have time. Roberto could be dying, right now.

"Ezaara."

"Thank you, Gret, but I'm sorry."

As Ezaara raced to Erob, Simeon's gloating echoed down the deserted tunnel. "Once again, little Gret, it's your *pathetic biased* word against mine."

The Wastelands

Tangerine sand, as bright as the orange on Ana's scarves, undulated in endless rippled hillocks. Ezaara's nostrils burned, just from breathing. Stinging sand grains whipped into her eyes, and sweat slicked her back. She'd always imagined the Wastelands as bleak, but this cruel land was also breathtaking. The rolling hills were etched with mysterious patterns from the wind's fingertips, and stretched so far they made her eyes ache.

"They're called dunes," said Erob, "those hills."

"It's hopeless, Erob. How will we ever find him?"

"Keep mind sweeping. Roberto's got to be somewhere."

"It's been two days. I haven't sensed a thing, except you. Apart from those tents near that oasis and a few Robandi tribes, the only thing we've seen is sand."

"Don't give up. We have to find him."

Hopefully alive. Although the longer they searched, the less likely that was. Ezaara gripped Erob's spinal ridge with tired fingers. Her throat ached and eyes stung—and it wasn't from the sand.

§

The heat pressed against Roberto, like a scratchy blanket. Despite the undershirt wrapped around his head and mouth, his throat rasped. He shook his waterskin. Not a drop left—he'd drained the last trickle hours ago. It was a miracle the paltry contents had lasted that long.

He dragged his heavy legs through the endless shifting sand, longing for the cool kiss of night—although dark brought its own challenges. Last night had been so cold, he'd been wracked with shivers by the time the sun had glared over the dunes, but right now, that would be better than being scorched alive. Ezaara's awful vision flashed through his mind: being burned alive by dragon flame. This furnace was burning his lungs—he was roasting alive, inside and out.

Shards! He had to pee.

Hope spurted inside him. Something to drink. By the Egg, had it really come to this?

He peed into the waterskin. Only a dribble, but it burned and his pee was so dark it was the color of this cursed sand. Shrugging, Roberto took a sniff, wrinkling his nose. Foul and stinking, but it was liquid. It could keep him alive. He raised the waterskin.

No, he couldn't drink it. Dropping the skin, he staggered toward the next dune. If only he could fly on Erob's back, traversing the desert by air. He blinked. Erob wasn't here, but something was clinking over the next dune.

His brain was so foggy, he nearly rushed straight up the sand. No! Caution. He dropped to his belly and crawled until he crested the hill. Robandi. Two feuding tribes. If he read the battle right, red headdresses were pitted against white.

A man ran a saber through the stomach of another, blood turning the amber sand to deep red. The man whirled, scarlet drops flying from his blade and slashed an arm, a chest, a face. Men, only men. Fierce, desperate, sabers flashing in the sun, until they were stained so red, they were too dull to flash. No cries, no yells or moans marked this battle. Feet muffled by sand, they fought with precision and uncanny silence, as if they were afraid of being heard. Only grunts and clashing blades scarred the stifling air, the strange silence as oppressive as the heat.

A man fell, throat slashed, his blood gurgling as his eyes turned lifeless.

Still on his belly, Roberto retreated down the dune, leaving a deep furrow. Curse this sand. He'd be easy to track. Scrambling to his feet, he turned to flee— and came face to face with two men with red headdresses whose white clothes were splattered with blood.

A grin flashed white in a dark weathered face. An instant later, a bloody saber was at Roberto's neck, its tip sharp against his skin.

He was their enemy. No sudden moves. Roberto edged his hand down his leg toward the blade hidden in his boot.

The pressure of the saber on his neck increased.

The other man flicked his sword across Roberto's fingers. Blood welled up across his stinging knuckles.

In a hiss of sand behind him, a shower of particles tumbled down the slope. Orange-clad camel riders were racing down the dune.

Shock registered on his captors' faces. One lunged at Roberto, sword slashing.

The pain was instant, blooming across his gut like a jellyfish unfurling thousands of stingers. Clutching his torso, he looked down. His clothes were sliced straight through, his guts spilling out of his broken flesh. He sunk to the sand, grasping at the edges of the wound, trying to hold the contents of his stomach together.

His gut rippled with fire. Lights ricocheted through his head. It was no use. In this blasted sun, his insides would dry out and disintegrate, as fragile as the crust of paper round the rim of a rice pot.

"*Ezaara!*" He'd never see her again.

Zaarusha

Zaarusha was wroth. That fanged Ezaara had risked the kingdom for infatuation. That silly volatile new rider. She roared, sending a sprinkling of shale tumbling down the mountainside. Undignified and irresponsible behavior for a queen, but she didn't care. Her rider was gone.

Gone. After eighteen years of waiting.

After loss and despair and deceit. Right when Zens was marshaling his armies.

Liesar alighted on the lip of Zaarusha's den and bowed her silver neck, her snout nearly scraping the ground.

"*The Queen's Rider is gone.*" Zaarusha knew the wave of despair she'd sent to Liesar would have left a lesser dragon cowering. But that's why she'd summoned Liesar. Not Ajeuria the Sly or Antonika the Stealthy, but Liesar the Strong. Liesar who'd arrived home last night with a sick girl from Lush Valley.

"*I know,*" was Liesar's reply. "*Erob melded with me as I was flying here and he was going south.*"

"*Erob told you, but deceived his own mother!*" Zaarusha snarled, blasting Liesar with a gust of fire.

Liesar stood solid, immovable, silver scales reflecting the flames. "*Yes, me. When you were enraged and would've killed Marlies, all those years ago, I ferried her away to Lush Valley to protect her lineage. I guessed correctly that your dragonet had passed his life force to her.*"

"*Don't remind me of your traitorous actions.*"

"*Traitor or savior?*" Liesar's turquoise eyes regarded Zaarusha. "*There are many facets to our actions, My Queen. My actions provided you with a Queen's Rider of exceptional capability, a rider as good as Anakisha herself.*"

"*A rider who has fled after her lover—a traitor!*" Zaarusha snarled, bunching her legs to pounce.

Liesar bowed her head, now submissive. That was better, the way a subject should treat a queen.

"*Shall we hunt them down and kill them?*" Liesar asked. "*Roberto, Ezaara—and Erob too? Would that avenge your wroth? Would that appease My Queen?*"

Zaarusha froze.

"Or would you rather listen to reason?"

Motionless, Zaarusha watched Liesar, feeling the timbre of her mind as she relayed Erob's message.

"*Tell My Queen and mother that I honor her and love her.*" A wave of love flooded Zaarusha's chest. That was Erob, loyal and true. "*Tell her Roberto is innocent, that he lied to save the Honored Queen's Rider, Ezaara, and that she fled to find him. There's a traitor at Dragons' Hold, but it's not Roberto or Ezaara. Someone is plotting to undo the realm. Someone who doesn't want Anakisha's prophecy to come true.*"

As much as she hated to admit she was wrong, Erob's words rang true. "*Why should I listen to his message?*" Zaarusha scoffed, but the heat had gone out of her words. It was all bluster.

Liesar, now grinning, knew it too.

The queen changed her stance, airing her wings. "*Let's hunt down this traitor before they do any more damage.*"

There was a rap at Ezaara's door and the pounding of hurrying feet in Ezaara's cavern.

Adelina burst into Zaarusha's den. "My Honored Queen, Master Jaevin is dead!"

Silent Assassins

Ezaara winced. *"No, Erob, we can't return without Roberto."*

"It's been days. We need more food," Erob insisted, flapping his wings, his shadow rippling over the wind-streaked orange below. *"Unless we find a food source here, we'll have to return to Naobia for supplies. We're no use to Roberto dead."*

"It'll take two days to fly to Naobia and back here. Anything could happen to Roberto in that time." Shards, they couldn't leave yet, not without him. Panic gnawed at Ezaara's gut. He'd die.

"Ezaara, don't despair. We have to eat. We're useless to him dead."

"And he's useless to us dead too!" she snapped.

Erob was silent, his slowing wingbeats speaking for him. Days of trawling the desert were wearing them down. They'd seen signs of skirmishes—ominous dark stains in the sand—and caravans of Robandi, but there'd been no sign of Roberto. What if he was hidden in a tent or a sandy grave?

"Sorry, I shouldn't be morose." She had to keep hoping. Roberto's face flashed to mind. His sardonic smile. His ebony eyes flashing as he laughed with Adelina. The way his arms flexed as he wielded his sword. The warmth of his torso as he adjusted her grip on her knife. His love—his mind-searing, heart-bursting, fire-in-her-veins love. He couldn't be gone. Mustn't be gone.

She sighed. *"All right, let's go back."*

Erob ascended to fly back to Naobia, the desert dropping far below them.

Ezaara stared out over the endless gut-wrenching orange, one last time.

There, what was that? Hidden over some distant dunes was a smudge. *"Look, Erob. Is that an oasis?"*

"I can't fly much longer without decent food." Despite his protests, Erob flew toward the blur of color nestled between orange dunes.

Their flight seemed to take forever.

"Yes!" A turquoise jewel was nestled in the sand, fringed by palms. *"Look, a lake, shade."* It was strange—all the other oases had been inhabited by Robandi tribes with their brightly-colored tents. *"You'd think an oasis this big would have people here."*

Erob didn't answer. His wingbeats were flagging and he was flying low. He banked and aimed for the lake edge.

"Unless we find food, we'll have to fill our waterskins and fly back over the desert and the Naobian Sea."

That vast ocean with its slate, lapis, cobalt and turquoise tones. She'd never expected the sea to be everchanging, writhing and seething far beneath them, whipping up white tips far out from the shore, sheltering enormous creatures that created dark blots, like ink stains, under the water. This life Zaarusha had given her was bursting with possibility. Except she didn't have Zaarusha anymore. She'd forsaken her dragon, her role and title.

And she didn't have Roberto. If she returned empty-handed, she'd have nothing.

"Let's rest and drink," melded Erob. *"It helps stave off dark thoughts."*

Ezaara stretched her mind out, reaching for Roberto. *"Roberto!"* Hundreds of times she'd tried mind sweeping, and hundreds of times there'd been nothing except the bite of windswept sand on her cheeks. Infusing every last scrap of her love into her message, she thrust out her mind again, *"Roberto."*

"E-zaa-ra ..." Faint and foggy, but it was him.

"Roberto!"

Nothing.

"Roberto!"

Again, nothing.

Had she imagined it? Was she sun-struck? Going crazy?

"No, I heard it too." Erob thudded to the ground, and staggered, his snout hitting the sand and wings askew.

Ezaara slid to the sand. *"Are you all right?"*

"Need to drink." Dragging his tail, Erob crawled to the water.

"Wait!" Ezaara called out loud. *"It might be tainted. Maybe that's why no one's here."*

Erob sniffed it. *"Seems fine."* He submerged his snout.

Ezaara followed, scooping crystal water into her mouth. It was pure, like fresh rain on spring grass. It beat the stagnant water from their skins. *"Erob, Roberto must be near. We can't leave."*

"We can eat and drink here. Look." Erob waved his snout at heavy clusters of dates hanging from the palms.

Ezaara roamed over to the palms, accidentally disturbing a herd of goats dozing in the shade. *"Strange. Goats, but no people."*

"*Maybe they're wild.*" As quick as a wink, Erob killed one and settled to feast.

They collected dates, Erob shaking the trees until the fruit fell down, and Ezaara gathering them into his saddlebags. She found an orange grove, the juicy fruit stinging her chapped lips as she wolfed it down. Why was this place deserted?

"*Look, footprints.*" Ezaara pointed at the churned-up sand near one of the groves. "*Lots of them.*"

"*I noticed camel prints from the air. Someone else must've been hungry.*"

"*Maybe Roberto was with them. Maybe they've just left with him …*"

"*Let's check.*"

They searched the perimeter of the lake, filling their waterskins. The whole time, Ezaara and Erob stretched their minds out to Roberto. There was no reply.

"*We heard him,*" Erob melded. "*He must be here somewhere. Be patient.*" He settled on the sand and she slid off.

Ezaara sank down, leaning against him. "*What if he's dead and that was his last cry? We've got to do something. To come this far …*" Her chest grew tight and she broke down, sobbing, burying her face in Erob's side.

§

A cool caress brushed Roberto's brow. A trickle of water slid down his throat. He swallowed, his gullet thick and clogged. A dull ache throbbed across his middle, laced with a filigree of dancing fire. Exquisite pain. Zens had taught him pain was exquisite and that there was an art to enduring it—Roberto had learned that the hard way.

His mind was slipping again. Faces flitted before him. Eyes, watching: Erob's golden ones, shining as they'd imprinted; Ezaara's sad green eyes when he'd been banished; Zens' giant yellow orbs, enticing him to cruelty, mocking him when he succeeded.

He *was* a mockery. He'd thought he could make a difference to Dragons' Realm, right his father's wrongs and help send Zens back through the world gate. But instead, here he was, banished and dying.

A gentle burble floated through his mind, like the babble of a stream, an accompaniment to the waves of fire rippling across his belly. If he lay perfectly still, would the water put the fire out? Only there was no water here in the desert, in the dark.

§

"*Ezaara.*"

Erob's sharpness woke Ezaara. Eyes gritty with sand, she rubbed them.

Then rubbed them again. This wasn't a nightmare. They were surrounded. Warriors were thrusting a nest of sabers at her throat and Erob's belly.

A tall warrior paced around the dragon, her kohl-rimmed eyes sizing him up. Ezaara followed her with her gaze, helpless. No wonder this oasis had been deserted. These warriors infested it.

"What are you doing here?" The woman's voice was soft, sibilant, like the hissing of wind on sand.

"Ah, Ezaara," melded Erob, *"I know these people. You'd better be polite."*

That sounded dire. Were they Robandi? Their faces and hands were sun-darkened like Robandi, but they were dressed differently—clad in gauzy headdresses, breeches and shirts the same orange as the sand. "We were refreshing ourselves at these beautiful waters." Ezaara inclined her head a fraction, as far as she could without being stabbed. "We also partook of your delicious fruit. Um, and a goat. Thank you for your hospitality." Shards, what was she supposed to say?

The woman hissed, "Seize the scorpion with the flattering tongue and confine her lizard." Swords flicked from her to Erob. Strong arms grasped Ezaara, removing her weapons in a heartbeat. "Now we'll find out what you really want," she whispered.

"We're seeking a friend," Ezaara said. "He may be injured. Dark hair, dark skin, black eyes."

Snorting, the woman whispered again. "Convenient, but not believable. That could be any Robandi. Take them below."

Below?

The warriors moved with lithe elegance and strength. They were women—all forty of them. They marched Ezaara and Erob at sword point to a grove of trees at the far end of the lake. Among the palms was a giant amber boulder with trees growing over it. A latticework of roots hung over the rock's overhang, enveloping it like a spider's web. Two figures stepped out from the overhang, their orange-and-brown-splotched clothing camouflaging them until they moved. They pulled aside some roots and the guards marched Ezaara down a tunnel leading underground.

"What about Erob?" she asked.

"He will be well-tended," a guard answered in a hushed tone.

So, the tall warrior didn't have a speech defect. All of these women whispered.

"Of course they do," melded Erob. *"They're the Sathiri, the Wastelands' infamous silent assassins. Whatever you do, don't mention men, especially not Roberto."*

§

Kohl-rimmed deep-brown eyes studied Roberto. The woman's skin was darker than his, the shade of rich pecans. Hawk-nosed, her face was a mask of tranquility. She was Robandi—and he was alive. High above her was a vaulted ceiling of amber rock. Still in the Wastelands, then. Fangs, his gut ached, a deep sharp throb that sent sparks of pain skittering across his skin whenever he thought of moving.

The woman lifted a cool compress to his brow, murmuring in Naobian, "Lie still. Rest."

As if he could go anywhere. Gods, he probably couldn't even sit up. More fire, pain. "Who—" His voice came out in a broken croak.

"Ssh. Let me tell you."

Roberto had heard similar accents from the Robandi traders in the Naobian markets. She held a cup of sweet cool water to his lips and he swallowed. Bliss. A faint smile traced her lips and she stood, moving with strength and calculated economy. Clothed in orange breeches, headdress and a loose shirt, a saber hung at her hip. A warrior, then.

Who was she and where were they? That babbling was still here. Slowly, Roberto turned his head, not wanting to risk stabbing gut pain. A spring was trickling out of the rock into a pool, feeding an underground stream. He hadn't dreamed the water. It was real.

"Robandi Duo slit your gut and left you to desiccate in the desert. The fools didn't recognize you were Naobian or a *dracha ryter*. How do you call this in your tongue?"

So, she knew what rider's garb looked like. "Dragon rider." Still croaky, but his words were now recognizable.

"Ah, yes, those magnificent beasts, so fierce in combat." A feral flash of teeth.

And she had an interest in dragons.

"Your road to healing will not be fast, but at least your fever has broken. Luckily, we found you and brought you here to the Retreat of the Silent Assassins." Fire stirred in the depths of her dark eyes.

The band of women, renowned for their fighting prowess, who sat in judgment over feuding Robandi tribes. Their skills were many. Ruthless, most trained from the age of seven, learning the spiritual and fighting arts. "And you are the Prophetess of the Robandi Desert?"

A nod.

An assassin prophetess. He coughed, his throat dry, gritting his teeth against the ache in his stomach. If he survived this, he'd never take coughing or laughing for granted again.

"Rest. It is your first time waking in hours. Do not strain yourself." She clicked her fingers, and a young girl of about thirteen approached his bedside.

There were other sounds, hidden by the spring: faint rustling, the chink of someone working. He lifted his head, stifling a groan of agony. Girls and women were working nearby, lit by shafts of sunlight angling through the ceiling. By the Egg, his guts. He'd never move again.

The prophetess frowned, voice stern. "Lie still. You must not rip the stitches."

The young girl lifted the cup to his lips, her fingers twisted and scarred.

"Little and often," the woman said to the girl. Then to Roberto, "Underestimate us at your peril. Every girl here is trained to kill." She slipped the knife out of his discarded boots, and stalked away.

There must've been something in the liquid he'd sipped, because soon Roberto was dreaming again. He hung in a dark void dotted with stars, body endlessly spinning. No matter how hard he tried, he couldn't move. Everything was numb—mind, body and emotions. Then he heard her.

"*Roberto,*" she called across time and space, her bright colors flashing through him. "*Roberto!*" Ezaara—the woman he loved. She'd brought vibrancy and meaning to his life, making him strive to be better.

He tried to answer, but his lips wouldn't move and his limbs were rubbery. He struggled against the darkness dragging his body down, down, spinning … He thrust her name outwards, *"E-zaa-ra,"* then he was gone, suspended in the void again.

§

Ashewar turned her head from the sleeping Naobian as footfalls approached. "Izoldia, have you secured that *dracha*?"

"The *dracha* escaped, my highly-esteemed Beloved One." Izoldia's bow was so low her nose nearly scraped the floor. "But it'll be back for food."

Her darling sycophant had hoped she wouldn't ask. "Trap the *dracha*. Or I'll be tossing your hide to the rust vipers."

"Yes, my Revered Prophetess."

Ashewar turned back to the Naobian. *Sathir* was strong in him. She sensed a ruthless discipline in his spirit, or perhaps it was a disciplined ruthlessness, a darkness. He would serve her purpose well. With this core of steel, his seed would provide good lineage. She surveyed the geography of his face: hollows under defined cheekbones, high brow, strong chin, dark lashes. It was a shame she wouldn't get to lie with him herself, but she had no need of more twisted progeny. Her loins had produced only bitterness: boys to be culled at birth and one daughter of inferior quality.

She needed good fruit. Strong female fruit, to be raised to carry on the legacy of the *Sathiri*. She'd selected ten protégés for the honor—women experienced in cajoling the seed from unwilling men. And when they were done with him, he would die. Just as he'd been about to die when they'd found him.

Izoldia appraised the male. "Good choice, Revered Prophetess. You show such excellent wisdom and foresight. He will give us many strong daughters."

"He will indeed. It's rare to find such a specimen, a man in his prime, on our doorstep. This is a good omen." She hesitated. Izoldia was tough, cruel at times, but that would serve them well: if the others begot boys, Izoldia would have no hesitation in feeding their bodies to the carrion birds. "Would you like to oversee the process?"

Izoldia's grin was fierce. "Thank you, Revered Prophetess. I'll make sure he complies and kill him swiftly afterward."

§

Roberto awoke with a start. "How long have I slept?"

"A day," murmured the girl, bunching her twisted fingers in fists and hiding them in her sleeves.

"Was that a sleeping draught? That sweetness?"

"It promotes sleep and healing."

His head was groggy, limbs still dead, but he was awake and his mind was his own. He'd dreamed of Ezaara, remembering the trial in horrible detail: Ezaara had believed him. Believed he'd poisoned Jaevin. By the Egg, that hurt— he'd only lied to save her. But even worse was the bleak expression on Adelina's face: eyes hollow, face drained of hope. He knew that look. He'd been beside Adelina when Ma had died from injuries inflicted by Pa.

In saving Ezaara, he'd abandoned his sister.

"You must get strong and heal quickly." The girl spoke quietly, her eyes slipping away.

Something in her glance sparked a memory: while he'd been dreaming, he'd heard Ashewar discussing him and harvesting some sort of fruit. What had it been?

Gods, his seed—they wanted to force him to give up his seed. Horror engulfed him.

When the girl offered him the sleeping draught again, he drank readily, falling back into the dark void.

Imprisoned

Guards marched Ezaara before the same imposing woman with kohl-lined eyes, now sitting on an ornately-carved throne. A prickle of dread ran down Ezaara's back. Every carving on her throne was of a woman killing a man.

"Your name?" the woman whispered, torchlight glinting off three diamond studs in her beaked nose.

"Ezaara of Dragons' Hold." She didn't belong there anymore, nor in Lush Valley—she was an outcast from the only homes she'd ever known.

"So, you are the new Queen's Rider, but where is your queen?" Even whispering, this woman was haughty.

The woman had heard of her, but Ezaara had never heard of these silent assassins. Not in Lush Valley. Nor at Dragons' Hold. "I have no queen," Ezaara mumbled, staring at the floor.

"Without a *dracha*, you are not much use. Unless you can fight?" The woman clicked her fingers and her assistants lunged, swords aiming for Ezaara.

She ducked, instinctively thrusting her arms up to block—but their blows never came.

"With training, you might amount to something," the woman hissed. "Izoldia, take her to the dungeon near the training room."

With a sneer at Ezaara, a towering barrel-chested assassin squeezed her arm.

"But I have to—"

"Silence," the burly Izoldia hissed. "You must not address Ashewar, Chief Prophetess of the Silent Assassins, until spoken to." She raked a dagger along Ezaara's arm. A line of red beads appeared. Ezaara sucked in her breath. That stung. Izoldia yanked her toward a narrow tunnel, more female guards in orange clothing trailing behind.

"Wait." The prophetess' eyes narrowed. "What is that pouch you wear?"

No, they couldn't take her healer's pouch. "My mother was a healer. I've learned some of her skills."

Ashewar snapped her fingers and a guard brought the pouch over for her to examine. "Hmm. Let her keep her pouch. She can heal cuts from training skirmishes. Now, take her away."

Roberto! Since they'd caught her, she'd forgotten to mind sweep. *"Roberto."* Nothing. But she wouldn't give up. He'd been alive a few hours ago. Why had Erob warned her off asking about him? *"Roberto."*

They went through a catacomb of tunnels and crossed a large cavern, where women were moving in an elaborate dance, swords and bodies flowing in time to some unseen rhythm. The guards paused at an adjoining cell, unlocking a door of iron bars.

Izoldia's fetid breath washed over her face. "If you're useless, Ashewar will give me the pleasure of killing you, but if you train hard, you'll become one of us." The guard shoved her, sending Ezaara sprawling onto a lumpy mattress against the rocky wall. The bars clanged shut.

Marching to the center of the cavern, the guards joined the dance.

So, this was their training area.

And hers. She had to survive until she could escape. Shrouded in shadows, her cell was barely longer than the mattress. Torches in the main cavern illuminated a spring near the front of her cell, flowing from the rock wall into a pool. Picking up a long-handled dipper, Ezaara drank. At least the water was good.

The women in the cavern moved in unison with supple fluidity, their robes swishing, feet slapping on rock and their sabers flashing. Their dance was beautiful, but their moves were deadly. Kill or be killed.

Ezaara stayed in the shadows, copying them. With no sword, she used the dipper, thrusting the handle at imaginary opponents. The assassins ignored her.

"Roberto."

"Don't give up," Erob melded. *"I think he's here. I've escaped, but I'll be back. Find him."*

"I'm imprisoned. I'll try." Ezaara kept at the killers' dance. Here, her right hand needed to be higher, her left leg more controlled. She danced. *"Roberto!"*

And danced.

An assassin's sword clattered onto the rock. A chain of echoes bounced around the chamber. Everyone froze. In a swish of orange gauze, Ashewar swept into the cavern, striking the offending assassin's face with her saber. The smack of metal against flesh echoed in through the cavern, ricocheting against the walls like a macabre drum beat. A bloody gash split the woman's cheek, but she retrieved her sword, slipping back into stance. Ashewar stalked out as the women continued, not missing a move.

Izoldia unlocked Ezaara. "You. Heal her." She stood over Ezaara while she rubbed healing salve onto the woman's wound, then marched her back to her cell. "If you don't shape up, you'll need more than healing salve when I'm through with you," she sneered.

Heart pounding, Ezaara slumped on the mattress, sweat beading her limbs and torso. It was hopeless. She lacked these assassins' control and finesse. She was weak from hunger. She'd never be good enough.

Roberto. Would he ever answer?

Across the training hall was a girl in the shadows, as still as a marmot scenting a predator. She was watching Ezaara, clumsily holding a silver dish. Her hands were covered by the ends of her sleeves. Maybe the dish was hot. The girl approached and passed the dish through the bars.

Dates, oranges and a grainy cereal containing smoked meat—not hot food. Then why had the girl covered her hands? "Thank you," Ezaara said.

The girl held a finger to her lips—a finger that was scarred and bent out of shape.

Silent assassins.

Ezaara took the dish, catching the girl's hand in hers. The girl shrunk back with terrified eyes, but Ezaara didn't let go. She set the dish down and examined the girl's fingers. Her fingers had deep scarring, as if by fire, all ten digits bent and twisted. The scarring looked like burns, but burns wouldn't melt bones and twist them. Had she been born that way?

Ezaara examined the girl's fingers, one by one, then pressed the tips with her nail to see if she flinched. She had some nerve damage. It'd be difficult to work with such fingers. Ezaara reached into her healer's pouch—thank the Egg, the assassins hadn't taken it—and pulled out a vial of piaua. Quickly unscrewing the lid, Ezaara tipped a drop onto the girl's smallest finger and rubbed it over the scar tissue.

A soft hiss escaped the girl. Her scars slowly faded into healthy tissue and her finger straightened. Wonder lit her features. Ezaara picked up her piaua vial to work on the girl's next finger, but she shook her head. Her eyes flicked to the dancing assassins and she motioned to the dish.

Ezaara scooped the contents into her mouth, then handed the dish back.

"I am Ithsar," the girl whispered.

"Ezaara," she whispered back.

"To complete the training, you must sense *sathir*, the energy of all living things, interwoven in the rhythm of the dance." With that, Ithsar melted back across the room and out the exit.

What did that mean? *"Roberto,"* Ezaara melded. No reply. She picked up her dipper and started the dance moves again. What was *sathir*?

The next morning, when Ithsar brought food, Ezaara healed another finger. In return, Ithsar mentioned the first step in sensing *sathir*: feeling your heartbeat in every movement, while reaching out to sense what was around you.

It took Ezaara hundreds of attempts before she could move in time with her heartbeat.

"Roberto." Would he ever answer? Was he alive?

When Ithsar came again, Ezaara was prepared. A drop of piaua, rubbed along her next finger, with a whispered question. "There is a man I seek: dark hair, with olive-black eyes and a tiny crescent-shaped scar on his cheek. Do—"

Ithsar's eyes flashed recognition. She stiffened and turned away, curling her healed fingers into her palms. Izoldia was approaching.

Picking up the dish, Ezaara used Ithsar as a shield to bolt some of her food, then made a show of chewing and eating while the small assassin waited.

With a hand signal, Izoldia dismissed Ithsar.

Ezaara practiced the intricate dance of killing again. For every ten beats of her heart, she sent out Roberto's name. It was easier now, the rhythm of the exercises counted in heartbeats gave a fluidity to her movements, but she doubted she'd sensed whatever *sathir* was.

That night, Ezaara jolted awake. A lamp flickered in the shadows across the cavern. Someone was sneaking around the perimeter, toward her dungeon. She grabbed the water ladle and slipped into the back of the dungeon, waiting in the deepest shadow.

As the figure came closer, she let out a breath of relief. It was Ithsar. Ezaara dropped the ladle and rushed to the bars. "What is it?" she whispered, mindful of the cavern's echo chamber.

"Thika is unwell." Ithsar set down the lamp. She drew a wan-beige lizard with dark stripes from the folds of her robe, cradling him on the underside of her forearm. Its head was nestled in her palm and tail curled around her elbow.

"Tell me about Thika."

"My father gave me Thika when he was a tiny lizard, only this long." She waggled her little finger.

"What's wrong with him?"

"I don't know."

Ezaara touched his dry cool hide. "Is he usually warmer than this?"

"Only when he basks in the sun or snuggles me. His skin can be fiery-orange, like Robandi sand, but today he's pale. Usually, he scampers around, catching midges, or crawling all over me. I found him limp in a corner and he hasn't moved since." Ithsar's bottom lip wobbled. "Please, use the juice. Help him."

She couldn't tell her only friend in this forsaken place that it would be a shame to waste piaua on a lizard, not when Ithsar cared so deeply for him. Ezaara reached into her healer's pouch. "Piaua doesn't heal everything."

Ithsar forced Thika's mouth open and Ezaara shook two drops of piaua into his maw. "There, he should be better in a few moments."

Ithsar stroked his skin. Moments stretched and there was no change.

"Ithsar, this juice cures most illnesses and heals many wounds, however it has limits. It can't treat infection or poison."

"Thika has been poisoned?" Ithsar's hand flew to her mouth. "It must've been Izoldia." She thrust Thika through the bars at Ezaara. "I know where the poisons and remedies are kept. I'll be back." Ithsar left the lamp and dashed away.

Ezaara sat on her mattress, stroking Thika. The lizard blinked and slumped on her lap. His hide reminded her of Zaarusha's—soft and supple. She released a long sigh, missing the queen.

Ithsar returned with a sack of earthenware pots. "I haven't done my poison training yet, so I'm not sure what is what," she whispered, her gaze hopeful.

"Let's see." Ezaara put Thika on the mattress and eased the sack quietly through the bars. Opening the pots, she held them near the lamp, examining the contents and sniffing each one. "I've never seen any of these before," she whispered.

"Thika was my father's. He's the only thing I have left of him." Ithsar's eyes pooled with tears.

"Is your father …"

"Dead? Yes. Ashewar killed him once they'd finished using him to breed. I guess I was lucky. He lived longer than most. I was nearly four when he died."

Ezaara took a sharp breath. "That's why there are no men here?"

"Ashewar hates men. She murders them once they provide enough offspring. Any man who comes here—" Ithsar's eyes flew wide. "I'm sorry. I—"

Oh, gods. They were going to use Roberto for *breeding*, then *kill* him. Ezaara's body ran cold. A gulf opened inside her, wide enough to swallow her.

Ithsar froze, her dark eyes huge.

"T-tell me." Ezaara tried to force a smile, but couldn't.

"You love this man with the olive eyes?"

She nodded.

"It is the new way of the silent assassins—since Ashewar destroyed the former leader and purged the ranks of men. I'm sorry …"

Breeding and murder. She had to get out of here with Roberto. She'd need Ithsar's help. "Where is he?"

"Under sedation while he heals."

"What's wrong with him? Is he poisoned too?"

"No, Robandi slit his gut in the desert."

Shards! The rock walls spun, then closed in on her.

"He is healing well, but it will be slow. Gut wounds are." Ithsar's eyes dropped to Thika and a tear tracked down her cheek. "I have no one else." Her whisper was barely audible.

Ezaara counted her heartbeats. She couldn't panic. One step at a time. First heal the lizard. Then Ithsar's fingers. Then plan an escape and rescue Roberto. And find Erob. Closing her eyes, she breathed deeply.

When she opened them again, there was a faint red glow around Ithsar. Must be the lamp light. She picked up a pot, sniffing the acrid black paste inside. When she held the pot near Thika, a sickly green shimmer enveloped the lizard and the paste. It disappeared when she moved the pot away.

"I think that one is rust-viper venom," Ithsar murmured.

Setting it down, Ezaara took another pot which also had a faint sheen of greenish light around it. "Is this special clay? Is that why the pots glow?"

Ithsar's face lit up. Her whisper was full of suppressed excitement. "*Sathir.* You can see *sathir.*"

"This light? *That's sathir?*"

Ithsar nodded. "If you can see it around the pots, that is a miracle. I can sense most people's *sathir* and Thika's. Some can sense animals and plants. Perhaps you have that gift." She held a pot near Thika. "Sathir shows the effect of things on one another. Here, what do you see?"

"Sickly green."

Another pot.

"A tiny thread of red."

"Red is Thika's *sathir* color. This substance strengthens his life energy, so it may heal him."

Rapidly, they tried the others, but only that one pot glowed red. Ezaara administered the liquid from the pot, a few drops at a time. Gradually, Thika perked up, his skin growing more orange with each dose. A wide ribbon of shining red connected him to Ithsar.

"His *sathir*, it's connected to you."

Ithsar grinned. "We are all connected to one another." The lamp sputtered. "I have to go." Ithsar shot to her feet and hid Thika in her clothing. Reaching through the bars, she gathered the pots up and shoved them in the sack. "Thank you."

"Wait." Ezaara grasped her hand and healed another two of her fingers.

"I must go. At dawn, the morning's training will commence." Ithsar rushed away, keeping to the perimeter of the cavern so her footfalls weren't amplified in the natural echo chamber.

Ezaara lay down, but before she could sleep, assassins filed into the cavern to perform their training rituals. She lay, watching through half-lidded eyes, seeing flashes of *sathir*. Maybe one day she'd be good enough to see more. But first, she had to escape and find Roberto.

Ithsar appeared, carrying a small dish of food, her hands hidden in the folds of her sleeves. "Give me the juice. I'll heal your friend and help you escape." Her murmur was barely detectable. Shielding Ezaara from view with her body, she held out her hand for the vial.

Five fingers healed in total and five to go. Ezaara could give Ithsar the piaua to heal Roberto, but the girl might use all of the juice on herself or her friends, saving none for Roberto.

She breathed, staring into Ithsar's eyes. One heartbeat.

Two. Three.

A connection, like a thread of color, wove between them, shimmering. The thread grew stronger, thicker, flowing between them. It felt right to trust this girl, as if their paths could influence each other's destiny.

"*Sathir* is strong between us," whispered Ithsar—she felt it too.

Ezaara handed Ithsar the piaua juice. "A few drops on the wound and two on the tongue. It's precious."

Ithsar retreated through the shadows.

Ezaara sank onto her mattress. She'd given her most precious healing remedy, the scarcest of her resources, to one of her captors. What had she done?

A Link Reforged

Roberto woke to the girl with the twisted fingers. By the Egg, he was sick of sleeping. The dark haze made his world turn upside-down and inside out. She lifted a cup to his lips. He shook his head. "Not the sweet water," he croaked.

"It will soothe you," she said, widening her eyes and shooting him a meaningful glance. She held the cup up, urging him to drink.

Strange. She meant something with that glance. Could he trust her? He took a sip. It was water, cool and pure, not tainted with the sickly-sweet draught that knocked him out. He gulped it down.

"Sleep now, while I change your bandages." That widening of the eyes again, with a casual glance at the other workers behind her. She subtly wriggled her fingers. Some of them were *no longer scarred and twisted.*

Roberto shut his eyes, feigning sleep. She peeled back his bandage, a twinge rippling across the dull ache of his wound. Something dribbled on his injury, burning. He nearly cried out, until he remembered the burn of Ezaara's piaua. Was it possible this girl had piaua too? Where from?

And then he heard Ezaara. Felt her.

"Roberto!" Vibrant colors flashed through him—with a potent wave of love.

"Ezaara!" He fought to keep an insane smile from his face. Ezaara was here. Ezaara believed him. Ezaara *loved* him. Every corner of his body was filled with light. He was a feather floating on the breeze, a bubble rising to the top of the sea.

The juice burned along his stomach. He opened his eyes. The girl re-bandaged his wound and shielded him from view as she leaned over, pretending to give him the cup, but slipping a drop of piaua onto his tongue. "For your insides," she barely whispered. "Ezaara is here."

"I know," whispered Roberto, smiling. He closed his eyelids, pretending to sleep.

§

It was him—Roberto! Her whole body was singing with joy. A rush went through her, like she was imprinting all over again. He was here. Alive. Ezaara counted her heartbeats, concentrating on *sathir*, but it was hard to focus, especially when Ithsar made her way across the training room holding a dish of sliced oranges. She was clever, curling her fingers so they looked unhealed.

"Quick, my mother is coming," Ithsar whispered.

Ezaara took the dish—and the vial of piaua hidden beneath the orange wedges. She pocketed the vial immediately, then sat down to eat her oranges while Ithsar watched, her face inscrutable.

Within moments, Ashewar, the chief prophetess of the silent assassins, appeared. So Ashewar was Ithsar's mother. Ugh.

The assassins turned to face their leader, right hands on sword hilts, left fists over their hearts. Ashewar strode through the room on noiseless feet. As one, they followed her, their bodies like the hands of a giant clock, always facing their master.

The chief prophetess stopped in front of Ezaara's cell. "Stand," she hissed.

Ezaara passed the dish of empty orange peels back to Ithsar and stood.

"You were asking about a man when you arrived," Ashewar said. "We have interrogated a Naobian man, found in the desert with his gut slit. He says you injured him in an attempt on his life." She shook her head. "To forfeit a life in the desert, without our sanction, is a grave crime, so you will be executed tomorrow at dawn."

"But I didn't—"

"Silence." Izoldia stabbed through the bars with her sword.

Ezaara leaped back.

Ashewar waved a hand at the assassins in the training area. "Choose who will kill you."

Ezaara's mind spun. She scanned the rows of stony-faced warriors. She pointed at Ithsar. "I choose her."

Ithsar's expression froze, her eyes piercing Ezaara.

Rage flashed across Ashewar's face. Her voice turned to ice. "Very well, Ezaara *formerly* of Dragons' Hold, soon queen of a shallow grave in the Robandi desert. May the buzzards pick your bones dry before they're bleached by our sun."

Ashewar gestured to Ithsar, and she joined the ranks of the trainees, keeping her fists in her sleeves to hide her healed fingers. She had no weapon.

Suddenly, Ezaara understood. She'd chosen the one assassin who couldn't properly wield a sword, disgracing both mother and daughter.

Izoldia bowed to the prophetess.

"Speak, Izoldia," commanded Ashewar.

Izoldia gave a nasty grin. "My Most Revered Prophetess, Ithsar may finally have her first kill." She barked out a harsh laugh.

The prophetess gave a curt wave, cutting her off mid-laugh. "This is Ithsar's last chance. If she is not successful in killing Ezaara, you will execute both of them."

§

In the deepest night, the faint slap of feet woke Ezaara. Someone was coming. She felt for her sword but, of course, had none. She got up and crept to the side of her prison, gripping the dipper.

A light flared. Ithsar was there, a tiny lamp in her hands. She unlocked the dungeon door and gave Ezaara a bundle of orange clothing. Hurriedly, Ezaara pulled the garments on over her own. Ithsar fastened an orange headdress over Ezaara's head, and darkened her face with earth. She passed Ezaara her sword and daggers. Then, tugging her hand, she led her into the training cavern.

"Where to?" Ezaara's whisper sounded unnaturally loud, reverberating in the chamber. No! She'd forgotten the echo effect in the middle of the cavern.

Ithsar's eyes flew wide. She doused the lamp, but it was too late. People were running along the tunnels toward them.

Grabbing Ezaara's hand, Ithsar dashed with her into the darkness. Heartbeats. Ezaara tried to focus on her heartbeat to stay calm and stop her breath rasping. But her traitorous heart boomed like banishment drums.

Assassins pounded the stone behind them.

Racing along the network of tunnels, Ezaara was soon disoriented.

Ithsar pulled her to the floor, whispering, "Lie down. Squeeze under this bridge. Don't move until I return."

Ezaara obeyed. She wriggled under some planks—a hand's breadth from her nose. Below, was the burble of distant water. Ithsar pushed her in further, then raced off to draw their pursuers away.

Moments later, footsteps thundered over the wood, so close their breeze brushed her face. Ezaara froze, counting her heartbeats until they passed.

Hundreds of beats after their steps had faded, Roberto melded with her. *"Ezaara, what's happening?"*

"I'm trying to escape."

"Me too, but—"

Ezaara tried to meld with him again, but couldn't. Time crawled as she lay, squeezed in that confined space. Her fingertips grazed slatted wood above her.

To her side, her other fingers met air. One wrong move and she'd tumble into the water far below. Swallowing, Ezaara kept counting.

§

Ithsar was used to hiding in the tunnels. Used to avoiding the unwanted gaze of her fellow assassins. Used to crawling into tiny spaces to escape their taunting. But she wasn't used to the new strength in her fingers, the strange energy that had surged along her half-dead nerves as Ezaara, she of the golden hair and green eyes, had *healed* her. Ithsar had never experienced such kindness from anyone. And although the *dracha ryter* from a far-off land had given her a vial of healing juice, Ithsar honored Ezaara, so she hadn't dared use any on herself.

So, Ithsar ran for her life and for Ezaara's. Having hands that didn't work well had helped her hone the rest of her body. Whenever she was off-duty, she practiced the *sathir* dance for hours on end, her limbs nearly brushing the walls of her tiny cavern. Her legs were strong, feet agile and her endurance was akin to the legendary *Sathiri*, who had established the ancient dance. Not that any of her fellow warriors realized. She'd hidden her prowess, deliberately acting clumsier than she was. Deliberately fooling everyone—especially her mother, Ashewar.

On through the dark, Ithsar ran, through winding tunnels to a hidey-hole they'd never suspect. When pursuers passed her, she doubled back until she reached an alcove near where the Naobian lay healing. *Healed.* She'd healed him. He of the dark eyes shining like ripe olives under the sun. No wonder Ezaara loved this man—it was evident in her *sathir* when she'd asked after him. And he had cried, calling Ezaara's name in his fever with such love, babbling about her color. The color, Ithsar had understood. Ezaara's presence radiated all the colors in her mother's prism seer. Another talent Ashewar was unaware of—Ithsar could *see* without a prism. And she'd seen a vision of these two *dracha ryter.*

The Naobian had also ranted about banishment, murder and poison. It appeared he'd saved Ezaara, the healer. For that, Ithsar owed him.

Ashewar planned to kill him.

But no, Ashewar would not kill this man, loved by her healer. Ithsar would see to that. He would go free to love Ezaara. Perhaps one day, she, Ithsar, would have a man like this, who called her name with a voice that ached with tenderness.

Her breathing now quiet, Ithsar stepped out of the alcove. The Naobian had only one person guarding him at night—but tonight it was Izoldia. Ithsar's birth defects meant she was smaller than other girls her age. Izoldia, the largest, had led the bullying, and was always the last to finish beating her—the most savage, the cruelest. Bruises, black eyes, and, later, cuts and burns had been Izoldia's mark—until one day, Ithsar had wrestled the brand off her and burned Izoldia, keeping her brutality at bay.

Ashewar, noticing Ithsar's hurts, had said nothing. Disciplined no one. If Ithsar had been the daughter of another assassin, Ashewar would've been ruthless in punishing Izoldia. But she wasn't. She was Ithsar, Ashewar's only daughter—the chief prophetess' malformed disappointment.

Perhaps Ithsar owed Izoldia, for driving her to artistry in *sathir*, for making her stronger than she otherwise would have been, but Izoldia had also twisted what the Naobian had said, conjuring up stories so Ezaara—*she of golden beauty* the girls called her in hushed whispers over their evening meal—would die.

Not while Ithsar breathed.

Opening the healing room door, Ithsar kept the anger from her face, instead, offering congeniality and supplication.

"What do *you* want?" Izoldia snapped.

"Did you hear the disturbance?" Ithsar asked, eyes downcast.

"You think I'd miss that lot, thundering around like a herd of Robandi camels?"

"I came to fetch you because you're much stronger. You'd be better at fighting an intruder than me."

Izoldia sneered at Ithsar, her chest swelling with pride, but then her eyes narrowed in suspicion.

Although she hated groveling, Ithsar had to be quick. She held out her twisted fingers, hiding the healed ones in her palms. "My hands … I'm useless, afraid …" She let her lip wobble.

"You miserable wretch, Ithsar. I should make you go and face the danger." Izoldia's bark was harsh, loud. She'd never been good at silence—gloating didn't sound right in a whisper. Izoldia got up, hand on her saber. "Watch that man."

The moment Izoldia shut the door, the Naobian's eyes flicked open.

"I am Ithsar," she murmured. "Ezaara's friend. I'll take you to her so you can escape."

"My hands and legs are fastened." His whisper was papyrus-thin. He was obviously used to stealth—good, that would serve them well tonight.

The ropes on his hands and feet were quick work for her saber. Ithsar thrust the cut ropes into her pocket and pulled some clothing and a headdress from a drawer. He threw them on. On close inspection, he wouldn't pass for a woman, but it was better than the *dracha ryter* clothes he wore underneath. She passed him his sword and dagger. They slipped out the door, sliding through the shadows along the walls and nipping into side tunnels or alcoves whenever someone neared.

Finally, they made it back to Ezaara, hiding under the bridge.

When she'd crawled out and they'd retreated to a nearby side tunnel, Ezaara whispered, "Ithsar, quick, give me your unhealed fingers."

In the darkness, something dripped onto Ithsar's fingers, then Ezaara rubbed the oil into her skin. The slow healing burn built until her bones were on fire and *moved and straightened*. An ache pierced her chest and her eyes stung.

She was *whole*.

Ithsar clutched Ezaara's hand for a moment longer, placing it on her wet cheek. "My life is yours."

The Naobian's hand rested atop theirs, enclosing them both. "Thank you, Ithsar," he whispered. "Thank you for risking your life to save ours."

They stood in the darkness, her and these two strangers, their breath flowing and ebbing together in the inky black. And then the vision descended upon Ithsar again—these strangers on mighty *dracha,* with *her* beside them on another. *Sathir* built around them, tangible, like a warm caress full of color and life, a force connecting the three of them. She belonged to these people. This was her destiny.

From Ezaara's soft gasp and the grunt the Naobian gave, they'd sensed it too.

Footsteps slid over rock nearby. They froze, waiting until they retreated, then Ithsar led them into a tunnel far away from the main thoroughfares. Winding under the heart of the lake, deeper and deeper into the earth, she took them toward a hidden exit on the far side of the oasis.

§

Roberto rubbed Ezaara's hand with the back of his thumb. Her palm was warm and soft in his as they followed the tiny silent assassin through the winding tunnel, guided by the light of her lantern. They stooped to avoid sharp rocks protruding from the ceiling and slithered over piles of rubble nearly as high as the tunnel itself. Thank the Egg, he could move again. Brilliant colors swirled at the edge of his mind—Ezaara was trying to communicate with him. How was he going to tell her? The assassins' sleeping draught had set all his old nightmares writhing and churning inside him. Perhaps it was better to get it over with. Letting his barriers melt away, he melded, *"Ezaara."*

"What's wrong, Roberto? Why won't you talk with me?"

She'd picked up on his emotions in spite of his effort to shield them. How could he ever protect her from himself, from the monster inside? He squeezed her hand. She was as bright as a thousand stars, her multi-colored light streaming through him. He reached for his resolve. *"Ezaara, I won't be coming back to Dragons' Hold with you."*

Her steps faltered. *"Why not?"*

Because his past had caught up with him. Because he'd lived a life before he'd become a dragon master. Because he feared Tonio was right: sooner or later, he could turn traitor. It was not only in his blood, it was in his past. Before Erob.

He tugged Ezaara forward, keeping pace with the assassin.

"I thought you loved me."

Pain speared through him. *Exquisite pain.* Shards, Zens' words were still shaping him. Would he ever purge the evil from his soul?

Escape

There was a ripple in the fabric of the *sathir*, a rip in the cloak that surrounded them. "What is it? What ails you?" Ithsar turned to the *dracha ryter*, holding up her lantern.

They were no longer holding hands. The Naobian's face was stoic.

Ezaara's … Ezaara's look haunted Ithsar. Hollow-eyed, bereft of hope.

"With such disunity, Ashewar will feel the disharmony and find us immediately. If you are to be reunited with your *dracha*, you must put this pain aside."

§

Dragons' Hold without Roberto? Every fiber inside Ezaara screamed. And she wasn't Queen's Rider anymore. Her life was meaningless. Worse than before she'd left Lush Valley. Then, she'd been ignorant of mind-melding, of the depth of love, the wonder of dragon flight, the *potential* of life.

She reached deep inside herself, stretching her mind out to Roberto, and showed him how to find *sathir*. He joined her and they found that place of peace, sensing the cord that bound them to nature, and to each other. And Ezaara found hope.

§

Ithsar's lamp shone on a series of hand and foot holds in the rock, leading up a chimney into darkness. Ithsar went first, Roberto next and Ezaara took the rear. Melding with Erob, Roberto was surprised Ezaara was also talking to him.

"*Erob, we're climbing out a tunnel on the other side of the lake, apparently near a cluster of date trees,*" she informed him.

"*Date palms? With hundreds of palms around, that should be an easy landmark to spot in the middle of the night.*"

Erob's wry response made Roberto's heart lurch. Could he take Erob away from Dragons' Hold? Would Erob leave his mother and kin? Or would he lose Erob, too? What about Adelina?

"*Stop disturbing the sathir with such morose thoughts,*" Ezaara melded. "*We'll sort out what we're doing once we're out of here.*"

She was right. He'd tell her everything when they got to Naobia. If they got to Naobia—there were still dozens of silent assassins to get past. His hands bit into dusty rock handholds. The footholds were gritty with stone particles, often making his boots slip.

Ezaara spat. *"Tastes great, thanks."*

He'd flicked dirt on her. *"Sorry."*

"I'd rather be underfoot than without you." Her response was glib, making him smile, despite his heaviness.

"Erob, we're nearing the top. Where are the assassins?" Roberto asked.

"Amusing themselves by thinking they're guarding me." Erob sent Roberto an image of him toasting an assassin on a talon. *"Only joking. They have me surrounded with their sabers."*

"Careful. I don't want you wounded. We have a long flight ahead of us."

"Yes," Ezaara chimed in. *"It's four or five days to Dragons' Hold from here."*

Roberto said nothing. Let her think she'd won. It would keep her happy for now.

Above him, Ithsar whispered, "We're here." She put out the lantern hanging on her belt.

There was a faint rustle. Foliage above them parted and the cool kiss of night air rushed in to meet them. Roberto climbed out to a sky scattered with stars, and date palms whispering in the breeze like hundreds of silent assassins. Moonlight cast a shaft of brightness across a lake. Beyond, a hillock was silhouetted among a fringe of trees. The sky was dark, but it wasn't long until dawn. They had to get out of here.

"Are you that lump in the trees?"

"A lump?" Erob snorted. The hillock on the other side of the lake moved. *"See that?"*

"Yes. We're straight across from you." Roberto grasped Ezaara's hand and pulled her out into the open. She stumbled on the edge of the chimney and he grabbed her to stop her falling backward. She landed with her cheek against his chest, and their eyes met. Dragon fire raced in his veins. His heart thrummed.

She was in his mind, against his body, her floral scent and her presence filling his senses. *"You can't deny what we feel."*

And he couldn't. He brushed his lips against her hair.

§

"No," Ithsar whispered, but it was too late. The Naobian's lips touched Ezaara's hair, lighting up the *sathir* connection between them like a million stars. Any assassin tuned into *sathir* would know where they were. So much for stealth.

On the other side of the lake, a sand-shifting roar split the air. A belch of *dracha* flame lit up the palm grove, and the mighty blue-scaled beast took to the sky.

He was coming. Both *dracha ryter* would be saved.

"Traitor." Izoldia stepped from behind a date palm, saber out.

Ithsar snatched her own saber and pointed it at the Naobian. "Now, you're coming with us!" she cried.

The Naobian spun, flinging Ezaara aside. He was fast. When had he unsheathed his sword?

"You," he spat at Ithsar, lunging at her. "You've outlived your usefulness."

He was absolving her of blame. Ithsar parried with her saber, letting it fly out of her hand as he struck, as if her fingers couldn't hold it. Izoldia wouldn't know any different.

The Naobian held his sword to Ithsar's throat. "Drop your weapon," he said to Izoldia. "Or the girl dies."

Izoldia threw her head back and laughed. "She's worthless. Kill her. It'll save me the trouble."

The slow burning anger that Ithsar had harbored all these years blossomed like a bruise, staining the *sathir* purple-black. The stain spread across Ithsar's vision, blotting out the stars, blotting out the date trees, blotting out Izoldia.

Ithsar had never deserved such scorn. Despite her deformed fingers, she had tried her best. Izoldia had seen to it that everyone despised her, including her own mother.

A breeze stirred at her feet, whirling the sand into a flurry. It rose, faster and higher around her, whipping her clothes in the wind. It shook the date palms, rustling their fronds and swaying their trunks. Thrusting out her anger, Ithsar's whirlwind made the date palm over Izoldia tremble.

A huge bunch of dates fell, hitting Izoldia's head, knocking her to the ground.

Instantly, the purple stain was gone.

The Naobian released Ithsar and spun, checking for more assassins. Ithsar could sense them across the lake, running toward them.

Ezaara rushed over to Izoldia. "She's unconscious." She hesitated for a moment.

"I'm sorry," whispered Ithsar. "I've never done that before."

"A good job you did," the Naobian said, putting a comforting hand on her shoulder.

Ezaara opened her pouch and took out a tiny sack of powder. "Ithsar, quick," she hissed, "fetch a little water."

Ithsar snatched the empty waterskin at her belt and collected water from the lake.

Ezaara threw a pinch of powder into the skin, and they held up Izoldia's head, letting the water trickle down her throat. Izoldia swallowed reflexively.

"This is woozy weed," Ezaara said. "It will make her sleep and leave her confused about what happened over the last few hours. She probably won't remember any of this."

Ithsar had been prepared to die to free these strangers. She let relief wash through her, not trying to control it. If anyone had seen the dark bruise in *sathir*, they'd believe the *dracha ryter* had caused it. She fished the ropes she'd cut off the Naobian's limbs from her pockets and thrust them deep into Izoldia's tunic. "Hopefully, they'll think she's a traitor who led you here."

The *dracha* bellowed.

"Fast," said the Naobian, "go back to your quarters through the tunnel."

Ithsar flung herself down the chimney, and he pulled foliage back over the entrance. Only when she reached the bottom and turned on her lamp did she realize she'd forgotten to farewell the *dracha ryter* and tell them about her vision.

§

With a flurry of wings, Erob landed. Roberto was liquid motion, snatching the dates that had hit Izoldia and flinging them into a saddlebag, then throwing Ezaara on Erob's back. He jumped up behind her, wrapping his arms around her waist, his touch kindling flames in her heart. Roaring, Erob took to the sky as the first rays of the sun turned the sand to honeyed amber.

Below, in the oasis, silent assassins waved their sabers, and a cry went up as Izoldia was discovered.

Ezaara squeezed Roberto's hand. She had to know. *"You said you weren't returning to Dragons' Hold, but it's not true, is it?"*

Roberto's arms tightened around her as if he was afraid to lose her. A wave of sadness hit her, and her throat tightened with grief.

The rumble of his voice carried through her back. "Let's enjoy the journey and talk about it in Naobia."

They didn't really speak much in their long flight across the dry and arid desert. Maybe she'd feel better when she saw the ocean again.

But when they reached the Naobian Sea, it was overcast. Instead of a sparkling jewel box of lapis, sapphire and jade, the sea was flat slate, its dark secrets roiling below the surface.

The day turned to dusk and darkness settled. Ezaara drifted to sleep, head against Roberto's shoulder, his warm arms around her.

She woke to that same slate sea rushing in to the Naobian shore. Today, Roberto would tell her why he wasn't returning. Ezaara felt emptier than ever before.

Naobia

The salty tang of the Naobian Sea woke old memories inside Roberto as Erob's wingbeats made currents, stirring wisps of Ezaara's hair against his cheek. She was breathing softly in her sleep, peaceful. He steeled himself against a wave of tenderness. Love led to heartbreak. He'd seen enough lives cut short by traitors like Amato. And he'd destroyed enough himself. It would be better to lose Ezaara now, before he destroyed her too.

There, it was time to face it. Amato, his father, had scarred him. Flying back to his homeland was like facing his past—the nightmares: his father, and himself.

It had started that night when he was ten.

Thirsty, he got up for a drink of water. His parents were yelling. They'd argued more since Pa had been lucky enough to escape from Zens. Adults didn't make sense—surely they'd be happier now Pa was home. Roberto crouched behind the bedroom door, listening. Adelina, only six years old, joined him, tucking her small hand in his.

"They're incompetent," Pa shouted. "The whole bunch of them. With wizards gone, they can't even protect our lands anymore. We'll all be destroyed unless we join Zens."

"Don't be ridiculous," Ma said. "Dragons have protected the realm for thousands of years."

"You ignorant fool, it's obvious." Wood splintered.

And splintered again.

Roberto's heart pounded. He put his arms around Adelina. She clung to him, trembling.

"Amato." Ma's voice was shaky. "What's happening to you? This is treason."

"Lucia, Zens makes sense. He has new blood and muscle at his command. He will win."

"How can you say that?"

"Lucia, my darling," Pa reasoned, sounding tender, "I'm only worried about the family, the littlings. I love you all so …"

His father wanted to follow Zens, the enemy of Dragons' Realm. Roberto pulled Adelina away from the door, taking her back to her bed. He was no longer thirsty.

Everything had gone downhill from there. Family life became tense and discordant, and his father, violent.

One day, after Roberto had fed the hens, Razo limped up to him, whimpering, trailing bloody footprints. Roberto knelt, patting his fur. "Hey, boy, what's wrong?" His dog's hind leg was gashed from haunch to paw, his tan fur laid open in a viscous slice of red.

Razo whined and sank to the ground, licking Roberto's hand. His leg was a mess. "Hang on, boy, I'll get Ma." Roberto spun.

"No, you won't." Pa's voice was dangerously soft. "Lazy dog, lazy boy. Both, good for nothing." Amato flicked a whip.

In a surge of anger, Roberto knew who'd hurt Razo. His fists balled. "What did he do?"

"Absolutely nothing. Should've been working, keeping the stock. Instead he was lying in the sun."

"That's not fair! You made him run those goats too far last night. He came home worn out." He gritted his teeth. "You're nothing but a coward, Pa. No one whips a good work dog."

"And no one whips a hard-working son," thundered Amato. He flicked his whip. The tip lashed out, striking Roberto just below the eye.

Razo leaped up, barking, to defend him. "No, Razo, no!"

Pa drew his knife and sunk it into Razo's throat.

Blood sprayed.

Over Razo's chest. Over Roberto's face and clothes and hands.

He knelt in the sun, blood dripping from his fingers, his chin. His dead friend. Roberto was numb with shock.

"Clean up this mess and bury him deep. Then you've got the hens to tend." Amato kicked the twitching dog with his boot and stalked off to the river to cleanse himself.

Roberto's tears mingled with the blood on his face, dribbling into his mouth. Chest heaving, he pulled Razo against him, crying until he couldn't cry anymore.

His mother arrived. Her warm arms folded around him, and she held him wordlessly until Razo's body was cold.

Ma's face was also streaked with red and tears. Adelina was clutching Ma's tunic, eyes red.

"Let's give him a proper funeral," Ma had said. "I'm sorry, Roberto, so sorry."

He and Ma were covered in blood and dirt by the time they'd buried Razo.

Along with his dog, he buried the playful innocence of his littling days and his love for his father.

It hadn't always been like that.

Pa had been loving and fun until his green guard troop had been captured by tharuks. All six riders were taken and enslaved, although their dragons escaped.

His ma, Lucia, had never given up hope that Amato would return, even though he was missing for nearly a year. Matotoi, Pa's dragon, had never stopped hunting for him, and one day, he brought Pa back, chasing the sorrow from Ma's face.

Roberto and Adelina were overjoyed. No one except Amato had survived. Naobia celebrated his return and mourned the loss of the other riders.

A few weeks later, Amato's angry outbursts began. Naobian leaders thought his rage would subside. It didn't.

Tharuks kidnapped settlers—one by one—from their fields, the woods or down by the coast. Over a year and a half, fifty or more disappeared, taken to rot and die as tharuk slaves.

No one suspected Amato. The best rider in the whole southern region, he'd been reinstated as the leader of the green guards, stationed in Naobia. Although his family life was tempestuous, Naobian leaders didn't want to interfere when Amato had been through so much and was valiantly trying to serve.

But Amato was addicted to swayweed and working with Zens and his tharuks.

"Roberto, would you like a ride on Matotoi?" Pa's eyes gleamed with excitement.

Ma was out with Adelina. Pa was in a great mood this morning.

"Can I? Really?" Pa's fiery green dragon, Matotoi, was the envy of all Roberto's friends.

Pa gave a belly laugh. "Why not?"

They made their way to the sacred clearing, where Matotoi was waiting.

A band of tharuks were waiting too. Pa held Roberto, while the beasts tied his hands and feet. He screamed and struggled, but Pa only laughed. "Come on, boy, do you want that ride or not?"

The tharuks gagged him and stuffed him into Matotoi's saddlebag, and Pa flew him straight to Zens, who trained Roberto as his protégé.

RIDERS OF FIRE

Sorrow ached deep inside Roberto. The things he'd done. The person he'd been. Hardly a suitable companion for a Queen's Rider who'd lived a sheltered life in Lush Valley. What had he been thinking when he'd admitted how he'd felt?

He hadn't—he hadn't been thinking at all. They'd simply melded, stripping away every pretense, revealing their love.

The cold gleam of the distant stars did nothing to light their way across the ocean. It would be a few hours until the sun rose, but Roberto didn't expect any warmth. Ezaara's hair stirred against his cheek again. He brushed his lips against the top of her head, one last time. Her love could never be his.

Dark Secrets

After visiting Naobia's early morning market, Ezaara sat with Roberto on a cliff, the churning tide smashing into jagged rocks below. Leaning against Erob, Roberto broke some bread and sliced a round of goat's cheese with his knife, passing some to her. After days of desert fare, the scent of crusty fresh bread made her mouth water. Although the cheese was creamy and mild, it was hard to eat with the unspoken question hanging between them.

After a few bites, Roberto said, "I have to show you something, and it's not very pleasant."

"What is it?"

"Me."

"Don't be silly. I'll always—"

"I can't come back with you, Ezaara." His face was etched with sorrow. "You won't understand my decision until you understand who I was. May I?" His hands hovered near her temples, his upper lip beaded with perspiration. He was nervous.

"Of course." Ezaara smiled, trying to make it easier for him. "It's all right. I'll always love you, no matter what."

"Maybe." His expression grim, he placed her hands on his temples.

Ezaara wanted to slide her fingers down his face and stroke his cheeks, reassuring him he was fine. Instead, she closed her eyes and focused.

Instantly, her stomach blossomed with pain.

"Pain is exquisite," a male voice said in her mind.

Sharp stabs pierced her legs. She screamed, but made no sound. A slow burn licked along her arms, and a vice tightened on her head, an excruciating ache throbbing through her skull. Her head was going to burst. Ezaara blacked out.

She came to in a dingy cavern, a man with bulbous yellow eyes looming over her. Zens. A huge tharuk thrust water at her and she drank, but the water coated her mouth with an odd tang.

Roberto's voice was gentle in her mind. *"Swayweed. Amato, my father, gave me to Zens, who tortured me, fed me swayweed and corrupted me."*

It felt real, as if it was happening to her, but she was reliving Roberto's memories.

Slammed against a wall, Roberto slid into a pile of filth, battered and bleeding. A nasty stench filled his nostrils, turning Ezaara's gut. A kick thumped his ribs. His head smacked a rock wall, and he blacked out again.

When he woke, Roberto struggled to his feet. "I won't. I won't do it." *His breath rasped, chest aching.* "I won't hurt people just because you want me to."

Zens gestured at a man in riders' garb, chained to the wall. "Are you sure, Roberto? I'd hate to force you. Just lay your hands on this dragon rider's head and use your new skills. A little pain will make him talk."

"No!"

"Very well." *Zens' silken voice caressed his mind. Roberto shuddered as Zens' eyes took on a feral gleam.* "You leave me no choice." *Zens turned to a massive tharuk with a broken tusk.* "Tharuk 000, bring in the others."

"Yes, beloved master." *000's red eyes gleamed and dark saliva dribbled off his tusks, splattering on the floor.*

Moments later, he was back with four littlings. Pitifully thin and hollow-eyed, they were about four to six years old. Littlings—slaving for Zens. The eldest had a festering lash mark on her cheek. Faces slack and expressionless, they were victims of numlock, wasted and broken.

What were they doing here? Did Zens want him to test them too? Well, he wouldn't.

"Place your hands upon that man's temples, Roberto. Extract the information."

"No."

"If you don't, I'll kill this girl." *Zens gestured to the blank-faced littling with the lash mark.*

It was an empty threat to bully him into submission. Roberto lunged for Zens' knife. "I'd rather kill myself than help you."

Tharuk 000 leaped between them and grabbed Roberto, tossing him against the stone wall, smacking his shoulder. That hurt.

"First, the girl. We'll see if he cooperates afterward." *Although Zens was mind-melding with 000, his voice slithered into Roberto's skull, battering him from the inside.* "Remember, Roberto, this was your choice. Now, she'll die, and it's your fault."

That's why the littlings were here. As hostages, to get him to cooperate. "No! Don't! I'll do anything you—"

000 raked his claws across the girl's throat. For a moment, her eyes flew wide. Blood welled along the gash, then spurted down her neck. Her mouth went slack and her head lolled to the side, eyes dead.

"No!" *Roberto screamed. Through his memories, Ezaara felt the scream rip through him, again and again.*

000 held his dripping claws to another littling's throat.

"Ready?" *Zens asked.*

Numb with horror, Roberto stumbled to the rider. He placed his hands on the man's temples and followed Zens' instructions.

Moons of Roberto's life passed in servitude. Amato visited, flashing gleeful smiles at his son's progress. Slaves died at Zens' hand, Roberto herding them, broken and bleeding, into Zens' cavern for mental torture—littlings, women and men.

Ezaara's gut churned with nausea. So young, only twelve. Roberto's hope died. His resistance was gone, and he did everything Zens commanded. He was a shell, obeying his masters' orders—almost eager for Zens' approval.

His subversion was sickening. Panicking, Ezaara dropped her hands from his temples and opened her eyes. Was this his horrible secret? Was Tonio right? Had he been a spy for Zens all along, only acting a role as master of mental faculties? Was Zaarusha right too? Had he been plotting to destroy her?

Roberto looked at her with strange intensity. "Are you all right?"

She shrugged.

"Let's continue. It's not over yet." His tone was flat, devoid of emotion.

He was as strong as the waves pounding the shore, as beautiful as the sparkling ocean she'd first traversed, and as dangerous as the gargantuan dark creatures that lurked in its depths.

He could destroy her.

Her stomach churned. "So how …?" She couldn't talk. Couldn't unsee those awful memories. The desolation, the torture and pain.

"How did I escape? Zens trusted me. It was his downfall," Roberto murmured. "Well, he trusted his ability to keep me under control. I had freedom to roam Death Valley because he knew the swayweed in my rations and numlock in my water would keep me subservient. After a year of slavery to him, things changed."

He placed her hands on his temples and his memories cascaded through her mind.

Roberto strolled through a horde of slaves, gloating at his ability to control them.

Ezaara recoiled. This wasn't the man she loved.

"Zens stole people and turned them into drudges, enslaving them physically and mentally, breaking their minds," Roberto melded with her. "*I had less numlock than the slaves, so I was capable of some independent thought and emotion, but not much.*"

His memories continued.

Roberto headed over the hill, coming out of the fog. His forehead prickled with sweat. He should go back. Zens could call upon him at any time, but he had the strange urge to explore. He trudged down the hill to a nearby valley, then over another hill. Something tugged him forward, further than he'd ever been since arriving at Death Valley.

Soon he came to a grassy valley of wildflowers with a stream running through it. Salt beading his upper lip, Roberto stooped to drink. His taste buds zinged with life. Fresh and pure, this water stirred distant memories in his fog-shrouded brain. Water was supposed to taste like this, not like the foul stuff he drank every day.

Scooping up handfuls, he swallowed greedily, drips running down his chin. He splashed his face, dribbled it over his hair, then drank again until his belly was tight.

Sudden cramps wracked his gut. Stumbling away, Roberto vomited behind a bush and kept on vomiting until he was dry retching. He spat and wiped his face on some leaves.

His gaze had cleared. Everything was more focused. The Terramites, the chain of mountains standing between him and the rest of the world, were pristine, snow-tipped and formidable, but his memory of life beyond those mountains was hazy.

Shards, he wouldn't drink Zens' fetid stuff anymore—it made his head foggy. From now on, he'd have fresh water. Zens didn't need to know. Taking the waterskin from his side, he tipped the tangy water out and rinsed it, then filled the skin from the stream. Ah, this felt good. He could slip out regularly and replenish his supplies. If he had to, he could alter the minds of those who noticed him leaving. As long as Zens or 000 didn't spot him.

Something blue flashed near the Terramites. A thrill ran through Roberto.

It flashed again, closer.

A dragon. Bright blue.

Roberto stole a glance back toward Death Valley. He was safe. No one could see them here. A surge of energy ran through Roberto as he and the dragon imprinted, breaking the hold of the swayweed and numlock. He had to leap upon this dragon, leave Death Valley and never return.

But Zens and Amato had threatened to kill Adelina if he left.

A rumble coursed through Roberto's mind, "Ah, Roberto, I'm Erob, named in your honor. You're my new rider."

Roberto stared into Erob's yellow eyes.

A yawning pit opened inside him as he remembered his actions among the slaves. "What have I done? Who have I become?"

"You've been a pawn in Zens' hands, twisted by him and your father, but you can be better. Become more, ride with me."

A strange energy thrummed inside his chest. He could feel his heart again. And hope.

But he'd been crossed by his own father. Maybe the dragon was tricking him too. "You think I'd believe you? Zens has helped me to become strong and powerful."

"Zens has shackled your true power, the power to lift mankind to a better place. Roberto, fly with me."

What if this was a devious beast trying to enslave him? Body trembling, Roberto fought Erob and the imprinting bond. "What about my sister? Amato threatened to kill her if I leave."

"I'll take your sister to a safe place, then meet you here at dusk in ten days. Drink only the stream water. Don't eat Zens' food." *The dragon's instructions blazed through Roberto's mind.* "Don't let Zens test you mentally, or he'll discover you're no longer under his influence. Being a dragon rider is your true destiny, Roberto of Naobia."

"And if I don't like this new life with you?"

"I'll return you to Death Valley."

"What if Zens suspects?"

Erob rubbed his eye ridge on Roberto's hand, and Roberto couldn't help scratching it. "You could come now."

Amato's angry face flashed before Roberto and he shook his head. "No, we must protect my sister."

"Here, take one of my scales. Eat a little each day. It'll give your eyes, skin, and fingernails a gray sheen, like you're numlocked, but you'll need to act sluggish."

Roberto stopped his memories. Ezaara reeled. So much information. So much hurt.

"Zens nearly caught me, but I pretended I had a belly gripe, blocking his probing mind with memories of nausea so he'd think I was too sick to eat," Roberto said. "On the tenth day, when I went to meet Erob, tharuk troops were combing the hills, so I had to sneak to the foot of the Terramites. Erob sensed me before I saw him. Under the cover of night, we escaped. He returned me to my home so I could uncover my father's treachery and bring him to justice."

"What happened to your father?"

"He was banished at his trial, but escaped on his dragon, Matotoi, who he'd turned with swayweed after he returned. My mother wouldn't tell him where Adelina was, so my father threw her off Matotoi's back onto some rocks. She never walked again." He stopped speaking, his throat bobbing as he swallowed. "She died a few moons later."

Ezaara gasped. "That's awful. Horrible."

"For a moment, my father was wracked with anguish that he'd hurt her. Matotoi felt his self-hatred, so he dived to the bottom of Crystal Lake, killing himself and Amato." Roberto gestured inland, his voice hollow, lifeless. "It's a short flight away, over those hills. Adelina and I used to swim there, but we haven't been back. The villagers searched for their bodies, but they were never found."

Her life in Lush Valley had been paradise compared to his. No wonder he'd been so distrusting when she'd first met him. His father had murdered his mother. Sure, it had taken moons for her to die, but he'd killed her. And tortured Roberto and sold him out.

If Amato wasn't dead, she'd finish him off herself.

"Ezaara." Roberto's voice pierced her thoughts. "I can't return to Dragons' Hold. I've been a traitor already, controlled by Zens, and I could fall again."

"You've turned your back on Zens once, proving you're true. If he ever catches you, you can do it again. You can resist him." Ezaara wanted to grab him and shake some sense into him. She hadn't come all this way, risking her life and giving up Zaarusha, only to have him give up.

Handel's vision flashed across Ezaara's mind: Roberto's face twisted into a cruel mask, lunging at her. She pushed the image aside. She wouldn't let that prophecy come true.

"Tonio's right." Roberto ran a hand through his hair. "Just say, they let me back as a dragon master again—if Zens gets hold of me and the information in my head, he'll learn enough to destroy the realm and its leaders."

"But you love the realm. You'll weaken the leadership if you're not part of it. No one has your mental talents. No one knows Zens' weaknesses better than you." She took his hand.

He pulled it away. "I can't go back. They think I was romantically involved with you. As a master, I'd be banished anyway."

"We didn't do anything! I was treating your wounds."

"But you weren't supposed to get off Zaarusha."

"I don't care if they know. I saved someone's life. Two lives."

"And endangered your own."

"So what?" Ezaara ripped a crust off the loaf and tossed it to some gulls that were wheeling and shrieking in the wind. They landed, squabbling over crumbs.

"Anyway, they think I poisoned Jaevin." Roberto uncrossed his long legs, scattering the birds.

"We know you didn't. There's a traitor at large at Dragons' Hold. If we don't find them, they may strike again. They may have already."

"No, they're better off without me, and so are you."

Ezaara threw her hands up. "Roberto, can't you see? I love you. I want you by my side."

"I'm not fit for you. You could do so much better. Besides my past with Zens, I'm a broken man. Even Erob tells me I don't trust enough."

"*True*," Erob interjected.

Roberto raised an eyebrow and gave a sardonic smile. "See?"

Ezaara took his hand again, rubbing the back of it with her thumb. "In time, you'll come to trust me, despite what's happened in your past. We can do this. Together."

He sighed. "I'm really not a fit companion for a Queen's Rider."

"Well, then, that's fine, because I'm no longer Queen's Rider. I gave up Zaarusha to come and find you."

His eyebrows flew up. His jaw dropped. "You gave up the queen for me?"

Ezaara nodded.

A tear ran from Roberto's eye. His voice dropped to a hoarse whisper. "You did that? For me?"

She stroked her finger along the track of his tear. "Yes, for you, Roberto of Naobia. You're worth it. But don't make me return alone."

§

Roberto was filled with a thousand swirling colors. Ezaara had chased away his darkness. She'd glimpsed the horror of his past and loved him anyway. *We can do this together,* she'd said. And he believed her.

"How can you want me, when you've seen what I've done?" His scarred cheek twitched where Pa had whipped him.

Her smile was like sunrise after a long night.

"With me no longer a master, and you no longer Zaarusha's rider, I don't know how we're going to get anyone to listen to us." Roberto sighed. It was worth a try. "If we're going back, it's time to hone your mental talents. I've designed training to help our riders beat tharuk mind-benders, but the council haven't let me test the training on my students yet."

"Why?"

"There are one or two masters who are resistant."

"Let me guess. Tonio?"

"No, he's for it." The spymaster was reasonable, except for his prejudice against him. Mind you, with his history, Tonio had reason. And someone had poisoned Jaevin …

"Roberto?" Ezaara jolted him back to the present. "What's a mind-bender?"

"Some tharuks can shape your thoughts, emotions or actions. They're called mind-benders. You can block them by keeping a fixed picture in your mind. The more detailed the image, the better. Picture something now, and I'll try to bend your thoughts."

Ezaara closed her eyes. There were dark circles under them. She was exhausted. The days in Robandi Desert hadn't been easy on her either. In fact, not much had been easy for her since she'd come to Dragons' Hold. Roberto placed his hands on her temples and accessed her thoughts.

She was imagining a bay fawn, sitting in sun-dappled light in the forest. He pushed the image away.

"More detail, Ezaara. Sounds, scents and sensations will all help."

Startled, the deer flicked its ears and raised its nose to scent the breeze rustling the nearby leaves. Roberto tried to push the deer aside. Not bad, a solid enough block against an average mind-bender, but not solid enough for him. He punched a hole in her image.

Flames danced in his head and heat rushed through him. He'd opened a floodgate. She was thinking about *him*—about how she felt. Shards! His arms ached to squeeze her against him, to lose himself in the touch of her lips, but he'd never be able to face Tonio with a clear conscience if he kissed her now.

§

"Ezaara, try again. Bring a little more life to it." Roberto's words floated through her. He'd pushed her image aside like a leaf in the wind. Oh, it had held for a few moments, before he'd shattered it.

Fire danced in her veins. With him, she felt so alive. So full of possibility and wonder. Strong.

He was only a hand span away, his breath caressing her cheek. Roberto closed his eyes, lashes dark against his olive skin as he slowly drew a deep breath.

He was struggling for control too.

His eyes opened and fell to her lips, lingering.

Every fiber of her being screamed out to kiss him. It was now or never. On tiptoes, Ezaara stretched up and brushed her lips against his. A jolt ran through her being. This was so right, so—

"No!" Voice hoarse, Roberto pushed her away. His face was tormented. "No, Ezaara."

Shame knifed through her. Oh, shards! Her face burned. "Sorry."

"Don't be. I just can't." Onyx eyes sad, he grimaced. "If we're returning to the hold, I can't kiss you."

"But you're not my master anymore." Ezaara thrust her desperate emotions deep, managing to stay calm. "We're free."

"Not if we're returning, we're not."

Ezaara wanted to throw herself on her knees and beg him for a kiss, but she could see conflict in every line of his body and hear chaos roaring in his head. Swallowing, she nodded.

"Go on, Ezaara, try again." Roberto urged her. "Use something you know well. Something deeply personal."

So, she did.

§

Shards, she was sly. Him, it was him. Seeing his own face, painted with the beauty of a skilled artist, made Roberto's breath catch. She saw him like this? Where was his hardness toward his father? His anger at Zens for shattering his core? Where was the broken man?

She showed him a face touched with compassion and admiration. A face that loved and cared and held human life precious. A face without the harshness he saw in his polished bronze mirror.

She brought out the best in him.

More reason not to kiss her now. To wait, and earn her love the hard way.

Face radiant, she stared up at him. Gods, he was tempted. *"Another picture. Choose something else."*

A cottage on a farm, nestled on the forest's edge, alps stretching to the sky. He shoved and pushed at the image, but it was anchored. It must be her home in Lush Valley. *"Well done; try something different."*

A tree, bark rough against her cheek as she hid from two boys below, hunting for her. Birds flitted through the branches, among rustling leaves. The scent of summer hung in the air. He tugged, pried, punched, but the trees and boys held fast.

"Excellent. We can practice more on the return flight."

She stood. "We should get back and warn people there's a murderer at Dragons' Hold."

"Ezaara …" Roberto hesitated. Her biggest stumbling block could be her loyalty to her friends. "I suspect Simeon and his family may be involved."

He hadn't anticipated the icy rage that flitted across her face. Her voice was deadly calm. "Whether the council accepts us or not, we can do better than warn them: let's hunt that traitor down."

Deadly Intent

Roberto had his arms around Ezaara as she slept, the warmth of her back seeping through his jerkin. His eyes were gritty and drooping, but he was too tense to sleep, despite the peaceful rhythm of Erob's wingbeats. The Egg knew what would be facing them when they arrived at Dragons' Hold. His whole life, he'd wanted to be a dragon master, but he'd gladly thrown it away to save Ezaara from banishment. He'd never expected her to sacrifice being Queen's Rider—it was nearly impossible to deny the bond between rider and dragon. But she'd done it—for him.

It had been a long hard flight and his backside was aching. Roberto shifted in his saddle. Erob was slowing.

The first rays of sunset hit the crags of Dragon's Teeth, making the snow-clad reaches catch fire. His breath caught. This is what he lived for. Flying. Nature in all its glory. And now, Ezaara in his arms, her breath rising and falling, and her hair smelling of the Naobian Sea.

She stirred and woke.

"Look," Roberto whispered. "Isn't it stunning?"

She exhaled, eyes wide at the sight. "Roberto, we can't let tharuks destroy this."

"They will, if we give them a chance."

"All this bickering and in-fighting … we've got to turn our gaze outwards and work to save the realm."

"If we regain our standing with the council …" He sighed. "One step at a time. First, we have to get there."

As they neared the ranges, blue guards took to the sky.

Erob melded. *"So, they're awake and alert. What do you want me to tell them?"*

"That they're a bunch of idiots for believing I was guilty."

"Well, you were pretty convincing," Erob replied.

"You didn't believe me. You knew I was innocent."

"Of course I did. You have a dragon of superior intellect."

"With a mild sense of exaggeration." Despite his trepidation, a chuckle broke from Roberto.

"And a wicked sense of humor. Don't forget the humor." A rumble rippled through Erob's belly. *"I'll manage them, shall I?"*

Ezaara broke in. Whenever she melded with him and Erob, it was like an extra string on Lars' harp, producing a new exciting thread in an existing melody. *"Remind the blue guards that they've pledged to serve our queen, and it's in her best interests to reunite her with the Queen's Rider. At least, I hope she wants to be reunited."*

"Did she banish you outright?" Roberto asked her.

Ezaara winced. *"Only because I went after you. But I'm glad I did."*

"Of course you are." Erob snorted. *"Neither of you are guilty. Which means someone else is."*

Erob melded with the blue guards' dragons. They were closer now, their talons visible. Were they coming to drive them off? Or to escort them into the hold?

Septimor, Seppi's dragon, roared, and Erob replied, a tremor running through him. *"We're to follow them to the council chambers."*

So, no longer outcasts, but not yet welcomed either. Well, that was better than being chased off outright.

"What's happening?" Ezaara straightened. *"I can't meld with Zaarusha."*

"That's strange." Roberto took his hands off her waist. "Maybe she's hunting or asleep."

Blue dragons flanked them on either side. Roberto gave Seppi a nod, and they flew on. When the peaks of Dragon's Teeth were below them, drumbeats started pounding.

"So much for a quiet entrance," Erob said.

"What's that drum signal?" Ezaara asked.

"Something's afoot," Roberto said. A repeated seven-beat rhythm. *"A death toll. Someone's died."* Shards! His breath got stuck in his throat. Adelina? Lars? Who? Another poisoning or an innocent death?

Ezaara sat bolt upright. *"Our traitor may have struck again."*

Seppi's grim expression conveyed similar thoughts. Erob swooped down, flanked by blue guards, and landed outside the council chambers. Roberto thumped to the ground with Ezaara and the blue guards close on his heels. They rushed into the chamber, drums reverberating through the stone.

No one was there. Two chairs were up-ended, the others pushed back haphazardly. Papers were scattered across the table and half-eaten food sat on plates. Cloaks were hanging on hooks, but there were no weapons in the weapons stand. The masters had left in a hurry, armed.

"Come on, we've got to find Lars," Roberto yelled to Seppi as he spun for the door.

Seppi grabbed his arm. "Not so fast, Roberto. Septimor's melding with Singlar to see if Lars wants you free or in chains."

That stung. And Roberto hadn't missed the fact that Seppi hadn't addressed him as 'master'.

Seppi's face blanched, right as Erob melded with Roberto, *"It's Master Shari. She's dead,"* said Erob. *"I'm sorry."*

Knees faltering, Roberto grasped the back of a nearby chair, the wood biting into his clenched hand. No, not Shari.

Her smile flashed to mind. When no one else had accepted him at Dragons' Hold, she'd welcomed him, trusting he'd changed when he'd imprinted with Erob. She'd stood up for him at his trial, seeing through his lies to save Ezaara. She was the closest thing to family he and Adelina had.

By saving Ezaara, he hadn't been here to help someone else he loved. Eyes stinging, he forced himself to speak. "Seppi, please ask Lars if I may see Shari."

Seppi waited a few moments, obviously asking Septimor to meld with Singlar, then replied. "Lars would like you and Ezaara in Shari's cavern, right away."

§

Ezaara glanced at Roberto's pale face as he gripped a chair. Shari had obviously been close to him. She kept trying to meld with Zaarusha as she and Roberto followed the blue guards down the tunnel, that strange drum rhythm echoing around them. *"Zaarusha."* Still no answer. Was the queen too angry to mind-meld?

They rounded a corner and met a troop of guards stationed outside Shari's door, swords drawn. "Halt!" A guard addressed Seppi. "Why are you bringing these traitors into the heart of the hold?"

Seppi nodded curtly. "Lars wants to see them immediately."

Moving aside, the guards opened the door, and they entered.

Face haggard, Lars was on his knees next to Shari's bed with his hand on her shoulder. He waved them in. Masters Tonio, Bruno, Aidan, Hendrik, and Fleur were in discussion, clustered at the foot of the bed.

Shari lay curled, with her hands around her stomach. Even in death, she was beautiful. Her braids were scattered around her face and across her pillow, their copper and silver fastenings glinting in the torchlight. Her dark eyes were blank, staring into nothing.

"We're not sure what caused her death," said Lars, voice husky. "But we'll find out."

Maybe the poisoner had struck again, not satisfied because Ezaara had thwarted their attempt on Jaevin's life.

"How's Master Jaevin doing?" Ezaara asked.

Lars' gaze was flat. "He's dead."

Ezaara's stomach jolted. "But I healed him. He should have been fine. What happened?"

"We don't know." Lars shook his head. "We've been trying to find out, but Master Fleur hasn't been able to get to the bottom of it."

Fleur chimed in, pointing at her and Roberto. "These traitors were banished for colluding to kill Master Jaevin. I told you Ezaara left a substance with Threcia, saying it was medicine, but it killed him. It was probably more dragon's bane."

Rising to his feet, Lars gave Master Fleur a withering look. "All masters, report to the main cavern to address the assembled folk. Tonio, you're in charge. Have your people circulate among the crowd and see if they can pick up anything. Fleur, once Shari's death has been announced, bring the other female master, Alyssa, back to prepare Shari for her death rites. Seppi, Roberto and Ezaara, you stay here. We have to get to the bottom of this before anyone else is killed."

Bruno strode across the room. "I'm not leaving you with two banished outcasts and only one blue guard for protection."

"Very well." Lars' gaze was icy. "Seppi, choose another blue guard to stay. Now, the rest of you, get to the main cavern." He glowered until Bruno left.

Roberto melded with Ezaara. *Bruno and Fleur seem very keen to have us out of the way.*

"And to tarnish our reputations," she replied. *I'm going to check something.*

But before she could move, Lars spoke, "Two Masters dead since you've been banished, so it obviously wasn't your fault. Roberto, I'm guessing you said you'd poisoned Jaevin to deflect the blame off Ezaara. You'd rather we lost a master of imprinting and mental faculties than the Queen's Rider, huh?" He shot Roberto a shrewd gaze. "We need to get to the bottom of this matter, then I'll have you both reinstated. But first, I need to know if you've been romantically involved."

"No, sir."

"Lucky we never kissed," Ezaara shot.

"Agreed." Roberto's answer was heartfelt.

"But you do care about her, don't you?"

A brief nod was the only sign Roberto gave.

"I'm glad you showed me how you feel or I wouldn't believe it," Ezaara said.

For a heartbeat, Roberto's cheeks took on a red tinge as he addressed Lars. "Tell us what happened."

The booming of the drums stopped, the air suddenly hollow.

Lars cracked his neck. "Jaevin's dragon, Vino, melded with Zaarusha and showed her Jaevin's dying thoughts. He insisted that you'd helped him to recover, then someone else had slipped poison into his evening meal. He had no idea who it was." Grief lined Lars' face. "I'm sorry. I owe you both my deepest apologies. Now we have to hunt down the killer before they strike again."

This was awkward. Ezaara had expected hostility or accusation, not contrition. "Thank you, Lars," she said. "There's something else that concerns me. I haven't been able to meld with Zaarusha since we arrived."

"When Zaarusha realized you two hadn't poisoned Jaevin, she barricaded her mind and hasn't let any dragons meld with her since," Lars replied. "Fleur's dragon, Ajeuria, insists that Zaarusha needs peace and quiet and that solitude will help her heal."

Odd. Ezaara would've expected Zaarusha to be angry, filled with fire and flame, not retreating in self-pity. Then again, Ezaara had never seen her heartbroken. Could Ajeuria be right? *"What do you think?"*

Roberto shrugged. *"I don't trust Fleur, Bruno or Simeon, but Ajeuria should be loyal to the queen."*

Ezaara's eyes were drawn to a bowl of half-eaten soup on Shari's bedside table. "Why was she eating here, not in the mess cavern?"

"She'd been feeling off-color, so she chose to miss tonight's council meeting and eat here." Lars pulled Shari's blanket up to her shoulders.

Except for her staring eyes, she could've been sleeping.

There was a knock at the door, and the guards let Fleur and Alyssa enter. While Lars and Roberto were greeting them, Ezaara used the opportunity to examine Shari's meal. She bent over, as if to tighten her boot, and sniffed the bowl. Odd. The soup had a strange but familiar scent. She quickly moved away before anyone noticed. Where had she recently smelt that?

"Alyssa and I will dress Shari in her ceremonial robes now." Fleur held the door open—a blatant invitation for Lars, Roberto and Ezaara to leave.

"Ezaara will be assisting you," Lars said firmly.

"But she's no longer the Queen's Rider—"

"It's tradition that all females on the council dress a deceased female master, you know that. I've spoken with Ezaara and deemed her fit. It's only a matter of time until she's reinstated as Queen's Rider."

"Very well. My son will be pleased to welcome her back."

In a flash, Ezaara knew when she'd smelt that weird flavor—Simeon's relaxing tea. That's why she'd vomited—Simeon had poisoned her, keeping her away from Sofia to create more prejudice against her. But why? What did Simeon have to gain?

It didn't matter. Simeon and his family couldn't be trusted. Roberto had never trusted him—said he'd had good reason not to. She'd been a fool, thinking he was sweet when she'd first arrived.

Lars turned to leave.

"Lars, I need to talk to you."

"What is it, Ezaara?"

Ezaara couldn't help shooting a nervous gaze toward Fleur. "Sir, I think I know—"

Fire blinded Ezaara's vision. Flames licked along her skin, making her flesh sear and blister. The stench of her own burning flesh filled her nostrils. Flames rippled over her jerkin, smoke searing her eyes. Her brain jangled, making her want to scream. No, she would not, could not, give in to this illusion. No dragon's vision was going to beat her this time.

Gasping, Ezaara fixed her home in her mind, picturing their shutters, the fields, the Alps rising far beyond the forest toward the sky. Flames flickered, threatening to burst through the cobalt sky. She focused. The sky was blue. Blue. The clouds, white and fluffy. The flames were an illusion. The day was warm. Birds were singing. Tomaaz was outside in the garden, tilling the earth. Her father was planting beets. Her mother was kneading a second batch of bread in their cottage, the scent of baking loaves wafting through their home. She would not let an errant dragon force her into submission through mind-bending. Squeezing her eyes shut, Ezaara went over every detail, a summer breeze kissing her face.

She relaxed. She'd won the battle.

"Ezaara, what is it?" Lars asked. "Are you ill?"

She opened her mouth, about to speak, when Roberto melded. *"Careful, Ezaara. Everyone is watching you, and it's obvious you've been attacked mentally. Stay cool. Don't give anything away."*

Someone had prevented her from sharing vital information with Lars. A bead of sweat trickled into her eye. Either Alyssa or Fleur via one of their dragons. She coughed. "It doesn't matter, Lars. It was nothing."

Fleur, it had to be. Ezaara melded with Roberto, *"Shards! Fleur's the murderer, and her whole family are in on it."*

"Come on," said Fleur, "we need some privacy to prepare Shari for her death rites." She waved the men out of the room before Roberto could answer.

"I'm sending Adelina to help you," Roberto melded from the corridor. *"I don't want you to be in there without support, but we need to catch Fleur in the act."*

"Thank you." Although relief washed through Ezaara, she kept her face neutral.

Fleur opened one of Shari's drawers and pulled out a pristine white tunic and breeches edged with golden dragons. "This is fitting for her final passage." She shook her head. "Such a tragedy that she's died so young. So much vitality snuffed out."

She sounded so sincere. The woman was demented.

Adelina arrived, her usual perky attitude missing. "Please let me know how I can help."

Fleur laid the robe on the bed and then turned, as if she'd just spotted the bowl on Shari's bedside table. "Oh dear, we can't have food next to the deceased."

"Why not?" asked Ezaara.

"Fleur is from Montanara," Alyssa answered. "Montanarians never leave food near those who die. It's considered disrespectful. Here, Fleur, let me get rid of it for you."

"No, I'll do it myself," she replied. "Alyssa, please show Ezaara how to wash and dress Shari. I'll be back shortly."

A chill shivered down Ezaara's neck. Fleur was trying to destroy the evidence.

Adelina whisked the bowl away before Fleur could reach it. "Master Fleur, allow me to perform this menial task. The dressing of a master is of utmost importance and must be performed by our distinguished master healer." Before Fleur could utter a word, Adelina slipped out of the room with the food.

"Excellent," said Alyssa. "It is fitting that you dress Master Shari for her death rites, Fleur."

"It would've only taken a moment," Fleur said stiffly. "But it's kind of Adelina to help."

"Roberto, Adelina is bringing poisoned food. Save it for their trial."

"Will do."

They disrobed Shari and washed her. Adelina returned and helped Fleur and Alyssa fasten her tunic and arrange her hair.

A knock sounded at the door. Ezaara opened it and nearly leaped backward when Simeon gave her a dazzling smile.

"Ah, My Honored Queen's Rider, or soon to be again, I'm sure." He bent and tried to kiss her hand.

Ezaara snatched it back. This creep had attacked her. Mauled her. She'd never noticed how slimy Simeon was: getting her onside at the feast; poisoning her with that tea; and driving a wedge between her and Roberto. He'd probably broken her cane, too.

"I do wish I could welcome you back to Dragons' Hold under more pleasant circumstances," Simeon continued. He turned to Fleur. "Mother, you're needed urgently. Someone is gravely ill. Please come at once." Fleur hustled out the door after him, without a backward glance.

Simeon and Fleur were up to something. Was Alyssa in on it too? Would she believe them if they told her? Or would she stop them from following Fleur?

Ezaara stared at Adelina, stricken.

Adelina gave a subtle wink. "My Honored Queen's Rider, you look weary. You must've had a long journey with my brother. Why don't you take some time to freshen up? Alyssa and I will keep vigil here overnight."

"I can manage on my own." Alyssa commandeered Ezaara and Adelina toward the doorway. "Shari was my dearest colleague." She backhanded a tear from her eye. "It's a privilege for me to keep vigil until her death rites in the morning. Adelina, you must see your brother. Ezaara, you need to be reunited with Queen Zaarusha."

As she and Adelina rushed out the door, Ezaara melded with Roberto. *Fleur and Simeon are up to something.*

I've been called away to a tharuk attack. Roberto sounded torn.

"Have you got any idea where they've gone?" Ezaara asked Adelina.

"Along this way, but I've no idea where they're heading," Adelina answered as they ran past the guards, along the tunnel. "While you were away, I've been volunteering in the infirmary. Over the past few days, I've taken a sample of every substance stockpiled in that alcove we discovered." She patted the bag she always wore, slung over her shoulder. "They're all right here."

"Good work. I may be able to identify some of them," Ezaara replied.

"While you were away, a girl arrived from Lush Valley. You may know her—Lovina. She was poisoned, but I healed her."

"Lovina? Here?"

"Apparently your brother helped her get here," Adelina replied.

Tomaaz—the first news she had of her family. "It'll have to wait. We have to catch Fleur first. Have you any idea who she'll target next?"

"If it was me, I'd go for the queen."

"Zaarusha!" No answer. *"Roberto, I can't meld with Zaarusha, and Fleur is prowling around with Simeon."*

"Find the queen!" Tension rippled through his thoughts.

A hollow pit yawned in Ezaara's stomach as drumbeats thundered down the tunnel. Her heart lurched. "Is someone else dead?"

"No, these drums are ushering in Alyssa's overnight vigil, the first phase of the death rites for Shari." Adelina's bag of supplies jangled as she ran.

Ezaara thrust her cavern door open. She and Adelina dashed through the archway to Zaarusha's den.

Her nest was empty.

"Fangs! Where could she be?" Adelina smacked her palm against her thigh twitch.

"I don't know!" Ezaara had to do something. *"Erob, where's Zaarusha?"*

"Rumors say she's pining for you, but I can't meld with her, and that's highly unusual. Years ago, when she was missing Anakisha, Yanir, and her dead dragonet, she isolated herself at the imprinting grounds."

"How soon can you get there?"

"The tharuk attack was a false alarm. We're coming, but we're still far away."

Ezaara whirled. "Adelina, take me to the imprinting grounds."

Adelina swiped a torch off the wall. "We're going to need this," she said. "It's dark where we're going."

They ran through the tunnels, past the main cavern where the rise and fall of voices and slow beats of the drums marked Shari's death.

"We should be there for Shari," Adelina slowed, her face torn.

"Shari's already dead. We have to help Zaarusha, and stop more murders."

As they rounded a bend in the tunnel, Gret stepped from the shadows. "Ezaara, you're back? What's wrong? Where are you two going?" Before they could answer, her eyes flicked to the torch. "The imprinting grounds? I just followed Fleur and Simeon to the grounds' entrance tunnel ... but there are no hatchlings up there now. What's going on?"

"Zaarusha is missing. We believe Fleur may want to harm her."

"Oh, fangs! Let's go." Gret ran alongside them, yanking another torch from the wall.

"How long ago did you see them?" Ezaara asked.

"Not long."

"They must have run the whole way," Adelina panted as they passed the infirmary and sped along the tunnel to a cracked wooden door.

Hinges creaking, Adelina yanked it open, revealing a steeply ascending tunnel. They stumbled up half-hewn steps, the flickering torchlight shadowing pitfalls that were a nightmare to negotiate.

On and on they went. *Zaarusha.* There was no answer, not a glimmer from the queen.

"How long is this cursed tunnel?"

"We're about halfway." In front of her, Adelina's torch moved steadily upward.

A sharp cry rang out from behind. Ezaara spun, nearly losing her footing. Gret was on the ground, clutching her knee. Blood dripped from a deep gash that cut through her breeches into her knee. Gret's torch rolled down the slope, coming to rest in a hollow, then guttered and died.

Ezaara knelt beside her. "Did you trip? I'll go and find your torch."

"Go on. I'll catch up." Gret's eyes reflected the light from Adelina's torch above. "You have to go. *Now*."

"She's right, Ezaara. We can't delay. Come on," Adelina called.

Torn, Ezaara dashed upward, leaving Gret injured and alone in the dark. It was wrong, on so many levels, for a healer to ignore an injury and abandon a friend.

Soon, air grew fresher. They were nearing an exit.

Adelina doused the torch, and they crept up the tunnel using their hands against the walls to guide them through the dark. Ezaara barked her shin against a rock, biting her lip to stop herself from crying out.

The exit led to a huge plateau, stars glimmering above. Brightly burning torches on the rocky walls illuminated a blood-chilling scene. Simeon was stroking a gray dragon's head, while Fleur tipped the contents of a large bottle into its maw.

Zaarusha!

Her stomach dropped. The queen's scales were dull gray. There was no iridescence, not a flicker of color in the torchlight.

"The queen is dying," Adelina whispered.

Ezaara leaped across the plateau, her feet seeming to grind against the stone forever, as if she was pushing her body through syrup. A sickly green glow emanated from the queen, although Ezaara knew no one else could see it. *Sathir.*

Washed-out-gray, Zaarusha swallowed the substance. The queen's head slumped to the ground and her body seemed to deflate—as if the life breath was leaking out of her.

It was no use. She was too late. *"Zaarusha!"* Ezaara's mind screamed.

Hundreds of dragons roared mentally in reply.

Except the dragon she loved.

"No!" With a bellow, Ezaara barreled into Fleur, knocking her onto the rock. Fleur kneed her in the stomach. Clawed her face. Ezaara punched her, but Fleur was stronger than she'd thought. As they rolled and thrashed, she caught glimpses of Zaarusha's scales, turning an ever-darker gray. With a desperate thrust, she flipped Fleur under her and drove her knee into Fleur's groin, pressing her weight on Fleur's torso.

Cool metal kissed her neck. "Not so fast," Simeon said, behind her.

The sword's kiss bit, cutting her skin. Warmth trickled down her neck, wafting the metallic tang of blood. A dark drop hit Fleur's cheek.

Fleur grinned. "Bleed, wench."

"Unhand my mother or my sword will bite deeper." Typical Simeon, lyrical, even when threatening her.

"Scum," she spat, releasing her grip on Fleur. "I don't know what I ever saw in you."

He yanked her to her feet, his sword rasping against her skin. She'd be no use to Zaarusha dead. Behind Simeon, a shadow slipped along the rocky walls. Adelina. Then another slower shadow. Gret. Ezaara had to keep Fleur and Simeon talking, to distract them.

Simeon pulled her to his side, eyes roving over her body. "Well, I certainly know what I saw in you," he sneered.

"What have you done to the queen?"

"Pretty face, but pretty stupid," Simeon said.

"Simeon," Fleur warned, scrambling to her feet and dusting herself off. "Finish her off. We need to go. Ajeuria will be here soon."

So that *was* who the burning visions had come from.

"I don't know—maybe I'd like to *play with her* a little first, mother. Ajeuria can carry three."

If they took her, she'd have no chance of saving Zaarusha. "Why? Why did you do this, Simeon?" she asked, stalling. "I trusted you. You could've wooed me and ruled beside me."

"And lose the power Zens will give me?" Simeon scoffed. "His vision of the realm is far superior to anything dragons can offer."

Violence and hatred and an army of monsters? Superior to dragons and bonded riders protecting a realm? Simeon was far gone.

Fleur strode to Zaarusha and placed her hand on the dragon's forehead. "She's waning. It shouldn't take long now. Soon the realm will have no queen." She grinned.

Guilt knifed through Ezaara. She'd chosen Roberto instead of Zaarusha, and now the queen was dying. "What are Zens' superior plans? If they're really that good, maybe I should join you. I don't want to be on the losing side. I've always liked you, Simeon."

"You really think I'm that dumb? I'm not going to fall for—"

Adelina appeared behind Simeon, driving her knife up into his armpit. He released his blade, crying out.

Pulling her sword from its scabbard, Ezaara leaped toward Fleur, but she was too late. Gret was already there.

Fleur and Gret's blades clashed and scraped as they fought, the sounds grating on Ezaara's bones. Gret's blade work was as good as ever, but her bloodsoaked leg slowed her.

With calculated moves, Fleur drove Gret past Zaarusha, pushing her ever closer to the cliff edge. Gret stumbled, but raised her sword to deflect Fleur's blow to her head.

Ezaara raced toward them.

Zaarusha! No one was saving Zaarusha.

"Ezaara," Adelina screamed.

Ezaara spun. Simeon was wrestling Adelina.

Flapping filled the air. She whirled again. Ajeuria dived at Gret, grasping talons outstretched.

With a desperate spurt, Ezaara shoved Fleur sideways, and dragged Gret back from the edge. Ajeuria roared, swooping down. Gripping her sword with both hands, Ezaara thrust it upward, aiming for the green dragon's soft belly.

A roar split the air. In a flash of midnight blue, barely visible against the dark sky, Ajeuria was yanked backward, screaming and twisting. Erob—with a death grip on Ajeuria's neck, Roberto flat against his back. The dragons writhed, plunging toward the valley below.

The air filled with the rumble of a rockslide. No, the flapping wings of a hundred dragons. Dragon cries ricocheted through her head.

"We're coming." Singlar.

"We heard your call." Septimor.

"Save the queen." Vino, Jaevin's dragon.

They were coming. All of the dragons of Dragons' Hold had heard her desperate cry that the queen was dying.

But only one person could save Zaarusha.

Ezaara raced over to Adelina's bag near the tunnel and snatched it up. Gret was still fighting Fleur. Adelina was battling Simeon. Roberto and Erob could be killed. Ignoring it all, she raced to Zaarusha.

Weak puffs of air issued from Zaarusha's nostrils. Ezaara laid her hands on the queen's skin. Nearly cold. Her scales were dark and flat.

Gods, gods. Please.

"Zaarusha."

Nothing, but she kept melding, talking to the queen. Focusing, Ezaara reached for *sathir*. A faint glimmering thread of life clung to Zaarusha—sickly green.

Hurry. Hurry. Her fingers fumbled as she opened the bag. No, she needed to see *sathir*. To be calm. Breathing deeply, Ezaara examined the bag's contents, pulling corks off jars and vials, and sniffing.

Woozy weed. Dragon's bane. Some foul-smelling green stuff. Clean herb. Rumble weed. More of that ghastly sleeping-draught poison. Clear-mind. The antidote to limplock. A little blue bottle of clear liquid. Bottles and jars of all shapes and sizes. How in the Egg's name could she know the correct cure?

Ithsar's lizard, Thika, came to mind.

Focusing on *sathir*, Ezaara held the bottle of the sleeping draught poison by Zaarusha's slumped head. A sickly green emanated from the bottle. The poison dimmed Zaarusha's life force. Good, hopefully the cure would show too.

She held up a vial of limplock remedy. Nothing.

The dragon's bane. Dimmer.

What about the woozy weed? Again, nothing.

Zaarusha's breathing was slowing, barely audible.

Around her, the sounds of fighting dimmed as she focused on the queen, willing her to consciousness.

Her hands shook as she held up item after item. The pale green thread faded until she could hardly see it. No, she was losing Zaarusha.

Wait, it was her. She'd just lost focus and couldn't sense *sathir*. She had to calm herself. There, the thread was back, but weak. There were now only three unidentified items left in Adelina's bag.

Ezaara held up a jar of Fleur's healing unguent. Dimmer and sickly green—so that was laced with weak poison too. She grabbed the next, a blue bottle, and held it near Zaarusha's head. A faint golden glow surrounded the bottle, connecting with Zaarusha's life thread, making it shimmer with gold light.

Just to be sure, Ezaara checked the last substance. Nothing.

Relief washed over her. She had the antidote. But how could this tiny bottle save such a massive queen?

Tooth & Talon

Roberto clung to Erob's back, his arms through the hand grips and legs cinched tight in the stirrups. His stomach somersaulted as Ajeuria bucked to free Erob's fangs from her neck.

Her tail lashed Erob's side, the tip slamming into Roberto's leg. He gritted his teeth, hanging on. Melded with Erob, Roberto felt Ajeuria's talons rake Erob's belly. The dragons snarled, twisting and thrashing.

Below, the pines were like an army brandishing lances at the sky.

"She can't hold out forever," Erob said.

"We don't have forever," Roberto melded. *"Any moment now, we'll be speared on those trees."*

Ajeuria blasted flame at Roberto as they plummeted earthward.

§

A hand grasped Ezaara's shoulder. "How can I help?" asked Lars.

"We need to feed this antidote to Zaarusha."

Nodding, Lars pushed Zaarusha's upper lips onto the sharp tips of her fangs, making the dragon open her maw reflexively.

Uncorking the bottle, Ezaara tipped clear liquid onto the queen's tongue. "And now?"

"Now, we wait." Ezaara focused on Zaarusha's life thread. Lars paced. She was dimly aware that the noises behind them were quieting. Soon, Zaarusha's life thread glowed golden.

"What's happening?" Lars asked. "Is it enough?"

The gold was fading. "No, I don't think it is."

Lars ferreted through the jars and bottles. "Is that all we've got?"

"Adelina found it. Tell her to fetch all the antidote she can find." She passed Lars the tiny empty bottle.

He glanced at the collection of vessels on the ground around Ezaara's knees. "How will she know which one we're looking for?"

"It has a distinctive smell."

Lars sniffed it, wrinkling his nose. "Indeed. We'll be back soon."

Ezaara stayed, hands pressed against Zaarusha's side. "*Zaarusha.*" No answer. The thread looked the same as it had a few moments ago. Her queen was still unconscious.

"*I love you.*" Roberto's words blazed through her. Piercing pines grew ever closer in the moonlight. The rush of air and wind. Bucking writhing dragons. Him, holding on despite his leg searing. "*Ezaara, I—*"

"Roberto!"

Ripping her hands from Zaarusha, Ezaara rushed to the edge and gazed down. There was a burst of flame below. A roar. Then nothing but blackness.

§

Adelina watched helplessly as Erob latched onto Ajeuria and the dragons plunged through the sky. Roars ripped through the night, tearing at her heart, making her chest tight. Shards, her brother. With a surge of energy, she drove her knife upward, slashing Simeon's wrist.

He dropped his sword.

She leaped through the air, flinging out her foot and driving it into his chest. He stumbled backward. She leaped and kicked again. Simeon went down.

Adelina jumped on him, twisting his arm up his back, and pinned him to the ground.

Moments later, blue guards arrived, taking Simeon off her hands.

"I've been attacked!" Fleur pointed at Gret and Ezaara. "They attacked a master. Seize them!"

The guards ignored Fleur's outraged cries as they held her arms fast.

"You may think you're clever, Ezaara," Fleur's voice glittered with malice as she addressed the Queen's Rider. "But there's not enough antidote in the whole of Dragons' Realm to save your queen."

Adelina shuddered as the guards bound Fleur and swept her off on one of their dragons.

She helped Gret up. "Are you hurt badly?"

Gret smiled through gritted teeth. "Been better. With our master healer poisoning the council, I'm not sure who's going to heal me."

"Come on, Gret. There are others on duty in the infirmary." A blue guard helped Gret onto his dragon.

With shaking knees, Adelina stumbled past Ezaara and Lars, crouched by Zaarusha's dull-scaled head, toward the edge of the plateau.

Lars waved a bottle. "Adelina, we urgently need to get more antidote for the queen."

Who to save? Her brother? Or her queen? Her queen who'd helped banish her brother. No one had believed him innocent except herself and Erob. Now he was plunging to the valley, risking his life for his queen again.

It seemed like hours since she'd discovered Fleur's stash of hidden remedies—and poisons. Numbly, she nodded and climbed upon Singlar. She'd see Roberto from the air soon enough—if there was anything left to see.

Lars climbed on behind her and patted her shoulder. "He'll be all right. He's an experienced rider."

But Erob was falling, not flying.

Singlar leaped into the sky. Adelina scanned the basin below, searching through the patches of moonlight and shadows for—there, a burst of flame, a roar, then nothing.

Gods, no! He'd been beaten, turned traitor, imprinted and saved, only to be banished, then return—and now this? It was too much. Tears tracked down Adelina's face, bitterly cold in the night wind. She clung to Lars' back, burying her face in his jerkin.

His voice rumbled through his back. "Roberto will be all right."

But his words were hollow. How could Lars know? Hope caught, half-formed in her throat. "Has Singlar melded with Erob?"

"He's trying." Lars pressed a bottle into her hand. "We need more of this stuff. You'll know it by the scent."

He was deliberately keeping her busy. Adelina uncorked the bottle and sniffed. Ew, gross. "Lars, I don't know if there's any more. Fleur said—"

"Hurry," Lars said, leaping down as Singlar landed outside the infirmary. "Zaarusha is dying."

Inside the infirmary, Kierion and a young girl were bandaging Gret's leg. No one else was around.

"Thank the Egg, you're here, Kierion," Lars said to him. "We need the antidote to a poison that's killing Zaarusha. Help us find it."

Kierion sprang to his feet. "What am I looking for?"

Adelina shoved the empty bottle under his nose. "Anything that smells like this."

"Phew! At least it's distinctive."

"You search out here. Lars and I will look in Fleur's secret stash." Adelina rushed Lars into Fleur's alcove. "I found that bottle in here."

They frantically rummaged through the shelves, opening bottles and jars and smelling the contents.

"Not this one." Lars set the bottle aside and snatched up another.

It seemed to take forever. The whole time, Adelina fought the dark panic rising inside her. Still no word of Roberto. "We've looked everywhere," she finally said. "There isn't any more."

Lars flung his hands out. "We'll turn the whole infirmary upside down until we find it. Then search the whole of Dragons' Hold. We have to save our queen." He strode out of the alcove.

Adelina hurried after him.

"Whoa, Kierion," Lars called. "You've torn the place apart."

Drawers were yanked open, mattresses and sheets had been ripped off beds, and Kierion was sprawled on the floor with his head and arms inside a mattress, ferreting around. He emerged, triumphant, hair full of straw, with bottles in his hands. "Look what I found!"

"We've no time to waste." Lars slashed the pallet open with his knife, and yanked back the straw, revealing a cluster of jars, bottles and tubs, each carefully wrapped in sheep wool.

"I figured Fleur would be more likely to hide stuff in a spare mattress than in the ones patients use." Kierion gestured to some pallets stacked against the wall. "There are a few more to check yet."

Adelina undid the corks and test-sniffed the contents. "None are the antidote."

Where was Roberto?

Surely, if he was injured, he would've been brought to the infirmary by now. Was he dead? Dread filled her like an ominous tide. "Lars, have you heard from Singlar yet?"

Grim lines tugging at his mouth, Lars shook his head.

§

Zaarusha's glimmering thread was fading, her breathing slowing again. The antidote had helped, but it wasn't enough. Melding with the queen wasn't working. Or with Roberto. Or Erob. *"Singlar,"* Ezaara melded, *"Zaarusha's fading again. Are Erob and Roberto all right?"*

"We're nearly there." At least she could reach someone. Within moments, Singlar landed at the imprinting grounds.

Kierion jumped off Singlar, cradling a bottle as tall as an ear of corn. "We found the antidote," he announced. "And lots of it."

How should she administer the remedy? All at once? In smaller doses? Too little, and they could waste the whole bottle in dribs and drabs, and not combat the poison. Too much, and it could kill Zaarusha.

"Adelina's stayed in the infirmary with Gret. Kierion will keep vigil with you over Zaarusha," Lars said. "I have to get back to the dungeons to help Tonio interrogate Fleur, Bruno and Simeon."

"Of course. Any word of Erob, or Ajeuria?"

"Not yet. We're not sure where they fell, but riders have gone searching. None of our dragons can meld with them at the moment." His glance slid away.

He feared they were dead.

Her stomach lurched. No, not Roberto.

Time for that later. She had a queen to save. Swallowing, Ezaara cupped the bottle in her hands and closed her eyes. She breathed deeply, sensing Zaarusha's life thread. Pale gold—no longer glimmering. Kierion held up Zaarusha's top lip so she could jam the bottle in a gap between her fangs. Ezaara dribbled liquid into Zaarusha's maw. The queen swallowed.

And again.

Ezaara waited, then dribbled a little more. The gold of the queen's life thread started to glow a little more. Last time she'd deteriorated a while later. If only Ezaara knew what Zaarusha's life thread looked like when she was healthy. She'd only ever seen it tonight, while her queen was dying.

Surely, Zaarusha needed more. Ezaara gave her twice as much as before.

The gold grew stronger.

After a while, it faded again. She still had most of the bottle left.

She doubled the dose again, and waited.

"Trial and error," said Kierion lightly. "You're doing well." He shrugged a shoulder. "You can tell me I'm being nosy if you want, or you can refuse to answer. I mean, I'm just curious ..."

"What is it?" Ezaara met his gaze.

"Well, at the trial, you were accused of loving Master Roberto." Kierion paused, awkwardly. "Is it true? Are you in love?"

Was Kierion Tonio's spy, gathering information against them?

It came in a flash—she didn't care what anyone thought anymore. They'd been banished. Roberto had had his guts slit like a rabbit. She'd saved him from murder. And now he was ... what? Dead? Alive? The dragon masters' opinions weren't important anymore. "Yes, I love him. But I've never acted upon my feelings." Thank the Egg, Roberto had stopped her.

"What does it feel like? How do you know ...?" Kierion blushed.

So, he liked someone too. "I imagine it's different for each person. For me, love is sunlight shimmering on water, dancing into the darkest corners of my soul." Despite her missing connection with Roberto, and despite Zaarusha's state, the thought of Roberto's love made hope grow in Ezaara's heart. She paused as Kierion nodded to himself. "How does it feel for you?" she asked.

Kierion started. "Me?"

She let a faint smile touch her lips. "Yes, you."

Blushing beet red, Kierion stammered, "A-as b-bright as an eagle's eye, as soft as the clouds and as if I'm about to burst with joy."

"Does the person you like feel the same?"

"Um, ah, I ..."

"The one you love doesn't know?"

He grinned and ducked his head. "No, not yet."

Under Ezaara's hand, Zaarusha moved. She had to focus. As Ezaara tipped the bottle, Kierion shifted his weight and bumped her. A gush of fluid rushed into Zaarusha's mouth.

"Oh, I'm sorry." Kierion's face twisted with worry.

Ezaara bit her lip to stop herself from yelling. It was too late. He'd wasted half the huge bottle. The Egg only knew what the effect would be.

Suddenly, Ezaara's mind was bathed with colors swirling in golden light.

"Ezaara?" the queen melded.

"I'm here, Zaarusha." A hot tear slid down her cheek. Then another. "Thank you, Kierion. Don't be sorry. I never would have given her that much at once, but it was exactly what she needed."

Kierion's face lit up like a fistful of candles.

"Ezaara." Zaarusha raised her head, voice shaky. *"Why are my littlings fighting?"*

Littlings? Ezaara frowned. *"You mean the masters?"*

"No, my son and daughter."

Her son? And—

Erob! Ajeuria! *"They're alive?"*

"And that master you're so fond of—Roberto's alive too."

A wave of relief whooshed through Ezaara, so potent she was glad she was kneeling.

"Sorry, Ezaara. I shouldn't have doubted you and forfeited your right to ride me." Zaarusha nuzzled her hand. *"How can you forgive me?"*

More tears slid down Ezaara's cheeks. *"I already have."*

"You've always trusted me, right from the moment you saw me, but I let my heart be darkened by aspersions from others. They convinced me you'd fooled me, and were still fooling me, even though I found no malice in your heart."

Ezaara flung her arms around Zaarusha's neck. Her skin was warm and comforting, like soft leather.

"Singlar tells me Bruno, Fleur and Ajeuria double crossed me. They must have fed Ajeuria swayweed." Zaarusha's hurt knifed through Ezaara. *"I'm supposed to be a queen of steel, tough but wise, but I've made so many mistakes, lost so many loved ones. I've just had you two unfairly banished. I lost my rider Anakisha, and my mate Syan and his rider Yanir."* Again, Zaarusha shared Anakisha falling into a horde of tharuks and the glittering black dragon and his rider rushing to save her, only to be caught as well. *"Your mother killed my dragonet before it was born."* A dead purple dragonet floated in a translucent golden shell. Deep sorrow permeated Ezaara, so strong her bones ached. *"Not only did I lose my baby, but, in my wrath, I lost two of my best masters."* Younger versions of Ma and Pa swam before her. *"And now these two."* Shari and Jaevin.

"And before you and I imprinted, I'd just lost my other son." An orange dragon was trapped by tharuks in the midst of battle. They dragged him away in a net, tail and talons trussed up, snarling and roaring. *"Is it so wrong that I don't want to lose Ajeuria too?"*

§

Roberto hung on as Erob straddled Ajeuria, pinning her body to the earth. She thrashed, but Erob tightened his jaws around the back of her neck. His earlier fang marks around her throat were oozing blood. Ajeuria's head slumped on the ground. She held still, but kept snarling.

Roberto slid down Erob's side and leaped down. *"Hold her tight, Erob."*

"I've got her. You should be able to find something out now, without having your pretty fingers snapped off."

"Pretty?" Roberto snorted. His nails had half the Robandi desert stuck under them. He laid his hands on Ajeuria's head. It took every scrap of concentration for him to delve through Ajeuria's mind, discarding irrelevant memories and looking for clues to Ajeuria's behavior.

He found a memory laced with hurt.

Ajeuria nuzzled Fleur. "You're wrong. Zens doesn't want what's best for us at all. I'd usually do anything you ask, Fleur, but I can't go against my mother or the realm."

"Come with me, Ajeuria," *said her rider*, "and I'll show you what great things Zens has in store for us."

Eager to please Fleur, and keen to convince her Zens was evil, the green dragon followed her rider into a barn. As the doors closed behind them, Ajeuria scented tharuks. "Fleur, beware!"

A net flew over Ajeuria, pulled tight by a horde of tharuks. "Run, Fleur!" *Her wings were bent back, squashed against her body, her feet snared in the net's ropes. The beasts yanked, tightening the net.*

Fleur laughed.

Anguish ripped through Ajeuria. Her rider had betrayed her. The more she thrashed, the more tangled the net grew. She flamed the ropes, burning through those near her snout. A brute shoved a spear into the skin below her eye. "Move again and I'll blind you."

They muzzled her. Then the tharuks twisted her tail, sticking it with spears and drove more spear tips into her belly. They fastened metal shackles around her limbs, tying them together with chains so short she couldn't move. Reduced to huddling with her legs bunched under her and her snout and tail tied, Ajeuria was miserable.

Fleur visited her daily, watching Bruno lash Ajeuria with a metal-tipped whip until she cowered. They starved her for days, until she was thirsty enough to drink anything.

One morning, Fleur arrived with a bucket. "We're so sorry to have treated you this way, Ajeuria. I was being influenced by Zens, but now I've seen that he's a destroyer. He tricked me into believing him. Will you forgive me?" *Fleur started crying.* "You're one of the last of a long line of royal dragons. I never should have treated you this way."

Hobbled and aching all over from Bruno's whip, Ajeuria stretched her neck out to nudge Fleur. "I forgive you. I'm sorry Zens duped you and Bruno. Untie me so we can escape."

Fleur undid Ajeuria's muzzle. "First, drink. You must be thirsty."

Ajeuria thought nothing of the odd tang in the water.

"Quick," *said Fleur.* "Someone's coming, let me put your muzzle on so they can't tell." *Once she'd fastened the muzzle, Fleur laughed.* "Enjoy your swayweed, precious mummy's girl."

Starved and half-crazy from being tied up for days, Ajeuria was furious—until the swayweed took effect, filling her with hatred for the very dragons she loved. From that moment, she'd carried out Fleur's commands.

"Ajeuria," Roberto melded, hands still against her head. "I'm sorry for what Fleur and Bruno have done to you." He had to check her reactions, so he reactivated the memory. Ajeuria trembled, whimpering with each remembered strike of Bruno's whip.

Bitterness ricocheted through Roberto. Amato had whipped him too and whipped Razo, destroying all his love for his father. Bruno and Fleur had mistreated a royal dragon, twisting her love and loyalty into cruelty and deceit. They'd broken her.

"Please, Roberto, help my sister," Erob melded.

"Some dragons never recover from swayweed, Erob."

"I know." There was an ache in Erob's words that made Roberto's eyes sting. How would he feel if this was Adelina?

Shari

The drums beat softly as riders gathered beneath the dawn-kissed tips of Dragon's Teeth. Roberto approached the clearing with the other members of the council. Surprise rippled through the crowd. He didn't care what they thought; he'd been reinstated as master of imprinting and mental faculties early this morning, and cleared of attempted poisoning.

Shari, dressed in white and gold, was lying on top of a wooden platform, on a mat of woven river reeds with four long ropes at the corners. Her arms were crossed upon her chest, her face peaceful and her dark braids gleaming in the early morning sun. She looked serene.

Too serene for Shari. Her eyes were closed, not sparkling with laughter, or warm with understanding. Her lips were still, instead of smiling or encouraging. The only master aside from Lars who'd welcomed him here, Shari had brought light to his early days at Dragons' Hold. Amid whispers, stares and ugly rumors, she'd championed him and Adelina. He'd been hollowed out with the grief of losing Ma, bitter against his Pa, and angry at the world. Shari's trust had sown the kernel of his own self-belief and given him the motivation to train hard and become a dragon master. Despite his past, she'd won the council over, insisting they give him a chance to train here on Erob.

Without Shari and Adelina's love, he would've been a broken shell, stranded on a beach of grief.

The drums stopped. The only sounds were the soft breathing of the crowd and the birds warbling.

"It's time, Ezaara. Do you remember what to do?"

"Yes." Short and simple, but accompanied by a wash of warmth and a blaze of color that took his breath away. He'd done nothing to deserve this amazing woman in his life, yet she was here.

"You've let down your barriers," Erob said. *"You can finally be yourself with someone other than me."*

"It's her. She makes it easy."

"Maybe being an ignorant settler from Lush Valley was an advantage. She had no prejudices."

"But I did. And yet she won me over." Roberto stretched, trying to ease the ache in his shoulder. The fight with Ajeuria had been brutal, but she was safely in a holding pen. Within days, they'd know whether the swayweed had permanently affected her loyalty to her queen and the realm.

Above them, Zaarusha spread her massive wings and took flight. The sun caught her scales. A pale gray sheen dulled their usual iridescence.

"My mother isn't strong yet," Erob commented. *"She needs rest so she can recover."*

Roberto nodded. They all did.

Zaarusha landed on the far side of the clearing beneath her den, and Ezaara dismounted. Her emerald eyes met his, and his breath hitched. She was gorgeous. Her hair hung in a honey-blonde silken swathe, catching the dawn light as she moved with grace through the crowd, head high.

People watched her, some gazes curious, some welcoming, others openly hostile. A far cry from the warm welcome when she'd first arrived at Dragons' Hold.

Ezaara melded. *"Are you all right? Any injures from yesterday?"*

"None that you can't heal. Ezaara, you saved our queen."

"Thank the Egg."

"No, thank you."

"Well, actually, I couldn't have done it without what Ithsar taught me."

"I'm glad there was some purpose in us going to the Wastelands." His skin still prickled whenever he remembered his slit gut and the assassins' bizarre breeding plans.

"Good morning, Honored Council Leader." Ezaara stopped in front of Lars, bowing. "As rider of Zaarusha, Queen of Dragons' Realm, I, Ezaara, request that you begin the death rites for Shari, Honored Master of Livestock, who has recently died at the hand of a traitor."

Murmurs erupted as people realized Ezaara had been reinstated as Queen's Rider—and Shari had been murdered.

"I would be honored," Lars replied.

The crowd quieted as Lars plucked at his harp. Face careworn, he sang of Shari's ancestors across the Naobian Sea. Weaving a spell around the listeners, Lars sang of Shari's life, her journeys, her brief sojourn among mages, and then of her imprinting with Ariana and coming to Dragons' Hold to prove herself.

Ariana threw her head skyward and howled.

Roberto's throat ached. Would Erob howl for him when he died?

"*Stop being so morose, or I'll howl right now,*" Erob said.

Roberto held back his tears as Lars sang of Shari's legendary gift with animals. But as Lars, gazing right at Roberto, sang about Shari's compassion for her fellow riders, tears ran freely down Roberto's cheeks, the sharp bite of salt on his lips.

§

Ezaara had never lost anyone she loved before, but it was obvious from Roberto and Adelina's reactions that they both had, and that Shari had been dear to them. Roberto's face was wet with tears as he cried unashamedly. To think this man had hidden everything behind a stone facade.

Shari's life-song danced among the crowd.

How would she die? Death had seemed so distant when she'd taken her vows as Queen's Rider. Would she plunge to her death amid a horde of bloodthirsty tharuks like Anakisha? Live her life enslaved to Zens like Roberto had been? Be murdered like Shari? Or killed in battle? Perhaps she'd die old, in Roberto's arms. Or would she, too, lose her life to a traitor?

For a moment, Handel's prophecy shot through her thoughts: Roberto's beautiful features twisted by hate, lunging at her. She shoved the image away. No, not Roberto. He would never harm her. He loved her.

Shari's life-song finished and the last quivering note of Lars' harp died.

"*When you die, I will sing of your courage, fearlessness and willingness to give everything for the realm and for the man you love.*" Roberto's thoughts brought a faint smile to Ezaara's lips, even as she shed a tear for this woman she hadn't had the chance to know.

The dragons of Dragons' Hold joined Ariana in mourning for Shari. Their eerie howls reverberated off the mountainsides, making Ezaara's arms break out in goose bumps. Since she'd woken, she'd maintained her awareness of *sathir*, seeing the queen's vibrant connection wherever she went. Now, she opened her mind.

A rush of color enveloped her. The deep blue of Erob, the shimmering purple of Singlar, Vino's vibrant red, and the brown of Ariana. Hundreds of dragons' life threads were there, dancing across her vision, weaving from dragon to rider. Their loss surged through her and, for a moment, Ezaara faltered.

"*This is why you're my rider. Feel them, understand them and honor them.*" Zaarusha strengthened her. Ezaara stood tall, letting their sorrow wash through her. "*You will lead the realm beside me with compassion, courage and strength.*"

Ariana took one of the ropes at the corner of Shari's reed mat in her jaws. Erob, Vino and Singlar took up the other ropes. As one, they rose into the air, Shari suspended below them. The underside of Shari's mat was decorated with a breath-taking picture of Shari riding Ariana into a sunset. The dragons flew higher until they were nearly level with the peaks of Dragon's Teeth, then headed out over the forest.

In a seething mass of flapping wings and scraping talons, the rest of the dragons took flight, heading after Shari. To Ezaara's surprise, they hovered below Shari's mat, heads facing inward, forming layers of glinting rings as the early morning sun caught their scales.

"What's happening?" she asked Roberto.

"Something beautiful." As Roberto melded, his life thread became visible—a strong dark blue river flecked with silver, flowing between him, Erob and herself—accompanied by a rush of love.

Trumpeting, Ariana, Singlar, Vino and Erob released Shari's mat.

Ezaara gasped as Shari's limp form plummeted earthward toward the layers of waiting dragons. As her body fell between them, the dragons shot flames from their open maws, setting her body alight. Aflame, she fell, through more circles of flaming maws.

Within moments, the flames died and nothing but ash was left, scattering above the forest on the breeze.

Traitors

A surge of pride welled inside Roberto—Ezaara was seated at the head of the granite horseshoe, next to Lars. Finally, after all this time, she was in her rightful place as Queen's Rider.

Ezaara wiggled her feet under the table. *"Do you like my shoes?"*

Roberto smiled. *"Very nice."* She was wearing the shoes he'd given her on race day. Thank the Egg, *she* wasn't on trial today.

The council chamber was packed. Most people wore black armbands, to honor Jaevin and Shari, and brightly-colored ribbons to show support for Zaarusha.

Lars rapped his gavel. "Unfortunately, today's proceedings are no cause for celebration. First, I must apologize to Ezaara, Zaarusha and Master Roberto for our mistaken verdict. They have been cleared of all wrongdoing. Master Tonio expresses his heartfelt apologies." He nodded grimly. "Earlier this morning, after Shari's death rites, the Council of the Twelve Dragon Masters reinstated Roberto to his position as Master of Mental Faculties and Imprinting. We now also appoint our Honored Queen's Rider as a member of the council. Although she is not yet fully trained, she has proven her capability."

Cheers erupted, then clapping. Someone whistled—probably Kierion.

When the room quieted, Lars continued, "It's a tragedy that Master Shari and Master Jaevin, two of our finest dragon riders, have been murdered."

Around the chamber, people raised their fists to their hearts and murmured, "May their spirits soar with departed dragons."

"Thank you for your solidarity in protecting the queen last night. We expect Zaarusha to recover fully," Lars said. "No doubt, the praises of Ezaara, Master Roberto, Adelina, Gret and Kierion will be sung around hearths for years to come. But now, we must deal with the traitors."

The doors to the council chambers opened with an ominous thud. Blue guards led Bruno, Fleur and Simeon inside. The shackles on their wrists and ankles clanking, Fleur and Simeon sat in chairs facing the council. Simeon hung his head, pretending remorse. Fleur's nose was in the air, her lip curled in a faint sneer.

Roberto snorted. They were as guilty as rats crushing thrush eggs.

"Please sit, Bruno," Lars ordered.

Bruno objected. "Highly Honored Master Lars, may I *please* have a word with you?"

Lars sighed. "Make it quick."

Some people muttered as blue guards hustled Bruno forward. Others were deathly silent, staring daggers at the traitors.

Only one seat away from Lars, Roberto heard everything.

"My wife and son acted without my knowledge," Bruno whispered. "I'm horrified by their actions."

Bruno was trying to save his own skin—the coward.

Ezaara mind-melded, *"You took their crimes upon yourself to protect me, but he won't protect his own flesh and blood."*

"He's a gutter-swilling yellow belly."

"I'm worried, Roberto. Perhaps he knows we have no evidence against him, only against his wife and son."

There it was: his fear laid bare. *"Let's hope Lars has found something."*

"Hmm." Ezaara sounded as doubtful as he felt. As long as Bruno was at Dragons' Hold, no one was safe.

After ordering Bruno to his seat, Lars outlined the charges against Fleur and Simeon.

"He hasn't charged Bruno," Ezaara said.

"Not a good sign."

Walking out from behind the granite horseshoe, Lars addressed the assembly. "Last night, I inspected the infirmary. Fleur has stockpiled poisons and destroyed most of our healing remedies. The deadly cache she has amassed is enough to wipe out our dragons and riders several times over. She poisoned our queen, fought our Queen's Rider, and we suspect she has murdered two of our masters." The chill in Lars' voice sent frost down Roberto's spine. "I've said enough. Now, our Honored Queen's Rider will speak."

Ezaara's chair scraped as she stood, face grave. "I was too new and naive to detect the trap that Fleur and Simeon laid for me. They undermined my role and tried to banish me, knowing Zaarusha would be vulnerable. When Master Roberto was banished for their crimes, I discovered his innocence and left to rescue him. Although I am glad I did, I give my deepest apologies for not being here to protect our queen."

"Stop this. It's not your fault!"

Ignoring Roberto, Ezaara continued, "They poisoned Zaarusha. They attacked me, Gret and Adelina. Ajeuria nearly killed Erob and Master Roberto."

"She did not. I'm much stronger than Ajeuria," Erob interrupted, melding with them both.

Still facing her people, Ezaara ignored Erob too. "We were lucky, but Master Jaevin and Master Shari were not. As the evidence unfolds, listen carefully and learn. Zaarusha and I never want traitors at Dragons' Hold again."

"Lying swine!" Fleur scowled. "This is preposterous. We've done our best for Dragons' Hold. She's the traitor."

Not letting Fleur's outburst faze her, Ezaara sat, composed and looking … well, regal. Her speech was a far cry from her first one here, during the feast. Her whole demeanor had changed. Had it only been four and a half weeks ago? *"Spoken like a true Queen's Rider."*

"Thank you."

Lars rapped his gavel. "I defer to our Dragon Corps Spymaster, Tonio, who will call our witnesses."

Tonio's dark eyes swept the chamber. "Our first witness is Adelina of Naobia." He nodded as Adelina stood. "Adelina, you came to me recently about something strange you'd found in the Queen's Rider's cavern. Please tell us."

"After Ezaara accidentally injured Sofia, Simeon gave her what he claimed was a restorative tea, but it contained a weak dose of skarkrak, a Robandi poison. It knocked her out, so she couldn't visit Sofia."

"How exactly did you recognize the skarkrak?"

"I smelt it as I emptied the Queen's Rider's vomit pail."

Amid a flurry of murmurs, Ezaara blushed bright pink. *"Great."*

"The scent of skarkrak was on Shari's soup bowl," said Adelina. "It was her last meal." Adelina produced Shari's dish from her bag, passing it to Tonio, who sniffed it and nodded.

Master Alyssa broke in. "When Jaevin died, Fleur disposed of his dishes, saying Montanarians didn't like food near corpses, but it was probably just an excuse to hide evidence."

Tonio gestured to a blue guard, who passed him a leather pouch. "This was found in the infirmary. Adelina, can you identify it?"

Adelina sniffed the contents of the package. "It's skarkrak."

"This is the same as the poison that was in Shari's soup. Thank you, Master Alyssa and Adelina." Tonio's predatory gaze swept over the traitors. "Most of you know the Queen's Rider had an accident at the knife-throwing range, but not many know that Ezaara injured Sofia because she was immersed in a violent mind-melded vision from Ajeuria. Ezaara, please explain exactly what happened."

Ezaara's voice shook as she spoke. Through her thoughts, Roberto saw flashes of fire and smelt the stench of burning flesh. Half way through explaining, she paled and gripped the table.

"Do you need fresh air?"

"No, I just need to get through this."

Sympathetic murmurs rippled through the crowd.

"She's lying," screamed Fleur. "Lying through her teeth."

Tonio shook his head. "Ajeuria was seen near the knife range. Our dragons witnessed the mental assault and have been on the alert since to find out who was responsible. When Ajeuria tried again last night, they recognized her."

"Fleur," Lars thundered, "we've mind-melded with Ajeuria, and she's revealed how you tortured her and fed her swayweed. You'd best stay silent until requested to speak."

Glaring, Fleur snapped her jaw shut.

"None of this has anything to do with me," Bruno whined.

Roberto's fists clenched. Bruno was right—it didn't.

"Silence, Bruno!" Tonio barked. "Kierion, you're our next witness."

At Tonio's taut nod, Kierion told everyone how Ezaara's cane had been snapped and hidden.

Fresh anger surged through Roberto. Simeon had ruined one of his mother's few remaining belongings.

Tonio continued, "Ajeuria's vision, the skarkrak and missing cane caused prejudice against our Queen's Rider, but she isn't the only one affected by Fleur's actions. Master Roberto has discovered another of Fleur's ploys."

Roberto pulled back his sleeve, revealing the wound that had never healed properly since the battle at River's Edge. "Fleur's famous healing unguent, used for years at Dragons' Hold, causes damage. Look." He walked through the chamber, showing the red lines webbing outward from his scar. "If you have a wound that Fleur's treated that hasn't healed properly, put your hand up."

Gasps ripped through the chamber as hands shot up.

"She's sabotaged our healing," someone cried.

Nodding, Roberto sat and Tonio started summarizing the evidence.

"Aren't you going to mention Shari's dragon?" Ezaara asked.

"You mean Ariana's belly gripe? No, we can't track it directly to Fleur." He sighed. "It's been a tough day. How are you feeling?"

"I should be asking you that after your fight with Ajeuria."

Revealing his feelings was strange after so many years of maintaining a tough facade. "I'm good, but this is taking ages. I wish it was over."

"Why? What's the hurry?"

"Then I can be with you."

Her surprise and pleasure rippled through him. *"Promise?"*

"A horde of tharuks couldn't keep me away." He stifled the urge to grin at her. Too many people were watching.

The doors burst open and Gret hobbled in, leaning on Ezaara's cane.

"Ah, I loaned it to her. Hope that's all right."

"Of course," Roberto replied.

Gret gazed at the packed room, her face reddening. "Sorry, I'm late! Master Lars and honored council members, I have evidence against Simeon, son of Fleur and Bruno."

Tonio paused, eyebrows raised.

Lars waved Gret forward. "Please proceed."

Gret limped through the onlookers to face the council. "I'm not sure if she told you, but the night our Queen's Rider left for the Wastelands, Simeon attacked her in the tunnels. His intent was to defile her. Our swords prevented him."

A chill ran through Roberto, and then the desire to drive his blade through Simeon's heart. *"Ezaara! When were you going to tell me this?"*

"I was too busy rescuing you," Ezaara snapped, a flash of Simeon's leering face and grasping hands shooting through him as she remembered. She paled. *"And it's not a memory I cherish reliving."*

Roberto seethed. That shrotty louse. *"Sorry, Ezaara, you need my understanding, not my anger."*

"Thank you." She bit her lip.

Shards, Roberto longed to shelter her in his arms—impossible with everyone watching.

"My Honored Queen's Rider, is Gret's accusation against Simeon true?" Lars' face was stormy. At Ezaara's nod, his piercing blue eyes cut Simeon to shreds on the spot.

Roberto rose. "If Simeon forced himself upon our Queen's Rider, then Trixia must've spoken the truth. He must've forced her, making her pregnant."

"Yes!" Gret exclaimed. "Trixia was innocent, but Simeon was not punished."

"You'd believe that whore, over the son of two dragon masters?" Simeon yelled.

"My daughter's not a whore!" Trixia's father rose from his seat, hands in fists.

"Yes, she is!" Fleur yelled back.

Lars rapped his gavel, but people were shouting, their outrage boiling over.

"Silence!" Lars bellowed, his icy gaze slicing through the crowd. "This is a trial, not a market place. Anyone who doesn't abide by the rules will be removed." As the crowd settled, he continued, "We have sufficient evidence against Simeon, son of Fleur and Bruno, and against Fleur, wife of Bruno, to banish them both. All dragon masters in accord, raise your hand."

One by one, the eight remaining dragon masters from the council of twelve raised their hands.

"Good, the voting is unanimous and complete. Simeon and Fleur shall be banished. Bruno, husband of Fleur and father of Simeon, please stand," Lars ordered.

Bruno's shackles clanked. He sneered at Simeon and Fleur as if they were dirt, then faced Lars. "I support my queen wholeheartedly, doing my best to protect her and Dragons' Realm. There's not a mark against me."

Fleur piped up. "It's true. My husband is innocent."

Roberto's heart raced and his hands curled into fists. Bruno was every bit as guilty as Simeon and Fleur. Surely they wouldn't get away with this?

Hendrik pounded the table with his meaty fist. "Bruno is my trusted and loyal friend. Not only my own, but also Jaevin's—may his spirit soar with departed dragons. I stand by Bruno and support him."

Lars gazed at Hendrik and Bruno intently.

Surely Lars didn't believe that? Roberto got up again. "Last night, Bruno sent Lars, myself and some blue guards away, to head off a so-called tharuk attack, while his wife and son were poisoning the queen. That was not a coincidence." He slammed his palms on the table. "Bruno is as guilty as Fleur and Simeon, and should be banished."

Tonio cut in, "To banish someone, we need evidence, not conjecture."

Roberto sat with a thud. That rankled. They'd wanted to convict Ezaara on less.

"Bruno is correct," Lars said. "In his entire six years at Dragons' Hold, there hasn't been a mark against him."

What? Couldn't Lars see how dangerous Bruno was? Ajeuria's memory of Bruno whipping her flashed to mind. He'd use that.

"But," Lars continued, "in his role as Master Seer, Bruno assured us all was in order. He caused us to doubt our own patrol leaders, while the tharuks made constant inroads into our realm, enslaving our folk, drugging them senseless, and starving them." He stabbed his finger toward Bruno. "You, Bruno, have not served us as master of prophecy. With the power vested in me as leader of this council, I demote you. You will no longer serve as a master on the Council of the Twelve Dragon Masters."

No! Lars had to banish him. Bruno was a snake lying in wait. He'd strike later. Hard, fast and venomous.

"Master Lars." Roberto rose. "I can test Bruno and discover any memories that betray his intent."

"That won't be necessary."

"But I also tested Ajeuria and—"

Lars cut in. "Roberto, you're obviously biased."

With good reason, Erob interjected.

I'm glad you see through Bruno, Roberto melded.

The door slammed open. Seppi, leader of the blue guards, marched through the crowd. Taking a pouch from his belt, he tipped the contents on the table. Rough yellow gems glittered in the torchlight. "The blue guards searched Bruno's possessions and found these."

"No!" Bruno lunged, shackles crashing against the granite table, as he grasped at the gems. Blue guards yanked him back and held him at sword point.

"They're obviously yours," Lars stated. "What are they?"

Bruno clamped his lips shut, glaring.

Roberto's breath caught. He'd seen those gems before. "Zens mines those stones," he said. "They're only found in Death Valley."

"So Zens is your paymaster, Bruno." Lars scratched his beard. "What exactly has he been paying you to do?"

Her face weary and grief-stricken, Threcia stood. "I believe Bruno poisoned my husband." She spoke softly, everyone straining to hear. "Jaevin told me how kind Bruno had been. On his way to collect the ceremonial swords in Ezaara's cavern, Jaevin met Bruno in the tunnels. Jaevin was called away to a tharuk attack, so Bruno offered to collect the swords and take them to our cavern to be kept overnight for the Queen's Rider's test." She shook her head. "He had access to the swords. I'd forgotten all about it until now, because I thought Roberto was guilty. It never occurred to me that a close friend would—" Tears tracked down her face. "Excuse me."

"Thank you, Threcia," Lars said.

Wearing her grief with honor, Threcia made her way to the door.

Lars turned to Roberto. "Test Bruno, now."

Blue guards held Bruno fast while Roberto placed his hands on his temples.

Bruno had barred his thoughts behind a dark wall. The scar on Roberto's cheek twitched where his father had whipped him. Sweat beading his forehead, he peeled back Bruno's defensive layer, a scrap at a time, until his memories were stripped bare. "Bruno poisoned the ceremonial swords and encouraged Fleur and Simeon to kill as many dragon masters and their dragons as possible," Roberto announced.

"You lowlife, using me and Jaevin!" Hendrik drew his sword and leaped at Bruno. Blue guards grabbed him, dragging him out a side tunnel.

The room burst into an uproar, people yelling at Bruno and his family, waving their fists and spitting.

Zaarusha bellowed and the other dragons joined in.

Lars rapped his gavel on the table, but it was lost in the uproar.

Roberto scooped the yellow stones back into the pouch and passed them to Lars. "For shards' sake, keep these safe."

Lars tucked them away and dashed forward to help the blue guards restore order.

Had Lars even heard him? In the chaos, Roberto didn't have a chance to explain that, from examining Bruno's memories, he now understood why the yellow crystals were more dangerous than Fleur's poison.

River of Sathir

Simeon leered at Ezaara, his gaze crawling over her body like a cockroach. It made her want to brush herself off. Or, even better, punch him in the eye so he couldn't stare anymore. Seppi yanked Simeon's head around so he couldn't see her and dragged him off. Other blue guards manhandled Simeon's parents out the door.

"Shards, he's a creep," Roberto melded. "*Always has been. I'm glad he's leaving.*"

"Did he really force himself upon that girl?"

Roberto's face was grim. "They never proved it, but ask Gret. Trixia was her best friend."

Lars dismissed the onlookers, who—some bandying insults about Simeon's family—trailed out the door.

Drumbeats boomed beneath Ezaara's feet. Banishment drums. She remembered Roberto's hateful expression and her horror at him murdering Jaevin.

"*Oops, you shared that memory,*" he said.

"Sorry." Ezaara shuddered. "*Banishment drums are always going to remind me of you being sent away.*"

"*To save you, I'd do it again, in a heartbeat.*"

"*Let's stay together instead.*"

"*Sure, right after we're done here.*" A rush of heat accompanied Roberto's words, making her blush.

Tonio's keen gaze sharpened, flitting between her and Roberto.

When the crowd had dispersed and only the council were in the room, Lars spoke. "This has been a difficult time. I'm glad Master Roberto and our Honored Queen's Rider have returned. We welcome Ezaara to our council. With two dead and two banished, we're now four masters short. Ezaara, would you mind overseeing the infirmary until we replace Fleur?"

"Yes, Lars, it would be my pleasure."

"Please urgently identify any poisons and antidotes. Fleur may have destroyed valuable remedies, so you'll need to build up supplies. I'll assign people to help." He glanced around. "Derek, as master of instruction, you'll take over Swordmaster Jaevin's duties until we have a replacement."

"Of course," Derek answered.

"Master Shari had several assistants, so I'll let them oversee her activities for now. Unfortunately, we have no one suitable to take the role of master of prophecy, so that post will have to remain empty." Lars' throat bobbed. "I am deeply saddened to lose two esteemed masters, as I'm sure we all are. Please comfort our riders and take care of our people."

Tonio nodded. "Zens has infiltrated our council once. He'll try to do it again. Report anything suspicious to me immediately."

"Any further questions?" Lars asked.

Everyone was too numb to say much, so Lars dismissed them.

Ezaara was bone-weary. *"Roberto, I'm so glad this is over. I could sleep for a week."*

"Later. Meet me in the orchard." Fire accompanied his words, leaping into her veins. Roberto's onyx eyes burned away her fatigue.

"See you there." Ezaara swept out the door upon the waves of drumbeats, Roberto at her side.

§

It'd been a long day, but there was more work to do. Lars put his gavel away and stood. He needed to see Shari's assistants. As the last of the masters drifted out of the room, Tonio sidled up to him.

"Come with me, there's something you need to see. Urgently."

Within a heartbeat, Lars was striding after Tonio to the landing outside. How could the sun shine so brightly over the basin when his heart was filled with sorrow? Two masters dead. Two more banished. And a royal dragon that might not recover from swayweed. "What is it, Tonio?"

"Look." He gestured toward Roberto on Erob, and Ezaara on Zaarusha, high above Dragon's Teeth. "Tell me what you see."

"Two highly skilled riders, but we knew that." Lars turned away.

"Look again."

Ezaara sat low on Zaarusha, Roberto mimicking her position on Erob. Simultaneously, both dragons swooped to the east, then spiraled down toward the orchard, replicating each other's movements with exact timing, as if attached by a giant piece of string.

"Have you seen dragons fly in such tight formation before?" The intensity of Tonio's voice made his spine prickle.

That's what he meant. Nodding, Lars replied. "Only two couples."

"*Couples.* Who?"

"Yanir and Anakisha, of course."

"And?" Tonio pressed.

Lars sighed. "Hans and Marlies. But that doesn't mean these two are mind-melding. Erob and Zaarusha are mother and son. Their bond is strong."

Tonio just arched an eyebrow.

"All right, so the riders might be melding, but that doesn't mean they're romantically involved."

"Blushing at each other in a council meeting isn't adequate evidence either, but the law is the law."

"Tonio, she's practically qualified," Lars warned. "We can't afford to lose another master, especially not the master of mental faculties and imprinting. Not when we need to perform mental tests on every newcomer to Dragons' Hold."

"Understood."

"This is one of those times when your suspicions must not result in action."

Tonio's gaze was stony. "Do I have to remind you of the only *other* couple that could mind-meld?"

Giddi and Mazyka—two of the most powerful mages the realm had ever seen.

"Mazyka was seventeen—like Ezaara," Tonio continued.

Impulsive and talented, Mazyka had quickly grown power-hungry and had encouraged her master to use his power in forbidden ways, nearly destroying Dragons' Realm.

Lars sighed. "Very well. Keep an eye on them, but do it yourself, not via one of your spies. Discuss your findings only with me."

"Will do."

"And Tonio," Lars cautioned, "Roberto is innocent of his father's crimes. This had better not be about you getting even with Amato."

Tonio's face tightened.

Lars shook his head and strode away.

§

Flying with Ezaara and Zaarusha was glorious. Every wing dip, each swoop and turn of their downward spiral were in harmony. Ezaara's laugh unfurled a coil inside Roberto that he'd held tight for years. Colors shot through him in a thousand tiny bursts.

He laughed too.

"So, you've finally found someone you can meld with, who loves you for yourself," Erob said. "Someone you can trust."

"I had no idea I could feel so happy. It's amazing."

"Caution, Roberto, you're both subject to the laws of the council."

"As if I could forget."

They spiraled down among the trees, the air sweet with the scent of ripe peaches. Erob descended to the grass, his legs bunching to soften the impact. Within moments, Roberto was racing to meet Ezaara. When they were barely an arm's length apart, they stopped, staring at each other.

Her eyes were green sea foam at dawn, churning with power and emotion. Her face was awash with tenderness. What had he done to deserve her?

She smiled. *"You're you."*

He swept her into his arms, burying his face in her hair and inhaling deeply. Light burst through him. This was so right.

§

Ezaara felt so alive. Every fiber of her being was singing. Roberto enfolded her in his arms, his onyx eyes full of wonder. The world shifted. This was where she belonged, right here.

"I'm glad Zaarusha chose you," Roberto's breath caressed her neck, making her skin tingle. He traced her cheek with gentle fingers, and tilted her chin. *"I love you, Ezaara, and always will."*

His lips brushed hers. Gods, they were so soft.

Ezaara slid her fingers into his hair and tugged him closer. *"And I love you too."* And then, she was kissing him back, her lips against his, millions of stars exploding inside her, shimmering with liquid light.

And then a strange thing happened.

The *sathir*, dancing around them—a myriad of colors from her, and midnight blue shot with silver from him—merged. At first, her colors swirled around his, then the blue seemed to absorb them, lightening and pulsing until they formed one river of brilliant light.

Fire roared through Ezaara and images flitted through her—from him, from her—weaving in harmony, a life-song of their short time together.

Roberto's eyes shone. *"I never dreamed love would be like this."*

Ezaara touched his lips with her fingertips. She felt, more than heard, the sharp intake of his breath. His eyes smoldered, burning through her, making her tremble. He crushed her body against the firm planes of his chest, then his mouth was upon hers again.

Her heart raced as she melted against him, running her hands over his shoulders and into his hair, pulling him closer.

"I love you," she groaned against his lips. Never had she imagined a kiss could feel like this.

"Take care, Ezaara," Zaarusha melded. *"Dragon above."*

Ezaara broke off their kiss, and glanced up. Antonika was circling the orchard.

"Don't worry." Roberto stroked strands of her hair back from her face. "Tonio's not riding her. She's alone."

"If she tells him, we're in big trouble."

"After everything we've been through, I don't care. We'll face that if we have to, but one thing I know: we'll never be ripped apart again."

This time, when he kissed her, fire seared her lips, burning a trail to her core, setting her soul ablaze. Their kiss was urgent, ravenous. Ezaara was lost in a sea of sensation as tendrils spiraled deep inside her, awakening feelings she'd never known.

Roberto pulled back, his eyes swallowing hers. He ran a hand through her hair. "I've never felt this way before."

"Neither have I."

"One day, when you're qualified, I'll ask Lars if we can be hand-fasted."

She smiled against his lips, murmuring, "Yes, one day." For now, they had these forbidden, hidden kisses.

Roberto kissed her once more, gently. "We'd better get back before someone misses us."

They walked hand in hand through the orchard, toward their dragons, their river of *sathir* dancing around them. Birds flitted in and out of the trees, feasting on peaches in the summer sun. A deep warm glow suffused Ezaara.

"Do you realize, it's just over one moon since you arrived?" Roberto asked. "We should celebrate."

"We just did." Ezaara giggled. Four and a half short weeks. A whole different life.

She was Queen's Rider. She'd finally earned her rightful place on Zaarusha's back, leading Dragons' Realm. And Roberto had earned his place inside her heart.

"*Help, Ezaara!*" The voice was faint, as if it was far away, with a familiar deep timbre.

"Handel?"

"*It's your father, Hans. He's dying.*"

Shock hollowed Ezaara's belly. No, not Pa. "*Where is he, Handel? What's wrong with him?*"

"*I'm bringing him to the infirmary.*" Handel's voice was fading. "*Please, you need to—*"

"Handel?"

No answer.

Roberto touched her face. "What is it?"

"Handel melded. My father's dying." What about her brother? If Pa was dying, where was Tomaaz? And Zaarusha had said Ma was off finding Zaarusha's son. Was Ma in danger, too?

Roberto enveloped her in his arms. "It's all right, Ezaara. We'll face this together."

"They're on their way here. I have to get ready." Her hands grew slick with sweat and her pulse thundered. Pa. Dying. How could she prepare when she didn't know what was wrong with him? She only had a few healing remedies—and Fleur's questionable supplies. "Roberto, I don't know what … how …"

Roberto took her hands, squeezing them. "Ezaara, if anyone can do this, it's you. I'll be with you, every step of the way."

Breathing deeply, Ezaara nodded. "Let's go."

They ran to Erob and Zaarusha, and took to the sky, soaring above the trees, their dragons' wings flipping in perfect synchronicity.

EILEEN MUELLER

DRAGON HERO

RIDERS OF FIRE

BOOK TWO

Prologue - Eighteen Years Ago

Marlies strode along the tunnel, torches flickering and shadows flitting across the stone walls. Although it'd been a long day in the infirmary, she had one more duty before she could sleep. Lifting her torch, she turned down the passage to the dragon queen's den.

Her footfalls echoed as she passed through Anakisha's empty sleeping chamber. Sadness washed through her. Had it only been two moons since they'd lost the Queen's Rider? It seemed longer. There'd been many people to mourn—and dragons. Marlies shook her head. Too many deaths in one battle; and more dead and wounded in skirmishes since. She walked under the archway into Zaarusha's den and placed the torch in a sconce.

Zaarusha, the dragon queen, was curled in her nest, her head tucked under a wing, and her tail snug around her body. She unfurled her wings, myriad colors flickering on her scales, like rainbows in an opal. A glint of gold under the dragon's haunches revealed her precious eggs. Zaarusha extended her neck, facing Marlies, her yellow eyes dull.

Marlies stretched out her hand to touch the dragon queen's snout, so they could mind-meld. She forced her thoughts to be cheery. The last thing Zaarusha needed was sadness.

"Thank you for coming," Zaarusha's voice thrummed in Marlies' mind.

"How are your dragonets doing today?"

"My babies are fine."

Babies. Marlies flinched.

"Only a few more weeks until they hatch." Zaarusha's sigh echoed like a rock clattering down a mountainside. *"Syan will never see our dragonets. I miss him: his companionship; flying together. Hunting."* The queen flicked her tongue out.

"Did anyone bring you food?"

"They did, but I had no appetite."

Marlies scratched the queen's eye ridges. "Would you like to hunt tonight? A meal would do you good. It's been a while."

"A week." The dragon's belly rumbled.

Marlies smiled. "You are hungry. Sorry, I couldn't come sooner. Several of our wounded have infections and fevers, so I haven't left the infirmary for days."

"I can always rely on you." Zaarusha gazed at her, eyes unblinking. "You'll take care of my eggs?"

"Of course. I'm not Syan, but I'll do my best."

"Remember not to touch them." Zaarusha butted Marlies' shoulder with her snout. "I won't be long."

"The fresh air will do you good."

Careful not to crush the eggs, the dragon queen rose to her feet and stepped out of her nest. She sprang to the open mouth of her den and, with a flash of her colorful wings, leaped off the mountainside and was swallowed by darkness.

Marlies turned back to the nest. Four golden eggs, as tall as a boy of ten summers, were nestled in the hay. The torch's flames made their translucent shells glow. Through the tough membrane of the eggs, dragonets were visible. The green flexed its wing nubs. Marlies held her breath, watching the magical creature.

"Zaarusha's babies." Unconsciously, her hand went to her belly. She swallowed. These were the last of the royal offspring. Syan, Zaarusha's mate, had been killed in battle. His rider, Yanir, too. Anakisha and Zaarusha had tried to save them, but Anakisha had fallen from dragonback, plunging into their enemies' hands. Zaarusha had still been carrying eggs, so, not wanting to risk the lives of her babies, she'd been forced to abandon her rider and her mate and return to Dragons' Hold.

For two moons, the Hold had been grieving—but no one as hard as Zaarusha. She whimpered when she slept, and keened by day. The only things keeping her clinging to life were her duty to the realm and the beautiful creatures moving within these fragile shells.

For Marlies, seeing the dragonets was like walking on glittering shards. Their beauty transfixed her but cut deeply. Married for three years now, she and Hans had no children. True, she was still young, only in her nineteenth year, but something was wrong.

Although she'd healed other barren women using herbal remedies, she couldn't heal herself. Only Hans knew the herbs she'd tried, the rituals by full moon and the tears she'd shed in his arms. And not even he knew of her bitter tears when she was alone. Every babe born at Dragons' Hold gave her reason to rejoice and cause for pain. Royal dragonets were no exception.

All gangly limbs and neck, the orange dragonet turned over. The deep blue dragon baby opened its jaws. The green wriggled. In the smallest shell, the purple dragonet was curled in a ball, its wings folded tight against its back. It was so delicate, so fragile, somehow endearing.

Her breath a whisper, Marlies watched it sleep.

It was still for a long time.

Perhaps it wasn't sleeping. Perhaps something was wrong.

Marlies moved closer, but recalled Zaarusha's warning. *"Remember not to touch them."*

As if it sensed her, the purple dragonet woke.

A faint humming came from the egg. Marlies' breath caught. She leaned closer, her nose a hand's breadth from the golden shell. If only she had her own babe to hold, to croon to. She caught herself humming back to Zaarusha's babe. Why not? She ached to have a baby. Why shouldn't she sing to Zaarusha's dragonet?

The dragonet pushed against the thin gold membrane, seeking her. First its snout, and then its body. Its crooning grew louder.

Was it calling her?

The dragonet's eyes pleaded with her.

Unable to help herself, Marlies sang a lullaby.

The baby dragon's music swelled, drawing Marlies closer, wrapping around her. The lonely, empty aching inside her eased. Her fingertips brushed the shell. She gasped in shock, but before she could draw her hand away, a heartbeat pulsed through the membrane, making her fingers tickle. Euphoria swept through her. Marlies laughed, like she hadn't in years.

The dragonet's humming rose in pitch then fell—it was laughing, as if they were sharing a joke.

Marlies lay her hands against the shell and closed her eyes, focusing on the voice and the pulse of the creature before her. Her hands filled with energy, her head with music. The stone floor swayed beneath her feet. Marlies felt as light as a petal drifting on a breeze, as radiant as a star.

The dragonet's pulse grew stronger, bounding against her hands. Energy ran up her arms to her core. Then it stopped.

Marlies' eyes flew open.

The dragonet was lying on its back, floating in the shell, its wings limp beneath it. She pressed her hands against the shell. No hum. No pulse.

"Please, please, no." Her voice caught. She rubbed her hands against the shell, willing the dragonet to move.

But there was only silence.

Stillness.

Nothing beneath her hands.

Marlies' mouth opened and shut. With a strangled sob, she fled.

Lush Valley

Tomaaz adjusted the sack of potatoes on his shoulder and stepped over a wayward chicken. He frowned. What was Lofty up to? In a corner of the crowded marketplace, Lofty had his head together with Old Bill and the pair of them were grinning like thieves. Rather Lofty than him. He didn't want to go near Old Bill. The only decent thing about him was his cloth—bolts of bright turquoise seascapes, blazing-gold-and-orange birds and strange creatures and plants—transported into Lush Valley from far over the Grande Alps. From exotic places Tomaaz had never been, like Naobia on the southern coast, Montanara or Spanglewood Forest.

One day he and Lofty would leave this valley and explore those far-off places. It's not like he planned to lug Pa's vegetables around for the rest of his life.

Old Bill shook Lofty's hand, while beside them, Bill's drab daughter was lost among the bright cloth, staring at her feet. That was nothing new. Lovina was always staring at the floor. Tomaaz had never heard her mumble more than a word or two. Oh well, he had more exciting things to do than keep an eye on Lofty.

Like delivering potatoes.

Tomaaz dodged a bunch of children playing tag, and headed for the baker's stall, passing over the sack. "These should be good for your potato patties, Pieter," he said. "Pa's given you our best."

"As always." Pieter chuckled, and carried the potatoes to his cart.

"Thank you," said Beatrice, Pieter's daughter, flashing a smile, then ducking her head.

Inhaling the aroma of pastries and pies, Tomaaz smiled back at her. With Pieter distracted, it was now or never. He raked a hand through his unruly blond curls. "Beatrice, would you like to go for a walk? Later? I—I mean, after you've finished?"

"I'd love to. I can bring you an apricot pastry if you'd like." Beatrice gazed up at him through her red lashes. "I made them myself."

Red. Even her lashes were red. And her cheeks now, too. Tomaaz grinned. Asking her had been worth the gamble—she liked him. "Thanks. I'll come by after we've packed up."

Her smile lit her eyes, making his day.

Humming, Tomaaz strode through the marketplace past Klaus' leatherwear stand. The enticing aroma of cheese melted on slabs of bread made his stomach grumble.

Whistling nonchalantly, Lofty fell into step with him.

Tomaaz rolled his eyes. "Come on, Lofty. Tell me, what were you and Old Bill up to?"

"Nothing." Lofty gave him that innocent look of his. "Just ordering more silk for Ma's scarves."

"Of course you were." Tomaaz snorted. They skirted a goat pen and wandered past a weapons stand, stopping to admire a knife.

"Such a beauty," Lofty said, weighing the knife in his hand. "But way too expensive." Suddenly, Lofty dropped the knife, sucking in his breath. "There she is. Across the square."

Lofty had a sixth sense when it came to Tomaaz's sister. Like a homing pigeon, he always knew where she was. It'd been moons since Lofty had admitted to Tomaaz that he liked his twin sister. And Lofty had been trying to catch Ezaara's eye ever since—usually failing.

"You're not going to tease Ezaara again, are you?" Tomaaz asked, shaking his head.

"No, you are!" Lofty beamed. "I've hit upon the perfect plan. You challenge her to a sword fight, and I'll swoop in and save her. She'll finally see me as a hero."

"I doubt it."

"Go on, do it for me." Lofty was eager, like a bird bouncing on its perch. "I've got to try something."

Tomaaz hesitated. "Here in the square? Feathers will fly if Klaus catches us."

"Beatrice will be watching."

Tomaaz hesitated. Lofty had him. "All right, but if this doesn't work, promise me you won't cook up any more mad schemes."

"I promise." Lofty's solemn look didn't fool Tomaaz one bit. "Come on," he said, "it's just a bit of fun."

Tomaaz led Lofty further away from Klaus' stall—there was no point in asking for trouble. They trailed Ezaara as she examined plaited onions and garlic wreaths.

"Go on, now," Lofty urged, "before Ezaara notices us."

Beatrice had a good view from here. It was as good a time as any. Tomaaz slid his sword out of its scabbard. The scrape cut through the buzz in the market square.

Ezaara spun, dropping her basket. In a heartbeat, her sword was in her hand, her blade gleaming in the sun.

She'd always had good reactions. People backed out of the way, clearing a ring around Tomaaz and his sister. He lunged, striking fast. Ezaara parried, then feinted, but it didn't fool him. He pressed forward with a series of quick strokes, driving her back toward an apple cart.

"Take five to one for Tomaaz," Lofty yelled among the clink of coppers.

That idiot! Betting against Ezaara wasn't going to win her over. Tomaaz lunged again. That was close, he'd nearly scratched her face. That wouldn't impress Beatrice or Ezaara. He thrust again, but Ezaara danced out of reach, then lunged back at him.

She must've been practicing. Her counterattacks were coming hard and fast. Tomaaz blocked with power, driving his sword against hers. Dodging, Ezaara bumped Bill's table and bolts of cloth went flying. She leaped over them, fleeing.

Tomaaz chased her.

She whirled to face him, blade high. "Seen any pretty girls today? Look, there's one behind you."

If she'd seen him talking to Beatrice, he'd never hear the end of it. Ignoring her jibe, he deflected her sword and attacked again. When was Lofty going to jump in? This wasn't supposed to go on so long. And surely Beatrice had seen enough by now?

"Any more bets?" Lofty called to the onlookers. He seemed more interested in taking coin than rescuing Ezaara.

Ezaara was slowing, tiring. Maybe that's what Lofty was waiting for. Tomaaz slashed his blade at his sister's torso.

Ezaara stumbled, landing on her knee. "Ow!"

Oh gods, hopefully he hadn't hurt her. "Ezaara, are you all right?"

Driving her sword under his arm, Ezaara tapped his shirt. "I did it!" she cried, leaping to her feet. "I beat you."

Whistles and yells erupted around them. She'd fooled him, but it was a fair win.

"Go, Ezaara!" Lofty called.

She was beaming.

Maybe Lofty's strategy, whatever it was, would work today.

Tomaaz glanced toward the baker's stand. Beatrice wasn't there. All this for nothing. Oh well, at least they were going for a walk together, later. For now, he had to make Ezaara feel good about her win.

"Aagh, beaten," he groaned, sheathing his sword, and wiping sweat from his brow.

"You chose to fight me here." Ezaara's eyes blazed.

She'd fought well.

Grinning, she stepped back, sliding her sword into her scabbard.

Around them, coppers changed hands. He caught a glimpse of Beatrice on the edge of the crowd, smiling at him. Tomaaz's chest swelled with pride. She *had* seen him fight. And it looked as if she was glad for Ezaara's win, too. Not only was Beatrice beautiful, she was kind-hearted.

Lofty clapped Tomaaz on the back. Then he kissed Ezaara, right on the lips. What? That wasn't what they'd agreed. The crowd *oohed*.

Old Bill nudged his way forward and gave Lofty a handful of grimy coppers.

Lofty punched his fist in the air.

That's what they'd been up to! Rigging the fight to make money. And probably betting Lofty would kiss Ezaara. Lofty hadn't had a chance to rescue Ezaara because she'd won in her own right, but he'd still embarrassed her. Ezaara would never fall for Lofty like that. Why couldn't he see it?

Yep, Ezaara's cheeks were flaming. And not from passion. She was mortified—and as mad as a bear with a toothache.

People scattered as Klaus barreled through the crowd. "Is that those twins again?" With a bellow like an ox, a girth to match a draft horse, and even taller than Lofty, Klaus was the settlement's arbitrator. "What's going on?"

"I'm off to get that knife." Lofty thrust a handful of coppers at Tomaaz and slunk away. Typical—always the first to plan trouble and the last to get blamed for it. But Lofty's adventurous streak appealed to Tomaaz. No one else here was half as fun.

Beatrice gave Tomaaz a wave and headed back to her pastries.

"Tomaaz! Ezaara!" Klaus faced them off, hands on hips.

Tomaaz pocketed the coins and squared his shoulders. People were staring at them, but he didn't care. Beatrice had seen him fight. "It's my fault," he said. "I challenged Ezaara."

"In the middle of the marketplace?" Klaus snapped. "You could have taken out a littling's eye."

"Our tips were corked and the blades aren't sharpened," Ezaara defended. "See?" She passed him her sword.

Klaus ran his thumb and forefinger along Ezaara's blade. "It doesn't matter. You shouldn't—"

"She tricked Tomaaz," Old Bill called out. "Fighting sneaky, like a dragon rider."

Why was Bill bringing dragon riders into this? The fool. Any mention of dragons was bound to get Klaus riled up.

Klaus spun on Bill. "If I hear you mention those filthy winged reptiles and their stinking riders again, you'll be getting acquainted with our jail."

Bill glowered.

Klaus stabbed his finger on Tomaaz's chest. "No fighting in the marketplace."

"Sorry, sir, it won't happen again." Tomaaz inclined his head. One day, he'd be free from Klaus' silly restrictions. One day, he'd see dragons for himself.

"They knocked over my cloth," Old Bill protested.

"Help Bill tidy up." Flinging them a stern glare, Klaus strode off.

Old Bill rubbed his hands together. "So, kissed by Lofty, eh?"

Tomaaz stared at Bill in disgust. "I can't believe you put Lofty up to that. I mean, he's liked her for ages, and now he's blown it. There's no way my sister's going to like him back now."

Ezaara rolled her eyes. "Would you two stop talking about me as if I'm not here?"

They'd cheapened Ezaara with those filthy coppers—and she had enough problems with her self-confidence already. Tomaaz tried to make light of it. "Come on, Bill, you should've bet Lofty a silver."

It didn't work. Ezaara turned her back on him and dumped a roll of cloth on Old Bill's trestle table. Bill's daughter, Lovina, ignored them all, her filmy gray eyes examining the frayed stitching on her tattered boots. Boots so fascinating, she'd probably missed the whole sword fight. Tomaaz tossed the remaining bolts on the table and left.

Walking a little straighter as he approached Beatrice's stand, he winked at her. Despite Klaus' bollocking, today was shaping up nicely. He passed Beatrice a copper. "I'd like a potato patty, please." Tomaaz grinned at Beatrice, whose cheeks pinked. Now, that was the way to make a girl blush, not by embarrassing her in front of a crowd.

As he took the patty from Beatrice, their fingers brushed, sending a thrill through him. Tomaaz's heart thrummed. He was loathe to go, but didn't have a reason to stay. So, he turned away, biting into his patty, savoring the salty cheese and paprika.

Ezaara was still hanging around the cloth stall. Old Bill was leaning over his trestle table, shoving something into her hands. She glanced around furtively. Then, cradling her palms, she stared down, face full of wonder.

What was he showing her? Bill was very interested in Ezaara today. Tomaaz ground the now tasteless patty between his teeth. One of Bill's customers bumped Ezaara and she shoved the object back at Bill and hurried away.

Scoffing the last of his patty, Tomaaz rushed after her, but the next moment, Lofty was there.

"Hey, Maaz, look at my knife. It's a real beauty."

The handle was bone, carved with interwoven vines. Tomaaz let out a low whistle. "Nice."

Lofty weighed it in his palm. "And it's beautifully weighted. Here, try." Lofty held the knife as if he was about to throw it.

"Watch it," said Tomaaz. "I don't want Klaus over here again." He took the blade. "Feels good. That should improve your aim."

Lofty nudged him, crowing. "At least, that's one thing I can do better than you!"

"True." Tomaaz passed the blade back, and Lofty rushed off to show someone else as Ezaara came out from behind the cooper's stall.

"There you are." Tomaaz approached her. "I was looking for you."

"Marco got a bleeding nose from Paolo."

Tomaaz rolled his eyes. "Those two again." The boys were always getting into scrapes.

"Now you sound like Klaus." Ezaara grinned. "They don't know the sharp end of a sword from a hilt, and Paolo swings way too hard. We should teach them."

"Good idea," Tomaaz said, tugging Ezaara toward their parents' produce stall. "Now, what was Bill showing you, on the quiet?"

Glancing around again, Ezaara whispered, "Cloth—speckled with dragons of gold and bronze."

"Contraband cloth? Lucky Klaus didn't catch you." What was Bill's game? "Be careful. Old Bill's bad news."

Ezaara's face was filled with longing. "Even if dragons are evil, the fabric was beautiful."

Tomaaz wrinkled his nose as they passed a pen of piglets. "Lofty says dragons are honored beyond the Grande Alps." Dare he tell her? Might as well. "One day, I'm going to look for myself."

She elbowed him, hard. "Someone will hear you."

"So what? I'm not going to live here forever, you know."

Her eyes flew wide. "You'd leave us?"

Tomaaz blew out his cheeks. "Don't know. Maybe."

Ezaara frowned. "That's why Lofty's ma wanted owl-wort—you and Lofty are planning to go tonight, right?"

Tomaaz laughed. "If only!"

"If you ever leave, take me with you." Ezaara's voice was fierce.

"All right." Tomaaz cuffed her arm. "But no running off without me, either."

"Never," Ezaara swore. They bumped knuckles, sealing their vow.

When they reached their family stall, Ma sent Ezaara off to gather more herbs in the forest. "I'll duck home and get some flatbread on the hearth before the fire's dead," she said.

Pa brushed his dark curls back from his forehead. "We've sold out sooner than I thought. How about a dip, Tomaaz?"

"Sounds great," Tomaaz replied. Good thing too: the coating of dust and grime he was wearing would ruin the impression he'd made on Beatrice. She was the prettiest girl in Lush Valley. For many moons, he'd been working up the courage to ask her out. Thank the gods, Lofty had dared him earlier, otherwise he'd still be wondering whether she'd say yes.

"Not so fast," Pa said. "First, take this last sack of carrots to the smithy."

Tomaaz wasn't in a hurry—Beatrice and Pieter always took their leftovers to the bedridden and widows after the market. And he didn't want to seem too eager to get clean—his family would tease the hair from his head if he told them he was seeing a girl.

"Sure, Pa." He shouldered the carrots and headed to the smithy. How many sacks would he haul and how many carrots would he harvest before he had a real adventure? Probably hundreds. Thousands. Tomaaz sighed, trudging away.

§

Hans floated on his back in the warm water. He and Marlies had discovered this swimming hole years ago, when they'd first arrived in Lush Valley and settled on their farm near the forest. It was his favorite place to bathe.

His son was scrubbing at his curls with more vigor than usual.

Hans raised an eyebrow at Tomaaz. "Going somewhere special later?"

"Just off for a walk."

Hans couldn't help grinning. Did Tomaaz think he was a fool? He'd taken so long delivering those potatoes, and it hadn't only been that sword fight with Ezaara that had delayed him. And he'd been as jaunty as a songbird when he'd returned. "I know market day's a welcome break, but tomorrow, we'll need to get back to harvest, Son."

"I know." Tomaaz dived under, then popped up, floating on his back, too.

Laughing, Hans waded ashore and dried himself. "Come on, we've got stock to feed before you go off on your *walk*." He pursed his lips, blowing Tomaaz a kiss.

"Hey!" Tomaaz swept his arm across the river's surface, spraying him. "You can feed the stock yourself, just for that!"

Hans laughed and tugged his clothes on. Marlies' flatbread and soup might be ready by the time they returned. He bent to tie his boots.

Was that a tingle in his chest? After all these years?

He'd never had *that* feeling since living *here*. He scanned the sky—as he had done every day since they'd settled in Lush Valley. The tingling grew stronger, pulsing across his ribs. The range and focus of his vision extended.

There, a flash in the distant sky. Moments later, he saw another.

Keeping his voice casual, Hans addressed his son, "Want a race through the forest to the clearing?"

Still in the river, Tomaaz grinned. "The loser cleans the dinner bowls?"

"You're on." Hans took off.

"Hey," Tomaaz called, splashing out of the water behind him. "Not fair!"

Hans threw caution to the wind, racing ahead.

The power in his chest intensified and he sped forward, leaping logs, charging through the forest. Liquid fire sang in his veins.

With his enhanced dragon sight, Hans recognized the mighty multi-hued dragon approaching from the north. The dragon was circling down toward … there, through the trees … his daughter! Shards! Zaarusha, the dragon queen, was coming for Ezaara!

No!

An eye for an eye, but this was crazy. If he could get there in time, perhaps he could reason with the dragon queen. He raced through the forest to the sacred clearing.

"No! Ezaara!" he cried out, as she jumped. Hans gathered his strength and sprang into the air. His fingertips grazed the tip of her boot as she shot skyward. He fell to the earth.

The dragon was too fast. She already had Ezaara.

Energy ebbed from Hans' body as Zaarusha winged her way toward the distant ranges. The dragon queen had found them. And Ezaara was gone.

What a price for an innocent mistake. His breath whooshed from his chest.

Several clear stones were scattered on the grass. He grabbed them, rubbing their smooth oval surfaces and pointed ends. Zaarusha had left him calling stones.

Twigs cracked and leaves rustled. *Someone* was coming.

Hastily, Hans pocketed the stones, mentally cursing the silly tales of dragons carrying off young maidens, made up years ago to keep young girls close to home. Such stupid tales might help folk guess what had happened.

Marlies broke into the clearing, breathing hard. "Hans! Where are the children? Tomaaz? Ezaara? Are they all right?"

"Zaarusha came. Ezaara's gone."

"No!" Marlies whispered, her face hollow. "My baby!"

Nearly seventeen, Ezaara was hardly a baby, but Hans felt the same—Zaarusha had raided their nest. "There may be hope yet. Zaarusha wants us to contact her." He showed Marlies a calling stone.

Marlies recoiled. "Contact her?"

Hans gripped her arm. "It may be our only chance of seeing Ezaara again."

Her breath shuddered. "Oh, Hans, what have I done? It's my fault. If only I hadn't touched her dragonet's egg …" She sagged against him.

Hans cocooned her in his arms. "You didn't know. It was an innocent mistake."

Marlies' turquoise eyes were heavy with tears. "I'll fix this. I have to. Please, pass me the stone."

"Don't be afraid." Hans tried to comfort her, in vain. If only he could stop his own heart from hammering like a battle drum.

§

Afraid? Marlies shivered. That didn't even start to describe the emotions rushing through her. She could still hear the dragon queen's shriek when Zaarusha had discovered her dead dragonet. Her roars had shaken the mountainside, setting off avalanches. Only the billowing clouds of snow had prevented Marlies and Hans being spotted as they'd fled Dragons' Hold on Liesar's back.

She couldn't guess what sort of punishment Zaarusha had given Liesar for helping them flee.

"Marlies." Hans' voice was urgent. "Quick, use the stone before Zaarusha's out of range."

Taking the stone from Hans, Marlies rubbed the flat surface. She gritted her teeth, straining to hold Zaarusha's face in her mind—a face she'd spent years trying to forget. A face that had stalked her nightmares.

Hans grasped Marlies' shoulder and mind-melded with her, giving her strength.

Even the breeze seemed to hold its breath as colors swirled across the crystal's surface. A shape formed—Zaarusha. Golden eyes regarded Marlies.

The pounding in her chest was so fierce, she was sure the dragon queen could hear it. Nearly eighteen years they'd hidden, burying their sorrow, and rejoicing in the lives of their children. Marlies dipped her head in a bow. *"My Queen."*

"Am I?" Zaarusha's voice rumbled through Marlies' mind like boulders shifting in a flooded river.

Marlies remembered the purple dragonet crooning to her, singing—then suddenly lifeless and dead, floating in its translucent shell. Pain stabbed at her. Her own pain? Or was she feeling Zaarusha's?

It made no difference; the royal dragonet was gone. Marlies fell to her knees, still clutching the calling stone. *"I'm sorry."*

"So am I." Zaarusha rumbled. *"Sorry my baby died."*

"It was an accident. I didn't mean to—"

"An accident that blessed you with fertility."

Marlies' throat tightened. *"I—I didn't know. I—"* Her tears fell onto the crystal, blurring Zaarusha's image.

"You fled—that was an act of cowardice."

She nodded. Zaarusha was right. Terrified of facing the dragon queen, she'd run, dragging Hans with her. *"I was horrified at what I'd done."*

"Yes, you killed my baby."

Her crime was out in the open, stark and raw. *"So, now I must pay for my cowardice."* Swallowing the lump that threatened to choke her, Marlies whispered, *"And that price is my daughter …."*

"No, your daughter is not a price. I need your bravery."

What sort of answer was that? *"I understand, Zaarusha. You want Ezaara. Your baby for my daughter."*

"No. It's Ezaara's destiny to be Queen's Rider. My dragonet blessed you with fertility in its dying moments and gifted Ezaara with special talents. Being Queen's Rider is her right, not a payment."

"I don't understand …"

"I need you, Marlies. My son is captive, held by Zens in Death Valley. Zens' tharuks are making inroads into the realm as we speak. I can't leave to save my son and I can't spare Tonio—the only other spy I'd trust to rescue him. Save my son, and I will forgive your recklessness."

Marlies held her breath. *"And if I fail?"*

"I hope you won't."

Marlies swallowed. If she failed, she'd be dead—murdered by Zens or his tharuks.

Her heart ached for Zaarusha. She'd not only lost her dragonet, she'd now lost a fully-grown son. Perhaps she could ease Zaarusha's pain—and her own. After all these years, the dragonet's blood still made her palms itch. Although nothing would ever cleanse her hands, she could do this. She'd slink into Death Valley and free Zaarusha's son, saving a royal dragon—and perhaps some slaves with him.

Still mind-melded with Hans, she sensed his alarm. *"I'll do it, Zaarusha. Please, tell me everything I need to know."*

Via the calling stone, Zaarusha shared an image with Marlies and Hans: a narrow mountainside pass winding down into an eerie mist-shrouded valley. Devoid of vegetation, the chasm looked as if it was waiting to swallow Marlies, to suck away her life. Marlies' stomach curled in on itself. *"I don't know this place."*

"It's Death Valley."

Hans' shocked eyes met Marlies'. *"It's changed,"* he mind-melded, *"but so have we in the last eighteen years."*

"I'm nearly out of range," Zaarusha said. "Marlies, do you accept this responsibility?"

"Yes, I do." The weight lifted from Marlies' shoulders, but another settled in its place—this task was no easy stroll through a flower-strewn meadow.

"Please, Marlies, return my son to me." The image grew blurry and Zaarusha's voice faint.

"Look after Ezaara," Marlies melded.

Colors flickered on the crystal, then it was blank.

Marlies exhaled. "She's right, Hans. I was a coward."

His green eyes blazed. "We can do this. I know we can."

"Hans, she didn't ask you."

"But I fled, too. Ezaara and Tomaaz are our children. We—"

"I have to do this, Hans. We've no choice. I can't sneak you and Tomaaz into Death Valley, and you know he won't stay here on his own. I have to go alone." Marlies whipped her knife out of her belt, brandishing it in the air. "I will fulfill your quest, Zaarusha, and reclaim our daughter," she called, throwing the knife. It sank to the hilt in the ancient piaua trunk, sap oozing out around the blade. "As the forest marks my words, we will be reunited."

Her oath, sealed with piaua sap, was binding.

Feet tromped through the trees, crunching the underbrush.

Hans spun. "It's Tomaaz."

Thank the Egg, Hans had dragon sight. It gave her a few moments to prepare. But how could she tell their son? After all these years, how could she admit what she'd done?

§

Tomaaz raced into the clearing. He gasped huge mouthfuls of air, trying to get his breath back. What was Ma doing here? "Ma, I thought you were baking bread? Pa, how did you run so—" He broke off. There was a dragon in the sky above the forest. A dragon of many colors. "A dragon? Ezaara and I were just talking about—" His mother's face was tear-streaked. "Why are you crying?"

Her knife was embedded in the old piaua on the other side of the sacred clearing.

"Your sister's gone," Pa said. "The dragon has taken her."

Pa wasn't joking. Not with him and Ma so worked up. Not with that dragon in the distance.

"Dragon! Dragon!" Cries rent the air.

"It's time we told him," murmured Pa.

Told him *what*?

"I know," Ma said, "but people are coming."

Voices yelled, "Dragon, over there."

Pa turned toward the trees. "They're on the stepping stones. Klaus is already across. We don't have long."

What? Pa could see through the forest to the river?

Pa gripped Tomaaz's arm. "You're all we have now. Do exactly as I say."

"What's going on?" A rock settled in Tomaaz's stomach.

"Don't breathe a word of Ezaara's disappearance. They'll be here any moment. Trust us."

"But—" Tomaaz nodded. He had no choice.

Pa pointed to the massive piaua. "Marlies, quickly."

Running to the tree, Ma yanked her knife out of its trunk and hid it in the leg of her breeches. Then she crushed a handful of piaua leaves, squeezing the juice into the gash on the tree's trunk. "I will fulfill my quest, piaua tree, and regain my daughter, as witnessed by thee." The piaua gave a shudder and the gash was gone.

Piaua juice was strong, but Tomaaz had never imagined it could do that. And Ma was a tree speaker, so why had she harmed the piaua?

Ma picked up some tiny leaves from the grass. "Owl-wort, for Ana. Ezaara must've dropped it."

"What's going on?" Tomaaz's voice cracked.

"We'll explain later, Tomaaz." Pa's green eyes were intense. "Don't mention Ezaara."

Tomaaz's throat felt raw, his chest tight. A dragon had stolen his sister, and he was supposed to do nothing? He clutched his sword.

Klaus burst into the clearing, a pitchfork in his hand. "Hans, did you see the dragon? Where is it now?"

"There." Pa pointed at a smudge flying toward the Western Grande Alps.

"It's gone," said Klaus, shading his eyes to see the disappearing beast. "What was the damage? What did it take? Are our children safe?"

"No damage," Pa replied quietly.

How could he be so calm?

"Tomaaz and I were bathing when we saw the dragon fly over the valley …" Pa's voice trailed off.

He was acting a part—*acting*, when Ezaara was gone. Tomaaz clenched and unclenched his fists.

"I saw it swoop," cried one man, waving a pike.

"Perhaps it took a deer from the forest," Pa said.

"It was pretty," murmured a littling.

Voices babbled. No one had seen it take Ezaara.

Eventually, folk turned back toward their homes, walking together, discussing stories of dragons. Pa and Ma chatted as if they hadn't a care. Tight-lipped, Klaus walked with them.

Tomaaz's world had turned upside down. His twin sister was gone. Gone. And his parents were hiding something.

"Where's your sister, Tomaaz?" Klaus asked. "I haven't seen her since the market."

Tomaaz's stomach twisted. He shrugged, not trusting his voice.

"Where is she?" Klaus turned to Pa and Ma.

"At home," Pa said. "She's not well."

Klaus looked wary. "She was fine at the market, this morning."

Pa nodded. "We suspect she has *pilzkrank*."

Pa was a sly old dog. It was a good ploy. Pilz looked remarkably like an edible fungus, but caused rapid, contagious infections. No one would come looking for Ezaara for days.

"Let us know if you need any help," Klaus said, his suspicions allayed.

"I will," Pa replied.

Why was Pa being so devious?

Klaus raised his voice to carry along the road. "An hour after dusk, we'll have a menfolk meeting in the square. Go home and check your stock to make sure the dragon hasn't struck. Women and children should stay inside and bar their doors in case the beast comes back. We need a plan to fortify Lush Valley against further dragon attacks."

People nodded and murmured, continuing along the road toward the village. Pa waved as the three of them turned down the track to their farm.

"Hans, I must get the flatbread away from the fire before it burns," Ma said.

Baking? Ma was worried about baking?

Pa nodded. "Tomaaz and I will check the animals and give them their feed."

A figure broke away from the folk to join them. It was Ernst, Lofty's father.

"Hans, trust you to get there first," Ernst exclaimed. "You saw the only excitement this valley has had for years. A dragon! Above Lush Valley! What was it like?"

Pa laughed. "A fearsome beast, but it was already far away by the time we got there."

Ernst slapped Tomaaz on the shoulder. "You're a man now, too, Tomaaz, so we'll be expecting you at the meet."

Hans nodded. "We'll be there."

Ernst left to rejoin the folk heading to the settlement hub.

"You'll have to come, Son," Pa said, "otherwise they'll be suspicious."

Usually Tomaaz would jump at the chance to attend a menfolk meet, but tonight all he wanted was the truth.

§

During the rounds of the animals, Tomaaz clenched his jaw so hard it ached. His sister was gone. They were obviously feeding the stock to stop the neighbors from being suspicious. Afterward, Pa insisted on harvesting more vegetables, then they made their way inside.

Ma was ladling soup into wooden bowls. "Eat up and we'll talk before you leave for the men folk meet."

"Soup?" A bitter laugh escaped Tomaaz. He strode over and shoved his bowl. It slid across the tabletop and thunked to the floor, splattering his mother's rucksack. "My sister's gone and you give me soup?" He glared at Ma. "And why is your bag packed? Are you going, too?"

Ma glanced at Pa. "It's time we told him."

Pa picked up Tomaaz's bowl and thumped it on the table. "Sit down, Son."

Instead, Tomaaz paced by the fire.

"Ma and I came to Lush Valley, years ago, to keep you and Ezaara safe," Pa said. "To give you a chance to grow up strong and learn survival skills. We chose Lush Valley, here among the foothills of the Grande Alps—"

"I don't need a geography lesson," Tomaaz snarled.

Pa ignored him. "Hemmed in by mountains and isolated from the rest of Dragons' Realm, Lush Valley's the only place where dragons are treated with suspicion. Across the rest of Dragons' Realm, folk respect the dragons who protect us."

"Protect us?" Tomaaz scowled. "That's not likely. One just snatched Ezaara." He picked up the poker and stabbed at the fire. Sparks flew up the chimney.

"Son, your mother and I are dragon folk." Pa paused. "Actually, we're dragon riders."

Tomaaz whirled, the poker clanging to the floor. "What?!" Dragon folk? Riders? They had to be joking. "What's that got to do with Ezaara?"

"Hear me out, Son." Pa broke off a piece of bread and chewed it slowly. The wait was agonizing. "It was years ago. When I met Marlies, she worked for Dragon Corps, a secret group of riders. She was a spy, a fighter, an expert in herb lore." He stroked Ma's hand. Her eyes glinted. "She rode a silver dragon named Liesar, whose eyes were bright turquoise—as your mother's now are, after years of riding her. Riders inherit other gifts from their dragons—sharpened senses and, sometimes, the ability to harness excess power. I was a dragon rider, too."

"And not too bad at it," Ma interjected.

Tomaaz snorted.

Pa's mouth grew tight. "Marlies and I fought side by side to defeat the tharuks that were trying to overthrow the dragons and enslave our folk."

Tomaaz stopped pacing. His neck prickled. "You fought tharuks? And Commander Zens?"

"Many times." Pa nodded. "We married. Together with our dragons, Handel and Liesar, we achieved joint mind-meld. All four of us could hear each other's thoughts. In the history of dragon folk, it had only happened once before." He squeezed Ma's hand. "I became the Master Seer—and Marlies, Master Healer—on the Dragon Council."

Tomaaz shook his head. This was all too much.

"We had every reason to be happy," said Pa. "Except one. We couldn't have children."

"We tried for years," said Ma, "but never conceived. Then there was a grievous battle. We triumphed, but Zens and his tharuks killed many—including the dragon king, the King's Rider, and the Queen's Rider.

"Zaarusha, the dragon queen, was carrying four eggs. In the aftermath of battle, amid our wounded, she laid them and brooded on her nest." Ma winced, lines appearing on her face. "One night I was looking after the eggs while Zaarusha was hunting …" She broke off, then blurted, "I killed a royal dragonet, Tomaaz. I accidentally killed one."

The fire crackled.

"I—I touched an egg when I should've known better." Her shoulders shook.

Pa put his arm around her. "But that's not all," he said. "Somehow, touching the dragonet's egg allowed the baby dragon to pass its life force to Marlies, healing her. Shortly after, she became pregnant and we had you and Ezaara." Pa ran a hand through his hair, tugging at his curls. "That dragonet sacrificed itself so we could have you."

The fire's flickering shadows danced across the lines on Ma's face. "But there was a price."

Ezaara—she was the price. "Will she survive?" Tomaaz's throat was so tight, his voice cracked. He slumped into a chair.

Ma placed her hand on his shoulder. "Yes, Ezaara should be fine. The price was my guilt."

Tomaaz shivered. The fire had dwindled. Red embers glared at him like angry dragon eyes. He threw a log on them.

Pa leaned forward. "Zens must have struck at the heart of Dragons' Realm for Zaarusha to *imprint* with Ezaara."

Tomaaz swallowed. So Ezaara had bonded with the dragon queen and flown away. So much for her promise not to leave him. That multi-colored beast hadn't stolen her at all. And that same beast's offspring was the only reason he existed.

§

"You're going somewhere, aren't you?" Tomaaz snapped, pointing at Marlies' rucksack. His jaw was jutting out, his body tense with accusation.

Marlies' family was being splintered, and her son's heart shattered, but she had to go. Zaarusha's son's life depended upon her. "I am." Marlies took a deep breath. "Years ago, I was too cowardly to face Zaarusha—even though I'd killed her baby. Now, I have to prove my loyalty."

"How?" barked Tomaaz. "By heading beyond the Grande Alps and rushing headfirst into a troop of tharuks?"

"Enough, Tomaaz!" Hans snapped.

"Enough? Ezaara's gone, now Ma's going, too!" Tomaaz leaped out of his chair, his hands clenched in fists.

"We hid in Lush Valley to avoid Zaarusha's wrath. Now that she's found us, there's no point in staying." Hans' eyes blazed like emeralds. "There's nothing left for us here."

"But Lofty, my friends …"

"He's right, Hans," Marlies said. "We've made a home here. It's hard to leave." Hans had been itching to leave for years, but her heart was breaking for Tomaaz. For the lies they'd told. "Zaarusha has asked me to find her son. Tomaaz, I have to rescue him for Zaarusha. I must clear my name." The weight of the dead dragonet had always sat on her shoulders. Now she carried the weight of more of Zaarusha's offspring. And if she didn't succeed, that weight would crush her. "I have to go tonight. Now."

"You, too?" Tomaaz stared at her.

She embraced him. He was so rigid with tension, it was like hugging stone.

Blinking back tears, Marlies picked up her rucksack and headed to the door. "I'm sorry, Son," she whispered.

"Just get Ezaara back." Tomaaz's voice was brittle, like shards of ice snapping underfoot.

Ezaara wouldn't be coming back. He didn't fully understand imprinting—the emotional and mental bond that compelled riders to be with their dragons. How could he? They'd never even talked about dragons.

Hans ushered Marlies outside, his hand warm in hers. Dusk had settled, giving her cover for her journey. They walked to the stable and saddled Star. Hans led the horse across the paddock to the copse.

"Here's your cloak. I wish I was coming with you." Hans embraced her. "Speed well," he said, kissing her.

Marlies wrapped her cloak around her. "My cloak always reminds me of Giddi," she murmured.

"Me too," Hans said. "May it protect you."

After kissing Hans again, she climbed upon Star, waved, and rode to the sacred clearing. Dismounting, Marlies bowed before the piaua tree, and placed her hands on its trunk, listening, sensing. The trunk thrummed beneath her fingers. The tree's leaves stirred, filling the air with a rushing sound, like a giant river cascading through a chasm. Marlies cocked her head, straining to hear the tree's message.

"Take my berries, witch of blue."

Piaua berries? Those were usually a last resort—only for the desperate. She shivered. Becoming a witch of blue had never been in her plans.

"Be quick. An enemy is approaching."

"Thank you," Marlies said, *"for the berries and the warning."*

She rose and plucked two stalks of berries, thrusting them into her healer's pouch. Marlies swung into the saddle, departing from the clearing as the crack of breaking sticks alerted her to someone's presence. She glanced back.

Bill was in the clearing with a crow on his shoulder. Staring after her with malice-filled eyes, he grinned.

Digging her heels into Star's sides, Marlies urged her on through the trees. She'd suspected there was something odd about Bill, the traveling merchant. Today he'd incited Lofty to wager and start a sword fight in the village that drew attention to her children's skills. As they'd cleared up at the market, Tomaaz had mentioned dragon cloth that Bill had shown Ezaara. And now, this. A prickle ran down her spine. Bill might be a tharuk spy.

There was a caw above her. A crow dived through the trees at her, circled, and flew off. Was it the same one that had been with Bill?

No, that was too strange. Marlies and Star galloped on.

Above the trees, high on the Western Grande Alps, something glinted. A beacon fire, in the pass—a warning that Lush Valley would soon be under attack. Torn between Zaarusha and her family, Marlies reined Star to a halt. Her chest tightened.

All those years ago, she'd fled Zaarusha's wrath, leaving death in her wake. Now she was abandoning her family when death would soon be visiting.

Death Valley

The creature licked his aching leg, trying to edge his tongue under the biting metal shackle. The dull throb returned the moment he stopped licking. Hunger gnawing at his belly, he limped through the gray haze to the mouth of his cave. He was wearing a furrow in the ground from his endless pacing.

Muffled scrapes reached his ears. Someone was coming. His nostrils flared. Human—sniff—and rotting rat. Daggers of sunlight stabbed his eyes. With a whimper, he pulled his head back into the shadows. A vague memory of days in the sun—sun that hadn't burned—stirred in his mind, then was swamped by gray fog again.

He growled, letting the rumble build in his throat. As usual, the human ignored him, shambling toward him with his meal—not that he'd call those putrid rat carcasses a meal.

Despite his disgust, he salivated.

Empty-eyed and slack-mouthed, the human dumped the meat in the glaring sunlight.

The creature tried to rear, but fell back when the shackle bit into his leg. Not noticing, the human shuffled off.

The creature lay on his stomach and edged toward the fetid stench, squeezing his eyes shut to stop the burn. Stretching his neck, he snapped up the rotten meat. Blinded and still hungry, he retreated into the darkness.

Scorned

Hans turned away from Marlies' departing figure, his neck hair prickling and senses alert. The farm was wrapped in night's shadows. He scanned the fields with dragon sight, but despite everything being peaceful, unease trickled down his spine. Again, he checked his land, then the copse and the river. Nothing there. Why were his nerves so jumpy?

He gazed across the grass, through the walls of his home. Tomaaz was jabbing the coals with a poker, but apart from his son venting his frustration, nothing was amiss. Just to be sure, Hans padded around the farm's perimeter. By the roadside, the carrot tops feathered in the breeze and the scent of rich earth rose to greet his nostrils, but his sense of menace lingered. Heading toward the fowl house, he kept an eye on the copse, in case of trouble.

His sense of danger grew.

A faint scrape sounded on the fowl house roof. Hans whipped around.

Bill landed on the grass, his knife flashing.

Hans gave a mental groan. He hadn't thought to look up at the roof. His senses sharpened. "Want to talk, Bill?"

Bill spat at Hans' feet. "Talk to the likes of you?" He wiped his mouth with the back of his hand. "Ha! I saw your stinking daughter, gone with the queen of flying lizards."

Had Bill been in the forest for Zaarusha's visit? Keeping his eyes on Bill, Hans edged toward a large stick lying on the grass.

"Suppose you think she's the new Queen's Rider?" Bill smirked. "Not if I have my way." His eyes gleamed unnaturally in the dark.

So, he'd recognized Zaarusha. Hans' muscles were taut, his gaze steady on Bill's face. "Oh?"

"Hah. Crows. I sent a crow to 458—the best tharuk tracker. Zens will have the entire army hunting your wife. The crow knows her, now."

Hans' blood froze, a chill creeping through him. He maintained a light tone as he edged toward the stick. "Why's that, Bill?"

"Your wife. You. Your daughter. All dragon riders, aren't you? Wait 'til Klaus and the settlement council hear about this. They hate riders and those hideous beasts. *'Protectors of the realm'* indeed." Bill added spittle to his sarcasm.

"As much as they despise tharuk spies?"

Bill snarled and leaped forward, slashing with his knife.

Hans lunged sideways and rolled. He leaped to his feet, grasping the stick.

Grunting in surprise, Bill glowered as they gauged each other, both looking for an opening.

"I know your dirty secret," Bill snapped. "Dragon lover!"

"Get off my land, Bill." Hans made his voice steely. He hefted his stick.

Bill gritted his teeth, eyes like fire on a blade. He darted for Hans' chest.

Hans swung his stick, connecting with Bill's knife. The blade arced through the air, landing on the grass. "I said, get off my land," Hans growled.

Bill snatched up his knife, spat at Hans, and ran off toward the settlement hub.

Hans frowned. Bill's eyes had shone with an oddly-familiar light.

He shrugged. It was probably nothing. Klaus' grandfather, Frugar, had been a dragon rider but he'd died in a fierce battle. His son Joris, Klaus' father, had been bitter about Frugar's death, turning everyone against the very creatures that protected the realm. As a result, Klaus and the entire settlement had grown up hating dragons. Where would Klaus' loyalty lie when he discovered his family had once been dragon riders?

Hans trudged inside, ready for his next battle. "Come on, Son. I know you don't feel like it, but we have to get to Klaus' meeting."

His back to Hans, Tomaaz stabbed the fire with the poker, then whirled, holding the metal rod like a sword. "I have no choice," he spat, throwing the poker.

It clanged against the hearthstone, making Hans flinch. "Tomaaz—"

A sigh hissed from his son's lips. "Don't panic, Pa. I won't tell your nasty little secrets."

"Thanks, Son." Not perfect, but it would have to do. "Let's go."

Tomaaz stalked toward the door, but someone knocked before he got there. He flung it open and admitted Ernst, his wife Ana, and son, Lofty.

"Evening," Hans said, wishing he and Tomaaz had more time to talk alone.

Ana closed the door behind them. "Hans, we'd like to support your family." Voice quiet, she raised a hand to cut off Hans' protest. "We suspect your lives aren't what they appear, but we'll stand by you. We agreed you should have this."

She gave Hans a brown velvet pouch. "It contains a few useful things, including my mother's magic ring, imbued with dragon power."

A magic ring of dragon power? Pocketing the pouch, Hans fought to keep the surprise from his face.

Tomaaz moved closer, shooting him a keen glance.

"If you're in a tight corner, with nowhere to go, rub the ring and say my name." Ana leaned in. "It's short for my mother's name, Anakisha, the last Queen's Rider."

"Thank you." A chill snaked down his spine. When Anakisha had become Queen's Rider, her children had already been scattered, far from Dragons' Hold, to keep their identities hidden. Now, Anakisha's daughter stood right here in front of him. Had been for years.

Ana studied him. "I see you knew her, or knew of her."

Hans felt naked—had their careful cover not fooled anyone?

"We've long suspected you and Marlies were riders," Ernst said, his shaggy eyebrows drawn into a frown. "We'd better get going. Klaus hates stragglers."

Tomaaz and Lofty were elbowing each other, heading for the door.

"Tomaaz, wait," Hans called. "Thank you, Ana. Ernst, we'll catch up with you." He shut the door behind them.

Kneeling before the fire, Hans whipped a knife from his belt and prized it beneath the loose stone at the front of the hearth. If anything happened to him, Tomaaz needed resources and a plan. Hans lifted the entire stone away. Reaching his fingers into the cavity, he angled them back toward the room. With a click, the floorboard in front of the fireplace sprung open.

Tomaaz knelt next to the loose floorboard as Hans pulled dark fabric from under the floor. "My dragon riders' garb. Marlies has hers with her." He showed Tomaaz a coin purse, then tucked the jerkins and breeches away again, and retrieved Ana's velvet pouch from his pocket. Placing the purse and pouch on top of his dragon riders' garb, he replaced the floorboard and wedged the stone back into the hearth. He kept his voice low. "If anything happens to me, take Ana's pouch and those silvers and head for Dragons' Hold."

"Where's Dragons' Hold?"

"North, past Montanara, hidden within a ring of treacherous mountains—impassable except by flying. Any dragon rider will take you there if you tell them you're my son." Hans sighed. "I hope it never comes to that."

Tomaaz stared at Hans, speechless, the crackling fire and their breathing the only sounds. Finally, he rolled his eyes. *"Ask any dragon rider?* As if I'd see one daily!" He stalked to the door.

Hans followed. He resisted the temptation to look back at the forest for a glimpse of Marlies. She'd already be gone. They walked along the road stretching south to the village. Ahead, Bill and his horse were a blot against the pale gravel. Around them, the Alps were tipped silver in the dark.

"You all right, Son?"

"Absolutely *fine*. Why wouldn't I be, with half our family gone?" Tomaaz's boot knocked a rock, sending it skittering along the road.

"Sorry, stupid question." Hans placed a hand on Tomaaz's shoulder, but his son shrugged it off, stomping angrily toward the settlement. "Tomaaz," Hans called, "I have to warn you."

His son turned back.

"Bill is out to discredit us. Be careful what you say tonight."

Tomaaz's only answer was the crunch of gravel under his boots as he jogged off to catch up with Lofty. Hans jogged behind him and soon they were walking with Ernst's family.

Raking a hand through his hair, Hans gazed out at the Western Grande Alps, Marlies' first destination, two days' hard ride away. Something on top of the Alps winked at him. He was about to turn away, but—

"Oh, shards! Ernst, Ana! A beacon fire." Hans broke into a sprint toward the village square.

"Pa!" Tomaaz called, racing to keep up, Ernst, Ana and Lofty running too.

Using his dragon sight, Hans evaluated the fire, a gleaming yellow spot between the silver snow-tipped alps. If was he judging it right, the fire was on the Western Pass. "Tharuks have attacked the Western Pass!" Hans yelled, spurting ahead.

He and Marlies had sheltered in this sleepy valley for too long, ignorant to the advances Zens was making. Hiding from their past, instead of owning it. Well, he'd make up for it tonight. He'd do what he could to save Lush Valley from the approaching monsters. If only he had dragon power, now, to speed his feet. At least his dragon sight was permanent, the result of him being Dragons' Realm's former Master Seer.

Fields and barns gave way to scattered houses. Soon they were dashing along streets lined with sleepy shuttered buildings, past corners where oil lamps glowed on posts. Voices drifted from the square. Hans rounded a corner—and stopped. The street was jammed with people. There was no way through.

"This way, Hans," Ernst called, wheeling toward an alley. They ducked behind a row of stores, leaping piles of refuse, and rousing dogs.

Hans followed Ernst and Ana between two buildings, Lofty and Tomaaz trailing them. They burst into the torchlit square among a crush of people.

There, at the head of the square, near the clock tower and village fountain, Klaus stood on the wooden stage, gripping the podium. "We must take precautions," he said, voice carrying across the gathered folk. "That beast will be back, and maybe more with it. We mustn't allow dragons to wreak havoc upon us."

An ocean of people stood between them and Klaus, but if they shouted a warning, they'd cause a panic, and people might be crushed.

Instinctively, Hans stood shoulder-to-shoulder with Ernst, and they pushed their way through the crowd. "Make way, please."

"We have to make sure our families are safe," Klaus called to the crowd, thumping the podium. "We need an army, especially archers, to protect us from vengeful dragons."

"Please, we must see Klaus urgently." More people moved. They had to barge past others.

Klaus was still talking as Hans climbed on stage and placed a hand on his shoulder.

Klaus lowered his voice. "What is it, Hans? Is Ezaara worse?"

By the Egg, he'd nearly forgotten their alibi. He hated lying. Hans shook his head. "Marlies has taken Ezaara to the healers at Western Settlement to see if they can help."

"I'm sorry, Hans." Concern painted Klaus' face.

Hans pushed on. "Klaus, there's a matter of utmost importance." People were pressing in against the stage. Many of them would hear, but Hans couldn't risk waiting. They had to fortify Lush Valley against tharuk attack. The best time to marshal their defenses was now, while everyone was gathered.

Hans pointed at the Western Grande Alps. "Klaus, that yellow light is a beacon fire. The dragon set a beacon pyre alight to warn us that tharuks are attacking Lush Valley." The moment he'd spoken, Hans knew he'd made a mistake.

A mask of fury snapped over Klaus' face. Men near the stage muttered indignantly about dragons. Other shook their fists.

Klaus jabbed a finger at Hans' chest, his voice rising. "Are you suggesting that *dragons* might warn us of attack?"

Hans wasn't suggesting it, he knew it, but he was no use to the realm imprisoned—and definitely no use to his family behind bars or burned at the stake. "You're right, Klaus," he agreed. "The guards at the pass could've lit that fire."

Eyes narrowed, Klaus scrutinized his face. "Then why did you mention dragons, Hans?"

"I'm sorry. With the stress of seeing the dragon today, I wasn't thinking straight."

Nodding, Klaus peered toward the west. "Beacon, you say? I can't see anything but stars."

Shards! He'd forgotten about his dragon sight! Could anyone else see the fire?

Ernst stepped closer, pointing at the pass. "There, Klaus, see that bright star, yellower than the rest? That's fire."

"Looks like a star to me," Klaus said, shaking his head. "Dragons and fire. What's gotten in to you, Hans?"

"Perhaps he's a dragon lover!" yelled a throaty voice.

Hans whirled.

Bill, stained teeth set in an ugly grin, leaped onto the stage. "Hans raced to that dragon," he shouted. "His daughter hasn't been seen since." He stabbed a finger at Hans. "How do we know the dragon hasn't taken her?"

Hans' breath caught in his throat.

"You're a dragon lover, Hans, aren't you?" Bill sneered. "Offering up your daughter as a sacrifice."

"Of course not. A preposterous notion!" Hans drew himself up straight. "That fire is a beacon, set by the guards to warn us that tharuks are invading Lush Valley." The crowd was riveted. Hans called, "We're under attack. We have to prepare!"

Murmurs crept through the crowd. Folk shifted uneasily. Good. They were listening.

"We need to protect our families and village," Hans urged them. "We must form an army to fight them, or we'll be overrun, slaughtered in our sleep or taken as slaves for Zens."

"The only thing that's attacked us is a stinking dragon," yelled Bill. "Hans *really* thinks a *dragon* lit that fire. It probably roasted the guards at the pass for dinner." His laugh rasped like a knife on a whetstone. "Tharuks have never come to Lush Valley!" Bill's eyes glinted yellow in the torchlight. "Why would they come now?"

People cursed Hans. "Dragon lover."

"Mud flinger!"

"No, you have to listen. I—" Hans started.

"Hans!" Klaus bellowed, rapping his metal gavel against the stone-topped podium. "You're inciting unrest and disrupting our citizens. I won't have these wild rumors."

Superstitious ignorant clods! It was a beacon fire. Way larger than men could light. Only a dragon could've built that pile and set it alight. Tharuks would swarm over the pass, attack Western Settlement, then head straight for Lush Valley.

Hans scanned the crowd: farmers, bakers, the odd smithy or warrior. Plenty were younger than Tomaaz. Many, too old to fight. Tharuks against them? Within hours, Lush Valley would be defeated.

"Arm yourselves. Protect your families!" Hans yelled.

"Order! Order!" Klaus bellowed. He smashed his metal gavel against the podium, sharp cracks ricocheting across the square.

The crowd quieted, but they were still restless.

Klaus faced Hans. "Go home, now!" His voice carried. "The shock of that shrotty dragon has addled your brain! Get out of here." He flung his arm across the crowd, pointing north, toward Hans' farm. "Now!"

Old Bill stepped aside to let Hans through, a smarmy smile plastered across his face.

§

Lofty elbowed Tomaaz, muttering, "Told you dragons were nothing to be feared. My grandma was Queen's Rider."

"And now my sister," Tomaaz replied glumly, traipsing home behind Pa and Lofty's parents. His life was getting more complicated by the heartbeat. It seemed like everyone in Lush Valley was hiding secrets.

"Your pa's excuse might've fooled the villagers, but not our family." Lofty nudged him again. "Hey, both of us have Queen's Riders in our families. Does that make us cousins or something?"

Tomaaz laughed. Trust Lofty to see the light side.

Up ahead, Pa was walking with Lofty's parents, his shoulders slumped. He was muttering to Ernst and Ana, and waving a hand toward the beacon fire.

"Do you think that's a fire, or is your pa crazy?"

Tomaaz shrugged. "He's always been able to see stuff in the distance."

"Tharuks must be coming, then. Can't wait to fight them." Lofty's grin lacked his usual bravado.

So, he was *scared, too.*

Tomaaz scuffed his boots in the gravel. "You know, we've been chaffing for adventure, but Ezaara disappearing and tharuks stomping into Lush Valley wasn't quite what I wanted."

"And I won't even get to kiss Ezaara again." Lofty sighed.

Tomaaz rolled his eyes, then stopped dead in his tracks. "Shards!"

"What?" Lofty raised an eyebrow.

"I forgot all about seeing Beatrice tonight."

"At least she'll still be here tomorrow, waiting for you."

As if Beatrice would wait for him …well, maybe—with her red hair and blushing cheeks. Tomaaz hadn't kissed a girl before.

"Come on." Lofty yanked him forward. "Let's see what our old men are nattering about."

They sped up.

"I'm sure Bill's a tharuk spy," Pa was saying. "His eyes were yellow, as if he's on swayweed."

Swayweed! Tomaaz's mind reeled. That was one of Zens' substances. It changed love to hate, and hate to love, breaking allegiance and loyalty, allowing Zens to force a bond with people who would normally hate him.

"I've often wondered about Lovina," Ana said.

"Now, *that* had never occurred to me," Ernst replied. "She could be numlocked."

"Marlies and I wondered about her being on numlock. Years ago, when Bill first visited Lush Valley, he asked Marlies to treat Lovina's slow-witted mind, but we couldn't pinpoint anything. Besides, he said she's been like that for years, so we thought we were being overly-concerned."

Lovina had never responded, just stared at them blankly. The *idiot*, some of the others called her when she turned up with Old Bill for market days. Poor girl, she'd never done anyone harm. But then again, she never did much good either. She just existed.

When they reached the turnoff to Ernst's farm, Ana cautioned them, "Keep your doors locked. You don't want to wake up in chains, being dragged away by tharuks."

Ernst shook his head. "It's the last thing any of us want."

"It's two days' fast ride by horseback from Western Settlement to here, and tharuks travel by foot," said Pa. "So, we should have a day or two to prepare."

"We'll talk tomorrow, see who we can get onside," Ernst replied.

Tomaaz bumped knuckles with Lofty, and Lofty, Ernst and Ana went along the road.

He and Pa were left alone, walking across the farm. "Ask me anything," Pa said.

Well, that was direct. Tomaaz released a gust of breath. "Why did you never tell us? You could've trusted me and Ezaara."

"I would have told you in a flash, if Klaus and his ignorance weren't such a danger. You saw them, tonight: their hatred; their close-mindedness." Pa shook his head. "Scared of the very creatures that have kept them safe for so long."

"Dragons haven't kept us safe! We've never seen them here."

"Dragons and riders patrol the outer rim of the Grande Alps, keeping the passes free of tharuks." Pa clutched his arm. "Something's happened. Something terrible caused that beacon fire. You and I must be prepared. We'll stand with Ernst and Ana and anyone else who'll join us."

They reached the house, and Hans opened the door, ushering Tomaaz inside.

Tomaaz sank into a chair by the hearth and tugged off his boots. "What made you and Ma become dragon riders?"

Pa tossed some kindling on the hearth, and kneeled to blow on the embers. "My mother was enslaved by tharuks." He blew again. The kindling caught, and the fire flared to life. "Dragons and riders battled to free fifty slaves. Only six survived. Most were too injured to go far. Others had been broken with numlock, their minds chained so they couldn't run to the dragons rescuing them." Pa tossed a small log on the fire. "My sister was one of the wounded. Whipped for defending my mother, she could only hobble. My mother ran, half dragging her, but a tharuk arrow hit Evelyn in the chest and she died in Ma's arms." A ragged sigh tore from Pa's chest. "A dragon carried them both away—Evelyn to her grave, and my mother home to us."

That was an awful violent death. How had Pa's mother felt, taking her dead daughter home?

"That day, I swore I'd become a dragon rider and fight tharuks." Pa strode to a drawer and pulled out their hunting knives, tossing one to Tomaaz. "Keep your weapons near when you sleep. If tharuks attack, we'll meet them head on."

Pa gave a grim chuckle. "I hoped that it would never come to this, but it's the reason Ma and I taught you and Ezaara to fight."

"You what?" Tomaaz gaped. "All those races, the endless archery practice, the sword fights, were a ruse to train us for combat?" He'd never thought their bouts were any more than fun.

"Think of it as preparation for life."

A life he'd never imagined. "How do you fight a tharuk?"

"Son. It's late. Tomorrow I'll teach you, Lofty, and anyone else who's keen, how to fight those monsters. The best we can do now is get some rest."

It took Tomaaz forever to get to sleep. When he finally drifted off, he dreamed of Ezaara, battling monsters from dragonback, high on a mountain pass.

Tomaaz awoke to pounding.

Tharuks! It had to be! Within moments, he had his sword and knives at his belt and was tying his boot laces. He rushed into the living room.

Pa was frozen, staring at the door. The wood was quivering under constant hammering.

"Tharuks?" Tomaaz asked.

Pa turned. "Villagers."

"So, you can see through wood?"

Pa nodded. "It's called dragon sight."

"You mean—"

Pa chuckled, striding to the door. "I saw you sneaking out to meet Lofty on many occasions!"

What next? *Nothing* was normal anymore. Not even Pa's eyes.

"Hopefully, the villagers have seen reason about the beacon fire and are here to train," Pa said.

"In the middle of the night?" Tomaaz grabbed his arm. "You saw how angry they were."

Pa shrugged. "Maybe they've just finished their meeting. You know how Klaus goes on." He opened the door.

It was only settlers, not bloodthirsty tharuks. Crowded around the door, a few were holding torches. Their faces were tight with fear. Behind them, a crowd spread across the grass, many in the shadows. There must be fifty people here—men, women and littlings.

"Good evening," Pa called.

Evening? It was after midnight.

The smithy stepped to the front. "Hans."

"It's been a big day," Pa said evenly. "How can I help?"

"You said you saw a beacon fire. That a dragon set it alight and tharuks are coming. We want to know more."

Tomaaz scanned the crowd. Pieter and Beatrice were here, too. He gave her a smile, but she looked too worried to smile back. Perhaps he could slip out and talk to her when they were done with whatever everyone was here for.

"Atop the Western Pass there's a pyre, always ready in case tharuks breach the pass," Pa replied. "I saw it burning. Tharuks might be here in a day or two."

The smithy jerked his head back toward the Western Grande Alps. "Why a dragon, Hans?" Eyebrows raised, his face was etched with curiosity. "Why not the guards?"

The moments stretched out like a man on a rack.

Would Pa tell them what he really thought? Surely not.

Then Pa answered. "The fire seemed a lot larger than a standard pyre. We saw the dragon yesterday. It flew in that direction. It seemed logical that the dragon could've spotted tharuks and tried to warn us."

"Logical?" A voice from the shadows cried in derision. "Since when is a friendly dragon logical?" Bill swaggered into the torchlight, his face contorted into a mask of hate. "Might be logical for a *dragon lover!*"

Someone jeered.

Hans held his hands up. "We must prepare for attack. Not fight amongst each other. We need to stand together against this outside threat."

"A threat you've made up," Bill sneered. "Tharuks aren't coming. The truth is that Hans gave his daughter to a dragon."

"Now, why would I do that?" Pa said, shifting his weight to move back inside the house.

The smithy stepped forward, poking a finger at Pa. "You tell us, Hans. Where's Ezaara?" His burly chest rose and fell. "We demand to see her. Prove Bill wrong."

"It's terrible," Pa said. "Terrible. She caught pilzkrank today and Marlies had to take her to the infirmary at Western Settlement."

"Why?" yelled a settler. "Marlies healed my boy of pilzkrank last summer."

That's right. Little Adam had eaten infected fungi last year and nearly died. Tension radiated off the crowd. Bill wanted blood. Tomaaz could sense it.

Pa's shoulders slumped and he gave a gutsy sigh. "Well, Ezaara was worse. We nearly lost Adam. I didn't want to lose her, so Marlies rode off this evening."

"So convenient!" Bill said.

Pa stepped inside, pushing the door shut. But the smithy was there, his weight heaving the door open and sending Pa sprawling on the floorboards.

Tomaaz's heart hammered.

"Seize him," Bill yelled. "We know what to do with filthy dragon lovers!"

With a cry, men surged into their home. The smithy dragged Pa out of the house by the ankles, his back and head thumping down the steps.

That had to hurt, but Pa didn't cry out. "Hey," yelled Tomaaz, drawing his sword.

He was instantly surrounded by a ring of men.

"Now, come on, Tomaaz," said Pieter soothingly. "You don't want to get hurt. We understand you standing by your father, but for now, you're innocent. Make one move with that sword and that's no longer the case." Although his tone was reasonable, the threat in his words was as plain as the sword in Tomaaz's hands.

Tomaaz couldn't help Pa if he was in jail too, so he sheathed his sword.

"Hand us your weapons, son," Pieter said.

Outside, the sound of a mallet cracked the air.

"I'm not your son," Tomaaz snapped.

"Nor will you ever be," Pieter barked back. "You're the son of a filthy dragon friend."

Fuming, Tomaaz shouldered through the ring and barged out the door, through the people milling outside their house. The smack of the mallet rang out. As he broke through the crowd, horror crept through Tomaaz's belly.

Two men had driven a stake into the ground. Others were piling dry brush around it. Pa was struggling in the grip of the smithy while four men gagged him and tied his hands and feet to the stake.

Gods, they were going to burn him. No trial. No witnesses, just a dumb pig-headed burning in the middle of the night. Tomaaz frantically scanned the crowd for Klaus. Nowhere to be seen.

There! A flash of red hair in the torchlight.

Desperate, Tomaaz ran toward Beatrice, seizing her arm. "Beatrice, please, fetch Klaus. Hurry."

Her eyes assessed him coolly. "Why, Tomaaz? Do you think you can talk your way out of this mess?"

"They're going to kill Pa." He clutched Beatrice's arm tighter. "Please!"

"He consorted with dragons! He deserves to die!" Beatrice spat on Tomaaz's hand. "Now take your hand off me or I'll scream, and they'll burn you too." Her face was twisted with venom, ugly.

Tomaaz dropped her arm, stumbling backward.

Someone shoved him. He fell. A boot thudded into his ribs. He scrambled to his feet and dodged through the crush of bodies. Over the backs of several brawny men, Pa was now gagged and tied to the stake, on top of a pile of tinder-dry brush. Men were throwing tallow onto the brush. One torch and Pa would be in flames—burning alive.

Tomaaz's skin crawled as he inched closer. He'd fight his way through, stick every man like a pig. He'd rather die than let Pa burn. He drew his knife from his belt.

As if he could read Tomaaz's mind, Pa's eyes widened, and he shook his head.

Pa didn't want him to fight? The idiot! Tomaaz slipped his knife back into its sheath, hand at the ready.

"So, who would like to see this dragon scum die?" Bill roared, leaping upon the brush and squeezing his fingers around Pa's throat.

Tomaaz's hand flew to his knife handle. One well-aimed throw and Bill would be dead.

"Don't you even think about it," a voice whispered, making his neck hairs rise. A blade pricked his ribs. Pieter.

"Wait," Ernst called, barging through the ring of men around the unlit pyre.

Where had he come from? He hadn't been here when the others had knocked on the door.

"We haven't heard any solid proof against Hans yet," Ernst stated.

"His daughter's gone," roared Bill, eyes glinting yellow. "No one's seen her since the beast appeared." The flickering torches cast demonic shadows across Bill's face.

"And his wife has left too," someone yelled from the crowd.

"He's a dragon lover," called a woman.

"Sacrificed his daughter to appease the beast!" screeched another

"That's just rumor," Ernst bellowed. "What will Klaus do, if he finds you've burned one of his best farmers because of gossip?"

"What will Klaus do if he finds out we've been harboring a dragon lover?" Bill bellowed back. "Burn him now and get it over with!"

More yelling broke out.

"Pieter," Bill called. "Come up here and show everyone the proof you have against Hans."

Proof? What had Pa left lying around?

"I'm a little busy," Pieter yelled back, the increased pressure of his blade making Tomaaz flinch. "But my daughter will bring it."

Men stepped aside to let Beatrice through. She stood in front of the stake, facing the villagers. From her pocket, she drew a scrap of cloth. "This cloth was in Hans' barn! It's covered with dragons—bronze ones, silver and red. This proves he covets dragons. Loves them!"

How had Tomaaz ever thought she was beautiful? Her face was full of hate.

"Show me that cloth!" Tomaaz shouted. "Let me see it."

"I, too, would like to examine it," Klaus said, and the villagers parted like wheat stalks before an ox.

Where had Klaus come from? Then Tomaaz spotted Lofty, panting, near where Klaus had been. No doubt Ernst, on the neighboring farm, had seen the villagers' torches and sent Lofty for Klaus.

Reaching the pyre, Klaus snatched the cloth from Beatrice. His face was thunderous. "Tomaaz! Come here!"

Pieter shoved Tomaaz.

He ran to Klaus, pushing through wide-shouldered men.

"Is this one of your pranks?" Klaus hissed. "Do you consider this funny?"

"No, sir." Tomaaz put his hand out for the cloth. Klaus thrust it at him. Tomaaz couldn't help his sharp intake of breath as he saw the pattern. "Bill was showing this cloth to Ezaara at the marketplace today. It's Bill's, not Pa's."

Klaus raised an eyebrow and plucked the scrap of fabric back. "Bill says it's your pa's and you say it's Bill's. Very convenient that you're blaming each other. And no one has yet cleared up the mystery of where Ezaara has been since your fight at the marketplace."

Holding the cloth high, Klaus turned to the crowd. "Whom shall I believe?"

The villagers yelled, waving torches.

Frantically, Tomaaz scanned their faces. "I know!" Tomaaz tugged Klaus sleeve. "Sir, I know how you can determine this!"

"How?"

Tomaaz gestured to a woman at the back of the crowd. "She saw Ezaara shoving the cloth back at Bill. She may recognize it."

Klaus motioned the woman forward.

"Tomaaz says you've seen this cloth before," Klaus stated.

She frowned, shaking her head.

"Earlier today, in the marketplace," Tomaaz interjected. "You bought a length of cloth from Bill, green with a wheat pattern."

"So I did." She nodded. "What of it?"

"Before you purchased your fabric, Ezaara was at the stand. Did you see her pass something back to Bill?"

"Oh, that!" Comprehension flashed over her face. "Yes, I did. She had her head down, fascinated with something she was holding. When she noticed I was near, she thrust a piece of material into Bill's hands, telling him, 'No, thank you.' I did wonder what had captivated her."

"So, do you recognize this fabric?" Klaus asked.

"It was black with gold and red, that's what I saw." The woman held out her hand. "Let me have another look."

Klaus passed her the cloth.

"Yes, it's definitely possible that this is the same piece I saw today."

"Possible," yelled Bill. "She's not sure. That's not proof! Not like we have against Hans."

Klaus narrowed his eyes. "What proof do you have?"

"Lovina," Bill called, charging through the crowd and dragging Lovina forward. Tomaaz winced. Bill's grip had to hurt. Sure enough, when Bill removed his fingers, the imprint stayed on her upper arm—her thin pitiful arm, covered in goosebumps. She was wearing her ragged shift—no protection against the chill of the night. "Lovina saw Hans' daughter leaving on that dragon," Bill said. "Tell them, Lovina."

She hadn't, had she? Tomaaz's pulse hammered at his throat. He met his father's eyes, bright over the gag.

Eyes downcast, Lovina murmured something incomprehensible.

"Go on, girl," Bill demanded. "Speak!"

Lovina opened her mouth, then shrugged and stayed silent.

"Girl, answer," Bill growled.

There was a threatening edge to Bill's voice that Tomaaz didn't like. Before he could think, Tomaaz blurted, "Tell the truth, Lovina."

From behind Lovina's matted hair, a glimmer of hope shone, then her face was blank again and she slumped.

Had he imagined that glimpse?

"Talk!" Bill grabbed the back of Lovina's dress. She pulled away and stumbled, the worn fabric ripping, leaving Bill clutching shreds.

Hands outstretched, Lovina fell. Tomaaz jumped forward, catching her. He gaped at her exposed back. A crisscrossed mess of wounds marred her skin where she'd been whipped. Fresh, red lacerations in raw flesh. Lash marks festering with crusty, flaking scabs. Pale-pink scars were layered over faded white ones.

Tomaaz stared in horror.

Shoving Bill aside, Klaus pulled Lovina away from Tomaaz, draping a protective arm around her. "We must find a healer," he croaked. "Lovina, who did this? Did Bill whip you?"

Lovina nodded, eyes flat.

"Did anyone else whip you?" Klaus asked.

She shook her head, greasy hair flopping around her face.

"Bill is sentenced to ninety days' imprisonment for whipping his daughter," Klaus's voice boomed. "Seize him!"

Bill lunged, snatching a torch. He threw it onto the pyre. "Dragon lover!" he screeched, racing off into the dark fields. Men sped after him.

For an instant, Tomaaz stood, rooted, as the pyre flared to life around his father's feet.

Flames licked Pa's boots. Pa tugged and jerked, but he was bound fast.

Tomaaz ran, stomping through the fire. He whipped out his knife and slashed at the ropes, but they wouldn't give. Angling his knife against the rope, he sawed. Sparks flew onto his breeches. Heat scorched through his boots. His legs were getting hot. Smoke smarted his eyes. He kept sawing. Just a few more fibers.

"Keep cutting," yelled Ernst, there beside him with Lofty, stamping at the base of the pyre.

"Help Tomaaz!" bellowed Klaus, throwing his jerkin on the fire to douse it. But the jerkin flared to life, flames devouring it.

Villagers jumped on the pyre, stomping on the flames.

Pa yanked and the ropes around his hands gave. He tugged his gag free, screaming as fire licked up his legs. Tomaaz stomped too, trying to see where Pa's legs were tied. Smoke stung, blurring his vision. In desperation, he slashed through the flames at the base of the stake.

Pa pulled hard. The ropes around his ankles gave way. He leaped off the pyre, stumbling onto the grass. Ernst chased after him, rolling him to douse the fire.

Then Lofty was there, pulling Tomaaz to the ground, rolling him, smothering the flames on his breeches. Until he felt the grass on his skin, he hadn't even noticed that the fabric had burned through. His legs were in agony.

But if his were sore, Pa's must be horrendous.

§

Hans groaned. Shards, his legs hurt. And his hands were throbbing, too. He lay on his side, his cheek in the damp grass, grateful for the cool relief. He'd been in worse scrapes and survived, although it had been a while.

Thank the Egg, Tomaaz had acted so quickly. He could still feel the vibrations of Tomaaz's sawing shuddering down the stake against his back. The wicked heat on his legs.

Hans gritted his teeth to stop himself from yelling as Ernst undid his boots and eased them off, but a groan still escaped him. The night air wafted over his searing feet.

"These won't be much use anymore." Ernst clucked his tongue, dropping the boots. "Thank the Gods, you had these on. Anything else and you wouldn't be walking for a moon."

The pain. Hans let out a long breath. Gods. And another.

Klaus' voice broke through. "Pick him up and take him to the house. Anyone with healing skills—or proof—may accompany us. We have yet to get to the bottom of this."

Hans groaned again. This wasn't over yet.

§

Tomaaz made his way back to the house with Lofty and Klaus supporting him on either side. Lovina followed them. They trailed Pa, who was being carried by the smithy and Pieter—the very men who'd wanted to burn him at the stake. Hopefully, they'd seen Bill's true colors and changed their minds.

Ana appeared, carrying healing supplies. "Are you all right, Tomaaz?" She took Lovina by the hand, bringing her along.

Through gritted teeth, Tomaaz attempted a smile.

"I'll need your ma's healing supplies, if you know where they are," Ana said.

He managed a nod as Klaus and Lofty helped him up the steps into the house.

Pa was on his bed, Pieter and the smithy pacing nearby like wolves.

"Over here." Klaus motioned toward Ma's side of the bed. "It'll be easier if you're both together."

What would be easier? Healing them? Or guarding them?

Ana seated the shivering Lovina in a chair in the corner and bundled a blanket around her. Klaus shooed Pieter and the smithy into the living area and took up vigil next to Lovina, leaning his bulk against the wall.

Tomaaz's shins and calves were red and blistered, but his feet had been protected by his boots. He grimaced at the raw flesh on Pa's legs and feet, covered with yellow blisters as big as eggs. Gods, how could his father walk, let alone fight tharuks?

Ana, Lofty and Ernst bathed Pa and Tomaaz's burns with wet cloths, cooling them. Then Ana smeared healing salve over the raw parts of Tomaaz's legs. Her touch bit into him like a nest of viscous ants. He clamped his teeth down on a stick, knowing Pa's pain was worse.

Ana moved to treat Pa. Pa lay there, groaning and grunting, drifting in and out of consciousness.

"Hans," Ana asked, "does Marlies have any piaua juice?"

No answer.

"Not sure," Tomaaz replied. "Her supplies are in the wooden chest in the kitchen." Was his pain ever going to end?

Ana left and bustled back in, beaming. "I found some piaua." She held up two vials of clear green liquid.

Only two vials. "Is that enough?" Tomaaz croaked.

Lofty gave him a sip of water.

Ana frowned. "We'll see." She approached him.

"No. Heal Pa. He needs it more."

She nodded and retreated to the other side of the bed.

Ana dribbled the piaua juice onto Pa's leg, then tried to smooth it into his flesh, but Pa screamed, twisting on the bed. His foot connected with Ana's stomach.

She cried out, but managed to hold the vial upright.

"Pieter, Smithy!" Klaus barked, coming over to pin Pa's shoulders. "In here. Restrain him."

The smithy held Pa's hips down. Ana wrapped bandages around Pa's ankles while Pieter had the awful job of holding them in place.

Brow beaded with sweat, his father moaned as Ana smoothed the juice into his burnt skin. Pa's wounded flesh shrank before Tomaaz's eyes, disappearing. The bulbous blisters shriveled and sagged, then vanished. Pa's moaning stopped. Where his burns had been was pale-pink skin.

Klaus exhaled. "No matter how many times I see it, piaua never ceases to amaze me."

Letting go of Hans, Pieter and the smithy murmured in assent.

Pa opened his eyes. "Shards, that stuff burns! Almost as bad as fire!" His chuckle died in his throat as he glanced over at Tomaaz. "My son, Ana. You must heal Tomaaz."

Ana held up a vial. "I only have quarter of a vial left. What will it be? Your hands? Or your son's legs?"

Pa held up his blistered hands, examining them as if they didn't belong to him. "I've had worse. I'll be fine. Heal him."

"Hans, I—"

"No," Pa bit out, "I want my son fit to fight tharuks when they arrive tomorrow." He glared at Klaus, his jaw jutting out.

Klaus shook his head, his mouth hardening in a grim line.

"Pa," Tomaaz said, his gaze landing on Lovina. "Lovina's back is worse."

Klaus nodded.

"Please, Ana, heal her," Tomaaz said.

§

Lovina stirred. The boy with the emerald eyes and golden hair had mentioned her. Impossible. No one ever noticed her.

Certainly not anyone that beautiful. She'd seen Tomaaz fighting in the marketplace today. Laughing. Confident. Hugging his sister.

He said it again. "Please, heal Lovina."

Lovina strained to see through the gray fog. He was staring right at her. She dropped her gaze. The only time anyone ever looked at her was usually right before they hurt her.

Uneven thumps reverberated through the floor.

It was him, hobbling over on wounded legs. Wincing, he lifted her chin with gentle fingers.

"Lovina." His breath brushed her cheek. "We'd like to heal your back."

She stared at him.

The fire crackled next door, the way the pyre had crackled before he'd saved his pa.

"Lovina, please, let us heal you."

She swallowed and bobbed her head.

"Good."

Lovina was bathed in the light from his smile.

§

Ana led Lovina out of the room, and Tomaaz sank back on the bed beside Pa. Those few paces across the room had taken more out of him than he realized.

If only there'd been enough juice to heal them all. But there wasn't, and Lovina's infected back needed more help than his legs. He was strong, healthy. He'd heal in a few days. She was frail, as thin as a wisp. Her dull gray eyes ate away at him.

"Lofty, please find something warm for Lovina to wear," he asked. "There must be something among Ezaara's things."

"Good idea, Tomaaz." Klaus' voice startled Tomaaz. He'd forgotten Lush Valley Settlement's arbitrator was there.

Pa sat up in bed, flexing his legs. "Klaus, we have to prepare against tharuks."

"I've had enough of you inciting people, Hans."

"They're coming, whether you believe it or not," Pa insisted. "Either we meet them prepared or pretend nothing's happening. It's your decision."

"I said, I'll not have you inciting rebellion."

"Klaus, see reason."

Klaus' face was a storm cloud. "I am seeing reason. I believe what I see. And I haven't seen a beacon fire or any sign of mythical beasts."

"Mythical!" Pa exploded. "I've fought those monsters, years ago, before I came to Lush Valley. Tharuks are no more mythical than a field of wheat. Look!" Pa pulled up his smoke-stained shirt to reveal a faded white scar across his belly. "Tharuk tusk! Now what do you think of that?"

Klaus shrugged. "Looks like an old knife wound to me."

"Klaus, you idiot!" Pa yelled.

He'd pushed it too far. Klaus face' went red and he hissed, "Smithy, Pieter, in here."

A moment later, their bulk filled the doorway.

"Hans requires a few nights in the cells to teach him civility and reason. Now that his wounds have been treated, you may escort him to jail."

Pieter and the smithy yanked Pa to his feet.

Ernst rushed in, placing a hand on Klaus' arm. "Klaus, please. Hans is an upstanding member of our settlement. He's had a few shocks today. First the dragon, then his daughter being ill, and now, almost being burned at the stake. I think he just needs rest."

Staring at Ernst as if he was vermin, Klaus said, "He'll get plenty of rest in jail. That will give us time to uncover more proof that he is, indeed, a dragon lover."

The crash of the front door made Tomaaz start. A man shoved his head through the doorway. "Klaus, sir, we've captured Bill and put him in jail. Says he wants to see his daughter."

"I'll not have that man go near Lovina again," Klaus said. "Help these two take Hans to jail. Not in Bill's cell, though. I'll not have murder on my conscience."

"Uh, sir, excuse me, but I'm suspicious of Tomaaz," Pieter said.

Klaus nearly snapped Pieter's head off. "What now?"

Tomaaz's heart thudded.

"Tomaaz offered to take my daughter, Beatrice, out walking." Pieter's glance slid over Tomaaz. "I believe he was trying to entice her into the forest to offer her to the dragon."

Throat tight, Tomaaz waited for Klaus' verdict.

In the next room, Lovina whimpered.

Glaring at Tomaaz, Klaus said, "You'll keep until morning." He swept out the door, announcing, "I've had enough! I'm going home to bed!"

Through Fog

After a hurried meal of flatbread, Lofty hoisted Tomaaz onto Sorrel, their tamest mare, then climbed into the saddle in front of him. Tomaaz felt like a littling, but he didn't protest. His legs were too sore to ride Sorrel on his own. He clung onto Lofty, each jolt painful, as they plodded along the road into the village.

Pa in jail. Ma heading for tharuks, and Ezaara riding a dragon queen he hadn't even known existed. Life was as slippery as the stepping stones in a flood. He shook his head, then wished he hadn't as the world rocked around him. He was weaker than a newborn colt.

As they passed by, mothers tugged their children behind them. Men glowered, folding their arms across their chests. Tomaaz's skin crawled from the heat of their stares. When they reached the jail, Lofty helped him down, and Tomaaz hobbled inside like an elderly man.

"Down the end, *dragon lover*." The guard spat on Tomaaz's boots.

It was all he could do not to draw his sword, but he was in no condition to fight.

"Easy," Lofty whispered behind him. "I've got your back."

Prisoners lay on wooden beds, warily watching them pass. In the distance, rough retching broke the silence.

"Got any food?" a dirty-faced man pleaded, poking his arms through the bars.

In the last cell on the left, Bill was crouched over a wooden pail, vomiting. "You!" He let out a string of curses, then bent over his bucket again.

The cloying scent made Tomaaz's stomach turn. Thankfully, he'd only had bread for breakfast. Lofty wrinkled his nose, and mimed gagging.

In the cell opposite Bill's, Pa was pacing. He hurried over to the bars. "Still in pain, Son?"

Tomaaz shrugged. "They treating you all right?"

Pa snorted. "Those sharding idiots will all be killed in their sleep."

"I heard that," called the guard down the hall. "Are you threatening murder?"

Pa leaned forward, speaking quietly. "You should've let yourself be healed yesterday. You can hardly walk. When tharuks arrive, you'll be easy pickings, Son."

"I had to help Lovina. You saw her back."

"Lovina?" Bill approached the bars of his cell. "Boys, where's my daughter?" He reached a grasping hand through the bars, beckoning to Lofty. "I helped you with those bets. Helped you get rich, I did. Surely, you can ask my daughter to bring me my favorite tea?"

Swayweed tea.

Lofty winked at him. "Of course I will, Bill." He turned back to Pa, rolling his eyes. "My father come to see you this morning?"

"Yes," Pa whispered. "He's recruiting those who will fight, but there aren't enough. See who you can find. Young, fit, strong. Although your Pa has never fought tharuks, he'll train them as well as he can." Hans shook his head. "If only I was out of here."

"What do you want me to do?" Tomaaz asked. "I could drill them in sword fighting."

Deep grooves furrowed Pa's forehead. "Not now, you can't. Go and rest in bed," he said. "Heal up before those beasts arrive."

Pa thought he was useless because he was injured. Tension coiled deep in Tomaaz's belly, like a tharuk tusk driving through his innards.

§

Gingerly, Lovina stirred, bracing herself. Bill's kick never came. Neither did his usual guttural shout. Something was odd. There was no dull ache in her back. No searing. No pain at all. Then she remembered.

Earlier today, Ana had healed her, telling her that not even piaua juice could erase such extensive scarring. It'd been years since her back hadn't been ripped bloody by Bill's lash. Every day she'd carried that pain. Some days it had swallowed her.

Now it was gone.

Her hand brushed against the softest fabric she'd felt since … distant memories tried to break through, like glimmers, but swirling fog devoured them. She sat up, rolling her shoulders, allowing herself to smile, a fleeting tentative thing.

The floorboards creaked. Through the gray shrouding her vision, a man approached, reaching out a hand. "It's all right. I won't hurt you."

Lovina flinched, pulling her knees up to her chest and curling in on herself. Bill had always said that, the yellow gleam of swayweed bright in his eyes as he raised the whip. She huddled against the wall.

The man placed something on the bed, then retreated. "The berries are for you. They'll help the fog go away."

The man must be lying. Why would he want to lift the fog? Lovina couldn't remember life without the debilitating blanket across her vision and mind. She peered through the gray at three burnt-orange berries, shriveled with age, on the quilt.

"I'll get you some water."

"No!" The whisper burst from her in a violent exhalation. She snatched the berries. They were dry—tiny nuggets of hope clutched tight in her hand.

What had Bill said? His water made her biddable. Obedient. Lovina snorted. Bill's water *enslaved her to his will*. This man had offered her water too. What did he want? She sat on the bed, gripping the berries, staring at him, fog weaving between them, keeping her newly-healed back pressed hard against the wall.

§

Lofty helped Tomaaz off the horse. "Why do you want to see Lovina anyway?" he asked. "I thought you liked Beatrice."

"Huh! Not anymore." The hurt of Beatrice spitting on Tomaaz still rankled, but it was nothing compared to what Bill had done to Lovina. "He deserves his hands cut off, Bill does." Tomaaz clenched his fists. "Treating his daughter like that."

"I doubt she's his daughter. They say tharuks often reward their spies with slaves from Death Valley."

"Death Valley!" Could Lovina really have been there? From living hell with Zens to further hell with Bill—a bleak existence. Tomaaz would never forget the blood-red, pus-yellow and faded-scar latticework across her back. Those whip marks were seared into his brain, hotter than the burns on his shins.

"She's in the littlings room," Lofty said as they crossed the threshold to his home.

Tomaaz hobbled past the kitchen table, toward the bedroom.

Ana closed a door with a click. Her shrewd eyes turned to Tomaaz. "You're here to see Lovina?"

He nodded, reaching for the door handle.

Ana placed a hand on his forearm. "Go softly. See if she'll take the clear-mind berries we gave her."

Clear-mind—to combat numlock. "I'll try." He turned the handle.

The room was bright with sunlight. The large bed for Lofty's three youngest brothers was pushed up against the wall. Lovina was scrunched in the corner, bleary-eyed, her face pinched with suspicion and fear.

Tomaaz closed the door and sat in a chair, resting his throbbing legs. So much mistrust. So tense and scared—not that he blamed her.

"Lovina," he scarcely dared breathe her name, afraid of startling her. "I trust Ernst and Ana. I've known them all my life. When I was small, we used to fish for freshwater lobsters in the creek. You know the ones?"

Her gaze flitted to the window, the door, around the walls and back to his face.

Her fear made his chest ache. He and Ezaara had grown up surrounded by love. Imagine living the way Lovina had.

Actually, he couldn't imagine it at all.

§

Tomaaz spun stories of sunny littling days in streams and forests, playing outdoors with his sister and friend. His gentle voice floated through Lovina's fog, his golden hair catching the sun. She leaned forward, straining to hear as he wove tales of the desert lands over the Naobian sea, the thriving metropolis of Montanara and the lush green flatlands past the Grande Alps.

The gray mists still swamped her, stopping her mind from forming pictures, but his words were soothing. Lovina's muscles loosened and she closed her eyes, listening.

"Lovina, do you want to be free of the fog?"

Hearing him rise, she snapped her eyes open. No fog meant feeling pain. She shook her head, gripping the berries tighter.

§

As a gold-tinged dawn tickled the treetops, Tomaaz walked to Lofty's house. Ana's healing poultice had helped his burns, but by the time he got there, his legs were throbbing.

Lofty craned his head around the door, a gaggle of littling brothers clutching his legs. "Tomaaz! How did you get here? Don't tell me you walked? Yesterday's horse ride nearly did you in."

Tomaaz shrugged. "Can't keep a good man down." He went into the house and approached Ana. "Has Lovina taken her clear-mind berries yet?"

"No, but she's awake. Maybe you could try again."

All he'd done was soothe her with stories. The poor girl needed more than that. She needed a real healer, like Ma. Shards, where was Ma? Heading straight for tharuks? He swallowed, hoping she was all right.

Lovina was hunched amid the crumpled bedding.

"Good morning, Lovina."

Head tilted, she started, a curtain of lank hair falling over her thin face.

Tomaaz sat down and started his story telling. He was soon interrupted by Ana, holding two bowls of steaming porridge laced with honey. After only eating flatbread for the last day, the aroma was like breathing in heaven.

"Thank you."

"See if you can get her to eat," Ana whispered. "She's so thin."

Tomaaz carried the bowls to Lovina's bedside, talking the entire way. "You must be hungry. This looks delicious. Here." He put her bowl on the bedside table, sitting near her bed. Then he picked up his spoon and dug in. "Mm, Ana makes the best porridge in Lush Valley."

Lovina shook the hair out of her face. She flared her nostrils, licking her lips. Her hungry eyes watched his spoon go from his bowl to his mouth and back, twice, before he realized what the problem was.

"Lovina, it's not poisoned." Using his spoon, Tomaaz ate a mouthful of her food. "See?"

She shook her head, glancing at her own spoon.

"And your spoon's all right too. Look." He used her spoon to take a mouthful from his bowl. "I can get you a fresh portion, if you want."

She snatched her bowl and spoon from him. Within moments, she'd downed a few spoonfuls and put the bowl down, clutching her stomach.

She'd eaten so little. What had Bill fed her? How had she survived?

§

Although Tomaaz's stories were funny, over the last eight years with Bill, the well of laughs inside Lovina had run dry. How could she ever feel anything again? Except endless pain and the weight of drudgery. And the gray, pressing her flat against the ground, all fire gone out of her, bending her to Bill's will.

Lovina's fog seemed thinner. Or was it because Tomaaz was so near that she could see the startling green of his eyes? He watched her, weaving a peaceful melody with his quiet words.

Then he stopped.

Beyond the window, birds called. The silence in the room stretched. His eyes on hers, Tomaaz slowly reached out. Lovina wanted to shrink back, but the kindness in his gaze pinned her.

"Lovina." His touch was gentle as he prized her fingers open. "Lovina," he whispered, "take the clear-mind and free yourself."

She shouldn't trust anyone, but she parted her lips and popped the berries in her mouth.

He took her cup of water from the bedside and drank deeply from it, then passed it to her. His message was clear: if it's poisoned, I'll die with you.

She clutched the cold metal of the cup and swigged water down her parched throat. It was cool, refreshing. Pure—not tinged with numlock, like the awful stuff Bill gave her.

Tomaaz smiled, sunlight catching in his blond hair. He leaned back against the wall, wincing as he moved his legs, and fell asleep.

Gradually, the fog drifted from Lovina's vision until she could see him clearly for the first time. His sleeping eyes were fringed with blond lashes and he was smiling faintly in his sleep. His tousled hair hung across his shoulders, which rose and fell as he breathed. His hands had callouses from hard work, but were clean, and his nails were neatly trimmed.

Lovina glanced at her own. The nails that weren't ripped and torn were pitted with black grime. Her hands were scarred where Bill had burnt her with hot coals when she'd been too slow making his swayweed tea. And she had callouses, too, many more than Tomaaz.

There was a slight change in Tomaaz's breathing.

Lovina looked up, trapped by his green gaze.

The fog on her feelings lifted, and something tight unfurled inside her chest.

Western Settlement

Tharuk 458 slugged back the last of its ale and stomped across the road to pee in the forest. At the sound of bird wings, it looked up. An old crow was flapping haphazardly, losing height. As it neared, the crow squawked Zens' two-note call. It wanted to talk. Stepping out onto the road, 458 held its arm out so the crow could land. The silly bird was so tired, it dropped in the dirt at 458's feet.

Picking the crow up, 458 touched its furry fingers to the bird's skull. Zens had drilled his tharuks for weeks, teaching them how to mind-meld with these daft birds. Sometimes their messages were garbled, but this crow's message was clear. *"Find this tall female with black hair."* The bird relayed the woman's image and scent through its memories.

Zens' stones did that. Implanted in the birds' heads, they allowed birds to mind-meld when touching someone, and enhanced these puny bird-brains' sense of smell—useful for a tracker. His nostrils twitched out of habit, trying to catch the elusive smell of this woman, but he couldn't. A dragon rider, she'd make a fine prize for Zens, alive or dead.

The bird croaked under its fingers. *"Alive,"* it melded. *"The spy said capture her alive."*

"Of course," melded the tracker. That still left scope for torture. After their troop's ruined infiltration into Lush Valley, he and his underlings had been killing time in the tavern, rather than returning to Commander Zens. Losing an entire troop on the Western Pass was not an incident Zens could laugh off. Hands would be severed. Yes, hands and feet, not just a harmless ear or toe. Heads could roll.

"Not finished," the bird croaked in his mind. *"This is the new Queen's Rider."*

A light-haired female shot into his mind. He knew that one—she'd been riding the beast that had slaughtered his troop, flaming them, high in the mountain pass, just two days ago. The crow squawked again. Another message? 458 kept his hands on the bird's head.

"The Queen's Rider is the dark-haired woman's daughter," the crow said.

Good, it would make the dark female's suffering even more enjoyable, knowing he was avenging his troops. *"Where is this dark-haired female? How can I find her?"* he asked.

"On her way here," the crow replied.

Thick globules of hunting saliva dribbled off 458's tusks. When she got here, 458 would be ready.

§

After two weary days, Marlies reined Star in near the ring road around Western Settlement. Her backside was aching, her back was sore, and Star needed a decent rest. While Star cropped tufts of grass at the forest's edge, Marlies dismounted and crept forward, peering through the foliage. On the other side of the road, bright lamplight shone through the windows of Nick's inn. Voices and laughter drifted through an open shutter. The clack of nukils meant a game was going on in the taproom. A cart rumbled along the road, loaded with hay, and a lone rider or two passed, making Star prick up her ears.

Marlies ate some freshweed to mask her scent, waiting for it to take effect. Her years of being a Dragon Corps spy for Tonio and Zaarusha had taught her stealth. That beacon fire had been a clear warning. Anything could be waiting.

When the road and the inn's grounds were clear, Marlies took Star into the stable yards, settling her into a stall, feeding and watering her and brushing her down. She scratched her mare's nose. "Thank you, girl." Her horse would never make it over the Western Alps, so she'd be going on foot from here. Star nuzzled her hand. Marlies gave her one last pat and, with stinging eyes, left the stables.

Ezaara was gone. As the daughter of a dragonet killer, she'd be facing scorn and prejudice. And Tomaaz and Hans would soon be in danger. She could lose everyone and still fail Zaarusha.

Zaarusha's words sprang to mind, making her insides churn. *You fled—that was an act of cowardice.* She had no one but herself to blame, and who was she to complain? The queen had lost everyone she loved: her rider, Anakisha; her mated dragon, Syan; his rider, Yanir; her purple dragonet; and now, the latest blow, her son.

Marlies straightened her shoulders. She had to try, for her queen's sake. And if she succeeded, somewhere out there, her silver-scaled Liesar was waiting. She slipped through the shadows to the back door of the inn and opened it a crack. Good, no one was around. She stepped inside. Now, to find Nick.

The kitchen door burst open, and a gangly figure bowled out, laden with platters. As the door swung shut behind him, his eyebrows shot up. "Marlies?" he whispered.

"Hello, Nick." He was leaner, but his eyes still danced with merriment, and that ropey scar from a tharuk's claws still twisted across his left cheek and down his neck. Twenty years ago, she'd managed to stop him bleeding out, but the result wasn't pretty.

"Wait here a moment," he said. "I'll be right back." As he opened the taproom door, the stench of rot wafted out. A guttural growl made her neck prickle.

Tharuks—here in Nick's inn. Years ago, Nick had been a loyal dragon friend. Had he turned? Half her instincts screamed to flee, and the other half said to trust him. Paralyzed, Marlies hesitated.

The taproom door opened and Nick came back out. "Let's get you a room before *someone* discovers you're here." He whisked her up the stairs and ushered her inside a room, closing the door behind him.

Weary, Marlies sank into a chair. "Since when do you serve *them?*"

Nick raised an eyebrow. "Since they turned up two days ago, telling me they'd kill my family if I didn't."

Two days ago—when Zaarusha had come. Was he telling the truth? "How many trackers, mind-benders and grunts?"

He grinned. "Just like the old days. Always sharp, weren't you?" His face grew serious. "Three tharuks: one tracker—a big mean-looking cur—and two dull-witted grunts. They're rooming downstairs." Nick leaned in. "A crow arrived yesterday and, since then, they've been asking around town after a tall dark-haired woman. They've checked every tavern in town."

Marlies frowned. "Tharuks have trained crows to carry messages?"

"There was no message tube tied to the crow's leg. My son, Urs, saw the tracker touching the crow's head. He thinks tharuks can mind-meld with them."

Strange. But then, why would Bill have been carrying a crow? And what about the bird that had swooped over her as she'd left Lush Valley? Bill's malicious gaze still made her flesh crawl. Could it have been his bird that Urs had seen?

"I'm sorry, Marlies, but there's worse news." Nick shook his head. "Since the tracker melded with that bird, it has been sniffing all around the village. I think it's got your scent."

A chill skittered across Marlies' shoulders. If tharuks took her, she'd never save Zaarusha's son. She stood, pulling her rucksack back on her shoulders. "I have to leave."

Nick put a hand on her arm. "Marlies, you look exhausted. Stay and rest. I'll drop some woozy weed into the tharuks' next ale."

This was it: she either trusted Nick or she didn't. Actually, she didn't have much choice. She was as worn out as Hans' holey old boots. She'd sleep with her dagger on her pillow tonight. Marlies slumped back in the chair. "And then what? I sneak out at the crack of dawn while they're still out cold?"

"Let me think about it. I'll meddle with their drinks, then bring you up some dinner. We can talk then."

"Be careful, Nick. Don't let them catch you."

When Nick left, Marlies locked the door and checked the window. It was a bit squeaky, but, in a pinch, she could jump to the ground. Leaving her rucksack packed and her dagger unsheathed, she rested until Nick returned with a plate of dark stew and mashed potatoes.

"The two grunts are out like doused lamps, snoring in the taproom," he said, passing her the plate. "The tracker's big, though, so the woozy weed it took may take longer to work."

Mouth watering, Marlies took a bite. "Oh, this is good," she gestured at the plate. "How much woozy weed did you give the tracker?"

"A double dose, but it only drank half."

"That might not be enough. I'll need to leave early. What's the fastest way over the pass?"

"The pass isn't the fastest route. Urs and I discovered a tunnel. It'll cut half a day off your journey and stop any crows or tharuks from spying on you."

"Sounds good. Where is it?" She dipped bread into her gravy.

"The entrance is above the tree line, behind a boulder shaped like a sitting dog. You'll see it as you emerge from the forest. We keep supplies in the first alcove on the right, and from there, you'd have a clear line of sight to the entrance. That is, if you can still shoot an arrow straight?" Nick's mouth twitched in a grim smile, his scar tugging at the corner.

"Of course I can, assuming I get out of here alive."

"Well, yes."

A big assumption, given the beasts downstairs and their infamous bloodlust.

§

Marlies sat up in bed, nerves jangling. Something had woken her. She cocked her head, but couldn't hear anything. The stench of tharuk slunk into her room. Slipping out of bed and into her boots, she snatched up her dagger and positioned herself behind the door.

A floorboard creaked. Someone shuffled along the hall. Then light footsteps came bounding up the stairs.

"Oh, there you are, sir," Nick's voice echoed down the corridor.

A low growl made the hairs on Marlies' arms rise.

"The kitchen's along this way, sir. I apologize, I know this place is a terrible maze, but you'll get used to it eventually." Nick was prattling like a typical innkeeper, distracting the beast. "Wait until you see what we have on the menu—eggs, chicken, fried potatoes. I can make something else if you'd like." Although his light footsteps were accompanied by heavier ones down the stairs, the stink still lingered.

No one would be safe until these beasts were destroyed. If she escaped, what would they do to Nick and his family? She couldn't have any more innocent deaths on her conscience. Marlies pulled the creaking window open and tossed her rucksack outside. Palming her dagger, she opened the door and slipped into the hall. She made her way to the top of the stairs and slid noiselessly down the wooden banister. As she landed, the tharuk spun. Marlies ducked under its slashing claws and plunged her knife into its throat. The tharuk slumped to the floor.

Another tharuk barreled down the hallway. "You!" it snarled, red eyes glinting as it raced after her.

Flinging the taproom door open, Marlies called to Nick, "Take your family and flee." Fangs! There was another one in here, sleeping. Marlies raced through the room. The beast lumbered to its feet, springing at her. She flung a chair through the window, spraying glass, then vaulted onto the table. The tharuk swiped, snagging its claws on the edge of her cloak. She yanked the fabric free, ripping a corner, and jumped out the window. Shaking the glass off her rucksack, Marlies grabbed her bow and quiver.

The tharuk thrust its pig-shaped snout out the window, grasped jagged glass shards and broke them off. Gripping the ledge with its claws, it surged out.

Marlies ran.

The snarling beast pounded after her.

She plunged into the forest. Growls ricocheted among the trees. What had she been thinking? She'd be dead in no time. Legs and arms pumping, Marlies raced. There, that knoll—if she could get a little height she'd be able to shoot. Scrambling up the hillock, she turned, nocking an arrow, and shot. Too wide. She nocked again. This time her arrow went through the tharuk's eye. Its roar cut off mid-bellow and it fell, black blood gushing over its snout.

The third one would be on her scent at any moment. Marlies fled up the slope, bashing her way through bushes until she found a trail. Roars echoed from below. It was coming.

§

One underling was dead and another was barging through the forest to head off the dark-haired female. 458 shook its head and roared. There were better ways to deal with humans. It hacked the hand off the dead underling, tattooed wrist and all, and tucked the hand into its pocket. The tracker stomped along the hallway. The innkeeper chose that moment to step into the hall. Perfect. Grabbing the innkeeper in a throttle hold, the tharuk squeezed.

The man's eyes bulged with fear and his throat gurgled.

"Hah, little human. You were hiding the woman. Who is she? Where is she going?"

"Don't know."

"No, *I* don't know." 458 tightened his hold. "But *you* do."

The innkeeper's face grew pale, and his eyelids fluttered. Although the angry burn in 458's blood demanded quenching, killing this cur was not the answer. The tracker slackened his grip, so the man could speak. "Talk, or your children will die."

That worked. The man squawked, "I—I've never seen her before. I have no idea where she's going or who she is."

458 dropped the human and ran outside. There was only one way over these mountains: the female would be heading for the pass. 458—swifter than other tharuks—raced for the mountainside. It couldn't track its quarry because it hadn't been able to scent anything since three days ago, when up in the pass, that dragon had burned its snout. Stinking dragon scum.

§

Clutching his aching throat, Nick raced to the kitchen, croaking for Urs. His son appeared, an axe in his white-knuckled grip.

"No, Urs, don't fight them. This is only the beginning. More will come. Esmeralda and the littlings are shoving supplies into the cart. Go, harness the horses. We're leaving."

"But those—"

"Just go." Nick indicated his scar, the thick rope that had tugged at his face and throat. "Quick! Go!" Urs knew what tharuks had done to him and Urs' mother, Lisa, his deceased first wife. May her soul soar with departed dragons.

Urs ran out the back door.

Nick wrenched a board off the pantry wall and retrieved his pouch of coins. Ducking into the bedrooms, he snatched up an armful of quilts and ran to the stables.

Urs was fastening the last harness. "Da, I found that woman's horse, and sent it back to Lush Valley."

"Thank you, Son." Nick flung the quilts in the back, where his wife and littlings were seated. "Lie down and stay still," he urged the littlings. Esmeralda threw the quilts over them.

Nick and Urs jumped onto the box seat. Nick snapped the reins.

When they made it to the ring road, he glanced up at the mountainside. The tharuk was a furlong below dog rock. Marlies was nowhere to be seen, but she was up there, all right. She'd been wearing one of Master Giddi's mage cloaks, which helped her blend in with her surroundings.

"Pa, look." Urs pointed.

Marlies appeared, just below the tunnel.

The tharuk surged upward.

Nick breathed a sigh of relief. That hadn't been an accident. Marlies had deliberately shown herself, luring the tracker on to buy his family time to escape. He touched his scar. He owed her his life—again.

§

Marlies ran into the tunnel. Not wasting precious moments to let her eyes adjust, she patted the right wall until she found the alcove, and went inside. There were Nick's supplies. But, from here, with light glaring from the cave mouth, she wouldn't see her enemy well.

She moved down the tunnel, finding another alcove. Here, she'd be able to see the tharuk in the dim without blinding herself. Marlies dumped her rucksack, nocked her bow and waited.

A faint scrape sounded outside the tunnel. Goosebumps skimmed her arms. It was coming.

If only Hans were here, he'd use his dragon sight to look through the rock, and mind-meld so she could see. Heart thumping, Marlies drew back her bowstring.

Another scrape. The light at the entrance was blotted out for a moment. There was a snuffle. The beast was inside, hovering around the cave entrance. It went straight to the first alcove. She'd taken freshweed in the forest, so it couldn't have scented her. Had Nick betrayed her? As she positioned her bow, the end scraped the wall. The tharuk tensed, then charged.

Shards, did it have night vision?

Marlies let an arrow fly. It bounced off the beast's armored vest. Too low. She nocked again and aimed at its forehead. The tharuk instinctively ducked and the arrow hit its arm.

The beast bellowed, its roars reverberating in the tunnel. The tracker lunged, claws out, its rot smothering her. Dropping her bow, Marlies drew her sword. As the tracker lunged again, she rammed the sword at its belly. But the sword bounced off armor.

Marlies struck again, a glancing blow off the monster's neck. The tharuk swiped, just missing her face. She danced out of reach. This couldn't go on forever—sooner or later it would kill her. Her foot hit the wall behind her. Trapped!

"Stupid human," the tharuk gloated. "I got you now."

Marlies leaped toward the beast, taking it by surprise, and rammed her sword upward into the soft flesh under its chin. The beast staggered, clutching at her blade. Using her weight, she drove the sword into its skull. She let go, kicking the beast in the stomach, and it fell, arms flailing, onto the stone. The tharuk twitched a few times, then lay still. Marlies palmed her dagger and leaned against the wall, catching her breath, waiting to see if it moved.

She counted a hundred heartbeats, then placed her foot on the beast's shoulder to tug her sword free. Slick with her enemy's blood, her boot slipped a little. It was dead, all right. After cleaning her sword on the beast's fur, she dragged the tracker into the alcove and grabbed her rucksack and bow, taking a moment to put a few of the beast's poisoned arrows into her quiver. She had to get a move on.

Nipping along to Nick's alcove, she looked inside and found food, water, and, of all the luck, dragon's breath, a rare mountain flower. When shaken, the petals emitted a soft glow. Thank the Egg, Nick was resourceful. She put half a dozen vials in her rucksack, and taking some twine, shook a vial, then bound it to her forehead. Tucking a couple of dried apples in her pockets, she took a swig of water from one of Nick's waterskins.

As she stepped out of Nick's alcove, rustling wings filled the tunnel. Bats? No, birds, from outside. Crows cawed, diving at her, talons out, sharp beaks pecking at her face. Grabbing her sword, Marlies swung it in an arc, knocking a bird to the ground. She yelled, swinging wildly and stomping.

The birds left in a swarm, dark shadows against the light as they fled.

Her dragon's breath light casting sinister shapes on the wall, Marlies ran deeper into the tunnel. It was only a matter of time before those crows reported her presence to other tharuks, or even to Zens himself.

Trapped

Marlies jammed the toe of her boot into a crevice and pulled. A few more handholds and she'd be out of this endless vertical shaft. Thank the Egg, she'd kept up her training, often journeying into the Grande Alps to keep her mountaineering skills sharp. Half the reason they'd trained Tomaaz and Ezaara in combat and archery was to keep their own skills honed—and because one day, she and Hans had hoped to ride their dragons with their family at their sides.

Mind you, she'd never see Liesar again if she lost her grip and plummeted to the bottom of this chimney. And it had been years. Every day she and Hans had lived in Lush Valley, they'd missed their dragons, trying to bury their grief in Lush Valley life. It had never been enough.

Marlies clambered out and sat, legs dangling over the black hole. Peering down, her light only illuminated a tiny part of what she'd just climbed. She sipped water and munched on flatbread and dried beef. It'd been four days since Ezaara had disappeared from Lush Valley, so she'd have arrived at Dragons' Hold yesterday. How was she finding it? Shards, she should have prepared her daughter better, should have taught her in dragon lore and protocol. She'd failed as a mother and a rider.

Sighing, she pulled her rucksack on and trudged upward, rounding a corner. Was it her imagination, or was it getting lighter ahead?

Around the next corner, it *was* lighter—the exit was near. She drew her sword, and made her way stealthily toward a cavern. The exit was half-obscured by bushes, light filtering through their foliage. A breeze wafted across Marlies' neck. She turned. Behind, in the left wall, there was a narrow aperture. Marlies stole over and squeezed through, dragging her rucksack in after her. Narrow steps led upward, giving her barely enough space to get through. She ascended, her sword at the ready.

The steps opened into a chamber directly above the exit cavern below, with a few holes in the floor. Sunlight streamed through a narrow slit in the far wall. The chamber was empty. Why go to all the trouble of having a secret cavern if there was nothing in it? Dragon riders had hidey holes all across the realm, but they kept them supplied with food, clothing and a few weapons. This one was no use to anyone.

A voice floated up from outside. Marlies nipped over to the slit in the rock. She was above the tree line, the forest sprawling past the foot of the mountain to the Flatlands, where her father had taken her as a littling. A rock slide slashed a scar across the greenery, and a goat track led to the shrubbery at the cave mouth.

Two tharuks were tromping up the trail, arguing. "What if crows were wrong?"

"Want to lose a hand?"

"No. Long climb. That's all."

"We climb because Zens. Want that troop leader report us?"

"Ah … no. I like hands."

The larger tharuk laughed harshly. "Then hold onto them." It gestured at the bushes. "Quiet. Nearly there."

The beasts were making such a racket. Marlies turned, evaluating the room. It wasn't useless, after all. Someone had designed it with kill holes, some angled toward the entrance and others to the rear of the cavern.

Taking owl-wort leaves from her healer's pouch, she chewed them, then Marlies laid the dead tracker's poisoned arrows next to two of the holes and a stone by another. She nocked her bow, careful not to touch the poisoned tip, and waited. Soon the owl-wort took effect, making her view of the dim cavern below much clearer. Her skin crawled with impatience until the tharuks rustled the bushes.

Rasping breaths and footsteps echoed in the tunnel. The large tharuk passed under the first hole. Marlies increased the tension on her bow. She waited. When the tharuk was under the third hole, she nudged the stone with her boot, sending it clattering into the cavern below. The beast whirled in surprise, giving Marlies a perfect shot. Her arrow zipped through the air and struck the tharuk in the temple.

"What was that?" its companion asked, entering the tunnel.

Marlies turned and fired down the front kill hole. Her arrow lodged in the tharuk's neck. Clutching at the shaft with its claws, it toppled to the stone.

She threw on her rucksack and fled down the stairs into the cavern. She removed the tharuks' bows from their backs, placing them in their paws. With any luck, someone might think these two had killed each other with their own arrows. Then again, maybe not—the crows and the dead tracker were damning evidence.

She shook her head. Years ago, dragons had kept Zens' tharuks confined behind the Terramites, the mountains between Death Valley and the Flatlands. Tharuks had only dared to make occasional forays into the Flatlands to plunder and enslave citizens of Dragons' Realm. Dragons had always driven them back.

Now, these brutes were everywhere.

§

Marlies froze among the foliage of a towering gum tree, glad she'd taken freshweed to stop the tharuks from scenting her. She pulled her camouflage cloak around her tightly, watching two tharuks stomp around the forest floor. In the four days since she'd left the tunnel mouth, it was the third time that they'd gotten this close.

"Always the same," snarled the hulking tharuk with a broken tusk. "Scent's gone again. Does that human fly?"

"Maybe," answered a runty tharuk, gazing up at the sky.

Broken Tusk cuffed Runty, sending it sprawling through the leaves into the trunk of Marlies' gum tree. "Stay there," Broken Tusk snapped. "Break time."

"W-we're not g-going to sleep, are w-we? If Zens c-catches us—"

"How would Zens know? I'm knackered. Shuddup. Move over." Broken Tusk kicked Runty, persuading it to shuffle over, then slumped to the ground, against the trunk.

"It killed two of us by that tunnel. M-might be dangerous."

"Don't be stupid. They was fighting. That female is gone. Now, sleep." Broken Tusk clobbered its underling, closed its eyes and was soon snoring.

Runty gibbered for a moment, then dozed off, no doubt lulled to sleep by the melodious cacophony Broken Tusk was conjuring through its piggy snout.

Marlies rolled her eyes. Charming! Trapped by snoring tharuks. There had to be a way out of here. She drummed her fingers lightly on the branch. A thrum answered her. She laid her hand on the smooth bark, inhaling the eucalyptus scent as the leaves around her rustled.

Be daring, be brave. Use my leaves to rid our forest of these vermin.

How?

Sacrifice is worthwhile for a greater cause.

An image of blazing gum trees appeared in her mind.

Oh shards, no. Everyone on the edge of the Flatlands knew that in intense heat, gums could combust due to the oil in their leaves. But to willingly offer? This tree was truly noble.

The tree gave an encouraging rustle.

It just might work. Extracting a fire bean and an arrow from her rucksack, Marlies plucked some gum leaves, crushing them and rubbing them along the wooden shaft of the arrow, coating it with eucalyptus oil. She wrapped more crushed leaves in a scrap of fabric from her healer's pouch, and tied it around the arrow head. Holding the arrow between her knees, she broke the fire bean against the leaf bundle. The bean ignited instantly, and the leaves flared. Snatching up her bow, she shot the flaming arrow at a pile of dry leaves, a distance from the sleeping babes. She snorted, baby monsters, more like. She wished them nightmares.

The leaves caught, but the tharuks kept snoozing. Shards, she didn't want the whole forest to go up in flames while they had their beauty sleep. Marlies dropped some leaves on the tharuks' faces. No response, except a giant snore from Broken Tusk. The leaf pile was blazing now.

Desperate, Marlies peeled long strips of loose bark from the gum branch and dropped them onto Broken Tusk's snout.

Broken Tusk spluttered, jumping to its feet. "Fire! Hey, lazy. Get up!" It booted Runty, and they both snatched up their water skins, rushing toward the flames.

It was in their best interests to put out the fire before the entire forest burned. Her work done, Marlies jumped into a neighboring tree and made her way northeast toward the Flatlands.

§

476 shoved the weakling toward the fire, bellowing, "Use your water first!"

"B-but I d-don't—"

"Now!"

The weakling threw water at the flames, a fly spitting against the wind—too little force and not enough fluid. Soon runt's skin was empty.

"Smother the flames with the skin," 476 roared, shoving the weakling closer, using it as a shield against the heat. The pathetic runt whimpered as it got close to the flames, shielding its face with the waterskin.

"Smother it. Too scared to use the skin? Use rocks, then." 476 picked up a rock, tossing it at the burning leaves. Soon the fire would be out of control and they'd have to flee, like beaten dogs. If they survived, Zens would murder them for losing their quarry. 476 cast around for something bigger to smother the fire with.

The weakling tossed a rock or two.

"Bigger. Get that boulder," 476 ordered.

The weakling tried uselessly to prize the enormous boulder from the ground with its claws.

Now, there was something that would smother the fire perfectly. 476 brought a rock crashing down onto the runt's skull, smashing its head against the boulder and killing it instantly. Then 476 lifted the weakling's body, almost hooking it on its broken tusk, and carried it to the burning leaves. It threw the body onto the flames, rolling it back and forth until the worst of the fire had died. The rest, it doused with its own waterskin.

By the time 476 was done, its paws were singed, its tongue was thick with smoke, and its eyes were stinging. The cloying stench of burnt gum clung to its nostrils, making it impossible to track anything. 476 hacked the burnt hand off its dead underling. It snarled, snatching up the waterskin and limping toward a river, so it could clear its senses, and track down whatever had started that fire—it must have been the prey they were seeking.

Captive

Two days in this rotting cell and still no chance of escape. Hans paced along the back wall: four steps north, four steps south, four steps north again …

Bill's constant melody of retching and ranting was wearying, but it least it was better than when Bill trembled on his thin mattress, howling. No one who ever witnessed that would want to take swayweed. But then again, no one ever took it voluntarily the first time—and once they tasted it, deep-seated cravings drove them mad. That sharding Zens was sly. He milked plants to subjugate everyone to his will. Thousands of Death Valley slaves under the control of numlock were testament to that.

His boots ground grit into the floor. He and Marlies had buried their pasts for too long. He was ready to fight Zens and his beasts, to reclaim everything Zens had stolen. To avenge those whose families and loved ones Zens had destroyed.

Hans slammed his bandaged knuckles against the bars. He'd tried reason. He'd tried the fear of tharuk attack, and now he'd had enough. "I demand to see Klaus. I demand a right to a fair trial," he shouted. He had to do something. Those monsters would sweep through Western Settlement and across Lush Valley, laying waste to everything.

The guard paced down the corridor, sword in hand, glowering.

"Please, listen to me," Hans pleaded. "Tharuks are coming. I have to help the township prepare."

The guard cocked his head, scratching his bristly beard. At last, he was listening.

"What a load of horse manure," Bill bellowed. "Dragon lover! Klaus wants you in here to stop you rabble rousing. Said as much. No one here respects a man who fed his own daughter to a fiery beast!"

The guard's teeth were a slash of white against his dark beard. He smacked his sword hilt against Hans' knuckles. "Oops, that slipped." He flashed a malicious grin.

Ignoring his throbbing hand, Hans threw himself away from the bars to jog off his fury along the length of his cell. After a while, he lay on his lumpy mattress and did stomach crunches until his face beaded with sweat. Then he lunged, using the air as his sword.

It was no use. He was stuck here. His heart was good, yet Ernst would never be able to train everyone before tharuks arrived.

The guard was speaking to someone. "I'll let Klaus know that you're consorting with the dragon lover again," he sneered.

Ernst came along the corridor. "Good day, Hans." He slipped a few rounds of flatbread and some cheese through the bars. "From Ana." He wrinkled his nose at the bitter stench of Bill's latest bout of retching. "Although you may choose to eat it later."

As if the biting stench would lift later. Shrugging, Hans bit into the bread, mumbling his thanks through mouthfuls.

"How are your hands?" Ernst asked.

"Much better. The salve helped. Tell Ana, 'Thanks.'"

"Nigh on thirty men now," Ernst whispered. "Training at your place these last few days. Handy, the size of your old barn; keeps prying eyes away. I've got about another fifteen in my barn, running them through basic weapon drills, like you advised."

So, forty-five fighters. "Dagger, sword and shield?"

Ernst nodded.

"Anyone good at knife-throwing?"

"My son, Lofty. Hadn't thought of that. We'll move onto it today."

Not thought of knife-throwing? The most basic training for all dragon riders? Hans struggled not to let his frustration show. "How many archers?" he asked.

"Not enough. Less than a handful." Ernst shook his head. "Seems Klaus warned them off us."

Hans' bread turned to dust in his mouth. "You'd think he wants to die at the hands of tharuks."

Nodding grimly, Ernst whispered, "Him and everyone else. Too stubborn for their own good. What should we work on next?"

"Spears for the front line."

Ernst had never faced tharuks before. He'd lived here in Lush Valley most of his life—apart from a short sojourn when he'd ventured beyond the Grande

Alps, had his eyes opened, and met Ana, bringing her back to raise a family in this little haven. A haven that was about to become a death trap.

There was so much to convey: the best defensive moves against tharuks; tharuk attack strategies; their most common tusk maneuvers; how to evade their crushing techniques; the right spots to aim arrows to avoid their matted fur; but most importantly, how to protect yourself from tharuk mind-benders.

Running his hand through his unruly hair, Hans opened his mouth, then hesitated.

Bill was hunched over a bucket, his back to them, but his retching had stopped. He was as still as a marmot, head cocked. Listening. Even now, he was spying for the tharuks.

Shooting a meaningful glance in Bill's direction, Hans still spoke quietly, hoping Bill wouldn't realize they'd changed their topic of conversation. "Tomaaz may need a hand to harvest the carrots and the last of the potatoes. It also wouldn't harm to kill a few chooks for smoking."

Ernst shot a glance over his shoulder at Bill before replying. "Very well, I'll be back later in case you think of anything else."

No! His chance to train Ernst was slipping away, all because of that cursed spy. "Ah, wait," called Hans. How could he give Ernst a clear message about mind-benders, without letting Bill know? "Um, Tomaaz … how's he feeling since he got burned?"

"Sore." His back to Bill, Ernst raised his eyebrows.

"No, I mean his emotions, his *mind*." Hans emphasized the key words with his hands. "I'm wondering whether he's *bent* out of shape, you know, with everything that's gone on."

A flash of comprehension lit Ernst's face. "Yes, he is. Poor boy. What could help him?"

Hans sat on the bed, leaning his elbows on his knees and wringing his hands together, as if he was anxious. Sure enough, Bill sneaked a glance. "His sister's sick. His mother's gone and I'm stuck in here. He must be miserable." He sighed, shaking his head. "Maybe he could think of a nice family memory. Focus on that if he can."

Ernst gave a barely perceptible nod. "I'll try, Hans. Like you said, it's a difficult time for the lad. I'll go now, and give him a hand, but I have my own farm to tend as well."

"Thank you, and thank Ana for the bread and cheese, too."

Bill swung around. "Food, you say. Did he bring food?" He crooked a bony finger at Ernst. "Come here. Give me some," he whined. "I'm so hungry. Wretched belly gripe has left me hollow."

"Give him this." Hans ripped off a piece of flatbread. Ernst took it to Bill's cell.

Snatching the bread, Bill stuffed half of it in his mouth and the rest in his pocket. He retreated to his mattress, chewing, his eyes faintly yellow from the remnants of swayweed in his blood.

They said that spies who'd been on swayweed for years could never completely rid themselves of its effects. Hans shuddered. Better Bill than him.

Ernst left and Hans resumed his exercises.

Bill got up and took the bread out of his pocket, ripping it in tiny pieces and placing it on the sill of his barred cell window.

A crow landed on the sill, plumage shining blue-black, and stabbed its beak at the bread. It eyed Bill as he crept closer to it, but it didn't fly away. Bill stroked the bird's head, crooning, as it ate the bread. Strange—Hans thought he caught his name and Tomaaz's in Bill's mad mutterings.

§

Tomaaz adjusted the boy's grip. "Lunge again, but this time, aim higher." He pointed to the boy's opponent. "And, you, block him with the flat of your blade, not the edge."

His burnt legs aching, he sat on a barrel and watched as the two lads, not even thirteen summers, clashed swords again. If these boys were their best hope of saving the township, then there wasn't much hope at all. With so many people training in their barn, the air was stifling. Tomaaz pulled a dipper from a pail and drank deeply. He brushed sweat from his forehead. Because of his injuries, being on his feet tired him out.

After getting Lovina to take clear-mind yesterday, Ana had insisted on bandaging another healing poultice onto Tomaaz's legs. Today, he'd made up a poultice himself, happy not to have Ana fussing over him. As the healer's son, he'd applied enough poultices for Ma over the years.

The dull clash of metal rang in his ears. A couple of girls in the far corner seemed to be getting the hang of their blades. In time, they could be promising. A shame they didn't have time.

Lofty clapped a hand on his shoulder. "Feeling all right?"

"It's good not to be in bed."

Lofty hooted. "And you used to like sleeping in."

"Only because you dragged me out every night, getting us into trouble."

Lofty indicated a pair of men, about their fathers' age, clashing swords, beyond the boys. "There's Murray and Kieft. Who would've known a couple of farmers could fight so well?"

Tomaaz pointed at another pair, the same age. "Or that *they* couldn't. An ox could wield a sword better."

Lofty snorted. "A shame it's an accurate description."

Tomaaz had to smile.

"Look, Pa's back," Lofty said.

"Hello, everyone." Ernst held up an arm. "May I have your attention?"

Weary fighters sat on the ground or in the hay at the back of the barn. Someone dropped a sword.

"Sheath your weapons," Tomaaz called, remembering his first lessons from Ma and Pa as a littling. "You must keep your blade on you." He stood, handing the pail to one of his new 'warriors', so they could pass it around and refresh themselves.

"I visited Hans today," Ernst announced. "He outlined the next steps in our training. Is there anyone here who's proficient in throwing knives?"

Lofty raised his palm, and another man did, too.

"Tomaaz will stay here and continue instructing you in swordplay, while Lofty and Francois take the ten of you who are best at knifemanship for knife-throwing, but before we get to that, there's something important I need to tell you."

Everyone ceased drinking or fidgeting. All eyes were on Ernst.

"Tharuks are vicious. I've only seen a few myself and have never had to fight them, but I have seen one gut a man with his tusks in an instant." Ernst's hand made a ripping motion over his belly. "Our best defense will be to stay out of their range, hence knife-throwing, spears and archery. If any of you can have a discreet word with an archer and convince them to join us, let me know. But be careful. Klaus has filled most of them with venom.

"In the short time we have, we can't prepare everything we'd like, but we can put guards around the perimeter of the village to raise the alarm. Those in outlying farms are welcome to bring their families to stay with me or Tomaaz at night for safety. During the day, your families can go back to their fields, but keep horses saddled and ready, or hitched to carts, so you can flee to the village square if you need to." Ernst took a deep breath. "Now I come to a more difficult task."

As if everything he'd already said wasn't difficult enough.

"There are a few types of tharuks. Trackers and mind-benders are most dangerous. Trackers hunt their prey over vast distances by scenting them. You'll know them from the dark saliva that dribbles along their tusks when they're hunting. Mind-benders have black eyes, instead of the usual red eyes, and drill into your mind, forcing you to follow their will."

A chill breeze snaked through the barn, making the sweat on Tomaaz's forehead prickle.

"Hans said that the secret to overcoming mind-benders is to focus on a memory or an object, pinning it in your mind in great detail. We'll practice now. Close your eyes, everyone."

Although it was useless closing his eyes in the middle of battle, Tomaaz shut his anyway.

"In your head, picture someone you love, a place you like to go, your favorite food, or a treasured possession," Ernst said.

The moment Ernst said *someone you love,* Lovina's face shot to mind. Weird, he didn't love Lovina. He was only helping her because—

A girl's voice broke through his thoughts. "Surely if we choose someone we love, the mind-bender could use that against us."

"Good point," Ernst replied. "Concentrate on an object. See how the light plays on it. Does it have a scent? How does it feel and sound? What are you doing with it?"

Tomaaz switched his thoughts to the trees at the back of the farm, where he, Ezaara, and Lofty had played when they were littlings. It had been Ezaara's favorite hiding place. Shards, how was she now? His twin's face filled his thoughts. It was suddenly difficult to swallow. They'd never been separated for more than half a day before all this craziness had happened.

"Hold the image in your mind, while I distract you."

He was thinking of Ezaara, not the tree. Tomaaz concentrated on the rough bark, the sunlight filtering between the leaves. Ernst bellowed. Tomaaz twitched and the tree was gone.

"Focus," Ernst called.

He tried again and again, trying to block out Ernst's loud noises. A girl shrieked. Tomaaz jumped to his feet, sword drawn.

Ernst held his hands above a girl sitting cross-legged on the ground. "It's all right, everyone. I just tapped her while her eyes were shut."

Laughter broke the tension.

"Now," said Ernst, "get back to fighting, but try and fight with the image in your minds, as if your life and loved ones depend on it."

Ernst took the first group of knife-throwing candidates outside, and Tomaaz stepped up to fight one of the girls, the tree firmly fixed in his head.

§

For a week, Tomaaz's home had been full of people every evening, all heeding Ernst's advice. Pa had predicted a tharuk attack within three days of the beacon fire. Disbelievers now had even more reason to jeer at him, but Pa had impressed upon Tomaaz, Ernst and Lofty that it was only a matter of time, so every space inside was spoken for. Tomaaz had given the beds to older couples, and the living area and hallway were full of bedrolls and blankets. Littlings jumped over people's legs, excited at so many people gathering.

Tomaaz approached Torston, one of the men cooking. "Could I get you more vegetables for that stew?"

Torston gave him a knowing glance. "We don't need them, son, but if you need some fresh air, how about taking some bread to Lofty?"

Tomaaz left the house and wandered toward the road, away from Lofty and the other perimeter guards. He didn't need Lofty's joviality or jokes tonight, just a bit of time to clear his head. The last twelve days had been a whirlwind: Pa nearly burned at the stake and being thrown in jail; Ma gone, perhaps in danger; Lovina's awful injuries; and Ezaara … shards, he missed his twin sister.

In the field near the roadside, the carrot tops feathered in the breeze. Tomaaz stared at the sunset's golden light playing on the greenery, losing himself for a moment.

Footsteps crunched along the gravel road. A figure was approaching, dressed in baggy breeches—a slim woman in men's clothing. Something about her seemed familiar, but with the sun at her back, he couldn't see her features.

She drew level and turned to him, her thin face tinged by the sunset glowing off the Grande Alps. The evening breeze tickled its fingers through her brown hair. Her eyes were blue and she had a sprinkling of freckles across her nose and cheeks. Her baggy breeches were rolled up and she was wearing an over-sized boy's jerkin. It was only as she nervously lifted a scarred hand to tuck a strand of her hair behind her ear that Tomaaz recognized Lovina.

He gazed at her mutely.

"I, ah …" She froze for a moment, eyes wild like a trapped rabbit, and then spun to go.

Tomaaz took her hand. Shock registered on both of their faces. They stood a few paces apart, he holding her hand and she, startled, staring at him.

He released her, his breath escaping. "Don't go!" he whispered. Had he scared her?

She nodded, waiting.

"Lovina, I—" How did you tell a girl who'd been beaten and abused for years that you were dumbstruck by her beauty? A girl who hadn't even trusted the people who'd tried to heal her. A girl who would need years to fully trust, if she ever could. His breath sawed in and out of him. The moment stretched, the tension in their gaze searing through him. "Lovina, I'm glad you're here."

She smiled, lighting up like a splash of water in the sun.

Last Stop

Crows were thick on cottage roofs on the outskirts of Last Stop. Marlies approached, her hair wrapped in a peasant's scarf, a long dress over her riders' garb and her rucksack hidden in a sack on her back with firewood poking out the top. Marlies adjusted the firewood. It was a flimsy disguise, but better than nothing. She had enough freshweed to last her a few more days, but she was still ages away from Death Valley. She'd need to find another way to evade the tharuks hunting her.

She kept to side alleys. Music filled the air, and laughter and merriment came from the center of town. Tharuks roamed the streets. Had everyone here grown used to the presence of these monsters?

Coming around a corner, she walked smack into a tharuk's back. "Excuse me, kind sir," she said with what she hoped was a Last Stop twang. She bowed, squinting in case it noticed her turquoise eyes.

The beast snarled through dribbling saliva. Its nostrils twitched. A tracker.

Marlies kept her head down, subservient and bowed over under the firewood. Her heart hammered. She thanked the Egg for freshweed, hoping hers was still effective. This was not the place to pick a fight.

"Doesn't look like the female," muttered another tharuk to the tracker she'd banged into.

The tracker deliberated, sniffing the air. It was surprising it could smell anything other than tharuk stench.

"It's tall enough, but it doesn't smell right," the tracker concluded.

"Move on."

Relief flooding her, Marlies moved past.

"Not so fast." A thin tharuk with black eyes stepped out from a bakery next to a cobbler's shop, blocking her way. "Where are you heading?"

Shards! A mind-bender. Marlies kept the cobbler's store foremost in her mind. "Need new shoes for my boy, sir," she answered, head down. She pulled an image of Tomaaz's face into her mind, as he'd looked when he was four.

"And the wood?" barked the mind-bender.

She could feel the mind-bender pushing at her thoughts, making her head spin. "To sell, sir, in the square." Not knowing what the square looked like nowadays, she kept the cobbler's shop in mind, and the torn feet of a Lush Valley littling she'd healed last week—and her fear of tharuks, just to be convincing.

"Very well," the mind-bender barked. "Get your weakling son some shoes."

The mind-bender shoved her. She stumbled, righting herself, then ran into the cobbler's shop. Marlies made a show of examining the shoes, then bought the cheapest littling pair in the store, fishing the coins out of her healer's pouch.

"A healer?" whispered the cobbler, eying her pouch. "Rare nowadays."

"Just an old pouch I found at the market."

"I'll trade you the shoes for a remedy. My wife has had a belly gripe for a week."

Marlies glanced at the tharuks loitering outside. Was he a spy? Would he sell her for a reward?

"Please," he pleaded.

She'd taken a healer's oath. How could she refuse? Marlies slipped him a measure of koromiko. "Cook this in water and have her drink the tea," she whispered. "Thank you for the shoes," she added loudly.

"My pleasure," he said. Then, making a show of polishing the shoes, he whispered, "Stay at The Lost King, in the square. I'd get a room now before it fills up for the harvest festival."

The Lost King? Was that some oblique reference to Syan, Zaarusha's dead mate? Or even Yanir, his rider? It might be possible. Last Stop had been named after Anakisha. On the way to her final battle, she'd stopped here, for reasons unknown. After her death, the villagers had renamed the town. Nodding, Marlies swallowed a lump in her throat and hurried outside, past the tharuks, now questioning other travelers. She made her way deeper into town through the throng of merrymakers in costumes and festive clothing. With so many tharuks here, why hadn't the villagers lit their beacon fire? She scanned the sky. No sign of dragons.

The square was a hubbub. Marlies picked her way past people dancing in time to musicians playing gittern and drums, and around pigs on spits, their fat hissing as it dripped into the fire. Scanning the square, she found a faded plaque, *The Lost King,* on an old stone building covered in ivy. Her first instinct was to avoid it, in case the cobbler betrayed her, but there were no tharuks near it, so maybe the cobbler was trying to help. She wound her way through the crowd. Hawkers called out, selling toys, sweets, crafts and stacks of firewood. Littlings ran through the square, playing duck and chase. Merry punters at trestle tables with tankards of ale laughed and slapped each other on the back. In a pit of sawdust, a wrestling match was in progress, the crowd cheering the winner on. There were so many people. Life in Lush Valley had been so very quiet.

Outside The Lost King, Marlies stopped a mother with a gaggle of barefoot children and discreetly gave her the shoes. She pushed the door open, and walked between strongwood tables toward a brown-haired young woman washing tankards.

The girl, not much older than Ezaara, finished drying a glass and greeted her. "Good evening, do you need a room for the night?"

There was something strangely familiar about the girl's face. "Yes, just one night, thank you."

Three tharuks burst into the taproom, the drumbeats from the square gusting in with them. "Beer, now!" one bellowed.

"Right away," the girl responded, drawing three tankards of beer from a barrel.

The beasts sat at the bar, their backs to Marlies. She retreated to an alcove at the side of the room to wait.

Soon the girl joined her. "I'm Kisha," the girl said, reaching her hand out to shake Marlies'.

Had she just flashed the sign of a dragon friend? Or was Marlies being fanciful, mistaking that quick flick of Kisha's fingers for something it wasn't? When extending her own hand, Marlies made the answering sign, and the girl nodded.

"You're in luck," she said. "We have two rooms left upstairs." She ushered Marlies to the second floor, a finger against her lips, pointing at some of the rooms. Dragon's teeth, tharuks must be staying here. "There's a tub in your room. Would you like a bath? And a meal brought to your room?"

Marlies smiled. "That would be lovely."

Kisha ushered her inside. "Make yourself at home." She left to fetch pails of hot water.

Once Kisha had filled the tub, she pointed to the bolt on the inside of the door, indicating that Marlies should lock it, and left.

Marlies checked the window. If she needed to, she could drop to the square and make a run for it. She stripped off and dunked herself in the warm water. It was tempting to relax and let her worries soak away, but she couldn't, not with tharuks downstairs. Although the festival was still going strong outside, a trickle of unease slid down her back. So, Marlies scrubbed herself, changed into fresh small clothes and pulled on her riders' garb and peasant dress, rubbing the grubby spots with a rag. She was done in less time than it took Tomaaz to wolf down a meal.

Someone knocked. "It's Kisha with your dinner."

Thank the Egg, it hadn't been a tharuk. She slid the bolt open. "Come in."

Kisha passed her a plate of bacon, eggs and thick slabs of cheese with bread. Marlies sank onto the edge of the bed, more than ready to eat, then sleep.

Kisha slid the bolt. "We must talk." Her eyes flicked to Marlies' healer's pouch. "Do you know the remedy for limplock?"

"Why?" Marlies narrowed her eyes. Limplock was one of Zens' poisons. Fatal. She'd had more than one dragon rider die before she'd learned how to combat it. "Has someone been poisoned?"

Kisha shrugged, waiting, so Marlies answered, "A blend of herbs and minerals combats Commander Zens' vile poison."

"And how does that blend look?"

"Yellow granules," Marlies replied. Years ago, she'd developed the remedy, but— "Why are you smiling?"

"Are you the Master Healer from Dragons' Hold?"

Marlies swallowed, trying to dislodge the lump in her throat. She'd never thought she'd ever be addressed as Master Healer again. Who was Kisha? Was she working for tharuks? A spy? Within a moment, Marlies' plate was on the bed and her dagger was at Kisha's throat. "Who are you? Tell me why you want to know." Shards, she should have laughed it off. Now she'd given it away. It had been so many years since she'd played this game—she was making too many mistakes.

Staying cool, Kisha murmured, "My grandmother was Anakisha."

So that's why she'd looked familiar. Marlies sheathed her dagger. "My apologies."

"Mine too. Years ago, my grandmother told me that there would come a day when she would depart to the great flying grounds beyond. May she soar with departed dragons." Kisha pulled up a chair and sat while Marlies continued her meal. "She came to visit my mother and me before her final battle."

Marlies inhaled sharply. "So, you're the reason she came to Last Stop? Why?"

"Anakisha had a vision. She told me that when I was older, you would visit me. She said to question every healer who came here, asking whether they knew the limplock remedy." Kisha chuckled. "Most of them had no idea what I was

RIDERS OF FIRE

talking about. Anakisha told me your name was Marlies, that you would come in a dire time. She mentioned your turquoise eyes."

Marlies' jaw dropped. Zaarusha must've known some of this. A dragon and rider didn't often keep secrets. Then again, maybe not. The Queen's Rider, Anakisha, had used the gift of prophecy, but not Zaarusha—unlike Hans and Handel, who both had visions.

Kisha drew a small piece of folded leather from her pocket. "This is from Anakisha. I've kept it all these years, since I was a littling." She passed it to Marlies.

Marlies unwrapped it to reveal a jade ring engraved with whorls.

"She said that if you were ever stuck in a dire situation, to rub the ring and say my name, *Kisha*. I hope it helps you one day."

"What does it do?"

"I'm not sure. I've never used it. My grandmother emphasized the danger in using this ring too often. It's for emergencies only."

Marlies tucked the ring in her breast pocket and hugged Kisha. "Thank you. I loved your grandmother very much."

Kisha blinked several times. "Me too. Where are you going?"

The more Marlies told Kisha, the more danger Kisha would be in if tharuks questioned her, so she kept her answer vague. "Across the Flatlands."

Kisha's eyes lit up. "We have a wagon doing deliveries in the Flatlands tomorrow. We can help you across."

Marlies hesitated. Would she drag the driver into danger?

"Our driver is experienced in avoiding tharuks," Kisha added.

Better than going on foot. "I'd love a ride, then," Marlies replied.

A tharuk bellow came from the taproom, "More beer!"

"Sleep well." Kisha rushed from the room. "See you in the morning."

After finishing her meal, despite the loud festivities outside, Marlies fell asleep. It was far from restful; she twitched and turned at every sound, dreaming of tharuks stalking her through *The Lost King*.

§

476 limped into Last Stop as dawn dragged its bloody claws across the sky. His crow alighted on his outstretched arm and showed him faces and scents of travelers who'd entered the village from the south yesterday. One caught his attention.

"That one," he said, seeing the crow's memory of a tall woman who was wearing boots under her peasant dress, instead of shoes or sandals.

It had been following large bootprints before the fire in the gum trees. This female had large feet—and no strong scent. Her head was wrapped in a peasant's scarf and she was carrying a sack of firewood—a sack large enough to hide something. 476 had to find her.

His crow perched on his shoulder, 476 tromped through the alleys toward the square. Spotting a troop of tharuks who were slumbering off beer—from the smell of their stinking breath—he roused a small one with a kick.

"Who is your overseer?" 476 snarled, spit flying off its broken tusk.

The small tharuk nudged a larger beast and it scrambled to its feet. Upon seeing 476's broken tusk, this overseer practically bowed.

476 smirked. There was value in having a reputation. "You seen this female?" he barked. His crow hopped onto his outstretched arm and let the overseer touch its head and mind-meld. Behind it, the troop rose to their feet, at the ready.

The overseer motioned a mind-bender forward to touch the crow.

Black eyes gleaming, the mind-bender said, "It's that female what wanted shoes. Let's visit cobbler."

§

Bloodcurdling growls woke Marlies. Leaping out of bed, she hastily fastened her sword belt and palmed her dagger, listening. Another growl came from below her window. Marlies twitched back a curtain. Shards, she'd overslept, lulled by a bath, hot food and a soft bed. Tharuks were swarming the square, hassling hawkers, overturning stalls and holding villagers at clawtip. Thank the Egg, only a few villagers were about.

Thumping sounded on the wooden door downstairs. Doors either side of hers bashed open, and snarls filled the hall. "She's here, somewhere," a tharuk roared. "Search!"

She had to leave to protect Kisha. Marlies threw on her rucksack. Sliding the window up, she clambered onto the sill, holding on to the lintel. Should she jump?

There was no way down. Cries rang out. Poised on the window ledge, Marlies had nowhere to go except sideways. The ivy smothering the inn was going to make it hard work. Her hands gripping the tiny crevices between the stones, Marlies edged along the building, picking her way around the leaves—until her foot got tangled in a vine. Nearby, a growl rumbled. Shards! A tracker was harassing a man right below her. If she dropped ivy leaves, it'd see her. Heart pounding, Marlies extricated her foot from the vine.

Reaching her arm around the wall, she found a handhold around the corner. As she swung her leg around, her rucksack threatened to drag her off the building. She grabbed another handhold, but her foot hit a piece of loose stone, dislodging it. The chunk of stone crashed to the ground, narrowly missing a littling. The boy stared up at her, opening his mouth to shriek. Marlies smiled at him, frantically shaking her head. Wide-eyed, he snapped his mouth shut.

Marlies nipped along the wall, hand over hand, making her way along a narrow alley. Her arms were burning and her legs shaking, but if she could just get around the next corner, she'd be above the stable yards at the rear of the inn.

Someone screamed. She whipped her head around to see a tharuk chasing the littling boy down the alley. Without thinking, Marlies let go, pushing off the wall. She landed on the tharuk's back. It hit the ground, snarling. Leaping to her feet, Marlies drew her sword. The beast slashed her leg with sharp claws. Pain lanced through her. By the Egg, her calf.

She lunged and drove her sword under the tharuk's arm, through its armpit into its chest. The beast shrieked and lay still.

Wiping her sword on its fur, Marlies said to the littling. "Go. Run and hide."

The boy scarpered.

Leg burning and blood soaking through her breeches, Marlies staggered to the stable yard and wrenched the gate open. Dragging herself inside, she closed the gate and leaned her forehead against it. She closed her eyes. That had happened so fast—one moment on the wall, the next with a slashed bloody calf. Taking a deep breath, she opened her eyes and pushed off the gate.

"There you are," rumbled a deep voice behind her. Thick arms wrapped around her middle and yanked her off her feet.

§

"I don't care about your sharding ethics, Marlies," Giant John said. "Now's not the time for principles. Tharuks will find your blood—especially if you haven't taken freshweed since yesterday. Take some now, get that stuff on your wound, and let's get out of here. Hurry."

Sitting on a pile of hay in the stables where Giant John had carried her, Marlies chewed on freshweed and dribbled piaua onto her wound, bracing herself against the burn. She didn't have time to stitch it shut—so it would leave an ugly scar. Marlies pressed the edges of the gash together, watching the skin knit over before her eyes. It'd been so long since she'd used piaua on herself, she'd forgotten the deep aching burn and tugging sensation as the muscles wove together again.

Giant John, looking every bit as formidable as he had years ago, scuffed dirt over her blood, and shoveled manure over it for good measure. It was good that her old friend was Kisha's driver. Giant John was good at keeping secrets—they'd worked together for years—and he knew how to evade tharuks.

Marlies wiped the dried blood off her leg and tucked the rag under a dry horse pat. "Now, what?" She chewed some more freshweed, to help mask her scent.

"It's good to see you again, too." Giant John grinned, then gestured at a wagon piled high with vegetables and ale. He flipped the side of the wagon down, revealing a hidden compartment under the floor. "Let's make some deliveries."

Marlies clambered in and he shoved her rucksack in after her. She was wedged on her side with her pack in front of her, but at least she could reach her supplies if she needed them. She checked her dagger was still in its sheath and laid her sword next to her rucksack. This was going to be a cramped and uncomfortable journey, but it was better than facing mind-benders and trackers.

"There's a trapdoor, bolted from the inside, in case you need to escape. If I drum my fingers, freeze. If I cough, we're in dire trouble. When I ask you a question, tap once on the wagon floor to answer yes, and do nothing for no. Got it?"

Marlies tapped once.

Giant John laughed. "Where are you headed?"

"Death Valley."

His eyebrows shot up. "You don't do things by halves, do you? Let's get out of here." He flipped the side of the wagon up. Bolts slid into place and Marlies was sealed in the dark. Giant John thumped into place above her. "Hear this?" Giant John asked, drumming his fingers on the wagon seat, then coughing.

Marlies tapped once and heard his dry chuckle and the snap of the reins. The wagon creaked across the yard, then the metal-bound wheels clattered along the cobbles in the alley. Each cobble jarred Marlies' body, and she was tossed from side to side. Giant John would be taking the winding back alleys. It felt like rushing through a chasm of whitewater rapids, clinging to driftwood. Good thing she'd used piaua—with an injured leg, this trip would be as bad as Death Valley itself.

§

Giant John left the cobbled streets of Last Stop and took a barely-used lane through outlying fields. The wagon rumbled along the dusty road, the horses' hooves clopping in time to a ditty running through his head. He casually scanned the surrounding pastures. No tharuks in sight—yet. So far, he'd gotten Marlies out of Last Stop without tharuks on her trail.

Soon, he'd meet up with the main road through the Flatlands. On horseback, he could've gone across country, but then, he'd hardly be smuggling Marlies across half the realm if he was on horseback, would he? Years ago, before she'd disappeared, he'd helped her on many of her clandestine trips, but that was before he'd had a family. Kisha had surprised him last night, asking for his help transporting Marlies and promising to send word to his wife. He hadn't risked his safety for years. His wife and littling needed him. He flicked the reins. Now, his routine trip into Last Stop had turned into an adventure—hopefully, one they'd both survive, although with Marlies heading into Death Valley, he wasn't so sure.

§

The compartment was hot and stuffy and Marlies' mouth was coated in dust. An odd rhythm sounded above her—oh shards, Giant John was drumming his fingers. She froze. The familiar stench of rot wafted through cracks in the wagon bed.

"Halt!" a guttural voice growled.

How could they halt when they'd already stopped? Typical tharuk, stating the obvious.

"Where are you going? What's in that wagon?"

"I'm delivering produce. Would you like some fine cabbage?"

"Got any meat?" another tharuk called.

"You heard. Any meat?" the first snarled.

The only meat was her, trapped in this shrotty cage. Marlies could practically hear the beast drooling.

"No, sir, but what about my finest ale?" Giant John asked.

Thunking sounded above her, then a barrel lid cracking open, followed by eager slurping and the scent of beer.

Stuck in a box, like the perfect prisoner, there was nothing Marlies could do. She was helpless while tharuks could be invading her home, attacking her daughter or torturing Zaarusha's son.

Giant John thudded back onto the wagon. So, this was how Giant John had planned to get her across the Flatlands—bribery.

§

A tharuk tracker, dribble sliding off its broken tusk, was standing apart from the troop, its black eyes piercing Giant John. His head spun. Repressing a shiver of revulsion at being mind-bent, Giant John imagined the beer—remembering its mouth-watering scent, the taste sliding down his parched throat to his belly. His stomach rumbled.

The brute snarled, breaking off its gaze, and thrust its way through the horde of tharuks crowded around the barrel. It shoved them aside and rammed its snout into some of Last Stop's finest ale.

Giant John snapped the reins, and they moved on. His trick with picturing the beer had incited the monster's thirst. Thank the Egg, that broken-tusked beast was behind him. Was the other half of its tusk impaled in someone?

They were only a few fields away when roars broke out. He snapped the reins and they picked up speed. Glancing back, he saw the tharuks fighting over the ale. What a waste of good beer, but they'd fallen for it. He only had a few barrels left and their journey would take days. What would happen when their supplies ran out?

He pushed the horses on, driving through the morning, keen to get to River Forks before nightfall and find a place to stay. The next day, they'd push on to Forest Edge and Waldhaven, where his friend Benji lived. It had been a while since he'd seen Benji, but he'd put them up for the night in his barn.

Mid-afternoon, Giant John stopped and stretched his legs. He was about to flip down the side of the wagon bed to let Marlies out, when a flurry of birds took off from the trees beyond the meadow. Something had disturbed them. A tharuk or a deer? Better to be safe than sorry. He drummed his fingers on the wagon side, then rummaged through a sack. Grabbing a couple of apples, he hopped back onto the seat and pressed on. They had to get to River Forks.

Bitter Truth

The sharp clack of dress boots echoed along the prison corridor. Visitors seldom came, except Ernst and Tomaaz. The pair had kept him posted, asked for guidance on training, and brought him decent food. Hans stopped his strength exercises and peered through the bars.

Klaus was striding down the corridor, stopping to mutter a few words with each criminal. Hans caught phrases such as, "few more weeks," and "got your just desserts," and "time will tell."

How many of these men and women had been unjustly imprisoned, like him? He'd never questioned it until now.

Bill hung his arms through the bars, rubbing his hands together as Klaus approached. "Master Klaus, so nice to see you."

Hands on hips, Klaus regarded him. "Despicable, Bill, whipping a daughter like that. You won't find any sympathy here. You'll be staying behind bars as long as I can keep you there."

"But Master—"

"Don't *Master* me!" Klaus' voice was low, deadly.

Bill slunk to the back of his cell.

Surely, Klaus didn't still think his opinion mattered to Bill?

Hans kept his gaze steady as Klaus faced him. "Good morning, Klaus."

"Yes, it is a good morning, a nice peaceful morning, like all the others this past week." Klaus shook his head. "No tharuks today, Hans. Or any other day for that matter. What do you have to say for yourself?"

Eight days in this dreadful place already, and still no attack. Hans had been pondering it all day, but he doubted Klaus really wanted to know. "Perhaps tharuk scouts slipped through, but were detained in Western Settlement."

"Perhaps there wasn't a fire, Hans. Perhaps you imagined it." Klaus' lip curled. "Perhaps it's been more peaceful because your children are no longer fighting in my marketplace."

Bill was leaning forward, listening. Every afternoon, crows visited his window sill for food, and let him pet them, while he whispered at them. As if he was reporting the jail's comings and goings.

Ridiculous. Hans collected himself. The boredom in prison was addling his brain. "Maybe." Klaus was never going to listen. Never going to prepare. But, then again, perhaps he was right. Maybe tharuks weren't coming. No, Hans couldn't risk it. They had to do whatever they could. "I'd rather prepare in vain than be caught unawares. These are our children and families, our neighbors, Klaus. Wouldn't you rather be cautious than sorry?"

"Well, I'm sorry I listened to you, Hans."

Listened? Hans crushed the desperate bark of laughter that threatened to break loose from his chest. Through the bars, he grasped Klaus' shirt. "Listening is training our warriors to fight tharuks. Listening is not caring what your father told you about dragons. He was wrong, Klaus. Your grandfather was a dragon rider—a fine rider, from what I've heard—and died saving a village. Your father turned against dragons afterward, injuring any dragons that patrolled Lush Valley. That's why they don't come here. That's why they set up a beacon system. Your grandfather Frugar would not want his sacrifice to be in vain. He'd not want you to risk the lives of your loved ones because of your father's bitterness."

For a moment, Klaus stared at him, shock etched on his face. "Unhand me, you poor deluded fool." He shoved Hans' hands away and stalked off.

Bill cackled with glee. "Good try, mate. Who'd believe that crock of dung? You've sealed your fate now!"

Hans stood, head against the bars, chest heaving.

Hunted

It had been good to get out of this forsaken wagon and stretch her legs last night, but now, after another day on the road, Marlies was weary. Strange how lying around fretting could tire you out. It'd been ten days since she'd left Lush Valley. Had more tharuks breached the pass? Were Hans and Tomaaz still alive? She rubbed her calling stone, but there was no hum or buzz. Hans wasn't using his, then.

Giant John, concerned freshweed wasn't enough, had stopped at a local sty, trading vegetables for a piglet and chickens. Now there was an ominous dripping near her feet. The stink of pig urine and manure made her gag. The animals' clucking and squealing hammered at her head. Thank the Egg, this prison wasn't forever.

No, she had to stop this fussing. Zaarusha's son and the hundreds of slaves in Death Valley were imprisoned, not her. She'd rather fly across the Flatlands on Liesar than stay in this shrotty wagon, but she hadn't earned back her right to fly. Manure and pig urine, she could handle. Marlies shifted to stop her belt from digging into her hip, then rummaged in her pack for an apple. She bit into it.

The wagon careened around a corner, then slowed, the horses trotting at a steady pace, hooves echoing off nearby walls. They were in a town. Marlies' nerves prickled. Perhaps there were mind-benders nearby. She submerged herself, going deep inside, so no one could detect her thoughts. She had to get to Death Valley as fast as possible, yet all she could do was wait.

§

Trickles of sweat ran down Giant John's back as he drove through Forest Edge. The village was quiet, too quiet. There were no children in the yards, no one on the street, and no livestock in the fields. Forest Edge had been abandoned. A stray chicken pecked at the dirt. A chill breeze rippled through the trees, making a door bang. Where had everyone gone?

Giant John flicked the reins, and the horses galloped out of town. Leaving the village, he spied movement in the trees, then a piggy snout and the glint of armor. A tracker, for sure. It must've followed them from Last Stop. He urged the horses along the road through Spanglewood Forest. Birds took to the sky behind them. The tracker was fast.

Giant John bolted along the track, driving the horses hard. They needed to shake the tracker before Waldhaven, so they could hide the wagon in Benji's barn. Although the tracker couldn't scent Marlies, it could track him and the horses.

Hours later, at the turnoff for Waldhaven, John relaxed his grip on the reins. He hadn't seen a sign of the tracker for a while, but they needed rest. Benji owned a small farm on the far side of the village. Straight through the center of town, and he'd be there. Giant John frowned. Everything was silent, just like in Forest Edge. Had everyone fled from here, too?

His wagon rumbled along the deserted street, around a corner. Except the street wasn't deserted.

Giant John gaped in horror.

People lay dead on the doorsteps. Bodies were scattered along the road. A man was hanging, gutted, from a tree. A littling's broken body had been flung onto a flower bed, her neck at an odd angle. Nauseous, Giant John pulled the reins, wheeling the wagon around, and made for the forest road. There was no refuge in Waldhaven.

§

Marlies' nerves jangled like an over-tuned fiddle. Something was wrong. The wagon swerved, throwing her weight into her rucksack. The horses' hooves thundered as Giant John pushed them into a gallop. The pig squealed. Branches struck the wagon, shudders reverberating through Marlies' bones.

Abruptly, the wagon halted. Marlies slid forward, her feet crashing into the end of the compartment. Outside, something creaked—a door? Giant John walked the horses forward, then stopped. He flipped the side of the wagon bed down and helped Marlies out.

They were in a barn. He shut the doors, while Marlies rubbed her legs and marched on the spot to get her circulation going.

When he turned back to her, Giant John's face was ashen. Tears tracked through the dust on his cheeks.

"What happened?"

His hands were trembling.

Marlies led him to a pile of hay. "Here, sit." She retrieved a waterskin from the wagon and held it out to him. "Have some, you'll feel better."

Mutely, he took the skin and drank. His eyes were dark, hollowed out with grief.

"What was it, John?" she asked gently.

"Bodies. No one left alive. Women, littlings, even tiny ones." He took another swig. "Rotting flesh in the streets and sprawled across doorsteps. All those lives …" His stare was blank—he'd be seeing it all over again, the way she'd seen the dead dragonet for years.

Marlies hugged him, and Giant John sobbed. "Benji, his wife and littlings …"

"Did you see them?"

"No."

"They may have survived, fled …" Or been taken as Zens' slaves. That would bring him no comfort. Marlies fixed some food—vegetables, bread and a cup of ale for Giant John. "Only one, mind you," she said as she passed him the beer. "We need our wits sharp."

"And our blades," Giant John replied, anger kindling in his eyes.

Good, better anger than hopelessness.

As they ate, their conversation drifted to other things. "It's the rift between mages and riders that's let tharuks get out of hand," Giant John said.

Marlies coughed on her bread. "What? They're still quibbling over the world gate?"

"Well, the wizards did let Zens through. It's their fault," Giant John said.

"But that was years ago. And no one suspected he was such a horror." He'd been ugly and misshapen, yet Zens had appeared peaceful.

Giant John took a sip of beer. "When Zens' hidden army of tharuks started capturing our people as slaves, we should have fought him, not each other."

"Surely the Council of the Twelve Dragon Masters has forgiven the wizards by now," Marlies replied. "They can't hold a grudge forever."

Giant John shook his head. "Forgiving is one thing, forgetting is another—they've done neither."

The mages had closed the world gate, but not without cost—many were stranded on the other side, locked out of Dragons' Realm forever. "You're not serious, are you?"

"As serious as I can be. Mages and riders haven't fought together since Anakisha's last battle." Giant John sipped his beer.

"Shards, those idiots! How can we withstand Zens without wizard power? Without mages, how can we be effective? Who, on the council, supports this?"

"Who doesn't? The mages are deep in Spanglewood Forest, or down in Naobia." Giant John gave her another bleak look. "I know you were in pain when you and Hans fled Dragons' Hold, but the masters who replaced you two are incompetent. Last time I was at Dragons' Hold, I tried to tell Lars and Tonio, but they didn't want to know." He sighed. "Because I'm still friends with Giddi, they don't trust me." His eyes seemed to accuse her of abandoning the realm.

Marlies' throat tightened with grief. "It wasn't only horror of killing Zaarusha's baby and Zaarusha's wrath that I fled from. There was the pain of losing Anakisha, other riders and their dragons. Many of the mages we lost were my friends too …" She broke off. It had all been too much.

Beneath his gaze, she straightened her shoulders. "We can't do anything about the past, just the future. I'm going to Death Valley to find Zaarusha's lost son. I owe her that. Will you help me get to the foot of the Terramites?"

"They're called the Terror Mites now." Giant John grimaced. "So, that's what you're doing." He hesitated.

She was asking too much. He had a family now. "Don't worry, I'll—"

With a flick of his hand, he cut her off. "I'll gladly take you. Sleep in the compartment, in case we're disturbed." He threw her a blanket. "I'll nap on the wagon." Giant John turned the horses around, so they were facing the barn doors. Harnessed to the wagons, they were ready for a fast escape.

Marlies climbed inside the wagon bed, cringing. If they were caught, her secret compartment would be a death trap.

§

476, the tharuk tracker, opened the door to the barn. The big dolt had been here, the male with the beer. Yes, there were wagon tracks and fresh horse dung. He could've scented him a valley away even without the wagon tracks to follow. The tracker sniffed around the barn. In the corner, it found breadcrumbs and an apple core, and everywhere was that elusive scent that he couldn't quite detect—the female. Somehow, she was masking her true scent. 476 couldn't say how it knew, but its instincts said the female must be traveling with the big man.

The prize was within reach. Zens would be very pleased.

Hah! The man would be an easy kill. The oaf looked thicker than a headless chicken—and being big, he was bound to be slow. Saliva dribbled off 476's tusks as it sped out of the barn, following the wagon's tracks along the road through Spanglewood Forest.

§

Giant John's supplies were pitifully low. All that remained was half a sack of vegetables and an empty beer barrel. He'd had to give everything else to a troop of tharuk trackers a while back, distracting them for long enough for him to ride off with Marlies. Oh, they'd questioned him about her, too. And those trackers had been coming *from* Death Valley. How had the news of Marlies traveled ahead of her? Giant John clicked his tongue against his teeth, encouraging the horses. His mares had done well this trip, but they were tiring.

He kept an eye on the forest, sure they were being followed. A shadow flitted through the trees, to his right, behind him. And again. Yes, it was a tracker. Might as well smoke the beggar out into the open. The next chance he had, he'd stop and invite the tracker to play.

Dread trickled down his spine. A hundred things could go wrong. Giant John mopped his brow. It was a chance he'd have to take.

§

The big oaf had stopped in a clearing and was standing on the wagon, rummaging in a sack of vegetables. Worse than a blind pig, the idiot had his back to a large tree with an overhanging branch.

The man's scent wafted toward 476.

476 slunk behind the tree.

Even better, the dolt was whistling. Good, that would cover the sound of its claws scraping against the bark as it scaled the trunk. The tracker crawled along the branch until it was right above the oaf, who was slicing an apple with a puny-looking knife.

476's nostrils quivered with excitement and bloodlust.

§

Giant John forced himself to slice an apple with neat methodical cuts, lifting the tiny blade between each cut to check the reflection of the branch above.

The tracker was there, waiting. He popped a slice of apple in his mouth, quickly chewing it. Shards, it would be a terrible waste to choke on a piece of apple in a fight. Another slice. The beast was crouching, ready to pounce. Giant John whistled a few more bars, then coughed loudly to let Marlies know there was danger.

Now! As the tracker leaped, Giant John turned, whipping his sword from his belt, raising it to impale the tracker on his blade.

Seeing his sudden move, the tracker twisted in midair. The blade barely sliced its arm. With a crash that shook the wagon, the tharuk landed on its feet, claws out.

An agile sod, this one.

Giant John had to keep the beast away from Marlies. Oh shards, this was the tracker with the broken tusk and black eyes. It could mind-bend. He mustn't think about Marlies. Jumping from the wagon, he sprinted across the clearing.

Stomping and rasping followed him.

Close—too close, he was breathing in the creature's rotty breath.

Pain sliced across Giant John's back.

He spun, droplets of his own blood flying, cherry-red in the sun. Giant John thrust his sword at the tracker, but it lunged low, grabbing his legs, slamming him to the ground. His sword went flying. Rolling, he leaped to his feet as the brute pounced right where he'd just been.

Giant John whipped a dagger from his sleeve. The tharuk sprang into the air, and snatched Giant John's other arm, wrenching it as it flew past him, spinning him off balance. Gods, this thing was fast, and cunning.

Giant John surged forward, aiming his dagger at the tharuk's neck.

The beast parried the blade with a flick of its arm and swiped at John's torso, raking its claws across his gut.

Giant John dropped his dagger and crumpled to his knees, clutching his stomach. The beast sprang, flinging him backward and pinned his arms with its claws.

Giant John tried to heave his legs up to dislodge the beast, but his middle burnt with fire, moisture leaking over his hips—blood, guts? He couldn't tell. Either way, his belly muscles were useless.

The tracker's black beady eyes focused on him. "Where is the female?" it snarled.

Dizziness swept over Giant John. He shook his head, trying to clear it. The irrational urge to tell this monster about Marlies filled his head. He fought, keeping an image of a sunflower in his mind, refusing to let the beast win. His forehead dripped sweat. Yellow petals, thick stem.

"Play with me, would you? Picking flowers?" The tracker drove a knee into his rib.

Giant John felt it pop. Smash. Another rib.

"Where is she?" The tracker's spittle flew into his face, making him want to gag. But he couldn't—oh gods, the pain was too much. And that awful dizziness. Focus on the sunflower—bright green leaves, yellow, dark center.

RIDERS OF FIRE

The tracker released its grip on his arms for a moment. Giant John snatched the tracker's fur, but it was too late, the beast's fingers closed around his neck. It squeezed. Giant John gurgled. Croaked. Black spots danced before his eyes.

"You got no chance," gloated the tracker. "I'm stronger. Smarter." It laughed. "Zens is making new creatures. To kill every male, female and small human. And all your stinking dragons. Gone. Just you wait."

Giant John tried to fight but could only gurgle. Darkness crept across the edge of his vision. The world spun.

With a fleshy thunk, a sword protruded from the tharuk's neck. Dark blood gushed over Giant John's head. Marlies' face appeared.

Giant John fainted.

§

Marlies kicked the tracker off Giant John and crouched by her old friend. "John! Don't pass out on me now. Come on!"

His eyelids fluttered.

Not waiting for him to rouse, she tugged up his blood-soaked jerkin. A gut wound, plenty of blood but no intestines, thank goodness. She whipped her piaua out of her healer's pouch and dripped juice along one end of the wound site, holding the edges together so his flesh could knit over. Giant John moaned at the burn, but didn't wake. She repeated the process until the wound was closed.

Lifting his jerkin, she saw mottled bruises spreading on one side of his chest. His throat was also bruised. Marlies dashed back to the wagon and grabbed her waterskin. As an afterthought, she pulled the trapdoor shut in the bottom of the secret compartment, and bolted it, then tugged the horses toward Giant John.

Sloshing water over Giant John's face, she woke him.

His eyes darted wildly, then his face brightened. "Marlies!" He spotted the dead tracker. "Thank the Egg! You saved me!" He tried to sit up, but winced.

"Ribs?"

Giant John nodded sheepishly. "Afraid so."

"Here, open your mouth." Marlies let two or three drips of piaua juice fall on John's tongue, then rubbed a little over the bruises on his throat and torso. "That should make it easier to move."

Soon, he could sit up unaided. He got to his feet and flexed his torso. "Piaua is amazing. Thankfully, you were here."

"Without me, you wouldn't be in this mess." She nudged the dead tharuk with her boot. A severed tharuk hand fell out of its pocket. "Ew, gross. We'd better get going in case its friends turn up."

"Ah, Marlies. We can't leave the body or the hand here. They'll be onto us in no time."

"Good, then we'll take them with us."

Giant John stuffed the hand back in the dead beasts' pocket and lifted its body. But when he flipped the side of the wagon bed down and stuffed the beast into the secret compartment, then gestured to Marlies to get in, she recoiled. "No, John, even I have limits."

"Well," he said, "this isn't one of them. I can't take either of you in the top of the wagon. If we're stopped, I'm a dead man."

She hesitated.

"Marlies, I have a wife, now. A wee littling."

"Fair enough." She sighed.

He stuffed some sacks next to the dead brute and wiped its blood stains off the floor.

Marlies climbed in, screwing up her nose. "Never thought I'd cuddle up to a dead tharuk," she muttered as he flipped the side up and locked her in. Brilliant, the tharuk's body was now blocking the trapdoor—her only exit if Giant John was attacked.

§

A while later, Giant John stopped the horses and let Marlies out of the wagon. They half-dragged and half-lifted the tharuk to the top of the ravine. Below, the Tooka river churned in a heaving white mass.

"On my count," said Giant John, adjusting his grip and using his thighs to lift the beast's torso while Marlies held the legs. They threw the beast into the river.

Its body bounced on a rock, then bobbed once or twice before it was swept down the gorge in a torrent of white wash.

Giant John turned to Marlies. She was heading into the jaws of the viper in Death Valley. He wouldn't wish that trip on anybody. "There's a steep chimney at the back of this cave leading to a goat track up the mountainside. The tharuks use a trail about twenty furlongs south of here. Just before Devil's Gate—"

"That's the pass into Death Valley, right?"

He nodded. "Before then, the tharuk track and your trail converge. You'll be sharing the way with tharuks, but the mountain's so steep, there's no other way up. I'd save your freshweed for then." He shrugged. There was so much more to say, so many memories they shared.

Marlies embraced him. "Thank you, John, for risking your life for me. Give my thanks to your wife. I'd like to meet her one day."

Chuckling, Giant John replied, "And I'd like to see your children."

Marlies smiled. "You may see one of them soon. My daughter, Ezaara, is now Queen's Rider."

"Queen's Rider?" Giant John gaped.

Marlies laughed. "Watch out, John, you might swallow a passing tharuk!"

He hugged her again. "Speed on wings of fire."

She snorted. "That would be nice, but Liesar isn't here, so I'll just have to use my feet." Marlies waved and entered the cave.

Giant John watched until she was out of sight, then unharnessed the horses, and took their saddlebags out of the secret compartment. He pushed the wagon to the edge of the ravine, and gave it a shove. It dropped, splintering into pieces on the rocks. The current tugged, sweeping some parts away and leaving others stranded.

The tracker's words echoed in his head, chilling him. *"Zens is making new creatures. To kill every male, female and small human. And all your stinking dragons. Gone. Just you wait."* Giant John shivered. New monsters? Someone needed to find out. Shards, he should've told Marlies. Was it too much to hope she'd stumble upon the secrets Zens was hiding?

After fastening the saddlebags on the horses, Giant John roped one behind the other and swung into the saddle. He took one last glance at the mountainside as the last rays of sunset melted into dark shadows, and muttered, "By the dragon's tail, I hope she makes it out again."

Tharuk Attack

There it was again—the slow creak of the prison door opening. Then soft footfalls.

Creeping to his feet, Hans felt in the dark for the jagged piece of wood he'd prized from his bed yesterday. As his hands closed around the makeshift dagger, a splinter drove into his palm. He clamped his teeth together to stop himself from grunting and stood with his back against the side wall of his cell.

At the other end of the prison, a strangled screech was cut short, followed by a muffled thump.

That was the guard out of the way.

Hans braced himself as the stench of tharuk wafted down the corridor, preceding a lumbering beast. It always made his stomach curl and brought back terrible memories. The sharp iron of their victim's blood was in his nose again, as he waited, silent, in the dark.

The gorge rose in his throat as the tharuk—a shadow in the darkness—stopped at the cell opposite.

Of course. They were coming to break Bill out. To use him as a pawn, once again. The crow had obviously passed its message on, somehow.

The tang of the guard's blood rose through the tharuk's stench. The monster must be covered in it.

With a jangle and a clank, Bill's cell door was open. A thud. A muffled groan from Bill, then his simpering.

"Oh, thank you, Master. I'm so grateful you came for me. Lovely to see you, absolutely lovely."

"Drink this," the beast growled.

Hans heard Bill chugging back fluid, then stumbling to his feet. Swayweed tea, no doubt.

"Ow, not quite so tight, Master," Bill said. "I'm coming with you, right now."

"Keep your voice down," the tharuk growled as it swept Bill down the corridor and out of jail.

For long moments, Hans waited, pressed against the wall. He cocked his head. There were no cries of alarm outside, no sounds of fighting. So, the beast had come to grab Bill ahead of the main attack.

Now, to get out of here, get weapons and defend the township. Hans reached his arm through the bars, stretching the wooden dagger toward Bill's cell in the dark. He waved the wood back and forth, until it thunked against the edge of the cell door, but it was too short to reach the keys. Hans turned back to the bed. There was plenty more wood where that came from.

Wait.

From outside the prison came stealthy whispers and the chink of armor. The reek of tharuk drifted through the window. There were no warning cries. Dread coiled through Hans' stomach. Tharuks were infiltrating the village, so Ernst's perimeter guards must be dead. If only Klaus had listened.

He needed more wood. Hans threw the mattress off his bed. The noise he was about to make could bring tharuks running, but if he didn't get out, he'd be trapped. Hopefully the racket would alert the settlers. Hans kicked the bed in the weak spot where he'd torn off his dagger. Just a thunk in the dark. He booted it again and again. The planks groaned but held solid.

"What's that?" a guttural growl rumbled outside Bill's window.

"Probably 731 smashing up the jail."

"But we weren't to start until—"

A scream cut through the air. Everything outside went mad: roaring, yelling, torches flaring through the barred window. Agonized screeches as tusks and claws met flesh.

It made no difference how much noise he made now. Hans jumped high, his boots smashing down on the bed. The wood groaned. He jumped again, thrusting his full bodyweight downward. With a jarring crash, the bed splintered. Pain sparking through his calf, he snatched up a length of wood and poked it through the bars. Erratic torches cast light through the windows, allowing him to skewer the enormous loop of keys onto the end of his stick. Hans jiggled them, trying to get Bill's key loose from the lock.

Through their cell bars, inmates cried out, then grew silent as they watched his struggle.

Hans jiggled the key again. The end of his stick broke off, falling to the ground, and the keys were still stuck in Bill's shrotty lock.

A deep snarl made Hans' neck hairs stand on end. A torch flared to life.

"Speed it, mate," someone hissed. "A beast is coming." The inmates disappeared from their barred doors, taking refuge at the back of their cells.

Hans thrust the stick through the key ring again, then yanked, hard. The key flew from the lock and the ring slid along the stick.

The snarls grew closer.

He didn't dare look. Hand over hand, he pulled the stick back through the bars of the cell. Another moment and the jailer's keys would be within reach. The light grew brighter. Hans clasped the jailer's keyring and glanced up.

The tharuk was stopping at each cell and lifting its torch high, sniffing the prisoners' scents.

A tracker. Hunting someone. Who in Lush Valley would be valuable enough to track?

A chill swept through him. A former dragon master and his family.

He had to get free before the beast found him. The scrape of the key as he slid it into the lock jarred his ears.

The tharuk was only a few cells down.

He turned the key, then stuffed them in his pocket. Let the monster think the door was locked. He lifted the stick, hiding it against his leg. A weapon, but a poor one. Before Hans could retreat to the back of the cell, the tharuk lifted its snout, nostrils twitching, and sniffed the air. The beast spun, long strings of dark drool dribbling off its saliva-coated tusks.

It stared right at him, a puckered scar under one of its red eyes. The beast's nostrils flared as it stopped at Hans' cell. It flexed its claws. "What's here, then? A former dragon rider, I believe?"

Bill had known and sold him out.

"You know what we do to dragon riders, don't you?" The beast's top lip curled.

Hans had seen tortured riders, hands missing, with strips torn off their backs and feet, left to rot in Death Valley. No way, not him. He lunged, shoving with all his weight on the cell door. It swung open, knocking the tharuk backward into Bill's cell door. The torch rolled along the corridor.

Hans ducked around his door. The tracker leaped to its feet, blocking Hans' escape. Hefting his stick with two hands, he drove it upward under the tharuk's chin. Blood rained over Hans. Impaled, the beast swiped at Hans, but the stick was too long, keeping its claws out of reach.

He pushed harder. The beast clutched at the wood, its eyes rolling back in its head. Black blood pumped from its throat. Soon the monster's head lolled to the side and its body went limp.

Hans let go, kicking the beast aside as it hit the floor.

"What was that?" a prisoner asked, face pressed against his bars.

"That was how you kill a tharuk. Aim for their throats or the weak spot under their chins." Breathing hard, Hans dragged the keys from his pocket. "Who wants to stay here and be slaughtered?" Silence. "Then will you help me kill these over-sized rats?"

Ragged cheers went up among the prisoners.

Hans unlocked the neighboring cell. "Release the others, grab some weapons, and meet me in the square." Most of them would flee, but some might help. Any fighters were a bonus.

Hans grabbed the torch and ran along the corridor, yelling his instructions to all the prisoners, then raced outside.

It was mayhem. People were fleeing. Beasts smashed buildings and homes. The few villagers fighting tharuks were armed with only pitchforks or spades, taking wild swings at the monsters. A pot flew out a window, hitting a tharuk on the head. Shrieks of pain filled the night.

A burly figure thundered toward him, lit up from behind by a home engulfed in flames. "Hans!" It was Klaus, his face pale and streaked with black tharuk blood. He shook his head. "I'm sorry, Hans. I should've listened. Here, your weapons." He threw Hans his scabbard and daggers.

Hans caught them, then whirled, drawing his sword to fight off a wiry tharuk. At his side, Klaus drove back a bigger beast with a bald spot above its eye. Hans feinted high. The tharuk looked up, and he drove his sword into its throat. No sooner had the beast hit the ground, three more replaced it.

Where were the blue guards and their dragons? Had they seen the beacon? With no way of knowing, Hans kept fighting.

§

There was a crash.

Tomaaz leaped off his bedroll, snatched up his weapons and threw his bow and quiver over his back. The front door was shuddering under the impact of—

Smack! Another blow shook the door in its frame.

Around him, people were rising to their feet, befuddled with sleep.

"Get to the center of the house," Tomaaz called. "Hide the littlings. Fighters, mark the entrances—the chimney, windows and doors." How had he come to be in charge? That was supposed to be Ernst's job, or Pa's.

There was a rush of activity behind him as people scurried around in the dark. Someone lit candles from the embers in the fireplace.

When the next whack on the door came, the floorboards shook as well.

Lofty and Kieft took the spots beside him, near the door. "There are six more at our backs," Kieft whispered. "In case any tharuks get through."

"What's that stench?" Murray covered his mouth with his hand.

"Stand fast," Tomaaz commanded. "Draw your weapons."

A sharp crack came from his parents' room, then the tinkle of shattering glass. Roars ripped through the rear of the house. The thwack of blades made Tomaaz's knees shudder.

"Stand fast. Someone else has it," he called.

A yell was cut off with a wet thump.

The front door shuddered again, then splintered, as a tree trunk smashed through the wood. Outside, there were raucous bellows.

Tomaaz sheathed his sword. Whipping an arrow from his quiver, he aimed toward the trunk protruding from the door. He'd only have one chance as the log was withdrawn, but a tharuk down was one less to fight. The log withdrew and Tomaaz loosed an arrow. A roar rang out. He nocked another arrow and let it fly.

Tharuks converged on the door. Tomaaz let one last shot fly, threw his bow across his back and drew his sword.

The door broke, showering the floor with wood. A piece smacked Lofty on the arm, then a wall of fur, tusks and claws poured over the threshold.

Tomaaz ran at them. A tharuk swiped, its broad furry arm bashing his sword aside. Tomaaz slashed at the brute. The beast swung at his head and he ducked, then counter-attacked. Fur flew. This stuff was like armor, thick and matted. He'd have to aim for a weak spot.

But the tharuk was a blur of tusks and claws, gouging and slashing. As fast as he blocked, the brute was there again, beady red eyes anticipating his moves. Tomaaz pushed himself harder, faster, driving the brute back toward the doorway, where more of their fighters had spilled past to battle monsters outside. He pursued the monster over the step. The beast stumbled, then drew itself upright, raising an arm high. Its sharp claws came down toward Tomaaz's head. Tomaaz swerved, and the beast's claws shredded the side of his jerkin.

Tomaaz swept in, driving his sword upward, under the tharuk's descending arm. Surprise flashed across the tharuk's face as Tomaaz's blade sank deep into the beast's armpit. The monster's roar nearly split Tomaaz's head.

He twisted the blade and dragged the sword downward, ripping a gash in the tharuk's side. The beast collapsed, sprawled across the stairs, staining them with its blood.

Pushing his foot against the monster's side, Tomaaz wrenched his sword free.

"Tomaaz!"

He whirled to face the chaos inside. Lofty was trapped by the kitchen table, holding off two tharuks.

Tomaaz rushed in. One of the beasts whirled and charged him. Tomaaz danced aside, striking at its neck. The beast flicked its head, its tusk catching Tomaaz's blade and ripping his sword from his grip. Tomaaz backed away, his foot hitting the hearth as the beast dropped its head to charge. He had to think fast.

The monster careened toward him. He grabbed the stew pot off the hearth and smashed it against the beast's skull, knocking the tharuk to the floor, unconscious.

Lofty was standing over the other beast, dark stains on his sword. He raised his eyebrows. "We did it. We got them all."

Fallen monsters lay among the shattered debris. People huddled in corners. Inside, there were no tharuks left standing. "Good job. I'll check the rest of the house. Meet you outside." Tomaaz picked up his sword and went through the back of the house, checking the bedrooms. No more beasts inside, and enough adults to take care of the wounded.

He and Lofty rushed out to help those still fighting tharuks. Even outside, the stench made Tomaaz want to gag. Raising their swords, they plowed into the fight, stabbing tharuks in the back of their knees, in the throat, or under the armpits, wherever they were most vulnerable. Back to back, they fought, battling the tusked beasts.

With a squeal, a boy went down. Tomaaz sprang to his aid, driving the tharuk off.

"They're getting away," Lofty called, slashing at a tharuk that had a torn ear.

The beast laughed.

Tomaaz jerked his head toward the village. A black swarm obscured the road—another troop of tharuks were heading for the town center. In the distance, a flicker caught his gaze. Buildings were burning!

"Pa!"

"Go," called Lofty. "We'll take care of these!"

Tomaaz raced down the road, his heart thundering. If tharuks breached the prison, Pa would be trapped. He veered off the road, running between rows of corn, across fields so he wouldn't be spotted.

Tomaaz was about halfway to town when he heard whimpering. He slowed. It was coming from behind a shed, so he crept along the rough wall.

"The girl, Lovina, where is she?"

Tomaaz froze.

It was Old Bill. There was a short cry, cut off by a slap. "There'll be more than that, if you don't answer now, boy!"

Lovina's lash marks flashed before his eyes. Tomaaz drew his knife and ran around the corner.

"Don't cut me anymore! Lovina's at Ernst's farm," blurted a boy, being held by Old Bill against the shed. The whites of the lad's eyes gleamed in the moonlight.

"You monster!" Tomaaz bellowed, running at Bill.

Bill flung the boy away, sneering, "And you're the scum spawn of a dead dragon lover!" He ran off into the dark.

Dead dragon lover? Pa? Tomaaz's heart lurched.

The sobbing boy crumpled to the ground. Tomaaz was torn. Should he chase Bill, look for Pa or check if the boy was injured? Sheathing his knife, Tomaaz knelt. It was one of the cooper's littlings. "Is that you, Paolo?"

The lad gazed up. "Tomaaz?"

"It's me. Are you hurt?"

"He cut my neck." Paolo whimpered.

"Show me. Where?"

Paolo guided Tomaaz's hand to a cut on his neck, about as long as his thumb, but thankfully, not too deep. Tomaaz ripped a strip off his tattered jerkin and gave it to Paolo. "It's only a flesh wound. You're a real warrior now. Here, hold this against it while we get you home."

"I thought I could fight," Paolo said, "so I sneaked out, but that bad man found me." He sniffed.

"It's all right," Tomaaz said. "These tharuks are tricky, so I'll get you home, but we have to be quick." They slipped across fields toward the cooper's yard, Tomaaz helping to keep the stumbling boy upright.

Suddenly, a light appeared. "Paolo! Paolo!" a woman's voice called.

Tomaaz stopped Paolo from replying. "Quiet! Tharuks will hear you," Tomaaz whispered. They'd hear his mother too. They rushed ahead, Tomaaz telling the woman to put out her lantern and keep her voice down. He explained what Bill had done. "Zens' tharuks are attacking the township," Tomaaz said. "Do you have weapons? People in your household that can wield a sword?"

RIDERS OF FIRE

The cooper's wife clutched Paolo to her side. "Yes."

"Then shutter your windows and bar the door and send who you can to help the village fight."

As the cooper's wife hurried Paolo to the house, Paolo begged, "Please, Ma, let me go to the fight."

A keening wind drifted through the trees. Tomaaz glanced at town, so close, then back to Lofty's farm. Bill was going after Lovina. He had to stop him. But Pa was stuck in prison. Or was he dead, as Bill had said? Shards, what to do? For an agonizing moment, Tomaaz was on the balls of his feet.

Then he raced to town. Lovina had Ernst and others to protect her. Pa only had him, and Pa might know how to save Lush Valley.

§

Tomaaz skirted around the main road to avoid the worst of the fighting. He ran past a blazing house and arrived at the jail, panting, the old burns on his legs throbbing.

The door was open. The guard was dead, throat slashed, his blood sprayed over the foyer. Sickened, Tomaaz entered the corridor and snatched up a blazing torch. Rows of cell doors stood ajar. He ran down the aisle.

So far, all empty.

Before Pa's cell, an enormous tharuk was sprawled against a barred door, a piece of wood sticking out from under its chin, sticky blood pooling around it.

Pa's wooden bed had been splintered, bits of timber scattered across his floor.

Tomaaz bent to examine the dead beast. So that's how Pa killed tharuks.

§

With Klaus' help, Hans had succeeded in rallying the villagers to take refuge in the square. They'd blocked off three entrances by piling furniture high and setting archers on nearby rooftops, but the monsters were still pouring in through the broadest street. While others staved off beasts with spears, Hans led fighters into the fray.

"Watch the tusks," he bellowed, slicing an unarmored tharuk's belly open.

"Look out for their claws!" Hans drove his sword into a tharuk's eye. "Hit their weak spots."

Around him, inexperienced fighters surged, some injuring one another while swinging at the brutes, but they hewed and cut their way into the enemy, desperate to protect their families.

Briefly, Hans wondered where Tomaaz was. Marlies. Ezaara.

Bodies hit the cobbles.

In the square, a couple of narrow alleys provided an escape route should the villagers need to flee. It was looking more and more like they'd have to. They were outnumbered, people falling like autumn leaves.

More tharuks kept streaming in. They had no chance. If dragons didn't arrive soon, the whole township would be lost.

§

Lovina huddled under the bed with the littlings. Crashes and grunts rang out around her. A dead tharuk thudded to the nearby floorboards, making the littlings tremble. Bellows came from the room next door, then, little by little, the noise receded and the fighting continued outside.

"Can we come out?" whispered the smallest.

"The monsters might hurt you, so we have to stay and be quiet," Lovina whispered.

The fighting sounded further away, now, but she'd promised to keep these children safe until their parents returned.

If their parents returned. She swallowed a bitter pang. Now that the numlock had lifted, her memories were trickling back. Strangely, the most distant ones had come first. The night she'd hidden in a closet while tharuks had ransacked their village looking for slaves. Da had not come back that night, and she and Ma were captured.

Arms around the littlings, she waited in the dark under the bed, trying to remember what had happened to her ma, but that memory was still shrouded in fog.

There was a clunk. Lovina's muscles tensed. Another clunk—the bump of wood on wood.

Was that a window flapping in the wind? She couldn't remember opening one, but with fighting going on, maybe someone else had. Perhaps she should close it in case a tharuk climbed in. Lovina waited, the window bumping softly against the sill a few more times.

Lovina eased her head out from under the bed. Oh, no: worn brown boots with tarnished buckles. Her heart froze. They were Bill's.

Bill grabbed a clump of her hair and pulled. Lovina resisted, clinging to the leg of the bed, but he yanked harder. A chunk of her hair ripped out, pain searing her skull. He grabbed another handful and yanked again, smashing her face against the frame of the bed. One of the littlings grabbed her legs.

Gods, no! If they hung on, he'd see them, hurt them too.

"It's all right, Bill," she gasped. "I'm coming out." Oh gods, don't let Bill think that was too easy and get suspicious. She shook her leg, getting the littling to let go, then clambered out.

Bill's eyes shone yellow in the candlelight.

Lovina cringed. She couldn't help it. Swayweed made him meaner.

He dragged her toward him by the hair, forcing her into a chair. He leaned over, his face in hers.

"What did I promise I'd do, if you ever ran away again?" Bill's breath made her eyes water. "What did I say?"

Last time, she hadn't got far. "B-break …" Lovina swallowed, unable to finish. She'd asked Ernst and Ana to help her get out of Lush Valley, but with Bill in jail, they hadn't thought it necessary. Why hadn't she left? Tomaaz's face flashed to mind. Where was he now? Nowhere. No one was ever there—except Bill.

"What did I tell you?" Bill asked, quiet menace in his voice.

Lovina hung her head.

The littlings shuffled under the bed.

"Um, ah …" She spoke loudly, so Bill couldn't hear them. "You said you'd break my bones."

His smile wasn't kind. "Good. You remembered. Now, let's get on with that. I'd hate to *break* my promise." Bill laughed at his own pun. Tying a length of rope around Lovina's wrist, he shoved her toward the open window. "I'm taking you somewhere we won't be disturbed. And if you make a peep, I'll be back to kill one of those stinkers under that bed."

Dread wormed through Lovina.

Bill picked Lovina up. For the sake of the littlings, she didn't struggle. He threw her out the window and jumped to the ground beside her. Stuffing a gag in her mouth and yanking her rope hard, he led her toward the trees by the river.

Turning Point

Panting, Tomaaz stopped outside Lofty's house, putting his hands on his knees to catch his breath. Ana and Ernst were tending the wounded where they lay. Others were still fighting tharuks in the neighboring fields.

"Where's Lovina?" he called.

"Safe inside," Ana answered, cleansing a gash in a man's shoulder.

"Did you fight Bill off?"

"Bill?" Ernst's shaggy eyebrows drew into a frown, as he cut a strip of bandage with his knife. "He's in jail, not here."

Tomaaz burst into Lofty's home and snatched up a candle. Muffled sobs came from Lovina's bedroom—the littlings' room. He dashed down the hallway and pulled the door open.

A dead tharuk lay on its side, in pooling blood. The bed was rumpled and a chair was overturned. A window flapped in the breeze. Maybe the sobbing had come from the next room. About to close the door, Tomaaz heard someone choking back a gasp.

He scrambled to his knees and lifted the bedding. Under the bed, Lofty's three littling brothers were squeezed hard against the wall, faces tear-streaked. "Hey," he called, setting the candle on the floor. "Come here, boys." He reached under and pulled them out.

Wait, blood on the bed frame. Long strands of brown hair on the floor. Tomaaz picked up some hair, and then more. "Where's Lovina?" His words were strangled. "Where is she?"

"Over there," said Deano, the eldest of the littlings. "I watched out the window."

Tomaaz rushed him to the open window. "Where did the man take Lovina, Deano?"

"By those trees," the boy said, pointing toward the swimming hole. "He tied her up."

No, while he'd searched for Pa, Bill had been snatching Lovina.

"Into the living room. Wait for your ma there."

He leaped through the window and sped across the field.

"Hey, Maaz!" Lofty yelled. "Where are you going?"

"Bill's got Lovina," Tomaaz panted, running toward the trees.

§

Blood slicked the pommel of Hans' sword, making it hard to grip, but he hacked into the beast. It dropped. Another surged forward to take its place. Feint, thrust, drive and sidestep. Lunge, deflect and aim … his sword hit home, piercing the soft skin under the tharuk's chin. The beast tottered and fell on its side.

With a screech, the cooper next to him fell, leaving his young son unprotected.

Hans swung to deflect the claws of a beast. He pushed past a furry back to pierce the armpit of a small tharuk with its claws raised over Paolo's head. The tharuk faced Hans, eyes blazing, angling its tusks at his face. Hans ducked, driving his sword into the beast's gut. With two hands and all his bodyweight, he pushed, feeling the pop as he pierced the tharuk's tough hide, but before he could drive the sword deeper, the brute grabbed him.

Hans dropped his sword, his arms pinned to his sides, helpless.

Then Klaus was there, ramming his knife into the tharuk's throat.

In a gush of stinking dark blood, the beast went limp. Hans kicked it backward, knocking another tharuk down. He yanked his sword from the tharuk's belly and nodded at Klaus. "Thanks."

"Back to the square, Paolo," he yelled to the boy. Then he and Klaus turned to keep fighting.

§

The sky was waning to pre-dawn gray when Tomaaz heard Lovina scream. Sword drawn, he ran through the trees.

"No, I won't come with you!" she yelled.

"Which bone shall I break next?" Bill laughed.

Tomaaz ran. There, through those trees.

Bill kicked Lovina in the stomach. She dropped to her knees, clutching her belly. Bill backhanded her. Her head snapped back, smashing against a tree trunk.

White-hot rage surged through Tomaaz. He pounded across the forest floor.

Lovina rolled out of the way as Bill aimed another kick.

Then, seeing Tomaaz racing toward him, Bill gave a guttural yell and leaped into the air toward Lovina.

"No!" Tomaaz's shriek cut the air. He was too slow.

Too slow to stop the full weight of Bill landing on Lovina's arm, boots first.

There was a crack. Bone jabbed through skin. Her face turned the white of solstice bread, and her eyes rolled back in her head.

Then, Bill was gone, dashing away through the bushes.

"Lovina." Tomaaz reached her, dropping his sword and falling to his knees. Her eyes flitted to him, beyond and back, breathing shallow. She murmured.

"What is it?"

"Behind you," she gasped.

Tomaaz turned.

"May I introduce you to my friends?" said Bill.

Four tharuks stood at his back, tusks gleaming in the sunrise.

§

Hans dragged his sword from a tharuk's throat and lifted it to swing again.

His legs were faltering, dog-tired. Usually at sunrise, even in battle, he felt a new surge of hope, but this was different.

Beside him, Klaus held the brutes at bay with a spear, jabbing them when they got too close. They were part of a ragged line, trying to hold back the flood of tharuks. Jammed between two rows of buildings edging the street, with archers positioned above, he'd thought they had a fair chance of repelling the beasts and securing the street, but he'd been wrong.

An arrow whistled past him, hitting a tharuk in the eye. It collapsed, knocking a fighter down. The boy lay there, trapped beneath the beast, too tired to move. Klaus swung his spear in an arc, allowing Hans time to get to the boy. He rolled the tharuk's body over and the boy dragged himself to his feet.

"Paolo, it's you! I told you to go back to the square."

"They killed my da. I want to fight." The boy brandished his sword, jutting out his chin.

"Then stick with me," Hans said, swinging his sword at another beast.

Paolo stuck a tharuk in the arm, but it wasn't enough. The beast swiped with his free claws, sending the lad flying, then picked up Paolo's sword and tossed it aside. It towered over the chalk-faced boy. Hans leaped over a body and rammed his sword through the beast's side. The tharuk collapsed on top of Paolo and, this time, Hans left the lad there. He was probably safer hidden under a tharuk than fighting.

Another man went down. This had gone on too long.

"Hans," Klaus bellowed. He was at the closest end of a line of spear wielders, struggling to keep the monsters at bay.

Near the far building, tharuks pressed forward. The foremost beasts were impaled on spears, but others pushed on, trampling their bodies and the fighters. Hans ran, sword out, watching in horror as his men screamed, then fell silent as they were crushed by stampeding beasts.

Volleys of arrows flew. Some tharuks fell, but more rushed over them, pouring through the gap.

"Retreat, retreat, they've breached the square!" He ran to retrieve Paolo, but was pushed back, in a crush of bodies, toward the square. "To me, to me!" he bellowed.

Klaus surged through the pandemonium, tossing aside a tharuk, but was swept up, alongside Hans.

When they arrived at the square, they tried, again, to form a front line.

"To us," Klaus yelled. "Regroup! Over here."

A ragtag bunch of fighters regrouped, but within moments they were shoved aside, each fighting isolated battles amid a sea of tharuks.

They had no chance. Absolutely no chance.

But at least Hans could take a few tharuks with him before he died. Ezaara, Marlies and Tomaaz flashed to mind. He hoped they were safe, but somehow, he wasn't sure anymore.

He hacked into the mass of fur in front of him.

Then, as if by magic, his arm was stronger. He swung his sword with more confidence. His legs moved faster, his mind was less sluggish. It was as if …

"Handel?"

"*On my way.*"

The warmth of his dragon's thoughts flooded Hans, giving him courage. If they could mind-meld, Handel must be close. He rammed his sword into a tharuk and hewed down another. "For Dragons' Realm!" he bellowed. "Stand strong and fight these beasts." The increased surge of energy came from Handel. Fire blazed in Hans' veins, and he slew tharuks with renewed vigor.

"*I hope you have company,*" he mind-melded with Handel.

"*Two full troops of blue guards.*"

At last, they had a fighting chance.

Wheeling blue dragons created shadows over the square with their enormous wingspans as riders shot arrows into screeching tharuks. Swathes of flame cut down tharuks that were chasing women and children.

Hans battled a huge tharuk, ducking claws and lunging away from the brute's tusks, his hair ruffling in the downdraft of the dragons' wingbeats. Funny that—the movement of his hair, right in the middle of battle. It felt so familiar, so right. Why in the Egg's name had he and Marlies hidden for so long in this backwater? This is what made him feel alive: dragon power singing in his veins; the knowledge he was needed to save lives. Never again would he hide for fear of repercussion. He'd gladly face Zaarusha, take her condemnation, and prove to her that he could still be true to the realm.

"To us!" Hans bellowed.

Lush Valley fighters took courage, joining Hans and Klaus, forming lines that blocked the streets. In the square, dragons flamed tharuks until they were piles of smoking flesh and char. That old familiar stench of burning fur hung in the air.

This was what he and Marlies were born for, not farming and living in terror of ever seeing a dragon again.

But not all Lush Valley citizens took cheer at seeing the dragons. Some ran squealing, looking for cover. Others were gibbering about the evil stinking dragons that were going to eat them.

Klaus shot Hans a grim look. "I was wrong, Hans."

Hans nodded, piercing the chin of a tharuk, leaping back as it fell. "Your father raised you that way, Klaus."

Klaus jabbed a tharuk with his spear, driving it back. Curiosity crept over his face. "So, my grandpa really was a dragon rider?"

A burst of flame hit a nearby tharuk. *"Busy chatting, are you?"*

Hans looked up, his breath catching. The last rays of sunrise hit his dragon's bronze scales, making them gleam like treasure. His throat ached at Handel's beauty.

"You're right, I am treasure. Nice to see you again, Hans."

"And you, too." A gust of Handel's affection blew through him, warming him. *"I thought you'd be angry at me for leaving."*

"For a few years, I was. But lately, I'd been hoping I'd find you again. Your daughter has created quite a stir." One of Handel's memories shot through Hans' mind: Ezaara flying a loop on Zaarusha, the crowd below transfixed, with those fierce mountain peaks of Dragon's Teeth standing guard in the background.

"Gods, I've missed Ezaara. And Dragons' Hold."

"Not for long. The blue guards will sort this mess out. You and I have places to be." Handel swooped.

"Klaus, the dragons want me to go," Hans said.

"My grandfather was a dragon rider," Klaus said, "so I'm sure I'll handle this. Just go."

Hans jammed his sword in his scabbard. Handel grasped his shoulders with strong talons, lifting him above the battle. Hans hung on, letting out a loud whoop. *"It's great to be back in the saddle."*

"You're not in the saddle yet. Give me a chance." Handel's chuckle fluttered through his mind.

Below, people and tharuks looked up, staring. "Keep fighting!" Hans bellowed. *"Handel, I should stay, help them. I can't abandon them now."*

"What could you achieve that two troops of blue guards can't deal with?" Handel ascended above the buildings. Thanks to the dragons and their riders—the battle had turned. Tharuks fled from the settlement, out across fields. Dragons were chasing them down, the blue guards' arrows finding their marks. In the fields near his home, Hans saw a flash of silver, then a spurt of flame. *"Liesar?"*

The tinkle of her laugh echoed in his mind. *"Yes, I'm here too, Hans. We must collect supplies and leave Lush Valley."*

Settlements often sent supplies to Dragons' Hold to support the riders who protected them. It made sense to take his produce. *"We can't leave without my son."* He showed them an image of Tomaaz.

"You're right, we mustn't leave him behind." Handel used that voice.

"What is it? What have you seen?" They shared the gift of prophecy, although Hans' was a little rusty.

"I'm not sure yet, but he's tied to the fate of the realm, just as your daughter is. Zaarusha's dragonet gave much more than either you or Marlies suspected." Handel dived, burning a tharuk.

Hans' face heated with shame. *"I'll stand and face the council. Marlies and I deserve that for running."*

"Yes, you will." Handel gave Hans time to digest that, before he continued, *"However, due to her folly, both of your children inherited gifts from Zaarusha's dragonet."*

"What gifts?" Hans' shoulders were beginning to ache where Handel gripped them.

"Time will tell."

For years, Hans had wondered how their farm looked from above, on dragonback. Now he knew. Handel spiraled down, depositing him on the grass. Liesar landed nearby.

Shards and dragon's teeth! The whole front door had been splintered. Dead tharuks were scattered across the fields. People were lifting wounded inside, exhaustion dogging their movements. At the sight of dragons, they stopped, fear and curiosity battling on their faces.

With blue guards scorching the enemy nearby, they probably realized dragons were on their side, but he had to reassure them anyway. "It's all right," Hans called. "The dragons are helping us."

A ragged cheer went up.

Where was his son? He dashed inside. "Tomaaz?"

His home was full of wounded, but his son was not among them.

§

Tomaaz slowly rose to his feet, taking a surreptitious step closer to his sword. So foolish to have dropped it.

"Give me back my slave, boy."

Bill's smile gave Tomaaz the creeps. It always had—there'd been good reason to avoid Old Bill, but with four tharuks at his back, there was no avoiding him now. For a moment, Tomaaz wanted to play for time, but what was the use? He was outnumbered and cornered—with a girl who was too injured to run.

He lunged for his sword, snatching it, and ran straight for Bill and the tharuks.

In an instant, Bill was behind the tharuks, shouting commands at the beasts.

A tharuk charged Tomaaz. He leaped aside, his tattered jerkin catching on the beast's tusk and tearing free. Claws swiped at him. Tomaaz thrust the tip of his sword at a brute's eye. And then he was surrounded. It was over before it really began, and Lovina was unprotected.

Bill lurched over to her, grinning.

Tomaaz swept his sword in an arc, trying to break through, then spun, protecting his back. The beasts laughed, throwing the odd swipe, taunting, taking turns playing with him. When they attacked, he'd be a goner, shredded by their claws and tusks.

Lovina's shrill scream made him whirl.

Bill was breaking Lovina's fingers. "I'll teach you, girl!" he snarled.

Roaring, Tomaaz pelted toward a tharuk, ramming his shoulder into its gut. The surprised beast fell backward. Strong furry arms grabbed Tomaaz from behind, pinning his arms at his sides in a bear hug. The tharuk lifted him from the ground, crushing the breath out of him. Tomaaz struggled and kicked. He tried to call to Lovina, but could only gasp.

Bill dragged Lovina along the ground by her injured arm. Her broken bone jutting through her flesh at an impossible angle, she fainted.

Oh gods, he'd thought he could protect her. Now they'd both die, a furlong or two from home.

The tharuks gathered around him, snarling. It was getting harder to breathe.

"I want a turn, too," one said. "When do we get to play?" An arrow hit the beast in the head and it fell.

With a whoop, Lofty crashed through the bushes. He let a second arrow loose. Another beast fell. Only two to go—and Bill.

Bill whipped out a knife, holding it to Lovina's throat. "Hurt another tharuk and the girl gets this."

Lofty raised an eyebrow.

Tomaaz shook his head. He couldn't risk Lovina.

The big tharuk holding Tomaaz spoke, its voice rumbling through Tomaaz's back like an avalanche, "Crush him, now."

The remaining beast swiped at Lofty, who whipped his sword out of his scabbard as Tomaaz watched—helpless, ribs and chest aching, lungs tight.

A downdraft stirred the foliage. Overhead, wings flapped. An arrow thwacked into Bill, and he dropped his knife, clutching his shoulder. A blast of flame shot from the sky, burning the tharuk fighting Lofty.

Above them, two dragons wheeled in the air—bronze and silver.

A bow twanged. The tharuk holding Tomaaz flinched and staggered forward a step. Tomaaz heard the zip of a second arrow, and the tharuk fell on him, pinning his legs to the ground. He shoved the dead beast off him and scrambled to his feet, taking a shuddering breath.

He raced to Lovina. Bill was gone, the only reminders of him a broken arrow shaft on the ground and Lovina's injuries.

The silver dragon roared, chasing Bill, shooting flame.

The bronze dragon landed between the trees as Lofty chased the last tharuk off. His father dismounted and was at his side in moments.

"Pa?" It took Tomaaz a moment to recover from the surprise. "Bill did this, Pa. He shattered her arm. I couldn't stop him." He'd made the wrong decision, looking for Pa when Lovina was in danger. "And her head …" He lifted her hair to reveal an ugly lump with a gash through it.

Pa placed a hand on his shoulder. "Son, how can we help?"

Lofty crouched next to him, putting a hand on his shoulder. "Yes, tell us what to do."

Years of healing at his mother's side kicked in. Tomaaz took off his jerkin, tearing what was left of it into strips. "Lofty, get me a short straight branch, about the length of her arm. Pa, cover her with something warm."

Pa strode to a huge saddlebag on the side of the dragon and came back with a blanket. He tucked it around Lovina's torso and felt her forehead. He sloshed some water from a waterskin into a mug and crumbled herbs into it, then took it to his dragon, who warmed the water with a small flame. Pa bundled another blanket under Lovina's head, and gave Tomaaz a pot of healing salve. "I'll give Lofty a hand with that branch. The sooner we can splint her arm, the better."

Tomaaz lifted the cup to Lovina's lips.

Her eyelids fluttered. "Tomaaz?"

"It's all right, Lovina. Bill's gone. I'm here."

A Narrow Escape

Marlies traipsed on through the dark, keeping to the goat track zigzagging among the trees in a steep climb. That chimney Giant John had sent her through, full of cobwebs and slithering things, hadn't been used in an age. It was good to be out of that shrotty wagon, breathing fresh air again. The moon slid above the tree line as if it had been waiting to greet her, reflecting off the snow higher up the mountain.

Were her family in danger? Was Ezaara fighting tharuks with Zaarusha? What about Hans and Tomaaz in Lush Valley? The beacon fire on the Western Pass had warned of an attack. She'd killed three tharuks at Nick's inn, but how many more were coming? She shivered, and it was nothing to do with the biting northern wind. Tharuks were smothering the people of Dragons' Realm like a thick suffocating blanket of evil, robbing innocents of free will and life. They were a scourge, a monstrosity created by a sick man. And she was heading straight to his lair.

In all her battles for the realm, she'd only seen Zens a few times, but every time, he'd made her blood run cold.

The trees along the track thinned and the mountainside grew steeper. Marlies pressed on. If she could make Devil's Gate when no tharuks were around … but she had no way of knowing what their movements were.

High above the tree line, looking over the Flatlands, Marlies swung her rucksack off her shoulder and took a deep draft from her waterskin. Here and there, between the dark carpet of Great Spanglewood Forest, the mighty Tooka River ran silver. By day, she'd see the distant peaks of the Grande Alps surrounding Lush Valley to the east, but the night had swallowed every trace of her family home. It was as if Lush Valley didn't exist and the last eighteen years had been erased. Here she was again, on a solo quest for Zaarusha.

No, she had *killed* the dragonet. And the new life she'd made had been shattered by her past.

An eerie howl rippled through the night. Wolves—in the trees behind her.

Shards! She was low on freshweed, so she'd skipped taking it and they'd picked up her scent. She was too far up the trail to run back to a tree. Marlies snatched a rope from her rucksack and sprinted up the hill, keeping an eye on the rocky mountainside.

Thank the Egg, the moon was up or she'd have no chance. There, that outcrop above the trail looked solid enough. She ran toward it, a howl sending gooseflesh along her arms. Marlies tied a dragon's hitch in the end of the rope and threw it at the outcrop.

And missed. The rope hit the ground.

A wolf ran out of the trees, growling. A lone wolf. Was it sick or crazed?

She threw the rope again. It sailed over the outcrop and caught. Oh shards, the wolf was getting closer, its gray pelt a flash against the dark trail. She tugged, tightening the hitch around the jutting rock. The wolf was so close, she could hear it panting.

Grabbing the rope, Marlies swarmed up the cliff. The wolf leaped, and its nose bumped her boot.

The wolf tensed its haunches, jumping again.

Thrusting her feet against the cliff, Marlies pulled hard with her arms, gaining height. There was a jolt that nearly yanked her arms out of their sockets. Marlies slammed against the rock, winding herself. The wolf was swinging in midair, growling, its jaws clamped on the rope. Foam speckled its jawline. It *was* crazed. If her hands were free, she could shoot it, but with it hanging onto her rope, she couldn't even tie herself up to free her hands. Marlies planted her feet against the rock face and hung on.

The wolf wasn't half as clever. It writhed and bucked in midair, thrashing its limbs.

Her arms burned. It was a sheer drop to a narrow trail then the valley below. If the wolf didn't finish her, the mountainside would. "Steady," she called, "or you'll have us both dead."

The wolf growled, its eyes mean slits.

Gradually, it stopped thrashing and hung on, its dead weight making Marlies' arms shriek with pain. This was beyond burning, beyond sore, her arm, shoulder and neck muscles spasmed, begging her to let go. It was only a matter of time.

The wolf dropped to the ground, snarling, and sat on the trail, waiting.

Marlies held onto the rope and, with the other hand, she pulled the rest of the rope up, jamming it between her knee and the cliff face. She rested for a moment, then freed her knife from her belt and hacked off the soggy end of the rope where the wolf's infested jaws had been. The last thing she needed was to become wolf-crazed.

Down on the trail, the wolf snapped up the discarded piece of rope and ran around in a frenzy shaking it. Then it slumped on the trail, gnawing.

How long would it stay there? Well, there was no going down. She pulled herself up until she could climb onto a narrow ledge. Her legs dangling off the edge, she secured herself to the ledge with her rope. If she fell, the knots would yank tight, making it impossible to get down without help. But at least she wouldn't be dead.

She glanced at the wolf. Oh, bad move. Her head spun. She didn't normally get vertigo. Probably a combination of tiredness and no food. But there was nothing she could do until the wolf left. She couldn't take her rucksack off up here. Exposed on the ledge, Marlies pulled her hood tight and tugged her cloak around her. She was sitting tight, stuck again. No one was coming to save her. No dragon would swoop down and pluck her from the ledge.

Oh well, she'd waited eighteen years in Lush Valley; she guessed she could wait a little longer. She wouldn't give up; she had to get to Death Valley and save Zaarusha's son.

Storm Brewing

"We're leaving, Tomaaz, and we're not taking a tharuk spy to Dragons' Hold," Pa whispered. He stood, bumping the table, rattling the weapons and tipping over a pouch of herbs.

"Lovina's not a spy. How could you even think that?" Tomaaz kept his voice low. If Pa kept this up, he'd wake her—asleep in Ezaara's room.

"I won't let you jeopardize the future of our family just because Lovina scrubs up well," Pa hissed.

"That's not on, Pa! You heard what she said!" Tomaaz whispered. He leaped to his feet, grabbing his chair before it fell to the floor. "You saw the lash marks on her back. Bill will kill her if we leave her here."

Pa picked up some smoked meat. "We can't take her with us. What if she's still under Bill's influence?" He shoved the meat in a sack.

"He abducted her. Tortured her. Beat her. She's not on his side. She's—" Tomaaz stopped, unable to speak as he remembered the bloody mess and infected scars on Lovina's back. And Bill smacking her head into that tree.

"Maybe this is what Bill wants—us fighting about her." Pa's breath was ragged. "I'll bet he wants her to sow unrest between us."

"It's not like that. Why can't you believe me?" Tomaaz pleaded. "Pa, it's my fault she's injured. If I hadn't searched the jail for you … if I'd followed Bill instead, he wouldn't have broken Lovina's arm or fingers."

Sympathy flickered over Pa's face.

This was Tomaaz's chance. "He's still out here. It's not safe for her in Lush Valley," Tomaaz said. "You know, you could ask Ernst and Ana what she was like—she's been staying with them."

"We'll see." Pa turned his back and busied himself with packing supplies. "Now that Lovina's asleep, it's time for a proper introduction to our dragons. Grab that sack."

Tomaaz had already met them, but seeing the dragons could soften his father's attitude, so he picked up the sack of food and followed him outside.

The bronze and silver dragons were curled up on the grass, sleeping in the sun. This close, it was hard to believe the size of them, and to get used to the others, blue wings spread, wheeling in the sky.

"Handel and Liesar are exhausted," said Pa. "They've come directly from Dragons' Hold—three days' flight away—and they got caught up for a couple of days in skirmishes in Western Settlement." Pa strode to the bronze dragon and put his sack of supplies into one of the dragon's saddlebags, which was large enough to hold a man—well, a small one, anyway. "Tomaaz, meet Handel."

Tomaaz nodded, putting his sack in the saddlebag.

"You can speak, Son. He understands you." Pa's eyes danced with amusement.

"You're joking, right?"

Pa placed Tomaaz's hand on the dragon's snout.

A deep voice rumbled through his head. *"Now, why would that be a joke? Think I'm too dumb to understand, do you?"* The dragon's green eyes regarded him, its diamond-shaped pupils narrowing to a slit.

Tomaaz's cheeks heated. "I–I didn't know. I thought—"

Warm dragon's breath gusted across Tomaaz's face and a strange sound echoed in his head, like stones skittering down a bank. Was Handel laughing?

"Of course I am."

"So, you're Pa's dragon?"

"No, Tomaaz. He's my rider." Handel winked at him. *"You don't have to speak out loud. While you're touching me, I can hear your thoughts—it's called mind-melding."*

Keeping his hand on Handel's head, Tomaaz let the memory of Bill attacking Lovina resurface. *"Can you help me convince my father that we should take her with us?"*

"She's important to you, isn't she?" Handel asked.

Was she? Tomaaz hadn't really thought about it. She just needed help.

"Well, you'll never find out if we don't bring her. I'll see what I can do."

"Tomaaz." Pa's voice made him start. "This is Liesar."

Tomaaz went over and laid his hand on the silver dragon's head. Like Handel's, her scales were smooth, warm and supple—like soft leather. *"My mother's your rider, isn't she?"* There was no mistaking those turquoise eyes.

"It's been a long time, but yes." Liesar regarded him. *"Greetings from your sister. She's doing well at Dragons' Hold."*

"Thank the Egg. I was worried about her."

"It's funny, you know," the silver dragon melded. *"You cuss like a dragon rider, even though no one in Lush Valley likes dragons or riders."*

"What do you mean?"

"'The Egg' and 'shards' refer to the legendary great Egg, from which Arisha, the Great Dragon, the mother of all dragons, was born. 'Sharding' is what happens when a dragon bursts forth from its egg." Liesar chuckled.

"Lots of people here speak like that."

"Ironic, isn't it?" The dragon yawned. "I'd better get some sleep. It'll be a long flight back. Make sure you leave one of my front saddlebags empty for Lovina."

"For Lovina?"

"Yes, you want her to come with us, don't you? She'll fit nicely in there."

"Yes, but Pa—"

"Handel's already convinced him." Liesar winked and went back to sleep.

§

Spreading her wings, Liesar ascended into the dark sky, sending a rush of cold wind at Tomaaz's face. Treetops flashed past. He turned to wave to Lofty below, his arm constricted by Pa's dragon riders' garb, but Lofty had already been swallowed by the night. They were so high. Going so fast. Behind them, a few isolated torches winked in the dark. That was all there was of Lush Valley settlement. Nothing else was visible in the dark—his lifelong home, his friends—everything had vanished.

A rush of dizziness hit Tomaaz, and he closed his eyes, gripping the saddle. Shards! If this was flying, Pa could have it. There was no way he wanted to feel this rotten all the time. Leaning low in his saddle, he focused on the silver dragon's neck scales, breathing slowly. He'd never had a great head for heights, but he hadn't ever felt this bad. Then again, he'd never been this high.

In the saddlebag in front of him, Lovina's eyes were shut. She'd woken late afternoon for a few sips of broth, then dozed off again. Even in sleep, her face was drawn in pain. Her knees were tucked up to her chest, her splinted arm resting on them. She started fitfully, muttering in her sleep.

Risking further nausea, Tomaaz leaned over and tugged her blanket up.

§

Hans hunched low in the saddle as Handel circled down and landed by the forest near Western Settlement.

"It's eating at you, not knowing how she is, isn't it?" melded his dragon.

"Yes, I have to know if Marlies is alive. I'll be back soon." Hans jogged off toward Nick's inn. He passed a few cottages, silent and empty. A door banged in the breeze.

On the outskirts of town, glass from the inn's shattered windows crunched underfoot. The front door was ripped off its hinges. Hans paused by the hollow doorway. This wrecked carcass had been home to Nick, Esmeralda, little Urs, and any other littlings they'd had. Using his dragon sight, he scoured the inn: no one alive but no dead either.

Sword drawn, he walked through the yard. The eastern wing was charred debris. The stable doors were smashed and the stench of rotten burned horseflesh hung on the air.

Hans melted into the shadows and raced back to the forest. As he barged through the trees to where Handel and Liesar were waiting, Tomaaz jumped up, nocking an arrow.

"It's only me," Hans called.

"Phew! You put the breeze up my spine, there." Tomaaz lowered his bow, then peered at him. "What is it, Pa?"

Was he that easy to read? Hans shook his head. "I went looking for an old friend. I was hoping he had news of your mother …"

"And?"

"His home has been destroyed and he and his family are gone," muttered Hans. "I can only hope he's fast enough that tharuks don't find him."

Their unspoken question hung thickly in the night air. *What about Marlies?*

§

After traveling all night, Tomaaz's backside ached. For the hundredth time, he adjusted Lovina's covers. At least he could stretch and move. She must be feeling worse, all hunched up in a saddlebag like that. Her face was so pale. The dark rings under her eyes hadn't improved, even though she'd slept for most of their journey.

For a moment, he compared her to Beatrice. She didn't have Beatrice's obvious beauty, but then he doubted she'd spit on anyone either. There was a gentleness about Lovina that surprised him. After so many years of Bill's abuse, he'd have expected bitterness or resentment.

She stirred. Her eyes opened, meeting his. She tried to talk, but only croaked.

Tomaaz leaned forward, holding the waterskin to her lips. "Here, you must be parched."

Lovina drank deeply. Wincing, she adjusted her position—no mean feat with only one good arm.

Tomaaz gave her some dried arnica flowers to chew against the pain.

"Look," Lovina said, gesturing with her healthy arm at the sweeping mountains behind them and the Flatlands stretching miles to distant peaks in the West.

A broad river divided the plains from a forest that spread to the feet of severe snow-clad peaks to the north—it looked like days of flight away. It was so vast and open after living between the Grande Alps.

"It's quite something," Tomaaz replied. "I've never been beyond the Grande Alps before."

"I have." Lovina was silent for a few moments. "But I've never seen any of it without fog. Not that I remember, anyway." She turned to him. "Thank you for giving me clear-mind berries."

"It was nothing." Heat crept up Tomaaz's neck.

"No," said Lovina. "It's everything."

§

They'd been underway for less than a day, when a chill wind rippled in from the west. Shading his eyes, Hans scrutinized the sky. In the distance, above the Terramites, a boiling stew of black cloud was thickening.

Handel and Liesar, we may have to take shelter. Years of being away from Dragons' Hold, and now, when they were only two days' flight away, they'd have to stop. *Or should we fly on, through the storm?*

Easy, Hans, Handel cautioned. *The girl's health is delicate.*

"Exactly why we shouldn't have brought her," Hans said.

"We have a duty to care for those wronged by Zens," Handel replied.

Hans sighed. He had no reply to that, and Handel knew it. *Are there any friendly way-stops nearby?*

Liesar answered, *Star Clearing should be fine. It's only a short flight, and I don't think our enemies have ransacked it yet. No one is likely to attack in a blizzard, so you'll be safe enough if Handel and I shelter in one of the nearby caves.*

It was good to hear her voice in his head. They'd lived too long without dragons. If only Marlies were here, with the four of them melding, he'd feel complete. But he had to stop second-guessing her decision to help Zaarusha. They owed the queen. *Handel, I haven't been able to see anything about Marlies yet. Have you had any luck?* Hans pulled his hood up against the cold.

I've seen some vague images, but nothing definite yet.

What were they?

I'd rather wait until I have something concrete, Hans.

Well, some things hadn't changed. Handel still hid portents of bad news.

§

Oh gods, Tomaaz was beautiful. His face lit with concern as he leaned over to tuck her in. The wind ruffled his blond hair and made his eyes shine.

But if Lovina wasn't mistaken, he was slightly off-color. Despite the wind blasting his cheeks, his face was pale; and every now and then, a shudder passed through him. He sometimes glanced at the horizon, but never down at the landscape, instead keeping his eyes glued to the dragon's neck—when he wasn't looking at her.

There it was again. He gripped the saddle harder, his knuckles turning white, panic flashing across his features. Poor guy.

Still, he was lucky to have parents and a sister. People who loved him.

"Are you all right, Lovina?" He held her forearm securely, easing the blanket out from under it, so it wouldn't hurt. Then he placed her arm against her body and pulled the blankets up over her. "Your fingers are so cold," he said.

As if she *mattered*.

"Thank you." She hadn't even realized her arm was half frozen until it was nestled against her—or that her bandaged broken fingers had stopped aching because they were so numb.

His soft smile made her feel cherished.

Stupid, stupid. He was just making sure she was comfortable. It was nothing special. Nothing personal. Just the healer's son looking after his charge. Lovina sighed. Life was one endless round of pain. And Tomaaz was no exception. As soon as she was healed, he'd ignore her, like everyone else did.

§

Tomaaz squeezed his eyes shut, clinging to Liesar's neck, trying to shake the dizziness. Liesar swooped. Not again. His stomach lurched, threatening to turf his lunch into the air—or worse, over Lovina. He swallowed back bile, stifling a groan. Thank the Egg, Lovina wasn't awake to see his discomfort. Actually, this was torture.

Lovina's lash marks flitted to mind. No, this was nothing. He had to face his flight sickness with courage. Sitting up straight, Tomaaz opened his eyes. Trees loomed and receded as Liesar executed a tight spiral.

He snapped his eyes shut again. Lovina was awake, watching him. He stifled another groan, not from nausea but from embarrassment. He'd fought tharuks, slain them, but couldn't stomach riding a dragon.

Her hand closed over his and she squeezed his fingers.

Tomaaz couldn't respond, his fingers grasping the saddle in a death grip.

With a whump, Liesar was on the ground.

After a few deep breaths, Tomaaz opened his eyes.

Pa approached and patted Liesar's hide. "Well done, girl, a lovely landing."

Right, absolutely lovely. Tomaaz swallowed, clearing the acid from his throat.

"How did you like flying?" Pa asked, eyes shining. "It's great, isn't it?"

"Sure," Tomaaz replied with fake enthusiasm. "Really great."

Lovina would know he was a hypocrite, but he didn't have the heart to tell Pa that flying wasn't for him. He'd go to Dragons' Hold to see Ezaara, but he'd never be a dragon rider.

Snowed In

The wolf had left a few hours before dawn. Any longer and Marlies would've frozen on that ledge. Dark clouds scudded toward her, their swiftness taking her breath away. Snow was coming—soon. The wind picked up. She tightened her jerkin and cloak and tugged on her gloves, then leaned into the wind, making her way through the snowy drifts across the trail.

Higher up, the wind howled and the snow drifts grew. She'd never make it to Devil's Gate today. Still, if she couldn't travel, neither could tharuks. Now, she desperately needed a place to hunker down.

Around a corner, the trail widened. A snowdrift as high as her shoulder was piled along the mountain's leeward side. This was as good a place as any. Taking off her rucksack, she retrieved a littling-sized spade. The Lush Valley blacksmith had made two of them for the twins when they were in their fourth summer. Shaking off a pang of longing for her family, Marlies dug a tunnel at the base of the snowdrift.

When it was the length of her torso, she lay on her back and wriggled into the narrow passage. She dug, angling upward to create a level sleeping chamber that could be warmed with her body heat. Her arms ached after the ordeal with the wolf, but she kept digging.

Thoughts of her family chipped away at her. Years ago, Dragons' Hold had been a political thorn bush. Ezaara was so impulsive. Was she stabbing herself on those thorns? Would she fail as Queen's Rider and be cast out?

And Tomaaz? As a littling, he'd brought her lame rabbits, butterflies with torn wings and friends with scraped knees, begging her, with tears in his eyes, to heal them. Now he was older, more resilient, but if tharuks attacked Lush Valley, would they shred him with their claws? Or would their brutality shred his heart?

She attacked the snow with her shovel. Her own desperation to have children had put her in this fix. If she hadn't reached out to Zaarusha's baby, hadn't touched what was forbidden, they wouldn't have been living in a sheltered backwater. Their children would have grown up at Dragons' Hold, strong and prepared.

Then again, if the dragonet hadn't blessed her with fertility, she may never have had children.

And she had.

Marlies had never known Ezaara was going to become Queen's Rider. In a moment of hope, she'd given Ezaara a name that had a syllable common with Zaarusha's name, but she'd never dared dream it would happen. She pushed the loose snow over her belly and out of the tunnel.

When Marlies scrambled out, the temperature had plummeted. Black cloud raced overhead. An icy blast hit her. She snatched up her rucksack and crawled back inside, dragging it by a strap. Marlies broke a fire bean and lit a candle, warming her numb hands over the meager flame.

Her stomach growled. She hadn't eaten since before dawn, and was exhausted, but she couldn't rest yet. She hollowed a shelf at the end of the chamber for her rucksack and sculpted the ceiling to prevent water dripping on her as the chamber warmed up.

Unrolling a tightly-bound oilskin, she laid it on the floor and put her traveling quilt on top. Marlies chewed a piece of stale flatbread. She had more bread, some dried meat and a few of Giant John's vegetables, but she didn't dare eat those now. She needed to save them for Death Valley in case Zaarusha's son was too weak to fly.

With her sword, Marlies created a small ventilation hole in the roof. The weather still raged outside, but the thick layer of snow insulated her against the storm, so it was only a distant hum.

Now, she'd talk to Hans. She took out her calling stone, rubbing it. The surface stayed cold and flat. Sighing, she burrowed into her quilt.

Hours later, Marlies was still listening to the drip drip drip of water from the ceiling.

She rolled over, trying to get comfortable, but it was fruitless. She was stuck again, helpless, not knowing what danger her family was in. Sitting here, she was unable to help Zaarusha or her captive son.

Unable to repay the blood debt she owed her queen.

Star Clearing

A blizzard raged outside, drifts piling up against the cabin. They'd barely made it here yesterday with enough time to unload the supplies and bring in firewood before the storm had hit. The upside was not being flight sick any more. Well, that and Lovina not being cramped in a saddlebag.

Pa had passed the time teaching Tomaaz and Lovina about Dragons' Hold and dragon rider history. He'd even mentioned the many safe caves scattered throughout the realm, supplied with food and gear for emergencies. But Tomaaz was itching for action. Being cooped up inside wasn't his idea of fun.

Neither was fighting tharuks, although Pa was keen to teach him about that, too.

"You're right, Son. The best place to wound them are the vulnerable spots where their fur isn't so matted, like their armpits, under their chins and behind their knees."

"Oh, and their eyes," Tomaaz replied, whittling a stick before the fire.

Lovina was in a chair, bundled up in a quilt, still pale and obviously in pain.

Tomaaz lifted a pot off the fireplace and tipped some water into a mug, adding herbs. "This pain draft might help," he said, setting it on a stump before her. "Just let it cool for a while."

She nodded, staring at the fire.

Had he done something to upset her? Was it her injuries, or was something else bothering her? Over the last few hours, she'd withdrawn.

Pa threw some onions into a pot with dried meat and herbs. "At Dragons' Hold, we'll eat better than this. You'll be trained up and tested as a rider. If you're lucky, you might imprint with a blue dragon and be called to the blue guards."

Him? Dragon rider material? Tomaaz doubted it. "Blue guards—like the ones now in Lush Valley?"

Pa nodded. "They're stationed in Montanara. A friend of mine was captain of the green guards in Naobia. Further to the west, there are red guards; and browns in the far north. It's essential that we patrol our borders to prevent enemies from taking the realm."

"If we have all these guards, how did Zens get so much power?"

"Zens is from a world with deep knowledge about how nature works, how bodies and minds can be controlled. He came through a world gate and began creating tharuks, sexless beasts, that he grows somehow, like we grow a plant from a cutting." Deep furrows ridged Pa's brow. "When I was on the dragon council, we had no idea how, but I'm hoping they've made some progress." He shook his head. "It's been twenty-five years since Zens arrived, and if we don't defeat him soon, we never will."

§

Lovina was sobbing. Pulling back his blankets, Tomaaz padded across the floor. He was halfway when the sobbing stopped. An unnatural stillness followed.

Should he comfort her or go back to bed? She obviously didn't want him to know she was upset, saving her tears for the middle of the night. The whisper of a tight inhalation—as if she was afraid to breathe—made up his mind. No one should live with that much fear.

Approaching the bed, Tomaaz sat on his heels, his face at the same height as Lovina's pillow. "I'm here. Lovina. You're safe."

Another tight sharp gasp in the darkness.

This might take time, and the fire had died completely. Tomaaz went back to his bedside and grabbed his shirt and jerkin, pulling them on. When he reached her bedside again, he whispered, "Are you warm enough?"

"Yes." Lovina's voice was so thin he had to strain to hear it.

Tomaaz sat by her bedside, waiting for her breathing to relax into a normal cadence. "How long did you live with Bill?" he asked. Not that you could call it living.

"Eight years."

So long—and they must've been nightmare years. But it made sense; they'd been bringing cloth to Lush Valley since he was about nine. "I'm glad you're not with him now."

"Me too. Um …"

He waited, but she didn't finish her sentence. "How can I help?"

§

Help? All he'd done was help her.

And she'd repaid him by dragging him out of his bed, so he could sit here, freezing in the dark.

"Lovina, what can I do?" He spoke gently, as if she was a precious vase that might shatter.

She wasn't precious. Already broken, she was far beyond healing. She'd never be whole again—no matter how gently he spoke or how tenderly he applied his healing herbs. Tomaaz, with the future shining in his eyes, could never put the shards of her life back together. The Lovina she'd been would never be there again. Although she was free, the fragments Zens and Bill had left her in were worthless, best crunched underfoot.

"Would you accompany me out back?" She coughed, embarrassed. She should go on her own; her legs weren't broken, only her arm.

A quiet chuckle escaped him. "Of course. Just let me grab some warmer clothes." He pulled on the heavy cloak he'd worn when he'd gone outside for more wood.

She got out of bed, and he passed her a jerkin, which she put on, leaving her arm out of the sleeve. He draped another cloak around her.

"No!" she whispered, shrugging it off. "That's your father's."

"He won't mind," Tomaaz whispered in the dark, pulling the cloak around her again, and tugging the hood over her hair. "He'll be happier if you use it than if I let you get sick."

Bill would've beaten her if she'd ever worn his cloak.

The coarse wool enveloped Lovina, an unfamiliar but comforting embrace.

"We might need these too." He grabbed his sword and a couple of blankets and guided her past his father's rumbling snores to the door.

The two of them slipped outside into the snow, tugging the door shut behind them. The chill wind was like an open-handed slap to Lovina's face. She pulled the hood closer against the swirling snow.

"This way," he said, taking her around the back of the cabin to the outhouse.

Thankfully, he was here. The air was so thick with snow, she probably would've gotten lost if she'd tried this on her own.

"Careful." He took her uninjured arm, guiding her over a solid lump in the snow—maybe a log. Everything was indecipherable in this land of dark and murky white.

It was a relief to finally get there and know someone was watching outside, and that she'd still be dry when she got back into bed—a luxury after sleeping on stone and dirt floors for years.

Once she was done, they started back, Tomaaz wrapping an extra blanket around her.

What were those shadows? They reminded her of—

"Tharuks!" he whispered, close to her ear.

§

Tomaaz's hand flew to his sword. Through dark flurries of snow, three or four shadowy figures were creeping up to the cabin door. The unmistakable odor of tharuk blew toward them. He couldn't attack. He had to get Lovina to safety. His arm tightened around her shoulders and he drew her away, toward the trees. Pa was still sleeping, but he couldn't go back for Pa. He'd made that mistake in Lush Valley. He could warn him, though. "Can you run?" he whispered in her ear.

She nodded, and they dashed away from the cabin. Tomaaz's boot hit a snow-covered stone. He lifted it and hurled it back at the cabin. It thunked on the roof.

Tharuks snarled, loud enough to wake the dead. Now, Pa had warning.

Tomaaz and Lovina raced off, snarls echoing through the trees behind them. At least one tharuk was following them. Thank the Egg, the wind was in their favor. The snow would erase their tracks, but the cold could kill them. Deeper into the trees they ran, zigzagging and leaping logs. Snow was falling in thick clumps. A roar penetrated the dark, but Tomaaz kept going, pulling Lovina after him by her good arm. She must be in agony, but, injured, she was no match for a tharuk.

They plowed on.

Dark shapes loomed ahead. Tomaaz slowed, placing a cautionary hand on Lovina's arm as they approached. The shapes turned out to be boulders.

"You shelter here while I get the tharuk," he whispered, leaving her under an overhang.

Lovina gave a mute nod.

Tomaaz doubled back and hid behind a broad tree. In the eddying snow and blasting wind, it was hard to make out the beast until it was near. Its head was down, snout to the trail.

Tomaaz waited until the beast had passed and, with the snow muffling his footfalls, struck from behind, jamming his sword into the back of the tharuk's knee. The tharuk didn't go down. It whirled, kicking snow in Tomaaz's face, and slashed at his torso. Tomaaz struck it on the hand, then went for a low strike, aiming at the soft tissue of the beast's belly. His blade bounced off armor. Avoiding the tharuk's claws, he lunged, driving his sword up into its throat, and the tharuk dropped, face first, in the snow.

The wind picked up, snow churning around him so he could hardly see, but finally he made it back to the boulders. Lovina passed him the blankets and he tied them around their shoulders. They were scant cover in a storm like this. Walking, he led Lovina, his other hand outstretched to prevent them from bumping into trees—or tharuks. What if there were more?

Lovina, stumbled, yanking his arm, and went down.

Tomaaz knelt beside her. "Are you hurt?"

She shook her head vigorously. "J-just t-tired." Her teeth were chattering, body wracked with shivers, and her hands were icy.

Tomaaz held them, easing her to her feet. "There's a cave around here somewhere, where the dragons are sheltering." He had to find them, so they could help Pa. "Handel and Liesar can breathe fire to warm us up. It'll be nice to be warm again, won't it?"

Lovina stared at him. "Do you know where the cave is?"

"Ah …" She'd seen through him. His bravado leaked away, leaving him flat. "No, but our only chance of staying alive is to keep moving."

§

It was like being in the clutches of numlock all over again: the gray obscuring her vision; the icy-cold nothingness inside her; the searing in her arm; the drudgery of one foot in front of the other, unable to think of much else. Right. Left. Step over a log. Right yourself from stumbling.

The only warmth had been the hand clutching hers. Dragging her forward when she could no longer walk of her own volition.

And now that hand was icy, too. Their blankets and cloaks were sodden, and they were chilled to the bone.

Still, Tomaaz pulled her on. She knew why: if he stopped, they'd never get up again.

Haven

The gray of dawn gave way to a gray wall of rock that rose above the trees to their right.

"There," Tomaaz croaked, pointing at the pockmarked rock face. A flock of ruby swallows soared out of a cave, their underbellies flashing blood red against dark wings.

Lovina didn't even look up.

His arm around her shoulder, they shuffled through the knee-deep snow. His shoulders sagged. Those caves were so close, but his legs were stone and feet were ice, making it a grueling task to get there.

The first cave they came across was at ground level and far too shallow, with snowdrifts piled high inside. There were a couple of caves up high, but Lovina could hardly climb. Tomaaz scanned the sky for dragons. If only he was a rider and could mind-meld with Handel or Liesar.

After stumbling further, there was an opening a few meters above them, half obscured by bush. It looked like there was a goat track to get up there.

"Lovina." Tomaaz peered into the cowl of her cloak. Her face was blank and eyes dark-ringed. "We might have found a place. Wait here while I check the track."

Her eyes darted to the trees. She nodded, hunching her shoulders and cradling her arm.

Tomaaz checked for tharuks, then pushed himself to scurry up the short steep slope to the cave. Shoving aside the brush, he entered. Snow had piled to one side of the entrance, but not very far. The rest of the cave was roomy and dry. Reluctant to leave Lovina alone any longer, Tomaaz rushed back outside.

She was gone.

Dashing down the track, skidding and leaving brown gouges in the snow, he followed her tracks. Behind a tree trunk, a shadow moved against the snow.

Lovina stepped out.

"Gods, Lovina, I was worried."

"Sorry, I was sheltering from the wind."

Tomaaz laughed. "I've found a cave. It looks great."

For the first time since they'd run away from the tharuks, she smiled.

§

It was hard going, getting up to the cave. Lovina dragged herself inside, hoping to find some warmth, but it was bone-numbingly cold. It was dry, though. Her foot bumped something in the dark and she stumbled. She ran her hands over a rectangular wooden box. She tried to lift it, but, with only one good arm, the box was too bulky.

"I've found a chest," she called.

Tomaaz came over. "Let me see." He dragged it to the entrance, opening a bronze latch on one side. "Lovina, you're fabulous. Look. This must be one of the safe caverns that Pa mentioned yesterday."

She inhaled sharply. This was better luck than a golden eagle, not that Lovina had seen one for years. The chest held dry clothes, tinder, a flint, candle stumps and some dried meat and fruit. Her mouth salivated at the sight of the food, and her hand shot out. She couldn't help it. She was starving.

"Here." Tomaaz passed her some dried peaches. "Have these for now, until we can get something warm into you."

The sweetness of the dried peaches made Lovina's mouth water, but her teeth were chattering so hard it was difficult to chew.

He dragged the chest back into the cave, and then struck the flint. It flared, and he lit a piece of tinder, holding it up so they could see their surroundings. "More luck." Beaming, he gestured at a blackened pot sitting in a crude circle of stones, and a stack of firewood against the cavern wall. "We'll have a hot drink in no time. Pass me that candle."

Tomaaz lit the candle stump and sat it on a high ledge, then gave Lovina a woolen undershirt and some breeches and a jerkin made of dark heavyweight fabric. "Um, you'll have to strip your wet things so we can dry them. If you go back there, I'll, ah … turn around and make a fire." He blushed, the tips of his ears turning red, then busied himself with the wood.

Still shivering, Lovina tried her best to pull her things off with one arm, but it took forever and she kept stumbling.

"Are you managing?" he called, as the fire flared to life and the wood took.

True to his word, he kept his back to her.

She grunted. "A few more moments." Abandoning all pretense at grace, Lovina sat on a cold boulder to tug her breeches up her numb legs one-handedly, and wriggled her way into her woolen undershirt. By then her arm was aching and she couldn't hold the jerkin to get her good arm into it. "Um … my arm?"

He was there in an instant, bringing her over to the fireside. He eased the jerkin over her shoulders and onto her good arm, and nestled her sore arm against her torso. "That'll stop your arm from being bumped." His cheeks flushed again as he buttoned the front with her arm still inside.

"Right, time for a drink." Snatching up the pot, he dashed out, returning with it half full of snow, and put it on the fire.

When the water was simmering, he added a few dried berries and leaves from a pouch in his pocket. Grinning sheepishly, he said, "Ma was always chiding me for leaving too many things in my pockets. Today, it's coming in handy."

A sweet aroma wafted from the pot.

Soon they were sipping from mugs they'd found on a ledge, the crackling fire throwing its warmth out like an embrace.

"Mm, what's this?"

"Soppleberry." He winked. "The rumors that soppleberry tea has magical properties are just gossip, but it does taste good."

"That's a shame, we could use some magic to turn those tharuks into rugs for our feet."

He chuckled, a dimple appearing in his cheek.

The sound warmed Lovina as much as the tea.

"Want another one?"

Their hands bumped as he took her mug.

Alarm shot through her. "You're icy. You need to get some dry gear on."

He shook his head grimly. "Not until I get more firewood, scout around for food and erase our tracks."

Her dismay must've shown on her face, because he hurriedly added, "Don't worry, I'll make sure I can still see the cave. You're safe here."

With him. Yes, despite her injuries and the tharuks hunting them outside, she was safer here than she had been in years.

§

Hard up against a trunk, tiny green shoots poked through the snow. Tomaaz pinched a tip with aching fingers and smelled them. It was bear leek. He uprooted some plants and stuffed them in his pockets, then covered the muddy hole with clean snow. They needed to find decent food, without leaving a trail.

Behind the tree trunk were some rabbit droppings—not yet hard, by the look of them. The rabbit's trail disappeared into a nearby burrow. The little blighter was coming out to feast on bear leeks, and there were plenty more, so it'd be back. If he could make a snare …

Plucking some brown dogsbane reeds, Tomaaz twisted the strands to form two thin double-ply ropes. Curse his fingers for being so numb—it was taking ages. He kept checking the woods and glancing back at the cave. It was quiet for now. The longer he was out here, the higher the chance of being discovered. And he'd freeze if he didn't get out of these damp clothes soon and into something warmer.

There, the ropes were done. He twisted them into a snare, fumbling to tie them, then fastened one end to a bendy branch that would provide great tension for his trap and tied the other end to a twig in the ground.

Carefully backing away so he wouldn't set the snare off, Tomaaz heard a loud crack. He spun, heart pounding.

It wasn't a tharuk. A branch, laden with snow, had snapped and hit the ground, leaving the sharp scent of tree sap. He had to get out of here, back to Lovina.

And find out if Pa was all right. Hopefully, he'd fought those tharuks off.

Tomaaz grabbed some branches out of the snow for firewood and, dragging a leafy branch behind him to cover his trail, retreated back toward the cave. Every now and then, he dropped a bit of bear leek, covering it with a thin layer of snow, hoping the pungent oniony scent would mask his trail. He kicked snow off the sides of the goat track into the furrow he'd left earlier, dragging the leaves over the top. It was a poor cover-up job, but his legs were heavy and his hands were numb to the elbows.

He paused at the entrance of their hideout. The fire was blazing. Lovina was standing at the rear of the cave, a charred stick in her hand, singing softly, with a beautiful clear voice that made his heart soar. She leaned in with unconscious grace, placing charcoal strokes to the boulder. She was drawing—with her good hand.

But what was she drawing? What had her so transfixed that she hadn't heard him?

He was intruding on her private moment. Tomaaz felt his cheeks pinking. Awkward, but fascinated, he stayed, afraid to move in case he broke the spell.

She added a few more lines to the stone, her body obscuring her art. Placing the stick against the wall, she rubbed at her stone canvas with her fingers, here and there, then stepped back. Still singing under her breath, she tilted her head, as if evaluating her picture. Her singing stopped, and she stood in silence for a long moment.

Tomaaz's arms were cramping with the effort of holding the firewood, and he was frozen to the bone, but moving now would be like admitting he'd been spying on her. Tomaaz cleared his throat.

Lovina spun, her coal-smudged hand flying to cover her mouth. "Ah, h-how did you go?" she asked.

He dropped the firewood in a heap and approached her, every step a leap across a chasm, his boots leaving pools of thawed snow in his wake.

The firelight painted her features with its golden glow. Silently, she watched him, forget-me-not blue eyes locked on his.

Tomaaz stopped close to her. Her eyes searched his face, brushing over every plane. No one had ever looked at him like *that*. As if she really saw *him*.

With a flash of insight, he realized that no one had seen her the way he was seeing her now, either.

He gestured at the stone. "Do you mind showing me?"

"It's nothing …" She shrugged nervously. "All right. You can see."

They both moved at once, bumping into each other. They stepped to the other side, bumping again. Lovina giggled and moved aside.

It was him. In charcoal, on stone.

She'd captured his tousled hair, the dimple in his left cheek.

"Do I really tilt my head like that?"

"Yes, and your eyes …"

He tilted his head. "My eyes, what?"

She scraped her foot back and forth on the floor, not meeting his gaze, and mumbled.

He tilted her chin, so he could see her eyes. "What, Lovina?" he asked so softly, he barely breathed the words.

Her forget-me-nots stared directly at him, and she whispered, "They're full of kindness. You look at the world with love."

Her scarred back flashed to mind. The blazing pyre with his Pa tied to the stake. And her refusing to testify against Pa, even though she knew Bill would lash her. "And you're brave. Courageous."

Her eyebrows flew up. "M-me? Brave?"

"Brave." He gestured at her art. She'd shown him a glimpse of her soul. Shown him himself, as she really saw him. "All those years with Bill, never giving up."

"My pictures kept me alive." A tear slid down her cheek. "In Death Valley, Ma died, Da, my brothers …" Lovina sniffed. "There was a tharuk …" she whispered.

Tomaaz stepped closer, angling his head so he could hear.

"… 274, his name was. He liked my art. I drew him little sketches in the dirt with my fingers, or on a scrap of hide with coal. Rabbits, squirrels, owls …. He gave me extra food, hid me when they were beating slaves." She shook her head. "My art kept me alive. Every day, I try to draw, thankful I survived."

He couldn't help it. Tomaaz's arms encircled her shaking shoulders, and he pulled her against his chest.

She gently pushed him away. "Tomaaz! You're freezing!"

"Oh shards! I'm making you wet." He waved her to the fireside. "Go and warm up while I get dry."

Grabbing some dry clothes from the chest, he went back to the boulder to get changed.

His charcoal face stared at him, smiling, eyes filled with tenderness. How had she captured that? Her art was stunning. Amazing. But nowhere near as incredible as her.

§

After all Tomaaz had done for her, Lovina couldn't sit idly. She put more wood on the fire and took the pot to the cavern mouth, filling it with clean snow. Pacing back to the fire, she caught a glimpse of his broad shoulders and muscled back as he tugged on a woolen undershirt. She glanced away, her cheeks growing hot, and tossed a handful of dried fruit into the pot of melting snow. That one glimpse had warmed her faster than any campfire.

Lovina bustled to the cave mouth. She dragged back one of the branches he'd fetched—her bad arm making her slow—and left it to dry by the fire. Her arm was aching, and her ribs, too, where Bill had kicked her. She'd healed before, though. Bill had hurt her more times than she could remember, layering pain upon hurt, gashes upon bruises. Lovina picked up the next branch.

Suddenly, Tomaaz was there beside her, picking up the rest of the branches and dropping them near the fire.

Now that she'd seen them, she couldn't help but notice his arms and back as he worked. Lovina stirred the fruit tea, biting her lip. He wasn't hers; never would be.

Tomaaz hung a sodden blanket over the half-open entrance. "To stop anyone seeing our fire," he explained. "The wool's dark enough not to be noticed." He hung the other blanket near the fire to dry and busied himself with the mugs.

"No," she said, taking the mugs from him awkwardly with one hand. "You sit by the fire. You're tired and cold."

He protested. She'd known he would. "You looked after me before," she said, setting the mugs on a rock. "Now it's my turn." She poured the water and fruit into the mugs and passed one to him.

He smiled, inhaling the steam. "I feel warmer already." His green eyes shone in the firelight, like those pearlescent-green Naobian seashells she'd seen in her travels.

Like he liked her.

But how could he? Her body would heal, but inside, she was broken beyond repair.

§

Cold stone floor. Glowing embers. Where was he? A scream jolted him into reality.

Lovina! He scrambled around the fire.

Still asleep, she took another deep breath. Gods, what if a tharuk heard her? He shook her shoulder.

Her eyes flew open, fear contorting her face.

"Lovina, it's me, Tomaaz. You were having a nightmare. Sorry, I thought someone might hear you."

"Tomaaz?"

He liked the way his name fell from her lips.

She sat up. Shuddering. "I was back in Death Valley. They were beating Ma …" A sob wracked her frame, then another.

Tomaaz stirred the embers with a stick, not sure what to do.

She kept crying.

He slipped an arm around her shoulders and pulled her tight against his side, cradling her head against his shoulder, letting her cry.

A Nasty Surprise

Marlies woke to the patter of drips from the ceiling. She'd been stuck in the snow cave for days. She wriggled the sword in the ventilation shaft to dislodge the loose snow. Something was different. She cocked her head. It was quiet outside; the storm had stopped.

She threw her things in her rucksack. She had to get out of here before tharuk patrols came over from Devil's Gate. Surely, she wasn't that far away now. How in the Egg's name was she going to free a captive dragon? Marlies sighed. She'd figure that out later.

She slid her rucksack down the tunnel mouth and kicked it out of the tunnel. Marlies scrambled upright.

A snarl sounded behind her. Whirling, she gripped her sword. Two tharuks were running down the trail at her.

Snatching her bow and quiver off her rucksack, Marlies nocked an arrow and shot. It flew straight into a tharuk's snout. It let out a roar of pain and clutched at the arrow, trying to yank it out. That would only make it angry. Loosing another arrow, she hit it in the head and it toppled across the track.

But now the other tharuk was nearly on her. Marlies leaped sideways. It slashed out, catching her shoulder and upper arm. Her sword arm throbbed, the cold air stinging the gashes.

The tharuk was on her again. Marlies cringed into the icy mountain face, cowering before the tharuk; a risky move, but a risk she'd take. As the snarling beast prowled closer, she gripped the rock and kicked out with both feet, sending the tharuk backward over the mountainside.

Marlies landed on her backside, her blood splattering the snow. She reached into her pouch and wrapped a strip of bandage around her arm. She had to go before more troops came. Retrieving her gear, and cradling her injured arm, Marlies stepped over the dead tharuk and started up the steep slope toward Devil's Gate.

Weathering the Storm

Lovina's nightmare kept them both up, talking quietly until dawn. Only then had she fallen into an exhausted sleep by the fire. Tomaaz dozed most of the day, half an ear open for intruders.

When he woke, he checked the snare, not expecting to find much after checking a few times the day before, but they'd been in luck. The fat buck soon ended up in the pot.

Tomaaz stirred the rabbit stew with a stick, then threw another handful of bear leek into the pot. His stomach grumbled, protesting at the wait. They'd exhausted the cache of dried food last night before they'd fallen asleep. He gave the stew another stir.

"It's a starry night. I think the storm has passed." Lovina was at the cavern mouth, peeking out the side of the blanket.

He nodded. "We'll leave first thing in the morning." There wouldn't be any fresh snow to cover his tracks outside. To stay any longer would be dangerous.

Lovina moved back toward the fire, wincing as she walked.

"I'll check your arm after we've eaten. How's your head?" The gash had healed well, forming a clean scab.

She shrugged her uninjured shoulder. "My head's fine, but if we open the bandage on my arm, it'll probably just get dirty. It's not as if we have clean cloths, here, or cleansing herbs."

"Good point. We'll check it as soon as we're back at the cabin."

He didn't dare mention his worst fears. Pa hadn't found them, and neither had the dragons. Each time he'd gone out yesterday to check the snare, he'd scanned the skies. Once he'd seen a distant dragon, and jumped and waved, but it hadn't seen him. He hadn't dared call out. Another time he'd seen a flash in the sky, but it had only been an eagle. Was Pa alive? Were the dragons still here? Or did Pa think they were dead?

And what about Ma, traversing the realm on her own?

Tomorrow they'd strike out and try to find the cabin, although in this vast forest, it was like seeking a thimble on the ground in a crowded marketplace. And if they found the cabin, what would they be facing? Pa's dead remains? A slew of slaughtered tharuks? Or Pa fighting beasts? He didn't want to burden Lovina with his worries, but if they couldn't find the cabin, what then? They'd be stuck, far from anywhere, stranded, without adequate weapons or food.

One step at a time. First, they'd eat, then sleep. The morning might bring new possibilities.

Lovina brought their mugs over. "I've searched for bowls in that chest, but this is all we have."

"They'll do fine." Tomaaz smiled, trying to put her at ease. "Unless you want to eat straight from the pot?"

"Without spoons or forks?"

He poured the thick stew. They held their mugs, blowing on the steaming contents.

Lovina's stomach growled.

"Sounds like a bear, sniffing out the bear leek," Tomaaz quipped.

She grinned. "If you'd told me two weeks ago that I'd be sitting in a cave today, free of Bill, eating rabbit stew, I wouldn't have believed it."

"You're safe now," he said.

"Tomaaz," she used his name again. With her accent, it sounded so exotic. "I know you must've traveled all over with Bill, but where are you from, originally?"

Lovina ducked her head. "Monte Vista."

"Where's that?"

"Northwest of the Flatlands, near the foot of the Terramites on the very edge of the Great Spanglewood Forest."

Tomaaz shrugged. "I've heard of the Flatlands, but—"

Lovina laughed.

It took his breath away. Musical and clear, he couldn't remember any other sound giving him such a light carefree feeling in his chest. He grinned. "What?"

"Lush Valley bumpkin!"

His grin grew wider. "Yeah, I know, I've never been out of Lush Valley."

"You're lucky. It's must've been a beautiful place to grow up." Her smile faded. "That'll all change now that tharuks have breached the pass."

"We have to stop them."

She nodded. "Zens' tharuks aren't kind, even to the littlings."

She'd suffered so much. She had no idea how brave she was.

After their meal, Tomaaz took down the blanket hanging above the fire and passed it to her. "It's nice and warm, a little smoky, but it'll be better than sleeping on the cold stone again." Would she sleep tonight? Or would her nights always be plagued with the terror of remembering?

She held the wool to her cheek. "I can't let you sleep on bare rock."

"Can't be helped. If I take down the other one, someone might see our fire. Or the smoke." With the entrance blocked, the smoke was funneling up through fissures in the cavern roof, getting lost in the mass of stone above them.

Lovina stared at her feet, her voice breathy. "We could share. It might help my nightmares go away." She looked up, her forget-me-nots pleading. "Please." Her voice quivered, a whisper sliding inside him, melting his heart.

An ache built in his chest. "Of course," he whispered back, stroking a strand of hair from her face. "Of course we can share."

They nestled near the fire, Lovina on her left side facing the flames, and Tomaaz snuggled along her back with his arm over her, careful not to bump her injured arm.

Sharing a blanket was a lot warmer than he'd anticipated.

Lovina hummed the melody she'd been singing while drawing him yesterday.

He propped himself up on one arm so he could see her properly. "Is that a Flatlander song?"

"Yesterday, I remembered Ma singing me this song when I was a littling." She rolled onto her back, smiling up at him. "I'm starting to remember things, Tomaaz."

Her hair gleamed in the firelight, all coppery hues, honey and burnished browns. Gods, she was beautiful. He lowered his head toward her, breathing in her warmth.

Then they were kissing.

§

Tomaaz's arms closed around Lovina, gentle with her injured arm, warm and reassuring. He'd come to mean so much to her, so fast.

His kisses trailed across her cheek, to her nose, her eyelids. "Brave," he murmured. "So brave and beautiful."

She'd never felt this. Never felt *treasured*. Never felt *home*.

§

In the wee hours, while the embers were still glowing, Lovina's sobs woke Tomaaz. "It's all right, Lovina, I'm here." Cradling her back, he curled around her.

Her cries subsided and she sighed in her sleep, her now-serene face lit by the glow of the embers.

He held her gently, careful of her injuries. She was precious, fragile but resilient. Beautiful, strong and vulnerable. Her trust was sacred, treasure to him. He'd do his best to protect her.

He propped himself on an arm, watching the cave entrance, keeping her safe while she slept.

§

Sunlight filtered through the flapping blanket, waking Tomaaz. It was hanging on an angle. Half of it had come down in the night, but it didn't matter, because they were leaving soon. He'd meant to rise earlier.

Wonder unfurled inside Tomaaz. His presence affected Lovina so deeply. His feelings meant so much to her, and hers to him. It was like unwrapping a gift and finding more than you'd expected.

And knowing you'd discover more each day.

The moment he stood, he missed her warmth. He tucked the blanket around her and stretched. There wasn't much point in making a fire. They had nothing to eat and weren't staying, and they could drink from a stream on the way. The water would be cold, but with the storm over, as long as they kept moving, they'd be warm enough.

While Lovina was asleep, Tomaaz changed back into his own clothes, the air warmer today, and repacked what he'd borrowed into the chest. He'd brought enough wood in yesterday to replace what they'd used, but couldn't do much about the food. Shrugging, he packed the mugs away and stood the pot on the cold fireplace. He donned his cloak.

There was nothing else to do except wake Lovina so she could get ready.

They needed to find their way back through the forest to the cabin. No small task. Shoving dreadful thoughts of Pa's fate out of his mind, he knelt by Lovina and kissed her cheek. "Good morning, sleepyhead."

She turned to him, smiling.

Was the stupid grin ever going to leave his face? He hoped not.

He helped Lovina up and passed her clothing to her, and she made her way to the rear of the cavern.

While she dressed, he strode to the cave mouth to take down the blanket. The trees below were bathed in sunlight and most of the snow had thawed. The goat track was now a trickling stream, edged in white. By tomorrow no one would know the storm had blown through.

Although he doubted he'd ever forget.

After scanning the sky for dragons, Tomaaz ducked back inside, twisting the blankets into snakes and tying them around his stomach, making sure he could still draw his sword.

Lovina approached.

He tucked her borrowed clothes back in the chest. Now that he was getting to know her, Tomaaz couldn't imagine life without Lovina, but he didn't want to scare her. With Dragons' Realm in upheaval and his family splintered, neither of them knew what the future would bring. He'd wait, perhaps talk to her later, when they were at Dragons' Hold.

Tomaaz took Lovina's hand and they left the cave. "The track's slippery; lean on me." The last thing he wanted was for Lovina to fall on her injured arm.

A furry mass hurtled toward them down the side of the cliff.

"Ambush! Back to the cave!" Tomaaz yelled, thrusting Lovina up the track.

He whipped his sword out, dodging the tharuk as it landed downhill, where he'd just been. The beast jumped to its feet, tusks trailing saliva. A tracker.

Another tharuk appeared between him and the cave. A furrow of mud showed where it'd been hiding, further up the bank.

A familiar voice sent a chill down Tomaaz's spine. "You two deal with him." Bill jumped out of the bush by the cave mouth, grabbing Lovina. He gestured at the blanket around Tomaaz's waist. "Thank you for the flag you left flapping in the wind. If it wasn't for that, I wouldn't have noticed your hideout."

Tomaaz had let his guard down.

Lovina kicked Bill's shins. Hard.

Bill grabbed her hair. She screamed, thrashing and punching, as he dragged her into the cavern.

"No!" Tomaaz rushed up the track, the tharuk barreling toward him.

Behind him, the tracker swiped. Tomaaz ran uphill, but there was nowhere to go. Pa had always said to fight smart, not hard, so Tomaaz whirled.

The tracker snorted, a huge globule of saliva flying off its tusks, and charged again. Right before impact, Tomaaz dropped into a crouch and sprung up, driving his sword into the beast's armpit. It roared and cuffed him across the head.

Reeling, Tomaaz stumbled, catching himself before he toppled off the cliff edge. He had to get past the other tharuk to Lovina. Tomaaz scrambled out of the tracker's way and raced toward the furry brute.

There was a shriek. Tomaaz's blood ran cold. "Lovina!"

Then the tharuk was upon him in a flurry of tusks and claws. He dodged. Ducked. Rammed his blade up toward the tharuk's throat. But the beast got him first, slashing his temple. Blood ran into his eye.

"Bleed," the monster snarled.

Temple throbbing, Tomaaz feinted, then leaped under the brute's arm, driving his blade into the side of its neck. The monster dropped. With a sucking sound, he yanked his blade out.

A bellow sounded from behind.

He ran up the slope, the tracker hard on his heels.

A thunderous roar shook the air and a whoosh of flame shot out of the sky. Dragons! Flaming the tracker! A stinking fog of burned fur roiled up the trail, enveloping Tomaaz as he made the top of the goat track and plunged into the cavern.

For a moment, it was too dark to see. A shove sent Tomaaz sprawling. Bill ran out the entrance.

Tomaaz got up, about to pursue him. No, he had to find Lovina.

She was at the back of the cavern, slumped below the boulder, her blood splattered over their picture. Her cheek was gashed. She was pale, her breath shuddering. Tomaaz scooped her up, cradling her against him, and carried her into the light.

"Lovina, Lovina." His throat was raw.

Her eyes fluttered. "Tomaaz?"

"It's me. I've got you." He propped her up near the cave entrance on the dry stone floor and examined her wound. The edges were tinged with green grunge. Bill's blade had been dirty.

Tomaaz slashed a strip of blanket with his sword and dashed outside to wet it in a clean patch of snow. Handel and Liesar were blasting flame between the trees below.

Lovina hissed through clenched teeth as he touched her cut with the icy cloth.

"Bill's knife was dirty. I've got to get the shrot out of your wound."

Lovina grimaced.

That stubborn dirt was mixing with her blood, traces of green spreading through the cut. Tomaaz tried his best to clean it, but couldn't get it all out. "You need healing salve and a bandage. I'll be right back."

Standing at the top of the goat track, Tomaaz cupped his hands around his mouth and bellowed for all he was worth, "Liesar! Liesar!"

The silver dragon wheeled, flying toward him. Thank the Egg, she was still wearing her saddlebags. She landed on the goat track, in a slushy splash, perching on the edge. The ground threatened to crumble under her weight, so Liesar kept her wings out, flapping to keep balance.

Ducking under her wing, Tomaaz used the straps to scramble up her side and open the saddlebag. "Healing salve, needle, squirrel gut and bandages. Lovina's hurt." He didn't have time to put his hand on Liesar's head and mind-meld with her, but she gave a displeased rumble, letting him know what she thought of Bill.

The moment he had what he needed, Liesar flew down to the forest.

Tomaaz smeared Lovina's cut with healing salve and pulled the edges together with a few stitches, glad Ma had insisted he learn some of her craft. If only they had piaua juice ... Never mind, he loved Lovina with every one of her scars and this scar would be no different.

Except that he was partly responsible for this one. "I'm sorry, Lovina. I should've kept watch. I should've thought—"

She pressed a finger to his lips. "Hush." Her eyes drifted shut.

In the end, it was trickier than he'd thought to put a bandage over her cheek. He had to wrap it right around her head. It looked terrible, but it would keep her wound clean while it healed.

The splash of boots coming up the slushy trail announced Pa's arrival. "Son." He gripped Tomaaz's shoulder. "Thank the Egg, we found you both. I've been so worried."

"We were outside when tharuks crept up on the cabin. We had to flee. Were you hurt?"

"A tusk to the leg, but I've had worse." He gestured at his bloodstained breeches. "At least I got three of them." Pa crouched next to him. "Lovina looks worse for wear. How's she doing?"

"Bill gashed her with a blade. I've cleaned it up and stitched it. Not much else I can do."

"Lovina will benefit from proper care at Dragons' Hold. The healers there are excellent." Pa smiled. "Well, they were when your ma was there." He picked up the healing supplies.

Tomaaz cradled Lovina in his arms and carried her down the goat track to Liesar, his boots sloshing through the runoff. "Hey, Lovina, wake up."

Her hand flew to her bandaged face, then she touched the skin above Tomaaz's eye. "You're hurt."

He'd forgotten all about the tharuk gashing his temple. "We'll have matching scars." He kissed her hair, not caring if Pa was watching. "Let's get you to the healers at Dragons' Hold."

Liesar knelt and Pa helped him get Lovina into the saddlebag. Tomaaz tucked the blankets around her.

"Hang on," Pa said, uncorking the healing salve. He smeared some over Tomaaz's wound. "It's just a superficial cut, but you'll be better off with some of this on it. There's food in there, too." He pointed at the saddlebag opposite Lovina.

"I'm glad you got Bill, Pa. He's done enough damage."

Pa shook his head. "We didn't. Bill escaped. Short of setting the forest on fire, Handel and Liesar couldn't reach him." He gestured at his bow, slung across his back. "None of my arrows hit true either, although I think I nicked his arm."

Tomaaz saw her charcoal drawing of them, splattered with her own blood. Bill marred everything beautiful. Ruined everything. Rage surged through him. If he ever saw Bill—

Pa placed a hand on his arm as Tomaaz was climbing into the saddle. "Let it go, Son. We have bigger fish to net. Bill's just one of Zens' pawns. If we can strike at the head, we'll kill all the arms."

"Good advice, Pa." Advice he wouldn't take. Tomaaz climbed into his saddle. The first chance he had, he'd make Bill pay.

Soldiering On

Huddled among boulders near Devil's Gate, Marlies had taken the last of her freshweed so she could stay undetected, but it was still risky being this close to her enemies. She kept her camouflage cloak pulled tightly around her, only leaving a gap for her eyes. This cluster of rocks looked like a giant's discarded playthings in the barren landscape, but made the perfect hiding place.

Tharuk troops were flooding through the towering icy walls—Devil's Gate—marching toward the Flatlands.

And, once again, she could do nothing but wait.

§

Wind howled between sheer ice walls of Devil's Gate. To Marlies' right, on the mountainside above, was a tharuk hut, occupied since dusk. They'd doused the light a while ago, but Marlies had waited before venturing into the pass. Now, she was half frozen, but it was better than being dead.

Creeping forward, Marlies was sure she stood out like a dark blot. Underfoot, the ice, scoured by the fierce wind, reflected the moonlight like burnished metal. She kept to the right wall where she was protected from the tharuks' view. Her boots slipped. Marlies thrust out her arms. Her sword arm hit the wall. It hurt. Had she opened up the wound again? Shards, there was a dark patch on the ice—her blood. She scraped at the wall with her gloved fingers, trying to remove it.

A guttural voice sliced through the night. "Where are you going?"

Marlies froze.

"To check the pass," another answered.

Tharuks, out and about! Their timing couldn't have been worse.

"The pass don't need checking."

"I saw a shadow."

"Get back inside. No wandering at night."

Feet crunched and a door slammed.

Crouched, Marlies waited, in case it was a trap. Then she hurried on, every squeak of her boots on the ice like a drumbeat in her ears.

At last, she was through the pass. The snow was churned up where many tharuks had passed through that day. She kept to their trail, hoping her boot prints would be lost among theirs. The only problem was, hers were going the wrong way.

You didn't have that problem on a dragon. How she ached to fly Liesar again. She would've been across the realm in a few days, instead of weeks of travel.

Her arm throbbed, but she plowed on through the snow. At least it was a fine night; she didn't have to battle through a storm like the one that had raged until this morning—although a storm would cover her tracks.

Near dawn, her head was spinning and her arm was throbbing. Tharuks would soon be on the move. She had to stop. She left the trail to explore. Further along the cliff, she found a cave with a narrow entrance, obscured by a rocky projection. Perfect.

Once inside, Marlies pulled out her bedding, laying it on the cave floor. She couldn't make a fire here. This was Zens' territory. But she could eat some cold food and dress her wound.

Shards, she was tired and dizzy.

Lying on her uninjured side, Marlies closed her eyes. Death Valley was waiting below. Tonight, she'd slip down into the valley, hide her rucksack and mingle with slaves to find out where the dragon was.

Insight

The creature was ravenous. It'd been days since the last putrid scrap of meat had been flung outside his cave. He paced, snarling as the chain tugged on his raw leg. Instinct pushed him to keep moving, despite the pain. If he stopped, he doubted he'd get up again.

He scanned the cave, but didn't dare venture outside to the pallid dawn. He'd tried going out at night, but even the moon had hurt his eyes. Venturing forth under the cover of cloud also hadn't helped—muted light still made his eyes ache. And sunlight made them sear.

Hours later, he was still moving, but slower. A faint scuff made him cock his head, nostrils flaring. Human. Bringing him his pitiful meal. He moved to the front of the cave, squinting in anticipation of the sharp light. But today, the sun only itched his eyes—it didn't burn or blind. Surprised, he opened them wider and went outside.

Before, everything had been a drab gray, leached of color—but now he could see.

He was in an arid wasteland, surrounded by stark hills. The human shambling toward him was barely alive—a thin young male with sunken eyes, holding a spade with a rotten rat on the end. The male stopped every few paces, breathing hard, the spade swaying.

The creature stood transfixed by that swaying spade. The rat's limp hindquarters hung off the shovel's blade, its tail dragging in the dust. With each of the human's uneven steps, the rat slid a little further. If the male stumbled, his next meal would land in the dust, out of reach.

Another step.

Then another.

The creature moved toward the dead-faced human until his leg ached from the chain's bite.

The male tossed the meat off the end of the spade, then put the blade on the ground and leaned on the handle, panting. After a while, he staggered away.

Lying down, the creature stretched its neck toward the stinking rat. He drew back his upper lip, wrinkling his nose, and snapped up the foul-tasting meat. Then he went into the cave to rest.

When he came out again, sunlight seared his eyes. Clawing at the cavern walls, he roared in agony, loosening showers of shale from the hillside. Then the creeping gray blindness took its toll and his mind was dimmed with fog again.

Now, he knew what caused it: he'd only seen clearly when he hadn't eaten for three days. The life-sapping blindness came from something in his food. There was no other explanation for his burning eyes or the blanket of gray shrouding his thoughts and sight.

He had to eat to survive this hell, but eating made everything more hellish. The creature limped past his dung pile, seething. Scheming.

Change of Plans

Lovina's broken fingers were aching. Strange, she hadn't noticed the pain over the last few days unless she moved them, and here she was, cramped in a saddlebag, not moving at all and they were throbbing. She raised her good hand. Come to think of it, so were her fingers on this hand. Her digits curved inward slightly, toward her palms. She'd probably strained them fighting Bill. But both hands? Maybe it was from being cramped in the same position for so long.

Tomaaz glanced down. "We'll stop soon so you can stretch your legs. Are you hungry?"

"If you feed me more, I'll burst." She wasn't used to eating so much, but from what she'd seen, Tomaaz could pack away an entire ox and still be hungry.

Lovina tried to shift, but cramps ran through her feet, her toes were stiff, and she was bone-tired. Weary in a way she hadn't been for years, despite no longer being under the influence of numlock. It must be the strain of the last few days. Or of the last eight years. Now that she was safe, perhaps her body was letting go.

She'd let go emotionally too. She'd never thought she could trust so fast, but Tomaaz had eased his way into her heart.

Hopefully he'd be around a while, not like all the people she'd loved and lost.

Although the trees whisked by beneath them, she barely saw them as her memories rose to the surface, finally freed from the grip of numlock and terror of fighting to survive.

Ma's face flashed before her, clutching her littling brothers as tharuks had dragged them from their home. They'd been reunited with Da as the entire village was driven over the Terramites, lashed by tharuk whips. Da's words now rang in her mind, *"Keep walking straight ahead. Don't look to the left or right. Don't stand out and you'll have a better chance of surviving. And always have hope: one day you'll escape."*

It was advice he hadn't followed. When his littlings had been whipped, he'd fought tharuks tooth and nail, grabbing their whip for himself and lashing a beast until he'd been pulled off and put to death. The last time Lovina had seen him, tharuks had hacked his hands off, then dragged his dead body to the flesh pile. Ma had hidden Lovina's face and the faces of her brothers in her skirts. But Lovina had peeked.

Tears slid down her cheeks.

And so it had been. Her brothers died too, then her mother, then all the settlers she'd known from Monte Vista. She'd become a nameless slave in a sea of lost people.

§

After two nights in the cave with Lovina, Tomaaz had forgotten about his flight sickness. But the flight sickness hadn't forgotten him. The moment Liesar had left the ground, his head had spun and his stomach had lurched. Thinking food might help, he'd eaten until he was stuffed, but that had made things so much worse.

The alps seemed just as far away as they had this morning. His nausea and dizziness made trees seethe, as if they were rising and falling beneath him. He clutched the saddle's pommel, battling a wave of nausea.

The sky was tinged with pink. A least it would be dark soon, and then he wouldn't be able to see as much. Hopefully they'd stop for a few hours of decent sleep.

"Not a fan of flying?" Lovina was awake again.

Tomaaz clenched his teeth, swallowing. "I'd rather walk."

"Then you'd never get to Dragons' Hold."

"I'm not sure I want to go." He gestured at Liesar. "I mean—"

"Feeling sick every time I rode a dragon wouldn't really inspire me to be a rider either. Although, you must want to see your sister."

Her last few words were wistful. All of her family had been killed in Zens' slave camps in Death Valley. "Yes," he said gently. "I'd love to see my sister." He took her good hand, rubbing his fingers across the back of it. "What about you?" It suddenly mattered what she wanted. His stomach lurched, and this time it wasn't from dragon flight, but from the fear of losing her.

She pulled her hand away, wincing. "My hands. They've been sore, cramping today, and now my calves are spasming. I think I need to stretch."

Tomaaz laid his hand on Liesar's hide. *"Liesar, we need to stop for Lovina."*

"Tell her I'll land when the trees thin out."

When Tomaaz relayed the message, relief washed over Lovina's face.

He'd have to watch her—she was obviously in more pain than she was letting on.

§

Tomaaz awoke, snuggled next to Lovina, with Liesar's wing draped over them. The night had started out differently. Pa had been next to Handel, Lovina next to Liesar, and he'd been on a bedroll in the open space between the two dragons. However, the moment Pa was snoring, he'd ducked under Liesar's wing to curl up against Lovina's back. There was no point in her having nightmares if he could alleviate them.

They'd both slept soundly all night.

Nearby, Pa was up.

Oh well, no point putting off the awkward moment. Tomaaz rested his hand on Liesar's belly. *"Thank you for sheltering us."*

"Any offspring of Marlies' is welcome to sleep under my wing." A tinkle sounded in his mind, like a clear high bell—she was laughing. *"And their friends, of course."*

Somehow, the word friend had a whole different meaning when Liesar pronounced it like that. Tomaaz's cheeks flushed hot. Liesar lifted her wing.

Pa's eyes swept over him, taking in his glowing cheeks, his arm draped over Lovina's hip, their proximity.

Well, Pa could think what he wanted.

"Are you two hungry?" Pa asked, holding out bread and sliced apples.

Tomaaz shook Lovina gently. "Wake up. Breakfast time."

She rolled over, grimacing. Her fingers were curled against her palms and, when she got up to walk, she hobbled.

"You feeling all right?" Pa asked.

Lovina smiled, but, to Tomaaz, it looked forced. "Just pins and needles. I'll be all right," she said.

But after a few hours in the saddle, with Lovina's arms and legs spasming, Tomaaz wasn't so sure.

§

The wind ruffled Hans' hair. After nearly eighteen years, he'd been surprised to slip so easily into riding Handel again, sensing his dragon's moods, easing back into the way they worked together as seamlessly as—well, as fabric without seams.

Nearby, Liesar was riding a thermal. On her back, Tomaaz was clinging to her saddle. He seemed to care about this pale slip of a girl, but Hans wasn't concerned. Tomaaz had liked the baker's girl just last week. At Dragons' Hold, there'd be plenty of attractive dragon riders.

"What do you think, Handel? Any pretty riders at the hold for my son?" Hans asked. *"Handel?"*

Something was off. Handel was avoiding mind-melding, a sure sign that he was having visions. *"What is it, Handel? You've seen a vision, haven't you?"*

"Yes, but there's no point in stopping. These forests are too thickly wooded to land."

It was a dire vision, if they had to land. *"Is everything all right at Dragons' Hold?"*

"Things haven't been all right at the hold since you left, but no, that's not it," Handel replied. *"I don't want to burden you before we can take action."*

Burden him? It was something personal. And taking action meant doing something other than flying to Dragons' Hold, so it couldn't be Ezaara. With a sinking hollow in his gut, Hans asked, *"It's Marlies, isn't it?"*

Liesar chimed in. *"You have to tell us. We have a right to know."*

"The visions were vague, but they've been getting stronger."

Not a good sign.

"Is this the one of Marlies injured?" Liesar asked.

"Marlies is injured and you didn't tell me?" Hans blurted out loud.

"It was always blurry, swimmy."

Uncertain, then. *"And now?"* Hans' heart pounded.

"Now, I see her dying. And it's not vague at all."

§

Liesar was descending. Tomaaz held on to the saddle, his stomach doing somersaults and his head spinning like a littling playing swing-about. Lovina gave him an encouraging smile—which made him feel like a total greenhorn. She touched his hand as Liesar spiraled down between the trees to a clearing, thick with thistles. He shut his eyes. Thistles or not, the sooner his feet were on solid land, the better.

Pa slid from Handel's back and raced over. His face was lined with tension. "Tomaaz, I need a word." He strode off so they could speak privately.

Tomaaz slid down the saddle, clutching at the straps. He bent, hands on his knees and sucked in a few deep breaths, then hurried after Pa.

Pa was pacing, ignoring the thistle thorns catching on his breeches.

Tomaaz narrowed his eyes. What was going on?

"I won't beat cream into butter, Tomaaz. Your ma's in danger."

Tomaaz inhaled sharply. "What's happened?"

"Handel's had a vision. Your mother is dying."

Panic surged through Tomaaz. "Where is she?"

"She's in Death Valley."

Death Valley! "Has she been captured? Is she a slave?"

"I don't know, Son." Pa tugged a hand through his hair. "I just don't know. Handel has seen her dying if we don't intervene."

"Then let's go. Now."

"Death Valley's four days' flight away." Pa laid a restraining hand on Tomaaz's arm. "Son, we need a solid plan. We can't take Lovina. She's in no condition to enter such dangerous territory."

It was like a punch to the gut. "But I want to save Ma."

"You can. *You're* fit to travel."

It took Tomaaz a moment. "No!" His mind reeled. "No, we can't leave Lovina here. That's crazy!"

"It is," Pa agreed. "That's not what I'm proposing. It's only a day's flight from Dragons' Hold. Liesar can take Lovina to safety while we rescue your mother." Pa held his palm up. "Neither you or Liesar like it, but there's no other way."

"I'm sticking with Lovina." Tomaaz broadened his stance. Pa could say what he liked, he wasn't changing his mind. "I'm not letting her travel alone."

"She won't be alone, Son." Pa said, sounding totally reasonable, as if he wasn't discarding someone Tomaaz cared about. "Liesar will protect her."

Lovina needed him. She had no one else. Tomaaz folded his arms across his chest.

"Tomaaz," Pa said, "Handel has told me that you're crucial to your mother's survival. I won't trade her life for a girl you hardly know. Your mother will die without *you*."

A girl he hardly knew? Her art. Her smiles. Her trembling body when her night terrors hit. He knew her, and he wanted to know more. He wanted to protect her. She'd been hurt before because of his mistakes.

But he couldn't let his mother die.

§

"I'll be back. Take care and speed well," Tomaaz whispered, his breath caressing Lovina's neck.

Lovina clung to him. Her broken arm, sandwiched between them, throbbed. This pain in her arm kept things real. Life was full of hurt, separation. Death.

Zens would kill Tomaaz too.

She squeezed her eyes shut, holding back hot tears. No one got out of Death Valley alive, unless Zens willed it.

"Lovina, you must have hope." Tomaaz pulled back to look at her.

Chill air snaked between them.

"You have to believe I can do this," he insisted.

"Do I?" Her voice came out flat. She willed herself to believe him, but his warmth was sucked into a dark cold whirlpool inside her.

"I have to try and save Ma."

She nodded. Family was family.

"Lovina," he whispered, "I want to stay with you."

Her heart leaped. Did he mean it?

He slid his arms from her shoulders, gazing at her.

No, he was memorizing her face—girding himself up to say goodbye.

On Fire

Marlies was burning. Everything was fire. The cave, her arm, her head. Groggily, she sipped some water, then fell back to sleep. Her instincts screamed at her to cleanse and dress her arm, but she was tired, so tired.

The walls spinning, she drifted off again.

§

Hans enfolded Marlies in his arms. It was so warm and comforting. She melted against him. But he was burning, licked by dragon flame.

No, her whole world was burning, filled with flame and fire.

Her skin was about to burst apart.

§

Marlies was damp with sweat. Her arm was on fire, hot and puffy. She still hadn't cleaned her wound. How long had she slept?

It was still daytime … no, she'd woken a couple of times in pitch black, so it had been night at some stage. Perhaps it was the next day? Or the day after? Shards, she must be sick if she couldn't tell what day it was. She sat on her bedding and pulled a vial of dragon's breath out of her rucksack to light the cave.

The makeshift bandage on her arm was covered in yellow crusted pus. Gods, she could've been out for days. She peeled the filthy bandage off her arm, gasping as it stuck to her flesh. The wound was red and swollen, festering. It didn't matter how tired and dizzy she was, if she didn't treat it, she would never get to Death Valley—or back to her family.

Marlies grimaced. She'd come so far. She was on Zens' doorstep, only a few hours away, and here she was, useless.

Her forehead was burning and her hands cold—sure signs that her fever was building again. She needed to make a feverweed tisane and brew some clean herb, but with only one candle and mug, she couldn't brew two things at once. Marlies settled for chewing feverweed leaves, not as effective as tea, and warming crushed clean-herb in a cup over the candle. It was best hot, but Marlies didn't have the luxury of time; she had to act before the next wave of fever hit her. It was a shame piaua wouldn't work on infections. A shame she hadn't cleaned and treated her wound when it had happened.

When the clean-herb was lukewarm, Marlies dipped a cloth in it and wiped out her wound, gritting her teeth to stop herself from crying out as she removed crusted pus and scabs. Her wound had swollen so much the hot red skin around it was tight and shiny. It hurt like molten metal. She let it bleed, hoping to purge the wound, then cleaned it some more.

Marlies threw the dirty bandage into a corner and washed her hands with the rest of the clean-herb. Shivering again, she bandaged her arm and got dressed again. She bit some hard flatbread, but it tasted like wood.

She wasn't hungry anyway, so she burrowed back into her bedding and dozed off.

Slipping Away

Wind rushed into Lovina's eyes, making them sting. The vast forest below turned into a blurry wasteland. The wind was causing her tears—only the wind. Tomaaz's face swam before her and she batted it away. Memories hurt. She'd learned that much in Death Valley.

Waves of agony spread up her arms and legs and across her torso.

Something was wrong: these sensations were more than pins and needles; more than spasms. Lovina's thighs and shoulders rippled with agony. Feverish, she drifted in and out of sleep, vivid nightmares clawing at her head.

She tried to pick up the waterskin, but her fingers were locked, bent like tharuk claws—and that was her good arm. The pain in her broken arm, spasming and hitting the side of the saddlebag, made her breath short and gaspy.

Tomaaz had put feverweed in her pocket—if only she could reach it. Her fingers scrabbled at the blankets, but couldn't grip—useless. Like a littling giving up in an avalanche, she slumped, drifting into another round of torture. Images washed through her mind. Zens beating children. Hurting her brothers. And always, that awful tank of his, waiting for her.

A Wing Down

"*Tharuk!*" Handel banked, tipping to the side, but a volley of arrows was flying right at him. He ducked and swooped.

Pain ripped through Hans' mind. "*Where have you been hit?*" he asked his dragon.

"*My wingtip.*"

"*Can you fly?*"

"*Not far. I can make it to that hill. There's a cave there where we can hole up.*"

"*Good.*" But not good at all. While Handel was healing, anything could be happening to Marlies. Hans rubbed the back of his neck. There was nothing he could do.

When they reached the cave, Hans sent Tomaaz off to catch some game, while he rubbed salve on Handel's wing and applied a healing poultice. "*Well, Handel, it's not too bad. Lucky the arrows weren't poisoned and you let me know quickly.*"

"*I'm sorry, Hans, it will delay us a few days.*" Handel butted him in the stomach with his head.

Hans scratched his eye ridge. "*Not much we can do about that. Except rest and heal.*"

Even as he comforted his dragon, Hans chafed to get moving. Every moment they delayed could cost Marlies her life.

§

Behind Tomaaz, Handel was resting on the grass, after a meal, gathering his strength for the last leg of the journey. Although his wing injury had delayed them three days, it had healed well, but they didn't want to take any chances when they were closer to Death Valley.

Pa placed his hand on Tomaaz's shoulder. "You're not enjoying this at all, are you, Son?"

Breaking a piece of flatbread in half, Tomaaz avoided Pa's intense gaze. "Racing to Death Valley to save my mother? No." He took a bite.

"Not that. Flying."

Pa had noticed? He chewed deliberately, giving him time to think. In the distance, the peaks of the Terramites lorded their grandeur above the forest.

In Zens' shadow, the birds were quieter, the forest subdued. He decided not to answer. "How much further?"

"Far enough, if you don't like flying." Pa shrugged. "You know, one of our dragon masters used to get terribly flight sick. As a trainee, the Master Archer, Jerrick, had no stomach for heights. He even barfed from dragonback once." Pa swigged from the waterskin.

"Thanks, Pa. Good to know." Just the thought made Tomaaz queasy.

Closing the waterskin, Pa cocked his head. "Jerrick overcame it."

Tomaaz paused. "How?"

"His friend Alfonso teased him, saying he'd jumped off his dragon to conquer his fear, but we could never get Jerrick to confirm or deny." Hans chuckled. "I can introduce you to him when we get to Dragons' Hold. Maybe he'll tell you his secret."

When we get to Dragons' Hold, not *if*. Interesting. So, Pa was certain they'd get out of Death Valley. Tomaaz had no idea how. From what Lovina had told him, Death Valley was like a fortress—difficult to penetrate and even harder to escape from.

"Any more news about Ma? Have you or Handel had any more visions?"

Face grim, Pa studied him at length, then said, "Yes, I saw her last night."

§

Hans hesitated. There was no point in alarming his son, but there was no point in lying either. In his vision, he'd seen Zens beating Marlies. She'd been in bad shape. Then he'd seen Tomaaz carrying Marlies' limp body. His throat constricted. He couldn't tell if she was alive or dead.

Death Valley was going to be harrowing. Tomaaz would see things that would haunt him for years. But it was worth it to save Marlies. He sighed and passed his son the waterskin. "Drink well; this may be the last untainted water you get for a while. Zens puts numlock in the water supply and in slaves' food."

Shards, what was he doing, taking his own son to Death Valley? Was he mad? The visions he'd had last night—and Handel's—confirmed this was the right course. He hated sending his son into the jaws of the wolf. The thing was, he hadn't seen *himself* in any visions. *"Handel, if we're wrong, I'll lose my family."*

"I know it's been years, but you used to trust our visions. You will *lose Marlies, if Tomaaz doesn't go."*

"And me?" Hans replied. *"What role do I play?"*

"I see nothing. No vision." Handel sent him a mental shrug.

His chest pinched. What if he lost Tomaaz *and* Marlies? Hans pulled out Ana's velvet pouch. Maybe Marlies wasn't in danger yet. Maybe it was yet to happen.

"I'd forgotten all about Ana's gift. What's in it?" Tomaaz asked.

Hans extracted some folded brown paper, opening it to reveal dried auburn berries.

"Clear-mind berries," Tomaaz blurted.

"If we eat them, the numlock won't affect us."

"But surely Zens will be able to tell."

"Yes, because our eyes won't have the gray sheen that Lovina's did, but …" Hans fished in the pouch again and pulled out a vial of gray powder. "Dragon's scale. A pinch of this should make your eyes and fingernails gray, then all we'll have to do is act slow and witless."

Tomaaz snorted. "About now, Lofty would be laughing, telling me I'm witless enough already."

Hans cricked his neck and forced himself to chuckle. "Check your fingernails regularly. Take more dragon's scale as soon as they start pinking. Don't forget. Your life depends upon it."

And Marlies' life.

Face earnest again, Tomaaz nodded.

"The biggest challenge will be to find Ma and get her out." Hans said, not mentioning the hundreds of tharuks at Zens' command. "We'll slip into the valley together, if we can, then join work teams and find out where your mother is. I don't like to say this, Son, but it might be best to split up." Pa passed him a clear oval stone with pointed ends.

"A calling stone …" Tomaaz eyes widened. "They're real?"

"They sure are. If we're separated, we'll talk each day at sunset. Just hold the stone in your palm, rub the surface and think of me. We'll be able to mind-meld across distances."

Tomaaz swallowed. "And if I'm caught?"

Hans gave him a grim smile. "Then I'll have to save you."

A Rude Awakening

Marlies heard muffled scrapes at the cavern mouth. Hans *was* here. She'd been dreaming of him and Handel streaking through the sky to save her. It must've been a rare prophecy, a vision.

"Hans?" she croaked, throat dry.

Boots struck the stone. She pushed herself to sit. A dark figure blocked the light at the cave.

"Hans, I—"

"Found you," a voice growled.

Marlies gasped. It wasn't Hans but a tharuk towering over her. She grasped her knife, but a furry hand closed over hers and squeezed until she dropped it.

The beast sniffed at her. "We've found the female Zens wanted," it called.

A smaller tharuk entered the cave. "Good. That makes up for losing the big male."

Could they mean Giant John?

"Pack this up," the large tharuk ordered. "Zens wants this one with belongings."

The wiry tharuk limped over to Marlies, and shoved all of her gear and weapons into her rucksack, while the big tharuk yanked her to her feet.

Although her arm was still in agony, it was better than before. Still, Marlies cried out. If she showed she was injured and weak, they'd think she wasn't a threat.

Soon she was outside, draped over the big beast's shoulder, her face pressed into its stinking fur. No wonder they'd found her. The snow was churned and splattered in blood all the way to her cave. It was amazing she hadn't been found earlier.

Marlies bobbed up and down as the beast strode along. At least she didn't have to walk to Death Valley herself now. Eventually, the motion of the tharuk's gait sent her back to sleep.

§

At dusk, Marlies' captors dumped her on the ground among stumpy bushes. Thank the Egg, they were below the snow line again. While the tharuks collected wood for a fire, she stretched and tested her injured arm. Better, but not good enough to fight with yet. She'd have to bide her time.

The small beast with a jagged scar across its snout approached, dumping her rucksack near her. "Eat." It nocked an arrow, training it on her. "Now."

Marlies drank from her waterskin, and fished out a piece of dried beef, one of Giant John's apples, now bruised, and some flatbread.

Scar Snout, the small one, tied her ankles and wrists tightly, and darted off into the bushes, returning with two squealing rats. It stomped on their heads, its heavy boots making a mess of the squirming creatures. It dashed off for more, amassing a pile of dead rats.

Soon the beasts were holding rats impaled on sticks over the fire. Sparks spat high into the dark and the rats' body juices sizzled over the flames.

Despite her revulsion, the aroma of char-roasted rat made Marlies' stomach rumble.

"Hold this," the large one handed his stick to Scar Snout, then turned and picked up a dead rat, biting into it and sucking the entrails out with a slurp. Blood dribbled over its snout and paws.

Marlies turned away, nauseous.

"Hey," yelled Scar Snout. "Don't eat them all. I want some, too."

"I'm bigger." After a thump from the big tharuk, Scar Snout was quiet.

Once the tharuks had finished slurping and crunching, she turned back to the fire in time to catch the end of a rat's tail disappearing into Scar Snout's mouth. "We're late. Zens will be angry," Scar Snout said, poking the embers with a stick.

"Weather was bad. And your fault. You searched by that river."

"I scented the large oaf. The one who gave us food. I went to look."

Marlies stiffened. Scar Snout had followed Giant John!

"Zens won't care. You didn't find anything."

"Actually," said Scar Snout slyly, "I found oaf's wagon. In the river. His horse's tracks went east."

"You didn't tell me." The huge brute clobbered Scar Snout, sending it sprawling. "I'm boss. You tell me everything. Hear?" It kicked Scar Snout along the ground. "The oaf would be valuable."

Marlies pretended to be asleep, watching through slitted eyes.

"We have the other one," whined Scar Snout, groveling.

The large tharuk grunted. "Zens will be pleased! I get a reward." A nasty rumble echoed from its throat, and it wandered over, nudging her with its toe. "This flesh must work hard. Or rot on the heap." The tharuks guffawed.

§

About mid-morning, the tharuks dumped Marlies on a foothill behind some scraggly bushes. The beasts crawled forward on their bellies to observe the valley below.

Marlies squinted through the sparse brush, the last sign of vegetation. Stretching as far as she could see were steep brown hills. An arid valley snaked between the hills toward the north, and haze clung to the hillsides. This was the destination Zaarusha had shown her—Death Valley.

Why were her captors being so stealthy? They were late back. Surely, these brutes would be in a hurry? Apparently not.

The large tharuk shoved a waterskin and a piece of bread into Marlies' hands and motioned for her to be quiet. She forced herself to chew slowly, straining to swallow each mouthful. Feeling this sick, how could she save Zaarusha's son, even if she did find him? And what of her family? Would she see them again?

Oh, shards, she'd forgotten Hans' calling stone in her rucksack. As soon as she was alone, she'd use it.

The tharuks stiffened and glanced at each other.

Then she heard it: a tharuk patrol was passing below—that's why her captors were hiding. The warmongering beasts would probably kill them and take her as their own prisoner. A shiver ran through her. Here, life had no value.

Once the patrol had passed, the tharuks backtracked to carry her down a steep ravine, out of sight of the main valley. The arid dust coated her nostrils and parched her throat.

She was alive. But for how long?

§

By afternoon, they'd reached Death Valley. Instead of taking her to Zens, the tharuks kept her out of sight and sneaked her up a side arm of the valley, riddled with caves. The tharuks took her into a cave and threw her on the stone floor. Landing on her injured arm, Marlies groaned.

"Give the female food," the large tharuk barked at Scar Snout.

Scar Snout passed her flatbread and the waterskin. "Eat, drink."

Thankfully, they'd brought her rucksack. She'd use Hans' calling stone as soon as they were gone.

The large tharuk grunted. "She won't go anywhere. She's too weak."

They left her ankles and hands bound and retreated.

RIDERS OF FIRE

Marlies lay down where they'd dropped her, biding her time. She was in no shape to walk far.

Maybe she could heal herself with the supplies in her pouch and talk to Hans.

Just as she was about to sit up, there was scuffling outside the cave. Marlies pretended to be asleep, her eyes thin slits.

Scar Snout slunk inside, toward her rucksack. The brute ferreted among her things, then, glancing at her, it hefted her bag over its shoulder and crept out.

No! Marlies wanted to scream. Clumsily, she rose to her feet and shuffled forward, the ropes biting her ankles. At the cave mouth, she peered around the rock and saw Scar Snout hiding her rucksack in a crack in the hillside. Dizzy and faint, Marlies slumped to the ground.

§

Behind a latrine, 316 turned the pretty stone over in its hands. Although the prisoner's rucksack now belonged to Zens, surely he wouldn't miss one little trinket? Checking that 555 wasn't around the corner, 316 absently rubbed the scar on its snout. It didn't need more scars from 555.

It rubbed the lovely stone. Swirling patterns formed on the surface. Fascinated, 316 polished it. The pattern eddied, forming a picture: a dragon of many colors.

The stone got hot. 316 bounced it from hand to hand, but its fur got singed. A roar pounded inside its head. Flame shot from the dragon's mouth into 316's face and the stone disintegrated, leaving its hands burned and charred.

The fur on its chin was smoldering. 316 batted at it, hoping it wasn't too noticeable. Someone was coming, so 316 ducked into the latrine.

When 316 came out, 555 was waiting. "There you are," its boss-tracker said. "I've been searching. You found oaf's cart. Zens is pleased. He reward you. Come."

316 nodded, his chin in his hand to conceal his burnt fur.

"Zens wants the prisoner's rucksack." 555 glared at 316.

Zens probably hadn't even asked for the rucksack. It was just 555 trying to get the treasure. 316 replied, "I don't know where the prisoner's bag is. Did you take it to Zens?"

555 smiled, tusks gleaming. "Come and get your reward."

Something in 555's smile made 316 shudder.

Dragons' Hold

Liesar flipped her wings, craning her neck backward to get a glimpse of the girl in the saddlebag. Pale face, eyes closed, breathing ragged. She couldn't see much else. The girl was probably unconscious. She'd tried rousing her by roaring, but Lovina hadn't responded. If Handel was flying with her, she could have asked him to fly close and monitor her health. But he wasn't. He was on his way to Death Valley with Tomaaz and Hans.

A cold ache filled Liesar's belly at the thought of Marlies dying. No, she couldn't die, not after all the years she'd waited to see her rider again. Not after her ferrying Marlies and Hans away to Lush Valley after the royal dragonet had died, so they could hide until Zaarusha's wrath grew cold and reason set in. Zaarusha had finally come around, thank the dragon gods, after a few miserable years.

Liesar battled a fierce headwind from Dragons' Hold, then flew higher, seeking a gentler current. Tomaaz liked Lovina. His affection ran deep. Lovina was precious cargo. Frail. Hopefully, not dying.

Liesar craned her neck again. She wasn't so sure.

Hours later, she alighted on a ledge at Dragons' Hold.

§

Standing in a corner of an empty training cavern, Adelina stared at Kierion. "Are you sure this'll work?"

"How many pranks have I pulled off since you've known me?" he asked.

True, he was good; that's why she'd sought him out. "We can't risk this going wrong. A girl's life is at stake."

Kierion's usually-merry eyes were somber. "That's why it has to look real. If I take my rumble weed, I'll be barfing so much that Fleur won't notice what you're up to."

"You mean you'd willingly vomit to help?" Not what she'd had in mind when she'd asked him.

Kierion's mouth set in a grim line. "I'm not letting Zens kill our people, and your brother's right: we can't trust Fleur."

Adelina swallowed. Fleur's evil lies had led to the council banishing her brother Roberto to the Wastelands.

Kierion squeezed her hand. "Don't worry, Ezaara and Erob will find Roberto." His cheeks pinked and he dropped her fingers. "Let's go. Gret will be wondering what's taking you so long."

Adelina retrieved some bread from the kitchens, then waited outside the boy's quarters while Kierion nipped in to retrieve his rumble weed.

"I've taken it," he said. "As soon as I eat, I'll be hurling."

She handed him the bread. "We'd better get to the infirmary quickly then."

He chewed it as they walked. By the time they got to the infirmary door, Kierion was clutching his stomach. Shards, his rumble weed *was* good. Adelina pushed the door open and brought him in. He doubled over, right in the doorway, groaning.

"Master Fleur," she called, "Kierion's sick."

"Basin," grunted Kierion.

"Here," called Fleur, snatching up a basin and running toward him. Once he had the basin in hand, Fleur led Kierion over to a chair. "Come and sit over here."

The moment he sat, Kierion deposited the contents of his stomach into the basin.

There were only two other patients in the infirmary, neither paying attention to Adelina, so she drifted to the back of the room, ducking behind a curtain into Fleur's secret alcove. She bent, searching through shelves full of pots of Fleur's stinking salve. Somewhere here, she and Ezaara had seen some vials nestled in sheep wool, in a little box. Ah, there was the box, at the back. She lifted Fleur's pots, careful not to let them clink against one another, and hid the slim box under her jerkin. She had to hurry. Lovina could be getting worse by the heartbeat.

"Hold on, I'll get you some soothing tea."

That was Fleur's voice, coming toward her!

"Master Fleur," Kierion called. "You should really look at this rash, in case it's not a simple belly gripe."

"Good idea," Fleur replied, her voice moving away. "How long have you had the rash?"

"Oh, let me think …"

Adelina peeked out from the curtain. Fleur's back was to her again, watching Kierion undo his jerkin so she could look at his torso. When Kierion started vomiting again, Adelina sneaked out of the infirmary. Now, to get the remedy to Lovina.

§

Lovina cracked her eyes open.

A young girl's face appeared above her, a girl with dark hair and black eyes—Naobian, from the look of her. Her forehead was lined with worry, but she had an overly-bright smile. "You're awake. Welcome to Dragons' Hold. I'm Adelina."

This was better than the boot in the ribs she usually got from Bill.

"How are you feeling?"

"Uh …" How was she feeling? She'd been drowsy for days. In the darkest moments, when her hands were cramped into painful claws, she'd despaired of ever drawing again. But now?

Lovina flexed the fingers on her good hand, the ones Bill hadn't broken. "They work," she murmured.

"Yes, they do," said Adelina. "What about the rest?"

"I can move my toes, too." Lovina straightened her legs and the arm that wasn't broken. There were no spasms. "Everything's a bit sore, but at least they're not cramping."

"That's good news," Adelina replied. "Liesar said you're from Lush Valley."

"My old master, Bill, was a traveling merchant, but yes, our last stop was Lush Valley."

Adelina's gaze was sharp. "*Master*?"

Lovina bit her lip, twisting the sheet in her fingers. "I—I was his slave."

Instead of scorning her, Adelina hugged her. "My brother was once a slave, too," she whispered. "We'll take care of you here. Do you know Ezaara, the Queen's Rider? She's from Lush Valley."

She was Tomaaz's sister, the pretty one, who could use a sword. Lovina nodded. "A little." Did she actually know anyone apart from Tomaaz? She'd been hidden behind a fog of numlock for too long.

Adelina raised her hand.

Lovina flinched.

"I'm sorry," said Adelina, "I was just going to tuck your quilt in."

"Sorry," Lovina mumbled. Her reactions to Bill were embedded, whether she was numlocked or not. She heard his voice all over again: *"You're useless. A good-for-nothing bag of skin and bones. The dung that a horse drops is worth more than you."*

Adelina placed a palm on Lovina's good arm. "Like I said, we're here to help you. Rest now, while I get you some broth."

Lovina nodded, drifting back to sleep.

Nightmares plagued her. Death Valley again, except this time it wasn't her but Tomaaz being whipped, his back laid raw under the lash.

A Risky Approach

After three nights in a cave, Pa had pronounced Handel fit for flight. Now, snowy peaks towered above Tomaaz, mist clinging to their tips. They were at the edge of Spanglewood Forest. Pa had said these woods were the seat of ancient wizard magic, whatever that was. It seemed Lush Valley had hidden more than dragons from its inhabitants. Handel shot down, making Tomaaz's stomach lurch. He clamped his eyes shut.

"Last stop before the Terramites," Pa's voice rumbled through his back.

Tomaaz cracked his eyes open. The ground was still rushing up to hit him, so he squeezed them shut again, waiting for the inevitable thud that meant his torture was over.

He was out of the saddle in moments. It was good to get down and stretch his legs again. He shivered. Zens was on the other side of that mountain range.

Pa passed him some dark thin leaves. "Freshweed—it'll mask our scent while we're sneaking into Death Valley. We won't need it once we're among the slaves."

"So, we're only half an hour away?" Too close—but then, everything was closer when you traveled by dragon.

Pa shot him a sharp look. "How did you know freshweed takes half an hour to get into your blood?"

Feeling sheepish, Tomaaz shrugged. "Um, Lofty liked to use it when we hunted."

"Typical Lofty," Pa chuckled. "This is deadlier than hunting rabbits. We'll creep along at the foot of the Terramites and approach from the north, way past Devil's Gate—the entrance that tharuk raiding parties usually use. Once we're in the valley, we'll mingle with the slaves, hopefully unnoticed."

"Sounds like a plan." They got back into the saddle.

Handel crept above the edge of the forest, hugging the steep sides of the Terramites, taking advantage of overhangs and rocky outcrops that would block him from view, gradually increasing in altitude until they were near the top.

"Nearly there," Pa said, glancing over his shoulder at Tomaaz. "Nock your bow."

They readied their bows. Tomaaz clung to the saddle with his knees, trying to stop his head from swimming. Focus—he had to focus.

They popped over the top of a ridge. There was a flash of snow, rock and sky, then they rapidly dropped back down.

"Shards," whispered Pa, "there's a new watchtower."

What had Pa expected after eighteen years?

"Only one tharuk guard," said Pa.

"Do you think it saw us?" Tomaaz asked.

"If it did, it'll be expecting a dragon," Pa replied, "so we'll take our chances on foot."

Handel landed and they dismounted. Pa patted the dragon's flank. "Handel says he'll wait nearby. I'll meld with him when we have Marlies. It may take a few days to find her."

Handel nuzzled Pa's shoulder, then with a whoosh of air from his wings, flew down to the Great Spanglewood Forest.

They crept up the barren rocky mountainside. Although the peaks to the north and south were higher and clad in snow, this ridge was dressed in only smatterings of white.

"Keep off the snowy patches, so you don't leave tracks," Pa warned.

They edged their way up. At the crest, beyond a rubble pile as wide as a meadow, was a crude watchtower, built of the same jagged bits of rubble. The tower had an open viewing platform with a wooden roof. A lone tharuk patrolled the platform, gazing down at Death Valley, its back toward them.

"There must be some way through all this rock to the valley," Tomaaz whispered. "Otherwise, why would they have a guard?"

Pa shrugged. "We might have to risk it and sneak past the guard. The tharuk's still not looking. See that gap in the rocks over there, by the tower? I'll find out where it leads." Before Tomaaz could protest, Pa ducked low, running along behind the rubble, toward the tower.

This was crazy! Tomaaz had thought they could sneak over the pile at night, or go around it, not head straight for their enemy's fortress. Bow in hand and keeping low, he followed Pa.

Pa reached the end of the rubble and stuck his head around the corner, then took a step into the gap. "Ugh!" He fell backward, thudding to the ground behind the rubble, his hands clutching his chest. An arrow protruded between his fingers.

He'd been hit! Tomaaz rushed over.

"Kill the shrotty beast," Pa gasped.

Peeking between some rocks at the watchtower, Tomaaz aimed an arrow, sighting the tharuk on the platform, and released.

Surprise flashed across the beast's face, then Tomaaz's arrow went through its eye into its skull. The tharuk toppled over the low wall and its body bounced down the slope.

"I've told Handel I'm hurt," Pa moaned between labored breaths.

Down the mountainside, Handel's bronze wings appeared.

Tomaaz dragged Pa further behind the rubble pile. The arrow was lodged in Pa's chest, above his heart. If it had been any closer …

Handel landed out of sight below the rubble heap. Tomaaz raced down, grabbed healing supplies from Handel's saddlebag and returned.

He gripped the arrow and snapped it off. Giving Pa the shaft to bite on, he dug out the tip with his knife. A fleshy sucking sound tore from Pa's chest as he wrenched the arrowhead free.

Pa pointed at the arrowhead, smeared with blood and green grunge. "Poison." He grunted. "Clean the wound."

Poison! Tomaaz stared at Pa's wound. Green slime coated the hole left by the arrow. Familiar slime—the same stuff that had been in the knife wound on Lovina's cheek. "What does it do?" Panic edged his words. He tore a strip of cloth from his shirt, and rubbed at the slime. "It's in deep."

"I know." Pa grimaced. "It's limplock. Dissolves in the bloodstream. Fever, nausea and gradual paralysis over five days. Try water."

Paralysis? Lovina! Her curled fingers and aching limbs. His head reeled.

By the time Tomaaz had snatched the waterskin, the stuff had mixed with Pa's blood, turning it muddy brown. He splashed water over the wound, then tried to staunch the bleeding with a wad of torn shirt.

"Son." Pa stayed his hand. "The antidote's in Ana's pouch." Breath short, he fumbled with his pocket. "Vial. Yellow."

Cries rose from the other side of the tower. Killing the tharuk had been a dumb move. More of them were snarling over the ridge.

Tomaaz tugged the pouch out of Pa's pocket and yanked it open, picking out a vial of yellow granules. "It's a quarter full. How much do you need?"

"One vial would cure me. This might get me back to Dragons' Hold."

"Y-you're going?"

Pa gave a shaky smile. "Save your mother." He squeezed Tomaaz's hand. "The vision wasn't of me helping Marlies. Only you. Now I … know why."

Tomaaz tipped the yellow granules into Pa's mouth, then he wadded a strip of his shirt over the wound and tied another strip across Pa's chest. He helped Pa onto Handel, strapping him into the saddle.

Guttural roars ripped through the air. Much closer. Tharuks!

Tomaaz slapped Handel's rump. "Go, Handel. Fly!" He dashed to the rubble heap, squeezing into a gap under some large boulders, and watched Pa and Handel winging high into the sky.

A tharuk yelled nearby, making Tomaaz flinch. "Over here. An arrow and rags."

"Got away on stinking dragon," replied another. "Filthy thing."

Through a crack between the rocks, Tomaaz watched the tharuks pick up the cloth, sniffing it. "Lots of limplock! Good. Another dead rider. 515 mixes limplock strong."

The other tharuk grabbed the arrow. "He be dead in two days. Rutting rider."

"Where's 515?"

"Dead as stone. Fell down the cliff. Stupid worm. Got shot by dragon scum." They guffawed.

"I have his bed."

"I take his slaves."

"No. Last time—"

Tomaaz shut out their crude bickering. Pa had said five days, but he was wrong. He'd be dead in two. Pa had no chance of getting to Dragons' Hold. No chance of more antidote. And what about Lovina? They hadn't realized she'd been poisoned. Had she found someone to treat her? Or had she died on the way? His mouth was coated in fine dust, making it hard to swallow.

He shoved his dark thoughts away. He had to believe Pa could get help. Had to believe Lovina was still alive. Ma was relying on him. He was the only one who could help her now.

§

Tomaaz didn't dare sleep for fear of tharuks finding him in the rubble pile. Thank the Egg, he had Pa's freshweed to save him from being caught. Under the cover of darkness, he left his bow and quiver in the rubble pile, and ate a clear-mind berry and some dragon's scale. Then he made his way down the barren hillsides, hiding behind boulders and traveling along ravines. No wonder they called this place Death Valley—nothing grew here except the odd scraggly bush. In the predawn gray, the whole place was bleak, not that the sun would make it look much better.

He stumbled along a ravine toward the main valley. An acrid odor hung in the air, and tendrils of fog leaked from splits in the cliffs. Breathing the stuff made his throat scratchy. As he neared the mouth of the ravine, the tromp of feet echoed off the valley walls. Stifling a cough, Tomaaz crouched behind a rock. Shards, he had to get this tickle in his throat under control or he'd give himself away.

A tharuk appeared around a bend, a group of slaves trailing it. They had to be slaves. They had that awful blank stare Lovina used to have, but worse. They shuffled forward, unsteady on their skinny legs. Wearing tatters, many of them limped or had festering sores. Their faces were the worst: hollowed out and empty.

A tharuk behind the group cracked a whip, raising a puff of dust. None of the slaves flinched.

Living with numlock had to be hell. To think, Lovina had—

A boy about his age stumbled and sprawled in the dust. The whip-bearing tharuk bellowed and turned away to yank the boy to his feet.

Now was his chance. Tomaaz darted into the crowd. Not a single slave glanced at him as he walked with them, letting his shoulders sag and his jaw hang loose.

Crack! Dust rose where the whip met the dirt.

It took all of Tomaaz's nerve not to twitch. He glanced at the slaves either side of him, then drooped his head. The stench of unwashed bodies and soiled breeches crept through his nostrils. He fought back a gag, breathing through his mouth, but the taste coated his tongue.

The valley widened, and the slaves slowed to pick up tools from various piles—shovels, spades, pickaxes and grubbers. Under the watchful eye of hulking tharuks armed with whips, those with pickaxes and grubbers traipsed into rifts in the hillside that oozed the foul-smelling mist. Tomaaz grabbed a shovel and followed a column of slaves heading further along the valley. They passed large sprawling buildings, outdoor cooking fires and a few caves with thick metal doors set into the entrances. Doors Tomaaz had never seen the likes of, with strange dials inscribed with numbers and long metal rods protruding from them. Locks?

Was Ma being held in one of these? Or was she another nameless slave traipsing to work on the valley floor or venturing into the bowels of the mountains? Was she even alive? She had to be. He hadn't come to this hell for nothing. He had to find her. The first opportunity he had, he'd slink off and look around.

"You lot!" the lead tharuk bellowed, "along here." It pointed up a valley branching off the main one.

The slaves trooped mindlessly after their tharuk leader into a stench-filled fug that made the inside of Tomaaz's nose crawl. Worse than the stench of the slaves, it was overpowering. Of course, no one around him reacted, all shuffling forward with their mindless gait.

They rounded a corner to a row of crude sheds, the stink making Tomaaz's eyes water. He stifled a groan. He'd chosen latrine duty.

Commander Zens

Days later, Marlies was still dizzy. Chewing herbs was helping the infection in her arm, but the thin gruel and mangy bread Scar Snout brought her each day weren't doing much to restore her strength. Her stomach was a constant gnawing hole. And this damp stone floor wasn't exactly paradise. She'd been tempted to use piaua on her arm, but she only had one vial left, and that was her only defense against Zens' torture.

Scuffing footfalls neared the cave.

Marlies lay down, pretending she was weaker than she was.

"You!" It was the tracker who'd caught her, the one with 555 tattooed inside its left wrist.

Scar Snout trailed it into the cave.

"Stand," 555 commanded.

Scar Snout cut the rope around Marlies' ankles.

The blood rushed into her feet, making them fuzzy and achy. Leaning against the wall, she flexed them.

"Human," 555 spat. "Zens wants to see you."

See her? More likely torture or kill her. Marlies staggered to the entrance.

"Pathetic!" 555 snorted. It threw her up onto its shoulder, and strode along the ravine.

When they reached the valley, a column of dead-faced slaves traipsed past them, staring at the ground.

She turned her head from side to side, trying to signal the slaves behind the tharuks' backs. No response. No one spoke or even looked at her. Gods, this was awful. They were shells, not registering what went on around them. Deep in the grip of Zens' plant extracts, they headed into caverns in the hillside.

"Stop wriggling!" 555 put her down. "Walk."

She shuffled along the bleak valley, between her two captors. The tharuks stopped before an iron door in the mountainside. Scar Snout restrained her, digging its claws into her arm to keep her still. 555 opened the door, leading Marlies into a tunnel that led past a series of wooden doors. Storerooms? Somehow she doubted it. Dungeons, more like.

At the end of the tunnel, tharuk 555 knocked on a large door. It was opened by an enormous tharuk, bigger than any she'd seen. Although this beast was furry, the inside of its arm was completely bald and emblazoned with a tattoo that took up its whole forearm: 000. Marlies knew tharuks had numbers on the inside of their wrists, but a whole forearm? Then she remembered Tonio the spymaster's lessons.

Zens' most formidable tharuk is 000, his first creation. Strong, cunning and possessing better mental faculties than all other tharuks, Triple Zero is like a son to Zens. Loyal and completely devoted, he's almost as dangerous as Zens himself. Zens' later creations are weaker specimens with only part of Triple Zero's talents. We suspect Zens made them that way to keep them subservient.

"Welcome," 000 smiled, showing sharp yellowed teeth and tusks.

Polite as well.

The tharuks pushed Marlies into a large chamber. Torches were blazing, their flames reflected on a smooth shiny rear wall. Metal implements with sharp prongs and jagged edges hung on the walls. Marlies' flesh crawled. These were the tools of a master torturer.

000 barred the door behind them.

A figure emerged from the shadows. Torchlight flickered over a bald head covered in blue-black stubble. His face was in shadow, but the bulk of the man was unmistakable—Zens.

"Good afternoon, 316 and 555," Zens greeted. "Returned from patrol with a little something, have you?"

"Yes, sir," 555 said, giving Zens an ingratiating smile.

Zens raised an arm, motioning Scar Snout forward. Zens' upper arm was as thick as a man's thigh, and his chest was a barrel, like Giant John's. "I hear you were delayed getting back," Zens crooned, pacing in front of the tharuk, his limbs moving with barely-restrained power. Above this thick malformed nose, his yellow eyes raked Scar Snout from head to foot.

The tharuk bowed. "Yes, sir. Found wagon in Tooka Chasm. All smashed."

555 cut in. "The big oaf went east on horseback. I told crows. Other troops will find him."

"Good, 555, you shall be rewarded." Zens' pupils dilated and he flicked a hand at 555.

Tharuk 555's eyes glossed over, unseeing, and a tusky smile broke out on its face. It stood motionless, gazing into nothing.

These creatures were completely under his control. It was sick.

316 spoke up, "Sir, I found trail. And wagon. Can I have reward?"

Zens turned his attention to Scar Snout. "Certainly." His smile gave Marlies the chills.

Scar Snout hopped excitedly from foot to foot, like an eager puppy. "The lake! Can I see pretty lake again?"

So, somehow, Zens gave them pleasant dreams.

"I won't have tharuks stealing from prisoners. That rucksack and the stone were mine." Zens stretched a hand out in Scar Snout's direction, fingers splayed. "Disloyalty cannot be tolerated."

The eagerness died on the little tharuk's face. Its eyes widened.

How had Zens known? Had 555 told him? Or had he seen Scar Snout's memories?

Slowly, Zens' hand tightened into a fist in midair. The tharuk's furry hands clutched at its neck. It gurgled and choked, then slumped to the floor.

Zens laughed, his thick corded neck rippling. "Triple Zero," he said, "Clean up, please."

"Gladly," 000 answered, voice dripping with relish. The enormous tharuk strode to the wall and selected an axe. Striding to the small tharuk, it hacked off its hand above the number on its wrist. Dark fluid pooled on the floor around the stump, near the tharuk's scarred snout.

Near the shiny end of the cavern, 000 pulled a lever, and the entire wall was flooded with yellow light. It was a glass wall, filled with fluid, holding trophies of Zens' kills. Hands. Feet. And smaller things —ears? Fingers and toes? 000 threw Scar Snout's hand over the top of the glass. It landed in water, its inky trail swirling as it bobbed on the surface, then sank.

Marlies retched, depositing her gruel and undigested bread at 555's feet. The tracker was oblivious, stuck in its dream world.

"Ah, weak stomach, little rider?" Zens crooned.

As tall as most men, Marlies had never been called *little* before. She rose from the floor. Now that she was closer, the malice in his gaze froze her marrow. Zens' irises were yellow, ringed with deepest blue. He smiled slowly, like a predator showing its teeth to transfixed prey.

She was not prey. "So, Commander Zens, we finally meet." She had to survive to find Zaarusha's son. Marlies planted an image firmly in her mind, holding it there.

§

"Tell me what you know." Zens mentally probed the woman's mind and found the holding cave. Gray stone, water dripping down the back wall. Clever, then, and a talented mind-blocker.

Zens had broken many riders. It only took a session or two of persuasion to get them gibbering the realms' secrets. This one would be no different. He flicked his hand, sending the woman flying across the cave and smacking into a stone wall. She slumped to the ground, dark hair splayed around her and her bandaged arm at an odd angle.

"Ready to talk?" he mind-melded.

No answer. She could hear him. He knew it. But he only got that same dank cave. Zens tugged on the air with his hand.

The woman slid across the floor toward him. Her head graunched and bumped on the stone. That should help her talk. He lifted his hand so her body rose into the air, all the while battering at her mind. Then he flipped his palm and slammed the woman face-first into the stone. Blood dribbled out from her face.

Still that same cave in her head.

This one had tenacity. What secrets was she keeping? Zens scratched his chin. He didn't have forever to mess about; he had to get back to developing his new beasts. Therein lay his hope. They would help him conquer the dragons of Dragons' Realm, not this stupid rider.

Then again, now that he'd softened her up, perhaps it was time to up his mental game.

§

Gray stone. Water dripping onto green moss. Sunlight angling in. Hard damp floor, cold. Marlies kept the cave in her mind, not daring to focus on the pain, the agony, the—

Stone walls. Hard floor. Gray, everything gray, even the bread. No, focus on the cave.

A chill started in her head, flowing down her neck and over her torso. Zens. She pushed the image of the cave back at him. The moss was lush and green, verdant—a sign of life in this awful bleak hell—so she kept the moss, the dripping walls, in her head. She would not let it budge.

"I know you can hear me. Can feel me," Zens' words slithered inside Marlies' head. *"Let go of the cave. Relax."*

A rush of cold engulfed her mind. Her head and neck. Her torso. Oh, gods, so cold, she was going to die. Marlies gritted her teeth. The cave. She kept it solid, despite him hammering her.

Then fire came. Flaming across her face, making the skin sear and bubble. The sensation was so strong, so real, Marlies bit her lip to stop herself from screaming. The stench of charred skin filled her nose. No! Cave. Gray. Stone. Moss. The fire washed across her, turning her body to cinders, leaving her gasping. Cave.

Then Zens spoke. "Take her away. No food or water for three days. That'll weaken her." His boots crunched on stone. He yanked her hair, pulling her face up from the floor.

Cave.

"Until then, *little one*," he sneered. Dropping her head, he left.

000 snapped its fingers and woke 555, who picked Marlies up, tossing her over its shoulder.

"Zens says this one is cunning," 000 said to 555. "Put her in a cave with a barred door."

555 carried her away, and still, Marlies kept the cave in her mind.

Sure enough, as they headed down the corridor, Zens tried battering her mind again.

The Creature's Ploy

Hunger gnawed at the creature's belly. For a week now, he'd thrown the human's putrid rats into a pile at the rear of the cave, where they'd lain stinking. Soon, live rats had come to gnaw at the carcasses. He'd snapped them up, still wriggling, crunching every last bit of tail and fur.

It had done little to ease his gnawing belly, but at least his senses were his own again.

Each time the food human arrived, the creature acted out its charade, squinting and groveling for putrid drugged rat as if it were a delectable morsel from a king's table.

Zens had underestimated him. One day he'd have revenge on this bunch of pathetic tharuks with their pitifully short claws and stumpy tusks. But it wouldn't be today. No rats had sneaked into his cave for a couple of days, so he was barely strong enough to stand. He had to eat, even if it was drugged food designed to torment him.

A faint whiff on the air—the human and his meal.

The rat landed on the dirt with a thump.

He snaked his neck along the arid earth to snatch his rotten flesh. The male stumbled and toppled to the ground, face down. Dead? The creature nudged him with his snout. Then growled, and nudged again.

The male dragged himself to his feet and shambled off, leaning on his shovel for support.

The creature doubted he'd see this one again.

Life in Death Valley

Tomaaz's shovel bit into the earth, the stench of the latrines making his eyes water. They'd made a pit that morning. Now, they were digging drainage ditches toward overflowing outhouses. They'd been at it all day, without food—only sips of tainted water from communal skins. With all the slaves under the watchful eyes of their tharuk overseers, he hadn't dared refuse the numlocked water.

It hadn't taken him long to learn that the tharuks called each other by the numbers tattooed on the bald spot inside their wrists. That's what Lovina had meant when she'd told him tharuk 274 had liked her drawings.

Tomaaz flung dirt out of the trench onto the pile behind him, and dug again. He was used to hard work. These slaves were, too. They dug without a word, blind to their surroundings. Even the littlings were silent, with hollow faces, skinny little arms, and legs as thin as wheat stalks.

Working next to Tomaaz was the boy who had stumbled earlier, causing the diversion that had let Tomaaz join the slave crew. He was pitifully thin, and so weak he lifted one shovelful for every six of Tomaaz's. Each time the boy threw the dirt out of the ditch, he leaned on his spade, panting, his shoulders jutting out like chicken wings, before he dug again. They were about the same height, but the boy's muscles had wasted and his cheekbones protruded from his gaunt face. Half his right ear was missing as well as two fingers on his right hand. It was as if he had half a hand. No wonder it was hard to dig.

In fact, many of the slaves had missing fingers or ears.

"You," snapped tharuk 568, flicking a whip in the air behind Half Hand. "Speed it up."

Half Hand leaned forward to dig, but stumbled, landing on his knees.

Tomaaz kept up a steady rhythm, not daring to lift his eyes as Half Hand got to his feet.

Another tharuk roared with laughter. "Problem controlling vermin, 568?"

568 reached into the pit and dragged Half Hand out by the scruff of the neck. "On his last legs." 568 shoved him back into the canal. "But he can dig more."

Half Hand sprawled face down in the dirt.

568 guffawed. "Get up and dig. Or it's the flesh pile."

Two canals over, slaves scrambled out of their trench. A man swung a pick. He swung again, breaching the latrine pit. There was a gurgle and a wafting stench as effluent flowed into the ditch and down the slope to the waiting pit.

Tomaaz fought back a gag, trying to school his features into blank dumb acceptance. He battled the tension that ricocheted through his limbs, making him want to flee, screaming, from this gruesome hell.

"Rest time," called the tharuk leading that slave gang.

The slaves collapsed where they stood, right next to the stinking canal. Other crews kept digging.

Great. One latrine was done and only about fifty to go. There must be thousands slaving underground. Soon, the sinking sun would touch the tips of the mountains, plunging them into shadow. The pit had taken half a day, and the canal had taken most of the other half. With around a hundred slaves working in five crews, perhaps they could manage ten latrines a day. That meant another week of this stuff. Tomaaz's mouth soured as he struck the dirt again. A whole day here without finding Ma. He'd planned on questioning slaves when he'd arrived—not knowing they'd all be muted by numlock, every heartbeat scrutinized by tharuks.

His drain had almost reached the latrine, and he was at the front of the line. Tomaaz gave a mental groan. He was actually looking forward to hitting sewage so he could rest. His life had been reduced to this—and he'd only been in this nightmare place for hours. It had to be worse for slaves who'd been here moons or years.

Anger burned in his empty stomach. Zens was a monster, ruining the lives of thousands. The worst were the littlings, no longer running in meadows, laughing or playing; just digging, heads down, like whipped dogs. And for what?

Zens valued something. Something above human lives. Something deep in those misty chasms in the mountains where hundreds of slaves had headed that morning.

Tomaaz's shovel hit softer dirt. Brown liquid seeped through the soil, trickling into the trench. He didn't dare risk saying anything, but he nudged Half Hand, before he loosened the dirt with a few taps of his shovel. A thin stream of sludge spurted out. He scrambled out of the ditch, half dragging Half Hand with him. The rest of the slaves climbed out, dropping their tools.

Tharuk 568 shoved a pick at Tomaaz. "Here, use that."

Tomaaz dragged his heels while the weakened slaves further down the canal climbed to safety.

568 narrowed his eyes, watching him.

Tomaaz's heart pounded as he leaned over the edge of the trench. Giving away that he wasn't controlled by numlock would mean losing Ma. He had to let the slaves around him suffer, or he'd be found out. Every nerve in his body screamed at the injustice. He swung the pick: once; twice. The dirt gave. Sludge spewed out of the gaping wound, flowing down the canal.

When 568 yelled, "Down tools! Rest time!" Tomaaz collapsed right next to his slave crew, not caring about the overpowering stench.

How had Lovina survived this?

§

Tomaaz scrubbed at the bottom of the cauldron to get rid of burnt-on sludge. The tharuk gruel had done little to fill his aching stomach or revive his weary muscles. Cramps ran down his back and his shoulders were more knotted than the old piaua trunk in the sacred clearing at home.

A whip-wielding tharuk paced nearby, scowling at him. "Scrub harder. It's almost sundown."

Giving a dumb nod, Tomaaz put his back into it. Gods, he was ready to fall into bed—if they even had beds here. He'd kept his eyes open, looking for possible places to keep a prisoner, scanning slaves' faces as he'd ladled out gruel, looking for Ma.

Nothing.

A whip cracked.

Tomaaz resisted the urge to snap his head up, raising it lethargically and gazing about with his jaw half open. Beyond the eating area, near a pile of rubble, a tharuk with a droopy eye towered over Half Hand, who was lying in the dirt with his shovel nearby. Odd—everyone else had returned their tools to the piles. What was he up to?

"Up," Droopy Eye bellowed, cracking its whip again. "Now!"

Half Hand dragged himself to his knees and heaved his shovel across the dirt, panting. Using the spade, he pulled himself to stand, then shambled a few steps, only to fall again.

Droopy Eye booted Half Hand in the ribs. "Get up, you mangy mutt! It's feeding time."

Tomaaz clenched the side of the pot to stop himself from running over. He had to bide his time. Find Ma.

The tharuk kicked the boy again. Blood trickled out of his mouth.

Half Hand was starved, weak and senseless. Anyone could see he was dying. The pot bit into Tomaaz's palms. Cords of muscle stood out on his forearms.

A whip cracked against the cauldron, making Tomaaz start. Furry hands grabbed his head, wrenching it around. "What's wrong? A bit twitchy?" Tharuk 568's fetid breath blasted his face. Tusks nearly scraped his cheek. The tharuk yanked one of his eyelids up and gave a satisfied nod. "Still numlocked. Good. Now, finish that pot."

Tomaaz thrust his arm back into the cauldron and kept his head down, scraping the ladle to loosen the last of the burnt crust. Thank the Egg, his father had given him dragon's scale to keep his eyes gray.

Above the prone figure of Half Hand, two tharuks were arguing. "You should'na kicked him."

"He wasn't moving," Droopy Eye growled.

"Probably killed him."

"He's fine. Look." Droopy Eye raised his whip …

One more lash would kill the boy. Tomaaz abandoned the pot, running, a croak escaping his dusty throat. Around him, time seemed to slow as slaves gaped and tharuks turned. He pretended to stumble and fall, then pulled himself up again. Shards, shards, shards! What had he done?

With a snap, a whip wrapped itself around his arm. Pain seared his bicep. Droopy Eye heaved on the whip, pulling Tomaaz toward him. Tomaaz stumbled, dragging on the whip as if it was hard to walk—as if they'd believe that, after his mad dash.

Droopy Eye and another tharuk grabbed his arms. A tharuk with a bent tusk thrust its snout into his face and, for the second time that day, Tomaaz had his eyelids pulled up and his eye color inspected. He kept his body loose, face slack. Bent Tusk fired questions at him and he stayed dumb, answer-less, except for an apathetic shrug of a shoulder.

"His eyes are fine," a huge brute snapped. "Doesn't have wasting sickness. Must be from last raid. Maybe not enough numlock." The beast pointed at 568. "You. Give him more. Keep an eye on him."

"Y-yes, overseer." 568 yanked Tomaaz's hair, pulling his head back and tipping a waterskin over his mouth.

Tomaaz spluttered, then gulped down tainted water until his bloated belly ached.

"Right," the tharuk overseer snarled at 568. "Replace the feeder with this dog." It kicked Tomaaz in the backside.

Then the overseer booted Half Hand in the head.

The boy twitched, his bloody head rolling to one side, then was still, staring at the world with open glassy eyes.

568 shoved Half Hand's spade into Tomaaz's hand, then drove his claws through the back of Tomaaz's jerkin, pricking his skin. "March. We're feeding the beast. Your job now. Morning and night."

Droopy Eye and Bent Tusk fell in beside 568.

His tail bone throbbing and back stinging, Tomaaz stumbled along the valley—driven by the three tharuks—without a backward glance at the dead boy.

§

Tharuk 568 jabbed Tomaaz's back and growled, "Go right."

They turned down another arm of the sprawling valley and headed between steep hills dotted with the stumpy thorn bushes. Once they'd gone a short way, a new stench greeted Tomaaz. Something putrid. His belly, distended with foul water, roiled. He gagged, but swallowed his gorge. He wouldn't give 568 another reason to stuff him full of Zens' tainted water.

Dragging his shovel, he shambled along until they reached a dead end—split into three short gullies by folds in the hills.

"Halt," 568 snapped. "Been here before?"

Tomaaz shook his head mutely.

"Left is human flesh. Straight ahead are dead tharuks. Right are animals." 568 yanked Tomaaz along while the Droopy Eye and Bent Tusk waited.

Earlier in the day, Tomaaz had dragged his shovel to prove he was numlocked. Now, he doubted he could lift it. He hadn't eaten properly; he hadn't slept; and he'd been digging all day.

Ahead, a tharuk was throwing mice onto a heap of dead animals—squirrels, birds, but mainly rats. No wonder the place stank.

"Get the beast food." 568's shove nearly sent Tomaaz sprawling.

568 speared a dead rat on its claw and crunched it down, tail flicking against its tusks.

Tomaaz pushed his spade into the heap, piling it with dead rats and a squirrel carcass.

"No. Squirrels and birds is for tharuks." 568 shook the spade, making everything but one rat fall off. "Not too much. Zens wants a hungry beast."

The tharuk tending the heap gave a throaty snarl, grimacing at Tomaaz. "An angry beast to feed." It sprinkled gray powder over the rat on Tomaaz's shovel. Shrugging at Tomaaz's lack of response, it spat. "Humans. All dumb."

With the rat balanced on the end of his shovel, Tomaaz followed 568 out of the narrow gully, past the heaps of rotting tharuks and dead slaves, hopelessness building inside him. Not only had he managed to get noticed by the tharuks, they'd singled him out for feeding some beast. He'd never had a chance to look for Ma—fat lot of help he was. The only chance he had of surviving this hellhole was to submit to the tharuks and hope he didn't run out of dragon's scale or clear-mind before he got out of here. He traipsed along, balancing the dead rat on his spade, arms burning.

The tharuks slowed. "It's your turn," said Droopy Eye. "Train the slave, 489."

Bent Tusk stopped, shaking its head, its face dark against the setting sun. "568's turn."

568 snarled. "Coward. I'm not going. I train him here." It shifted from foot to foot, then grabbed Tomaaz's shoulder. "Go to the end." It pointed up the narrow side valley. "Caves up there. Beast in large cave." 568 flashed sharp teeth. "Drop rat outside cave. Watch beast eat. If you throw wrong, you go get rat."

"Don't do that." Droopy Eye gestured at the scar pulling its eye down. "I did. Look what happened."

The other tharuks guffawed.

Tomaaz swallowed, trudging away. He turned a bend. Out of sight of the tharuks, he scurried further along the canyon. The sun was dipping below the hills as he reached the end of the gully, swathes of shadows creeping across his path and shrouding the cave entrances. The largest cavern was a dark maw in the shadowy hillside.

The rattle of a chain and a growl made Tomaaz's neck hair stand on end. He was no longer alone. Snatching the rat by the tail, he flung it through the air toward the gaping hollow.

The snap of jaws and crunching told him all he needed to know. The beast had caught its meager meal.

There were caves on either side of the beast's. Hopefully, the creature's chain wasn't long enough to reach them. Tomaaz ducked into the cave on the right, the one furthest from the beast, and pulled the calling stone out of his pocket. He sunk to the cavern floor, leaning on the rough wall. Rubbing the crystal vigorously, he kept Pa's face in his mind, staring at the flat surface. It was too dark to see anything. He could hardly see his own hands, but he had to know if Pa was still alive. Rubbing again, he willed his father to answer.

The crystal grew warm in his hands, then glowed. A vibrant sunset rippled across its surface, casting light around it. Pa's face came into view. "Pa," Tomaaz whispered. He was alive, thank the Egg. His breath whooshed out of him in relief.

His father's words drifted through his mind. *"Tomaaz, did you make it down to the valley? Have you found Marlies?"*

"Yes, I'm here. No sign of Ma yet."

"Handel says she's captive. Been beaten. You have to …" Pa winced as a spasm wracked his face.

"Pa, are you all right?"

"I'll be fine. Find your ma."

"I'll sneak out tonight and search for her." His voice caught. "Pa, the poison—they said it was a strong dose. That you'll die in two days. You have to get help."

Pa managed a grimace as another spasm wracked him.

Tomaaz peered at the image of Pa glowing in the dim cavern. Sweat beaded Pa's face and his skin was ashen.

A low rumble skittered through the wall behind Tomaaz's spine, making his skin crawl. He turned.

A hand span from where he'd been leaning was a hole in the wall the size of his head. Bathed in the glow from the calling stone was a large gray eye with a slitted pupil, watching him.

The glow on the stone was fading. Tomaaz raced for the entrance. The beast growled. Its chain clanked. Tomaaz ran back toward the waiting tharuks, its roars echoing behind him. Just before the bend in the valley, he heard the tharuks snarling at each other about who was going to fetch him. He slowed to catch his breath, then slumped and shuffled around the corner. No! He'd forgotten his shovel. Hopefully his captors wouldn't notice in the dark.

568 yanked his arm, dragging him down the valley. "Stupid slave. You dropped the spade."

§

The sprawling buildings Tomaaz had seen when they entered the valley turned out to be the slaves' sleeping quarters. 568 took Tomaaz's crew to the closest one. They were each given more numlocked water as they filed inside. Crammed with dirty pallets and sweaty unwashed bodies, the place reeked. Tomaaz shuffled forward. Imitating the slaves who collapsed, dragging tattered blankets over their bodies, he sank to his knees on a filthy pallet, hoping it wasn't infested with lice or vermin. He pulled the thin blanket over him. The moment his head hit the fabric, his eyes drooped.

The last time he'd slept had been in a cave with Pa and Handel, two days ago, high above the forest. He'd had no idea how beautiful that landscape was. How great his freedom had been.

Tharuk 568 grunted and slammed the door. Its footfalls crunched along the valley.

Struggling to stay awake, Tomaaz gazed around the room. Candle stumps flickered. One guttered and died. Its life was snuffed out, just like Half Hand earlier. Had the same happened to Ma? Was she lying dead somewhere on the ground? Did that boy have family who didn't know where he was? Or had they all died here, too?

A hollow ache gnawed at Tomaaz's belly as he drifted to sleep, but nightmares of tharuk whips yanked Tomaaz awake. Around him a hundred sleeping slaves wheezed and muttered. A lone candle was still burning, so he couldn't have slept that long. Outside, feet stomped toward the sleeping hut.

The door opened and a tharuk held a torch high. "All good here," it growled.

"Of course," another tharuk answered. "Numlock keeps slaves easy."

"We got to check," said the first. "I not give keepsakes for Zens' tank."

Lovina had mentioned a tank, too. What was that about? And where was Zens?

"Let's go. Check the other sheds." They closed the door, their voices getting fainter as they moved away.

How soon would they be back? Should he slip out now? No, he didn't know their routine. Tomaaz lay in the dark, counting his breaths.

Sure enough, after about three hundred and fifty breaths, the tharuks returned, chortling at a joke. The door opened, the torch flared in the room, then they were gone again. Rising to a crouch, Tomaaz took his boots off and tucked them under his blanket, leaving a lump in the bed. The crude wooden floor was cold on his feet, but his socks would be quieter outside than boots. He didn't have long.

Tomaaz eased the door open and stepped outside.

Dim moonlight filtered through the mist wisping from the cracks in the hills as Tomaaz picked his way past the eating area and the cold fire pits. Sticking to the shadowy cliffsides, he soon reached Half Hand. Tomaaz rolled him over. The boy's skin was pale in the wan light, and his eyes glassy. He felt for the pulse at his throat, just in case. Dead.

He'd had to check. Could he bury him? No, the tharuks would get suspicious if the body disappeared.

Besides, he had to find Ma. He couldn't get sidetracked by some slave he didn't even know.

But that was the problem. Tomaaz wanted to help them all—to free these poor people from this living, dying hell. Straightening, he sighed and cast about. Where could Ma be?

"Strange scent," a tharuk's voice carried across the valley. "Someone outside."

"I not seen anyone, 701."

"Course not. *You're* no tracker, 131. Let's get one."

A tracker! Panic clawed at Tomaaz's throat. He had to hide, but the voices were between him and the sleeping shed. There wasn't another shed nearby—only a rubble pile and the boy's body.

He took off his shirt. Kneeling, he unbuttoned the boy's shirt, and slipped it on. Then he put his shirt on the boy. Hopefully, that would disguise his scent. He ducked in among the rubble. Whatever Zens' slaves were doing in the hillside, it produced a lot of debris.

Tomaaz's heart pounded as the tracker traced his scent to the dead boy.

Moonlight glinted off the tracker's tusks as it cast about, circling the rubble pile. "Lost the trail," it snarled. "Scents are mixed. Are you two skiving off patrol?"

"No. Slave stole his shirt," muttered a tharuk. "One slave is thinking."

"Zens will be angry," said another. "Should double their numlock."

"Zens must not find out," the tracker agreed. "I mix strong numlock tonight, so no one will know. Now, get back to patrol."

The tracker took one last sniff, and the beasts moved on.

So, trackers were smarter than the usual tharuk grunts. With a tracker on the prowl, it was too dangerous to keep searching for Ma. Sweat slicking his brow, Tomaaz sneaked back to the sleeping shed.

Piaua's Promise

Marlies hadn't had food or water for a day and a half. Her head was throbbing, her face was swollen, and every time she moved, fire shot through her ribs. Even breathing hurt. She'd tried to get out of the barred door, but … oh, shards, she was exhausted.

"Zaarusha," Marlies murmured, "I've failed you." And she'd failed Hans, Ezaara and Tomaaz …. Maybe, if she slept, she'd feel better.

A while later, Marlies woke—not better, but worse.

Zens was right: if he tortured her again, she'd crack. In fact, if he visited right now, she didn't have the strength to put up a fight. She no longer knew the latest secrets of Dragons' Hold and the Council of the Twelve Dragon Masters, so that wasn't a danger, but Zens would find out about her family. And Zens never did things by halves. He'd discover Ezaara was the new Queen's Rider. His tharuks would hunt down Ezaara and all Marlies' loved ones and murder them all.

Marlies would never let that happen.

With sudden clarity, she understood why Zaarusha's dragonet had sacrificed its life so she could have the twins.

Sometimes, it was worth it to give your life for others.

She reached into her healer's pouch and silently thanked the piaua tree as she pulled the stem of blue berries out. No one was coming to save her. No one even knew of her plight. She would never be able to repay Zaarusha. It was time to become a *witch of blue*.

A tear tracked down her cheek.

Marlies ate the berries and tucked the stem back in her pouch.

A Terrible Discovery

Tomaaz tossed and turned all night, his belly rumbling. He woke before dawn and chewed clear-mind berries and checked his fingernails. Still gray, so he could wait a while with the dragon's scale. Thankfully, he hadn't been searched, or his remedies would have been found. Perhaps he should hide them somewhere. Or would a tracker sniff them out?

Tharuks roused the slaves and dosed them up with numlocked water. Chunks of rock-hard bread were their breakfast fare. Tomaaz nearly broke his teeth on them, but at least they filled his belly more than the sour gruel they'd had the night before.

568 hauled Tomaaz out of the eating area. "Get your shovel. Feed that beast. Then off to latrine duty."

It sent him off with Droopy Eye, who had the number 1666 tattooed on its wrist.

Over a thousand tharuks. What hope did he and the other slaves have against so many? There were more slaves, but, numlocked, they'd be mowed down like wheat in a hurricane.

Tomaaz took a shovel from the tool heap.

"No, you don't," said 1666. "Get your old shovel from the beast."

The last thing Tomaaz wanted was to visit that beast twice.

"I got a better idea." Droopy Eye grinned, baring its yellow teeth. "Use your hands."

Tomaaz shrugged and allowed himself to be escorted to the stinking animal heap. Once again, a tharuk was sprinkling a rat with gray powder. Numlock? Why would they keep their own beast numlocked?

Tomaaz grasped the tail of the rat and carried it, holding it away from him. Its fur was dark with grunge and flies buzzed around its caved-in skull. The rat's jaw hung open like a slack-mouthed slave. Although Tomaaz tried to breathe through his mouth, he could *taste* the putrid stench.

Once they turned off and got to the bend in the beast's gully, Droopy Eye lagged behind. "Off you go. I wait here. No mucking about. Don't forget that shovel," the tharuk snarled, cracking his whip. "Or you'll feel this."

Relieved he was alone again, Tomaaz loped along the gully floor. The distance seemed shorter, now that it wasn't dark. Soon, he was facing the three caves at the end of the canyon. Protruding from the cave mouth on the right was the handle of his spade. He must've dropped it when he'd spoken with Pa.

A chain clanked.

Tomaaz steeled himself. All he'd seen of the beast so far was an eye.

A low snarl built, echoing off the gully walls, building into a growl.

Tomaaz's skin prickled.

Within the cavern, something lurked in the shadows. Something huge. Coming his way. A blunt head appeared, its serpentine neck snaking along the ground. Shoulders emerged, towering above Tomaaz. The whole creature was gray, its eyes covered in a thick gray film. It bared its fangs, snarling.

Lovina flashed to mind. Before—with Bill. And after.

The creature's powerful limbs flexed, bringing it closer, saggy folds of gray skin dragging at its sides. It tilted its head, squinting. It moved again, the chain clanking. It was captive, too. The powerful creature was a washed-out parody of a dragon. Nothing like Handel, Liesar or the blue dragons he'd seen in Lush Valley.

Then again, Pa had said Zens could grow tharuks, breeding them without parents. Had he grown this beast too?

If so, why was he keeping it numlocked?

Tomaaz flung the rat, and the beast raised its head to catch it, snapping it down.

"I'm sorry it's such an awful breakfast," Tomaaz crooned.

It was a prisoner, just like him. Perhaps it was smart. Tomaaz kept talking, low sweet murmurs, like he was soothing an angry dog. The beast tracked him with its filmy eyes as he retrieved the spade. Squinted at him as he placed a few clear-mind berries onto the blade and held it out. Tomaaz's legs shook as he approached. How far could the beast's chain reach?

The gray beast's nostrils quivered. It snaffled the berries and licked the spade.

"I'll be back later," Tomaaz crooned.

The beast stood staring as he retreated down the gully.

He was getting distracted again—today, he had to find his mother.

§

The creature cocked his head, nostrils flaring as it scented the new human. This one smelled strangely familiar, yet the creature knew it had never come across this particular male before. It sniffed again. This new man carried the scent of an old friend with him. Nostrils still quivering, the creature strained to remember his friends. Hazy memories of blue and green and vast open spaces flickered at the edge of the fog, but couldn't break through.

Then the male started to talk. Not the harsh bellows of his tormentors, but a soft cadence that rose and fell like a gentle breeze. Squinting against the harsh sun, the creature tried to see through the fog.

The human was approaching. Offering delicious-smelling berries.

The creature gobbled them down, pining for more, then watched the male depart.

§

Tharuk 555 hurried along the ravine. 000 had told it not to feed the female prisoner, but 000 hadn't meant to forget the prisoner completely. 555 was sure Zens wouldn't like that. But then again, with 316 dead, it'd had more work in the mines. Then there'd been an unruly slave to deal with. It jiggled the key in the lock. Bars clanked against stone as it opened the door. The prisoner was still asleep.

555 kicked the female's ribs.

No cry, no twitch.

This one was hardier than it'd thought. The tharuk bent, shaking the woman's shoulder. Her head rolled toward him, eyes open and glassy. Her lips were tinged blue.

Dead—the prisoner was dead.

It'd never get away with hiding the body. 316 had hidden her rucksack and look how that had ended. 555 would have to take her to the flesh pile, then report to Zens.

§

Bone-weary, Tomaaz shoveled his evening gruel into his mouth. Occasionally, the spoon missed, hitting his jaw or cheek. Was he numlocked? No, after days of digging latrine canals, exhaustion was making him clumsy.

Or shock. Tharuks had been especially vicious today, whipping and beating slaves. More than one had died. The overseers had barked at the crew leaders to drive their slaves harder, even though people were dropping around them. 568 had even whipped littlings.

Now the tharuks were standing in a group, grumbling.

"Zens got bad news," said 568. "That's why overseers whip."

"Kill more slaves. They will speed up," reasoned Droopy Eye.

"Zens can chop their hands off," snorted another and they all guffawed.

As if that would help anyone dig faster.

Tomaaz blanched and slipped a clear-mind berry into his gruel, scoffing it down, just in case. He checked his nails. After this morning's dragon scale, they were gray again. Three mind-numbing days in this place and he hadn't found a trace of Ma. He couldn't give up. Last night, Pa had looked worse. Frustration welled inside him, then sputtered and died. It took too much energy. He slurped his gruel, then picked up his shovel.

"Hey, you!" 568's whip flicked Tomaaz's calf, stinging. "Take that stinking corpse. To the pile." The tharuk gestured at Half Hand, who'd lain there for two days.

Dead, while Tomaaz wore his shirt. Flies buzzed around the body, flitting into Tomaaz's face as he picked up the boy. He huffed, trying to blow them away without tharuks noticing.

"Take your shovel," yelled 568. "Feed that beast. Or *see* Zens."

The way 568 said *see* made Tomaaz's back prickle.

Half Hand was all poky bones and saggy skin, but Tomaaz still staggered under his weight. His head spun. Their meager rations would make anyone weak.

568 hadn't requested a tharuk escort, so Tomaaz shambled off on his own.

Along the gully, he passed slaves, eyes empty and slack-faced, returning from depositing the dead. When he got to the flesh pile, bile rose in his throat at the stench of decomposing bodies. A little girl lay on the heap—she'd been two canals over, whipped, for stopping to pee. The second lash had done her in. The hand of a tiny littling peeked out from under a man's corpse. It wriggled. Gods, was the littling still alive?

Sharp teeth and a twitching nose poked out from under the hand, followed by a rat's body and long tail. No, the littling was dead, now a rodent's feasting ground. A crow cawed, landing on a body and pecking at its eyes. Tomaaz hissed and waved his hands, but it just hopped over to another body. Nauseous, he averted his eyes, carrying the boy to the edge of the heap.

"I'm sorry," Tomaaz murmured. "Sorry you had to die here, so far from family and fresh air." He lay the boy on the earth, to the side of the pile, refusing to toss him on a heap, like a discarded vegetable scrap. Did this boy have family? Had they died too? Or were they at home where the earth was fertile and green, while he'd wasted away in this land of dust, dirt and death?

His eyes stung.

He was the only one not drugged, among thousands. It was hopeless, searching for Ma.

The stench of death clawed at his nostrils, forcing its way down his throat, making him gag. He fought it, then gave in, retching until his guts were empty.

Wiping his hand on the back of his sleeve, Tomaaz rose, and turned to take one last look at the boy.

His breath caught. Oh, Gods. It couldn't be.

Under a man's body at the top of the pile, sticking out at eye level, was a boot bearing the mark of the Lush Valley cobbler. A boot just like his.

"No!" Tomaaz whispered.

He scrambled up the bodies and rolled the man away. Glassy turquoise eyes stared lifelessly from a pale face, framed by dark hair congealed with blood.

He'd found Ma.

Hope Awakened

Hans was over the Great Spanglewood Forest, only a day's flight from Dragons' Hold, but it felt like years away. He clung to the saddle, arms and hands spasming. His legs had the tremors. An anvil was pressing on his chest, making him gasp sips of air. Another shudder ran through his body. The breeze pricked his sweaty skin.

He had to face it: he was dying. Tharuk poison was killing him from the inside out.

He scrabbled in his pocket with cramping hands and pulled out a calling stone. The angular one—Marlies' one. He rubbed it. The stone flared, then crumbled into ash in his fingers. So Marlies' calling stone had been destroyed. By Zens? Tharuks? Or had it been an accident? He shoved his fingers at his pocket, missing. Then tried again, more slowly. On the third attempt, he extracted Tomaaz's calling stone and rubbed it … nothing. He tried again … nothing. Afraid he'd drop it in midair and have no means of communicating with his son, he shoved it back into his pocket.

Gods, he wasn't going to make it.

"*Hang on, Hans,*" Handel melded. "*We're not too far away.*"

"Too far for me," Hans said. "You'll be returning on your own. Give Ezaara my love. Tell her to get Tomaaz and Marlies." Shards, how awful. He'd never see his family again. A spasm seized his chest, making his whole torso convulse. Hans gritted his teeth until it passed.

"*Think,*" said Handel, beating his mighty wings. "*Think, Hans, there must be something we can do.*"

A vision shot through Hans' head, of him riding Handel into battle with Ezaara at his side on Zaarusha.

"No, Handel, it's not possible." He gritted his teeth as another spasm hit him. "That's not prophecy, just wishful thinking."

But it felt like prophecy. That same sense of mystique washed over Hans, as it always did when he saw the future.

"*Think back over your life, Hans. There must be some way we can save you. A different remedy? A place we can go … I'm not giving up on you, so soon. We've barely flown together.*" It was obvious that Handel had run out of ideas.

Flashes of his life appeared before Hans' eyes: Marlies crumpling in his arms when she'd killed Zaarusha's dragonet; fleeing Dragons' Hold; their wonder at their newborn twins; Tomaaz and Ezaara as littlings, laughing; Ezaara's first arrow hitting a clump of grass; Ezaara and Tomaaz fighting in the marketplace the day Ezaara had imprinted with Zaarusha—the last time he'd seen her; Ana giving him the little pouch; tharuks attacking Lush Valley; Lovina and Tomaaz on Liesar.

"*There!*" Handel latched onto one of his memories, showing it to him again. "*What did she say, Hans? What did Ana say when she gave you that pouch?*"

"I don't know." A spasm ran across his face. The sun was too bright. All Hans wanted to do was close his eyes and …

"*And fall to your death. Hans! Pull yourself together!*" Handel roared, the rumble jolting him back to reality. "*Ana. Think.*"

Ana's words sprang to mind. "She said, if I'm in a tight corner, to rub the ring and say her name. Her mother was Anakisha."

"*Anakisha's ring? She gave you a ring of power, Hans. Use it! Now!*"

Hans drew in a strangled breath. The pouch, where was it? He fumbled, taking it out of his other pocket. As he was untying the strings, it slipped. He snatched it, cupping it against his leg, and grabbed it with both hands so it wouldn't drop.

The trees below were tiny twigs against a ribbon of blue.

"*Don't get distracted, Hans, put the ring on.*"

Hans jammed it on his finger. "Ana," he called, rubbing the jade whorls. "Help me."

The forest, sky and distant ranges disappeared.

Hans and Handel were suspended in a tunnel of billowing clouds, bathed in golden light. A woman moved toward them in a flowing white gown. Strange, she was transparent, the glowing clouds showing through her. As she approached, Hans recognized her.

"Anakisha! I thought you were dead."

She spoke in his mind. "*Zens entered Dragons' Realm in my reign, so I am trapped in the land between life and death, only able to pass on and join Yanir in the great flying grounds when Zens and his evil are purged from Dragons' Realm.*"

"Where are we?"

"*The ring creates a realm gate, similar to a world gate, but you can only travel within Dragons' Realm.*"

The possibilities were endless.

"No, Hans, not endless. Every time a realm gate is used, the walls of the gate grow weaker, creating a ripple in sathir, the energy of life. Zens senses those ripples. If he takes advantage of them and encroaches the walls, he'll be able to move throughout Dragons' Realm at will. Imagine the danger."

Hans swallowed, his throat tight, as another spasm wracked his body.

"Only use the ring in dire circumstances," Anakisha warned. "Never for convenience."

"Help, Ezaara!" Handel called. "It's your father, Hans. He's dying."

"It's no use calling Ezaara, she can't hear you." Desperation was making Handel do ridiculous things. His daughter couldn't meld with a dragon other than Zaarusha.

A dark ripple flashed through a cloud, like lightning in a stormy sky.

"What was that?" Hans asked Anakisha.

"A crack in the wall. Hurry. Where do you want to go?"

"Dragons' Hold." Gods, he could hardly hold on.

"Safe travels," Anakisha said.

With a loud crack, the glowing clouds disappeared and Hans and Handel were suddenly above Dragons' Hold.

"Welcome home," said Handel, satisfaction radiating from him.

Hans was about to reply, but he blacked out.

§

Ma's body was still warm. Tomaaz's heart hammered. He held his fingers under her nose. No breath. He felt her neck. No pulse. Dead, dead, dead. Oh Gods, he was too late to save her. A sob burst from his throat. Tomaaz cradled her against his chest, staggering over the dead bodies. Under his boot, a rat squealed and scurried deeper into the pile. He shuddered. He couldn't leave Ma here as fodder for rats or carrion birds. He half-slid down the flesh pile, his mind in a frenzy. He had to get her out of here. Take her somewhere. Give her a decent burial.

There was plenty of dirt near the latrine pits. No! No! He wasn't burying Ma near a pile of human excrement. Not anywhere here. He'd take her back to Lush Valley. Wait for Pa, and take her back. But where could he hide her until then?

Tomaaz's boots hit solid ground. Backhanding tears, he slung Ma over his shoulder and picked up his shovel. As long as he was feeding the beast, he'd have freedom. He snorted. Confinement to a lousy valley under duress was not freedom.

He traipsed to the rat pile, his shoulders bowed under Ma's weight. Dark sorrow clogged his throat, making his breath come in gasps. Thank the Egg, the rat tharuk had finished duty. Scooping rats onto his shovel, Tomaaz headed toward the main valley. He'd tell any tharuks he saw that Ma was a dead slave; that he'd dump her on the pile once he'd fed the beast. Even so, he stuck to the lengthening shadows.

His legs were boulders, weighing him down. Perhaps Pa was dead, too. Lovina had also been limplocked. And Ezaara? What if everyone he cared about was dead? What then?

Weighed down with his mother's corpse, Tomaaz trudged up the branch toward the beast's cave. Although he didn't encounter any tharuks, he could hear them further along the main valley, whips cracking as they mustered slaves to the sleeping huts.

Rounding the bend, Tomaaz stumbled along to the dead end. The beast growled softly, sticking its head out of its cave as he approached. Barely glancing at the creature, Tomaaz threw the rats at it, then carried Ma into the neighboring cave. Here, she should be safe.

He gently laid Ma on the floor near the far wall. Stroked the matted hair back from her face. Oh, Gods, this was real. He bowed his head to her chest and put his arms around her, sobs tearing from him.

Tomaaz wasn't sure how long he cried, but suddenly there was snuffling at the hole in the wall. A tongue flicked through.

Shards, the beast. It might make a ruckus and bring tharuks running. Sighing, Tomaaz pulled some clear-mind from his pocket, placing it on the tip of the shovel, and held it by the hole. The beast made short work of the berries, then shoved its eye against the aperture, observing him. Was the gray film over its eye growing thinner? Probably just his imagination. It was hard to see in the half dark.

Tomaaz took out his calling stone and rubbed it. Nothing. Dread rushed through him. If Pa was dead, there would be no chance of getting Ma out of here—no chance of saving himself.

He should get back. Tharuks might notice he was missing. But somehow, nothing mattered anymore.

Tomaaz lay on the cold stone floor next to his mother's corpse, staring into the dark.

§

Dawn stole through the cave, waking Tomaaz. His mouth was dry and his hands and feet were numb with cold. Blearily, he gazed at Ma, his thoughts pushing through sludge. It was hopeless. He rolled over and drifted back into a nightmare-plagued sleep.

A grunt woke him.

Tharuks?

He fumbled for the shovel. There, near the hole in the wall. Tomaaz lurched over and grabbed it, then faced the cave entrance.

Another grunt—behind him.

He spun. It wasn't a tharuk, just the beast, watching him again. "Hungry?" Tomaaz's voice cracked. "I don't have any food, but here you go, have these." He passed the beast some clear-mind. He didn't have many berries left, but who cared? Maybe it would be better to be numlocked than stay alert in this hell, with death lurking in every shadow.

He tried the calling stone again. No luck. He was on his own. Putting the stone back in his pocket, Tomaaz caught a glimpse of his pink fingernails. He took a pinch of dragon's scale and went back over to Ma in the corner.

How had she died? He touched the blood-encrusted gash on her head. Wait. Her skin was *still warm*.

His breath hitched. Impossible.

Tentatively, Tomaaz touched her neck, then slid his hand under her jerkin to touch her shoulder. Definitely warm. But then why were her lips and fingertips blue, her eyes glassy, and face as white as goat's cheese?

He splayed one hand by her mouth and nose, the other on her torso, waiting. Was that a faint tickle on his hand? There, a minuscule movement in her chest? Hard to tell. He held his own breath, waiting. Again, the softest whisper of breath on his hand, the barest movement of her torso.

His fingers moved to her neck. He cocked his head, concentrating. *Please.* There, a slight tremor against his fingers … it seemed like forever until he felt it again.

Shards! Ma was alive.

She was existing on a few shallow breaths and a faint heartbeat, but barely. He had to act fast or he'd lose her.

Tomaaz lifted her jerkin and found her healer's pouch at her waist. Pulling out her remedies, he piled them on the floor, looking for something that might help. Clear-mind berries wrapped in brown paper, dragon's scale, owl-wort, warm weed, dragon's breath, healing salve and … what were these? He held up a stem with two dried blue berries on it, and nubs where other berries had been plucked.

Piaua berries—they looked different, dried and shriveled, but they had to be piaua. He'd never seen another plant with blue oval berries with pointed ends. Right at the bottom of Ma's pouch, he found a slim vial of clear light-green fluid—piaua juice. A memory flashed through his head.

Ma was crouched near the base of the piaua, her hands on the trunk, whispering solemn words. A sudden strange breeze stirred only the piaua's leaves. A rushing sound, like a thousand waters, whooshed around the clearing. There was silence as the tree's leaves stilled. Ma spoke again. Again, the piaua's leaves moved and the rushing resumed.

Even though they were only littlings, Ezaara had been the first to realize what was happening. "Ma's talking to the tree," she said. "The piaua is answering."

Tomaaz and Ezaara watched Ma harvest piaua juice from the tree's leaves.

"I'm hungry. Can I eat those blue berries, Ma?" Tomaaz asked, pointing at the pretty oval berries with poky ends.

"Tomaaz," Ma said, taking his face in her hands, "you must never eat those berries. They're dangerous. Promise me, both of you, that you'll never touch them."

They nodded.

"Can I feed them to tharuks?" Ezaara asked. "Will the berries kill them?"

That made Ma laugh. "And have them in comas? Yes, you can."

He hadn't understood what comas meant, but he was still hungry. "What about the juice? Can I drink that?" Tomaaz asked.

Ma knelt in the grass with them, among the wildflowers. "Piaua juice can heal anything except poison, but there is a cost. Every time we use the juice, it steals life force from the piaua trees. If we guzzle down piaua juice, then the mighty piauas scattered across Dragons' Realm will fail, and we will have no healing remedies for our people. That's why the juice is sacred, and only a tree speaker can harvest it."

"I'm going to be a tree speaker when I grow up," Ezaara declared.

"Me too," Tomaaz said.

The berries caused comas. Is this what had happened to Ma? Did a coma slow your body down until your breathing and heartbeat were barely there? If piaua berries had caused this state, then perhaps the juice could cure it. It was worth trying, as piaua was a strong remedy for many things.

He had to try.

Resting Ma's head and shoulders on his knees, Tomaaz uncorked the vial and parted her lips, dribbling piaua juice onto her tongue. Nothing happened.

He dripped more juice into her mouth, careful not to spill any. Piaua was best a few drips at a time, but usually it worked faster than this. Maybe it wouldn't be enough. Tomaaz dribbled a little more, counting his heartbeats to stop himself going mad with frustration. Maybe nothing would heal her.

Please, please. Tears rolled down his cheeks. She had to make it. He couldn't bear it if she didn't. He'd already lost her once, yesterday. He kept at it. The vial was now only half full. He gave her more.

Her lips. Something had changed. Tomaaz inspected them. He couldn't be sure, but was the blue fading? Two more drips. He checked her hands. Yes, her fingernails had lost some of their bluish tinge. He let out a slow breath. The piaua was working, but did he have enough?

Soon the vial was empty. Ma's pulse was stronger, but still not normal. A tinge of color crept into her cheeks. Tomaaz sat, cradling her head, his knees numb, waiting. There was nothing more he could do except wait and hope.

§

A snort at the hole in the wall made Tomaaz jerk awake. His legs were dead under the weight of Ma's head and shoulders, and he was fighting to stop his head from drooping again, but he didn't want to move and disturb Ma. Sometime while he'd dozed, her breathing had deepened. Her chest was now rising and falling regularly, thank the Egg.

Another snort. He turned, rubbing his stiff neck. The beast was watching him again. The gray film over its eyes had thinned, showing a glimmer of startling green. Tomaaz tried to speak, but his throat was dry.

Gods, he hadn't eaten or drunk for hours.

Ma's hand twitched. Then her foot. A gusty sigh shuddered through her, then another. Her eyes fluttered, then flew wide, alarm shooting across her face.

"Ma," Tomaaz croaked. "It's me, Tomaaz."

"Tomaaz?" Her voice was fragile.

"Yes, Ma, I'm here to take you home." How, he had no idea.

"Ezaara?"

"I haven't seen her." What had happened to Ezaara? "Don't worry about that now. Let's get you better." Shards, he had nothing to feed her, no water. Nothing to keep her warm, not even a blanket.

Her eyes drifted shut again. He shook her gently. "Ma, I'm going to find you water and food. I'll be back. You'll be safe here." Nodding, she curled up and went back to sleep. Tomaaz hovered, unsure about leaving her.

There was another snort at the wall.

"Keep an eye on her," Tomaaz said to the beast.

The large green eye winked.

Tomaaz nearly jumped out of his skin. Snatching up his shovel, he rushed down the valley.

§

The noon sun broke through the mists, beating down on Tomaaz. Panting, he paused at the junction to the main valley. He was much weaker than he'd realized. He had to eat—soon—and source some food for Ma. Oh, and feed the beast. With Ma hiding next to the beast's cave, the last thing they needed was a roaring ruckus to bring tharuks running. Whips cracked to the south, near the latrine pit. Tomaaz headed north toward the eating area. If he was caught out of place, he'd be whipped, but he'd also be punished if he collapsed from exhaustion in the latrine ditches.

To Tomaaz's surprise, the area was full of milling slaves. He'd never been feed here at noon, but by the look of their pickaxes and grubbers, these were the crews that worked in the mountainside. Tomaaz casually deposited his shovel and lined up with them. These slaves were covered in grime and fine yellow powder. They smelled of the mist that leaked from the crevasses.

Many of them had fingers, ears or hands missing. One had his nose cut off, leaving a gaping scar in his face. Coughing and wheezing punctuated their sluggish movements. The little girl in front of him hacked, spitting up dark globules of phlegm. Those in line shuffled forward, hands out, to grab chunks of hard bread from the numlocked serving slaves. As the girl took her bread, she coughed and fell, her crust flying into the dust at Tomaaz's feet. She lay on the ground hacking. Then she stilled, eyes rolling back in her head.

Tomaaz took his bread from the server, then picked up her piece, slipping it into his pocket. Gods, stealing bread from the dead to feed Ma. What would he stoop to next?

The slaves ground to a halt, waiting for the tharuks to act.

A huge tharuk flicked its whip, striking a man, who yelped. Still gnawing their hard crusts, the crowd parted to let the beast through. The tharuk booted her in the neck. Her body slid, rasping against the dry dirt, her head lolling at an odd angle.

"Dead," the tharuk pronounced, its red eyes scanning the slaves.

Although Tomaaz's belly grumbled, he suddenly had no appetite.

The tharuk pointed a stubby finger at him, its claw a whip's breadth from his face. "You! To the flesh pile. Take this human scum."

Tomaaz bent to retrieve the girl. Shards, he could hardly lift her. Last night, he'd carried Ma without a problem, but now he was too weak.

"Move it." The tharuk glared at him, whip poised.

Slinging her over his shoulder, Tomaaz staggered off. A tharuk hovering over a crude bench holding waterskins motioned Tomaaz over. "Slave, drink. Water makes you healthy."

Healthy? Hardly. Tomaaz put the girl down and drank the numlock-tainted water, not stopping until the waterskin was nearly empty. The tharuk turned its back to give water to other hapless slaves. As Tomaaz picked up the girl, he slipped the mostly-deflated waterskin up the back of her shirt, and tucked her shirttail into her breeches. There, that should hold it. Now he had food and water for Ma. He lifted the girl and trekked off to the flesh pile. The water had eased his dizziness, even if he still had no idea how to get out of this gray hell.

Tomaaz laid the girl near Half Hand, at the mercy of the crows and rats. He slipped the waterskin out of her shirt and under his jerkin, waving flies off the girl's face. Yesterday he'd been horrified at the flesh pile, but now, seeing and smelling death felt normal.

It scared him. He was losing himself.

The tharuk at the rat pile laughed when Tomaaz turned up. "Dumb human. No shovel. Forget to feed the beast? It will be hungry. Might eat you."

Hands full of rats, Tomaaz traipsed back along the valley to see Ma.

The beast was deep in shadow and ignored the rats he threw at the cave mouth. Tomaaz shrugged and went to Ma, wiping his hands on his filthy breeches. The eye was watching at the hole in the wall. Once again, it winked, then the beast's chain rattled and it moved away.

Had it really stood guard over Ma the whole time he'd been gone? He must be going crazy.

He managed to rouse Ma, sitting her against the cavern wall. Softening the bread with water, he fed it to her and gave Ma clear-mind to counteract the tainted water. Then he ate his own bread.

"How are you feeling?"

"A bit better, but still tired. Thank you, Tomaaz." Ma's eyes filled with tears. "I've failed Zaarusha. I never found her son."

§

Standing near Tomaaz above the ditch, a littling was scraping loose dirt into a pail with her tiny hands. Her efforts were pathetic—she dropped more than she filled—but if she stopped work, she'd feel the lash. Slack-jawed, a woman with one ear watched the littling. Her mother? It was hard to tell when everyone's faces were grimy and their eyes gray.

Tomaaz swung his pickax, hitting the dark dirt of the latrine pit. Sewage gushed into the ditch. His gut roiled. He was never going to get the stench out of his throat.

Suddenly, the littling was hanging over the sewage ditch. Her fingers scrabbling, she slipped lower. Tomaaz lunged for her arms, but the littling slithered through his hands, plunging into the sewage. The muck closed over her head, suffocating her. With a wail, the woman shoved past him and threw herself in, choking as she submerged. Tomaaz reached out, but a whip cracked, biting into his shoulder.

568 towered over him, whip poised for another strike, as the sludge-covered bodies were swept toward the pit.

Tomaaz wanted to snatch the whip off 568 and thrash every tharuk in sight, but Lovina's family story flashed to mind: her father had died retaliating against tharuks.

If he died now, no one could rescue Ma. He slumped to the ground, forcing himself to let the tension drain from his body. Numb with shock, Tomaaz sat staring until tharuk 568 cracked the lash overhead, driving their crew over to dig the next ditch.

§

Tomaaz thought he was used to death, but the revolting images played over and over in his mind all day—first the littling, then the mother. He should've been faster. Should've lunged further. Or jumped in. Now they were dead. Gods, he hated this place.

Shoulder still sore, he slurped his evening gruel, spitting out a weevil, and managed to surreptitiously snag another crust of bread for Ma from the mining crew's lunch barrel. There was a chill in the air tonight. He had to get her a blanket. But how? No one was near the sleeping sheds, so he couldn't just wander in and get one. And with trackers about, he didn't like his chances of sneaking out tonight. He gazed up at the gray sky. Was it actually gray? Or was it just that stinking mist coloring the air?

Shambling to his feet, Tomaaz collected his shovel and went to feed the beast.

When he reached the caverns, the beast was at the hole in the wall again, watching over Ma. It gave him the creeps. Was it protecting her or observing prey? Whatever it was, it was intelligent. After eating the clear-mind berries off his spade, it retreated.

He woke Ma. "Are you all right?"

"Fine." She gave him a weary smile.

He passed her the bread and sat quietly as she ate and sipped from the waterskin.

"Bad day?"

He nodded. "The carnage here makes me sick."

"Zens has gotten worse."

He nodded. "I have a calling stone. Pa will expect me to talk to him near sunset." Soon. What if Pa was dead? He'd cross that bridge when he came to it. "What happened to your head?"

"Zens." She shrugged. "I knew if I didn't do something he'd torture me to find your identities and kill everyone I loved."

"So, you took piaua berries?"

"That way I still had a chance of being found." She squeezed his hand.

"And your arm?"

"I hurt that on the way here." She winced. "Sometimes, we can't fix everything, Tomaaz."

"I know. I wish—" Clenching a fist, he punched the wall. The ache in his fingers felt good. It *should hurt,* being here day after day, watching people die. "Everything in this forsaken valley is gray. The people, the food, the air, their faces, their corpses … and the way I feel inside."

Ma chewed on her lump of bread.

"If only I could do something to get out of here."

"You can," she said. "Speak to Pa, then I'll tell you where they hid my rucksack."

Ezaara

Ezaara and Roberto sped across the orchard on Zaarusha and Erob. They'd just been kissing in the orchard. Forbidden kisses. Still officially her dragon master, Roberto could be banished to the Robandi Wastelands for kissing her.

He'd been banished before, and captured by the Robandi assassins in the Wastelands. She'd gone to save him. They'd come back to Dragons' Hold last night to find Zaarusha poisoned and two dragon masters dead. The queen was straining. She wasn't strong yet. Not after being poisoned with dragon's bane. Thank the Egg, they'd found the remedy.

But now, it was life or death again—not Ezaara's or her dragon's, but her father's.

"*What did Handel say?*" Roberto mind-melded.

They left the orchard behind, speeding over the fields toward the granite crags of Dragon's Teeth—the vicious peaks surrounding the basin of Dragons' Hold.

"*He said my father was dying. That I should prepare.*" Ezaara clenched her hands around Zaarusha's spinal ridge. "*Which doesn't help, if I don't know what's wrong with him.*"

An image of Pa's tanned face shot through her head, curly dark hair, green eyes gleaming as he shared a joke. He was so full of life. She'd learned many of her combat skills from him. A pang of loss hit her. This was the first she'd heard of her family since imprinting with Zaarusha and leaving Lush Valley on dragonback.

"*Zaarusha, I didn't even say goodbye.*" A lump constricted her throat. Shards, what if she never saw him again? Or Ma and Tomaaz?

"*Imprinting is like that. It changes lives.*" Zaarusha, the dragon queen, sent a wave of warmth through her.

"*I know, but if he's dead—*"

"*I can't see them,*" Roberto melded, turning his head to scan the ranges to the west.

"*Handel will be here soon enough,*" Zaarusha replied. "*Then we'll know.*"

Erob flipped his midnight-blue wings, Roberto leaning into his neck as he shot up the cliff. "*Where to?*" Erob asked. "*The infirmary or Zaarusha's den?*"

"*Infirmary*," Ezaara replied.

"*If Fleur left anything of worth.*" The venom in Zaarusha's tone hit home.

Yes, what if Fleur, the traitorous master healer, had destroyed the remedy her father needed?

"*May the rust vipers of the Robandi Wastelands destroy her and her family,*" Roberto snapped.

There was a loud crack and a bronze dragon appeared above the ledge to the infirmary, a rider slumped over his back.

"Pa!" Ezaara's voice echoed off the mountainside. How in the Egg's name had Handel appeared in midair like that?

"*Dragon's claws and fangs! Never seen that happen before,*" Roberto said.

Handel dropped to the ledge, bunching his legs to soften the impact. Still, Pa's body slipped as he landed.

"*Zaarusha! Hurry!*"

Ezaara slid out of the saddle and raced over. Roberto was already there, untying Pa's harness. His midnight eyes flashed with sympathy as he lifted her father down.

Gods, Pa was pale. He was breathing, but barely.

Roberto lifted him into the infirmary, stepping over slashed mattresses and bottles and jars strewn on the floor.

Dropping some herbs onto a table, Adelina, Roberto's sister, rushed over. "Sorry, we haven't finished cleaning this mess up yet. Kierion's gone to— What's happened? Who's this?" Dark smudges ringed her eyes.

"Ezaara's pa," Roberto said as he eased Pa onto a bed.

Pa's hands were curled into fists, his wrists bent at odd angles. His arms were bunched across his torso, as if he was having a spasm. Ezaara picked up his hand to uncurl his fingers, but they were rigid. She felt his pulse. "He's still alive, but it looks like he's frozen in the middle of a fit."

Roberto and Adelina exchanged a meaningful glance.

"What?" Ezaara shot. "What aren't you telling me?"

Roberto nodded at Adelina. "It's limplock. Do you have any remedy?"

Ezaara had never heard of limplock.

"I'll get it." Adelina dashed into a curtained alcove. She reappeared a moment later with some vials of yellow granules. "I remembered you telling me about limplock, in Naobia, Roberto, when you returned from Death Valley. Lucky you did, because a girl from Lush Valley arrived while you two were away, and she'd been limplocked, too."

Lush Valley—Ezaara's home. "Who was it?" Ezaara asked, examining a vial.

"Lovina. You must know her. She's a friend of your brother's." Adelina uncorked a vial.

Lovina? Old Bill's daughter? She'd never been a friend of Tomaaz's. But who knew what had happened since she'd left? "How do we give this remedy? Mix it with water?"

Roberto shook his head. "Like this." He leaned over Pa, prizing his jaw open, and nodded at Adelina. "Slowly."

Adelina shook a few granules onto Pa's tongue, while Ezaara held Pa's hand, stroking his clenched fingers. No matter how she tried to straighten them, the moment she let go, they cramped. She felt Pa's pulse again. It was fast and thready.

"Giving him the remedy too quickly could damage his nerves," Roberto explained. "Limplock paralyzes the body slowly over a few days. It starts at the hands and feet and works its way deeper, until the heart finally stops beating. It's good your father got here in time."

"In time?" Ezaara tried to swallow. "You mean it's not too late?"

"I hope not." His midnight eyes blazed. "We'll do whatever we can."

Pa's jerkin was stained with blood and a dried green substance. Ezaara gently eased the fabric back, examining a wound above his left breast. "An arrow got him." She pulled some clean herb out of the healer's pouch at her waist and set about treating his injury, while Roberto administered the limplock remedy.

There was a knock at the infirmary door. Adelina went to answer it.

Already, Pa's breaths were deeper, more rhythmic.

A thin girl entered the infirmary, ducking shyly behind a curtain of pretty brown hair. "Oh, you're busy," she said, backing toward the door. The girl's blue eyes flew open. "Ezaara?" She glanced at the bed. "What happened to Hans?" she cried, rushing forward. "Oh, limplock. That's awful. It hurts so much."

"Lovina?" It couldn't be. This pretty girl with soft brown hair and blue eyes was Old Bill's daughter?

"Hello, Ezaara." She spoke quietly and leaned over Pa, taking his other hand. "Did Bill hurt him, too?" She rubbed Pa's hands. "My hands were cold when I was limplocked."

It was the most Ezaara had ever heard Lovina say. "Looks like an arrow got him in the chest." Ezaara hadn't been thinking—she should have asked Handel what had happened. Oh, shards, she hadn't even thought of Handel. *Handel, are you all right?*

"I'll go and check on Handel, shall I?" Roberto asked aloud, tucking a blanket over Pa. It was going to take some getting used to him hearing what she was thinking. He passed the remedy to Ezaara and headed to the ledge outside.

Pa's fingers tightened convulsively on Ezaara's, then loosened. His feet twitched, then relaxed.

Relief rushed through Ezaara. "It's working."

"Keep giving him the remedy until the vial is gone or he'll slip backward," Adelina said. She bustled around the infirmary, starting to clean up the mess they'd made last night when she, Lars and Kierion had been searching for the remedy for dragon's bane to heal Zaarusha. "Let me know if you need anything."

Lovina's clear blue eyes met Ezaara's. "Do you know your mother and Tomaaz are in Death Valley? I think that's where your father was hurt."

Ezaara gasped. Death Valley? Things were much worse than she'd thought. "Are they still alive?"

Eyes sad, Lovina just shrugged.

§

Hans woke—if you could call it waking. Everything swam before his eyes and he was as groggy as a hatchling. His leg had a tingling sensation—that's what had yanked him from deep slumber. He ran his hand down his leg. It ached; well, everything did. His limbs, his chest ... that's right, he'd been on Handel heading for Dragons' Hold.

He turned his head against the pillow. Sprawled on a bed next to his was Ezaara, sleeping.

His daughter, at last. So, he'd made it to Dragons' Hold.

"Of course you did," Handel harrumphed from somewhere nearby. *"Did you think after all these years, I'd let you down?"*

"No, but I let you down when we fled."

"At first, I was angry, but that faded after a few years. I missed you. Liesar never told me where you were until we had to rescue Lush Valley from tharuks. Welcome home."

They were in a cavern similar to the old cavern he and Marlies had lived in, next to the infirmary, at Dragons' Hold. The walls blurred. He closed his eyes for a moment, fighting the urge to drift back to sleep. Something made his leg tingle again. Oh! Thrusting his sore clumsy fingers into his pocket, he pulled out his calling stone, fumbling as he held it up. That's what had woken him.

Tomaaz's face lit up the surface of the stone, his voice echoing in Hans' mind. *"Pa, I've found Ma."*

He had, all right. Images of Marlies flitted through Hans' head, the way Tomaaz had seen her. Pale, blue-tinged lips and lying deathly still. Hans' throat choked up. Another image followed: Marlies' eyelids fluttering as she gazed up, then drifted back to sleep. So Tomaaz had saved her. He'd got there in time.

"Thank the Egg, she's safe with you."

"When can you meet us, Pa?" Tomaaz looked gaunt, worn out.

Hans tried to smile, but he was so exhausted, he wasn't sure if he'd managed. Tomorrow? No, that was too soon. He didn't even know if he could walk yet. *"Two days? Can you hold on that long?"*

"I'll meet you at sunset on the hill north of the watchtower, as we arranged." Tomaaz hesitated, then blurted out, *"You still look sick, Pa. You sure you can come?"*

"Need rest," was all Hans could croak out. His fingers were aching from holding the small stone.

"I'll take care of Ma. Don't you worry," Tomaaz said. *"Gods, I'm glad you're alive. Have you seen Lovina?"*

"Not yet, but they say she's recovered."

"Good. Ezaara?"

"Yes," Hans mumbled, losing his grip on the stone as his eyelids closed.

Revelation

The sun would soon go down. Tomaaz could hardly restrain his excitement. Two days and he and Ma would be out of there. He left the beast's branch of the valley, making his way south to get her rucksack. Tomaaz tucked his shovel behind a boulder and broke into a run. The cliffs were pockmarked with caves.

Shards, he wasn't used to running. Tomaaz slowed to a walk.

Two guttural voices drifted toward him. Hiding in a short tunnel in the hillside, Tomaaz wished his pounding heart would quieten.

"Her rucksack is not there. Where's it gone?"

"316 was with her. Maybe he took it."

"Slimy runty worm. Good that 316 is dead." A tharuk chortled.

Tomaaz pressed his back flat against the tunnel wall as two lumbering tharuks passed. He held his breath, poised to run in case one was a tracker.

Their voices faded as the beasts went into the main valley.

Phew! That was close. Heading up the ravine, Tomaaz took the branch to the right, counting the caves in the northern wall. There was the one Ma said she'd stayed in, slimy and damp. The tharuks had probably searched there. Three caves further … there, that was it. In the cave, behind a rocky outcrop, was Ma's rucksack. Tomaaz slung the straps over his shoulders and made his way back to the main valley.

But when he got to the boulder, his shovel was gone.

Shards! Those tharuks had found it. They'd have a tracker here in no time. Unless they thought a slave had left the shovel on the way to the latrines. Should he go back and hide the pack, in case he was seen? Tomaaz eased his head around the corner, surveying the valley. No one was in sight. It was only a short run back to the branch that led to Ma and the beast. Should he chance it? If he didn't take the pack to Ma now, he may not get another chance. Especially if a tracker was set loose.

Keeping to the shadows cast by the hills, Tomaaz shot up the valley. His legs were weak and his breath rasped, but he made it to the side branch without seeing any tharuks. He pushed himself further, way past the bend, running until he reached Ma.

He dropped the rucksack near the entrance to her cave. "Ma, I've got to get back before the tharuks miss me."

Her reply was drowned out by the rattle of a chain. The beast sprang out of its cave, blazing bright orange in the rays of the setting sun.

Orange? Yes, and those were the same green eyes that had been peeking through the hole, watching over Ma. But how?

A thrum ran through his mind. Warmth spread across his chest. A rush of energy enveloped him.

The folds of what had been saggy gray skin by the creature's side were now orange. They flexed and spread into wings. The beast *was* a dragon.

The thrum turned into words inside his head. *"Thank you for feeding me those berries, Tomaaz."*

"I, ah—you're a dragon."

"And you're now my rider."

An image of him flying above Death Valley astride the orange dragon shot through Tomaaz's mind. He felt like a mighty eagle soaring above the valley—free and powerful. "Whoa, that would be amazing."

"It will be, when we finally fly together, free of this hell."

"How can we get you out of here?"

"You don't have to speak, you can share your thoughts and feelings."

That's right, he'd done this before while he was touching Handel and Liesar. *"Like this?"* With a whoosh, something rushed through him, making him want to dance and yell with joy. He approached the dragon, holding his hand out. The dragon bowed its head and sniffed his chest, butting him gently. Tomaaz scratched one of the dragon's eye ridges. Its scales were warm and supple like worn leather. A rumble issued from the dragon's throat, like a cat purring.

§

Marlies woke. Her head was clear for the first time in days. She sensed something familiar. Dragon energy? No, not in Death Valley. Unless … Slowly, she got to her feet and, leaning on the walls with her uninjured arm, made her way to the mouth of the cavern. For a moment she was blinded—it'd been so long since she'd seen daylight.

Then her eyes adjusted.

Tomaaz was outside, standing spell-struck before an enormous orange dragon. In her fever-induced dreams, she'd imagined a green eye staring through a crack in the wall. But no, she hadn't imagined it. That green eye belonged to this bedraggled dragon in front of her son.

She slumped in relief. They'd done it. They'd found Zaarusha's son. She'd nearly died, but she'd repaid her debt to Zaarusha. Well, almost. She still had to get them all back to Dragons' Hold.

The poor thing looked half starved. Tomaaz had lost weight too. They were so absorbed in each other, they hadn't seen her. They were imprinting. She shook her head. This was more than she'd ever dared hope for. Both of her children were dragon riders. Marlies swallowed the lump that rose in her throat, and blinked her pricking eyes.

Perhaps she could help them strengthen their bond. Supporting herself against the wall again, Marlies went back into the cave to retrieve something from her rucksack.

§

Behind Tomaaz, Ma chuckled. She was leaning against the rocky face outside her cavern, holding something out. "You're imprinting, Tomaaz. You may want to feed your dragon. Here, from my rucksack." She passed him some dried meat.

Tomaaz took it. Shards, it smelled good. The dragon's nostrils flared and twitched. Its tongue tickled as it licked his fingers.

"Tasty," it mind-melded.

"And here I was these past few days, thinking you were going to eat me." Tomaaz laughed, really laughed, for the first time since Ezaara had left Lush Valley. So, this is why Ezaara had left. This inexplicable intense rush of feelings, this sensation that you could soar forever, this bond and feeling of rightness. *This* was imprinting. His chest swelled as if it would burst from happiness.

"So, this is Zaarusha's son," Ma said. "What's his name, Tomaaz?"

The dragon's green eyes regarded Tomaaz. *"From now, I am called Maazini, in honor of you."*

"He says his name is Maazini, to honor me. What does that mean?"

Ma sighed. "I wish we could have taught you this when you were young, Tomaaz. When a dragon and rider imprint, their names share a common syllable, so he's changing his name to match yours."

"I am grateful that you gave me clear-mind."

Tomaaz's chest swelled with pride. This mighty creature was grateful to him. He rubbed Maazini's nose.

Maazini butted his chest again. "*Hide your mother in my cave. I'll keep her safe.*"

"Before you go back, have something to eat." Ma held out some dried meat and an apple. "But be careful. Too much food might make you vomit."

Tomaaz bolted the salty meat, then finished the apple, seeds and all. He'd taken good food for granted all his life, but never again. "Here, let me help you." He shouldered Ma's rucksack and helped her through to Maazini's cavern. At the back of the cave, Maazini's chain was fixed to the wall. Tomaaz yanked at the thick links, pulling with all his bodyweight, but they held firm.

"*I already tried that, but all it did was chafe my leg.*" Maazini snorted. "*Did you really think you were stronger than me?*"

"No. So, how can we get you out of here?"

"*If I knew that, I'd be gone already,*" Maazini replied. "*I guess I'm stuck here.*"

"No! Pa's coming tomorrow night. I won't leave you behind."

"*You might have to,*" said Maazini. "*A dragon never willingly sacrifices his rider.*"

§

It didn't matter how much Marlies slept, nothing lifted her bone-deep exhaustion. She nibbled on stale flatbread, but food didn't really help much either. Doubt nagged at her. What if she never fully recovered from using piaua berries? As a healer, she'd treated people that couldn't shake the effects of sudden illness—people who dragged themselves through life without energy or vitality. She didn't want to be like that. Pushing to her feet, she forced herself to pace the cavern and keep her muscles active. She needed a task, something to take her mind off her physical state.

Her pacing took her past Maazini. Zaarusha had wanted her to rescue him, but unless they could get his chain loose, there wasn't much chance of that. Perhaps she could pry one of the links open. Rummaging through her pack, she hunted for her knife, but it was gone. That clumsy tharuk had left her bow and arrows and food, but taken her knives and the calling stone. Where was the logic in that? Maybe it assumed she couldn't use an arrow at close range. More likely it didn't think she'd seen it hide her pack.

Maazini lifted his head.

There was one job she could get done while she waited here: it was time to face her past. She approached Maazini, laying her hand on his head so they could mind-meld. "*Maazini, I am thrilled that you have imprinted with my son. May your bond grow deep and be long-lasting.*" Like her bond with Liesar—who'd risked her life to help her and Hans flee from Zaarusha's wrath. Marlies hadn't seen her dragon for years, but she had no doubt that they were still bonded.

"*I recognize the timbre of your mind,*" Maazini replied. "*You seem familiar.*" He cocked his head, gazing at her with solemn green eyes. "*Have I met you before?*"

Only when he was a shell-bound dragonet.

Zaarusha's purple dragonet sprang to mind, floating dead in its translucent golden egg. Marlies gasped, yanking her hand off Maazini's forehead. Oh Gods, had he seen? Would he hate her for killing his sibling? She shrank back, Zaarusha's words echoing in her head: *You fled—that was an act of cowardice.*

She'd lived the last eighteen years in hiding. Would she live the next twenty the same way?

No, she couldn't let cowardice color her actions—not anymore. Holding the image firmly in her mind, Marlies took a step toward Maazini and laid her hand on his snout.

Seeing her memory of the dragonet's death, Maazini flinched. "*That was you!*" His tail twitched.

"Yes, it was me. *I'm sorry I killed your sibling.*" Marlies bowed her head, waiting for his wrath.

"*His name was Dyanmar,*" Maazini said, his voice rumbling in her mind. "*As dragonets, even when shell-bound, we are linked, sharing thoughts and memories, and having access to the memories of all our dragon ancestors since the First Egg. I sensed you through him.*"

"So that's how you knew me." The bitterness of her actions stung afresh.

"*Yes. My brother recognized your gift of healing, because he, too, was a healer. He saw a vision and knew your line was destined for great things. So, he sacrificed himself, passing his healing energy through the shell of his egg to heal you, so you could have children.*"

Marlies gasped. "He knew what he was doing? He willingly *died for me and my children?*"

"*Yes.*" Maazini tilted his head. "*Tomaaz reminds me of Dyanmar, but I can't understand why.*"

"What do you mean?"

"*I'm not sure. There's something about him …*"

That wee dragonet had sacrificed his life to help her. She hadn't murdered him. It had been his choice. The mantle of pain and regret that had nearly suffocated her slowly eased from Marlies' shoulders.

§

Yelping, a man was cowering in the corner, a tharuk looming over him. Under his blanket, Tomaaz gripped his pallet, trying not to act, for Ma's sake. The fabric ripped beneath his fingers. He thrust his hand inside, grabbing a fistful of straw, the ends poking into his palms, trying to restrain himself from leaping up to help. Then he sighed in relief as the tharuk turned away from the man, yelling for everyone to get up.

They traipsed to the eating area and chewed their crusts of stale bread. Another day in the latrines. He was so exhausted, he could crawl back onto his pallet and sleep for a week.

"If only I could lend you energy," Maazini melded, *"but I'm too weak, now."*

"If only I could set you free."

"We'll find a way."

Tomaaz didn't reply. How could he? He'd been racking his brain all night and hadn't come up with a way to free Maazini.

"Get to work, you lot," 568 bellowed.

Slaves went to the tool piles.

"You," 568 bellowed again, pointing at Tomaaz. "Feed the beast. Now. Zens wants that beast soon."

Zens wanted Maazini. No! Pa was coming tomorrow night. If they left Maazini behind, he'd be doomed. Tomaaz plodded to the tool pile.

At his feet was a thin saw. Its curved handle was hooked on the stem of a shovel. No one was watching. Casually, Tomaaz stepped on the saw blade and yanked the shovel handle, snapping the blade. He dropped the shovel, letting it clatter to the pile to mask any noise. Used to clumsy slaves dropping tools, the tharuks didn't even look his way. Tomaaz bent to grab the shovel and tucked the broken saw end into his boot. At last, a chance to free Maazini.

§

555 stood before Zens, head bowed.

555 was trusty, a lot better than his sneaky underling, 316, had been. Then, why wasn't the prisoner's rucksack where 316 had left it? Zens sent the image to 555 again—the image of the crevice he'd seen in 316's mind before he'd killed him.

"I checked there, sir. This morning," 555 replied. "There's nothing there. Just 316's scent and some scuff marks."

Zens pried through the beast's mind, but found nothing untoward. "A rucksack can't just disappear!"

000 shot him a mental message, *"Perhaps another patrol member moved it. I'll question them tomorrow morning. We'll find it then."*

"Good idea," Zens said. "Now, I must get back to my new lovely."

000 guffawed, just as keen as him to unleash their new lovelies on Dragons' Realm.

§

A young boy was working next to Tomaaz in the latrine pits that day. He was slow, stumbling under the weight of the dirt. Young, but so weak and wasted.

"Faster," 568 barked.

The boy twitched, dropping half his dirt, then scrambled to get it back onto his spade.

"Haul him out," 568 called to Burnt Face.

Burnt Face dragged the boy out of the ditch, bellowing, "Boss said, *work faster. Do it.*" The tharuk sent the boy sprawling into the ditch, then jumped in after him, raking his back with its long claws.

Tomaaz bit back a gasp.

Four gashes slashed the boy's back, blood seeping into his ragged shirt.

Dark spittle flew from Burnt Face's tusks. "Get moving. Work faster. All of you."

Tomaaz bent to dig, keeping an eye on the boy. Whenever the tharuks' backs were turned, he steadied the lad to stop him falling. Soon the lower half of the boy's shirt was drenched in red. Splatters covered his breeches. Ragged breaths hissing from his chest, the boy kept digging. The tharuks ignored him, targeting other slaves.

Tomaaz's gut churned. Tomorrow he'd escape, leaving all these poor folk behind. Most of them would be dead within moons. It didn't matter to Zens. He'd just send his raiding parties out to abduct more.

If he got to Dragons' Hold with Maazini, Tomaaz would petition Maazini's mother, the dragon queen, to save these people.

That evening when he fed Maazini, Ma showed him the chain. "I've sawed halfway through the metal loop that hooks it to the wall," she said. "If tharuks come, Maazini will stop them from getting in here to check, and tomorrow, I'll keep sawing. When is Hans coming?"

"Sunset." Had she forgotten already? He'd only told her yesterday. She was still pale, with dark smudges under her eyes. Her face was gaunt. Those piaua berries had knocked her about badly.

"I'll take care of her," Maazini melded, sending a wave of affection through him.

Feeling Maazini's powerful emotions every time they melded was amazing, but it took some getting used to. Tomaaz rubbed the dragon's snout and went back to the sleeping hut.

That night, Tomaaz was woken by whimpers. A puppy? He rubbed his eyes. No, he was in Death Valley. There were no puppies here.

In the sputtering candlelight, he glanced about the hut. The boy who'd had his back raked by Burnt Face was huddled on his pallet, moaning, biting his fist so he wouldn't make too much noise.

The stomp of tharuks alerted Tomaaz to approaching guards. That was odd. It was taking them longer than usual to get here. A tharuk flung the door open. The whimpering stopped. Tomaaz shut his eyes as the tharuk strode among the pallets, then stomped off, slamming the door behind it. Tomaaz heard it laughing with the other monsters as they continued on patrol. He could hear them better than usual. Weird—unless imprinting had sharpened his hearing. Maybe it was possible. Pa had said dragon riders received talents from their dragons. Maybe great hearing was one of them.

Breath hissed through the boy's teeth. Moans racked his little body. Poor thing. Tomaaz pulled on his boots and made his way between the pallets to the boy. The littling froze as he approached.

Tomaaz laid a hand on the lad's shoulder.

He flinched.

"I'm not going to hurt you," Tomaaz whispered. "There's a healer in Death Valley. Can I take you to her?"

No answer.

The candle hissed and flared. The boy was terrified, the whites of his eyes gleaming.

"It's all right. I'll carry you, but we'll have to be quick."

The lad gave a sharp nod.

Tomaaz scooped him up, careful not to touch his wounds, and cradled him against his chest. Starved, the boy was lighter than half a sack of carrots. Shards, what he wouldn't give for a carrot now—or even a bite.

Nudging the door open, Tomaaz peered outside. No tharuks around.

He was halfway through the door when a guttural voice startled him. "Why are you creeping around?"

Tharuk! Tomaaz froze, scanning the valley, but couldn't see anyone.

"Want to trade? You can have it for six rats."

Somehow, Maazini *had* sharpened his hearing. Much further along the valley, to the north, a door to a sleeping hut was ajar. Tharuks were inside talking. He hoped neither were trackers.

"Hungry, are you?" A guffaw. "Two rats. It's measly. Could find a better one myself."

"Four rats."

Hurrying on, Tomaaz kept to the shadows, his pounding heart marking each soft footfall.

There was a snarl. His body tensed. It was just those tharuks, fighting.

The boy's eyes were wide, fixed on Tomaaz. He was grimacing against the pain, teeth digging into his lip to stop himself crying out.

At last, they were speeding along Maazini's branch of the valley.

"Tomaaz, I sense you." It was Maazini mind-melding. "*Stick to the shadows. There are tharuks patrolling the hilltops tonight.*"

"Shards! That was close. *I was about to start running out in the open.*"

"*Easy does it. Take your time and be stealthy.*"

A wave of soothing calm spread through Tomaaz. How did Maazini do that? Calm his emotions and ease his pounding heart?

"*Years of training. Stealthy, now.*"

Although the boy was light, Tomaaz hadn't had decent food in days, and he was tiring. Just as he was near the bend, a rock skittered down the hillside above him, landing right next to him. He stopped, waiting in the shadows for what seemed like forever, before he moved on.

Slower than a snail, he made his way toward his waiting dragon, creeping along the hillsides, arms burning with fatigue.

A short distance from Maazini's cave, the dragon melded again. "*They're gone, but be cautious, just in case.*"

"How can you tell?"

"*Their scent, but my best sense, by far, is my hearing.*"

That explained his newfound skill.

When he edged into Maazini's cave, Ma was waiting.

Maazini moved to the cave mouth to block them from view as Ma pulled out a small vial that shone in the dark, quickly shrouding it in cloth so only a sliver of light shone on the boy's wounds.

She inhaled sharply. "Place him face down on my blanket," she whispered, laying her tiny light on the floor and rummaging in her healer's pouch.

Tomaaz sank to his knees, still cradling the boy. The lad clung to him, casting fearful glances at Maazini.

"It's all right, he's my friend," Tomaaz whispered in his ear. "He'll protect you from tharuks."

The boy went limp in his arms. Tomaaz placed him on the blanket and tousled his hair.

He kissed Ma on the cheek.

"Go," she whispered. "Get back before they miss you."

§

A face swam into focus. Blonde hair. Green eyes.

"Ezaara?" Hans asked.

A cool hand touched his forehead. "Pa, you're awake."

Hans tried to sit up. Shards, his limbs ached something fierce, and his chest was sore.

Ezaara pushed him back down. "Relax. It's going to take time to recover."

"Ezaara." His voice came out croaky. She passed him a cup of water, and he drank. Then she hugged him, avoiding the wound in his chest.

He winced anyway. "Sorry, still a bit sore."

"Of course you are." Her brow tightened.

In all his years of using dragon sight, he'd never seen anything as welcome as her sitting here, looking every bit a dragon rider. Actually, the Queen's Rider. "So, how are you finding Dragons' Hold?"

"A lot has happened since I got here. I'll fill you in later. But first, Lovina says Ma and Tomaaz are in Death Valley." Her voice was tight with concern.

Hans nodded. "They are." He spared Ezaara the details: the haggard expression on Marlies' face and how gaunt Tomaaz had looked after only a few days. "How long have I been here?" His memory was hazy. He'd floated in and out of consciousness.

"Since yesterday afternoon. You slept all night."

Well, not all night—he'd woken to talk to Tomaaz. He tried to gauge what time of the day it was from light filtering in through an unshuttered hole in the rock face, and failed. "How late is it now? I have to contact Tomaaz at sunset."

"A couple of hours until then. Pa, you're going back, aren't you? To Death Valley."

He nodded and squeezed her hand. "I have to bring your mother and Tomaaz home."

"It'll be dangerous."

"I'll be fine. I—" He sighed at her stubborn expression. "Yes, it will be dangerous. But I'm going as soon as I'm able. Tomorrow."

"Good," she said, "then, you won't object to me healing your chest with piaua juice."

"Piaua? But that's only for grievous injuries! Marlies would skin me alive for using it on a non-fatal wound."

"You'll be facing hundreds of tharuks. Our entire family is depending on you and you can't even shoot an arrow properly with that hole in your muscle." Ezaara folded her arms. "I'm not having you go back there to get shot again. Or worse."

It was true. He drew his bowstring with his left arm. His wound would hamper him. He hesitated.

She pounced. "Great, I knew you'd agree." As quick as a hare, she tugged his bandage open, and uncorked a vial of pale green piaua juice. Raising an eyebrow, she asked, "You're fine with this, aren't you? I mean, you want the best possible chance of saving our family, don't you, Pa?"

Hans sighed. "When you put it like that … yes. Go ahead." He held his shirt open.

"This won't hurt a bit."

He snorted. "That's not what Marlies says."

Ezaara flashed a feral grin. "It may burn a *little*."

He burst out laughing. "Ow, my chest hurts when I laugh!"

Tharuk Crackdown

The door of the sleeping hut flew open, bashing the wall. Tomaaz jerked awake, bone-weary.

568 and Burnt Face marched into the room. "You check the small male. I'll wake the others," 568 said, hefting a stick as thick as Tomaaz's bicep. It strode among the pallets, whacking slaves.

Their yelping woke the rest.

Burnt Face stomped about the room, muttering, "Skinny rat must be somewhere."

He was looking for the boy, and it was obvious the lad was missing. His blanket was hanging off the end of his bloodstained pallet.

Burnt Face halted by the mattress, sniffing at the blood. Tomaaz's brow prickled with sweat. He fought not to shiver; to look dull-witted and numlocked.

"Hey!" Burnt Face called. "Small one is gone." His head swiveled and his nose twitched. "Get a tracker."

Shards!

"Not now. Get these slaves to work," 568 snarled. "Or Zens will *reward* you."

"N-no. N-not a reward." The tharuk's scar spasmed.

It would've been funny if Burnt Face hadn't looked so petrified. Zens had created these monsters, but they were terrified of him.

"Go on." 568 waved his stick at Burnt Face. "Feed them. Get them to work. I send tracker to flesh pile for the boy."

Burnt Face herded the slaves out of the hut, tossing chunks of hard bread after them. The slaves scrabbled in the dirt to retrieve the tough crusts. It was the strongest emotion Tomaaz had seen from them, apart from the mother throwing herself into the sewage canal. He shuddered.

Sharp claws poked through the back of his jerkin. "Shivering? Got a chill?" Burnt Face thrust his snout over Tomaaz's shoulder.

His stomach churned at the beast's rat-laden breath. Tomaaz lunged among the slaves to snatch bread. He sat on his haunches in the crowd, gnawing at the hard chunk until Burnt Face looked away.

That was close. He had to keep his emotions locked away until they left this hell.

Tomaaz checked his fingernails. A faint pink tinge was showing on the edge of one nail. His dragon's scale vial was with Ma. How long before his eyes turned green? By sunset they'd be gone. He couldn't risk discovery now.

Two tharuks were gesticulating by the tool pile. Tomaaz wandered through the milling slaves, until his enhanced sense allowed him to hear what the tharuks were saying, then he sat down to finish eating.

"This saw blade is broken," said a tall gangly tharuk.

"Probably old."

"No, it's new. From our raid last week."

"You sure?"

"Look. See notches on handle? This is saw eighteen. A new one." The tharuks leaned in, examining the saw handle. "Wasn't broken two days ago."

"Where's the rest of blade?" the other tharuk asked, rummaging through the saw pile and searching the nearby ground.

"Missing," Gangly said in a rough undertone. He scanned the slaves. "One of them might have it."

"No. They numlocked. We'll check the mines. Don't want Zens' *reward*."

"I checked. It's not there."

"We look again. This morning." The tharuk scratched the matted fur on its neck. "Then we check the slaves."

"Don't tell 568," said Gangly.

"Course not."

Now they were looking for the boy *and* the blade. Tomaaz had to return the blade or all the slaves would be at risk. No, he couldn't. Ma hadn't sawn all the way through Maazini's chain yet. He swallowed down the tasteless pap, kept his eyes lowered, and shuffled over to get his spade to feed the beast.

A crack sounded in the air and a whip struck him. He staggered, pain blooming across his back.

568 glared at him. "No! Not feeding beast today. Zens says feed beast later."

Latrine duty first, then. If he was lucky, the stench of the sewage would stop him from being linked to the boy. Shards, his back stung. Cool air nipped at his skin. The whip must've broken the fabric. Tomaaz dragged his shovel, shoulders slumped.

As they filed past the water station, Burnt Face was towering over a short tharuk, 216. "Gone? What you mean, *gone*?" Burnt Face growled.

"I counted them. One is missing," 216 said.

"When you count waterskins last time?" Burnt Face's red eyes gleamed.

"Uh, th-three days ago." 216 cowered.

Burnt Face's scar contorted with anger. The tharuk slashed out, leaving three bloody gashes in 216's forehead.

"Count skins every day," Burnt Face roared. "Take 216 to Zens."

Two burly tharuks dragged the screeching underling away.

It was his fault. He'd had to steal that waterskin to keep Ma alive. That poor tharuk. Hang on. These beasts enslaved people and killed them. He sneaked a glance at the retreating tharuks, who were dragging 216 inside a metal door between two deep fissures. So that's where Zens was.

568 cracked his whip, herding the slaves to the latrines.

The slave crews settled into digging ditches again. The lash wound on Tomaaz's back burnt every time he bent to dig. He'd maintained his position at the head of each ditch he worked on, *lucky* to be the slave that let sewage flood the ditches. By being careful, he'd saved a few lives while he'd been here. His thoughts flitted to the boy with Ma.

"Maazini, how's the boy?"

"In pain, but remarkably brave."

He was glad he'd found Maazini. All of this would be worth it, if they could free him.

A tharuk ran into the latrine area, panting, and reported to 568. "The small male is not there," it said. "I searched the flesh pile. It is gone."

568 turned to Burnt Face, barking, "Gather the guards."

Burnt Face brought most of the tharuks from each crew toward the latrine Tomaaz was working on, leaving only the overseers to guard the ditch diggers.

Now would be the perfect time for a slave rebellion. They were all armed with shovels and outnumbered the tharuks. Tomaaz sighed. Numlocked slaves weren't capable of rebellion. He threw another shovelful of dirt out of the trench.

The tharuk group gathered in front of 568.

"Small male human is missing. Not on flesh pile. Not in sleeping hut. Where is it?"

His troops shook their heads, shifting from foot to foot.

"Something is wrong," snarled 568. "Did one of you eat it?"

Tomaaz's flesh crawled. Tharuks ate people?

The underlings shook their heads again. "Not eat humans," one said. "Commander Zens kills us if we eat them."

"No humans." 568 nodded. "Waterskin is missing. Anything else?" His red eyes scrutinized the tharuk guards.

Tomaaz kept digging, tossing dirt. The slaves were oblivious. At the crack of an overseer's whip in the next trench, Tomaaz forced himself to breathe steadily, and tossed another spadeful of dirt.

"Tell me!" 568 barked. "Or straight to Zens."

"A blanket, sir," a tharuk muttered. "Missing from the hut. Two days ago."

"Anything else?" 568 thundered, claws extended.

They knew about the blanket, the boy, the waterskin …

"A saw snapped. Half blade is missing."

"What?" 568 roared, wheeling to grab the beast's leather tunic. "When?"

"184 was with me," the tharuk gibbered.

Tharuk 184 spoke up. "Found out this morning. Just checked the mines. Still missing."

They'd discovered every single thing he'd taken. Who would have known this ramshackle valley was so organized? Tomaaz's breath hissed as he worked. His scent would be on the boy's bed. The boy's scent would be all over him. Could a tracker find his trail or had he masked it? Only one way to be sure.

Tomaaz was nearly at the end of the ditch. A few more shovelfuls and he'd hit the latrine pit. He tossed another spade of dirt. He dared a quick glance around. No tharuks were watching. He tossed out two shovels of dirt in rapid succession.

"We have tharuk traitor," 568 said, "or slave spy. Get a tracker!" it bellowed.

A tharuk ran off to the main valley.

"Report back," 568 barked at two burly tharuks. "What happened to 216?"

"Zens took a hand," one answered.

"Good. Keeps you all honest." It laughed. "If tracker not find spy, everyone can hunt."

The tharuks laughed raucously.

The violence in their guffaws raised the hairs on Tomaaz's neck. His spade hit the dirt in front of him. A trickle of sludge crept out of the pit. Tomaaz nudged the slave behind him and scrambled out of the ditch. Slumping on the freshly-tossed earth, he waited until everyone was clear, then leaned over, whacking the pit wall with his spade. Not too hard, that should do it. Only a trickle of sludge leaked out.

"Get in and finish it off!" bellowed a tharuk, breaking away from 568's group. "Move it!"

Wearily, Tomaaz clambered back into the ditch. He had to time this right.

He hit the wall with his shovel, twisting it. A spurt of sewage shot out, hitting him in the chest and splattering his breeches and spade. Tomaaz scrambled out of the ditch as the whole wall caved in under the pressure of the pit's stinking contents.

"Rest time," thundered the tharuk.

The slaves from Tomaaz's crew flopped to the ground. He leaned back on the earth, stinking of excrement, breathing through his mouth to avoid the stench. That should mask his scent.

A swarm of tharuks reported to 568. Their black eyes flitted across the slaves, and their tusks gleamed with trails of dark saliva. "We scented bloody bed. Two strong scents. One toward Zens' beast."

"Maazini, is your chain cut?"

"Yes. I'm ready and waiting for you."

"The tharuks know the boy is with you. Get him and Ma out! Quick, before they come for you."

Without Maazini, Tomaaz would never get out of there. Not with suspicious trackers prowling. He'd become another lump on the flesh pile. But he didn't want the boy's life and Ma's life on his conscience. Or Maazini's. *"Go, Maazini, go."* Tomaaz stared blankly at the sky.

No answer from Maazini.

No trace of dragon above the hilltops. Not even a silhouette of a wingtip.

"Go, Maazini, don't be a fool. Save them while you can."

Although he couldn't hear Maazini's voice, Tomaaz could *feel* him. Stubborn refusal trickled over him, like a littling stamping its foot for a toy.

Tomaaz sighed. *"Get out of here, Maazini."*

"There's still time. Be careful, Tomaaz. If they suspect you, they'll kill you."

"I know, but I don't want any of you to die."

Maazini gave a mental snort.

Trackers scoured the edges of each ditch, sniffing at the slave crews, working their way closer. Tomaaz's crew was still on break, so he couldn't do anything to release the dread building inside him. Could trackers smell fear? Perhaps they'd sense his heart pounding.

"Stay calm," Maazini mind-melded.

Soothing energy washed over Tomaaz, but it wasn't enough to calm his racing heart.

"Stand up!" barked Burnt Face.

The slaves scrambled to their feet.

Trackers roamed among them, black eyes flitting from slave to slave, and snouts twitching.

A small wiry tharuk stopped by Tomaaz. "This one," it barked. "This scent goes to the beast."

His ploy with the sewage had been for nothing. The beast had still recognized his scent.

568 laughed. "Of course. That human feeds beast. But did it take small male?"

The trackers clustered around Tomaaz. Claws out, their nostrils quivered, snouts thrust in his face.

"Can't tell," muttered the wiry one. "Too dirty."

The others nodded and broke away, stalking among the slaves.

Tomaaz held in his sigh of relief, only letting his breath escape slowly.

A heartbeat later, 568 was in front of Tomaaz. "Time to feed beast." He motioned to Burnt Face and Wiry. "Come. Feeding time." His laugh was laced with menace.

"Maazini, I'm coming, with three tharuks. Escape. Now. Take Ma and the boy." The tharuks behind Tomaaz prodded him with their claws. His nails! Oh, shards! They were pinking at the edges. What about his eyes?

The tharuks marched him to the rodent pile.

"Feed beast well today," 568 said. "Zens wants to play with beast tomorrow."

Thank the Egg, they were leaving. Tomaaz piled his shovel with rats and a dead bird. *"Maazini, get out of here."* He didn't dare look up. But there was no flap of wings, no gust of wind to signify a dragon flying above them. And no flash of orange. *"Escape, you silly dragon,"* Tomaaz melded, pleading, *"please, go."*

Too soon, they rounded the bend in Maazini's branch of the valley.

The cavern mouth was dark. Tomaaz shambled forward, 568 right beside him, while Burnt Face and Wiry hung back.

An earth-shattering roar ripped through the air, and Maazini lurched out of the cavern, chain rattling and sagging gray wings drooping at his sides. His scales were dull gray. *"Dragon's scale works wonders,"* Maazini melded.

Tomaaz stared blankly.

"You look like a numlocked slave," Maazini said in his head.

"Feed it," 568 growled.

Tomaaz tossed the rats at Maazini's feet and retreated.

Tharuk 568 turned to Wiry, the tracker. "Smell the small male?"

Wiry shook his head. "Nothing new."

Your mother's very clever. She gave the boy freshweed. See you here tonight. Maazini retreated into his cave with the rats.

§

Zens thrust his hand in the air and, with his mind, overturned a table. Then he flipped his hand over, turning the table back onto its legs. Then he did it again. It wasn't enough. He sent the table smashing into the wall, where it splintered, broken pieces clattering to the floor.

Now, *that* felt better.

A waterskin missing. A blanket. The prisoner's rucksack. A hacksaw. It could only mean one thing. The ex-rider wasn't dead. He scanned through 555's memories.

Glassy-eyed, the woman stared at him vacantly, her lips blue-tinged. She looked dead all right, but there was only one way to appease his sneaking suspicions.

He addressed 000. "Triple Zero, search the human flesh pile. Make sure the ex-rider is still there."

§

Tomaaz turned over the corpse of a littling. Vacant brown eyes stared up at him from under matted blonde hair. He swallowed. Only four or five summers old, her skin was smudged with grime and yellow dust. She'd been in those bitter-smelling mines. She should have been free to romp in meadows, play with chickens and pick flowers, not waste her life underground.

"Find the female," 568 barked at the slaves, searching through the human flesh pile. "Tall. Blue eyes. Dark hair. Keep looking."

Zens was looking for Ma. Did he really suspect that she was still alive? Or was he just eliminating her as the cause of the missing things?

Tomaaz turned over a woman with dark hair. Her face was bruised, marred by viscous claw marks. She had blue eyes. He waved an arm and 568 came over, dragging a small tharuk with him.

"Is that the one?" 568 snapped at the small tharuk.

The beast shook its head. "Our one is taller."

It was right; Ma was taller. Tomaaz turned back to his sickening task, sifting through littlings, men and women. All these lives ending here, in Death Valley. It was hopeless, daunting.

RIDERS OF FIRE

They had to fight back. Free slaves. End the terror caused by Zens.

It was nearly evening. Soon they'd stop for gruel. He smothered a cynical snort, not daring to let the tharuks notice. He'd never thought he'd ever look forward to that sloppy weevil-infested muck. But after he'd eaten, he could feed *the beast* and escape with Maazini, Ma and the boy, to meet Pa and Handel.

Way before mealtime arrived, 568 ordered them back to the latrines. Tomaaz had never been so glad to shovel excrement.

Closing In

Tomaaz didn't dare strain the weevils or cockroaches out of his evening gruel. Hundreds of tharuk guards were scrutinizing the slaves' movements, hovering over them like giant vultures. Burnt Face had been staring at him all afternoon, red eyes slitted in concentration, as if their earlier trip to Maazini had cheated him of a chance to have *fun*.

Tomaaz kept his eyes hooded and his face slack. The tips of all his fingernails were now pink, so he kept them curved around the base of his bowl as he drank his soup from the rim. Something wriggled in his mouth. A weevil? A roach? Red eyes bored into him. He fought his gag reflex, swallowing the squirming insect.

Shards, he hated this place.

He washed the insect down with another gulp of gruel and shambled to the dish barrel to dump his bowl. Then he sat, away from Burnt Face's gaze, to await his next orders. It wasn't long until sunset.

He'd be leaving all these people behind, condemning them to this horror. Why did Zens have slaves? The latrines crews weren't important; they were only servicing the latrines for the hundreds of slaves that disappeared into those crevasses in the hillsides. Tomaaz had never seen what came out of the earth, and there was no way he'd find out now. He was leaving.

A scream cut through Tomaaz's thoughts. Tharuks were still observing them, so he tightened his muscles against the urge to look. But it got harder to act numlocked when another scream was followed by grunts of pain and cries. More than one person was being hurt.

Slowly, as the slaves around him shifted, Tomaaz adjusted his position to see.

Burnt Face and a few other tharuks were kicking slaves—not littlings or the elderly, but able-bodied men and women. Each time a tharuk kicked a slave in the gut, their fellow guards observed the slaves' reactions.

Tomaaz sucked in his breath. They were testing to see if everyone was numlocked. If they didn't find anyone, they'd probably start on the littlings.

This was his fault. If he hadn't stolen those things, the tharuks wouldn't have known he was here.

"Maazini, they're hurting the slaves to find me. I should give myself up."

"No!" Maazini roared in his head. "*Stand strong. We'll come back and hunt down Zens and free the slaves. Your ma, the boy and I need you.*"

Burnt Face was closer now, kicking a man, four slaves over. Through hooded eyes, Tomaaz watched the slave moan and curl in on himself. The man hadn't tensed as the tharuk had neared, and he hadn't made any move to defend himself. Acting numlocked was going to be harder than he'd thought.

Burnt Face skipped a littling and kicked a woman in the stomach. She sprawled on the ground, whimpering, then curled up, holding her middle. The tharuk's stench wafted over Tomaaz as it swung its boot at Tomaaz's neighbor.

It turned to him.

Tomaaz didn't dare look up. *Relax, relax, relax.*

Burnt Face's boot connected with his gut in an excruciating thud. Pain bloomed through his middle. He flew backward, sprawling on the ground. He gasped for air, letting out a moan, and curled up. He couldn't breathe, couldn't breathe. Gods, his stomach *hurt*.

"*Tomaaz!*" Maazini mind-melded, his concern spiking through Tomaaz's head.

Two tharuks loomed over him. Yanking him to his feet, they held him up. He tried to hunch over to ease the pain, but they refused to let him, pulling him by the shoulders until he was dangling from their sharp claws, his feet hanging in the air. "*Maazini, they know. They've found me.*"

"*Stay calm,*" Maazini melded.

"You," Burnt Face bellowed, "feed the beast."

The tharuk followed Tomaaz as he stumbled toward the tool pile, clutching his stomach with one hand, and picked up his shovel.

"Fall in," Burnt Face called, gesturing to other tharuks, who formed a wall behind Tomaaz. Wiry, the tracker, was among them.

His pain receded to a dull ache as they marched him along the valley, prodding him with their claws and breathing their foul stench over him. "*Maazini, coming now, with five tharuks. Tell Ma.*"

"*We're prepared.*" There was malice in Maazini's tone.

He hefted rats off the rat pile. Maybe with a dragon on his side he had a chance.

But Ma was weak, the boy too, and Maazini wasn't in the best shape either. The tharuks escorting him were carrying quivers and bows. Their arrows could be drenched with limplock. All he had was a shovel. He'd be lucky to get any of them out of here alive.

"Keep moving," 568 growled, hurrying him along.

They were trying to catch him out. He shambled along, as if he couldn't go any faster.

"Faster," Burnt Face roared.

Tomaaz ignored it.

They rounded the last corner in the waning light. The entrance to Maazini's cave was shrouded in shadow. The dragon was nowhere to be seen. Tomaaz's neck hair prickled. It was a dead end. The only way out was on dragonback.

Moving forward like a numlocked slave, Tomaaz staggered to the mouth of the cave, holding out his shovel of rats.

Burnt Face hung back, pushing Wiry forward. "You! Go too."

With the tracker breathing down his neck, Tomaaz's chest was tight. He threw the rats. They thudded to the stone. With a roar, Maazini leaped out of his cave, brilliant orange, his chain rattling.

Wiry twitched.

"Coward," barked Burnt Face. "It's chained up."

"It's orange! Not numlocked," Wiry snapped, lunging at Tomaaz.

With a roar, Maazini flew at Wiry. Dropping his spade, Tomaaz ducked and rolled. Maazini swung his leg at Wiry's head. The chain whipped around the tracker's neck. With a yank, Maazini pulled it tight, strangling the tharuk. Maazini kicked out. Wiry flew through the air, his corpse knocking Burnt Face to the ground.

Maazini pounced on another tharuk, crushing it with his jaws and flaming its corpse.

"Get them!" yelled Burnt Face, jumping to its feet.

Scrambling up, Tomaaz snatched his shovel and hefted it in front of him as a tharuk charged. He whacked the brute in the neck, but the shovel blade bounced off.

The beast swiped with its claws, raking Tomaaz's side. His ribs stinging from a flesh wound, he danced away, swinging his spade again. Shards! If only he had his sword.

"*Their matted fur's like armor*," Maazini melded. "*Try its head. Fur's thinner there.*"

RIDERS OF FIRE

Another tharuk ran at Maazini. The dragon pounced, shredding the tharuk's torso with his talons, spilling its stinking guts.

568 lunged at him. Raising his shovel high, Tomaaz brought it crashing onto the monster's skull. It stumbled, then lunged again, scratching his face. Tomaaz whacked its head again.

Groggy, the beast reeled and fell. Tomaaz brought his shovel smashing onto its head one last time, and the beast lay still.

Everything had gone quiet. Panting, Tomaaz looked up.

Burnt Face was facing him, bow nocked, with an arrow pointing straight at his heart—an arrow dripping with green grunge. Limplock.

Maazini was silent, crouched near the cavern, haunches tense, his green eyes slits. His tail twitched. Tomaaz's heart pounded as his eyes flitted from Maazini to Burnt Face.

"Beast move and male dies. Zens *play* with him." Burnt Face laughed, his tusks gleaming in the last rays of the sun.

Shards, the sun was setting! Pa was on the far hills. No chance of getting there, now.

Maazini's low growl bounced off the canyon walls. The tharuk overseer increased the tension on his bow.

Oh gods, this was it.

With a shout, the boy ran out of the cavern, rushing at Burnt Face. Eyes wide in surprise, the tharuk swung its bow toward the boy. No! Tomaaz closed his eyes. There was a hiss of an arrow releasing.

No! Not the boy. Tomaaz's eyes flew open.

Burnt Face was toppling to the ground, an arrow embedded deep in its eye.

Ma ran out of the cavern, her rucksack and quiver on her back, and her bow in hand. "Quick, Tomaaz! Get on Maazini! Grab the boy."

Tomaaz scooped up the lad, running to the dragon, and threw him up onto Maazini's back. Ma was in bad shape, breathing hard. He gave her a leg up behind the boy, and then climbed up in front and clung to Maazini's spinal ridge. Skinny arms wrapped tight around Tomaaz's waist.

"Hold on." Tomaaz called. *"Fly, Maazini, fly."*

The hills were swarming with tharuks. Beasts were vaulting over rocks, charging down the sides of the canyon toward them.

Tensing his haunches, the dragon sprang, flapping his wings. *"I'm not so strong,"* Maazini said. *"Numlock, no food for weeks …"*

They slowly gained height, but Maazini was right, he wasn't strong. The combined weight of the three of them was too much. Melded, Tomaaz could feel Maazini straining, the drag on his muscles. The tips of his wings were dangerously close to the canyon walls.

Arrows hissed past Tomaaz. *"Oh, shards, Maazini! Their arrows are limp-locked. Don't let them hit you!"*

Maazini swerved toward the opposite wall, tilting. The boy's arms tightened around his waist. Tomaaz hung on as the chain on Maazini's leg whipped out toward the hillside.

With a roar, a tharuk leaped off the hill, grabbing the chain. Maazini lurched, losing height. He beat his wings desperately as they plummeted toward the canyon floor. With a roar, he strained upward. Slowly, too slowly, they gained height. Tharuk arrows zipped past them.

Maazini grunted. Melded, Tomaaz felt his dragon's searing pain. *"Are you all right?"*

"Arrow. Chest," Maazini replied, tipping from side to side.

"It's not far, just to that ridge. Pa will meet us." But what then? How could Maazini ever make the arduous flight back to Dragons' Hold?

"Tomaaz, below," came Ma's urgent cry.

He whipped his head around. What? Maazini lurched again. Then Tomaaz saw it. Climbing up Maazini's chain was a tharuk, a knife between its teeth. Its red eyes gleamed as it pulled itself up the chain. *"Maazini, tharuk on your chain!"*

"I … know …" Even Maazini's thoughts sounded weak.

§

The tharuk was clambering up the chain, pulling the dragon off center and dragging him down. The hillsides were swarming. If she didn't act soon, Marlies could kiss her son and Zaarusha's goodbye, and forget about saving this slave boy, too. As soon as that tharuk slashed Maazini's gut with his knife, it was over.

Pushing the boy forward against Tomaaz, she urged, "Hold on tight."

Marlies leaned sideways, increasing the grip of her legs on the dragon's sides. "Swing the chain, Maazini, so I can shoot," she yelled, nocking an arrow on her bow.

The dragon tipped. The tharuk on the chain swung out beneath her. She released the bowstring. Her arrow went wide and the tharuk swayed back under the dragon, out of sight. She nocked another arrow. The dragon was flying erratically, affected by the tharuk's weight.

The chain swung again. The tharuk was hanging on like a roach, climbing higher. Her next arrow missed, too.

Gritting her teeth, she leaned out further, her injured arm screaming in protest as she fitted another arrow into her bow. The chain flew out. Holding on with one arm, the tharuk grabbed its knife from between its teeth to plunge the blade into Maazini's belly. Marlies fired. The arrow struck the tharuk's forehead. Maazini rocked as it plummeted to the ground.

Marlies slipped sideways. Hands grasping at smooth scales, she plunged after the tharuk.

§

"No!" a scream tore from Tomaaz's throat as Ma dropped earthward.

Maazini dived. A whump shook Tomaaz's teeth, then his dragon flapped, rising in the air again. *"I caught your mother, but I need to land. Soon."*

"Is she all right?"

"I can feel her heartbeat."

Tharuk arrows rained around them. Maazini zigzagged back and forth up the hillside, ducking the tharuks' shots. Zings of pain shot through Tomaaz's mind as three more arrows met their target, lodging in Maazini's hide. They drew level with the hilltop, in clear sight of tharuk archers.

"Go, Maazini, go." Tomaaz willed his friend to fly faster, higher, anywhere but here.

An arrow zipped straight for him. Tomaaz ducked. The arrow hit Maazini's neck. The dragon bellowed, gusting flame along the hillside, scattering the tharuks.

Finally, they shot above the ranges, into a sky of blazing orange sunset. Tomaaz yanked the arrow out of Maazini's neck, and ripped the sleeve off his shirt, wiping at the green grunge on the wound. Despite his efforts, limplock was rapidly dissolving into Maazini's bloodstream. With flagging wings, Maazini made his way across Death Valley to the western range of the Terramites.

Below, a battle horn echoed in the valley. Tharuks spewed out of the mines and caverns, racing up the hillsides. Shards, they were fast. Where was Pa? By now, Handel's bronze form should be clearly visible. He scrabbled in his pockets for his calling stone. It wasn't there; he'd left it with Ma. No healer's pouch either.

He clung tightly to Maazini's spinal ridge as the dragon headed toward the watchtower.

"Maazini, avoid the tower, it's full of tharuks with more poison." He shared the memory of Pa being injured.

Maazini bellowed. *"Done."* He swerved toward the hill beyond. *"Can't fly much further."*

"Land behind that pile of rubble."

The battle horn rang again. Tharuks were swarming over the neighboring hills, around the watchtower. Some aimed arrows at them, but they fell short. Thankfully, none were on the hill they were heading to. But it wouldn't take long for them to get there.

Tomaaz strained his eyes. Where was Pa?

"Tomaaz! I can't hold on. My talons are cramping. I might drop your mother!"

§

"I have to go, Ezaara." Deep lines etched roads of weariness in Pa's face.

She hugged him. He still wasn't fully recovered, but thanks to the piaua, at least he had a fighting chance. She pulled back and looked at him again. No, he didn't have a fighting chance. She could be sending him to his death. But how else could they save Ma and Tomaaz? "Pa, there has to be a better way. You'll be facing hundreds of tharuks on your own."

He laid his hands on her shoulders, looking her straight in the eye. "We've been over this, Ezaara. I can get there within moments, sneak in and then bring them home. I shouldn't be gone long at all."

"Zaarusha and I could come."

"Not with the ring, you can't. You know that."

And if she rode behind Hans, there may not be space for Ma and Tomaaz, especially if Ma was injured. Ezaara shoved her fists in her pockets. "Give them my love."

Pa smiled. "Tell them yourself when we return." He hugged her again and climbed onto Handel.

"I'll take care of them all," Handel melded with Ezaara, letting Pa hear.

"Please do."

Pa shot her a surprised glance. "You can meld with Handel, not just Zaarusha?"

"I can meld with all dragons."

He raised his eyebrows. "Just like Anakisha. I'll be back soon." He slipped a jade ring from his pocket, rubbed it and called, "Ana."

With a loud snap, Pa and Handel were gone.

Dread dogged Ezaara's steps as she paced on the ledge. Below, dragons flew about their business, people harvested crops in the fields and gathered fruit from the orchard. Ezaara's feet pounded out an anxious rhythm.

Roberto arrived. "Adelina's got a few supplies ready in the infirmary, in case they're injured when they return."

He stood near her, but didn't touch her. A dragon was flying past, carrying Lars, head of the Council of the Twelve Dragon Masters. Ezaara took a step back, distancing herself from Roberto. Lars mustn't suspect a thing.

"*If* they return," she replied. Ezaara's chest ached. Pa didn't stand a chance. She'd probably just seen the last of her family.

§

Golden clouds surrounded Hans and Handel, making Handel's bronze scales gleam. Strange, Handel wasn't flapping, just hanging in midair with his wings outspread.

"*Last time, you were too sick to notice,*" Handel said.

Anakisha appeared before them. "*Hello, Hans. Someone must be in grave danger for you to be traveling with the ring again so soon.*"

Hans nodded. "Marlies and my son are stranded in Death Valley. Marlies has been deathly ill."

"Very well." Anakisha's eyes were sad. "*Is Death Valley your destination?*" Hans kept a picture of the hill north of the watchtower in his mind. "Here," he said. "Thank you, Anakisha."

Past Handel's wingtip, a dark ripple moved through a cloud, like a fracture in an icebound lake.

A snap rang out. Anakisha and the golden clouds disappeared.

§

Hans and Handel appeared in the air with a pop, behind the mountain just north of the watchtower. Handel flew cautiously, zigzagging his way up the mountainside.

"Right, here is good, Handel. It's only a short way to the top."

"*I'll take shelter behind those rocks further down,*" Handel replied.

"If you stay still, they may mistake you for a boulder."

Handel snorted. *"Me, a rock? An inanimate lump of stone?"* As Hans dismounted, Handel blew a gust of air over his head, ruffling his hair. *"You're lucky that's not flame,"* his dragon huffed.

"That would definitely disrupt your disguise." Hans chuckled, taking his bow and quiver from Handel's saddlebag. *"I'm good."* He scratched Handel's snout. They'd fallen straight back into their old pre-battle banter. It used to help calm his nerves, but today was different—today he had to free his wife and son.

Handel curled up behind the rocks, his snout at ground level so he could peep around some stones.

"You're right, Handel, you don't make a fantastic rock, but if anyone gets close enough to see you, it'll be time to fight them anyway."

A mental snort was Handel's only reply.

Hans picked his way to the crest of the hill and peered over the ridge. Like the other mountains along this end of the Terramites, there were unnatural rubble heaps on the top. Years, ago, Zens had started mining these hills. The rocks were probably the resulting debris. But why here, at the peak of the mountain? It made no sense.

A battle horn made Hans' blood run cold. On the next hill, tharuks were swarming the watch tower, nocking bows and firing. More tharuk archers raced along the ridges. Below, in the valley, it was mayhem. Tharuks were shooting at the sunset, but their arrows were falling back to earth, some wounding their own troops.

Hang on, the tharuks were all firing at one point. Something orange that he'd hardly noticed against the blazing orange and gold sky.

It was a dragon. Carrying something in its claws. Something it nearly dropped, then grabbed again at the last moment.

"Hans!" It was Marlies, melding. *"Hans, where are you? Maazini can hardly hold me."*

Hans used his dragon sight. The dragon was struggling to hold Marlies in its talons. A rider was on its back. *"Fly for the rubble pile north of the watchtower,"* Hans melded. *"I'm hiding here. Where's Tomaaz?"*

The dragon pitched; Marlies' legs slipped out of its talons. Gods, if she fell, she'd land in a writhing nest of tharuks.

"Handel, now!" Hans yelled, racing toward his dragon.

Handel unfurled, sprang into the air and landed nearby. Hans vaulted into the saddle. The mighty bronze's legs bunched, and they were airborne, racing toward the orange dragon. *"Meld with him, Handel."*

"I am. He's exhausted, malnourished and limplocked."

"Can he gain any height?"

"I've told him to try. If he drops Marlies, we'll swoop in and get her."

Shards. *"Handel, can you fly faster?"*

Handel beat his wings, hard. Hans' hair was flat against his head as they raced toward the dropping dragon. Its wings were slowing. Marlies slipped.

She was hanging onto the dragon's leg, dangling like a target beneath it.

Another battle horn blew. Arrows zipped at Handel from the watchtower. He ascended above them, but the orange dragon couldn't.

"Can we get in low, Handel, and grab her off him?"

"Too risky. We'll put him off and may lose all of them. He's barely staying in the sky as it is. We're going to have to guide him in."

"Marlies, can you hang on?"

"Hope so."

Belching flame at any arrows that came near, Handel flew alongside the orange dragon. The poor thing's limbs were spasming and tail flicking erratically, but he kept flapping until they were near the rubble pile. Marlies curled her legs up as he glided over the pile, preventing them from being bashed on the rocks. Then she dropped, rolling down the slope.

The dragon landed near her, wings draped over the ground, sides heaving. Arrows bristled from his side, dripping limplock.

Handel landed upslope. *"Maazini needs space."*

What was Marlies doing? She'd pulled Tomaaz and a boy off the dragon and was sending them uphill. Tomaaz sped up, carrying a lad so skinny there was hardly anything to him.

"What are you doing?" Hans asked her.

"If Maazini can't make it, I want Tomaaz alive. Take him home, Hans."

"No. Not your guilt again. You don't have to sacrifice yourself to pay for that dragonet. Marlies, come home." Hans helped the boy up behind him. "Hold on," he said, wrapping the boy's bony arms around his waist.

"I told Zaarusha I'd save her son."

"How? He can't fly."

"Don't know," Marlies said. "Something will come to me."

Hans gave Tomaaz an arm up. He sat behind Hans, sandwiching the boy between them. "Pa." He was skinnier and out of breath.

"*Marlies, you fit on Handel, too.*"

"*He'll never make it with four of us. Not that far.*"

"*I have a ring that helps me travel instantaneously between locations. A jade ring. Come with me. I'll take you home.*"

"*A jade ring? I have one too, etched with whorls.*"

Hans drew in his breath. Could it be true? Could there be two? He shared what the ring looked like.

"*Exactly,*" Marlies replied.

Before Hans had time to explain how the rings worked, Marlies yelled, "*Hans, behind you!*"

Hans whirled.

Tharuks poured from the rubble pile. The rubble must be a mine exit. They raised their bows. Some threw rocks.

Hans reached for his bow, but had to duck to miss a poisoned arrow. Handel sprang into the air.

Tharuks tugged at the rocks. With an ominous rumble, half the rubble pile seethed and crashed down the hill toward Maazini.

"Maazini," Tomaaz hollered.

Maazini strained his legs. He flapped. He bunny-hopped. Rocks crashed into his hind legs as he struggled to lift off, then he was airborne, raining precious dragon blood on the heaving avalanche below.

"*It's now or never!*" Marlies melded. She screamed, jerking as an arrow hit her arm.

Hans rubbed his ring. "*Ana,*" he called, staying melded with Marlies, providing her with a vision of Dragons' Hold.

"*Kisha,*" Marlies cried in his head.

The two names formed a whole—Anakisha, the former Queen's Rider.

Reunion

Ezaara paced in the infirmary. "Pa said he wouldn't be long." Because traveling with the ring held danger for the realm, she, Pa and Roberto had decided to keep the ring secret.

"It normally takes days of flight to get there," Adelina said.

"Four days, actually," Roberto mind-melded with Ezaara, before answering Adelina. "Hans will be back soon. He's taking a shortcut."

If Pa made it at all. Ezaara's chest tightened. Hopefully he wouldn't be alone. There was so much riding on Pa's trip. If anyone messed up, she'd lose everyone she loved. Well, nearly everyone.

Roberto met her eyes. *"Your pa has experience. He'll bring them home."*

Ezaara masked her fears, hiding her thoughts. Until a few weeks ago, Pa hadn't ridden a dragon for eighteen years. What if he made an error? What if he was too late? "Shards," she said. "Where are they?"

"Dragon injured," Handel's voice was stronger than she'd expected. They must be close. *"And riders, too."*

Who? Who was hurt? "Roberto, Adelina, there are riders and a dragon hurt."

A whump sounded on the ledge outside the infirmary cavern, then throaty whimpers of an animal in pain.

§

One moment they were in Death Valley and the next they were floating above the clouds, awash in gold light. Maazini and Handel were suspended in midair without flapping, as if time stood still. A willowy transparent woman floated toward them and communicated with Ma and Pa, without words. Somehow, Tomaaz knew his parents were mind-melding with her.

With a loud snap, they appeared above a basin ringed with sharp mountains.

"Wel … come home." Maazini melded, landing on a ledge below them, his wings drooping on the rock floor.

Ma slid off Maazini's back and staggered into a gaping cavern mouth at the back of the ledge.

With a whump, Handel landed beside the orange dragon. Tomaaz slid down, racing to Maazini's side.

The dragon groaned. His talons were curling in on themselves. His legs spasmed and twitched, and his tail thrashed.

Pa clambered off Handel and pulled the boy into his arms. The lad was bleeding. Probably an arrow.

"Tomaaz," Pa said, "Ma's getting Maazini some limplock remedy. I'll take the boy to the infirmary, just in here. What's his name?"

"I don't know," Tomaaz said. In the face of starvation and whippings, names hadn't been relevant in Death Valley.

Tomaaz rubbed Maazini's neck. *"Hold on, Maazini. Hold on, we're home."* His throat was tight. Maazini was slumped on the ground, his eyes glassy. His scales were losing their bright orange hue. Tomaaz sat near Maazini's head, rubbing his snout. Instead of being warm, Maazini's scales were cool. No! His dragon had turned himself inside-out to save his family. To save him. To help the boy. Tomaaz had endangered Maazini by finding Ma, by bringing the boy with them, by trying to help too many people at once.

"Never..."

It was just one word, and Tomaaz heard it. *"Hang on. Ma's a healer, she'll know how to help you."* No answer. *"Hold on, Maazini. I can't lose you, not now when I've found you."*

Ma stepped up beside him. "Tomaaz," she said, her voice taut. "Push his lip onto his tooth to open his jaw."

Tomaaz snapped to his senses. He could help. Tomaaz pushed Maazini's soft flesh onto his bottom fangs—hard.

Maazini's jaw dropped.

"Now, feed him this." Ma uncorked a vial and shoved it into Tomaaz's free hand. He upended the contents into Maazini's mouth.

"Not so fast."

"Ma, your arm. You're bleeding!"

She gave Tomaaz a grim smile and shook some fine yellow granules onto her own tongue, then passed him the vial. "Give him the rest of these." She passed him the vial and two more. Then she used her knife to free the arrows from Maazini's hide, wiping the poison from his wounds with a cloth.

"It's too late for that, isn't it, Ma? Most of it is in his bloodstream."

Before Ma could answer, Pa rushed out of the cavern. "Marlies, go inside and let Ezaara tend to you. You're in bad shape."

"I'm fine."

"No, you're not."

Ma squeezed Tomaaz's arm. "Give him the other vials, a little bit at a time. Mind-meld with him. We don't want to lose him." Pa led her inside. Handel settled on the far side of Maazini, pushing against his side to hold his thrashing limbs still.

Tomaaz cast out his mind. *"Maazini, come on, talk to me."*

Nothing. He swiped a tear from his cheek. Then another. *"Maazini, we haven't escaped Zens and Death Valley to let you die. You're home, here with friends now. Your ordeal is over."* A sob broke from him. *"You're safe. Safe at Dragons' Hold, Maazini … Maazini!"*

Silence. Except for the hammering of his own heart.

Tomaaz tipped another vial, a bit at a time, onto the dragon's tongue.

"Maazini, I can't face it, not without you."

A huge dragon landed, its scales shimmering with many colors. It nudged his arm with its snout. He placed his hand upon its head.

"Thank you for bringing my son home." This must be Queen Zaarusha. *"I am indebted to you, Tomaaz of Lush Valley. I'm calling more dragons and their riders to form a healing circle."*

"A healing circle?" Tomaaz croaked.

"It's the best chance he has, along with that remedy for limplock." Warmth and comfort flooded him as she spoke. *"Keep feeding him that, Tomaaz, and meld with him. Hold him here. If he can hear you, he won't want to leave his new rider. Help him stay strong."*

Maazini was anything but strong. Rubbing Maazini's eye ridges, Tomaaz reached out with his mind again. Opposite Handel, Zaarusha nestled up to Maazini, holding his rear limbs still, although his tail still thrashed. She draped her wing over Maazini's back, the tip touching Handel.

Pa returned, sucking in his breath when his eyes grazed Maazini's pale gray scales.

Liesar landed. A tall man with dark hair and black eyes strode out onto the ledge. Moments later, a midnight blue dragon dropped to the ledge. The man nodded. "Tomaaz, I'm Roberto, and this is Erob." He gestured at the blue dragon. "We've come to join the healing circle. Keep one hand on his snout and the other on my shoulder."

They made a circle of dragons and riders, touching hand to wingtip around Maazini. The only sounds were the slap of Maazini's tail on stone, and the hiss of dragons breathing.

"Stay melded with your dragon," Roberto whispered to Tomaaz. He cleared his throat. "Let's begin."

Tomaaz searched for Maazini's thoughts. Nothing.

There was a faint hum in his mind. Pa and Roberto had their eyes closed, deep in concentration. The dragons' eyes were slitted and their focus was on Maazini's head. For many heartbeats, they stood, silently touching one another.

Tomaaz's fingertips tingled, then buzzed.

Then energy flowed up his arms, across his chest and through his fingers into Maazini. The waves grew stronger, pulsing through him to the wounded dragon. *"Maazini, we're here. Maazini, stay with us … Maazini, can you hear me?"*

Suddenly, Tomaaz's veins were burning, fire coursing through him, like when he'd imprinted with Maazini. He was no longer tired, exhausted, beaten down or in pain.

Roberto spoke. "Pass your energy to Maazini. Feed him. He needs this life force."

Tomaaz pushed the energy out of him, imagining a huge torrent like a river of fire flowing through his hands into his dying dragon. *"Maazini, stay. Maazini, I want to fly with you, to go back to Death Valley and rescue those slaves. Maazini, I can't do it without you."*

A faint peach tinge crept across Maazini's scales. It was working. A strangled sound broke from Tomaaz's chest; half sob, half laugh. Tomaaz fed more life force into his dragon. *"Maazini?"*

"To … maaz." It was faint, but he was there.

Tears rolled down Tomaaz's face. *"Shards, I thought I was going to lose you. Hold on. We'll get you out of this yet."*

§

Ma was sleeping and so was the boy.

"They should be fine for a little while," Ezaara said to Adelina, glancing at the ledge outside the infirmary. Roberto had melded, letting Ezaara know they were using a healing circle for Zaarusha's son. "Do you mind if I—"

"Go," Adelina said. "I'll keep an eye on them. It's *your brother*, Ezaara." She gave a tired smile, shooing her out.

Ezaara stepped softly to the cavern mouth. What she saw stole her breath: a ring of dragons and riders, joined at hand and wingtip around a pale-orange wounded dragon. But it wasn't that.

It was the *sathir* dancing from wingtip to hand, coursing along the bodies of the riders and dragons into Zaarusha's wounded son.

Multi-colored light streamed from Zaarusha's wings, combining with Handel's bronze and Erob's midnight blue light on one side and Liesar's silver on the other. The strands of *sathir* wove in a river of color, flowing through riders and dragons until it reached Tomaaz, brilliant orange light pouring from him into his dragon. Grateful for the gift of seeing *sathir*, or life energy, Ezaara mentally thanked Ithsar, the desert assassin, for teaching her.

The dragon's scales grew brighter until he was glowing a healthy orange.

§

"Safe."

The word shot through Tomaaz with such power that he broke the healing circle and crumpled to his knees, flinging his arms around Maazini's neck.

Maazini lifted his head and nuzzled Tomaaz's ribs. Soon his dragon was asleep.

Pa hugged him.

Roberto extended his hand. "Well done." His dark eyes shone with approval. "There's someone here who'd like to see you." He gestured toward the cavern mouth.

"Ezaara!" Tomaaz bounded over to her and wrapped her in his arms.

She was crying and laughing all at once. "Thank the Egg, you're home."

"Home?" he said. "I guess it is now."

She wrinkled her nose. "Phew! What's that smell?"

Tomaaz let go of her. "It's the stink of Death Valley."

She slugged him. "Whatever it is, get rid of it." Ezaara wasn't laughing any more. A tear on her cheek, she hooked her arm through his, leading him into the infirmary where the boy and Ma were sleeping.

He needed to bathe. He couldn't risk carrying the stench of slavery and death to Lovina.

§

"I told her to wait in the mess cavern for you." Ezaara pushed Tomaaz toward a huge archway.

Tomaaz hung back.

Everything was strange here, all caverns and tunnels. And what if Lovina didn't feel the same anymore? It was one thing to kiss someone when they'd rescued you and you were stranded in a cave alone, but Lovina had been at Dragons' Hold for two weeks. What if she liked someone else?

"What if she doesn't?"

"Maazini, you're supposed to be resting."

"And you're supposed to be seeing Lovina. Handel told me all about her."

"Well?" Ezaara folded her arms and raised an eyebrow. "Cold feet? Or worried that your bath didn't purge the stink?" She grinned.

Oh, shards! First his dragon, then his sister! Tomaaz strode inside without another word to either of them.

The place was deserted. She wasn't here, after all. He sighed. All that worry for nothing.

Then he saw her: back hunched over a table in a far corner. Two bowls of soup were before her and a pile of bread rolls in a basket. Two bowls—one for him. She *did* want to see him.

She turned. "Tomaaz?" Her voice was tentative. Her face lit up, like moonlight in a forest, full of wonder and soft secrets.

Rushing toward her, Tomaaz couldn't help grinning.

She held a hand up, stopping him, before he could hug her. "I—I—" she stammered.

"What is it?" He took her hand, enclosing it in both of his. "Lovina, what is it?"

She burst into tears. "No one else has ever come back."

§

Tomaaz had come back to her. He was here. And he still liked her. Bill was wrong. She wasn't a heap of horse dung.

Tomaaz wrapped his arms around her. "You have me, Lovina. You'll never have to be alone again."

She leaned into his chest, enveloped in his arms, and cried.

He brushed his lips against her hair, murmuring, "It's all right. You're safe now."

She wasn't just safe, she was happy. And that made her cry even more.

Until his stomach rumbled.

She laughed and tugged him over to the table. Tomaaz stood there, staring at the food, nostrils flaring.

"I know." She smiled. "There's nothing like the smell of real food after Death Valley, is there?"

"So *good*," he moaned, sinking into the chair opposite her.

She pushed a bowl of soup toward him. "I don't know if it's still warm."

"Doesn't matter," he said, picking up a spoonful of soup and tasting it. "Oh," he groaned, "this is delicious."

"I would've said that about dishwater after Death Valley." Even Bill's food had been a jump up from Death Valley. Lovina passed him the bread rolls.

His hand closed over hers. "This is paradise, *being here with you*." His green eyes searched hers.

She ducked her head. "I'm just not used to—"

He nodded, waiting. "Not used to someone loving you?" he asked, finally, stroking her hand with his thumb.

She nodded. Yes, that was definitely going to take some getting used to.

§

The ceiling swam in and out of focus. Marlies rubbed her eyes. Her arms still ached, despite the limplock remedy. She'd never imagined feeling so tired. Was this what the wasting sickness was like? Those patients had complained of bone-weary exhaustion.

"Zaarusha would like to see you," Liesar melded.

It had been wonderful to see her dragon again, her silver scales gleaming as they'd first greeted one another. Now it was as if they'd never been apart.

"I'll bring her," Hans replied, wrapping a warm robe around her and lending her an arm to help her out of bed.

Marlies smiled. He was enjoying mind-melding with Liesar and Handel again. Save some masters on the council, few here would remember that the four of them could meld. She leaned on Hans as they made their way to the ledge outside the infirmary.

Zaarusha furled her wings and strode toward her. Marlies held up her hand and the queen lowered her head so they could touch. *"Ah, Marlies. I'm so happy you're back with us."*

"It's good to be back," Marlies replied. Zaarusha's scales were warm under her hand. Or was she just cold?

"Thank you for returning my son. This journey has taken a toll on you. You've sacrificed much. I'm sorry you've suffered." The queen sent a gentle wave of peace through her.

"But now I can stand tall before my people and the council once again," Marlies said.

"You can indeed."

Marlies bowed her head to hide her tears.

Giant John

Giant John lay still in the underbrush, his blood pulsing at his temples. Hopefully, he'd crawled far enough into the thicket not to be seen.

"Big one in here," a guttural voice yelled. "Search."

There was a crash to his right, then another. He forced himself not to move. Nearby, a branch hit a bush, trapped in its springy foliage. Then a log landed on another bush, crushing it. These hardy bushes could only withstand so much.

If he crept forward, the tharuks would see the bushes move. If he broke out, they'd surround him. For now, it'd be best to sit tight and hope they didn't hit him. There were a few more crashes, then nothing. Giant John strained to listen, but everything had gone quiet. Too quiet. No bird calls. No rustling of animals. Everyone was hiding from those stinking predators. He caught a waft of tharuk stench, carried on the breeze. Giant John waited, his pulse hammering.

Behind him something crackled. The tang of smoke caught in his nose. They were burning him out!

Elbows striking sharp stones, he dragged himself along on his belly. With a whoosh, the bushes behind him caught alight, smoke billowing overhead. Good, that might disguise his movements. With stinging eyes, Giant John raised himself on his hands and knees and crawled faster. The fire was building, a wave of heat at his back. Soon it would engulf the whole thicket.

His knees ached and his palms were scratched and torn. Rasping, John pushed on. Not far to go now. Behind him the fire roared. Sweat dripped off his forehead, stinging his eyes. He blinked to clear his vision, but the smoke was too thick. Oh gods, he was going to cough. Or burn. Too late for stealth now. Under the cover of heavy smoke, Giant John rose to his feet and bashed his way through the chest-high undergrowth.

Over the roaring of the fire, tharuks yelled.

They'd spotted him, but they wouldn't take him alive. Giant John broke from the bush, his feet pummeling the stony clearing. Yells rang out behind him. Through tearing eyes, he saw a tharuk charging at him. Giant John swerved, the beast's claws raking his side. Despite the pain, he raced on, the tharuk snarling at his back. He took a giant's leap onto an enormous boulder at the edge of a chasm.

Far below, a river raged. He risked a backward glance at the tharuks swarming after him, fire crackling at their heels.

Giant John sprang high into the air and dived toward the black churning water. The rocky walls of the chasm blurred as he sped downward. Then he hit the water, the impact knocking the air from his lungs. His body went numb with cold, and he was swept under.

Blackness surrounded him. His lungs burning, Giant John kicked upward, breaking the surface for a gasp of air, only to be sucked under again, dragged by the swift current toward Tooka Falls.

Giant John battled the current. Grabbing hold of a log, he clung on, panting. The roar of the falls filled his ears. If he could get on top of the log, it could help him ride the falls, otherwise he'd be shredded on the sharp rocks at the falls' entrance. He grasped at a branch protruding from the top of the log, and tried to pull himself up, but the log kept spinning, dumping him underwater. He gave up, wedging himself between the log and one of its branches.

Above the falls, tharuks were running along the cliff top. Giant John ducked. An arrow thunked into the log where his chin had just been. He grabbed a quick breath before the current swept him past the rocks, over the edge of the falls. Amid a torrent of water, he lost hold of the log and plummeted toward the churning white mass below.

Pounded by water, he hit the surface, smacking his ribs on the log, the force of the falls driving him underwater into darkness. His body was buffeted, swept along in the murk. Giant John couldn't tell up from down. He'd heard terrible tales of people being swept below Tooka Falls, then popping out again, downriver. Those who fought usually drowned.

Holding air in his screaming lungs, he forced his body to go limp. Eventually, he'd find his way to the surface—unless he got snagged on tree roots.

There was a dark shape on the water. The log. He'd ride it downstream. Suddenly, the surface was pebbled with splashes, tharuk arrow shafts cutting through the water. With burning lungs, Giant John popped up for a breath and dived before the next spray of arrows.

He'd been teased for his large stature as a littling—a largeling, they'd called him—but his strong limbs and lungs made him a powerful swimmer. The river swept him downstream.

It took forever to get to Horseshoe Bend.

It was nearly dusk when he arrived.

Giant John was shivering as he clambered from the water, stepping on tendrils of willow leaves to avoid leaving boot prints in the mud. Growls and cries rang out from the opposite bank. Tharuks were attacking villagers at Spanglewood Settlement, but he couldn't stop to help. He had an important message to get to Dragons' Hold. The fate of the whole realm lay in that message. He'd let Giddi know about Spanglewood, so he could send aid.

His widowed mother was at Horseshoe Bend village, only moments away, but Giant John couldn't stop for anyone. He had to get his message through. He vaulted the fence and ran through the trees. Shards, his sodden clothing and waterlogged boots weighed more than an ox, making it hard going, but he smiled, feeling the magic of the Great Spanglewood Forest around him.

By the time he reached Giddi's cottage, his limbs were weary. He rapped on the door—three short raps and two thumps. Giddi's dog, Mischief, barked, then whined.

Giddi opened the door a crack. Light spilled into the dark woods. "John! You're as wet as a drowned rat! Come in."

Giddi was the only one who ever called him John; to everyone else, he was *Giant*. John stepped inside and Giddi embraced him, not bothered by his dampness.

"Tharuks are attacking Spanglewood Settlement. We have to send help."

Giddi nodded. "Starrus and Benno and some warriors from Horseshoe Bend left a while ago, so they should be there by now. Come and sit by the fire."

John sighed. Glancing at the cold hearth, he grinned. "It's good to see you. It's been too long."

"It has." The mage flicked his fingers. Green wizard flame shot from his hands. The wood in the hearth caught, flames licking up the chimney. Giddi hung a pot over an iron bar and swung it over the fire. "We'll get you out of those wet clothes and some stew into you, then you can tell me why you've come." He opened a cupboard. "Here are your things."

John took his fresh clothes. "Thanks for hanging onto them for so long."

Giddi arched a sardonic eyebrow. "It's not as if they'd fit anyone else."

John chuckled and stripped off, drying himself on a rough wool blanket. As he dressed, the aroma of stew filled the cabin.

Giddi ladled him a bowlful and pulled some chairs over to the fire. "Now, tell me how you got those bruises all over your ribs."

Between spoonfuls, John recounted his travels with Marlies, his journey back, and how that tracker had boasted of Zens' new plans. When he recounted his dive into the Tooka chasm and swim down the falls, Giddi raised one of his famous bushy eyebrows, but said nothing until he'd finished.

"It sounds like you need rest and a good horse, so you can get to the blue guards and on to Dragons' Hold." He picked up John's clothes, running his hands over them as he spoke. Steam wafted off the garments. "You can take Midnight all the way to Montanara. She's fast and will find her way back here." Giddi folded the clothes.

"Hang onto them. You never know when I'll be in a tight spot again."

Giddi laughed. "I've got you out of enough of those, but you've saved my hide, too. Remember that first battle against the tharuks at Horseshoe Bend? Zens had just come through the world gate and made those foul creatures. We had no idea what we were up against."

"Or how long these battles would go on."

John sipped his wizard tea. "Gah, what's in this?"

Giddi chuckled. "I forgot you hate fennel and aniseed, sorry. It'll help you heal from the inside." Giddi hesitated.

"What is it?"

"If I'm not here next time you come, you know where your things are, right?"

"Why wouldn't you be here?"

Giddi shrugged, his eyes flitting away. "We live in perilous times."

There were only two reasons Giddi would leave his cottage in the woods—war or death. John cracked his knuckles. Unless Giddi was thinking of going through the world gate after Mazyka? Surely not. When he sealed the world gate all those years ago, Giddi had promised Anakisha never to open it again.

§

Giant John and Midnight left at dawn, traveling hard all day, through the night and throughout the next day. Many of the villages they passed in Spanglewood Forest had tharuk outposts nearby, their ominous presence cloaking the land with Commander Zens' evil shadow. Whenever possible, Giant John skirted around villages, taking back trails through the forest. Midnight was fast, surefooted and didn't spook easily, but a short way from Montanara, as they joined the main route, she started rolling her eyes and snorting.

A rotten stench drifted across the track, and a tharuk tracker stepped out of the trees, blocking the trail. "You," it snarled, tusks glistening with dark saliva. Its nostrils dilated, scenting him. "We seek big man. Like you. Where are you going?"

"Home to Montanara." Giant John pictured a cottage on the town outskirts, where his friend lived, keeping the image firmly in his mind, in case a mind-bender was near. Sure enough, a second tharuk stepped out of the trees, its black eyes narrowed on him. Then a third, neither tracker nor mind-bender, just a red-eyed grunt.

The mind-bender approached. Giant John's thoughts swirled. He held onto the image of his 'home', fighting the rush of terror the beast sent at him.

His fears had been realized. Word had gotten to these troops that other tharuks had been hunting him. How? Apart from sleeping at Giddi's, he'd traveled non-stop since Tooka Falls. It was almost as if they had messenger pigeons. There was movement among the trees as more tharuks sneaked through the woods to surround him.

Digging his heels into Midnight's sides, Giant John yelled, "Go!"

She leaped ahead, charging at the tharuk tracker, striking him in the chest with her hoof. The tracker rolled aside, and the trail was open.

"Go, Midnight," Giant John yelled, snapping her reins.

Midnight surged forward.

The tracker roared. His troops pounded the forest floor behind them. Giant John leaned low against Midnight's neck, urging her on. She galloped along the trail through Spanglewood Forest. Low-hanging foliage whipped against Giant John's face and slapped against Midnight's flanks.

She powered onward, her thundering hooves drowning out the sound of pursuit. It would be dark soon, but Giant John suffered no illusions: trackers only needed scent, not light, to hunt down their quarry.

By the time they stopped in a meadow outside Montanara, the evening's shadows had crept across the fields. Midnight's sides were heaving and her head drooped. Giant John let the reins hang slack, but she had no energy to eat. He slipped off her back and patted her neck. Her flanks steamed in the cool night air. He tugged the reins, pulling her head down.

Giant John breathed a sigh of relief as she lipped the grass, ripping it out of the earth. He waited for her to eat, then walked her to the stables. On Montanara's outskirts, he'd often stabled his own horses here and frequented the tavern next door. But tonight, he wouldn't be stopping for an ale. The tavern was humming, and the fewer who saw him, the better.

Giant John opened the gate to the stables. Giddi had sent a messenger bird to warn the owner that they were coming, so the front stall was empty and supplied with clean hay. He unbuckled Midnight's saddle and hung it up. Patting the mare fondly, he left, easing the gate shut behind him. He had a hard trek by foot over the snow-clad mountains before he reached the blue guards near Dragons' Hold.

A burst of raucous laughter came from the tavern as a patron stepped outside to pee. Giant John melted into the darkness. He'd have to push himself hard. No doubt, that tracker was still on his trail.

§

Bill fastened his breeches, grinning at the large figure disappearing into the shadows. That very evening, he'd received a message from a crow about a large man *wanted* by tharuks. By mind-melding with the crow he'd seen the man they wanted—someone with the same gait and stature as the huge man sneaking off into the forest.

The crow's troop would be here by morning. Zens would reward him well for this information. Bill licked his lips and went back inside for another ale.

The next morning, when the troop arrived, Bill stepped out of the tavern. "I have something for you," he said, addressing a tracker. The sheer power in the brute's gaze was enviable. Pride surged through Bill. To think he was on the winning side, the side that would rule the whole of Dragons' Realm. He bowed. "A crow told me last night that you're seeking a large man."

The tracker grunted, narrowing its eyes.

"Bill, at your service." Bill revealed the inside of his left elbow. "He went toward the river."

The tracker inspected Bill's elbow, then barked at his underlings, "Tie the spy up and take him back to Zens with the others. 764 and I will find the giant." The tracker spun and sped off toward the river, nostrils quivering.

Two grunts bound Bill's hands, but Bill didn't fight. He was going to his beloved master. Zens would give him a fine reward for such a big prize.

A New Path

Tomaaz scrambled out of bed and raced to the slave boy. Eyes still shut, the lad was convulsing and shrieking, sheets twisted around his thrashing limbs. The poor littling hadn't slept through once since they'd arrived back. In Death Valley, none of the slaves had screamed at night. But then again, they'd been numlocked.

Tomaaz shook the boy awake and gathered the lad in his arms. "It's all right, you're safe." Picking up a blanket, he sat in the chair Hendrik, the master craftsman, had brought them. With curved beams under the legs, it rocked back and forth.

"Perfect for getting babes to sleep," Hendrik had said.

This boy was no babe, maybe eight or nine summers old, but he was as thin as a twig with legs that looked like they'd snap if the wind blew too hard. The boy shuddered. Tomaaz nestled him close and tucked the blanket around his bony frame. He rocked him, smoothing the hair back from his face.

Those haunted lake-blue eyes stared up at him.

"So, what's your name?" Tomaaz asked for the hundredth time. Despite being here a few days, the boy still hadn't spoken. Tomaaz talked to him, telling him stories, keeping his voice low so he wouldn't wake Ma and Pa in the next room. Ma still needed rest, too.

Finally, the boy drifted to sleep. Tomaaz tucked him back into bed and lay down on his own pallet. There were hundreds of slaves, like him, in Death Valley.

§

Tomaaz helped Lovina onto Maazini's saddle and swung up behind her. "Just a short flight."

"It's nice not to be in a saddlebag." She turned to him, their noses nearly touching, and brushed her lips against his.

"I didn't expect that."

She laughed.

"I love your laugh."

Her face grew warm. No one had *ever* said anything that nice. "Thank you."

He wiggled his eyebrows, making her laugh again.

So, this was what happiness felt like, this bubbling inside.

He touched the new scar on her cheek. "All right, Maazini," he said aloud, "let's go." He wrapped his arms around her, cradling her broken arm.

"Wait!" Lovina turned to him again. "Don't you get flight sick anymore?"

He grinned. "No, I don't."

"What happened?"

"Maazini happened. He's changed my life. And so have you." Tomaaz patted the dragon's flank.

Maazini bunched his legs and leaped off the ledge, his wings still furled tight against his sides. They plummeted like a stone, Lovina's stomach dropping. Then the mighty orange dragon unfurled his wings and caught a warm thermal current, spiraling upward, to carry them high above the valley. Dragons wheeled in the air at the far end of the basin. The wind sifted its fingers through Lovina's hair.

"Maazini says, welcome to your new home, Lovina." Tomaaz's arms tightened around her as they headed across the basin.

The air was fresh. Tomaaz's warmth was at her back, pristine snow flecked the mountaintops, and a lake glinted below in the forest. Her heart soared.

"Welcome to your new life," he murmured in her ear.

§

"So, how are you feeling, Master Healer?" Hans asked as they entered their new living quarters, just off the infirmary.

"I'm not sure, Master of Prophecy," Marlies replied. The weight of her new responsibility had yet to sink in. "Strange, I never thought the council would reinstate us. I thought we'd shattered that egg long ago."

"So did I." Hans shrugged. "With the other masters banished, they don't have much choice."

"Thanks a lot!" She smiled, hugging him.

He squeezed her hand, then pulled an armchair over for her.

"I'm not an invalid, Hans."

"No, but now we're together again, I have a chance to spoil you."

And to humor her. Mind-melding meant he knew exactly how worn out she was.

Hans produced a paper package from his jerkin pocket and passed it to her.

She unwrapped it. "Oh, Hans, a butter cake?" Her mouth watered.

"Cook said that anyone who rescued Maazini deserves more than a butter cake. Go on, try it."

She broke a piece off for Hans, then bit into the creamy cake.

"Blue guards are coming," Liesar announced, breaking into their thoughts. *"They're bringing a man who's been cut up by tharuks."*

Marlies sprang to her feet. "Hans, prepare a bed, bandages and—"

"I know the drill."

They ran through the infirmary, Hans stopping to prepare, while Marlies raced out to the ledge. Liesar took to the air. Far off, specks of blue were growing larger—two dragons were approaching.

Liesar flew out to meet them. *"Marlies, Hans,"* she melded, *"it's Giant John, and he's pretty gashed up."*

Shards, she'd led him to being hurt. No, she had to stop thinking like this. *"Hans, I'm going to need help lifting this one."*

The blue dragon landed. Marlies stared at her gashed and bloody friend. "I hope you've got the piaua juice ready," she said to Hans. "John's going to need it."

§

"Order!" Lars, the leader of the Council of the Twelve Dragon Masters, rapped his gavel on the granite table.

Roberto pulled his chair into the horseshoe-shaped table. A few straggling masters took their seats. The new master of prophecy and master healer weren't here yet. "Where are your parents?" he asked Ezaara.

"Zaarusha says they're coming."

Two more seats were empty: those of the recently-murdered masters. *"May Shari and Jaevin's spirits soar with departed dragons,"* Roberto melded to Erob.

Erob grunted.

"A matter of grave importance has come before us," Lars said. "Zens is creating new beasts. Rumor says they'll be able to slay dragons."

Roberto's belly tightened. New creatures?

Murmurs rippled around the room.

"Just let those beasts try," Erob snarled in Roberto's mind. Behind him, the dragons' talons scratched stone.

"A trusted witness heard tharuks gloating about these new beasts," said Lars. "We plan to counter their attack."

Battle Master Aidan spoke up. "What are these beasts like? Are they armored? Do they have weaknesses? How many of them?"

"I wish I knew." Lars combed his fingers through his beard. The doors to the chamber room swung open. "Ah, we may have more answers now."

"There they are." Ezaara's relief rushed through Roberto as she glimpsed her parents, but then it died. *"Who's that with them? Poor guy."*

Ezaara's parents helped a huge man through the door. Marlies had obviously treated his wounds, but his fresh scars left no doubt that he'd been mauled by tharuks.

"Welcome to Dragons' Hold, Giant John," Lars said. "Or should I say, welcome back? It's been a few years."

More than five, since Roberto had never seen him.

"Seppi," called Tonio, the spymaster, getting up. "Fetch him up a chair."

Seppi found two armless straight-backed chairs, pushing them together side by side. The man sat, his bulk taking up both.

Marlies and Hans took their seats behind the council table, and Lars motioned Giant John to speak.

Giant John's breath was ragged in the quiet council chamber. "I've traveled non-stop since Tooka Falls, where a tharuk tracker boasted that Zens is creating new creatures." He took a few slow breaths, then continued. "These beasts can destroy dragons and people. Zens wants to control everyone in Dragons' Realm."

Tonio paced between Giant John and the table. "What can you tell us about these beasts?"

"Zens is creating them," Giant John replied.

"What sort of beast are they?" Tonio's dark eyes scanned the man's face. "Flying, crawling, slithering? Or some strange otherworldly creation, like tharuks?"

"I don't know—only that they'll fight dragons." Giant John winced, rubbing his side.

"How many?"

"No idea."

"What more can you tell us?"

"I really don't know anything more." The Giant slumped.

Tonio placed a hand on his shoulder. "Thank you, Giant John."

Marlies and Hans stood and started to escort him to the door.

"Not so fast," Tonio said. He wheeled to face the council. "We need more information. Someone has to collect it."

"I'm not sending anyone into the jaws of that viper," Lars snapped.

"Me, neither." Tonio held up a finger. "But, we have several people here who have been to Death Valley and survived."

Roberto's blood ran cold. He'd left Death Valley behind and come here. Turned his life around. He wasn't going back, no matter how desperate for information Tonio was.

Lars' voice took on a hard edge. "Exactly who are you thinking of, Tonio?"

The masters shifted in their seats, eyes touching on Roberto then flitting away.

"We have the slave boy," said Tonio, counting him off on his thumb. "And—"

"Who can't speak," interrupted Lars, "so he's no good."

Tonio nodded, and kept going, "and Lovina, the girl who was enslaved to the traveling merchant—"

"She's terribly thin and suffering from maltreatment," said Marlies. "She's in no condition. That would be her death sentence."

"And there's you," Tonio said, turning to Marlies, and counting off his third digit.

Hans bristled, but spoke quietly, "My wife hasn't recovered yet, either."

Tonio held up his last two fingers. "That leaves your son, Tomaaz, and Master Roberto."

There it was; out in the open. Tonio had resented Roberto's tenure here at Dragons' Hold ever since he'd been appointed as master of mental faculties and imprinting. The best way for Tonio to be rid of him was to send him straight back to Zens.

"No, they can't send you," Ezaara melded.

"That's right, they can't," Roberto replied. *"I won't go."*

"No!" It was Marlies, standing right in Tonio's face. "Tonio, I've lived my life. I've done my dues. Send me, not two young ones who haven't had a chance yet."

Tonio lay a hand on Marlies' shoulder and shook his head. "You're not well enough yet, and besides, we need a talented healer here at Dragons' Hold."

"As if they don't need a master of mental faculties and imprinting!" Ezaara melded. *"Without you, they wouldn't have unearthed the traitors!"*

Lars' lips were pursed. "Zaarusha, honored Queen of Dragons' Realm, what do you think?" He strode to the back of the room and lifted his hand to her lowered head. After a few moments, Lars said, "Zaarusha is concerned that Zens may slaughter more of her citizens and loyal dragons. She would like more information, so we could minimize the danger."

Roberto's queen needed more information. He had pledged to serve her, to fight and defend Dragons' Realm. "I'll go," Roberto said.

Ezaara's gasp was audible to every ear in the room.

Tonio shot him a sharp glance. "Thank you, Roberto."

There was a knock at the door. The blue guards opened it.

Tomaaz strode in, Maazini behind him. Giant John sank back into his chair, and Marlies and Hans moved to stand on either side of their son.

"Erob, you sly dog, you just had to tell Maazini, didn't you?" Roberto asked.

"He is my brother, Roberto. Besides, Tomaaz has grit. I want you to have a good traveling companion."

Roberto snorted. *"You're the only traveling companion I need."*

"What about me?" Ezaara broke in. *"I'd rather help than lose you all."*

"I'll go with Roberto," Tomaaz said. "We have to kill Zens."

"We're not looking at killing Zens, now," Tonio said dryly, "although if you get the chance, we'd be highly appreciative." His lip curled in a sneer.

A titter ran around the room.

One by one, Tomaaz stared the masters down. "I've just been in Death Valley," he said. "I've seen the starvation, the beatings, the senseless suffering. I've seen our people robbed of their minds, their will to live. I'm not afraid to go back."

"Well spoken," said Roberto.

The spymaster pursed his lips. "You need to leave by nightfall."

Roberto rose to his feet. Tomaaz met his eyes, nodding.

Lars' smacked his gavel on the granite. The meeting was over.

EILEEN MUELLER

DRAGON RIFT

RIDERS OF FIRE
BOOK THREE

Six Weeks Earlier

Lars smacked his gavel on the granite table. "Queen Zaarusha and the Council of the Twelve Dragon Masters are in accord." His voice was crisp in the tension-filled silence of the council chamber. "It is imperative that we understand this new threat to our dragons and our people. Master Roberto and Tomaaz will infiltrate Death Valley to discover what manner of new beasts Commander Zens is developing. We must know how they'll attack Dragons' Realm. You'll leave tonight." He gave Roberto and Tomaaz a grim nod. The other masters' eyes slid away. No one envied them this job. "We thank you both," Lars said. "Our spymaster will instruct you further. I hereby end this meeting." The council leader gave another sharp rap of his gavel.

Everyone flooded toward the doors.

Master Marlies approached Lars. "Please, Lars, this is madness. Let me go in their stead."

"The queen's decision is final," Lars said, ending the discussion.

Thumping his fist over his heart, Roberto bowed to the dragon queen, then followed the other dragon masters and Tomaaz toward the chamber's exit. His head reeled. How had that happened? How had he agreed to return to Death Valley? Last time he'd been there, Commander Zens had broken him. He'd become a monster, a pawn in the hands of the enemy. A powerful pawn.

He shuddered, remembering the people he'd killed while under Zens' power. If it hadn't been for his dragon, Erob, he'd still be Zens' prisoner, living in a drugged fog of numlock, subservient to Zens' will. *"I'm so glad you found me, Erob."*

"Don't go all mushy on me, now," Erob mind-melded. *"Mushy is the last thing you need to face Zens."*

"I don't want to go back and face my worst nightmares," Roberto replied.

"Worse than nightmares," Erob said. *"People wake from those."*

Roberto sighed. He'd just promised Zaarusha, his dragon queen, he'd return to that arid hell, but right now, he needed time alone to think.

Ezaara, the Queen's Rider, was inside the huge double doors, chatting with the Master of Flight, Alyssa. The elegant flight master tipped her dark head back, laughing. Torchlight played across the highlights in Ezaara's honeyed hair. How could he leave her when their love was so new and bright, and head to Zens' soul-crushing slave camp? She furtively mind-melded, while nodding at something Alyssa was saying, *"Roberto, you don't have to go."* Jade eyes met his, full of concern.

His heart jolted. Gods, what had he done to deserve her? Every time he looked at her, he felt the wonder of a new dawn in spring. *"I wish I didn't have to, Ezaara. You heard Tonio and Giant John. Zens is creating a new type of monster, something that can destroy dragons. We have to find out more."*

Someone tapped Roberto's shoulder. "Roberto, a moment, please."

It was Tonio, the spymaster.

"Ezaara, I'll meet you in the orchard in an hour." He had to hold her one last time before he left. Burn their time together into his mind for the bleak days ahead.

"Of course. I look forward to it." She was swept outside amid the flow of masters and dragons.

"I'll be on the ledge," said Erob. *"Watch your step with Tonio."*

Tonio waited until everyone had left, then pushed the huge double doors shut with an ominous thud. He paced before Roberto, boots snapping on stone.

Roberto drummed his fingers against his thigh. So little time left with Ezaara. "Lars wants us gone by nightfall. I don't have much time to prepare. What is it you want?"

Wheeling, Tonio grabbed Roberto by the shoulders, slamming him against the rock wall. "Antonika was flying the perimeter of the basin earlier. She saw you kissing the Queen's Rider in the orchard, *Master* Roberto." He spat on the rock beside Roberto's face. "You're her master. The law says you should be banished for this crime."

Roberto clenched his jaw. So, it had finally come to this. "You've always had it in for me, Tonio. You tried banishing me using Fleur's false evidence, and now this."

"How long has this affair been going on?" Tonio snapped.

Roberto's blood boiled. Who was Tonio to dictate who he could and couldn't love? Ezaara had nearly died for him. Had given up her role as Queen's Rider, had risked everything she loved to save him. And the law said he couldn't kiss her? Roberto's mind raced. Antonika's memories could be used as evidence, but having recently lost four masters from the council, Dragons' Realm was in a precarious position. They couldn't afford to banish him now. He had nothing to lose by being honest.

"Just that one kiss in the orchard. She's nearly qualified—Lars said so himself. She saved the queen's life, for the sharding Egg's sake." Roberto's breath sawed in and out of his chest. "And mine." Tonio's eyes narrowed, and he jabbed a finger at Roberto, but Roberto cut him off before he could start. "And maybe she saved your life too, by catching the traitors you failed to detect."

That last bit was too much. Tonio's dark eyes flashed.

Roberto had never noticed the similarity before, but Tonio looked just like Roberto's abusive father, Amato, with his calculating Naobian eyes. Shards. He shouldn't have goaded him.

"I could have your head for this, sent to the Wastelands on a platter," Tonio snarled. "However, this trip will probably kill you." He shoved his finger in Roberto's face. "Find out about those new creatures, Roberto, and get out. If you get stuck in Death Valley, we won't be coming after you."

Roberto pushed off the wall, forcing Tonio to take a step backward. "So, you can forgive Marlies for killing a dragonet, but not me for being Amato's son? What is it that Amato did to you, Tonio? Why do you hate me so much?"

Pain flashed across Tonio's face. Stiff with rage, he stalked out.

§

With Tomaaz and Roberto about to leave for Death Valley, and everyone buzzing around preparing, no one noticed Ezaara slipping out to the infirmary ledge. Her boots crunched in the snow.

Pa's dragon, Handel, was resting, his tail curled around his huge bronze body. Pa and Handel had the gift of prophecy. If anyone knew the outcome of this trip, it would be them. Thank the Egg, Handel was alone. She couldn't risk telling Pa how she felt about Roberto.

"Handel, please tell me," Ezaara mind-melded. *"Will Roberto and Tomaaz be safe in Death Valley?"* She hid her feelings for her master so Handel wouldn't know.

Handel snorted. "*Death Valley is always dangerous. As Queen's Rider, you should know that.*"

"I'm asking about this specific trip. Will anything happen to them?"

He huffed, his breath stirring up dust. "*You thought I could conjure up a quick prophecy to reassure yourself about your master and your brother? These are perilous times, my Queen's Rider. You heard the council. Commander Zens is creating new monsters to overthrow us—worse than tharuks—beasts that can easily kill dragons. We must know everything we can about these new enemies.*"

"I know, it's just that—"

"*You want reassurance, comfort, and safety.*" Handel's tail twitched. "*Nowhere is safe. Not even Lush Valley, now that tharuks have breached the pass.*"

Why wouldn't he answer her? "Handel, listen."

"*No, you listen. I've recently returned from the edge of Death Valley and fought Zens' tharuks. I wouldn't wish that experience on anyone.*" He leaned his head down. "*I can show you, but don't blame me if it's not what you want to see.*"

Although she could mind-meld with any dragon without touching them, when she'd last touched Handel, it had prompted a rush of prophetic visions. Ezaara put a hand on Handel's hide. This time, there was a single vision. One she'd seen before: Roberto's face was a mask of hate as he lunged for her—

Ezaara yanked her hand away.

Handel blinked his emerald eyes. "*This may not come to pass.*"

"A vision so strong? I've seen it twice now…" Her stomach clenched. Roberto hurt her? No.

"*All right, so maybe it will happen.*" Handel twitched his scaly shoulders and wrapped his tail around his body.

No. Ezaara refused to accept it. She clung to a sliver of hope. Roberto loved her. Surely, he would never harm her. She shuddered, staring down at the dark forest in the basin of Dragons' Hold.

§

Zaarusha landed in the orchard, the draft from her wings making the autumn leaves flutter. Ezaara slid down to the ground and patted her side. "*Thank you.*"

The dragon queen furled her wings and went over to nuzzle her son, Erob, resting on the grass.

Roberto took Ezaara by the hand and led her under an apple tree. His onyx eyes blazing, he pulled her into his arms. "I swear it, Ezaara. I swear I'll come back to you." He buried his lips in her hair, kissing the top of her head.

Ezaara's heart banged against her ribcage like a battle drum. "*So many things could go wrong,*" she mind-melded. "*Why did you volunteer? Zens could kill you.*"

"*Someone's got to go. I know Death Valley.*"

"*Yes, and Zens knows you. He'll chew you up and spit you out before breakfast.*"

"*Ezaara—*"

"*I don't like it.*" She mind-melded with the queen. "*Zaarusha, tell him he can stay.*"

Zaarusha replied, "*Roberto and Tomaaz are the logical choices.*"

The sadness in his dark eyes made her breath catch. Neither of them wanted him to go, but he would serve their queen.

"Let's enjoy our time together," Roberto said. They sat on a log and he fished in his pocket, pulling out a purple pouch of aged velvet. "This is for you." He passed it to her. "Go on, open it."

"Thank you." Ezaara hadn't expected a gift. She loosened the silken drawstring and tipped up the pouch. A crystal teardrop on a fine silver chain slid into her palm. She held it up. The teardrop twirled in the sun, casting tiny rainbows across Roberto's face. "It's beautiful."

"My mother gave it to me before she died. It belonged to my grandmother. Ma said it was magic, although she never used it."

"Magic? What does it do?"

"I'm not sure, but I wanted to give you something special. I hope it'll comfort you while I'm gone." His fingers traced her cheek, lingering. "Besides, I wouldn't want you to forget me."

Forget him? He was seared into her soul. "It was your mother's. It should go to Adelina."

"Ma gave Adelina another heirloom. This one's mine—and now it belongs to you."

The crystal hummed beneath her fingertips. "That's strange. It's vibrating." She closed her palm around its smooth, comforting surface. "You won't be here for my name day tomorrow."

"You're seventeen summers tomorrow? I'm sorry." His eyes were tinged with regret.

She shrugged. "I have something for you too." She pulled a crinkled green ribbon out of her pocket and passed it to him.

His eyes widened. "I gave that back to Adelina when I was banished."

And Adelina had thrown the ribbon in Ezaara's face, blaming her for her brother's banishment, because the ribbon Ezaara had given him had constituted a vow between Queen's Rider and her trainer—that he would pledge his life to protect Ezaara.

And he had. He'd taken the blame when she'd been framed for murder, knowing she'd never survive the Wastelands and the Robandi desert assassins.

"When I gave you this ribbon, I didn't know it formed a pledge. Did you realize?" she asked.

"I suspected."

"Then why did you take it?"

"Because I wanted to protect you." His midnight eyes flashed.

"Even though you were being so arrogant?"

"Like this?" Roberto straightened, staring down his nose at her, and curled his lip. "Yes, my *Queen's Rider*," he said in that sarcastic cold voice he was so good at.

She whacked him, smiling. "Don't ever do that to me again."

Roberto threw back his head and laughed. Grinning, he took the crystal, his fingers tracing delicately across her skin as he fastened it at her nape. She leaned against him. He wrapped his arms around her and whispered, "I'll remember our time together, and I'll come back to you as soon as I can."

"I'm worried. What if Commander Zens—"

"I won't let anything keep me away from you. You've given my life meaning." With Roberto's thoughts came a powerful surge of emotion that left Ezaara breathless.

"You feel that strongly about me?" she asked.

"You know I do."

He kissed her. Not like their first kiss, just five days ago in this very orchard. This kiss ignited a slow flame that burned inside her, like a beacon for him to come home to.

His face grew serious. "Before I go, I need to teach you two more mental techniques. In Naobia, I taught you to fixate, to block a mental intrusion by fixing an image in your mind, but there are two other techniques that are just as valuable: submerging and the silent witness." His voice rumbled through her head, *"You're outnumbered. Tharuks are hunting you."*

Roberto's midnight eyes seemed to swallow her. Gods, she could lose herself in them. She had to focus.

Suddenly, tharuks were in her mind, firing arrows and gashing people with claws. Tusks dripping blood, they tracked her scent through the forest. Fear ratcheted through her. How did he do that? Kick an image into her head so powerful she wanted to cower?

Roberto's voice was gentle. *"How can you prevent them from finding you?"*

"Take freshweed and hide." Ezaara's voice shook, even though she knew these horrific beasts weren't the real thing. *"Hopefully, they'd pass me by. Especially if I doubled back. My scent …"*

A tharuk loomed in her mind. Smaller than the others, with black eyes, it seemed to stare right through her. A vice tightened itself around her head, the way it had in Roberto's memories. A mind bender. "No," Ezaara cried out. Shards, this was crazy. It was only a mental image. The monster's roar ripped through her head, and she hunched, hands over her ears.

Roberto was doing this. No wonder he hated his talents. No wonder Tonio feared him.

"You'll recognize mind benders because their eyes are black, instead of red. Mind benders can find you by sensing your thoughts—unless you submerge by going so far inside yourself there's no trace of what you're thinking." The tharuks in her head disappeared. *"I'll demonstrate. Stay melded and notice the difference."*

Ezaara closed her eyes.

Roberto's mind was vibrant. His thoughts faded, slipping away like water through fingers, until they were barely a whisper. Then, like a candle snuffed out by a draft, he was gone.

Ezaara cast out her mind. Strange, usually Roberto slammed a wall between them when he was blocking her, but there was nothing. She opened her eyes.

He was still there.

"How?"

"Peel away your mental habits—your anxieties, thoughts, fears and passions—and reach a state of calm. Go to the true center of your being and remain still for as long as you can."

"Sathir." That's what he meant. *"Feeling the connection with nature and becoming one with it."* She'd done this in the desert.

"Sathir is life energy."

Ezaara shrugged. *"To the silent ones, sathir* also means reaching a meditative state."

"Try." The sun cast a golden sheen on Roberto's skin. His voice was soft, eyes warm. His mind, sharp.

Ezaara submerged by sensing *sathir* and finding her still place. Roberto probed. He found her several times, when she was distracted by his dark eyes or soft laugh.

She sighed. "It's not exactly easy with you loving me."

"It's not going to be easy in battle, either." He raised an eyebrow. "Try again."

Twice, he couldn't detect her.

"Better. Now, I'll teach you the hand signals."

"Hand signals?"

"I've developed signals for each of these mental techniques, for communicating when a mind bender is near. A subtle circle with the thumb means fixate." Roberto flicked his thumb around in a small circle.

She copied him. "So, this is fixing an image in my mind?"

"Right, and a twitch of your middle finger is for the silent witness, and lifting your smallest finger is the signal to submerge."

"I think I've got them." Ezaara demonstrated each gesture. "Thumb circle for fixate, small finger for submerging, and middle finger for silent witness—whatever that is."

"We'll get to that in a minute. The last signal is a flat hand, palm down, telling you to flee immediately."

"Flat hand, flee. I hope I never need it."

"So do I. Now, the last thing is the silent witness. You need to mind-meld with me, without leaving a trace of your own thoughts. I'll show you."

"How would that be useful, melding if you can't hear my thoughts?"

"I'll show you. There are two parts of your mind that are active in mind-melding, the part that reaches out to make a connection, and the part that produces thoughts. To perform the silent witness, you need to make the connection, but shield your thoughts. Observe."

Roberto placed his hands upon her temples.

She was in the sacred grove in Lush Valley again, the alps rising high above the forest, and Zaarusha overhead. Sunlight blazed through her—she was imprinting with the queen.

Roberto murmured in her mind, *"I hope you enjoy this experien—"* His voice was gone.

"Roberto, are you still there?"

In a swirl of colors, Ezaara was swept up onto Zaarusha's back and, heart pounding, flew away from her family.

"Could you sense me?" Roberto gently brought the experience to a stop.

"Only at the start."

"You try."

Ezaara melded with Roberto. His mind was buzzing. He and his sister Adelina were swimming in a sparkling sapphire lake. She raced him, diving deep and entering a long channel in the rock. Roberto swam strongly, chasing Adelina, and they both came up inside a cavern, gasping for breath. "I love it here." Adelina grinned.

"I know. Pa will never find us here," Roberto replied.

"If we ever have to run away, I'll meet you here."

Shards, what a life, scared of their own father.

"Silent witness," Roberto melded. *"Submerge."*

She quieted her thoughts, striving to become a silent witness.

"Ezaara, you're like an iron fortress standing in my path. Be gentle, simply fade away."

Ezaara blocked him out, but the vision of Adelina died.

"Try again."

Perhaps it was like sleeping or dreaming, just relaxing and letting her mind slip away.

"That's it. You disappeared." He broke mind-meld. "You could still see my memory, right?"

"Phew, that's easy, but still really hard work." Ezaara wiped her brow. "Now that we've mastered the silent witness, how do tharuks mind bend?"

"Using the silent witness lets you sense what someone's thinking, unobserved. Mind benders inflict mental violence and terror. I won't teach anyone those techniques. It was bad enough having them thrust upon me."

"So why are you teaching me?" she asked.

"As Master of Mental Faculties and Imprinting I have to test people on trial. If you could perform tests too, we'd have a better chance of discovering spies and traitors, and if anything happened to me, my skills wouldn't be lost. I've been trying to convince the council to train more people, but they're too scared of mental powers."

So that was it. "You're teaching me because you might not come back."

Roberto's eyes slid away. "There is that," he finally said, meeting her gaze. "These tools are valuable. I don't want them lost."

"And I don't want to lose you."

His eyes burned through her and he bent his head, kissing her again. Their *sathir* swirled around them, enveloping them in a protective cocoon—his dark blue flecked with silver dancing with her vibrant colors.

Roberto smiled. "Now, let's compose ourselves and go back to face the council so Tomaaz and I can receive our final instructions."

Unbidden, Handel's vision rushed into Ezaara's mind—Roberto lunging at her, his handsome face twisted with hatred.

She clamped down on the vision. No, Roberto would never harm her. He'd nearly given his life for her, bleeding out on the desert sands with a gut wound inflicted by feuding Robandi. This awful prophecy had to be wrong. But Ezaara couldn't help the dark feeling rising inside her. As Roberto took her hand and they walked back to their dragons, a shiver snaked down her spine.

Dragons' Hold

Tomaaz was slumped in the saddle, his head leaning on Maazini's spinal ridge, clinging on with aching arms. How many days had they been flying? It felt like forever. His hip throbbed like someone was pounding it on an anvil, the pain making him dizzy. His throat was parched and his stomach twisted with hunger, but he had no food and he was too weak to reach for the trickle left in the waterskin.

Ahead, moonlight glanced off snow-clad slopes. Maazini beat his wings, ascending a mountainside. Tomaaz's eyes blurred and drifted shut, darkness claiming him.

The dragon's voice rumbled in his mind, jolting his eyes open. *"Tomaaz, we're nearly there."*

Tomaaz dimly registered the glance of moonlight on snow. If that was snow, he should be cold, but he was burning up, limbs trembling as he clung to his loyal dragon.

Lovina's face swam before his eyes, and he reached out to stroke her cheek, slipping sideways.

"Tomaaz!" The sharpness of Maazini's tone snapped him out of delirium.

They swooped over a mountain peak, and plunged down the other side toward a dark forest. His head spun. Maazini headed across the basin, backwinging alongside a ledge. Grunting, the dragon scrabbled on the rock for a foothold, scattering shale and snow down the mountainside. *"We're at Dragons' Hold."*

"Made it ... we made it." Tomaaz fumbled to untie the saddle straps around his waist—the only things that had stopped him from sliding out of the saddle. Sweat stung his eyes as his fingers fumbled with the knots. And then he was free.

"Easy," Maazini cautioned as Tomaaz gritted his teeth and hoisted his good leg over the saddle.

Red hot pain seared like a poker in his hip, rippling up his side. He clamped his teeth down and drew blood, salty and wet. He sucked down the moisture. Jaw clenched, he slid out of the saddle, breaking his descent with the straps.

"Ugh. Ah—" He landed on his uninjured leg. Leaning against Maazini, he struggled for breath. He had to see Ezaara, pass her a message. He haltingly put some weight on his injured leg, but his hip, awash with fire, gave out. Tomaaz slipped and struck his head on the stone floor, and everything went black.

§

Screams sliced through the night, waking Marlies. Throwing back the covers, she dashed to the next room, where her son Tomaaz usually slept. There, in the flickering candlelight was the nameless slave boy, thrashing in his tangled bedsheets. Marlies shook him awake. Scooping him into her arms, she carried him to the rocking chair. He was so light, the weight of a young littling. She settled in the chair, tucking a blanket around him.

He stared up at her, his eyes wide with terror.

The poor thing. Since Tomaaz had rescued him from Death Valley, he'd never slept through once, constantly plagued with night terrors. What had the poor boy been through? How many years had he lived there, and how had he survived? Most died within months of arriving, through starvation, sickness, sheer exhaustion or from the tharuks' brutal beatings—Death Valley had earned its name, thousands of lives over.

She smoothed back his dark hair, rocking and crooning. Although he'd been at Dragons' Hold over a moon and a half, he still hadn't spoken a word. They had no idea whether his family was alive or dead, how old he was, or even what his name was.

"It's all right," she crooned, as she rocked him to sleep. "You're safe."

His eyelids fluttered and closed. Soon his breathing was peaceful. Her own time in Death Valley was plaguing her too, Zens appearing in her dreams to mock and taunt her as he threw her around the room using the power of his mind. And now, Tomaaz, her son, could be facing that same horror. She pulled a calling stone from her pocket and rubbed the flat side of the oval crystal. Nothing happened—no flicker; no image of Tomaaz's face. He hadn't contacted them for a week, now. She grimaced and stowed the crystal.

Rocking this boy reminded her of her twins when they'd been littlings. Tomaaz had always rescued injured insects and woodland creatures. Ezaara, on the other hand, had helped her with the healing arts since she'd been old enough to pick herbs.

A while later, Marlies carried the boy back to bed and tucked his covers around him. If she was lucky, he'd sleep through the rest of the night.

Marlies padded into the bedroom to Hans' soft snores, his dark curls outlined on the pillow in the candlelight. He'd flown patrol tonight and was exhausted. She was just climbing back into their bed, when Liesar, her dragon, mind-melded. *"Marlies! A wounded rider's in Zaarusha's den."*

"Tell Zaarusha I'm on my way." Marlies threw a warm jerkin on and raced through the infirmary next door, snatching her supplies, then out to Liesar's den.

Marlies picked up the dragon's enormous saddle. "What's wrong with the rider?"

"He's unconscious and there's a lot of blood," the silver dragon replied. *"Marlies ..."* Liesar turned her turquoise eyes to her, lowering her head. *"It's Tomaaz—Maazini's not sure if he'll survive."*

Dropping the saddle, Marlies swung onto Liesar's bare back, her heart smacking her ribs like a battering ram.

§

"Ezaara!"

Ezaara woke, sitting bolt upright in bed. Strange, she thought she'd heard two voices in her head—not just Zaarusha's, but also Maazini's. She must've been dreaming again. Nightmares of Tomaaz and Roberto had been bothering her since they'd left for Death Valley six weeks ago. She snuggled back under the covers.

"Ezaara!" This time it *was* Maazini and Zaarusha.

She yanked back the covers, shivering in the chilly air. *"What is it?"* she mind-melded with both dragons at once.

Zaarusha answered. *"Your brother's injured, here in my den."*

Gods, no. Ezaara shoved her feet into her boots and her jerkin on over her nightdress, then snatched up her healer's pouch and ran from her cavern to Zaarusha's den next door.

Torchlight illuminated a horrifying scene. Her brother lay unconscious on the stone, blood seeping from his side. She knelt down and placed her fingers at his throat. He was still breathing. Heart, still beating. Around his hip, his blood-soaked breeches were in tatters. She pulled the fabric back.

Her hand flew to her mouth. Tomaaz's right hip was a gaping hole of torn and bloody flesh. His hip joint was shattered. Fragments of splintered bone gleamed in the torchlight among congealed blood and pus.

By the First Egg, no. Ezaara turned away, dry retching. *"Zaarusha, call my mother!"*

Zaarusha bent over Ezaara, nudging her with her snout. *"The master healer and Liesar are on their way. Are you all right?"* Behind Zaarusha, Maazini was slumped on the snow.

"I'm fine. Please organize someone to take care of Maazini." Ezaara turned back to her brother. Feeling his scalp, she found a gash where he'd whacked his head on the stone floor. There were also grazes on his arm, right thigh and side.

Liesar landed with a whump. Ma leapt to the ground and sprinted over.

Ezaara gestured to Tomaaz's hip. "This is the worst, Ma. He has a gash on his head, but—"

"We'll have to move him off this cold floor." Ma's face was creased with worry. "You take his shoulders while I support his injured hip and legs."

Tomaaz was a deadweight, leaving a bloody trail behind them. Despite Zaarusha's efforts to calm her, Ezaara's heart pounded, mind racing. As they lifted Tomaaz onto her bed, he came to, shrieking in pain. Ezaara's stomach wrenched.

Ma's forehead was slick with sweat as she barked instructions. "Make some woozy weed to knock him out again. Fetch powdered slippery elm bark, bone-knit, and piaua juice. Fast!"

Ezaara grabbed the items from her supplies and brewed the woozy weed tea, feeding sips to Tomaaz until his eyes rolled back in his head and he slept.

Grunting, Ma extracted splinters of bone from Tomaaz's hip wound with her surgical knife, her hands a bloody mess. "Grab that bowl," her mother snapped. "Three measures of slippery elm to two of bone-knit and a few drops of piaua."

Ezaara's hands shook as she measured the powdered bone-knit, spilling some.

Ma grabbed Ezaara's wrist, Tomaaz's blood trickling down Ezaara's arm. "It's all right, Ezaara, we can do this." Her voice was steady, but anxiety puckered her brow.

Do what? Help him die without pain? Amputate his leg? Keep him alive so he could never walk or run again? Ezaara nodded, not trusting her voice, and mixed the powder and liquid to form a thick paste.

"Add a little more bone-knit." Ma placed a few shards of Tomaaz's shattered bone into a dish, arranging them in some order. "Piaua juice restores life, but the slippery elm and bone knit helps glue the bone back together, giving the restorative juice something to work with. The more pieces of bone we can stick together, the better." Ma dropped two last bits of Tomaaz's bone into the dish. "Ezaara, fasten his limbs to the bed so he doesn't thrash."

Eyes pricking, Ezaara bound Tomaaz's arms and legs. She checked his heartbeat, then mixed the ingredients in her bowl. The substance changed in texture, taking on a pale bone color. When the paste formed a thick clump, Ma scooped the substance out of the bowl and pushed it into the cracks in Tomaaz's hip. "Bring that torch closer, please." She painstakingly stuck pieces of his ball joint back together, adjusting them, and pushing them into place, until only a thin coating of mixture held them.

It took forever.

Ezaara kept checking Tomaaz's pulse and breathing. His vibrant orange *sathir* was steady.

At last, while wiping away the excess mixture, Ma said, "That's all the largest pieces taken care off. The challenge will be getting the splinters back in."

"Do you think you got them all?" Ezaara asked, holding up a candle so Ma could see.

Ma picked up a splinter. "There may be shards that have been washed away. Maybe tiny particles have caught in his muscle or connective tissue. That'd give him trouble later. We'll just have to do our best."

Fitting the splinters back in took longer than the initial pieces of bone.

When she was done, Ma called Liesar.

The silver dragon snaked her neck through the archway of Ezaara's cavern. *"It's all right, Ezaara, we've done this before, years ago. It's unnerving, but might help."*

Might help?

Liesar stretched her neck down to Tomaaz's wound, blowing over it. Her hot dragon's breath solidified the ball joint and smoothened Ma's work, hardening it into a slick replica of Tomaaz's bone.

An odd scent filled the cavern. *"Zaarusha, have you seen that before?"*

The dragon queen peered through the doorway. *"Anakisha, my former rider, had me use similar techniques,"* Zaarusha melded. *"But now, I leave healing to the healers."*

"Anakisha taught me this after a battle," Ma said. "We saved the leg of a young boy whose kneecap had been shattered. It's not always perfect, but it's better than amputation." She shook her head at the mangled flesh of her son's hip. "Mind you, it's not always successful. Pass me my surgical knife."

Ezaara passed the knife.

"We can't have jagged edges catching in his flesh." Ma scraped Tomaaz's new ball joint with her knife, clearing the debris away from his wound.

The blade rasped, setting Ezaara's teeth on edge. Tomaaz's eyes fluttered and he moaned and his head thrashed. They'd been working on him so long, the woozy weed had worn off. Ezaara clenched her teeth and held his hand. Even with his arms bound, he gripped her fingers so hard her eyes smarted.

"Could you bring me some piaua, clean herb and cloths?" Slumping into a seat, Ma wiped her forehead. "The bone's fixed now, but his muscles and connective tissue have taken a hammering. We must staunch the bleeding."

Ezaara gestured at his mangled flesh. "At least the blood has washed the pus away." She passed Ma clean herb and placed her fingers on Tomaaz's throat. "His heartbeat's weakening. His *sathir* is fading." Ezaara's own heart lurched. Even though Ma had fixed his hip, he could still die from shock and blood loss.

"Quick," Ma said. "The piaua, before he loses more blood."

They treated the wound with piaua juice, layer by layer, the flesh healing before their eyes. Tomaaz's breaths were shallow and rapid.

"I thought I knew a lot of healing remedies, but I've never seen anything like that new bone," Ezaara said.

"The piaua will help his nerves to regenerate," Ma explained.

Ezaara bit her lip.

"What is it?" Ma asked, setting the piaua vial aside.

"Will he be able to walk again?"

Ma shrugged. "We'll have to see." Ma stitched the hip wound shut, sealing it with piaua.

Ezaara parted Tomaaz's hair and applied a few drops of piaua to his head wound.

Ma snipped the stitches on his hip, tugging them free, then checked his pulse. "His heartbeat is stronger, but still rapid. We'll need to keep him warm. Hopefully the shock isn't too much for him." Ezaara covered Tomaaz with some blankets.

"He's not out of the woods yet, is he?"

Ma shook her head. "No, he's not, but there's nothing more we can do." She sank into a chair and patted the seat next to her. Ma's arms and hands were splattered in blood. Ezaara fetched her a bowl of water, asking Zaarusha to warm it. They cleaned up their hands, the area and the wound site.

"What now?" Ezaara asked.

"We wait until he revives and see whether it's worked. In the best case, he'll walk with discomfort. In the worst ..." Ma sighed, patting Ezaara's hand. "I'll sit with him. Why don't you take a breather?"

Ezaara walked outside through Zaarusha's den, where the dragons were sleeping.

Zaarusha opened an eye as she passed. *"Maazini's not injured, just exhausted."*

"Any word of Erob?"

"Not yet. Maazini was too tired to make much sense." The queen's eye drifted shut.

The cool air out on the ledge dried the sweat on Ezaara's brow, making it stiff with salt. She leaned against the stone wall, her hands clenching the fabric of her jerkin. Where were Erob and Roberto?

She shuddered as her nightmares replayed in her mind: Commander Zens torturing Roberto. Screaming, his handsome features were twisted into a mask of pain, his olive skin crusted with blood.

No. It was just a nightmare. She'd find out the truth when Tomaaz or Maazini woke.

Roberto would be fine. He was resourceful, clever. He'd survived being captured by Zens before. Him and Erob might be flying home now, just hours behind Maazini.

Ezaara sank to the snowy ledge, not caring about the chill.

Soon, the first rays of dawn hit the peaks of Dragon's Teeth—the ring of mountains surrounding the basin of Dragons' Hold—setting them on fire. Ezaara scanned the skies. No dragons.

Roberto's face flashed to mind, his ebony eyes tender as he'd kissed her, vowing to return. No one knew they were promised to each other. No one must know. As master of mental faculties and imprinting, he was forbidden to love his trainee. Not that she'd be his trainee for much longer—she was nearly qualified.

She touched the crystal teardrop at her neck. A memory cascaded through her mind: Roberto nearly plunging to his death when he and Erob had fought Ajeuria.

Her gaze swept the empty snow-covered basin. What if Roberto didn't come back? A chill climbed Ezaara's spine. What if he was already dead?

Footfalls echoed behind her. Ma was approaching. Ezaara's backside was freezing. How long had she been sitting, lost in her thoughts?

"Tomaaz is stirring," Ma said.

Ezaara nodded and followed Ma into her cavern. The scent of clear-mind infusion hung in the air. Ma must have steeped the berries to wake her brother. Pa was sitting by her bed, his brow furrowed, watching her brother.

Head tossing, Tomaaz was moaning and muttering in his sleep.

Ezaara patted his hand. "Tomaaz, it's all right. You're safe at Dragons' Hold. It's me, Ezaara."

His eyelids fluttered, then flew open. "Ezaara, I've failed," he rasped. "Commander Zens has captured Roberto."

War Council

"Ezaara, did you hear me?" Tomaaz asked, grasping her hand. "Roberto's been captured by Commander Zens."

Ezaara was lost for words. Her mind spun. Roberto was captive. Surely Zens would kill him.

"What happened, Tomaaz?" Pa asked.

"We were leaving Death Valley when tharuks attacked us. They forced Erob to the ground and dragged Roberto away. Maazini flamed tharuks and I shot some, but they drove us back with limplocked arrows."

"When?" Pa asked.

"Five days ago." Tomaaz looked at Ezaara. "Roberto had a message for you: something about his mother saying, *teardrops amplify thoughts*. Erob told Maazini to tell the Queen's Rider."

What did that mean?

Probably that she should hide her sorrow so no one knew how she felt. Ezaara resisted the urge to clutch her necklace. No one must know it was from Roberto.

"Make any sense?" Ma asked.

Ezaara shook her head. She didn't dare tell anyone.

"Um, Ezaara, do you mind letting go of my fingers?" Tomaaz asked. "You're crushing them."

She glanced down—she had his hand in a death grip. "Sorry," she said, releasing his fingers. "I'm so relieved you're home. We need to sort out how to retrieve Roberto, but first, how's your hip?"

How was she sounding so normal, so in control? Ezaara wanted to scream, rage, and pound the stone walls with her fists. Zens had nearly broken Roberto last time. She shuddered, remembering the awful memories he'd shared when they were in Naobia. Shocking, violent memories that had taken weeks for her to push to the back of her mind. And now Roberto was in that monster's hands again. Ezaara clutched the crystal teardrop at her neck.

"Let's see if you can stand. Hans, give him a hand," Ma said. "Now, Tomaaz, flex your leg like this …"

As Ma tested Tomaaz's reflexes, Ezaara went to the other side of her cavern to get changed. *"Zaarusha, notify the dragons that I'm calling an urgent council meeting."* She couldn't turn up in her nightdress and jerkin. She dressed mechanically, fastening her healer's pouch at her waist. Instead of tugging her boots back on, she selected the shoes Roberto had given her for their race. Light and supple, they were hand-painted with a likeness of Zaarusha soaring over a lake, her colorful scales reflected in the water.

"Everyone's been roused and is on their way, except Tonio, who will be a little late."

So, the spymaster was off on business again. Ezaara was almost relieved. Tonio wasn't exactly her favorite dragon master.

Ma had Tomaaz on his feet. He was still a little unsteady.

He needed a cane. Ezaara's hand automatically fastened around the walking stick leaning against her wardrobe. Roberto had carved it for her when she'd twisted her ankle. Her throat grew tight. Even when she'd mistrusted him, he'd been caring. She held the beautiful handle, carved with herself upon Zaarusha, and offered it to Tomaaz. "Would this be helpful?"

Tomaaz took the cane. "Thanks, Ezaara."

Ma nodded at Tomaaz. "Your range of motion is pretty good, and the wound has healed well, but it'll feel odd while your muscles adjust to the new joint. Do you have any pain?"

Tomaaz screwed up his nose. "No pain, but it does feel weak, as if it might give out. The walking stick will be great."

"I know you haven't slept much, Tomaaz, but we've called a war council," Ezaara said. "They'll need to hear your report. Are you up to attending?"

"I haven't had a chance to see Lovina or the boy yet. How have they been?"

"Both thriving," Ma answered. "They'll keep another hour or so. They're probably fast asleep anyhow. You should attend the council first."

"Of course he should," Ezaara snapped. "We need to know what's happened." Oh shards, she sounded ratty. She had to do something or she'd crack.

Tomaaz gave her a long look, then nodded. "I'll come."

"I'll bring him. Maazini is exhausted."

"Zaarusha says she'll take you," Ezaara said, striding to the door. "I'm walking. I have an urgent errand on the way." She went into the corridor and closed the door.

"Ezaara?" Zaarusha asked.

"I can't stand it, Zaarusha. I have to do something or I'll go mad."

Ezaara started running, feet pounding the stone. She ran away from the council chamber, toward the main cavern, then took the left corridor down to the storerooms. A slow burn built in her muscles. She reached down deep, seeking *sathir*. The air shimmered with a thin ribbon of multi-colored light. That was her connection to Zaarusha. She strained to feel the deep blue of Erob and Roberto. Nothing. She wanted to scream, but didn't dare, so instead, she exhaled forcefully, sucking in great gulps of air. Fire leapt into her veins—she was harnessing her dragon's power. She sped through the dark subterranean tunnels.

"*Run like the wind,*" Zaarusha mind-melded. "*Tomaaz and I have just arrived, but not everyone's here yet. You have a few moments to purge your sorrow before you face the council.*"

"*Thank the dragon gods, you understand.*"

Comfort washed over Ezaara, but she shrugged it off. Pushing her muscles until they seared, she ran past the door to the dungeons. At last, she came to a staircase winding up to the rear exit of the council chamber—the exit the guards had manhandled Roberto out of when he'd been banished. Ezaara raced up the stairs until her head spun and her legs trembled. A few steps from the top, she mind-melded, "*Zaarusha, is everyone there yet?*"

"*Two more to come: Jerrick, and Tonio—who'll be late.*"

Ezaara sat on a step and leaned back against the wall, taking slow deep breaths. Nothing had changed. Roberto was still Zens' prisoner. But at least she no longer felt like screaming or punching something. She stood, smoothed her jerkin and opened the door to the council chamber.

Lars, leader of the council, gave her a quizzical look as she entered and took her seat beside him at the arch of the horseshoe-shaped granite table. Near the wall behind the table, the dragons crouched, scales gleaming in the torchlight. There were no natural windows in this chamber.

"*You're looking much more settled,*" Zaarusha melded.

"*If only I felt it.*"

Seven people were at the table, including Lars. Five seats were still empty. Two masters—Shari and Jaevin—had recently been murdered. Tonio's seat remained vacant, and Jerrick, the master archer, wasn't here yet. The last empty spot was Roberto's, which made Ezaara swallow, but she quashed her feelings. Now was not the time for emotion, only for action.

Tomaaz was in a chair, leaning against the wall, his chin on his chest, dozing. He'd grown thinner in Death Valley again, his cheeks gaunt and eyes ringed with exhaustion. Ma and Pa, recently restored as masters, kept glancing at him and murmuring to each other.

The huge double doors flew open and Master Jerrick entered, folding his gangly frame into his chair. "My apologies for being delayed. There's been an uproar among the archers."

"An uproar?" Lars asked.

"Yes, I'll need to get back and sort it out. I hope we won't be too long."

Lars rapped his gavel on the table.

Tomaaz twitched and woke, his gaze meeting Ezaara's. He stretched his leg, testing his hip.

"I declare our council meeting open," Lars said. "I call upon our Queen's Rider to speak, as it was she who summoned us."

All heads swiveled to Ezaara.

For a moment she felt that old feeling of inadequacy she'd had when she'd first arrived at Dragons' Hold. But, no, she was the Queen's Rider. She'd earned her dues—fighting tharuks, rescuing Roberto from the Wastelands, and saving Zaarusha from traitors' poison.

She stood and met each master's gaze. Pa's eyes were warm and encouraging. Ma's were grave. Ma knew what they were here for, and the horrors of Death Valley.

Even though Roberto was in danger, there was still hope for him yet—Ma had confronted Zens and made it back. "Esteemed council members, I apologize for calling a meeting so early in the morning. As you can see, my brother has returned from Death Valley. However—"

The exit door behind her clicked shut and Tonio slid into his seat. "Apologies, my Queen's Rider." He gave her a curt nod, then his eyes flitted around the room, taking everyone in.

Ezaara continued, "However, Master Roberto has been captured by Commander Zens. We believe he is being held captive. We need to determine how to free him."

Murmurs rippled around the table.

"I call upon my brother, Tomaaz, to report." Ezaara sat.

Lars gestured at the spymaster. "Master Tonio, as Tomaaz was on your assignment, perhaps it's best if you question him."

Tonio rose. Pacing to the front of the table with panther-like grace, he gestured Tomaaz to stand.

Leaving Ezaara's cane against the wall, Tomaaz walked to the front of the council table with a slightly uneven gait.

With the tiniest twitch of his brow, Tonio glanced at Tomaaz's leg. "Before we discuss Roberto's capture, perhaps we can see what you gleaned during your time in Death Valley. Did you manage to infiltrate Zens' slave camp?"

"Yes, Roberto and I entered Death Valley separately. We met up every few days to compare our findings. But you need to understand, because the slaves have numlock in their water, they're incapable of coherent speech or thought. So, there's no gossip. I couldn't quiz anyone about what they'd seen or heard. They're like blind, mindless sheep."

Tonio nodded. "Did Roberto find out anything about these new monsters?"

"Roberto got into a mining crew and went deep into the hillside to dig up yellow crystals."

"Yellow crystals?" Lars asked. "Zens paid Bruno in yellow crystals. Roberto told me they were dangerous. Did he tell you anything about them?"

Ezaara tapped her forefinger on the granite table.

That's right. During the traitors' trial—when Bruno and Fleur and their son Simeon had been banished for poisoning Queen Zaarusha—a sack of Zens' yellow crystals had been found among Bruno's possessions.

Tomaaz shook his head. "I have no idea what they're for."

Tonio resumed his questions. "How was Roberto caught?"

Ezaara gripped the table.

"Roberto said he'd found important information and wanted to get back to Dragons' Hold," Tomaaz replied, his voice hollow. "We sneaked out of Death Valley to meet our dragons, but tharuks ambushed us, firing arrows at Maazini and Erob. A tharuk pierced Erob's belly with an arrow with a rope attached to it. The beast yanked on the rope, tearing Erob's skin and forcing him to land. Maazini flamed some tharuks, but they were shooting limplocked arrows at us, so we had to retreat or I could've lost my dragon, too.

"After dark, I slunk back to find Roberto. As I was descending the hill into Death Valley, tharuks launched a pile of boulders at me. I had no chance. My hip was crushed. Tharuks rushed to finish me off, but Maazini …" Tomaaz's swallow was audible in the quiet chamber. "Maazini swooped down to grab me in his talons." Tomaaz's leg faltered.

Ma and Pa leaped up to bring him a chair, and Pa helped Tomaaz into it. "Maazini landed near Erob, and I managed to drag myself up into the saddle so we could fly home."

"So, neither of you found out *anything* about Zens' new creatures?"

Was that contempt in Tonio's voice? Ezaara bristled.

"Roberto may have found out something, but he didn't have a chance to tell me."

"Was there anything that seemed contrived about his capture?"

Silence struck the cavern.

Tomaaz stared at Tonio. "Are you implying that Roberto *wanted* to be caught by Zens?"

"Please answer my question."

"With all due respect, Master Tonio, are you mad? Who in their right mind would let tharuks rip their dragon's belly open, injuring their best friend? And who would want to help Zens?"

"We've just had traitors do exactly that, Tomaaz," Tonio replied sternly. "Before you arrived here, Bruno and Fleur, masters on this council, maltreated Ajeuria, our dragon queen's daughter. They were influenced by Zens. And they tried to poison Queen Zaarusha. We don't yet know if they've influenced Unocco, Bruno's dragon, but I suspect they must've or they wouldn't have gotten away with everything for so long. Now, answer my question: did Roberto appear to be complicit in his own capture?"

White-knuckled, Ezaara's grip on the tabletop tightened, the granite biting her palms.

"Of course not," Tomaaz yelled, leaping to his feet. He gasped, clutching at his hip, and fell back into his chair.

Ma rushed over. "Are you all right?"

Tomaaz waved her off. "Just a twinge."

Ma stalked over to Tonio. "My son came home last night with his hip joint shattered. It was touch and go, but we managed to heal him. I've recently been in Death Valley. Zens threw me around the room with the power of his mind. I nearly died."

"Why would anyone willingly go to that monster?" asked Pa, shaking his head.

Tonio bristled. "Not willingly, Hans, but under coercion. Zens weaves some sort of magic over people. He turns them. Roberto has been his protégé before. It could happen again."

Ezaara felt nauseous. She'd seen Zens' cruelty through Roberto's memories. "This has gone far enough," she said, snatching Lars' gavel and smacking it on the table. "I called this meeting to make rescue plans for Roberto and Erob, not to hold a trial for a crime a master hasn't committed. The Egg knows we've had enough of those lately." She shot Tonio a venomous look. He'd been instrumental in having Roberto unjustly banished to the Wastelands.

Tonio gave a cool smile, his dark eyes flashing. "Very well, my Queen's Rider." He turned to Tomaaz. "Please inform us of Erob's whereabouts and the extent of his injuries."

"Erob is near Death Valley along the border of Great Spanglewood Forest."

"South of Monte Vista?" Tonio asked. "Or north of the Tooka River? I hope he's not anywhere near those shrotty wizards."

"Maazini knows the location," Tomaaz replied. "He'll show any dragon how to get there. I'm worried about Erob. He's been lying there with his gut slit for five days now."

"We must rescue Erob at once," Lars interjected. "But it'll take a few days to reach him. He could be dead by then."

Pa spoke. "Actually, Marlies and I have rings of power that can get a rider and dragon to any destination instantaneously."

"That's impossible, Hans," called Aidan, master of battle.

Ma interrupted. "Master Aidan, not only is it possible, I've used one too. That's how we escaped Death Valley."

"I'd heard that after Anakisha's last battle—may her spirit fly with departed dragons—the two rings of power were lost," Tonio said. "Now you're telling me you have them? Did you steal them when you fled Dragons' Hold eighteen years ago?"

Ezaara held her breath. That dirty spymaster was using every lowdown tactic, reminding everyone of how Ma had accidentally killed Zaarusha's dragonet.

Ma met his gaze evenly. "The rings were not lost, Tonio, but given to her progeny who were scattered throughout Dragons' Realm. Her daughter recently gifted one to Hans, and on my way to Death Valley, Anakisha's granddaughter gifted one to me."

Pa nodded. "Although Anakisha's rings of power create realm gates for travel within Dragons' Realm, every time a ring is used, the walls of the gate grow weaker, creating a ripple in *sathir*. Zens senses those ripples. We've been warned that overuse could risk Zens discovering the gates."

"The result would be disastrous," Ma said. "Imagine Zens appearing anywhere without warning. He could even breach Dragons' Hold."

Ezaara shivered. Behind her, dragon talons scratched stone. "So, now we can get to Erob, who will go?" she asked.

"I will," Tomaaz replied.

"Not with your hip, you won't," Ma said.

"If I wasn't your son, would you object?"

Ma pursed her lips. "Yes, but I know you're too stubborn to listen. Please rest for a few hours before you leave."

"I'm going with Tomaaz," Hans said. "I know how the rings work."

"Then it would seem you're well-suited to lead the rescue, Hans. There's still one problem." Lars gazed around the table. "Any ideas about how to retrieve a dragon with a gaping belly wound?"

One problem? What about retrieving Roberto? Ezaara's hand went to the crystal teardrop at her neck. If they didn't get Roberto back, this wouldn't be the only teardrop at this table. "I have a solution," she said, keeping her face devoid of the rage churning within her. "Roberto had a secret."

"Only one?" Tonio asked snarkily.

Resisting the urge to punch the spymaster, Ezaara continued, "Roberto was a great fisherman, catching the fish for all our feasts." Nods and murmurs of assent rippled around the table. "He and Erob used nets, not a spear. If we can't heal Erob in Spanglewood Forest, we could place the nets under his wounded belly and lift him home."

"Anyone else with a better suggestion?" Lars scratched his blond beard as he gazed around the silent table. "Good, that's settled. It'll take two large dragons to lift Erob, though."

"Handel's large enough," Hans said.

"Zaarusha is the largest of all," Ezaara chimed in.

"You'd risk our Queen's Rider and the queen?" Tonio asked, shooting Lars a meaningful look.

Lars gazed at Tonio, some hidden meaning passing between them, then turned to Ezaara. "If Zaarusha is willing, I agree."

"Of course I'll rescue my son," Zaarusha melded with Ezaara, then roared her assent for the council.

Lars raised his gavel.

Ezaara placed her hand on his arm. "Master Lars, before we adjourn, there's a matter we haven't settled. How are we going to retrieve Master Roberto?"

"If he wants to be retrieved," Master Tonio muttered.

Ezaara stood. "I was in this room when Roberto refused to go. He finally agreed, in order to serve his queen."

Zaarusha roared her confirmation.

Again, meaningful glances shot between the council leader and the spymaster. What was going on?

"We need our master of mental faculties and imprinting. We must save Roberto from Zens," Lars said. "But now that he's in Zens' hands, we'll need to take precautions. I don't want more riders or dragons captured. We've only just rescued your mother and brother, Ezaara."

As if the council had helped. Pa had rescued them himself, without the council knowing what was going on. "I disagree," said Ezaara. "We must retrieve Master Roberto as soon as possible."

"Roberto went there on your behalf and now you're abandoning him?" Tomaaz jabbed a finger toward Tonio. "We have to get him out."

"And we will," Tonio placated, "as soon as we've brought Erob back. He'll have information that will be vital to rescuing Roberto. I suggest you all leave as soon as possible."

Hopefully, they wouldn't be too late. Erob could already be dead.

Lars raised his gavel, but Ezaara's chair legs grated across the stone as she stood, drowning out the council leader's words. She stalked from the meeting room, fuming.

There was no way Commander Zens would let Roberto escape after he'd thwarted Zens' last attempt to make him his protégé. Would Zens try to bend Roberto to his will again? Or would he kill him outright?

If no one else was prepared to save him, she'd go herself.

Prank Gone Wrong

Lars shook his head. Ezaara had done well in saving Queen Zaarusha recently, but it was downright rude of her to stalk from the meeting before he'd officially closed it. And with Roberto in Death Valley, it wasn't as if he could have a word with her master to make sure she obeyed protocol. Guilt needled Lars. Was Roberto all right in Zens' hands? Tonio did have a point: Roberto had survived Zens last time, and he could still be gathering information. Alternatively, he may even be on his way home now. No point rushing in when a man didn't need rescuing.

But on the other hand … Lars didn't want to consider the alternatives.

However, Erob was a different case altogether. The dragon was obviously stranded and injured.

Lars stowed his gavel in the cubbyhole under the table and glanced up at the nearly-empty council chamber. Why were Jerrick and Derek hanging around? That's right; Jerrick had mentioned a problem with his archers. "Master Jerrick, what was the uproar with your archers this morning?"

Jerrick cracked his knuckles. "All of our arrows are missing, Lars. I've searched high and low and can't find them anywhere."

"Do you remember where you last had your quiver? I'm sure it will turn up soon if—" Jerrick was frowning at him like a brewing storm. "What is it?"

"Everyone's arrows, Lars. Well, nearly all of them. Each archer has two arrows left in his quiver, and the rest are gone."

"All of them?" Lars scratched his beard. "Have you searched the armory?"

"All gone too."

"The blacksmith and fletcher?"

"They both said a lad collected the arrows due for the armory, but they never got there."

Derek, master of training, added, "And no one knows who collected them or took the other arrows from the armory."

They'd never guarded the armory. No one except dragon riders could access Dragons' Hold, so why bother? "Do you suspect a thief? Who?"

Derek grimaced. "There's been growing rivalry between the young sword fighters and Jerrick's archers—arrow flingers, they call them. I suspect my charges have hidden your arrows."

My charges, Derek had said, although they wouldn't have been his if Master Jaevin hadn't been murdered by Bruno and Fleur—those traitorous vipers.

"Mine call yours blade thrusters," said Jerrick, shaking his head. "How can they face tharuks if they can't even cooperate? This is the last thing we need with war coming."

"They'd defend each other's backs if they were in a tight spot," said Lars. "But you're right—their timing is lousy. And this ridiculous rivalry has gone far enough. Find out who the perpetrator is and send them to me."

§

"It's been five nights, Adelina. Five nights of awful nightmares that Tomaaz has been wounded and dying." Lovina backhanded a tear from her cheek. "I've barely slept and I'm so worked up, I can't eat." Her eyes were underscored with bruise-colored shadows. Although she'd gained weight since arriving at Dragons' Hold two moons ago, she was still so thin that there was barely any flesh on her bones.

Adelina could understand Lovina's agitation. Hearing about her friend's nightmares did nothing to calm her own growing anxiety about her brother, Roberto. He was the only family she had. For the hundredth time, she questioned why Tonio had suggested he go back to Death Valley with Tomaaz. Sure, there was the obvious rumor that Zens was breeding new monsters that could fight dragons, but did Tonio have an ulterior motive? He'd never liked Roberto—or her. In fact, he was pointedly rude to them.

Putting her arm around Lovina's shoulders, she said, "I know I'm not much comfort, but if you'd like to sleep here on the couch, I'll be nearby. Maybe that would help you get some rest."

Lovina turned her blue eyes to Adelina. "That would be great."

Adelina fetched some blankets. "Here, it's cold. You'll need these."

Tugging the blankets over her, Lovina curled up on the sofa. "Thanks," she said. "I haven't had a friend since I was a littling." She drifted to sleep.

Shards, how awful, spending your life in Death Valley and then as a slave to one of Zens' spies. Lovina was lucky to be alive. If it hadn't been for Tomaaz, she wouldn't be. Adelina jumped into her own bed and lay staring at the stone ceiling. The thing was, Roberto had been on her mind since … she counted back the days. Five days, too. Was it a coincidence or had something happened to him?

Hours later, rapping at the door woke Adelina.

Tomaaz stepped inside.

Bleary-eyed, Lovina sat up on the couch, her face breaking into a smile. "Tomaaz, you're back."

But Tomaaz didn't smile and run to hug her. He gave her a short nod. Face grave, he walked stiffly into the cavern, holding himself as if he had an old leg injury. "Sorry, Lovina, first I need to talk with Adelina."

Adelina's heart cracked. Her hands grew clammy. She sank into a chair, eyes fixed on his somber face.

Tomaaz took her hand, his fingers like icicles, but nothing compared to the icy shivers that ran down her arms. "It's Roberto, isn't it?" Adelina squeaked, throat tight.

Tomaaz nodded. "Zens has captured him. I'm sorry."

The room seemed to still. Tomaaz continued talking, explaining how her brother had been captured, but his voice was muffled, far away, as if someone had stuffed Adelina's ears with sheep wool. Her mind spun. Roberto. With Zens again. Zens would be doubly vigilant this time—and four times as mean. Roberto already had enough scars from Death Valley. How could her brother survive? She stood, feet like lumps of wood, and walked to the door.

"Adelina, shall I come with you?" Lovina asked, rising.

Shaking her head, she fled into the corridor, Tomaaz's protests echoing along the rock walls.

Adelina ran to Roberto's cavern. Here, she'd find comfort. Here, she'd find Erob. She dashed through to Erob's den. It was empty. "No, not Erob, too," she gasped.

Adelina sank to the stone. For years, she'd dammed up sorrow, putting a bright face on life. Through her father's betrayal, through him selling Roberto out to Zens and causing her mother's death, she'd tried hard to be cheerful for Roberto's sake. He'd borne the brunt of their father's treachery and it had broken him. But he had been her mainstay, and now, he was gone. Hugging her knees and burying her head in her arms, she let her tears come.

§

Despite him calling after her, Adelina had fled. Tomaaz stood in the doorway, staring down the tunnel. Should he follow her?

A gentle hand rested on his arm. "She needs time, Tomaaz, just like I'd need time if it was you who hadn't come back." Lovina's cornflower-blue eyes looked up at him.

He nodded. He'd talk to Adelina later. He stepped back inside.

Lovina had changed in the six weeks he'd been gone: her face had almost lost that gaunt haunted look; her skin glowed; and her hair was glossy and healthy.

"Do you mind?" he whispered, his hand hovering above her hair.

She closed her eyes and flung her arms around him, and he ran his hand over her hair, her back and then hugged her—the way he'd dreamed of hugging her every day he'd been in Death Valley. Her hair had a floral scent, and her body was warm against his. He'd been cold for weeks. Blankets in Death Valley had always been thin, and although it wasn't snowy like here, the nights had been bitterly cold and much of the valley shrouded in shadow, even during the day.

Lovina's back trembled under his hands, then shook. She was sobbing.

He pulled back, and tilted her chin. "Lovina?"

"I'm great," she said between sobs. "I couldn't be better. I'm just so glad you're home."

He pulled her back into his arms, rubbing his cheek on the top of her head. He'd never thought of anywhere except Lush Valley as home, but she was right—Dragons' Hold was his new home. Now that he'd imprinted with Maazini, it was the best place for him to live, but what about her? "Lovina, is this your home too?" he murmured.

Through tear-filled eyes, she smiled. "Yes, Tomaaz, it's my home too."

"Then why are you crying?" He stroked her cheek.

"I had the most terrible dreams for the last five nights. Always the same. You were trapped under a landslide with tharuks swarming down a hill toward you. I'm so glad they're not true. So glad you're safe." She sniffed. "And when I paint, the pictures come out the same as my dreams—you injured, lying under rocks."

So, they were tears of relief. "Five nights?" It was five days' flight to Death Valley. "Lovina, your dreams were true. I was trapped under some boulders five days ago, but Maazini freed me."

"And you weren't hurt?"

"Ma healed me. My hip was shattered." Tomaaz tilted his head. There was more to her than met the eye, but then, he already knew that. "You might have the gift of prophecy."

RIDERS OF FIRE

"Me?" Her eyes flew wide.

"It's possible. You dreamed of something that happened. You should talk to Pa. He has visions and dreams too. His dragon Handel does as well."

Lovina pulled his arm, leading him toward Adelina's couch, but he resisted. "Lovina, there's something I have to tell you."

"What is it?"

"I'm not here for long. I have to go back and help Ezaara and Pa find Erob. He's wounded and can't fly."

"Erob?" Adelina's voice came from behind them. "Erob's wounded? Where is he?"

"Near Great Spanglewood Forest," Tomaaz replied, turning to face her.

"Oh, that's only a day's flight away. Good." Although her eyes were red-rimmed, Adelina had an overly-bright smile stuck on her face.

"It's further," Tomaaz said. "He's on the other side of the forest, near Death Valley."

"I don't care how far it is. I'm coming too," Adelina said stubbornly. "No one's going to rescue Erob without me. My brother's dragon is the only reason I'm alive. My father would've given me to Zens too, if it hadn't been for Erob. He hid me in a cave while he freed Roberto from Death Valley."

Tomaaz nodded. "Roberto and Erob both care about you. Roberto made me promise I'd look after you if anything happened to him."

"If he cares about me that much, he can just sharding-well come home, then, can't he?" Despite Adelina's brave words, her bottom lip trembled.

Lovina hugged her. "Do you want me to stay with you?"

Adelina waved her off. "No, I'm fine. I have things to do."

She was anything but fine, but she shooed them out the door. As they left Adelina's cavern and walked along the tunnels to his family's quarters, Lovina slipped her hand into Tomaaz's. It felt so natural and right. He smiled at her. "Your arm's not splinted anymore. How's it feeling?" Her bruises had also faded and her cuts had healed.

"A lot better. Marlies has given me exercises to strengthen it."

Every time he looked at her, wonder bubbled inside him. "What about your drawing? Have you done any more pictures?"

She ducked her head and blushed. "A few."

"Can I see them?" He could hardly wait. Looking at Lovina's art was like seeing a hidden landscape within her.

Her face grew even redder. "I, ah ... well, some might be of you."

Oh. He hadn't expected that. Tomaaz chuckled, trying to put her at ease. "Only some? I was hoping they all were."

That made her grin. He squeezed her hand, and they approached his cavern. He hesitated. Lovina hung back too. Eyes locked, they spoke at the same time.

"Do you mind if—"

"Is it all right—"

They laughed nervously.

Tomaaz slipped an arm around her waist and touched his lips to her hair, then pulled closer. "I don't mind at all," he whispered.

Her eyes roamed his face and fell to his lips. Her breath caressed his cheek as he leaned down. And as his lips touched hers, Lovina gave a tiny gasp—the sweetest sound Tomaaz had ever heard.

Then they were kissing. That same wonder bubbled up inside him, like a glorious secret bursting into the sunlight. This was home. This woman, right here, was where he belonged.

Tomaaz drew back to look at Lovina. She was still so physically fragile, yet so strong to have survived Zens' slave camp and years as Old Bill's slave. Abused and drugged by Bill, she'd hidden behind a drab curtain of lank hair, tatty clothes and been dazed by numlock. She'd barely spoken a handful of words in the years he'd known her. Until he'd helped her escape Bill's clutches. Then, little by little, he'd grown to know her. His heart stuttered when he thought of how hard her life had been, how lucky he was to have her, how easily she could've been killed. "Lovina, you're so beautiful. I …" He shook his head staring at her, unsure of what he wanted to say. "I, uh, I've never felt like this about anyone before."

"Neither have I." Her cornflower eyes caressed his face, then she frowned.

"What's wrong?"

"I'm remembering you, so if Zens catches you when you're rescuing Erob, at least I'll have my memories."

He hugged her again, fiercely. "No. I won't let Zens ever separate us. I'll be back. I'm coming home to you."

They entered Tomaaz's family's cavern, next to the infirmary.

"Hello, Lovina." Pa embraced him. "Son, well done, getting home. Lars has told me to let you rest for a few hours and that we'll head out at dusk. I guess you'll want to see the boy?"

Tomaaz nodded. "How's he been?"

"Still has broken sleep." Pa shrugged. "Not much we can do about that, but your mother's trying her best. I've taken him out on Handel a few times, and he seems to like that, not that he's spoken yet."

"Even after all these weeks?"

"He's still mute," Lovina said. "I've spent quite a bit of time with him while you've been gone."

Pa nodded. "You've done a great job, Lovina." He gestured through their caverns toward the mountainside. "He's out on the ledge with Handel now."

Lovina hung back, hesitating.

"Come on." Tomaaz took her hand and they walked past the two smaller sleeping caverns, through the living chamber, to the ledge outside.

The boy was resting against Handel, eyes closed, the wan sunlight bathing his features, an arm flung over Handel's foreleg.

While they were in the council meeting, Maazini must've flown the short distance here, because there was a hillock of orange scales beyond Handel's tail. Tomaaz melded, but Maazini was sleeping too deeply to rouse.

As they approached, the boy's eyes flew open, and he threw his arms up protectively, as if someone was about to beat him.

"It's all right. It's just Tomaaz. He's come home to see you," Lovina crooned, slowing her pace.

The boy's eyes widened. He scrambled to his feet and shot toward Tomaaz, like an arrow to a target. Flinging his scrawny arms around Tomaaz's ribs, he burrowed his head into Tomaaz's midriff.

"Whoa," Tomaaz said, ruffling his hair. "I'm glad to see you too, buddy." He hoisted him up off his feet and hugged him, then he strode over to Handel, placing a hand on his warm scales so he could mind-meld. *"He seems to like you. Are you all right for us to sit here too?"*

"Sure, Tomaaz. Welcome back to Dragons' Hold." Handel lowered his neck, his keen green eyes regarding him.

He and Lovina sat, leaning against Handel's back. Tomaaz cradled the boy on his lap, keeping his voice low as he spoke to him. "I'm so glad to see you. I know I've been gone a while and you must've been worrying about whether I'd come back. I'm home now."

Tentatively, the boy reached his palm up to Tomaaz's face and cupped his cheek.

Lovina sucked her breath in. "That's the first time he's done that," she said.

"You know you're safe with us, don't you?" Tomaaz asked. The memory of the boy's beaten and bloody back flashed to mind. He'd been so frail and light, lifting him had been less effort than carrying a small sack of carrots as Tomaaz had smuggled him out of the slave's sleeping quarters, past tharuks, to the cave where Maazini had been held captive. And now he had to rescue another dragon. "You know how we saved the orange dragon, Maazini?"

The boy nodded.

"Well, there's a blue dragon, Erob, who's been injured by tharuks, just like you were. I know I've just returned, but I need to help save him, so I'll be leaving again soon."

The boy shook his head, his hands clutching at Tomaaz's clothes.

Tomaaz hugged him tight again, gazing at Lovina over the boy's head. "I'm sorry, buddy. I have to go again, but I'll be back."

His whole life had become one long series of farewells and danger.

Wizardry

The chill seeped through Fenni's breeches, slowly making his backside numb. He'd thought his folded cloak would combat the cold, but he'd been here so long the snow had penetrated the thick layers. Trying again, he held his hands a body-width apart, green sparks flitting between them. His brow furrowed in concentration as he drew his palms apart. Bright green sparks flew from hand to hand. Fenni smiled. Just a little wider now. He pulled his hands further apart. With a fizzle, the sparks died, leaving him with nothing but air between his palms—and cold air at that.

Dragon's manky breath! What would it take to get this right? He kicked a clump of snow onto the thin layer of ice coating the stream below. The ice broke with a satisfying crack. He held up his hands again.

Snow or no snow, he would not give in. He was never going to pass wizard training and be able to battle tharuks if he couldn't master fire. His uncle's dead face haunted him—he'd been mauled by tharuks and his death had been ugly. Fenni had vowed to become a mage and avenge him, but the last wizard trials had been a catastrophe. Every other first-year wizard had conjured fireballs except him. Sure, he'd been good with other elements, like wind and water, but he had to control flames too—and real green wizard flames, not just lousy sparks. Wind and water wouldn't kill a tharuk.

Hands apart, he tried again. Sweat rolled off his brow as a thick cord of sparks flowed between his palms. This was much better. He willed the sparks to grow, focusing his mind as his wizard master had taught, although that never usually worked for him. When his hands were as wide as he could hold them, he pushed them inward, trying to compress the sparks into a flame.

He let out a gasp as a burst of fire shot out of his fingers, forming a fireball that roiled between his hands, tongues of green wizard flame licking hungrily at the chilly winter air.

"Ha, ha. I've done it!" Fenni crowed. "Now, Master Giddi will be proud of me."

"Will I?" came the austere voice of his master.

The fireball shrunk and zipped over Fenni's shoulder, shooting into the master mage's outstretched hand. Master Giddi extinguished it with his long bony fingers.

Fenni gulped. His secret was out. "That wasn't me, was it?" he asked.

"No, that wasn't you, Fenni." Master Giddi raised one of his bushy eyebrows—the ones everyone likened to hairy caterpillars. "But you're close."

No closer than he was nine moons ago. Fenni hadn't deliberately told any lies, just left out the details, and always insisted on practicing alone. He rose to his feet, shaking off his cloak, and kicked some snow at a tree trunk.

Those hairy caterpillars now pulled down into a thunderous scowl. Master Giddi's voice was deadly quiet, almost sinister. "So, all these moons when you've been practicing fire, you haven't even made a flame?"

"A tiny burst or two."

"Why didn't you tell me?" Giddi thundered. "I could've helped you. Fool. Now the mage trials are upon us in a few days and you're not ready."

"A few days? But spring equinox is three months away."

Master Giddi pursed his lips, the familiar sign that a lecture was coming. "Not any more. I just got a messenger bird, so I was coming to tell you the news. With war looming, the Wizard Council's moved the trials to winter solstice. We need everyone qualified to fight tharuks. We're leaving for Mage Gate at first light tomorrow." Master Giddi pointed at Fenni, sparks dripping from his fingers. "You've wasted nine moons of your training. You led me to believe your fire skills were fine." He spat in the snow. "I thought by now you'd be conjuring up walls of flame, or even a fire dragon. That you'd have something worthwhile to show for all those hours." Master Giddi's sparks coalesced into a plume of flame. "Do you know what your biggest weakness is?"

"My fire skills." Fenni sighed. It was out now. Soon, everyone would know.

"No, it's your pride. You worry too much about what others think."

Shame washed over Fenni. He'd been embarrassed about his lack of skills, but it was nothing to how he felt now.

"So, now that you're ready to learn, hold your hands out and close your eyes. Cast out your consciousness. Sense the forest around you," Master Giddi said, as if Fenni was a littling, not nearly eighteen summers old.

Fenni thrust his senses out. Cold feet, rustling leaves …

"Feel the energy in the core of your being, right down through your feet, connecting with the earth. Sense each tree; the forest as a whole; how everything vibrates with nature's energy. When you feel that familiar hum of *sathir* …"

Fenni opened his eyes. He hadn't ever told anyone, but he'd never felt the hum that everyone talked about.

The wizard cocked a bushy eyebrow at Fenni and stared at him for a long moment before saying, "That doesn't work for you, does it?"

"Feeling nature's energy? No, it doesn't. Never has."

"You told me you'd mastered it privately. Why in the Egg's name didn't you say something earlier?" Master Giddi snapped. "Stretch a hand out."

Fenni sighed. "With all due respect, Master Giddi, I don't see how—"

"Quiet." The master mage's voice was soft, but, as usual, held power.

Fenni obeyed, holding a hand up, flinching as Master Giddi touched his freezing little finger with his bony forefinger.

"Feel that?"

Fenni's finger was buzzing. "Yes, I do," he said. Amazing, it was like a hive of bees in his fingertip.

"And this?"

A vibration traveled down his finger into his hand, making his palm tingle too. "Incredible. How did you do that?"

"Now …" The master mage lifted his finger into the air and Fenni's finger was pulled up, as if they were attached, until his arm was stretched high. Giddi curled his own fingers into his palm and put them in his cloak pockets.

Lucky for some, keeping their hands warm.

"Now, close your eyes again and sense the forest," Master Giddi said.

The air around Fenni's fingers seemed to pulse with life. Weird. *Is that what other mages felt?* He forced his senses out further, and bit by bit, the hum of the earth vibrated through him. Energy radiated from the strongwood trees, making his skin hum. A creature lumbered through the forest nearby and a surge rushed through him. Fenni snapped his eyes open and let out a whoop. "I can do it. I can feel *sathir*."

Master Giddi threw up his hand, motioning him to be quiet.

A chilling snarl rang out. Something crashed through the bushes toward them.

"Tharuks," hissed Master Giddi. "Hide."

Fenni scaled the nearest strongwood and pulled his invisibility cloak around him. Not that it would do much good. His footprints in the snow were a dead giveaway.

Master Giddi scrambled up after him, but instead of hiding himself in his cloak among the branches, the master mage stood on a sturdy branch, parting the foliage to get a better look.

Piggy snout twitching, a tharuk lumbered into view. On two legs, its matted fur prevented it from succumbing to the cold. The beast followed Master Giddi's prints toward the tree, then took a running jump, launching itself at the trunk. Claws sprang from its fingertips in midair. Gripping the bark as it landed, the beast swarmed up the strongwood, the stench of rot wafting over Fenni. His heart pounded.

Invisibility cloak be cursed. Fenni grabbed his bow, nocked an arrow, and fired. The shot thudded into the strongwood's trunk, next to the tharuk's hand. Master Giddi flung flames at the beast, but the foliage was in the way. Fenni shot another arrow, hitting the tharuk's arm. It shook the arrow off like a mosquito. Beady red eyes boring into Fenni, it swung onto his branch, tusks drooling dark saliva.

His flame had to work. Now. Fenni desperately tried to sense nature's energy. He held up his hand to blast a fireball at the tharuk. Green sparks dribbled from his fingers onto the branch, sputtering out—useless.

A fireball flew past the tharuk's ear. Master Giddi was aiming at the beast, but the tree trunk was in his way. Master Giddi thudded to the ground, bellowing at the tharuk. The beast ignored Giddi, lunging toward Fenni.

He scrambled further along the branch. Master Giddi shot an arc of green flame toward the tharuk. It ducked, flinging itself onto its stomach, pulling itself along the bough after Fenni.

The branch was getting mighty slender, bowing with their weight. Fenni clambered as far as he dared. He fished his knife out of its sheath and flung it at the tharuk just as a fireball blasted the creature off the branch in a trail of flame and smoke. Fenni's knife thunked into the branch. The tharuk thudded to the snow.

Heart booming like a drum, Fenni peered down at the dead beast. There was a smoking hole in the side of its torso. The stench of burnt hair and flesh drifted up. He wrinkled his nose and swallowed. That had been a sharding close call—he could've been dead meat, like his uncle. "So that's why mages have to master flame," he joked shakily.

Master Giddi gave the beast a nudge with his boot, then looked up. "Indeed," he replied. "And the sooner you do, the better."

§

Hours later, Fenni was in Giddi's cabin playing with a tiny green fireball that shot erratically between his fingertips. Surely, now, Master Giddi would be impressed.

Suddenly, the fireball darted at the master mage's face. Giddi caught it, snapping his fingers shut around it. Face grim, he raised one of those infamous bushy eyebrows at Fenni.

"Ah, sorry, I, um ..."

"Not good enough. You think you can kill a tharuk like that? Come on, Fenni, focus. You need drive, precision and more flame. You'll set half of Great Spanglewood Forest alight if you don't master this. If you can't control your own flame, the Wizard Council will never let you loose."

Face growing hot, Fenni scuffed his boot on the floorboards, not meeting the master wizard's eye. Shards, he'd been doing so well.

"You got distracted and thought of me, so that's where your fireball went. That won't do in battle. Now, go and practice outside in the clearing, so you don't burn my cabin down. I'm not losing my home to a fledgling wizard."

Fledgling? Even though he knew Master Giddi was goading him, Fenni rose to the bait. "I'm not a fledgling and you know it. I've passed my first trials. I only need to master the fireball."

"Good, you've got two days."

"But two days is—"

"Yes, I agree, way too long for an experienced wizard like yourself, so I'll give you a day and a half. Now, outside. Get practicing."

"A day and a half?" Fenni spluttered. He strode across the threshold, pulling the door shut. Shards, he'd never do it.

"Yes, you will. And I want your fireball looping among those trees without damaging a leaf." Master Giddi's voice sounded in Fenni's mind.

Fenni spun, jaw dropping and pushed the door open. "How did you mind-meld with me?"

Eyes crinkling, Giddi laughed.

"Can you teach me?"

"Maybe. Master your fireball."

"With only two days until trials, I won't even have time to sleep," Fenni grumbled.

Giddi chuckled. "Nothing like a little focus to hone skills. I'll check your fireball tonight."

"Tonight." Fenni snapped his jaw shut and stalked out the door, leaving it open to the snow.

"Yes, tonight. There's more advanced fire training to master, too."

Oh shards, he'd fail his trial.

Snake-tongue

"You fool," Lars yelled. "All my archers without arrows for half a day. What would've happened if we'd been attacked?" His piercing blue eyes raked Kierion from head to foot.

"I didn't think of that, sir." Kierion made himself meet Lars' scathing gaze. "It was meant as a prank." He had to tough this out or the council leader would think even less of him. Playing the fool was one thing, but Kierion prided himself on not being a coward.

The whole of Dragons' Hold had been in an uproar that morning when the dragon masters had discovered the arrow flingers had lost their weapons. Well, not all of their weapons. He'd left an arrow or two in each archer's personal quiver, but he *had* cleared out the weapons store. Their panic had shocked him out of his playful mood.

"Imagine tharuks swarming over Dragon's Teeth and us sitting here weaponless."

"I can't really imagine that, sir," Kierion said. He'd been such an idiot. He just hadn't thought. "I mean, those mountains are the guardians of Dragons' Hold because they're impenetrable, but what if our riders had been called away to Montanara or to a village because tharuks had attacked? We could've lost lives as a result of my prank." His neck grew warm as shame washed over him.

Lars' eyebrows shot up in surprise. "So, there is a brain rattling around somewhere in your skull." He shook his head, sighing. "It seems we have three issues here: the longstanding rivalry between sword fighters and archers; your inventive nature; and the grave danger we're all facing." He thrummed his fingers against his breeches.

Grave danger? Well, that was the tharuks. But inventive nature? No one had called him inventive before. A fool, yes. A prankster, too. Growing up on a farm on the outskirts of Montanara, he'd been known by the locals for his high jinks. He cocked his head, waiting for his inevitable punishment.

Lars' eyes narrowed as he appraised Kierion for more agonizing moments.

Kierion's spirits sank into his boots. He'd been hoping he'd come to the council leader's attention so he could be in the next crop of trainee dragon riders. He sighed. There was no way that could ever happen now. He'd intended to retrieve the arrows before the council found out. But apparently, they'd all been up at the crack of dawn for an emergency council meeting. Thank the Egg, no villages had been attacked. It had seemed like such a fun idea, but he really had been stupid.

"I can't let an action this foolhardy go unpunished. You're on kitchen duty until further notice: an hour before dawn and two hours after dusk. No skipping classes or any training, or your hours will be doubled. You must also fulfill all of your usual duties. I assume you had help from other *blade thrusters* to carry out this *prank*?" Lars spat the word prank, as if it was dirty.

It felt strange hearing their nickname, *blade thrusters*, roll off the council leaders' tongue—young and petty. "Um, yes, a few people helped me." He didn't dare mention that every trainee blade thruster had been in on the gag.

"Good. Then, unless you want to be stuck on kitchen duty for months, you'd better get them to own up and help."

Months? Kierion swallowed. Who'd willingly want to scrub Benji's smelly old soup cauldrons for months?

"The more of your accomplices that help, the shorter your kitchen duty will be." Lars held up a finger. "And don't let me catch you doing anything stupid again."

Kierion nodded. Months of kitchen duty. There had to be a way out of that.

Lars shot Kierion another piercing gaze. "Where are the arrows?"

With Lars grilling him, it was hard to swallow. "Um, up on Lookout Peak."

"Lookout Peak?" Lars frowned. "Surely you mean halfway up? Not at the top?"

"Ah …"

Lars shook his head. "You never do things by halves, do you?"

"Not usually, sir. Ma taught me that if a job's worth doing, it's worth doing well."

A chuckle escaped Lars. The council leader was enjoying watching him squirm. But then Lars asked, "Tell me, how did you get all those arrows up Lookout Peak? Did a dragon help you?"

"Oh, no, sir. I'd never involve a dragon, sir. Some of the blade thrusters—ah, sword fighters—collected the arrows with me during dinner time, then one helped me bring them up the peak."

Lars' brow furrowed. "But how did you get them up there? It's a steep climb."

"We dragged a sledge."

To Kierion's surprise, Lars burst out laughing.

He shifted from foot to foot, unsure what to make of the leader's outburst.

"What did the archers do to deserve having all their arrows stolen?"

Before he could think, indignation had Kierion blurting it out, "Those arrow flingers filled our scabbards with honey, sir, so we couldn't draw our swords. Took hours to clean up the mess."

"Indeed." He scratched his beard. "I'll definitely shorten your tenure in the kitchens if you manage to get your *enemies* to front up to kitchen duty too." Lars stabbed a finger at him. "But remember, the archers are *not* your real enemies. Tharuks are. Those same *arrow flingers* may save your lives in battle. From now on, I want to see teamwork."

That would be impossible. "Yes, sir, I'll see what I can do."

"No, Kierion, don't just try. Make it happen. Now, go and retrieve those arrows."

Kierion nodded. What else could he do? If he didn't want to lose his chance at being a dragon rider, he had to find some way of breaching the growing rivalry between the arrow fling—no, the archers and the sword fighters. Rivalry he'd been happy inflaming. He turned to walk from Lars' cavern.

"Before you go, Kierion, there's one thing I've been meaning to ask you."

Kierion turned back. "Yes?"

"Is it true that, back in Montanara, you strung a whole flock of chickens up a tree without harming any of them?"

Kierion groaned inwardly. So that gossip had spread to Dragons' Hold too. His face grew hot. He met Lars' gaze anyway. "Yes, sir, I did."

Lars laughed. "Brilliant, absolutely brilliant. Now, go and fetch those arrows back before I get Singlar to flame your breeches."

As Kierion shut Lars' door, the council leader was still chuckling.

Great. Scaling two hours up Lookout Peak to retrieve the sledge full of arrows was going to be easy compared to convincing both the arrow flingers and the blade thrusters to do weeks of kitchen duty—and learn to work well together. But Lars was right. They needed to fight tharuks, not each other.

§

Lovina and Gret were about to enter the girls' sleeping cavern when a sharp voice echoed down the corridor. "Ezaara as Queen's Rider? That's the biggest joke I've heard in years. She doesn't deserve the title." Lovina put her arm out to stop Gret from rounding the corner and pressed her finger to her lips. Gret raised her eyebrows and they huddled against the stone wall to listen.

"But Zaarusha chose her," said a young voice.

"Don't be stupid. We all know Ezaara's not the rightful Queen's Rider. It contradicts Anakisha's prophecy."

"What do you mean? She imprinted with Zaarusha."

"How do we really know that? She could have fooled the queen. Anakisha's prophecies have never failed, therefore Ezaara *can't* be Queen's Rider."

Lovina turned to Gret mouthing, *'What?'*

"Come on, we're going to be late to training." Footsteps approached.

Gret yanked Lovina back down the tunnel and around a corner. "There's somewhere we can talk along here." They jogged further until they were outside Ezaara's cavern, then Gret pulled Lovina down the Queen's Rider's tunnel and into a hidden alcove opposite Ezaara's door, barely large enough for both of them.

"I never knew this was here, and I've often visited Ezaara."

"Erob showed me this place."

Lovina arched an eyebrow. "A dragon couldn't fit in here."

Gret chuckled. "By mind-meld. He asked me to watch Ezaara one night. I caught Simeon trying to sneak into her chamber."

"Thank the Egg, him and his parents have been banished. What's this prophecy Sofia was talking about?" Tomaaz had said she had the gift of prophecy. Maybe she could learn something. A tiny bud of wonder started to unfurl inside Lovina. Could she—Bill's useless slave, less than the dust under his feet—have a valuable talent? If she did, she could contribute to Dragons' Realm. She wouldn't be a nobody, shackled and beaten; she could be special—like Anakisha.

Gret snorted. "Anakisha prophesied about the next Queen's Rider. There's a verse or something. Apparently Ezaara doesn't fit the criteria."

"Why?"

"Ssh."

The other girls were barreling past on their way to training. "I'll beat you all at knife throwing," Sofia said, her cruel laughter hammering Lovina's ears like a woodpecker.

When they were gone, Gret said, "Look, it's some old prophecy made almost twenty years ago. But I know Ezaara's the true Queen's Rider. I've seen her fly. I've seen her with Zaarusha. Besides, Master Roberto tested her—he'd know if she was fake." She shook her head. "I'm not sure how much use prophecy is.

The last master of prophecy was hopeless, and Anakisha's prophecy is a stupid legacy that makes people argue. Come on, we'd better get to class."

Gret had a point. Lovina's shoulders slumped.

"Hey, what's up?" Gret said as they walked to class. "Don't worry, Sofia's wrong. Ezaara's fine as Queen's Rider. That prophecy was dumb."

Exactly. The bud of hope inside Lovina withered.

Erob's Rescue

Tomaaz and Pa were finally ready. Ezaara patted Zaarusha's side. *"You've been very patient."*

"I'm itching to get my son," the queen replied.

"You ready?" Pa asked, seated on Handel. Tomaaz was wedged in behind him. Maazini was too exhausted to come with them, his orange scales pale, even in the blazing sunset.

Ezaara patted Zaarusha's saddlebag. "Healing supplies, fishing nets, and I also brought a waterskin, in case Erob's thirsty."

Boots thudded in Handel's den, and Adelina ran onto the ledge. "Lars finally said I can help rescue Erob." Her cheeks were pink and voice breathy.

Ezaara melded with Singlar, Lars' dragon. *"Is Lars all right with Adelina coming along?"* she asked.

"He relented a few minutes ago. It seems she wore him down," came the old dragon's sardonic reply.

Ezaara sent him a mental chuckle. Good. It made sense Adelina was coming. Besides being Roberto's sister, Adelina knew Erob the best. Although how she'd convinced Lars, Ezaara had no idea. "Adelina can ride with me," she said.

Zaarusha extended a foreleg to help Adelina climb up into the saddle.

"We have to get Erob to safety as quickly as possible," Pa said. "Ezaara, please give Adelina some freshweed too, to mask her scent." He nodded at Adelina as she stuffed the bitter leaves into her mouth. "We've all had ours. Remember, Erob is our goal. If tharuks are around, we'll communicate via our dragons to decide our strategy. If Erob's gut is too badly injured, Ezaara may need to stitch him up temporarily before we move him. Before our dragons mind-meld with Maazini to get Erob's exact location, does anyone have questions?"

"Yes," said Adelina. "Why aren't the council rescuing my brother?"

Hans frowned. "As far as I understand, the council wants us to retrieve Erob first, then we'll use the information he has to free Roberto."

Thank the Egg, Adelina had asked. Ezaara was half crazy with worry.

Ezaara, Zaarusha and Handel mind-melded with Maazini.

Ezaara was hit with Maazini's sense of bone-weariness. Then she saw Erob, his head slumped on stony ground near a glade of trees. The side of his belly was ruptured. In her mind's eye, they ascended and Erob grew smaller. It wasn't a glade of trees he was lying near; he was in a clearing in a vast forest—Great Spanglewood Forest—with mountains rising a short distance away.

"Those are the Terramites," Zaarusha said. "He's very near Death Valley. There are bound to be tharuks nearby."

"Then we'll deal with them," Handel snarled.

Ezaara held up the ring Ma had lent her—Anakisha's ancient ring of power. "Are you ready, Pa?" At his nod, she slipped the ring on her finger, rubbed it, calling, "Kisha."

"Ana," called Pa, rubbing his ring.

With a pop, Dragons' Hold disappeared.

Suddenly, they were in a tunnel of billowing clouds, bathed in golden light, their dragons suspended in midair. A willowy woman in a white gown approached, the clouds visible through her transparent figure. Ezaara recognized her from Zaarusha's memories—Zaarusha's last rider, Anakisha, who'd died in a desperate battle years ago.

Zaarusha crooned a bittersweet melody of love and loss.

Anakisha smiled, mind-melding with all of them. *"The years have treated you well, Zaarusha. Thank you for bringing your new rider and Hans to see me."*

"It's good to see you again, Anakisha." Hans said. *"My daughter, Ezaara, is yet to fully qualify, however, she's doing well."*

"It's pleasing to see Zaarusha so well loved." Anakisha nodded at Ezaara. *"Remember, only use these rings of power in dire need."* A dark shadow rippled along the tunnel wall.

"We're in need. Zaarusha's son, Erob, is dying," Ezaara melded.

Zaarusha rumbled, showing Anakisha their destination.

Her ex-rider smiled. *"It's wonderful to see you again, my friend."*

With a crack, they were above Great Spanglewood Forest. The sinking sun splashed its blood-red rays over the jagged Terramites. Roars ricocheted off the trees. Burning torches blazed. Tharuks yanked on chains, dragging Erob's limp body across a stony clearing.

Ezaara readied her bow, mind-melding with Erob. Nothing. A faint blue thread of *sathir* was all she could sense. *"Zaarusha, I can't talk to him."*

"Neither can I, but I can talk to them," she snarled, diving at the tharuks. Fire gusted from her jaws, sweeping a group of beasts off their feet and leaving them

smoking. An arrow whipped past Ezaara's cheek as Adelina let one fly. A tharuk fell, the shaft embedded in its eye.

More tharuks ran from the trees, aiming arrows. Ezaara loosed an arrow, hitting a tharuk in the chest. It stumbled, crashing to the stone.

Handel roared past, chasing a group of beasts.

Arrows rose in the air, whistling toward Zaarusha's wing, dripping green gunge. *"Look out, limplock."* Ezaara shrieked.

The queen swerved. *"Thanks."*

In Erob's wake was a trail of churned-up earth and stones where the beasts had dragged him. A wide swathe glistened in the setting sun. *"Zaarusha, lower, I need to see what that is."*

Zaarusha swooped low, heading over the trail, blasting flame at the monsters in her way. Her fire illuminated an ugly sight. A wide slick of Erob's blood marred the ground, leading to an enormous rent in his belly. His pale, moist entrails glinted. Ezaara's hand flew to her mouth as her gorge rose.

"Pull harder," yelled a tharuk troop leader, his bellow carrying above the mayhem.

The beasts heaved on the chains. Erob's belly skin split further, the gaping wound growing with each tug.

"They're killing him," Adelina screamed in Ezaara's ear. "We have to stop them."

Zaarusha swooped lower, slashing tharuks with her talons as she sped toward her son.

Adelina's arms loosened from around Ezaara's waist. Chill air rushed across Ezaara's back. Adelina dropped off Zaarusha. With a crunch of stone, rolling to stand, Adelina was running to Erob, sword out.

"No, Adelina," Ezaara cried.

Handel swooped. Stones crunched as Tomaaz dropped to the ground and pelted after her. Handel flew above them, blasting tharuks with fire, clearing the way to Erob.

Zaarusha whirled to flame a new troop of beasts that burst from the trees. Ezaara nocked and fired, felling tharuks as fast as she could, but more kept coming.

The queen grabbed the trunk of a young tree and wrenched. Roots ripped from the earth. Rocks and clods fell from the tree's tangled roots onto the tharuks, knocking some out. She swung the tree, sending tharuks crashing to the rocks. With a roar, Zaarusha dropped the tree onto the beasts, trapping most of them beneath it.

Opening her jaws, she blasted fire. The branches caught. Flames licked along the trunk, incinerating the beasts in a column of fire that rose to meet the bloody-red sky. Through the stinking smoke, Ezaara aimed at two tharuks that had escaped, felling them with her arrows.

Zaarusha wheeled back to Erob.

Near Erob's head, Tomaaz was hacking at a tharuk. Its claws swung near his face and he jumped back, his spine against Erob's snout, then lunged.

With a half-snarl-half-shriek, the tharuk fell, an arrow in its neck. More arrows flew from Pa's bow, hitting tharuks in the arms, thighs and head. Handel spun to the beasts yanking the chains.

"Move dragon," yelled a large tharuk, waving a torch.

Tharuks yanked the rope around Erob's neck. The momentum swung Erob's head across the stones, knocking Tomaaz to the ground.

Adelina jumped in, slashing her sword across a tharuk's neck. Its head flew to the ground in a spray of black blood.

"Let's clean up this mess," Zaarusha snarled. She swiped at the tharuk leader, impaling his neck on her talon, then ripped his head from his body, tossing the remains into the trees. She roared, swathes of fire cutting down the tharuks tugging on Erob's neck chain. Handel attacked the beasts yanking the other chains.

"Not too close. We'll burn Erob."

"Retreat," a tharuk yelled. The remaining tharuks dropped the chains, fleeing for the forest. Handel chased them with tongues of fire.

As the sun dipped behind the Terramites, Zaarusha landed near her son. *"Hurry, Ezaara."*

Erob's deep blue *sathir* was weak and flickering. Even though his sides barely moved as he breathed, the sharp imprint of his ribs pressed against his skin above the gaping rent in his belly.

No, not Erob. They'd journeyed for days together, searching for Roberto in the Robandi desert. His dry humor had stopped Ezaara from going crazy. Losing him would break Roberto's heart.

Handel thumped to the ground, stones flying. "Tomaaz, Adelina," barked Pa. "Stay vigilant. Swords at the ready." He rushed over. "What can I do to help?"

"Bring me torches, as many as you can."

Adelina ignored Pa, flinging her arms around Erob's scaly neck. "Come on, boy," she said, voice shaky. "Roberto needs you. I need you. You can't die on us. I refuse to let you." Even in the torchlight, it was easy to see Erob was dying. The ragged wound was as long as a man, and oozing guts and yellow pus.

Zaarusha butted her head against his snout, but Erob didn't respond. Her sorrow washed through Ezaara.

"Pa and Tomaaz, ready the nets. Adelina, tell Erob to hold on."

Ezaara sloshed water over Erob's intestines. If they dried out, they'd crack and there'd be no saving him. Luckily blood seepage had kept them moist. She dampened a clean cloth and held it against his gut, pushing it back inside the wound. "Adelina, hold his skin together, please."

Adelina pressed the cloth over the end of the wound, holding Erob's gut in. Ezaara threaded her needle. If she didn't stitch him temporarily before they moved him, his gut would split wide open, spilling his intestines. Erob didn't even flinch as she jabbed the needle through his tough hide. Sweat beading her forehead, she tugged the edges of the wound together in long uneven stitches. Adelina moved along the wound as she worked, holding the edges together.

Handel stalked the clearing. Tomaaz and Pa prowled around, bows nocked, keeping an eye out for tharuks.

"Monte Vista, where I grew up, is an hour's flight away. We're near where I first met Handel." Pa's brow furrowed as he paced past Erob.

A few weeks ago, Pa had told Ezaara the story of how his sister, Evelyn, had been killed at the hands of tharuks near the foot of the Terramites. Was Pa remembering his sister too? She jabbed the needle back through Erob's skin.

At last, Ezaara was done. "His guts are on the inside now. Let's get him back to Dragons' Hold."

Erob. Please, son, wake up," Zaarusha begged. Her desperate attempts to meld with the dying dragon yielded nothing.

Ezaara strode to Erob's head. "Adelina, hold the corner of his lip up." She jammed a vial of piaua between his fangs and tipped. Erob swallowed. Thank the Egg.

"We have to get the nets under Erob," Ezaara said. "Zaarusha, Handel, if you roll him, we can slide them under halfway, then we'll have to roll him back to pull the nets through. Hopefully the stitches will hold."

A gust of air few from Erob's nostrils. *"Ezaara?"*

"Erob, You're awake."

"Barely," he answered weakly.

Ezaara's eyes stung. *"We're using Roberto's fishing nets to carry you home."*

"A dragon-fish?" Erob attempted a weak chuckle, but it turned into a splutter.

"More like a fish out of water," she answered, motioning the others into place. *"We have to move you to get the nets under you. It'll hurt, but please hold on."*

"Now," Ezaara commanded.

Zaarusha and Handel squatted and pushed against Erob's side, rolling his injured belly off the ground. Still melded, Ezaara felt the wave of pain rippling through his wound. Scrambling between their limbs, Adelina, Tomaaz and Pa unrolled the net, pushing it under Erob's belly as far as they could.

They gently lowered Erob back down onto the nets.

"The hardest part will be to hold him while we pull the nets through," Ezaara said. Tomaaz, Pa and Adelina joined her on the other side, faces grim in the flickering torchlight.

They positioned themselves, ready to grab the nets as Handel and Zaarusha rolled Erob. The dragons shoved.

"I see the nets." Tomaaz darted under Erob's belly to grab one end. Pa, Adelina and Ezaara crawled under to help. Crouched under the dragon's bulk, groping for the nets in the dark, Ezaara realized what a far cry this life was from the innocent sheltered life she'd led in Lush Valley.

"A far better life," Zaarusha mind-melded. *"What you're doing now matters. You've already saved the lives of many—including mine and Roberto's."*

Ezaara could feel the strain of lifting Erob in Zaarusha's thoughts. *"Can you hold him?"*

"Only for a few moments longer."

"The dragons need us to be quick," Ezaara said, tugging a length of net and flattening it.

"My part's done." Adelina scrambled out of the way.

"Mine too," Pa called, crawling out between Handel's limbs to safer ground.

"This end's stuck," Tomaaz called. "Ezaara, can you give me a hand?"

Ezaara slipped along to his end of the net and yanked it. *"Handel, Zaarusha, a little higher."*

The dragons strained and pushed Erob further.

Erob let out a moan that made Ezaara's skin crawl. "Shards, we're hurting him."

"Fast!" Zaarusha's mental voice trembled. *"I can't hold him."*

Ezaara yanked. Suddenly, the net was free. She sprawled on her backside under Erob's descending belly.

"*Move. I'm slipping,*" Zaarusha barked, talons scrabbling in the stones.

Tomaaz's strong hands pulled Ezaara backward as Erob's bulk landed right where she'd been.

Gasping for breath, she stared at Tomaaz. "That was close."

He nodded and swallowed. "Dragon squash—never grew that on our farm, did we?"

Behind them, twigs cracked and a low snarl came from the trees. As quick as a starving dragonet, Adelina snatched up her bow and fired. A yell sounded. Pa nocked his bow, too, aiming for dark shadows among the trees. Handel gusted flame at the tharuks.

Zaarusha mind-melded, "*Ezaara, we have to go.*" She snatched up the net on one side of Erob. "*Handel, take the other side. Ezaara, tell everyone we're leaving.*"

"To the dragons. Let's go," Ezaara yelled.

Pa and Adelina ran to Handel, but a beast leaped out of the trees, straight for Tomaaz. He slashed with his sword.

Shards! More tharuks were nearly upon him. Ezaara fired an arrow into a beast's neck, then slung her bow over her back and ran at the tharuks. She swung her sword, connecting with flesh, fur and bone. More and more beasts were pouring out of the forest. "Tomaaz, too many tharuks. We have to go." Ezaara ducked a tharuk's claws and parried. "Hurry, now."

They raced to Zaarusha, two tharuks on their heels. As they scrambled onto Zaarusha's back, Handel blasted the beasts.

Roars and snarls broke out as tharuks ran at them.

Handel and Zaarusha grasped the net on their respective sides of Erob's body and flapped, lifting him off the ground. "*Quick, the rings. He's no lightweight,*" Zaarusha melded.

Ezaara and Pa rubbed the rings, calling Anakisha's name. With a pop, the snarling beasts and smoldering tharuks disappeared.

Anakisha floated toward them, surrounded by golden light.

"*Liesar, we have Erob,*" Ezaara mind-melded.

"Quick, Anakisha, to Dragons' Hold," Hans called. "Erob is dying."

§

Marlies paced on the ledge outside the infirmary. Her needles and squirrel gut thread were ready on a small table. She'd also prepared clean herb infusion—which Liesar kept warming every time it cooled—vials of piaua, and limplock remedy in case Erob had been poisoned. All they needed now was Erob. What was taking Ezaara, Tomaaz and Hans so long? With instantaneous travel, they should've returned ages ago. The torch stuttered in a chill wind that rippled across the basin. She stopped to gaze out over Dragons' Hold.

Something strange was going on. A dragon master was stuck in Death Valley, yet no rescue party had been sent. The council hadn't refused to rescue Roberto, but they hadn't acted yet. Why would they leave one of their own, a master with highly valuable skills, in Death Valley? She tugged her jerkin closer around her and went into their quarters next to the infirmary to fetch a cloak. Cold affected her more since she'd returned from Death Valley two moons ago. And fatigue.

Lately, she was always tired.

When she'd taken the blue piaua berries and sunk into a deep coma to prevent Zens from torturing her, she'd never realized that it would leave her with bone-deep tiredness that she could never shake. On the outside, no one guessed. Since she'd been reinstated as Master Healer, she fulfilled her duties, but exhaustion dogged her. Throwing her cloak over her shoulders, Marlies paced through the infirmary.

"*Marlies, Erob's coming,*" Liesar melded from the ledge.

Marlies strode out to the ledge. What she saw made her blood freeze.

Erob was suspended in the nets between Handel and Zaarusha, but below him hung a tharuk. Clinging to the bottom of the nets with one hand, it was sawing at the ropes with its dagger. Any moment now, Erob would plunge to his death.

"*Liesar, there's a tharuk on board.*" Marlies ran to the infirmary, snatched her bow and arrows. "*Tell Handel and Zaarusha to hold right there. I'm getting weapons.*"

"*Done.*"

She raced back to the ledge. Shards. In the flickering torchlight, with the dragons fighting to keep Erob aloft, the tharuk was swinging like a rag doll. She couldn't get a clean shot.

The beast drew its dagger back and plunged it into Erob's belly wound. Erob bellowed in pain.

Marlies loosed her arrow.

The tharuk thudded to the ledge, its knife skittering across the stone. Marlies kicked the monster's body off the ledge and it thunked down the mountainside to the basin.

The fraying nets ripped.

"*Support Erob,*" she melded to Liesar.

Liesar dived under the hole in the net, using her body to help ease Erob to the stone.

Ezaara sprang down off Zaarusha. "He has a belly wound, blood loss, is dehydrated and may have an infection."

Erob was listless, his scales fading. "Ezaara, check the rest of his body for wounds or arrow marks in case he's been limplocked. I need water."

"I'll get some." Adelina dashed into the infirmary.

"What should I do?" Tomaaz asked. Shoulders slumped, he looked ready to collapse.

"Go and lie down and rest that hip," Marlies said, taking the water from Adelina.

She dampened the wound. It was a ragged gash, weeping yellow pus. Marlies cut the stitches with her surgical knife. Ezaara bathed Erob's exposed gut with clean herb. Marlies lifted back the edges of the wound and swabbed the pus away. They made a good team, working quickly and efficiently. If she wasn't Queen's Rider, Ezaara would have made a wonderful healer.

A low growl built in Erob's throat.

"Adelina," Marlies said, "please soothe him. The last thing I need is an irate dragon thrashing around."

The young girl placed her hand on the great blue dragon's snout, eyes shiny with tears. Zaarusha crooned to her son, resting her snout on his shoulder. Soon, Erob's growls turned to whimpers.

Hans and Ezaara kept Marlies replenished with clean herb, but Ezaara seemed distracted and pensive.

"*Hans,*" Marlies mind-melded. "*What happened tonight? Ezaara seems off-color.*"

"*I expect she's just tired. We fought off a couple of tharuk troops.*"

"*Maybe that's it. Pass the piaua, please.*" Marlies wasn't convinced. Something was eating at her daughter, but she had bigger things to worry about with a dying dragon on her hands.

Death Valley

With every swab of Erob's belly, every dose of clean herb, and each drop of piaua, Ezaara wondered whether Roberto had similar wounds. Was he lying somewhere in Death Valley, his blood staining Zens' floor? Was Zens battering his mind and crushing his will?

Zens delighted in brutality. Each moment in the evil commander's presence lessened Roberto's chance of survival.

She couldn't delay any longer. If the council didn't want to act, then she would. *"Zaarusha, you saw tharuks dragging Erob across jagged stones. They nearly killed him,"* Ezaara mind-melded. *"They'll kill Roberto too. I can't leave him with Zens."*

"My son is gravely wounded, Ezaara."

"We'll go when Erob has been healed. I still have Anakisha's ring, so we'll be quick. No one will miss us."

"Mother." Erob's voice was weak in Ezaara and Zaarusha's minds. *"Save Roberto … please."*

"My heart is heavy, Ezaara," Zaarusha said. *"Roberto's already offered his life twice for us: once when he was banished in your stead; and again when Ajeuria attacked me. We'll go, and answer to the council once we fetch him home."* Zaarusha placed a wing over Erob's back, protectively. *"But before we do, we must participate in Erob's healing circle."*

"Of course. I'd do anything to help Erob." Ezaara burned to leave, but they couldn't abandon Erob.

They all stood around Erob in a ring, dragons interspersed with their riders, hands on hides, with Marlies touching Erob. Ezaara watched Handel's bronze *sathir* stream through Hans and into Zaarusha, whose multi-colored energy soared around Ezaara, then flowed into Liesar, mingling with her silver glow. Silver light flowed through Ma's hands into Erob. His scales grew darker, healthier. His *sathir* deepened in color until it was midnight blue.

After what seemed like forever, Erob opened his golden eyes, fixing them on Ezaara.

Ezaara mind-melded with him. *"Thank the Egg, you're better. We're going to get Roberto, in secret. What do you know that could help us find him?"*

Hope gave Erob's voice strength. *"They took him over Devil's Gate. That's all I know. Find him, Ezaara and Mother. Find my rider."*

Ezaara inclined her head, and she climbed upon Zaarusha.

"Ezaara," called Ma. "You look tired. Do get some rest."

"Good idea. Thanks, Ma," Ezaara replied. A great idea, but not one she'd be using tonight.

Zaarusha leapt off the ledge and they flew across the dark basin. Ezaara chewed some freshweed while they soared, waiting for the blue guard patrol to fly past. When no one was watching, she rubbed Anakisha's ring, whispering, "Kisha," and they disappeared.

Once more, they faced Anakisha.

"Anakisha, we have to find Master Roberto," Ezaara said, sharing a memory of his face. *"He's in Death Valley. Please send us near Devil's Gate."*

With a crack, Zaarusha and Ezaara appeared above a mountain with a crude watchtower on it.

"This is Devil's Gate." Zaarusha said. *"Your mother sneaked past here, injured, only to be captured down the other side. I'll drop you on the next peak over."* Zaarusha winged away.

Tharuks shouted below.

"Do you think they've seen us?" Ezaara asked.

"For your sake, I hope not." Zaarusha landed down the far side of the next peak. *"Just in case, wear the cloak Roberto gave you,"* the queen said. *"It's magicked. When you pull it around you, you'll be invisible and leave no scent."*

Ezaara pulled the cloak on, hugged Zaarusha's neck, and sped up the slope.

Zaarusha took to the sky. *"Find Roberto, Ezaara, but remember, if it gets too dangerous, get out."*

Near the crest of the hill, Ezaara dropped to her belly and crept forward, peering between rocks at two tharuks warming their hands over a fire. Slinking off, she picked her way through the snowy terrain down a rocky trail.

A guttural voice cut through the night. "Bill sees shadow in sky. Now we climb up here. Not fair. Our patrol finished."

Tharuks were coming up the trail. Ezaara slunk behind a rock, pulling her cloak around her, heart pounding. Old Bill from Lush Valley had been a tharuk spy. Were they talking about the same Bill?

"Quiet," snarled another tharuk, tromping uphill. "Bill will hear you. Want Zens' *reward*?"

"Not reward. Not me. After reward, 378 dead."

"Said quiet." A grunt of pain followed.

An answering roar came from up the trail. Close, too close. She was trapped between two groups. Gods, she needed a better hiding place. Ezaara scurried, half sliding down the track. Perhaps there was somewhere around that next bend.

An overpowering stench wafted on the breeze—tharuks were around the next corner. What was that shadow on the cliff? She scrambled over to a deep fissure with dirty churned-up snow at the entrance—well-used, but her only chance.

A spine-chilling snarl echoed from around the bend. Neck hair standing on end, Ezaara plunged into the fissure, tugging her cloak around her.

Inside, candle stubs flickered in recesses in the rock, casting light and leaping shadows. A tunnel network led deep inside the mountain. She dashed on. What in the Egg's name was she doing? She could be heading right for Zens.

A guffaw echoed off the rock behind her, answered by snorts and heavy boots.

Ezaara raced deeper into the tunnel, squeezed into a crevasse, and froze, tugging her cloak around her. Not a moment too soon.

"Troop, stop," a tharuk bellowed. "Tracker come here. Smell something?"

Snuffling came from the fissure's mouth. "No, sir," a throaty voice replied. "Just rats, like always."

Rats, just what she needed. Thank the dragon gods for freshweed and her cloak.

Hours passed. Every time Ezaara was about to sneak out to find Roberto, boots echoed along the tunnel.

It must be deep in the night by now. She had to find another exit, and find Roberto. Ezaara crawled deeper into the tunnel. Chinks in the left wall spilled light, illuminating a fork. Scraping her hands and knees, she headed along the left passage. At least she could see along here. The tunnel narrowed.

A scream rent the air.

Her blood froze. Roberto.

His next scream made her scalp crawl.

She pressed her eye to a chink in the rock. A wall of dark fur was in front of her, its edges limned in yellow light—a tharuk. The beast raised a whip and lashed out.

Roberto's scream ripped through Ezaara. She bunched her fists.

The beast struck again with the lash, and Roberto grunted in pain.

"Enough fun for tonight, Triple Zero," an icy voice said. "Tomorrow, we'll play with your sharp little toys."

The tharuk laughed.

Zens—she was sure of it. His voice gave Ezaara icy chills. This was the sadist who'd thrown Ma around the room with the force of his mind, breaking her will to live. He'd ruined Roberto's childhood, scarring him. And destroyed thousands of her people. The man who enslaved innocents. The man who'd created an army of monsters.

And Roberto was with him.

Fear crept its icy fingers up her spine.

Ezaara submerged her thoughts, going deep within herself. Thank the Egg, she'd practiced every day since Roberto had taught her.

The tharuk stalked across the cavern. Now she could see. Roberto was chained by a wrist and ankle to the rock, his head lolling on his shoulder.

000 hung its whip on the wall next to spiked metal implements and wicked knives—*its sharp little toys.*

A beautifully-manicured hand came into view, palm facing Roberto. Although the hand was body-lengths away, Roberto's head shot back, slamming against the wall, his eyes bulging. He thrashed, gurgling, grasping at his throat.

Ezaara clamped her teeth on her lip, drawing blood. Her knuckles scraped stone.

"See, Roberto? I control the very air you breathe," Zens said in a silky-smooth voice. He stepped into view, his back to Ezaara. "I say whether you breathe. When I've broken you, I'll determine what you think. I'll own you. And you'll do my bidding." He dropped his hand, the muscles in his arm and broad back flexing with latent power.

Roberto gasped, gulping in air, his eyes roaming the cavern.

Zens tilted his bald head, the light catching his sallow skin. "Think you're clever, do you?" asked Zens. "Not clever enough, son of Amato." He lingered over Roberto's father's name, giving Ezaara the creeps. "You can't mind block me forever. I'll break you, just like I did before."

Zens addressed the tharuk. "Triple Zero, if he blocks you tomorrow, play a little longer." He waved a hand at the rack of blades, some as tiny as Ezaara's little finger and as slim as needles; others large enough to cleave a man's head from his shoulders.

The tharuk picked up a needle as long as Ezaara's forearm. "Perhaps this one, boss."

"Yes, yes. Now, let's check on our lovelies—our hope of destroying Dragons' Realm."

A door thunked, a key scraped in a lock, and Roberto was alone.

But not entirely alone. She was here. For long moments, Ezaara watched her lover from the chink in the wall. His rider's garb was in tatters and crusted with blood. Lash marks were visible through the holes in his clothing, red and bloody, on his chest. New welts, open and raw, rose on his shoulders, blood welling from them. His face was haggard and bruised and his grimy hair was plastered to his head.

But it was Roberto, the man she loved.

Dare she mind-meld? Would Zens sense her? Had he already? He could be laying a trap for her, right now.

She couldn't sit here, paralyzed by fear. She had to try something. Tentatively, Ezaara stretched out her senses to mind-meld with Roberto. She slammed into a rock wall—he was mind-blocking with an image of the cavern.

He turned his head, gazing around, his movements clumsy, as if he was punch drunk. His eyes rested on the chink in the wall. For a moment, he stared right at her. Impossible. He'd never be able to see an eye through a crack from so far away. Had he sensed her trying to meld?

Roberto bent his chained wrist so his palm was horizontal to the floor. The fingers on his hand stiffened—the signal to flee. Was it her imagination? Had she made something out of a random movement?

Again his head tossed and turned, then his fingers flipped out, flat. Flee. The third time Roberto made the signal, he muttered something that sounded like *now*, as if delirious.

He wanted her to leave. She must be in danger. Maybe Zens had sensed her after all.

But what could she do against tharuks as brutal as 000? Hundreds of them. Probably thousands. She knew where Roberto was. She'd report to the council and come back with reinforcements. They'd get him out.

One last time, Roberto made the signal to flee, then his head sagged like a rag doll.

Ezaara didn't dare mind-meld to tell him she'd be back. Zens might sense her.

She crawled back along the tunnel, throat tight and eyes burning. If they didn't rescue Roberto, Zens would kill him.

Discoveries

"I've never seen anything like it," Benji, head of the kitchens, said. "I've had so many trainees turning up for kitchen duty that I've sent half of them down to sort the storeroom—and that's both sword fighters and archers."

"What?" Lars replied. He'd never anticipated that.

"It's Kierion. Apparently, he told them all that if they helped in the kitchens, they had more chance of being chosen as trainee dragon riders."

"That scoundrel." Lars laughed.

"Is it true?"

"It had crossed my mind that those who accepted responsibility for that prank might have enough integrity to become riders." How had Kierion guessed his intentions?

As if reading his mind, Benji said, "I tell you, that one's ahead of the bunch. It'd be good to harness some of his excess energy."

Lars gave a wry smile. "I trust you'll keep him busy enough to stay out of trouble. How's tension between the sword fighters and the archers? Are they spitting at each other over the cauldrons?"

"Kierion gave them a pep talk. Told them it's tharuks they should be fighting, not each other. Said he'd been a fool to hide their arrows. Now they're working hand in glove."

As Lars was shaking his head in amazement, someone knocked on the door.

"Come in," Lars called.

Jerrick, master of archery, came inside. "Lars, did I miss something? Has the council instigated a new training schedule?"

"Why?"

"This morning, the trainee sword fighters turned up for extra archery practice. And my trainee archers have doubled their sword practice, fighting the … ahem, *blade thrusters*, as they call them." Jerrick shrugged. "A wise move. They could all do with extra cross-training, but I just wasn't aware it was happening."

Neither was Lars. Must be Kierion's work. Inventive indeed. That young man had leadership potential. Benji winked. He knew it was Kierion, too. Lars cleared his throat. "Yes, I've assigned Kierion to train the blade thrusters and arrow flingers to work as a team."

"That irresponsible cur that hid all of our arrows?" Jerrick blustered. "Why he's—"

"Effective?" Lars asked dryly. "A brilliant leader?"

Jerrick stopped in his tracks. His open mouth broke into a grin. "Effective. If he's the one behind this, he's sharding amazing!"

§

Adelina patted Erob's blue scales and rose from sitting between his front limbs. Worry had gnawed at her stomach, keeping her awake. As dawn's early rays had crept onto the ledge outside the infirmary, she'd faced the wan sun, hoping it would warm her, but nothing could melt the chill inside her.

Except Roberto's return.

He'd been her anchor for so long. Protecting her when Pa had wanted to beat her. Taking beatings for her, hiding her from Pa. Even diving with her in Crystal Lake to wash her fear and worry away. Then there was that awful year when her father had kidnapped Roberto and given him to Zens. Her skin still crawled at the thought of her father willingly giving her brother to that brutal monster. Roberto had come back changed. Nightmares had plagued him. Anger had stalked him. But when Pa had broken Ma's back, Roberto had loved her and nursed her until she'd died.

Since then they'd only had each other—and Erob.

Adelina had been awake since yesterday morning. A whole day and night of knowing Roberto was in danger, and doing nothing. If Erob was well enough, they'd fly off and search for him. Although his belly wound was mended, he'd lost a lot of blood. It could be days until he'd have the strength to fly.

There was a whump and a flurry of snow on the ledge as Liesar landed with a goat's haunch in her jaws. Handel and Liesar had agreed to take turns hunting for Erob.

Watching dragons eat might put Adelina off her own breakfast. She stamped her frozen feet. She'd head to the mess cavern. She wasn't going to be any use to anyone cold and hungry.

"Hi, Adelina." Mara and Leah were coming past the infirmary, so she fell into step with them. A few years younger than her, they were both orphans too. "What was it like?" they asked, eyes wide. "They're saying you're a real hero now, because you fought tharuks and rescued a dragon."

"A hero, huh? Says who?"

"Kierion."

Adelina rolled her eyes. "Since when did you two take anything he says seriously?"

The girls giggled. They all went into the busy mess cavern. Happy chatter from the kitchen punctuated the hum of conversation and the clatter of people eating.

Mara leaned in. "Since Kierion's prank with the arrows, it's so jolly in the kitchen because everyone's helping."

Worry about Roberto had driven Kierion's hoax from her mind. "So I heard. You two find seats and I'll get breakfast for us." Adelina lined up and served dollops of porridge into three bowls, and then grabbed jam and fresh bread. Taking her laden tray, she threaded her way through the crowded tables to join the girls at their table in a corner. Thank the Egg, Mara and Leah had left her a seat that faced the wall. The last thing she felt like was plastering on a smile for the world.

Leah spread jam on her bread roll.

"How's it going?" Adelina gestured at Leah's hand. Tharuks had nearly severed her finger when Septimor had brought her to Dragons' Hold over two moons ago. Ezaara had had to finish the job.

Leah flexed her remaining four fingers. "Great. It's strange. Sometimes my missing finger gets itchy or tingles, but apart from that, I manage just as well with four. I'm lucky it wasn't my thumb. You know …" Leah's face was pensive.

"What is it?"

The girl blushed. "Well, you and Ezaara did such a good job of healing me from limplock that I wanted to ask you whether you'd teach me more." Her eyes shone.

"I can't teach you much, and Ezaara is probably too busy."

"Oh." Leah bit her lip.

"You should ask Master Marlies, the healer," Adelina said. "She's looking for a new trainee."

"Me?"

"Yes." Adelina nodded. "I know you're young, but you have a keen mind, good hands and you work hard. I bet you'd learn really quick."

"Good hands?" Leah stared at her stump of finger.

"Yes, despite your missing finger."

Mara elbowed Leah. "Go on, talk to the master healer."

Leah took a bite of her bread. "All right, I will."

If only Adelina's own problems were as easy to solve. Her brother was missing. No one wanted to rescue him. Why hadn't they gone already? She'd speak to Ezaara about it after breakfast.

A brittle voice from the table behind her cut through Adelina's thoughts. "Ezaara isn't the rightful Queen's Rider. I tell you, it goes against Anakisha's prophecy."

Adelina raised her eyebrows at Mara and Leah.

Mara mouthed *Sofia,* and kept eating.

"Ezaara's not of Anakisha's bloodline. I told you, the prophecy says one of Anakisha's kin will rule here at Dragons' Hold."

Adelina rolled her eyes. Not that old line again. Sofia's babble was getting really old, fast.

"But Master Roberto tested her," said another girl.

"Ssh, someone will hear you," Sofia snapped. "Who says his test was true? You heard them at his trial. Even Master Tonio wasn't sure whether he was lying. Roberto could've pretended Ezaara had imprinted well. You know he used to work for Master Zens."

That sharding cow. Here was Roberto, laying his life on the line for the realm, and she was spreading lies about him. Adelina placed her fists on the table to stand up and blast Sofia, but Mara widened her eyes and shook her head.

Adelina hesitated. What more was Sofia saying? She stayed seated, chewing her bread, although it had lost its taste.

"For Zens? That's terrible. But Zaarusha chose Ezaara."

"That's what Ezaara told us," Sofia replied. "Now quiet, I don't want everyone to—"

"Hey, there's Adelina," a male voice hissed. It was Alban, Sofia's lover.

Adelina faked a laugh, grinning at the girls. "That was a great joke. Tell me another."

Thankfully, Mara and Leah caught on quickly, and giggled.

"What's big as a dragon but weighs nothing?" Mara asked, wiggling her eyebrows.

"I don't know!" Although she was seething, Adelina forced mirth into her voice. "I give up. What's as big as a dragon but weighs nothing?"

"His shadow."

Adelina and Leah laughed again. "That was bad," said Adelina, turning to Leah. "Do you have a better one?"

Behind them, chairs scraped as Sofia and her gossips got up to leave.

"They've gone," breathed Mara. "I'm sorry you had to hear that."

"You mean it's not the first time they've said those things about my brother?"

Mara broke crumbs off her bread roll, not meeting Adelina's eyes.

"No, it's not," said Leah. "But I'd ignore them."

Adelina glanced behind her. Although the rest of the mess cavern was still busy, the few tables nearby had emptied out. No one could hear them, but still, she whispered. "No, don't ignore them. Listen in, then let me know what they're saying."

"But Alban …" Leah murmured.

"Is he hurting people?"

"Not sure, but there was a rumor that Sofia asked him to punch a girl."

"When did that happen?"

The girls shrugged. "It might just be a rumor," Mara said. "Is it true Ezaara knifed Sofia?"

Adelina sighed. "Yes, but it was an accident. Fleur's dragon, Ajeuria, was on swayweed and sent Ezaara a vision of her being blasted by a dragon. It was so real that Ezaara thought her skin was on fire. She stumbled and her knife went into Sofia's leg."

"How could a dragon meld with Ezaara without her touching it?"

"She has special gifts. She can meld with any dragon, but not many know that, so keep it quiet. That's one way we know she's Queen's Rider. Besides, my brother doesn't lie."

Leah still looked uncertain.

"What is it?"

"Did he really work for Master Zens?"

"Only because he was drugged with numlock and forced to, but Erob saved him." Adelina shivered, remembering Roberto's screams through her bedroom walls when he'd returned to Naobia.

§

Marlies stifled a yawn, and placed her hand on Erob's forehead so she could mind-meld with him. His scales were a healthy hue, but a little cool. *"How are you feeling?"*

He opened an eye, his lid sliding over his slitted pupil. *"A bit better. Still weak."*

"Sleep, then."

"Thanks. I was until you woke me." His lid closed again.

She checked Erob's wound again. There was a slight mark along his scales, but otherwise not a blemish. Piaua juice was incredible. What they'd do without it, she had no idea.

After rescuing Erob and helping heal him, Hans had collapsed in bed. Marlies had been tending the blue dragon and the patients in the infirmary on her own—even though she'd also hardly slept. She wasn't as hardy as she'd been when she left Lush Valley a few short moons ago. Death Valley had dealt her a raw card. But at least she was alive, with her family. More than she could guarantee for Roberto.

Strange, she'd expected Ezaara to pop in by now. She was probably sleeping too.

Marlies threw some blankets over his back, and then more on each of his limbs. If she could help him conserve heat, he'd use his energy for healing. Behind him, Maazini snuffled in his sleep. She threw some blankets on him too.

Liesar landed on the ledge and came inside the overhang where the dragons were dozing. *"You've been up all night and half the day. You need rest."*

"Soon." A knock sounded at the door. "Come in," Marlies called, going back inside the infirmary and pulling the door shut. Although there were two exhausted dragons on the ledge, Erob was out of danger and it was freezing. She'd wake Hans so he could rug up and take the next shift, watching him.

A young blonde girl entered the infirmary, the one whose finger Ezaara had amputated. She was older than a littling but not a fully-fledged teen yet, shy wee thing. What was her name again? Lara or Lexi—no, Leah, that was it. "Good evening, Leah. How's your hand?"

"F-fine, M-master Healer Marlies," Leah replied.

From memory, the girl had been orphaned. Perhaps she needed someone to talk to. "I'm just making a cup of tea. Would you like one?" Marlies tipped water from a waterskin into two cups and passed Leah one.

"Thank you." Leah clutched her cup, knuckles white.

Leah was either really nervous or freezing. Either way, tea would help. "Come with me." Marlies walked to the ledge and opened the door to a chill wind. She mind-melded with Liesar. *"Be gentle, she's just young."*

"I'm nothing but gentle," Liesar replied.

"Especially when you fight tharuks." Marlies held out her cup.

Liesar sent hot gusts of air over Marlies' cup until the water was steaming.

Leah's eyes nearly fell out of her head. "Liesar warms your tea? Doesn't her breath burn your hands?"

"She has great aim—and because we mind-meld, she'd know if she hurt me. She feels what I feel."

"That's handy. Does she help you heal people?"

"She helps heal other dragons."

"And I sterilize your surgical knives, don't forget to tell her that. And I fetch injured dragons' riders." Liesar ruffled her neck scales.

"I wish I was a healer." Leah's eyes shot wide open and she gasped. "Oh, sorry, I meant to ask you nicely. I mean I—"

Marlies laid her free hand on Leah's arm. "You want to be a healer?"

"Yes. Ezaara and Adelina helped me so much when they healed me from limplock. I would've died without them. That's why I want to help others."

The Egg knew she could do with help. With hardly any healing supplies and no decent assistants except Ezaara, Adelina and Tomaaz—who all now had other responsibilities—she'd been run off her feet whenever there was a tharuk skirmish. Lars had assigned a couple of people, but they'd been more hindrance then help, so Marlies had suggested they work with the master craftsman. Marlies nodded. "Very well. Here's your first lesson. You'll often need to heat water for herbal infusions, like feverweed tea or koromiko for belly gripes. Hold your cup by the handle only. Don't put your hand around the base."

Leah held her cup out, as instructed.

"Now, the trick is to stand absolutely still so Liesar can aim. That will prevent you from being burned."

The silver dragon rumbled her approval as she heated the water. *"Not a twitch. She'll be steady in emergencies."*

Hans came to the doorway, tugging on his riders' jerkin. "Oh, tea? Could you make me one too?"

Marlies nodded at Leah. "That's your second assignment."

While Leah went inside to fetch another cup, Marlies said quietly to Hans, "I thought Ezaara would have come to see Erob by now."

Hans arched his eyebrows over his emerald eyes. "Hasn't she been in yet?"

"No," Marlies replied. "She must be sleeping."

Someone else knocked on the door. Adelina appeared on the ledge with Leah. "Do you know where Ezaara is?" she asked, frowning. "I thought she'd be here."

"She's not in her cavern?" Marlies asked.

"No, and no one's seen her for hours."

§

"Do you want to sit with us at lunch?" Gret asked after their combat session in the training cavern.

Lovina shook her head. "I'll be along a little later." Gret and Adelina always respected her need for space, never questioning her when she escaped the busy tumult of Dragons' Hold for a little peace.

Lovina wandered through the tunnels aimlessly. She longed to see Tomaaz again, but he'd been so pale and tired when he'd returned from rescuing Erob, she'd insisted he get some sleep. Hours later, he was still sleeping. When he'd gone back to Death Valley, she'd been sure he'd become another of Zens' victims, thrown on the flesh heap to rot. She hadn't dared hope he'd survive. Hope hadn't helped her family. Hadn't helped her hold onto anyone she'd loved.

There. She'd admitted it. She did care for him—loved him. He nurtured something precious inside her.

Lovina suddenly realized that her feet had automatically brought her to the infirmary and Tomaaz's family quarters. Oh well, since she was here, she may as well visit Maazini. Opening the door, she entered the infirmary. She'd stayed here for her first two weeks after arriving at Dragons' Hold—she'd been so ill and broken. Two patients lay in beds sleeping, so Lovina gave Marlies a small wave.

"Tomaaz is still sleeping," Marlies said quietly.

Lovina nodded and made her way through the rows of beds, and opened the door to the ledge outside. She tugged her jerkin shut, put on her gloves and pulled up her collar against the cold.

Erob's sleeping form greeted her. Beyond him, Maazini was also asleep. Lovina sighed. She couldn't wake them; they, too, needed sleep. This particular ledge was large enough for several dragons, providing necessary space to bring the wounded in from battle. A deep overhang provided shelter for the sleeping dragons and many more, if need be. She walked out from the protection of the overhang, her boots crunching on snow, and stood near the lip of the ledge.

When she'd first come here, two moons ago, she'd seen a verdant basin below, nestled among a ring of icy peaks. Dragons of every imaginable color had wheeled in the sky, looking like a scene off one of Bill's bolts of cloth. An orchard of laden fruit trees had edged a patchwork of fields, hemmed in by a vast forest to the north. It had taken her breath away.

Now, shrouded in snow, with the lake glinting silver in the wan winter sun, the evergreens dusted with fine powder and the fierce peaks of Dragon's Teeth standing like guardians, protecting her from her old life outside, Dragons' Hold had a special type of pristine magic to it. A beauty that still made her breath catch.

Was that because she'd spent so many years in the arid waste of Death Valley—and then more in the grip of numlock, with a gray fog over her eyes and mind, preventing her from seeing the world's beauty? She'd traveled the length of Dragons' Realm, a slave to Bill—a merchant and tharuk spy—and yet she'd barely noticed any of it.

Out of the thousands of inhabitants she'd encountered, Tomaaz had been the only one to see her, to wake her from her living nightmare and fight for her to be free. She automatically flexed the arm Bill had broken. It was healthy again, not quite as strong as her other, but it would recover. Although she'd never be rid of the whip scars on her back, they would fade. She would not let Bill damage her for life.

Nearby, Singlar, Lars' purple dragon, sprang from a ledge. Her fingers itched to paint the dragon's majestic wings, limned in light as it flew over a waterfall that tumbled down an icy slope.

"Beautiful, isn't it?"

Lovina spun back to the arch. Erob and Maazini were both still asleep. The voice had sounded odd, like she'd heard it in her head, not with her ears. Had one of the dragons mind-melded with her? She shrugged it off. She'd probably imagined it.

"I'm over here. The other way."

She spun again. On the other side of the ledge, beyond Erob and Maazini's sleeping forms, under the overhang where the mountainside blocked the snow and sunlight, deep in shadows, was a green dragon. The dragon stretched its limbs and paced past the others toward her. As it stepped into the sunlight, its scales glinted like emeralds. Lovina had seen dragons before, but not like this, full of majesty, glory—and deep sadness.

The creature bowed its head gracefully before her. *"Lovina …"*

The voice *was* in her head. She hadn't been mistaken. The dragon's tones were like sweet music that welled inside her. Sunlight played across its hide, turning the green into wondrous shades: moss, fresh mint, new spring grass, evergreens, emeralds and baby ferns in woodlands. If only she had her paintbrush and a palette of colors.

The dragon gazed at her with deep blue eyes.

A rush of wonder engulfed Lovina. Warmth spread through her. A sense of belonging.

"Will you be my rider?"

"*Me?*" Even as she asked, Lovina was drawn forward. She placed her hand on the dragon's head. Its skin was warm and supple. "*I'm not up to this. I'm untrained. Only a slave.*"

"*Then we are well suited. I, too, have been enslaved by Zens.*"

She barely dared breathe. "*You, too?*"

"*But now I am free. And so are you. Come, fly with me.*"

The music inside her grew until she was swept up, leaping onto the dragon. Its haunches tensed and with a flip of its wings, they were airborne, high above the basin, spiraling up toward the peaks. Something loosened inside Lovina. It had started with Tomaaz, and, now, it loosened further. Carefree and unfettered, she laughed.

The dragon chuckled in her mind. "*Lovina, for years I was miserable serving a master who had chained me with swayweed, making me hate the ones I loved. I was powerless, but now we can make a new life.*"

"So that was the source of the sorrow I sensed in you," Lovina replied. "For eight years, I was numlocked, beaten and abused. My home was burned and my family killed."

"*I am now your family. Dragons' Hold will be your home.*"

The music swelled inside Lovina, bursting into brilliant harmony. She'd never felt like this before. Never had such a sense of belonging.

"*I was called Ajeuria, but now I will be known as Ajeurina, in your honor.*"

It was an honor. "Ajeurina," she liked the way it sounded. Like a new start. So, this was Erob and Maazini's sister—all three were Zaarusha's offspring. Fleur, the former master healer and traitor, had been her last rider. "*Why don't you show me my new home?*" Lovina asked.

"*That would be my pleasure.*" A deep wave of Ajeurina's satisfaction flowed through Lovina, driving away the cold and making her tingle with warmth. Ajeurina dipped her wings and they shot over the basin toward the distant peak of Fire Crag.

Stuck

By the time Ezaara made her way to the mouth of the crevasse to sneak back out of Death Valley, it was broad daylight. Shards, how long had she been holed up watching Roberto? It was one thing to slip into Death Valley wearing an invisibility cloak at night. It was another to walk out among troops of tharuks in broad daylight. Should she chance it?

No, she'd be handing Zens her head on a platter. Roberto's hand signals had said to *flee,* not to find Zens and join him in the dungeons.

The stomp of tharuk troops echoed from the main tunnel down the crevasse Ezaara was hiding in. She huffed her breath out, crept further into the crevasse and wrapped her cloak around her. She couldn't go too far in. Roberto was obviously afraid Zens would sense her. Hastily, she chewed some freshweed. She'd have to wait this out like a brooding dragon, but at least she could disguise her scent. Then she submerged her mind, the way Roberto had taught her, and waited.

§

"*Roberto, I know you can hear me.*"

Roberto groaned, but not too loudly. He couldn't show any weakness or Zens would exploit it. But he was weak. Weak from 000's latest torture and from Zens' relentless mental battering. Even when Zens wasn't in the cavern, he bombarded Roberto with insidious thoughts.

"*I will* beat *you. I'll break your mind and body. You have no hope. Soon, I'll be your master.*"

Even though it was cold, sweat rolled off Roberto's face as he gritted his teeth and held an image in his mind that Zens couldn't use against him: the wall of this cavern. He blinked with his good eye. The other eye was swollen shut and his face was stiff with crusted blood. He tried to stretch his cramped shoulder, but the metal shackles only bit harder.

So, he did what he'd been doing for days, he stared at the wall, noticing every bump, pit and crevice in the flickering torchlight. Deep underground, it was hard to figure out how long he'd been here, but something different had happened recently …

As his good eye roamed over the wall, he spotted a tiny chink, and suddenly, he knew what it was. Someone had been here.

He clamped down on that thought. Quashed his feelings. He mustn't give Ezaara away. If Zens slipped into his mind unwittingly, he'd know she'd been here. He submerged his thoughts, going deep inside himself, so Zens couldn't detect him.

What had Zens said about the new creatures? Nothing more than he already knew: a threat to Dragons' Realm and dragons. But what Zens didn't know was that Roberto had discovered the location of his new lovelies.

If he could get out of these chains, he'd come back with reinforcements to destroy them.

Surprises

"What is it? Do you know?" Lofty asked Kierion as they walked toward the main cavern.

Kierion shrugged. Lars had said there was an important announcement this afternoon. He had a fair idea what it might be. He leaned toward Tomaaz's best friend, who'd arrived a few weeks ago while Tomaaz was still in Death Valley. With his love of adventure, Lofty had become one of Kierion's stalwart supporters, and had helped him drag the sledge full of arrows up the mountainside. Not that that particular prank was anything to brag about anymore. "Well, I may be wrong, but—"

"But what?" Lofty's keen eyes flitted down to Kierion.

Shards, the man was tall—no wonder his nickname was Lofty. "Battle's coming. There are many young dragons of imprintable age …" He let the words hang, so Lofty could draw his own conclusion.

"Imprinting with dragons?" Lofty grinned. "Do you think we stand a chance?"

Kierion shrugged. He'd been telling everyone that if they did kitchen duty, extra training and cross-drilled, sharing their fighting skills, they'd have more chance of becoming dragon riders. It made sense—but he hadn't exactly asked Lars' intentions. He huffed his cheeks out. "Dunno," he said truthfully. "Could be anything. It might not be imprinting."

"Imprinting?" someone behind them asked. "Hey, Kierion said we're imprinting." Murmurs rippled through the trainees behind them in the corridor.

"Great, we might imprint a dragon, just for scrubbing a few pots."

An arrow flinger piped up. "Pot scrubbing for a dragon? Beats trading blows with you blade thrusters."

Kierion groaned. It wasn't exactly like that. You couldn't force imprinting. Now he'd done it again. His big mouth was always getting him in trouble.

Lofty slugged him on the shoulder, grinning again. "What color will your dragon be?"

Kierion rolled his eyes and entered the main cavern. Lars swooped through an entrance on Singlar's back. The purple dragon landed on the rock stage. Two more dragons shot into the cavern, their wingbeats stirring the trainees' hair—Reko, a blood-red dragon carrying Derek, the master of instruction; and the maroon Lysika, carrying Alyssa, master of flight. More people flooded in behind Kierion—kitchen workers, smiths from the forges, littlings, mothers, and dragon riders in their riders' garb.

The hubbub was incredible. Murmurs of *Kierion* and *imprinting* rebounded around the cavern, spreading like wildfire. Kierion tried to shrink in on himself, hoping Master Lars wouldn't notice him, but he was swept forward with the crowd, who were clamoring to get a good spot by the stage.

Lofty clapped him on the shoulder. "Hey, great spot. We'll hear everything here."

They were so close, Kierion saw a smattering of snow on Master Lars' blonde beard as he dismounted. The council leader cocked his head, listening to the crowd's murmurs. His piercing blue eyes lanced through Kierion.

Kierion's face burned. Right now, he must be about as red as Reko's scales.

Lars held up his arm and the crowd quietened. "Thank you for attending," Lars said, his voice carrying across the crowd. "As you know, tharuks are growing more brazen, attacking villages and murdering our people. Hans, our master of prophecy, believes that things will soon come to a head. Within weeks, we may be in an all-out war with Commander Zens and his unnatural creatures.

"We must marshal our forces. Many of you will be aware that we have young dragons who are now mature enough to imprint. We often let this happen spontaneously, as dragons meet suitable people, however, time is not on our side. Tomorrow, Alyssa will accompany selected trainees to the imprinting grounds."

A cheer rang out. Lofty pounded Kierion on the back. The trainees closest—both blade thrusters and arrow flingers—joined in, whooping. Kierion risked a quick glance at Lars. Shards, the council leader was looking right at him.

Lars raised his hand for silence again.

Even when everyone was quiet, their excitement still bubbled like an underground spring.

Master Derek stepped forward, unrolling a scroll. "Master Lars and I have made a list of prospective riders—those we feel are ready for this opportunity. As I read your names, please join Master Alyssa on the stage so she can brief you. If your name isn't read out, don't be overly concerned. There will be more chances to find the dragon meant for you."

The crowd whistled and cheered.

Kierion didn't join in. He'd always wanted to be a dragon rider. What if his name wasn't on the scroll? A dragon rider had to be trustworthy, not a jokester. Had his pranks killed the chance of achieving his lifelong dream?

§

Adelina's mind reeled as she slumped on her bed. When she was a littling, she'd secretly believed that one day she'd become Queen's Rider. Zaarusha hadn't imprinted after Anakisha's death, waiting years for that one special person. Adelina had known it was her—all it would take was one look into Queen Zaarusha's eyes.

After their father killed their mother, Roberto had brought her to Dragons' Hold. She'd met Queen Zaarusha—and nothing had happened. No whoosh of emotion. No instant mind-meld, no rush of energy the way Roberto had experienced when imprinting with Erob. She'd been inconsolable, crying for days. Roberto had comforted her, telling her one day she'd find another dragon. But she didn't want another dragon. She wanted the queen.

Years later, Adelina had been prepared to hate Ezaara—but the ignorant tear-streaked girl she'd met in the Queen's Rider's chambers, trying to put a brave face on for the world, had touched Adelina's heart. Instead of her scorning Ezaara, they'd become good friends.

Earlier today, Master Derek had read Adelina's name from his scroll. Master Alyssa had briefed them about imprinting protocol. They'd meet the dragons tomorrow.

She didn't want to be Queen's Rider anymore, but maybe she didn't want to be a rider at all. Adelina had gotten used to Roberto and Erob being her only family. What if she imprinted and it changed things? What if she didn't imprint at all? And, if she did become a dragon rider, would Zens target her too? He'd turned her father and her brother against Dragons' Realm before. What if he caught her?

Adelina shuddered. She punched her pillow, then threw it against the wall. The truth was: she missed Roberto; she was worried about him; and every day that the council delayed made her anxiety grow.

Mind you, if she imprinted, she could go after Roberto herself…

Now there was a thought.

Someone rapped on her door. Adelina started guiltily. Silly, really, no one could hear her thoughts—although that would change if a dragon chose her as its rider.

Gret came in. "Oh? You're going to bed? But it's so early."

"Uh, yeah, I'm tired." She faked a yawn, hoping Gret would get the hint.

But Gret wasn't that stupid. She sat on the bed next to Adelina and squeezed her hand. "I know you're missing Roberto," she said, as if all Adelina's cheery smiles and reassurances over the past few days had been transparent.

"Miss him? Why, I'm as happy as a lark. Now there's no big brother to boss me around." She smiled brightly, but her voice trembled, giving her away.

Within a heartbeat, Gret was hugging her as fat tears rolled down her cheeks.

"That's better," Gret said, pulling back when Adelina stopped sobbing. "You can't bottle everything inside you."

"Why not? I did for years." Adelina gave a weak smile. "I wish there was something I could do. It seems wrong, getting on with normal life while Roberto's captive." She sighed. "Why did you come to see me? Are you nervous about imprinting tomorrow?"

"No." Gret's brows were pulled into a frown and her mouth was grim. "I have bad news. Snake-tongue's spreading rumors about your brother."

Adelina rolled her eyes. "I heard her at breakfast this morning. She hasn't been the same since Ezaara injured her. Not that I blame her. I'd be angry if the Queen's Rider knifed me."

"We both know it wasn't Ezaara's fault. Anyway, I think we should talk to Lars. It's getting serious. There are rumors that Alban's threatening girls who won't side with Sofia against Ezaara."

"We'll need evidence."

"I know. I'll keep an eye out." Gret stood. "Are you sure you don't want company?"

"Thanks for the offer." Adelina preferred being alone. It was easier to carry her grief without someone watching. She had too many hurts in her past to lump them all on a friend. Too many secrets. That's why Roberto had given her a cavern of her own next to his when he'd become master of mental faculties and imprinting. She gasped. "Usually it would be Roberto's job to test each imprinting bond …."

"But he's not here," Gret said. "Don't worry, Lars and the council will rescue him soon. And just think, tomorrow you may be a dragon rider." Gret smiled.

"Thanks." As Gret left, Adelina faked one last smile for her friend. That was why she needed Roberto. Her brother got her, because he was hiding the same dark family secrets.

§

Gret was nearly at the girls' cavern when Sofia and Alban stepped out of the shadows.

"Visiting Adelina, were you?" Sofia sneered, her teeth glinting in the torchlight. Behind Sofia, Alban was a wall of muscle, oozing menace.

"None of your business." Gret's hand hovered near her sword hilt. She was an ace with a sword and everyone here at Dragons' Hold knew it. That's what came of being the Montanarian swordmaster's daughter.

"I'm surprised you'd hang out with the sister of a traitor," Alban said, his hand sliding to his knife hilt.

"Really, Alban? A knife against a sword? You've got to be joking," Gret said scornfully. "And I didn't pick you to be so stupid. Master Roberto was declared innocent. Fleur, Bruno and Simeon were banished as traitors, remember?"

"Everyone knows Roberto mind-tricked the council into letting him back."

Gret laughed and pushed her way past them. Her back crawled. She had the urge to spin and parry, just in case. But she didn't. Pa had taught her never to show a weakness.

"Gret," Sofia called.

Gret turned.

"We were just kidding." Sofia licked her lips, eyes darting. "Joking around. You know, like one of Kierion's pranks."

"No," said Gret, "not like Kierion's pranks at all—they're funny."

§

Tomaaz woke late. A candle burned in the sconce and the slave boy was fast asleep in the bed across from him—peacefully. Shards, he'd slept all day. How was Maazini? What about Lovina? He'd barely spoken a few sentences with her since he'd returned from Death Valley.

He threw back the covers, pulled his riders' garb on and went into the infirmary. Pa was sitting, reading by torchlight. A couple of men were sleeping in the beds lining the walls.

"Good morning, Son," Pa quipped. "Nothing like greeting the dawn."

Tomaaz snorted. "Or the sunset, in my case. How's Maazini?"

"Still sleeping. He and Erob have dozed most of the day."

"Like dragon, like rider," Tomaaz replied, striding past the beds to the door. He took a torch from a sconce by the door and went over to Maazini and Erob, curled together for warmth under the protective overhang. Huffing out clouds of breath, Tomaaz held the torch high and walked around the dragons, looking them over. Their scales were resuming their healthy vibrancy. Another day or two and they'd be well enough to fly. He didn't meld with Maazini. After everything they'd been through, sleep was the best thing for both dragons.

Stomach rumbling, Tomaaz wandered to the edge of the ledge. There were dragon prints in the snow and small boot prints—Lovina's. She must've come out here for peace. Ma had mentioned that the infirmary ledge was one of Lovina's favorite spots. By the Egg, he was hungry. Not surprising after his time in Death Valley. Perhaps Lovina was in the mess cavern.

An hour later, Tomaaz was back on the ledge with a surprise for Lovina in his pocket. No one had seen her all day. He lifted the torch and examined her boot prints. It was possible she'd been taken somewhere by dragon. Shrugging, Tomaaz grabbed a spare blanket from the infirmary and settled on it, leaning against Maazini's hide.

Tomaaz awoke to a thump and a spray of snow on his face.

Lovina was clinging to the back of a green dragon, eyes bright in the torchlight with a grin as wide as Dragons' Realm. He raced over. The tips of her long hair were tinged white with frost. Her lips were wind-chapped, and her cheeks and nose were pink from the cold, but it wasn't her coloring that looked so different.

Lovina was beaming. Radiant with joy. He'd seen her first shy smiles, heard her hesitant laugh, but it was nothing like the musical burst of laughter that burst forth from her now.

"Tomaaz, meet Ajeurina."

Ajeurina? Didn't she mean Ajeuria?

Maazini lifted his head. *"No, Tomaaz, my sister imprinted with Lovina, so she's modified her name."* He burrowed back down against Erob and promptly fell back to sleep.

Tomaaz caught Lovina as she slid off Ajeuria's—no, Ajeurina's—side.

She flung her arms around him, burrowing her freezing cheek against his neck. "Tomaaz, I never thought I'd become a dragon rider." She looked up at him, eyes bright.

He pulled the heart-shaped pastry wrapped in waxed cloth from his pocket.

"Thank you." Lovina traced the pastry heart with her finger. "And I never thought I'd love such a thoughtful man."

Love? Tomaaz's heart soared.

Return

"Zaarusha is missing?" Lars asked Tonio. "Why didn't someone tell me earlier?" They were on the ledge outside Lars' cavern, grabbing some fresh air.

The spymaster shrugged. "I'm just reporting what I know."

Lars snorted. "Come on, Tonio, what do you think's going on?"

"Well, no one's seen Ezaara either …" Tonio pursed his lips, leaving his words hanging in the chill evening air. The spymaster paced, his boots crunching in the snow. Icicles hung down the sides of the overhang, reflecting the flickering torchlight. Beyond, snug in the shadows, Singlar was sleeping, his tail wrapped around his huge body. "They could be running an errand. Or …" Tonio splayed his hands.

Lars knew where this was leading. Tonio's dragon, Antonika, had seen Roberto kissing Ezaara in the orchard. He shook his head. "No, even Ezaara is not fool enough to dash off to Death Valley on her own. Besides, Queen Zaarusha is more seasoned than that."

"She was fool enough to go to the Wastelands and rescue Roberto," Tonio said. "Why not Death Valley? I'm telling you, Lars, that man has been having an affair with his student—our new Queen's Rider. His punishment should be banishment. Death Valley's as good a place as any." He snapped an icicle. The glittering shard in his hand, Tonio stalked off.

Lars gazed over the basin. Surely Roberto wasn't stupid enough to be romantically involved with his trainee? But then again, Tonio had insisted that Antonika share her memory with Lars. When she'd shown him Roberto kissing Ezaara, it definitely hadn't been a perfunctory kiss. But could he blame them? Roberto had been to hell and back, even had his gut slit in the desert to protect Ezaara from wrongful banishment. Then they'd returned just in time to save Zaarusha from being murdered. No wonder the queen's loyalty overrode her duty to the council.

He wanted to give Roberto a chance. His rotten father had corrupted the boy, but he'd pulled through and become an irreplaceable asset. No one had his mental talents. It was scary, how he could manipulate people's minds to find out what he needed.

What terrible price had he paid for his formidable skills learned at Zens' hands? He never discussed his time in Death Valley, except to say that Erob had freed him. But, when he'd first arrived and been rejected by the council, Lars had heard him screaming in the night, tortured by his demons—demons that could destroy Dragons' Realm if that talent was used by Zens.

An affair with the Queen's Rider …?

Hmm. Maybe Tonio was right: the law was the law. No master was allowed to have an affair with his student. Look where that had gotten Dragon Mage Giddi. His student, Mazyka, had nearly destroyed Dragons' Realm.

He shook his head again, this time sadly. Despite his sympathies, as the council leader, he had to be firm.

There was a loud crack. A dark shape appeared in the sky, blotting out the stars.

§

Ezaara and Zaarusha appeared above Dragons' Hold. *"Shards, Zaarusha, I never meant to be gone an entire day."*

"Me neither. Not much we can do about that now."

"Agreed. We need to see Lars."

"He's seen us already," Zaarusha rumbled in Ezaara's mind. *"That's his cavern."*

A figure stood on a ledge below, limned in torchlight. Ezaara rubbed her cold hands. *"Let's pay him a visit."*

"After that, you should eat," Zaarusha replied.

Ezaara's belly rumbled, but food was the last thing she felt like with her fresh memory of Roberto, battered and bloody. She mind-melded with Singlar, who was curled up on the ledge. *"Please let Lars know that Queen Zaarusha and I would like to visit."*

"He's already expecting you," was Singlar's reply.

Zaarusha swooped through the cold night air to land neatly on Lars' ledge.

"Greetings, Ezaara," Lars said. "We've missed you today."

Ezaara dismounted and shook Lars' hand. The council leader's eyes were as cold as the icicles behind him.

"You're freezing," said Lars. "Let's discuss your recent whereabouts inside. With war looming, the last thing we need is our Queen's Rider getting ill."

Was that concern or a reprimand? Either way, Ezaara didn't like Lars' tone. She wasn't only *our Queen's Rider*—the council's property, to do with as they saw fit. She was Ezaara of Lush Valley, Zaarusha's rider. She had a say in her life. If they hadn't learned that after wrongly trying to banish her and getting Roberto nearly killed in the Robandi desert, then they had a thing or two to learn. "Thank you, Master Lars," she said demurely. "That would be nice."

Zaarusha chuckled. *I see you can manage him on your own. I'm going hunting. I'll be nearby if you need me.*

A fire blazed in Lars' hearth, the smoke funneling up a natural chimney in the rock ceiling. Ezaara took off her gloves and held her numb hands out, sitting in an overstuffed chair near the fire.

Lars sat in the chair opposite her.

"Come, Ezaara, you're positively blue," Lydia said, bustling over with a warm cup of herb tea and a plate laden with cookies. The scent of cinnamon wafted over them. Ezaara's mouth watered. She loved the winter delicacies, made with ground almonds and egg whites.

"Would you like one, Ezaara?" asked Lars.

He was playing the congenial host. Would he be that congenial when he found out where she'd just been? Ezaara was about to pick up a cookie but changed her mind. She wasn't a littling, to be plied with treats then told what to do. "Maybe later. Business first." She leaned back, crossing her long legs. "Do you know where I've been?"

Lars replied, "Please, tell me."

"Death Valley, to see Master Roberto."

"I thought so," Lars replied.

So, it wasn't a surprise. She'd thought she'd been so stealthy.

He leaned forward. "You didn't actually see him, of course, you're just speaking figuratively."

The memory played out in her mind again: Roberto, bloodied and torn, chains clanking. Ezaara swallowed. "Yes, I saw him." Shards, her voice was husky. She mustn't give away her emotions or Roberto could be banished all over again.

Lars' eyebrows shot up in surprise and he choked on his cinnamon star, taking a gulp of tea to wash it down.

She put steel into her voice. "He's being tortured. Zens has him in chains and is probably beating him again as we sit here, having tea and cookies." She was doubly glad she hadn't eaten one.

Still coughing, he asked, "How did you slip in?"

"The same way Tomaaz and Roberto got in last time." Ezaara carefully placed her tea on the table. "Now that I know where he is, he'll be easy to rescue.

With two or three dragons and a few riders, we'd be in and out in no time." She had no idea how to get into Roberto's prison—a minor detail.

Lars took a long draught of tea, eyes regarding her over the rim.

There was a sharp rap at the door, and Lydia admitted Tonio. He barreled into the room. "Lars, Zaarusha is back. I suspect Ezaara was in Death Valley. None of her family know—" His words dried up. A mask of superficial cordiality snapped over his face. "Good evening, my honored Queen's Rider."

"Good evening, Tonio." Ezaara nodded, deliberately dropping off his title. "Yes, I have been to Death Valley."

"And?" The spymaster's gaze was genuinely curious.

"And we need to rescue Master Roberto before Zens kills him."

"You're assuming a lot, Ezaara." Tonio's voice was silky, laced with steel.

"You sent Roberto to Death Valley."

"He agreed to go."

"He's a valuable member of our council," Ezaara snapped. "We need him back."

"Valuable?" Tonio asked softly, eyes glittering. "To whom?"

Chills raced down her spine. He knew. Antonika had told him. Ezaara turned to Lars. "Lars, I may have come here as an ignorant girl from Lush Valley, but I'm now the Queen's Rider."

"And I'm the leader of the council," he replied, mettle in his blue gaze. "May I remind you that your training as Queen's Rider will only be complete after the dragon races."

Ezaara stalked back outside to the snow.

§

Lars met Tonio's gaze. "If she leaves for Death Valley again, she could jeopardize Queen Zaarusha's life. I want eyes and ears on her at all times. Ensure she stays at the hold."

Tonio's dark eyes flashed. "Yes, Master Lars. I'll see to it." His boots clicked on stone and he shut the door.

Lars dropped his head in his hands. He'd expected Ezaara to be contrite, not attack him and the council, but after everything they'd put her and Roberto through, he couldn't blame her. So, why had he been so harsh?

Because Tonio's endless goading and insidious comments were eating away at him—that's why. Yet Tonio was hardly impartial where Roberto was concerned.

Lydia came over, putting her arm around his shoulders. "I heard all of that. Tough situation."

"In the name of the sharding Egg, Lydia, I don't want to condemn Roberto, but I have no choice. He and Ezaara are in love."

"Do you remember when we fell in love? she asked softly.

"Yes, I do." He chuckled. "Your father wasn't very happy, was he?"

"No, the last thing he wanted was me hand-fasted to a dragon rider." She leaned in to kiss his cheek. "But we defied him and ran away to be together. It took years for him to forgive us. Do you regret it?"

"No, but this is the Queen's Rider," Lars said.

"Even more reason to let her lead the way she wants to," Lydia answered.

"Tonio willingly sent Roberto to Death Valley. We know he has an ulterior motive."

"His grudge is influencing him," said Lydia. "Amato hurt him grievously, but Amato's been dead for years. And Roberto is not his father." Lydia retreated.

Lars stared into the crackling fire. Tonio was a sharding good spymaster and his instincts were usually right. As council leader, his hands were tied. The law was the law. He had no choice but to act upon Tonio's counsel.

STRANGLETON

Fenni shivered as the chilly air brushed his naked skin. Narrow shafts of moonlight cut through the trees, illuminating a white quilt of snow that hugged the ground all the way to the edge of the river.

Master Giddi stowed Fenni's clothes in their tent under the strongwood trees. "Master your magic to warm yourself," he said, coming back to the river's edge. "Fenni, this is all about control. If you can master this, you can do anything with fire. Harness *sathir* and shape it to your needs."

His need was to kill tharuks. Fenni glanced over his shoulder, just in case.

"It's all right, there aren't any monsters around," Master Giddi said.

That was a relief. Being caught naked by tharuks wouldn't be fun. Lit by the moon, Fenni's breath gusted out of his lungs in a silvery cloud. He lifted his ribs. Air rushed into his lungs, filling them. Now was as good a time as ever. He plunged headfirst into the dark water.

The shock nearly knocked the air from his lungs, but he held it in, warring with his instinct to scramble out. *Master your magic to warm yourself?* Master Giddi was crazy. The only thing he'd master was his death.

Warmth flickered inside Fenni, spreading outward from his core to his limbs. Impossible—unless … yes, it was Master Giddi, helping him combat the freezing river.

Hair swirling in the water, Fenni felt the *sathir* in the river's fish and plants, and harnessed the energy. Soon, green flickers shot from his fingers and a fireball grew between his hands. Fire underwater? Not as impossible as he'd thought. A fish, attracted by the light, shot past him. Fenni's fireball died.

"*Concentrate!*" Giddi's reproach blasted through his mind.

Fenni kicked up for the surface. His head broke into the chilly air.

"A fish? A fish knocked you out of your rhythm?" Giddi boomed.

Thank the Egg, no one was around to hear him. Highly embarrassing.

"What if you lose focus when you're facing a stinking tharuk? Get back underwater."

Fenni gulped in air, and dived back under, starting over. First sparks, then a fireball. He played, shooting fire between his hands. Not bad.

"Bring it to the surface," Master Giddi mind-melded.

It was strange hearing the master mage's voice in his head. Rumors said Giddi could mind-meld with anyone and any dragon—that's how he'd received the title Dragon Mage.

Fenni pushed the fireball out of the river, into the air, but it vanished.

"It takes high-level mastery to switch between elements," said Master Giddi. "Down you go again."

Weeds swirled around him as he settled on the riverbed. Flame it, he had to prove himself. When his fireball was a seething mass of molten flame, he kicked off the bottom. Weeds brushed his legs as the fire roiled, shooting toward the surface. He could do this.

Something yanked Fenni's legs, nearly pulling his hips from his sockets. Tendrils were tangled around his calves. He kicked, but the weeds gripped tighter, dragging him down. His lungs strained. Was Master Giddi testing him? Using *sathir*, he thrust the fireball upward. It broke the surface then fell back, sizzling in the water. He'd done it. Now, Master Giddi would free him.

The stranglehold on his legs tightened, his flesh searing. Fenni snatched at the tendrils, trying to pull himself free. More weeds snaked out of the murky water, wrapping around his arms, his chest and neck. His chest spasmed. He was losing air. This was no test from Master Giddi. It was a strangleton.

Reeled down like a hooked fish, Fenni thrashed. The monster plant's grip constricted, threatening to squeeze the last air from his lungs. Fenni tensed his chest. His muscles burned, screaming at him to open his mouth and breathe in the muddy water. By the dragon gods, he'd never avenge Uncle Fennock now. Desperate, he flung his remaining firepower at the strangleton before everything went black.

§

Light sneaked through a chink in the tent door. Fenni rubbed his eyes and tried to sit up, but pain shot across his chest and back. He pulled back the covers and lifted his shirt. Angry red marks scored his chest and sides, and he ached all over.

On the bedroll next to him, Master Giddi stirred. "About time you woke."

Not a word about what had happened. Shards, his master was tough. "That was a strangleton. I nearly drowned."

"Your fireball was a great signal. Good thinking. I was fighting a tharuk tracker or I would've got to you quicker. Sorry." His master tossed him a pot of healing salve. "Here, rub this on your chest and legs. I'll do your back when you're done."

Fenni smeared salve on his chest, breathing in peppermint. "Last night, you said there were no tharuks around."

Giddi's gaze was fierce beneath his dark, bushy eyebrows. "Well, I was wrong, wasn't I?" He rolled up his bedding with sharp angry movements, muttering, "Often happens, sometimes with disastrous consequences. You're lucky you're alive."

"How?" Fenni massaged the salve into his aching legs.

"You seared the thing's tentacles off with fire, but I had to fish you out." Giddi tied his bedding with a short length of rope. "You've mastered fire, by the way. Although more practice never hurt anyone. Let me look at your chest." Master Giddi grunted and lifted Fenni's shirt, prodding his livid bruising. "Luckily, nothing's broken. How are you feeling?"

"Sore." Fenni sighed. "I messed up, didn't I?"

"To the contrary. I'm happy with your progress. You survived a strangleton—something few can claim." Giddi shooed Fenni out of the tent and rolled up his bedding.

Fenni chuckled. His master must be concerned if he was packing up his gear.

Giddi's head appeared at the tent door. "If you're laughing, you're well enough to help. Here, throw these in the saddlebags."

Fenni caught the bedrolls, groaning.

"And while you're at it, give me a hand to roll this tent up." Giddi snapped his fingers at their fireplace. Within the ring of stones, green wizard flame licked at the wood, and soon, a fire was blazing.

Fenni filled a pot at the river and put it on the fire, sprinkling oats, herbs and cheese chunks in the water.

"That'll be a hearty wizard porridge, Fenni," Master Giddi mumbled, shaping the fire's flames into dragons, their fiery tongues licking at the base of the pot until the porridge was bubbling.

"How did you do that?"

"This?" Master Giddi waved a hand and the fiery dragons circled the pot and disappeared in a shower of sparks. His control over mage flame was absolute. "Years of underwater practice."

Fenni sighed. He was such a raw beginner. At the last trials, he'd covered up by excelling with water and wind, but he couldn't do that now. These wizard duels were his final trial. If he didn't show he'd mastered fire, the wizard council would never let him fight tharuks on his own.

After they'd eaten, they swung onto their horses. "We'll be at Mage Gate later today," Master Giddi said. "You can practice on horseback on the way. But whatever you do, don't harm the spangles. They don't like rogue mage flame."

"So it's true." Fenni trailed Master Giddi through the trees. "There *are* spangles in Great Spanglewood Forest."

"Of course there are, my boy."

At seventeen summers, Fenni was hardly a boy, but he wasn't about to argue. "And is it true they're magic?"

"Aye." Master Giddi guided his horse to the foot of a hill.

Rocks rose steeply on either side of the trail as they started the trek over the pass that cut through the northern end of Great Spanglewood Forest. Fenni glanced behind them as they left the tree line. Spangles? Then how come none of the trees glimmered the way the legends said they would? Was his master telling him a tall tale? Or was he serious?

Gossip

Ezaara's body slammed against the wall, the back of her skull cracking on stone. Hot blood trickled down her neck. She woke, soaked in sweat, panting.

She clutched the crystal at her neck—warm against her fingers and skin. Soothing. Her nightmares were so vivid—as if she were living them. But in them, she wasn't herself. Her hands were different. Her limbs were rangier, and she felt more solid. Like she was experiencing the world through someone else's body.

She was so tired. Zens stalked her dreams, never letting her sleep—but it was nothing compared to what Roberto would be going through. She had to convince the council to rescue him before it was too late. Ezaara flipped back the covers and got out of bed, shivering in her sweat-drenched nightdress.

"You need a hot bath to soothe you," Zaarusha melded. *"The council members are still sleeping, so you have time."* She snaked her head through the archway and shot flames at the pile of wood under Ezaara's bathtub, then breathed on the water and the outside of the metal tub.

"Thank you, Zaarusha, you take such good care of me." Ezaara rubbed Zaarusha's snout.

The queen butted Ezaara's stomach. *"You're doing your best to take care of Dragons' Realm. I need you at my side."*

"And I need Roberto at mine."

"We'll get him, but I'd rather have the sanction of the council than have you fighting them. If we're going to defeat Zens we need to be united."

Ezaara pulled off her nightdress and climbed into the steaming water. "And if they won't rescue him?"

"They will." Zaarusha's scales bristled. *"And if they don't, we'll go together."*

An hour later, Ezaara was seated in the council meeting. Absently, she clutched her pendant. It was cool now, not warm at all. Roberto's bloodied face flashed to mind.

Tonio's gaze sharpened, resting upon the crystal at her neck. "That's an interesting bauble. Where did you get it?"

Everyone stared at her necklace. Ezaara didn't like his carefully-casual tone. She tucked the necklace back under her jerkin. Had Tonio recognized the Naobian craftsmanship? Did he suspect Roberto had given it to her? "My jewelry is immaterial to the matter at hand. We've called this council meeting to discuss rescuing Master Roberto from Death Valley."

"Thank you, my honored Queen's Rider." Lars nodded, formally. "Erob is home, as we desired, however, he's still recovering from his injuries. This afternoon, when he's rested, Master Tonio will mind-meld with Erob and Maazini to gather information regarding Roberto's capture. This is of utmost priority."

The spymaster nodded. "My honored Queen's Rider and council, we must rescue Master Roberto as soon as possible."

Ezaara's jaw snapped shut. She'd been ready to fight them, all her arguments lined up: how Tonio had insisted Roberto go; the value of Roberto's role on the council; how she could guide them to the right place in Death Valley …

Now Tonio agreed with her?

Lars nodded. "I concur. All in favor of Roberto's rescue, raise their hands."

Everyone's hand shot up. Good, the decision was unanimous. They could leave after Tonio had melded with the dragons. It would be best to sneak in after dusk, like she had yesterday. Maybe they needed more invisibility cloaks. Who would be the best to go? And how many? Just a few so they could still sneak in, but enough so that if they were discovered they could fight their way out.

"How will we rescue him?" asked Aidan, the battle master. "We can't afford a heavy loss."

True, but he spoke as if Roberto wasn't a loss already. Yet every day was empty without him.

"Agreed. It's imperative that we prepare for war," Lars said. "We must also qualify the Queen's Rider. Our people need confidence that she is at the helm, leading us."

Leading? What a joke.

"We'll have our official race in six days and Ezaara's feast afterward," Lars continued. "That'll give the new riders time to practice flying. Meanwhile, we have the imprinting ceremony today. Because Roberto, our master of mental faculties and imprinting, isn't here, Ezaara will need to greet the new riders and help Master Alyssa train them."

Alyssa smiled. "Ezaara, your help would be valuable. As one of our most accomplished riders, you must pass on your knowledge."

Master Aidan steepled his fingers. "Yes, we need our new riders ready for battle. We don't want them or their dragons injured."

"We must develop their sword and archery drills," said Derek, master of instruction. "And dragonback archery. If they can see Ezaara, one of our newest riders, excelling, it will inspire them to train harder."

"This makes sense, Ezaara," Zaarusha mind-melded. *"We must better our chances in this upcoming war against whatever Zens will unleash on us."*

"But wait," said Master Tonio, eyes on Ezaara again, "We seem to have forgotten the Queen's Rider's request. When will we rescue Master Roberto?"

"Why, after the race day feast," said Aidan. "Training our new riders must be top priority, and ensuring the Queen's Rider qualifies."

Tonio smiled. "Great idea."

What? He'd manipulated the council into delaying. That shrotty weasel.

Lars rapped his gavel. "It's decided, then. In six days, after the feast, a small group will travel to Death Valley to ascertain how we'll rescue Master Roberto."

Around Ezaara, masters rose. Ma rushed over and kissed her on the cheek. "I must go, honey. I have to check Erob and Maazini."

Ezaara nodded. "Master Lars," she said, keeping her voice down. "The race is in six days. Anything could happen to Master Roberto in that time." There, that was just about right—concerned, but not brimming with emotion.

Lars gazed at her frankly. "I understand your concern, but if Zens had wanted to kill Roberto, he would've done so already. We have a war to prepare for. Master Roberto would want us to focus on the realm first, him second. As Queen's Rider, I'm sure you understand balancing the needs of thousands against one. We will rescue him. It's just going to take a little longer than you'd like." Lars patted her shoulder, as if she was a littling. "Let's prepare for imprinting. There's a lot to do." He followed the others out of the chamber.

Ezaara slumped back into her chair, studying the flecks in the horseshoe-shaped granite table. She'd been played by an expert. By agreeing with her so early in the council meeting, Tonio had disarmed her. Surprised, she'd laid aside all her carefully prepared arguments. And then he'd tromped in, making sure everyone was busy, preparing for war.

They'd promised to rescue Roberto in six days. She'd make sure it happened.

"Ezaara."

She snapped her head up, unaware that anyone had remained in the chamber. "Pa?"

He paced to her chair. "You don't seem yourself. I know you've the realm on your shoulders."

She sighed. "Yes, there's that."

Pa put an arm around her. "I missed you yesterday. Where were you?"

So, Lars and Tonio hadn't told anyone else.

"Zaarusha and I had urgent business."

"You could've told—"

"The dragon queen approved my whereabouts," Ezaara snapped.

His face fell.

Oh shards, she hadn't meant to hurt Pa. "How's Erob?" she asked, softening her voice.

"Exhausted. He's lost a lot of blood." Pa rubbed his hands on his breeches. "That necklace Tonio mentioned, may I see it?"

It was a gift from Roberto, personal. She hadn't meant to wear it outside her jerkin. "Uh, I'd rather not, if you don't mind. It's just a trinket."

"A trinket? I doubt it," Pa replied. "It looked like Anakisha's dream catcher."

"Anakisha's dream catcher? No, I'm sure you're mistaken."

"It went missing years ago. The wearer can tune into another's mind while they're sleeping, sensing their thoughts." Pa shook his head. "Whoever gave it to you must've stolen it."

"I don't think—"

"Or perhaps they bought it from a market," he said hurriedly. "I didn't mean to disparage anyone. It could be an imitation. Who did you say gave it to you?" His brow furrowed.

"I didn't." Ezaara faced Pa, forcing herself to breathe steadily.

"You may be Queen's Rider, Ezaara, but you're still our daughter." Pa shook his head sadly and left.

"I know." A tear slid down Ezaara's cheek as the double chamber doors boomed shut behind him. "But there are some things I can't even share with you," she whispered.

§

Lovina held the boy in her arms. the steady motion of the rocking chair comforting him. His body was all sharp angles and poky bits, but then again, so was hers. You didn't bounce back overnight after years as a slave in Death Valley. She hummed a Flatlander tune under her breath, the one her mother had sung when she was little. Slowly, her memories were returning.

Tomaaz was out flying, training on perimeter patrol, so he'd asked her to sit with the boy.

"You're so patient," Ajeurina melded.

"That's what he needs. It's hard adjusting to all the sights and sounds after being numlocked." She gave the rocking chair another push. *"And to being loved."* That had been strange, but now a dragon in her head?

"If I ever catch Bill or those tharuks that beat you …." Ajeurina shared an image of furry bodies being tossed into the air.

She smiled. Even though Ajeurina was in the den next door, outside the infirmary, they'd been chatting for most of the morning. The lad had been sleeping better since Tomaaz had come home, but still hadn't spoken. Lovina kept humming Ma's tune, breaking into the words on the second verse. The lad's lake-blue eyes were fastened on her face the whole time.

"I'm going to hunt. Would you like to come?"

"I don't think the boy would like it."

"You could always ask him."

"Good idea." Lovina stopped singing. She was about to speak when the boy placed a hand on her cheek and hummed the refrain.

Hope surged in Lovina's chest, making her want to shout with joy. "You want me to keep singing?"

Eyes solemn, he nodded.

She hummed a few more bars, and he joined in. "So, you know this song?"

Another nod.

Lovina barely dared breathe. "Are you from the Flatlands, too?"

"Yes." His whisper was barely audible

"Which village?" She held her breath.

"Waykeep," he croaked, his voice rusty.

A small village smack in the middle of the Flatlands, at the crossroads. She brushed his hair back from his eyes. "Do you remember your name?" If they knew his name, maybe they could find his family. With his family, he'd have a better chance than she'd had.

"Taliesin," he murmured.

§

Adelina paced in her cavern. The world was too small, too confined. She wanted to hammer the stone and burst through the mountain. Grief and fear sunk their talons into her innards, twisting them. She needed to run, scream—something.

Shards, she was supposed to be at the imprinting grounds soon. No dragon would choose her. Zaarusha hadn't. What if she just wasn't dragon rider material?

Roberto had always told her she'd find a dragon, but with him captive to Zens, the world felt like a dangerous place, a place where the future couldn't be trusted, where her smile wasn't bright enough to overcome her troubles.

Dragon's claws! Now she was sniffing. Adelina backhanded a tear and tugged on her boots, yanking the laces hard. Zens had ruined her family: stolen her father, her brother, her mother's life and now her brother again. But what could she do? She was just Adelina, the little sister of a master on the council. She'd never be able to make Dragons' Realm a better place. For years she'd fooled herself that her smile and her bubbly attitude would make a difference—and it had, for Roberto, during his darkest moments. Now, he was gone.

She flung herself on her bed. The last thing she felt like was seeing a bunch of people. And that was saying something. Usually she, Kierion and Lofty were the life and soul of the party.

Adelina pummeled her pillow. Moping wasn't going to fix anything. She'd find a sharding smile if it killed her. She strode to her door and flung it open, coming face to face with Mara, who had her hand raised to knock. Leah was behind Mara, brow creased with worry.

"Oh, uh, come in," Adelina said.

"Adelina, we're glad you're here." Mara dragged Leah through the doorway. "Snake-tongue's gossip is getting worse."

Adelina pulled them inside, then shut the door. "What's going on. Is it about Ezaara?"

Mara's eyes were wide. "Yes, Sofia is saying she's vicious and can't be trusted. There's talk of how she attacks trainees with knives and worse." Mara nudged Leah. "Tell her what you heard."

Leah nervously tucked her blonde hair behind her ear. "You know I'm helping the master healer in the infirmary now, right?"

Adelina nodded.

"Ezaara came in, looking for healing supplies this morning. After she left, a patient said Snake-tongue had told him Ezaara had poisoned the queen herself, only pretending to rescue her."

A surge of hot rage blasted through Adelina's chest. "Lies! I helped the Queens' Rider save Zaarusha. I was with Kierion when he found the remedy." She wanted to punch Snake-tongue's smarmy face. She and Sofia had been good friends until the accident. Overnight, everything had changed. It was awful, like Sofia had been magicked into being nasty.

"Kierion found the remedy?" asked Leah.

"Ezaara figured out what remedy was needed and sent Kierion to find more, but that's not the point," said Adelina. "That guttersnipe is ruining everything."

"We have to do something," said Mara.

The door burst open. Gret and Lovina barreled in. "Oh, sorry, we didn't realize you had company," Gret said.

"What is it?"

"Just something we heard." Lovina's eyes flitted to Mara and Lara.

"It's all right. They were just letting me know the latest gossip that Snaketongue was spouting."

"Oh, good," said Gret. "That's what we wanted to see you about too. Sofia's saying Ezaara poisoned Zaarusha."

"The girls said so. Keep your eyes and ears peeled. Once we know what's going on, we'll tell Lars."

"We have to write down what's been said," Gret said. "Lars always wants evidence."

Mara and Leah nodded. "We can do that," Leah said. "I'll get a quill and paper from the infirmary."

"Right, we'd better get to the imprinting grounds or Alyssa will be wild." Adelina gazed at Lovina, suddenly awkward. How awful. Her and Gret were in the imprinting group but Lovina wasn't. "I'm sorry, Lovina, I wish you could come too."

Lovina's thin face lit up, like sun reflecting off a lake. "I don't need to. I imprinted with Ajeurina yesterday. I'm already a dragon rider."

Gods, in her self-pity-fueled state, Adelina hadn't even realized.

Dragons

Master Alyssa raised her arm, motioning for the trainees to be quiet.

Kierion elbowed Lofty. "Ssh."

The hubbub in the training cavern died down.

"I apologize on behalf of Roberto, master of mental faculties and imprinting. He cannot be here today. As flight master I am here in his stead."

There'd been rumors that Roberto had been away on council business. Kierion hadn't seen him for at least a moon and a half. Tomaaz had been with him, but he'd recently returned, so surely Roberto would be back soon.

Adelina and Gret hustled in, late.

Kierion winked to greet Adelina. She barely raised an eyebrow in return. Over the last few days, she'd been distant and withdrawn—ever since the prank with the arrows. Was she mad at him over that? Surely not. Maybe Adelina was missing her brother. Or maybe she was mad at him for something else. Kierion racked his brains to think what he could've done to annoy her, but came up blank.

He yawned. Doing double kitchen duty and extended training was wearing him out. Shards, everyone was raising their hands and he hadn't been paying attention. He shot his hand up, too, so he wouldn't stand out.

"All right, Kierion," said Master Alyssa, waving him to the front with a flourish. "You may demonstrate first."

Demonstrate what? Kierion shot a panicked glance at Lofty, who mimed eating. What was that about?

"Please, Kierion, show the class how it's done."

He thought fast. "Perhaps you could recap the step beforehand, Master Alyssa, just to refresh everyone. And then I'll show them, of course."

Alyssa laughed, shaking her head, her dark plaits swinging. "Recap imprinting? I don't think you were listening."

If word of this got back to Master Lars, he'd be dragon toast. What should he—

Lofty was surreptitiously miming eating again.

Of course! Kierion pretended to place something on his palm, and held it out flat. "Although it's not necessary, feeding a newly-imprinted dragon helps to cement your bond. Hold your palm flat, like when you feed a horse, or toss scraps into the air for the dragon to catch." He mimed tossing food to the trainees. Lofty caught an imaginary morsel, chomping it down. Oops, they'd better not get too carried away. "Is there anything else, Master Alyssa?"

"Thank you, Kierion." As he re-joined the class, Master Alyssa added, "Of course, I asked you all that quick question for Kierion's benefit, because he wasn't listening. Pay attention now, all of you, please."

Lofty sniggered. "She got you there."

Ears hot, Kierion nodded, not daring to take his eyes off their instructor.

"The imprinting grounds are a place where many dragons and riders can meet to see if they form an instant bond. Not everybody will bond with a dragon today. Remember, imprinting can happen anywhere, anytime." Alyssa paced before them. "For example, Ezaara and Zaarusha imprinted in the forest in Lush Valley, an area dragons hadn't visited for years."

One of the arrow flingers put up his hand. "Is it true that people from Lush Valley used to hate dragons?"

"Yes, many years ago they had a settlement arbitrator who had a grudge against dragons, so he raised his son and grandson in the same vein. Once our honored Queen's Rider imprinted, dragons went back to Lush Valley to help save its people from tharuks. They understand our intentions are good now. Ezaara and Zaarusha have changed Lush Valley attitudes for the better. Let's hope the outcomes of your bonds with your dragons are as productive. Any more questions?"

Soon, they were heading along the tunnels to the old door that led to the imprinting grounds. Kierion had only been there once before, when he'd helped save Zaarusha from poison, and he'd flown up, so he'd never seen this narrow tunnel.

Lofty was at Kierion's side as they negotiated the uneven rocky stairs that wound up through the mountain. Torches sputtered in their sconces, the light flickering over the trainees in front of them. Some had been training for months, like Sofia, Alban, Gret, Henry and Rocco. Others were only new, like him and Lofty, but they were all here for one thing: dragons. With tired legs, Kierion trudged upward, yawning again.

"Too much kitchen duty," Lofty teased.

"Well, you're helping in the kitchen too. Aren't you tired?"

"No, I snatch a snooze between training and dinner."

"Brilliant. Why didn't I think of that?" Ahead of him, a girl stumbled. Kierion leapt forward to steady her.

"Thanks, Kierion."

Thanks to his arrow prank, everyone knew his name, but who was she?

Behind him, Lofty was now walking with another trainee. "Do you mind if I pass?" Kierion flashed a smile at the girl and she let him past. He bounded up the stairs and caught up with Adelina, falling in alongside her. "Bit of a steep climb, isn't it?" he asked.

"I hadn't noticed." Her voice was flat, disinterested.

So, she *was* mad at him. Kierion sighed. "Whatever I've done, I'm sorry, Adelina. Sometimes I upset people without realizing."

She stared at him. "Not everything's about you, Kierion." She pushed up the stairs, past people, to get ahead.

What? For a moment, Kierion stopped, dumbfounded. Someone behind bumped into him. He spurted up the stairs after her, saying, "Excuse me," and "Thanks for letting me pass," until he reached Adelina.

Something glimmered on her cheek in the torchlight. She was crying.

So, it wasn't about him. Something must be up with her brother or a friend. Or maybe she was just sad. Kierion walked with her in silence up a few more stairs, then gave her hand a quick squeeze to let her know he understood. To his surprise, she gripped his hand fiercely, not letting go as they wound their way upward through the stone.

Something splashed onto the back of his hand. Another tear. He squeezed her hand tighter and kept walking. As it started to get lighter, she gave him a wan smile and whispered, "Thank you."

Adelina released his hand, scrubbing her cheeks with her sleeve, and pasted a bright smile on her face. "I'm all right now."

Who did she think she was fooling? She looked terrible.

Then her face changed. Eyes bright, she smiled—a genuine smile. "Can you feel it?" Adelina asked, her voice filled with wonder.

What? Kierion shrugged.

And then he felt it. His tiredness vanished. Excitement pulsed through his veins. He wanted to run straight up the stairs onto the plateau.

"It's the dragons. Come on." Adelina snatched up his hand again, and they raced up the stairs.

Out on the plateau, Kierion's heart pounded. The sky beyond was filled with flapping wings, sinuous necks and dragon maws shooting tiny flames of excitement. Scales flashed in the sun: emerald, copper, scarlet, violet, mustard, orange, blue and more. The whole sky seethed with color.

With thuds, dragons landed in the snow, flurries eddying with their wingbeats.

And then Kierion saw her. His dragon. His heart exploded wide open, and a rush of love enveloped him. He was swept up in a river of feeling, his feet moving effortlessly toward this golden-eyed beauty out on the plateau. Her purple scales glinted with gold specks as she approached him.

"Kierion, you were born to be my rider."

No one had told him that imprinting was like this—a rush of emotion so intense, it could sweep you away; a harmony so sweet, you could cry; a dragon so exquisite, you'd give your life for her. *"How did you know my name?"*

"Since your prank with the arrows, all the dragons know your name. It caused quite a stir, you know."

Kierion's ears went red, yet again. *"What's your name?"*

"I shall now be named Riona, in your honor—because it's an honor to have a rider like you."

"L-like me?"

Then Kierion had the oddest moment of his life—and he'd had plenty of odd moments. He saw himself as Riona did: tall, lean, with a shock of blond hair and blue-gray eyes. Pretty sea eyes, his Ma had called them. But it wasn't his features that were strange; it was his face, etched with love as he gazed at his new friend.

He touched her snout. Her scales were warm and as supple as worn leather. He scratched her eye ridges, and she thrummed, like a purring cat. A shot of vicious pleasure ripped through his mind with an image of Riona devouring a cat. Her lip curled back and her fangs glinted.

"You're smiling." Kierion laughed. "You have a sense of humor, too."

"And I like pranks, as much as you."

Master Alyssa approached, holding a bowl of meat scraps.

"Thank you." Kierion held some out for Riona.

Her snout tickled his palm as she snaffled them down. *"Come on, Kierion, let's fly."*

Riona's impatience thrummed through Kierion. Stepping upon her extended foreleg, he climbed onto her back. She had no saddle, so he settled into a soft hollow between her spinal ridges and hung on tight. Riona's haunches tensed, coiled with energy.

A voice rang out over the plateau. "Please wait before you fly."

It was Ezaara, flying on Zaarusha, sitting tall in the saddle, holding a stick high in the air as the queen landed on the plateau. Hang on, there was something familiar about that stick. Kierion squinted against the sun. It was the cane Roberto had carved for Ezaara.

Riona's body trembled beneath Kierion, full of suppressed energy. Other new riders were straddling their dragons, perched in the snow, ready to fly. With one short call, Ezaara had stopped them all.

"Welcome to the ranks of riders of fire," Ezaara said. "In time, you'll learn to harness the energy from your dragon to enhance your abilities. Some of you may inherit their gifts too. Use what they give you wisely. Now, before you fly, you must all pledge to serve our Honored Dragon Queen, Zaarusha, and Dragons' Realm." Ezaara held her staff high again.

Voices fired up, everyone chanted, "We pledge to serve our Honored Dragon Queen, Zaarusha, and Dragons' Realm."

"I pledge to serve my queen, Zaarusha, and Dragons' Realm," Riona said at the same time.

Zaarusha roared, accepting their allegiance.

A ripple of pride flowed through Kierion from Riona. He chuckled. *"Your emotions are so glorious. You make the colors in my life brighter."*

"You inspire them, Kierion. Everything feels richer since we've imprinted. I can't help sharing that with you." Again, a rumble built in his mind.

At the back of the plateau, Sofia and Alban were perched on dragons, scowling.

Kierion couldn't imagine them pledging to anyone. Sofia had been as sour as an unripe grape lately, and had poisoned Alban's attitude, too. Behind them were the trainees who hadn't imprinted yet, most trying bravely to smile and failing.

"Before you fly, please introduce your dragons to us," the Queen's Rider requested. "We'll start with Gret."

"Gret and Hagret." Gret was sitting on a scarlet dragon.

"Adelina with Linaia." Adelina sat smiling, on a fine blue mount, whose scales changed from light to dark as she moved.

"Lofty with Itziga."

Their names didn't match. Murmurs immediately broke out among the new riders.

Ezaara raised her staff again. "I know it appears Lofty is breaking the naming convention between rider and dragon because their names don't have a common syllable, but he isn't." Ezaara laughed. "His true name is Fritz. My brother Tomaaz nicknamed him Lofty, back in Lush Valley because he's so short."

The towering Lofty, short? Everyone laughed. Lofty grinned and gestured at the next rider to continue.

It wasn't until Ezaara laughed that Kierion realized something was wrong. When she'd arrived at the hold, Ezaara had laughed easily. Now it was forced. Dark shadows smudged her eyes, her shoulders were weighed down and her smile was brittle.

"Kierion with Riona." He inclined his head.

Riona roared, and a tremor ran through him. *"I want to fly,"* she said.

"Not long." As more riders introduced themselves and their dragons, Riona's impatience grew, making Kierion itch to get going.

At last it was Sofia's turn.

"Sofia and Aria." Sofia's dragon was also purple, but not as beautiful as Riona.

"Aria sings," said Riona. *"When she was tiny, her voice was awful, but now she's quite melodious."*

"Really? I didn't know dragons could sing."

"Alban and Banikan." Alban was on an emerald dragon.

Hopefully, he'd be sent off to the green guards in Naobia. Kierion was sick of his scowl.

Raising a hand, Master Alyssa called, "Now fly. Trust your dragons. We'll see you in the training cavern after dinner."

Flapping, roars, and whoops filled the air as dragons launched into the sky.

Instead of leaping after them, Riona strode to the edge and dropped down. The mountain face whooshed past. Wind tugged at Kierion's hair. The snowy clearing rushed closer. His stomach plummeted.

Riona flapped her wings to break their fall, and soared over the basin. Above them, dragons were blurs of color in the sky. Riona caught a thermal and spiraled up toward the snowy peaks. Kierion was filled with a rush of energy that took his breath away. Every wingbeat sent a tremor of joy through him. Shards, he felt so alive. He'd never be the same again.

So that's why riders said life wasn't worth living if you lost your dragon.

Mage Gate

Fenni and Master Giddi traveled over the rocky pass and down through foothills. "Try that snow drift," Master Giddi ordered.

Flame blasted from Fenni's fingertips, shooting under the foliage of two strongwoods to hit the snowy hump. His fireball sizzled, melting the snow and revealing a rock.

Giddi grunted. "If you can manage that from horseback, you might have a shot at doing decently on dragonback one day. Try that stump."

On dragonback? That would be awesome. Fenni flung out his hands, but his fire fizzled out on the side of the trail. Oh, shards, his flame still wasn't reliable.

A bushy eyebrow raised. "Keep practicing."

"I've never seen a mage on dragonback." Oh, what a fool. He was speaking to the dragon mage himself. "Sorry, I meant—"

"Don't worry so much, Fenwick. Of course you've never seen a wizard on a dragon, but years ago, we rode behind dragon riders, blasting tharuks with wizard flame while riders shot arrows." He sighed. "It'll never happen again, in your lifetime." His master gave such an ominous scowl that Fenni didn't dare ask anything else. They rode on in silence, Master Giddi deep in thought with his bushy eyebrows pulled down.

When they entered the northern part of Great Spanglewood Forest, the woods were carpeted in deep snow. The horses trudged on until they arrived at a wide snowy clearing, sliced through the middle by a fast-moving stream. The far side was edged with tents, a stable and cabins with green mage smoke curling from their chimneys.

Master Giddi chaffed his hands together. Fenni's behind was saddle-sore and his shoulders ached from flinging flame all day. If only he could rest.

Wizards dotted the clearing, shooting flame at targets, and dueling each other with snow, water or flame. Thick vines wrapped themselves around one woman's legs, and a magical gust of wind knocked a man down. Bolts of light flashed from trees and mages conjured magical shields to protect themselves. A group were gathered by a cauldron over an outdoor fire, brewing a smelly concoction that wafted plumes of blue smoke.

Master Giddi and Fenni walked their horses through the low point of the stream, then dismounted and led them toward the stable.

"Hey, it's the dragon mage," a group of Naobian mages called out, waving at Giddi.

"Master Giddi." A Naobian, a couple of summers older than Fenni, with broad shoulders and long black hair broke away from the group. His skin was tan, and his eyes were a startling blue—not typical for a Naobian. He was a flashy type, wearing three earrings—turquoise, jade and garnet. "Jael of Naobia." He held his hand out to Fenni.

Fenni shook it. "Fenni of Montanara."

"Ah, so you're Fenni?" Jael smiled. "I'm helping you train, right?"

Fenni shot a querying gaze at Master Giddi.

Giddi gave a sharp nod. "Ah, right. Forgot to mention that."

Jael pounded Master Giddi on the back. Master Giddi embraced him.

His gruff old master hugging someone? Fenni's boots nearly flew off in surprise.

"So, I got your messenger bird," Jael said. "I've brought the herbs with me. You say the former master healer is back at Dragons' Hold? What's she like?"

Master Giddi grinned. "You'll meet her later. First, Fenni needs a little practice with underwater fireballs."

"Sure, come with me." Jael led Fenni past a blonde mage aiming her hands at the snow. Light shimmered from her fingers and snow was swept from the ground, exposing the lush grass beneath. A flurry formed, then thickened, growing into an impenetrable wall, blocking their way. The wall iced over, solidifying.

"Ah, Velrama, could you please let us through?" Jael asked with a laugh.

"Sure." The blonde girl shot a bolt of green flame at the wall. The snow in the center sizzled and melted, creating an archway for them to walk through. On the other side of the wall was an old mage with snowy hair and a beard threaded with brightly-colored mage crystals—turquoise, green, red and purple—that indicated his rank as a senior wizard master.

"You're Giddi's lackey, aren't you?" The mage's gaze was so intense, he could've peeled skin.

What had he done wrong? Fenni drew himself up, and met the master's eye. "Yes, sir, the dragon mage is my master." That ought to impress him.

The wizard's lip curled and his nose wrinkled in distaste. "Don't miss the choosing pouch ceremony at sunset or you'll forfeit your place in the trials."

Fenni and Jael made their way into the woods. "Who was that old grump?"

"Master Starrus," Jael replied.

"*That* was Master Starrus?" Fenni had heard of the high master on the Wizard Council. "He'll be judging the trials tomorrow?" The Egg help him—he was going to need it if that sour man was determining whether he passed or not.

Jael's bark of laughter startled a deer, its white tail flashing as it fled. "One of the reasons you need more practice."

The stream met a broad river that wound between the trees. Although the edges were crusted with ice, the middle still flowed. "Let's work here," Jael said.

Fenni took off his cloak, but Jael stopped him from removing more clothing. "You won't have time to take off your clothes in battle. Do you really want to face tharuks naked?"

"Good point."

"Go on, then, jump in."

"But—"

"Come on, my feet are getting cold. We Naobians are used to the sun."

As if Jael would get cold in his fur-lined leather boots. A thousand questions flooded Fenni's mind. Who was Jael? What if there was another strangleton? Why had Master Giddi abandoned him to a stranger, nearly the same age as him?

"Now, Fenni. We can't miss the choosing pouch." Sparks flew at Fenni's boots.

Fenni dived into the icy water. Reaching out with his mind, he ignored his sodden breeches dragging him down, and drew on the *sathir* of the river flora and fauna. Sparks flaring at his fingertips, he tried to warm himself. Shards, this was colder than Spanglewood River. Much colder. Icy water pressed in on him, chilling him. His chest constricted in panic and the air whooshed out of his lungs. The sparks at his fingertips died. Fenni burst above the surface, face dripping. He'd failed again.

"Don't let the cold put you off," Jael barked.

Under he went, but the chilly water stole Fenni's breath again—and again.

Finally, Jael motioned him over to the bank and hauled him out. Instead of berating him, Jael embraced him.

What? When Jael stepped back, Fenni's clothes were dry and he was toasty warm. "That's great."

"Sit."

Fenni parked his rump in the snow.

"Here, eat this." Jael gave him some dried beef to chew on. "What's stopping you?"

"My breath," Fenni answered between bites. "It's just so sharding cold, it steals my air. It's panic, I guess."

"If you can manage fire across all mediums, you can manage anything. Master Starrus has a grudge half the length of Dragons' Realm against your master. Tomorrow, he'll do anything to make you fail. You have to try harder for Giddi's sake."

For Giddi's sake? What about his own? What about vengeance for his uncle's death?

"Your weakness is your fear, but you need to master it. What's the worst thing that could happen to you in that river?"

"I could die of cold. Drown. Get caught by a strangleton. Eaten by a muncher."

"I did a *sathir* sweep of the river when we got here and couldn't sense any munchers or strangletons. Besides, Master Giddi would blast my britches if I let you die. Now, anything else?"

"I, ah …"

"Good, then get back in the water." A fireball flew from Jael's hand, right at Fenni's head. He ducked, scrambling back into the river.

Fenni came up spluttering a few more times, but by the end of the afternoon, Jael had Fenni shooting fireballs at him from underwater, while he perched high in a tree. Finally, Fenni clambered from the river, shooting volleys of fireballs.

Jael easily caught every one of them. "Not bad," he said. "Now dry yourself."

How? Fenni had never done that with magic.

The icy wind cut through Fenni's clothes, making him shiver. Jael leaned against the trunk of a strongwood tree and chewed on another piece of dried beef. "You must be freezing," he said, watching Fenni with those strange blue eyes.

Despite shivering, Fenni's mouth watered. "Could I have a piece? I'm starving."

"Once you've earned it." Jael's earrings caught the sun, sparkling blue, green and red.

That wasn't fair. All Jael had done was sit around on his behind, barking commands, while Fenni had been using firepower all afternoon—freezing his backside off. Who did he think he was? Why, he was just a jumped-up trainee, only a year or two older than himself. "Why, you—" Hey, what was going on? Steam was rising from his clothes.

"Well done. Now, finish the job off without getting angry." Jael tossed him a strip of beef.

Fenni caught it. The steam dissipated. Cold seeped back into his skin. Without getting angry? Fenni created an internal rush of energy, similar to the sensation of being angry, but without the emotion. His clothes were dry in a heartbeat.

"You're a fast learner." Jael passed him his cloak. "Now, let's get back for the choosing pouch. I'm dying to see who you'll be dueling."

"Hey, thanks. My cloak's warm."

"You deserved that for putting up with me for so long." Jael cocked his head. "Great stamina. You probably didn't realize how many hours we've been at this."

The sun was low and the woods were shrouded in early evening shadows as they arrived back at the clearing. Mages stood in a circle in the snow with a fat sack in their midst. The blaze of sunset peeked through the trees.

"Just in time," whispered Jael at Fenni's side.

From across the clearing, Master Giddi mind-melded. *"Jael says your control was exemplary. Well done. Now that you can control fire underwater, you should be able to control it anywhere."*

A gentle glow spread through Fenni at his master's praise, but he'd missed what Master Starrus was saying.

"… and may the best opponent win," Master Starrus finished.

"The feathers will determine your dueling partner," Jael whispered. "Watch, here they come."

"What? We never did that at the last trial." Maybe because Master Starrus had been away.

Jael's only answer was an infuriating grin. Did that guy never stop smiling?

With a flourish, Master Starrus struck the sack with his staff.

The string on the mouth of the sack unraveled. A giant plume of fluff burst from the sack, flying up into the air, an explosion of color in the blazing sunset. Master Starrus waved his staff and the plume dispersed. Feathers of all colors swirled around the clearing in a madcap dance. Emerald, lapis and amethyst feathers spun through the air, landing in mages' hands. A gold sparkling feather shot past Fenni. A pair of peacock feathers angled themselves and flew like arrow shafts, one straight into the hands of a girl next to Fenni, and the other, to a boy across the clearing.

"Peacock," the girl crowed, racing across over to the lad, who was standing dumbstruck, admiring his feather.

"So, I have to catch one?"

"No, the feathers will find you. They're imbued with magic to sense what your weaknesses are and who your best opponent would be." Jael chuckled. "I wonder who I'll get this year."

"This year? How many trials have you been at?"

Jael gave that casual shrug of his. "A few."

"Like, how many is a few?"

"My parents are both mages, so I've been trialing since I was a littling."

"Whoa, you must be good. I've only been training for—"

A long-plumed silver feather dropped down past Fenni's face and hovered in the air in front of him. He stood gobsmacked, staring at it. The feather bobbed up and down impatiently. When Fenni didn't grab it, the silver quill twisted, poking his chest.

"Hey, stop that." Fenni snatched the feather. A thrill of magic ran through his palms and the feather flopped, lying flat against his palm. "Jael, what did—" Fenni's words died when he saw a matching silver feather in Jael's hand. Oh, shards. He was pitted against Jael—a mage with years of experience—but at least he was pitted against someone his own age.

A sudden silence enveloped the clearing.

Fenni spun. Master Giddi and Master Starrus were standing in the middle of the ring, both holding orange feathers as long as his arm. Overhead, stray feathers floated in the air, defying the chill breeze skittering through the trees. Master Starrus glowered at Giddi, then waved his staff. The stray feathers formed a plume, then rushed back into the open sack. He thumped his staff on the snow and the sack closed, tying itself shut.

Master Giddi regarded Master Starrus, face impassive. "So be it," he said, his quiet voice carrying in the silence. "I'll duel you at sunset tomorrow." The last rays of the setting sun were swallowed by darkness.

§

The next morning, Fenni was observing Master Giddi forming magical ice daggers and plunging them into tree trunks, when a mage ran into the clearing. "Dragon. A dragon's coming."

"Defensive positions," Master Starrus yelled. "Non-combatants inside."

A few mages scrambled up trees, at the ready. More took positions around the clearing. The others rushed to the cabins.

Fenni had been about to run after them, when Jael laughed, nudging Master Giddi. "All this over a dragon? Ridiculous. In Naobia we get along with the green dragons and their riders."

Giddi just arched one of his bushy eyebrows.

"You know those eyebrows are famous across Dragons' Realm," Jael said. "They're so versatile—a twitch for every mood."

Giddi guffawed, his laughter booming across the clearing.

The mages on duty shuffled from foot to foot as a silver dragon swooped across the trees, its wings catching the sunlight. Its beauty made Fenni's breath catch in his throat. It spiraled down to land gracefully in the snow.

"Time you fetched me those herbs, Jael, and bring some cups too," Master Giddi muttered, sending the Naobian trainee off to the cabin.

Giddi paced over to the dragon. With a flourish of his cloak, he bowed. "Liesar, it's an honor to see you." He cocked his head, then laughed.

He must be mind-melding, sharing a joke with the dragon. The dragon turned its eyes on Fenni, staring straight at him. Its slitted orbs were a beautiful deep shade of turquoise, like the wizard crystal he'd receive if he passed this trial.

"One moment." Master Giddi waved a hand at the mages on duty. "These visitors are mine. No need to stand sentinel. Go back to your duties."

"But Master Starrus said—"

"But Master Starrus, nothing," Giddi boomed. "I won't have my personal visitors being treated like enemies. This rider and dragon protect the realm, like we do. Now get back to work." He flung a flash of wizard fire at a mage in a tree.

Wizards scrambled out of the trees and fled to the large cabin.

"Good riddance," muttered Giddi. "Marlies, how are you? John told me you were back in the saddle."

"So Giant John has been gossiping again, has he?"

Back in the saddle? She was dismounting, sliding down the dragon's side to the snow. The rider was tall, old enough to be his mother, and she had eyes the same shade as the dragon's.

"Oh, Giddi, it's so good to see you." She embraced his master, and not only for a few seconds.

Was this an old lover of his master's, or a good friend? Embarrassed, Fenni coughed.

"Seems we're causing my trainee discomfort." Master Giddi ceased embracing her, and turned to him. "Fenni, this is Marlies, master healer at Dragons' Hold. It's been eighteen years since we've seen each other. Marlies, Fenni."

Not an old lover, then, just a friendly reunion.

They shook hands, and Marlies smiled. "I have a son and daughter about your age," she said. "Good luck in your trials."

"So, the rumors are true. You did have twins," Giddi said.

Marlies nodded. "Although not without a cost." She shook her head, sadness in her eyes. "But that can wait. Do you have the healing supplies?"

"Yes, I got your messenger bird. I had enough time to ask the Naobians to bring supplies from the South. There's not much growing around here at the moment." He gestured at the snow-blanketed earth. "Uncanny of you to remember where the wizard trials are held, especially after all this time."

"I never forgot a thing, Giddi, even after all those years of hiding."

Hiding? This woman was brimming with secrets.

"Couldn't have been much happening in Lush Valley." His voice grew urgent. "You were needed here all along, Marlies. The realm needs Hans, too. I'm glad you're back."

"And the realm needs you, Giddi," Marlies said softly, placing her hand on Master Giddi's arm. "Even though you've given so much."

To Fenni's surprise, his master didn't shake her arm off, or bluster, or even flinch. He stood there, gazing at the sky, eyes shiny with tears, while Marlies waited silently beside him. At long last, Master Giddi shook his head, his face lined with deep sorrow. "The past is over and we must both move on."

She nodded.

Giddi cleared his throat. "So, what's the first order of the day?"

Who was she, to bring back such sad memories that even the toughest wizard had tears in his eyes? The only emotions Fenni had seen his master show were mirth, frustration or his blustery gruffness. He hadn't known Master Giddi had a tender bone in him.

Jael returned, holding two bulging sacks. "Your herbs, Master Giddi. I have another sack somewhere."

"Not mine," Giddi answered, waving a hand at Marlies. "Master Healer Marlies from Dragons' Hold, this is Jael of Naobia. How about you brew us a cuppa, Jael?" Master Giddi and Marlies each loaded a sack into the dragon's saddlebags. They went over to a log, the silver dragon included. Giddi flourished his hands and the snow dissipated off the fallen tree in a cloud of steam. As Marlies sat, Master Giddi observed, "Your cloak is ripped."

"It's only a corner. I was fighting a tharuk in Western Settlement and its tusk got caught." She shrugged. "The tharuk came off much worse."

RIDERS OF FIRE

This rider looked weary. She must be tougher than she looked.

"I'll make you a new one, although invisibility cloaks take a while. What else do you need?"

Marlies hesitated. "You. At Dragons' Hold."

His master's face shuttered. "Marlies, I'm not coming to Dragons' Hold."

"Giddi, the realm needs you. With this rift, we won't withstand Zens. Our young trainees need to ride together, fight together, like we did."

Jael poured water from a waterskin into three mugs, and Liesar opened her maw and breathed over the cups. Soon they were steaming. Fenni added soppleberries to the cups, passing them around.

"No, Marlies. Those days are over."

"But dragon riders need wizards. We need to work together. The whole realm will be overrun if we don't defeat Commander Zens and his tharuks."

Master Giddi shook his head, bitter lines etched in his face. "I'll do more harm than good."

"No, Giddi. We're older, wiser. We won't make the same mistakes."

"Leave saving the realm to the young. We're still trying to undo the damage I caused."

"You caused? It was Mazyka's mistake, not yours." Marlies drained her cup and handed it to Fenni. "I'll see you soon, to collect my cape. I don't care about history, Giddi. We have to stand together." She climbed upon Liesar and flashed Giddi a smile. "Don't give Starrus too much of a hard time. Leave him some vestige of pride." She waved at Master Starrus, who was scowling from a window. Her mighty dragon tensed its haunches and leaped into the air.

Fenni's hair stirred in the breeze from the down-thrust of the dragon's wings. Gripping Marlies' cup, he frowned. Mazyka was the wizard who had opened the world gate and let Zens in. Why was Master Giddi shouldering the blame for her actions?

Jael shook his head grimly.

Master Giddi kicked the log. "Sharding dragon riders. To the Egg with the lot of them," he cursed.

His voice shot through Fenni's mind. *"No gossiping. Keep your trap shut."* Not a muscle twitched in his master's face. Not an outer sign he'd mind-melded with Fenni.

Fenni gazed at the silver dragon's blazing scales as it grew ever smaller in the sky.

§

Wizards ringed the clearing, perched in trees, sitting on the roofs, and gathered in a group at the edge of the forest, but not too close—no one wanted to get caught in the crossfire of a wizard duel. They'd been watching for a while now. Fenni's stomach was as a pond of frogs. Soon it would soon be his turn.

Velrama, the blonde who'd made the archway in the ice wall, was pitted against an older boy. She was good, blocking every flame the boy threw.

"Hey, Sorcha, you're being bested," someone called.

Face red, Sorcha flung a fireball at Velrama's knees, but she froze it with a wall of ice. His blush deepening, Sorcha shot a plume of flame at her. She caught it and flung it back. Scowling and gritting his teeth, he threw a giant fireball that exploded over Velrama's head, raining molten fire.

"Enough." Master Giddi's bellow shook the air. He raised his hands and doused the fire, then flung a hand at Sorcha, throwing him across the clearing to land in a snow drift.

Master Starrus shook his head. "Sorcha of the Flatlands, you know the purpose of the wizard trials is to demonstrate control over your power. Today, you lost control. Even though you have demonstrated great ability, you have failed. Velrama of Last Stop, your control in the face of his anger was exemplary. Master Reina will present you with your wizard crystal."

Sorcha clambered to his feet and stomped into a cabin, slamming the door.

The woman from the Wizard Council placed a leather thong with a turquoise crystal around Velrama's neck. Fenni wanted a crystal so badly, but his flame was still erratic. How in the Egg's name was he going to show his skill against Jael? He mustn't lose his temper, no matter what Jael flung at him. Or he'd never get to fight tharuks.

Master Reina called the next contestants. It was a routine demonstration with carefully-conjured and defended flame. No one wanted to repeat Sorcha's mistake. At the end, both contestants were awarded turquoise crystals.

"Jael of Naobia and Fenni of Montanara," called Master Reina from a table where she sat with the other two members of the Wizard Council—Master Starrus and Master Hemlon, a rotund wizard with hairy ears.

Fenni's palms were sweaty as he stepped forward. Although he'd spent a few hours with Jael yesterday, he hadn't seen him in action, so he had no idea what the Naobian was capable of.

"Now, remember, Fenni, play to your strengths," Master Giddi said.

Jael's master was nowhere to be seen. In fact, Fenni didn't even know who it was. Poor Jael. At least he had Master Giddi to support him. "My strengths? What are those again?" Shards, those frogs in his stomach wouldn't settle.

Giddi chuckled. "You're a fast-thinker. Trust your instincts and make sure you—"

A horn cut off Master Giddi's words. Well, that advice was as good as useless, wasn't it?

Fenni sensed the *sathir* in the forest and drew the energy inside himself. He flung his hands. Bolts of flame flew from his fingers, straight at Jael. The Naobian conjured up a thick ice shield. Sweat beading on his forehead, Fenni shoved his flames through the ice, melting it. Rivulets of water ran down Jael's shield. This was easier than he'd thought. Any moment now, he'd blast through.

Jael barely moved, but the water froze again. The shield thickened.

The Egg save him, no matter how much fire he threw, Jael's shield stayed intact.

Jael tilted his head. A flurry of snow swirled at Fenni's feet, then melted, turning to a pool of slush. Icy water trickled through Fenni's bootlace holes. He ignored it. Jael was trying to distract him. Fenni blasted the shield with more power.

The shield collapsed. Fenni's flame shot at Jael. Yes. He'd done it. Holding up his hand, the Naobian doused Fenni's fire before it reached him—and smiled. Jael was playing with him.

The earth underfoot churned with the slush to form mud. A gale-force wind blasted Fenni face-first into the mud puddle. Crows and hoots of laughter rang out.

"Go Jael," someone yelled.

"Show that Northerner how we duel."

Kneeling, Fenni spat out mud, grabbing handfuls of snow and scrubbing his face. His belly burned with anger. How dare—

No, he couldn't go there. If he lost his temper, he'd fail.

Fenni drew himself up to full height and pulled *sathir* inside himself until his whole body was humming and his fingers pulsing. Snow swirled around Fenni, but he ignored Jael's attack. He tugged a vine from a tree behind Jael. He'd bind Jael the way the strangleton had bound him. The vine whipped from the tree, wrapping itself around Jael's torso, trapping an arm against his side. Surprise shot across Jael's face.

Hah. A one-armed wizard—that would serve him right.

Jael flung his remaining arm out. Snow hit Fenni, knocking him back a step, his footing slippery in the mud. Pulling more sathir, Fenni channeled the energy into a vortex, flinging a whirlwind at Jael. Jael stumbled, but his laughter echoed around the clearing as he spun the vortex, aiming it at the ground. The wind ripped through the snow, spraying white as it plowed toward Fenni—and knocked him down.

Shards, he'd been knocked down twice. Would he qualify? Fenni's dreams of fighting tharuks flashed before his eyes. He saw Uncle Fennock's dead body all over again, his cousins' tears tracking down their faces. He'd vowed he'd grow up to be a mage and smite those awful beasts.

Jael's vines froze and shattered, debris flying.

Fenni scrambled to his feet and created a wall of mage fire.

His forehead glistening with sweat in the green firelight, Jael waved a hand. Fenni's flames fizzled and died. A plume of green mage fire arced through the air, right at Fenni.

Flaming shards. Desperate, Fenni flung one hand up to create an ice shield, and pointed his other hand toward the forest, searching for something, anything. A massive spiderweb, as wide as three men, hung between two trees. He squeezed his fingers into a fist. The web coalesced into a sticky mass, which he flung at Jael. The spiderweb wrapped itself around the Naobian mage. Jael's fire guttered and fizzed out, and Jael fell to the ground.

He'd done it. He'd knocked him over—

Jael wasn't moving. Murmurs rippled around the clearing. Oh gods, had he killed him?

Fenni ran over, kneeling by Jael, just as Master Giddi reached him. Jael was pale, eyes shut, his chest rising and falling with rapid gasps. "He's still breathing," Fenni cried. "He's not dead."

"I should hope not," said Master Giddi. "Get him out of there, quick."

Fenni used mage power to tear the spiderweb free and send it hurtling back into the forest. He shook Jael awake and helped him sit up. "You all right?" He didn't look all right. He was still gasping for air. "I'm sorry. What happened?"

"It's nothing." Jael waved a hand, trying to laugh it off.

Master Giddi kept his voice low. "Jael's mother was killed by a venomous gargantula when he was very young. Ever since then, he's been terrified of spiders."

Fenni hadn't known, but everyone would think he'd exploited Jael's fear. His face burned with shame. Surely, he'd failed his trials.

"Thanks, Giddi," Jael snapped. "That's not something I want everyone to know."

"I've blown your secret. I'm sorry." Fenni slumped.

Jael shrugged. "Too late now."

Fenni helped him up and the crowd cheered. They stood, awaiting Master Starrus' verdict.

"Master Jael, you dueled well, testing our trainee's fire skills. We hope you have recovered."

Still pale, Jael nodded, giving a tight smile.

Wait. What had Master Starrus said? "Jael's a master?" Fenni asked. He'd had no idea.

Master Giddi twitched an eyebrow. "That's why I let him train you."

"Not that it did any good if I've failed my trials," Fenni said, sighing.

"What do you mean?" said Master Starrus. "You exhibited control. You had no idea that the spiderweb would affect Master Jael like that." He passed Fenni his turquoise crystal. "Now, you're qualified as a wizard and have been endorsed by the Wizard Council. You may fight tharuks and use your powers to protect the realm."

Fenni slipped the leather thong over his head, the crystal resting against his chest. Jael pounded his shoulder, his turquoise, jade and garnet earrings flashing.

"Hang on, those are your wizard crystals."

Jael nodded as the crowd cheered and Master Giddi raised both of his infamous eyebrows in approval.

§

The sun sank behind the trees, shadows chasing its fiery rays from the sky. Wizard fires burned on stakes around the clearing, the makeshift torches casting a green hue on the snow and the onlookers' faces as they huddled near the cabins. Whispers and murmurs rippled through the crowd.

In the clearing, Master Giddi and Master Starrus were poised like dragons about to pounce.

The horn blew and the whispers died.

Fire arced from both of Master Starrus' hands. Master Giddi twitched a finger. It sputtered out before it hit him.

Face red, Starrus aimed a firebolt at Giddi's chest. The dragon mage caught it, extinguishing it.

Using both hands, Starrus drove a wall of fire at Giddi, then lifted it, arcing the crackling green blaze through the sky.

Dragon's Eggs, Starrus had lost control. People screamed and ducked. Fenni's heart hammered like a smith at an anvil.

"No." Master Giddi's strangled cry ripped across the clearing. A plume of fire shot from his hands, illuminating everyone's faces in a blinding flash.

The two fires slammed together, forming a molten green ball bigger than Master Giddi's cabin. Heat pressed down on Fenni. The onlookers fled. The fire erupted into a geyser of flame, shooting skyward, lighting up the entire clearing and surrounding forest.

"You fool," Master Giddi cried, waving his hands. In another flash of light, the fire disappeared.

Master Starrus was flat on his back in the churned-up snow, jaw slack.

What had that dragon rider, Marlies said? *Leave Starrus some vestige of pride.* Although Giddi had won, he'd definitely lost her challenge.

Giddi strode over to Starrus. "You'd risk the entire Spanglewood forest, the spangles and every mage in Dragons' Realm just to prove yourself? You're more of an idiot than I'd suspected." He spat in the snow near Starrus' face and stalked off into the forest.

Rumors

Adelina was sewing an old pair of breeches, when someone knocked on the door.

Linaia, napping in the den adjoining her, melded instantly. *"Do you want me to eavesdrop and ensure you're safe?"*

Adelina smiled. "No, I've managed this far without a guardian. I'll be all right."

"Up until now Roberto has protected you. He's not here, so it's my turn." Linaia stayed melded.

Adelina opened the door to Mara and Leah.

"Can we see your dragon?" Mara asked.

"Your dragon?" Linaia huffed. *"I'm not your dragon. You're my rider."*

"Sure, come and meet Linaia," Adelina showed the girls through her cavern out to Linaia's den.

"Dragons' tails. She's huge," exclaimed Mara.

Linaia preened her sapphire scales.

"Not as large as Erob," said Leah knowingly. "He's staying on the infirmary ledge, and he's huge."

Linaia stuck her snout in the air. *"Size isn't everything."*

"You're so lucky." Mara stretched her hand toward Linaia. "May I?"

"Yes, I'm sure Linaia won't mind you petting her."

"I'm not a dog, you know," melded Linaia, woofing in Adelina's mind.

Adelina stifled a chuckle as Mara rubbed Linaia's nose. Linaia snorted. Mara jumped back.

"Come on, I'll get you a drink." Adelina fetched three cups of goat milk, adding dollops of honey. Linaia warmed them. "These may be a bit hot." Adelina passed them their cups. "Linaia is still learning."

"Huh. What about you, new rider?"

She bit back a smile. "And I'm still learning too. Come on, it's cold. Let's go inside."

The girls went in and sat in comfy chairs, sipping their drinks.

"We came to tell you something, Adelina." Mara nudged Leah. "Go on, tell her."

Leah leaned forward. "It's a little awkward. It concerns your brother."

Adelina dropped her cup. It shattered on the stone, milk splattering her boots. "Sorry, I—"

"Thought it might be true," said Mara, eying Adelina and the shattered crockery. "The council haven't announced anything, but people are saying he's working with Zens."

Anger surged through Adelina. "Roberto would never work for that murderer." Again. She hoped. No one was supposed to know where Roberto was. Had word got out? Or was this just another lie spread by Snake-tongue?

"We know he wouldn't," said Mara. "He's a good man …" She blushed.

Adelina wanted to roll her eyes. Not another girl who admired her good-looking brother.

"We don't believe he's with Zens," Leah said, "but we think we know where he is."

"Where?" Adelina blurted. Shards, first dropping her cup, then thinking out loud like a littling. Where was her usual composure?

"Seppi, head of the blue guards, came to the infirmary earlier today, and told Marlies he'd seen a Naobian in the northern end of Spanglewood Forest, near Dragons' Hold."

A Naobian. So, it could be anyone. Tomaaz had said Roberto had been captured by Zens. Adelina's hopes deflated. "Thanks."

"There's more," said Leah. "He has long hair, like Roberto."

Maybe he'd escaped. How could he have gotten across half the realm? Probably not by dragon or he would've come straight to Dragons' Hold. "What was this Naobian doing?"

"The guard saw him in the forest."

"Why was he telling Marlies?"

Leah blushed again. "Well, I shouldn't really have been listening, but a while ago she told him to keep an eye out for Naobians in that part of the forest. And after she found out, she left on dragonback. She only just returned. I was on duty in the infirmary, so I couldn't tell you earlier."

Why? Why was the master healer looking out for Naobians? Unless Roberto had escaped. It was possible. They were trying to keep morale up, so no one was supposed to know that her brother was captive except her, Tomaaz, Lovina and the council. Adelina shook her head. "I'm sorry, girls. Master Roberto is on an errand in another part of Dragons' Realm, so it must be another man. Thanks for letting me know."

Leah slumped.

Adelina patted her shoulder. "It was good that you came to me. Don't worry, the next information you bring me will probably be very valuable." She waved a hand. "Roberto's always here and there doing business for Master Lars. Sometimes he's gone for weeks on end. People often gossip about him."

After the girls left, she saddled up Linaia. *"Where to, Adelina? Do you want to look for your brother?"*

"Of course. But we don't even know if it was him."

"I melded with Septimor, Seppi's dragon, and he showed me where he saw the man."

"He did? Could you show me?"

"It's only a short flight from Dragons' Hold." Linaia showed Adelina the image Septimor had shared with her. It was early morning, on the cusp of dawn. A man wearing a cloak was sitting in a strongwood grove. He did look like Roberto from above. Her heart pounded. He looked up as Septimor flew overhead, but the dragon's shadow prevented Adelina from seeing his features. *"Septimor has seen him in the same spot at dawn for three days running."*

It *could* be Roberto. He was about the right build and height, and his hair was a similar length.

But then again, it could be anyone.

If she talked to Marlies, she'd forbid her to go. Adelina climbed into the saddle. "We can't leave Dragons' Hold, I've only been a rider for a day. Lars would kill me."

"If he killed you, he'd have to find me a new rider, silly." Linaia's chuckle reverberated through Adelina's mind. *"I often fly beyond Dragons' Hold on my own. I see no difference in taking you."*

It was tempting, but what if something happened to her? "We shouldn't go on our own."

"Bring a friend. We can slip out before dawn and be back for breakfast."

Adelina laughed. The tightness she'd felt in her chest for days eased. Even if this Naobian wasn't Roberto, and even if she didn't go, it was good to be planning something. If—and it was only an if—she did go, who could she take? Ezaara would have to tell the council. Gret was too straight-laced. She needed someone who didn't mind bending rules.

"Linaia, let's pay Kierion a visit."

§

"Zaarusha, I'm going outside for a break. Please tell Reko to let Master Derek know I'll be back soon." Ezaara walked out of the main cavern, leaving the dueling trainees under Master Derek's supervision. Her breath huffed in the cool air. She stretched her arms and cricked her neck.

Scales flashed in the sky. *"Hello, Antonika."* Lately, every time she looked up, Tonio's dragon was flying overhead. At first, she'd thought it a coincidence, but now she was sure Antonika was dogging her steps. She shrugged. What else could she expect from the spymaster's dragon? She was one of Tonio's sets of eyes and ears.

Nightmares had kept her up half the night again. She was drained after instructing the new riders with endless flight and stunt training, weapon drills and combat skills. She didn't know what was worse—the constant need to put on a brave face or the horror-filled nights. Both left her chaffing at the bit to get Roberto.

A dragon shot out of the cavern, its massive multi-colored wings catching the sun. Soothing warmth washed through Ezaara. *"Don't worry,"* Zaarusha melded. *"Only five more days until the council gets him."*

Five days that stretched into forever.

§

Lovina passed Tomaaz Maazini's saddlebag, her eyes bright. "And then Taliesin told me he'd had nightmares for the five nights before you came home, just like I did. The poor boy."

"Is that so?" He was listening, but distracted by the malicious gossip he'd heard about Ezaara in the mess cavern. Someone at the next table had said Ezaara was a mage and had magicked the council members to let her be Queen's Rider. Ridiculous. He threw the saddlebags over Maazini's back. His dragon stood so Tomaaz could fasten the straps.

Ajeurina nuzzled Maazini. The siblings were happy to be reunited after her being on swayweed and Maazini being Zens' captive. Roberto was still in Death Valley. Shards, it'd been five days since Tomaaz had returned. The council had to do something.

"When I told Master Hans, he said Taliesin might also have the gift of prophecy."

"What?" Now Lovina had his full attention. "So, both of you have the gift?"

"Don't you see? Taliesin and I both had nightmares about you being hurt—from the day you were attacked until you got home. Once you were healed, they stopped."

Tomaaz rubbed his hip. Thank the Egg for Ma and piaua. "So, is Pa going to train you both?"

She nodded. "Your pa says, at the beginning, its usual to have visions or dreams about people you know. The trick is to train yourself to seek visions about the realm. Apparently, it's like casting a fishing net in the ocean, instead of using a line in a pond." She shrugged. "I'll learn."

"I'm sure you will. You're so talented." He squeezed her hand. She was finding her place in the world. No longer a slave, she was an artist, a dragon rider, and now, a visionary.

Maazini snorted impatiently. *"Well?"*

"Ajeurina wants to fly, too. We'd better go before they take off without us." Lovina laughed.

Her laughter made him smile. They climbed into their saddles. Maazini bunched his legs and leaped off the ledge. A thrill coursed through Tomaaz. His heart stuttered and his stomach dropped as they swooped over the forest, Ajeurina and Lovina at their side. The wind tugged Lovina's hair from her braid and pinked her cheeks. Today she was absolutely radiant. Since imprinting with Ajeurina, her smile had gone from being shy to courageous.

Their dragons flew out over the basin. Soon, duty would call, but for now they had time together.

§

On the ledge outside the mess cavern, Tonio interrupted himself mid-sentence and pointed over the basin at Maazini and Ajeurina. "Look at them, Lars."

Maazini tilted his wing and banked, before descending. Ajeurina mimicked him a heartbeat later.

Lars sighed. Not this again. "I know what you're going to say—but this doesn't prove anything."

"Ajeurina is a half a wingbeat behind Maazini," said Tonio. "Tomaaz and Lovina are sitting differently, moving out of sync, so it's obvious they're not mind-melding. The dragons are close, brother and sister, to Zaarusha and Erob's mother and son partnership, but it's all four melding together that made those other partnerships so incredible. Hans, Handel, Marlies and Liesar. And Yanir, Syan and Anakisha and Zaarusha. You've seen them fly. Seen them think in battle; their speed and efficiency were a strategic advantage."

"Yes, they had an advantage." One Tonio and Lars had been envious of. Lars' Lydia hadn't imprinted and Tonio's wife was dead. But that jealousy didn't give Tonio license for a vendetta. This whole business was growing old. "And?"

Tonio whirled, eyes stormy. "Master Roberto was kissing his trainee. Antonika saw it. Dragons don't lie. We've both seen them fly together. The four of them were mind-melding."

"Master Roberto is stuck in Death Valley, and—"

"Where he belongs," snapped Tonio. "Amato's spawn is rotten to the core. Corrupting trainees, influencing the Queen's Rider. I bet Zens is training him again, right now."

Lars sighed. "Isn't that all the more reason to rescue him?"

"What? Because our lovesick Queen's Rider is missing him?"

Lars shrugged. No, because he was a valuable master on the council, but telling Tonio that would only antagonize him. Tonio had never wanted Roberto to become a master. It always came back to him hating Amato.

Tonio leaned in. "Roberto may have even persuaded Ezaara, using his mental talents. Who's to say it's genuine affection and not mental force that's making her nag us to rescue him."

Lars had never considered that. Until this was cleared up and the dragon race was done, he had no choice but to leave Roberto where he was. His conscience pricked, but at least it was better than Roberto being banished outright. This way there was still hope. He shook his head. That was crazy. Since when was being captive to Zens called hope?

Vengeance

It must be night again. 000 and Zens were gone and the torches had burned low, the sole indication of time passing in this underground hellhole. Roberto cricked his neck. At least, only one of his hands was chained.

He pulled on a thread in the cuff of his jerkin until a clear-mind berry popped out. With clumsy fingers he slid it off the thread and ate it—his only defense against Zens' numlocked water. His grimy, blood-coated fingernails were starting to pink again. Reaching into a discreet pouch along the inside of his belt line, Roberto extracted a pinch of dragon's scale and ate the gray powder. That should keep his fingernails and eyes gray, disguising the fact that he wasn't numlocked.

He let his mind back up to the surface and reached out with his senses.

Ah, peace. Zens must be asleep. It was the only time he didn't torture Roberto mentally. He tried to wet his cracked lips, but his tongue was parched. 000 would bring water in the morning. There was nothing to do, except wait and enjoy the peace while Zens slept.

His body was one dull mass of aches, with sharp pain in his ribs when he moved. He cast his mind out. What was that? Not a tharuk—the sense of intelligence was too keen. Not a slave—there was no numlock at play in this mind. By the shards of the First Egg, he was mind-melding with Zens. Roberto was about to withdraw when an image hit him.

Zens was having a nightmare.

He was trapped in a dark space, pushing against two heavy doors, a crack of light shining between them. Locked, the doors wouldn't budge. Zen slammed his body into them, panic tightening his chest. He couldn't get out. He pounded his fists against the wood.

Hang on. They were small fists, like a littling's. In this dream, Zens was young.

Something thudded into the doors. Zens sprang back, hitting his head on a wall, and slid down, whimpering in a corner.

He was in a tiny dark space, like a cupboard.

"Shuddup, scummy kid," someone bellowed.

Fear spiked through Zens' belly and he trembled, huddling in the corner. Flashes of a face shot through his mind, too fast for Roberto to grasp. Zens sat for hours, fear building, his stomach a grinding mass of nerves. Gradually, a new sensation fought with his fear. Zens struggled to hold his bladder, but failed. Whimpering, he wet himself. His sobs were heartbreaking. Skin burning, he sat in his damp breeches for hours, waiting. Eventually, he fell asleep.

Zens pried his eyes open, wincing as the harsh light hit him.

"Not again, you stinking whelp." Large arms yanked him out of the cupboard, dangling him in the air. A huge man with malicious yellow eyes snarled, "You'll be cleaning that stink up yourself."

Zens' surroundings were strange. Whatever world he came from, it was nothing like Roberto's.

Zens was in an enormous room with metal walls as shiny as a newly-forged blade. Strange tabletops and work benches lined the walls, littered with vials, glass tubes and stands. Something bubbled in a glass pot on a benchtop. The fire underneath it was not powered by wood, but came out of a metal stand with a red tube attached to it.

What sort of wizardry was this?

A metallic scent hit him. A human body lay upon a bench, cut open, flesh peeled back, with the entrails showing. Along the back wall were huge glass urns containing liquid, with creatures swimming inside them.

Breathing ragged, Roberto broke mind-meld. If he wasn't careful, he'd give himself away. Once he'd controlled his shock, Roberto slipped back into Zens' mind.

The man threw Zens into a metal tub, mounted in a bench. Zens pushed a shiny handle and water came out of a spigot. He bathed himself in warm water.

More wizardry.

After he'd bathed, Zens pulled on a suit of soft fabric.

"Done, are you?" said the yellow-eyed man. "Now clean up that mess."

The man shoved some rags and a clear bottle—too light to be glass—into Zens' hands. The boy stumbled to the cupboard to clean up his mess.

The stench of stale urine and blood made Roberto's empty stomach roil.

Zens squeezed a handle on the neck of the bottle and a fine spray shot out of the strange spout-shaped lid. When he was done, Zens threw away the rags. "Sorry, Papa."

The man towered over him. Eyes slitted, he backhanded Zens so hard his jaw snapped shut.

Zens bit his tongue, the coppery tang flooding his mouth. He curled in a ball, blows raining on his head. Blinding flashes of pink and yellow seared through his mind.

Roberto snapped mind-meld. Nausea hit him as his memories of Amato beating him resurfaced. He almost pitied Zens, until he remembered the countless slaves he'd murdered and villages he'd razed in his quest for power. He tried to moisten his lips again, and failed.

Should he dive back in? What if Zens woke?

Despite his trepidation, Roberto slunk back into Zens' mind, a silent witness to his worst nightmares.

The man kicked Zens in the gut. He retched on the floor, clutching his abdomen. Dark blood flew out of his mouth as he vomited, splattering the cupboards under the benches.

Aiming a final kick at the boy, Zens' father spat on him. "Clean your filth up." He left the room, slamming the door.

The scene of Zens' nightmare changed.

Zens was in the center of a group of littlings, taunting him and jeering.

"Your father smack your nose in?"

"How'd it get half way across your face? Fall off a roof again?"

"You're uglier than ever—suits you."

Shame knifed through Zens. He lashed out with his fist and connected with someone's stomach. As cries broke out, he fled along a shiny metal corridor. Flexing his fingers, he shook his hand, but the pain felt good. Better than cowering in shame.

A new memory surfaced.

A thin dark-haired woman was seated on a high stool at one of the workbenches in the room where Zens had wet himself. "This won't hurt a bit," she crooned, strapping Zens' arms, legs, chest and neck to a worktable. She tightened the bands and gave him an acrid red drink, cradling his head as he swallowed.

Sweet dreams flowed through him—of sunny beaches edged by vast forests full of colored birds. Zens reveled in the air's salty tang, the cool water lapping around his ankles and the sun on his skin.

Something pricked the soles of his feet. Heat surged through them, building until his feet were blazing hot. His body convulsed. The bands cut into him. Small, neat stabs of pain trailed up his legs. Fire seared his veins. He was burning up. He screamed for help, "Mama."

"You're all right, darling," responded the dark-haired woman, her eyes cold as she plunged needles into his arms.

His arms were on fire. His chest, his belly.

She stuck a needle into his neck.

His head throbbed with heat. "No, Mama," Zens whimpered, over and over.

The woman stalked from the room without a backward glance.

Zens twisted and writhed but couldn't escape the burning.

An age later, the fire ebbed and he collapsed like an empty sack. Everything went black.

Had Zens stopped dreaming? Gods, his parents were devils, evil torturers.

Light entered through a narrow window high in a wall. Dawn was breaking. Zens was still strapped to the table. His body ached all over. What had his parents done to him this time? Darkness clawed inside Zens, robbing him of hope.

Muted voices sounded. Large metals doors were flung open. His parents entered. Zens' mother flicked a tiny lever in the wall and white light flooded out of strange globes in the ceiling.

Zens' eyeballs were on fire. He squeezed them shut, trying to stamp out the burning with his lids.

"Open them," barked his father, his voice grating, hurting Zens' ears and head.

Zens opened his eyes, but the light burned them. Through a film of tears, he faced his parents, still bound to the bench.

"Oh, God." Zens mother recoiled. "What have we done?'

"He's a monster." Even his father looked shocked.

"What have we done? This experiment was supposed to give him extraordinary mental powers to help subdue our enemies, but look at him."

"As ugly as sin." His father grimaced.

"Papa," Zens' littling voice shook. "Mama?"

His mother turned on his father, lips tight with rage. "I told you we shouldn't use that DNA, but you wouldn't listen."

Roberto had no idea what she was talking about, but Zens seemed to.

"Mama," Zens whimpered. "What is it?"

His mother held up a mirror. Zens' eyes had become enormous yellow orbs. His head had grown and his neck had thickened. All of his hair had fallen out. He was ugly. Uglier than ever before. The bullies would never stop taunting him.

"Let me go," he yelled, bucking against his restraints.

"You're uglier than a scum-sucking dog, but it might have worked." His father's smile sent chills down his neck. Turning to Zens' mother, he said, "Let's test his powers."

Zens lay helpless, crying, on the workbench.

Zens' dream flipped to the same corridor where Roberto had seen him being taunted.

He was surrounded by a crowd of littlings.

"Your eyes are big and yellow. Did your daddy's experiment go wrong?"

Experiment? That word again. Its meaning eluded Roberto.

"Your body's huge. How did you get so big?"

"Yeah, what have they been feeding you? Pig slop?"

"Your ugly nose is still squashed, though—that's how we recognized you." A girl shoved him.

A rush of power coursed through Zens. He pointed at the girl, and squeezed his fist. The girl gurgled, clutching her throat. Her eyes rolled back in her head and she collapsed.

At last, it was his turn to be strong. Zens laughed—his voice rumbling out of his bull-like chest.

The others fled, screaming. Rejoicing in his power, Zens dropped another two before the corridor was empty.

Zens' memories flashed by: jabbing animals with needles in his parents' metal room; slicing samples of their tusks, fur, and flesh; setting the samples into fluid-filled jars; watching them grow; all the while, making notes.

He was following in his parents' footsteps—bending nature with strange magic. A blur of images passed before Roberto's eyes, then one came into focus.

Zens was older, hauling a furry, tusked creature out of an enormous jar and helping it stand. Its nose was snout-like and its beady eyes, red. A tharuk.

Elation surged through Zens. He'd done it. He hugged the beast. "Welcome to my world, 000. Together we'll strike our enemies."

The tharuk growled, rubbing its head against Zens' palm. Zens laughed, patting it.

Footsteps and voices echoed outside the room. Zens thrust 000 into a metal cupboard to one side of the entrance doors, sending it mental instructions.

Roberto flinched. Surely, he'd misunderstood.

The door flew open and Zens' father entered. "Still mucking around? You'll never amount to anything." He spat in Zens' face.

"It's not his fault. We ruined him. Can't you give him a break?" Zens' mother pleaded, wringing her hands.

"Mother, come and see what I've made." Zens called her over, taking advantage of her soft spot for him. "Here, in this jar." He escorted her toward his jar nearest the cupboard.

Falling for his lure, she came closer. "Has one of your pets grown, dear? Do show me. It's a shame you can't go to school anymore, but after you harmed those boys … let me see. It doesn't look much larger."

The cupboard doors flew open. 000 burst out, roaring. It lunged at Zens' father. Grabbing him in its strong arms, it squeezed his ribs until they punctured his clothing, blood soaking his shirt. 000 twisted the carcass. It slashed the man's neck open with his claws. It ripped his belly open with its tusks, flinging entrails over the room.

'Enough," called Zens, "Now it's mother's turn."

Her screams were silenced as the tharuk ripped her head off with a sweep of its claws and smashed it against the metal cupboards, splattering gray tissue over the walls.

§

Zens woke with a pounding headache. His nightmares had been riddled with memories of his parents. When the nightmares came, they came hard and fast—always about their experiments. "Your father and I bred you as a living experiment," his mother used to say, filled with pride, as they'd meddled with his DNA. Idiots. That had been their downfall. They'd changed him so his mental and physical powers had exceeded theirs. And his lust for power. They'd only wanted to control the world, whereas Zens was determined to rule other worlds as well his own.

At least, that had been his plan until that master wizard had shut the portal.

A shame, really. Limitless planets were out there, waiting for him—if he could only escape this backward realm, and those stinking flying lizards. Without them, he'd be in charge already.

He walked down the tunnels and took the passage that spiraled down to his lab. Opening the stone door, he walked through the anteroom and inspected the glass vats in his underground laboratory. The whole lab was powered by methimium. By accident, he'd found the valuable energy source, here, in this corner of Dragons' Realm, along with enough vassals to mine it. At least they were now spending their pathetic lives on something useful.

Reaching into a bowl on the lab bench, he sprinkled the finely-ground yellow crystals onto his tongue. The bitter taste permeated his mouth, bringing back foul memories of when his father had first started feeding him the stuff. He swallowed it down, craving more of the power it gave him.

Zens flicked a switch and yellow methimium-powered light flooded the vats. His lovelies were coming along quite nicely. Soon, he would overpower those vile dragons and put the entire population to work in his mines. Then, when the next mage opened a portal, he'd return to Earth and create methimium-powered weapons that would bring mankind to its knees.

§

Roberto snapped mind-meld and hunched over, dry retching. Even though he hadn't eaten for days, his stomach heaved again and again. Although Amato had abused Roberto and sold him to Zens, who'd tortured him and broken his mind and will, never once had Roberto imagined inflicting that sort of damage on his father. He drove the ghastly images from his mind.

Zens must never know he'd seen his parents' abuse, the bullies, or him killing his mother and father. Zens would kill him outright.

Roberto now knew Zens' biggest weakness. A weakness Zens probably didn't realize he had. A weakness Roberto might be able to exploit to get out of here.

But if Zens dug through his mind and found out how he felt about Ezaara, he'd also know Roberto's weakness. He slumped against the wall, exhausted, mentally burying his memories of Ezaara.

§

Zens' skull-splitting headache was brought on by the memories of his parents' torture. Torture in the name of science. Torture that had made him the powerful being he was. Torture that had made his life on Earth miserable.

There was one remedy for his headache.

He entered the cavern adjacent to the lab, where 000 was working, and where he performed his own experiments. "Triple," he said.

His beautiful first creation turned to him. "Yes, beloved Master?" 000 asked.

"It's time for a killing spree."

"I'll find you some slaves," 000 said, "and bring them to your chamber." He stalked from the cavern, his boots echoing with menacing thuds down the tunnel.

Zens laughed. Today was getting better already.

Kierion's Folly

The torch in her cavern was burning low when Ezaara got in, peeling off her damp jerkin and stamping her cold feet.

"You're out late. It's way after midnight."

She started. She hadn't seen Tomaaz, sitting in the shadows. "Hey, how are you, Maaz?" She'd been out, stunt-riding Zaarusha.

He unfolded himself and approached. "That's what I wanted to ask you. Nightmares again?"

She shrugged. "Every night. And you? Why are you up so late?"

"I don't know. Restless." He shifted from foot to foot.

Perching on the bed, she removed her boots, and pulled on a fresh pair of woolen socks.

"You're Queen's Rider," Tomaaz said. "You can meld with any dragon. And you're a great healer. But I don't know what my role is here."

It wasn't like Tomaaz to doubt himself. Something must be eating at him. "You're incredible. You saved Lovina, Ma and the boy from Death Valley."

"Taliesin's his name—he's talking now."

"That's good. While you were off saving lives, all I've done is sit at Dragons' Hold."

"And go to the Wastelands to save Roberto. And save Zaarusha from poison."

"We do what we can for those we love."

"Exactly." He sat on her bed beside her.

She knew her twin. "Is this about Lovina?" she asked. "You love her, don't you?"

His voice softened. "I do." He stared at her. "And you, Ezaara? I guess I can't ask you that question."

He knew she loved Roberto. They'd never been able to hide much from each other. "We have to save him," she whispered.

"We do," said Tomaaz. "I feel terrible for leaving him behind." He patted her hand. "Only four more days and we'll return with the strength of Dragons' Hold at our backs. I wish we could go now."

Ezaara nodded, throat too tight to speak.

Tomaaz walked to the door and put a hand on the handle. "Believe me, Ezaara, every day he's there kills me. It's not fair that I'm at home with my loved ones while he's subjected to the dragon gods know what."

Exactly. When Tomaaz shut the door, Ezaara lay on her bed, staring at the cold stone ceiling.

§

By the time dawn touched the tips of Dragon's Teeth, Kierion and Adelina were far from Dragons' Hold, skimming over the northern part of Spanglewood Forest. The peaks protecting Dragons' Hold were distant sentinels behind Kierion's back. There was nothing quite like the thrill of flying above the realm while the sun bathed the snow-dusted trees in its glow.

Kierion mind-melded with Riona, *"Where did Septimor see Roberto?"*

"Just below this ridge, in the trees." Riona shared Septimor's memory.

Adelina hadn't said exactly where Roberto was supposed to be or what he was doing away from Dragons' Hold, just that he was on *council business*. But Kierion wasn't stupid. She was holding something back. Since Tomaaz had returned without Roberto, she'd been troubled. Even Erob was back, although he was still resting on the infirmary ledge. It didn't take a genius to figure out that Roberto had been attacked by tharuks. Maybe he was missing. Rumors said he'd gone rogue, but Kierion didn't believe Roberto would desert Erob.

Linaia and Adelina swooped down the ridge. Kierion followed on Riona, the rising sun making the gold highlights in Riona's purple scales blaze. Exhilaration swept through him. He'd never imagined flying could feel like this—the wind in his face, the peace so high above everything, or the love he'd feel for such a magnificent beast.

"You're not such a bad beast yourself," Riona said.

Kierion grinned.

Their dragons dived between the trees, banking steeply to prevent their wings from hitting foliage. Riona and Linaia settled onto the ground, furling their wings against their sides.

"We'll search for him by foot," Adelina called.

"Good idea. The trees are too dense to scout by air." Kierion took his bow and quiver from Riona's saddlebag and checked his sword was secure in its scabbard. He slid to the ground.

"Look." Adelina pointed to boot prints in the snow. "Maybe that was him."

The prints led deeper into the forest. Kierion nodded. "As good a chance as any. Let's go."

Their boots crunched through the snow as they wound between the trees. Kierion was bursting with curiosity but he waited until they'd walked a while before questioning Adelina. "So, what's Roberto been doing away from the hold so long?"

Adelina's shoulders tightened. "Stuff."

"Come on, Adelina. Something's been eating at you."

She raised a sardonic eyebrow. "Oh, has it? Then why don't you tell me what it is?"

Kierion shrugged. "Erob was hurt, so tharuks must have attacked. Is your brother hiding somewhere, or injured?"

Her face paled.

Oh, shards. He'd blurted it out without thinking about how she'd feel. "Come on, Adelina. You know me. You can trust me." He pounded his fist against his chest. "Always."

She bit her lip and kept trudging after those darned boot prints.

They probably weren't Roberto's. If he'd been hurt this close to the hold, he would've signaled a blue guard to collect him, surely. Unless he was hiding from the council. Kierion hurried after Adelina, then fell into step beside her, passing her an apple from his pocket.

She cradled the apple in her palm, murmuring something so quietly, he missed it.

He kept his trap shut and ears open, not biting into his apple in case he crunched too loudly and missed what she said.

Sure enough, after a few more paces, she spoke again. "He was on council business, you know. I wasn't lying." He nodded, and she kept talking while they walked. "Roberto and Tomaaz were sent to infiltrate Death Valley. As they were leaving, they were attacked and Roberto was captured."

"By tharuks?" He could almost smell the pungent stench of the tusked beasts.

"Now Zens has him." Her dark eyes were pits of despair.

Kierion had never seen Adelina so down. He'd do anything to make her brown eyes dance again. "When the blue guards said they'd seen him, they said he was healthy, right?"

Her eyes slid away. So maybe that was a lie. But dragons didn't lie and Riona had shown him this place. He pushed back a branch so she could pass. Snow slid to the ground. "Adelina?"

Her lip trembled. "The council didn't tell me to collect him at dawn. I-I heard a rumor that there was a Naobian in the forest. I j-just wanted to see if it was him … whether he'd escaped."

So, he'd been duped. By a friend who was desperate to find her brother.

Tears glimmered in Adelina's eyes. He put his arm across her shoulders, following the prints. "Come on," he said. "We've come this far. We might as well find this Naobian. Hopefully it is Roberto and he's escaped."

"You don't think it's possible." Adelina shrugged off his arm and glared at him, fists on hips. "He's done it before, you know."

"What?"

"Roberto. He's escaped Death Valley before. And you know Tomaaz has."

That's right, Tomaaz had crept in and rescued Maazini. "I didn't know Roberto had been there."

She nodded. "And Lovina. She was a slave in Death Valley for years. Then there's the boy Tomaaz brought back." Chin up, she stared at him fiercely, daring him to disagree.

That was four people who'd made it out. "And Marlies," he said. "The master healer was there too. So, there's a high chance this Naobian could be Roberto. There aren't that many Naobians in these parts." His eyes slid to her dark hair and tan skin. Foot in mouth time again. "Well, except you," he said. "Come on. Let's find him." Searching had to be better than arguing.

They ducked around a tree trunk. Adelina wrinkled her nose. Kierion hadn't imagined the stench of tharuk—it had been real. A spine-chilling growl ripped between the trees. Instinctively, Kierion snatched his sword from his scabbard. Curse the Egg, he should've nocked an arrow instead. He could have shot that brute running at them. Too late now.

Kierion ran to meet the monster as more tharuks broke from the trees. Adelina's arrow twanged through the air and struck the beast in the eye. It toppled to the snow. Kierion spun, claws raking past his head. He plunged his sword under another beast's upraised arm. The monster howled and lunged at him. Driving his sword hilt deep into its body, Kierion ducked, its tusks just missing his head as the tharuk crashed to the ground. Black blood gushed onto the snow.

Kierion kicked the tharuk over and yanked his sword from its body. It twitched. Quick as lightning, the tharuk's eyes flew open and it whipped its legs around, sending Kierion flying into a tree trunk. His side throbbing, he scrambled to his feet. The tharuk was on its knees, clutching its wound, struggling to stand. Kierion charged, aiming his sword at the beast's neck, and hacked off its head. Stinking blood sprayed him.

"Kierion." A shriek rang out. Adelina.

He whirled.

Adelina was up a tree, shooting arrows at beasts prowling around the trunk. A tharuk sank its claws into the bark, ready to climb the tree.

No, not Adelina. Sticking his fingers into his mouth, Kierion whistled. The piercing tone cut through the tharuks' snarls. They spun to face him.

"Hey," Kierion yelled, "I just killed your friend." He waved his blood-stained sword. "Who's next?"

The tharuks charged.

"Run," Adelina screamed.

Kierion's quick-fire instincts had him running before he could even think. He pelted through the trees, leading the beasts away from Adelina.

Their stench wafted after him, their boots thudding through the snow.

Shards, they were faster than he'd expected.

§

Adelina fired at the tharuks chasing Kierion as he disappeared into the trees, bravely drawing the beasts away from her. Her arrow flew into the rear tharuk's neck, felling it. All those hours Roberto had drilled her at the archery range were finally paying off.

One of the tharuks whirled back to its dead companion. It roared and ran toward her tree. Adelina fired another arrow and another, but the beast zig-zagged, nipping in and out of the trees to avoid her shots.

Suddenly, it was below her, sinking its claws into the bark.

Heart thudding, she aimed. The foliage deflected the arrow, and it hit the snow. The tharuk climbed closer, its snarls turning to grunts as it hefted itself onto a branch, making the tree shake.

Adelina's next arrow got embedded in a branch. The fetid stink of tharuk wafted up to her.

"Got you." It grunted, heaving itself higher. Adelina stowed her bow on her back and climbed. If she got high enough, the furry brute would be too heavy for the branches. She scrambled up, pushing off with her legs and yanking her bodyweight up with her arms. As she reached for another limb, her bow snagged on a branch. Shards, she was suspended by her bow and her arms. Kicking with her legs, she tried to find a foothold so she could disentangle herself.

A raucous guffaw came from below. The tharuk climbed onto the branch she'd just been on, making the whole tree shudder. Adelina kicked out as it snatched at her. Her boot struck its head. The tharuk roared and grabbed her legs, yanking hard. Her arms were just about pulled from their sockets. Thank the Egg her bow was snagged, or she'd be in its grip already. Adelina tried to free her legs, but the tharuk yanked again.

The branch snagging her bow snapped.

Adelina fell in a tumble of branches, limbs and tharuk, bashing her body, arms and head. She landed in the snow, winded. The tharuk fell beside her and rolled to stand. Adelina whipped her dagger from her boot, and scrambled up, facing the beast.

§

"Kierion, run into that clearing and I'll help you," Riona called in his head. *"I can't see through the foliage. I might burn you instead of those monsters."*

Kierion couldn't see a clearing, let alone think. The tharuks were practically breathing down his neck. One snagged his archer's cloak, but he ripped free. His feet churned up snow as he twisted and turned through the trees, trying to dodge the tharuks. *"Help Adelina."*

"My duty is to you, Kierion. You're my rider," Rona replied.

"Forget your sharding duty." A tharuk swiped at him, and he spurted ahead, heart pounding. Dragon's claws, that was close.

"Linaia is with Adelina." There was a pause.

"What is it? Is she all right?" Kierion faltered.

"Get the human," a tharuk bellowed.

Another tharuk leapt on him. They crashed to the ground.

Riona's roars ricocheted through the forest. Flame blasted from above, but it couldn't penetrate the foliage, only singeing the treetops.

Kierion palmed a dagger from his sleeve and thrust it at the tharuk's chest. It slid off the beast's leather breastplate. The tharuk's claws gashed Kierion's side. He struggled to free his dagger, but it was trapped beneath his enemy's body. The beast grabbed his neck, digging its claws into his flesh. Warm blood ran down his throat as the beast squeezed.

Kierion gurgled, his airways tightening. The tharuk's weight pressing down on his chest didn't help much either. Desperate, he yanked the dagger out from between their bodies and whacked the tharuk on the skull with the handle.

The beast growled and squeezed harder. Kierion thrashed, hitting the brute again.

The rest of the tharuks formed a ring around them. Guffaws rang out. "Go, 1777. Get the runt."

"Throttle the human."

"Choke harder."

"Riona," Kierion called.

Above the tharuks' heads, wings swooped. Riona's mighty talons grasped a young tree, wrenching it from the earth. The tharuks stopped laughing and spun. Riona swung the tree through the air, clods flying from the roots, smacking a tharuk with the trunk. Others scattered. 1777 loosened its grip on Kierion's neck. Kierion jammed his dagger into the soft tissue under the beast's chin. The tharuk slumped, blood gushing over Kierion's jerkin.

He rolled, thrusting the hulking beast off him, and ran, gasping. Snarls echoed through the forest. His side throbbing and bruised throat aching, he slipped in the churned-up snow.

Behind him, Riona swung the tree trunk. *"We must get back to Adelina,"* she melded.

"Is she all right?"

Once again, she was peculiarly silent. Something was up. Being a prankster, he recognized the complicit silence of his dragon—better to say nothing than reveal what was going on. Kierion rounded a grove of trees.

A group of tharuks jumped out from behind the bushes.

Shards, they'd sneaked up from another angle. He darted away. The Egg knew what direction Adelina was in.

The tharuks were gaining on him. Not again. His legs were tiring. There was no way he could outrun them. Climb a tree? Trick them somehow. Shards, his throat hurt. Every gasp of air was agony. The stench of the beasts enveloped him. Their breath rasped in his ears. Dragon's claws.

A tharuk with a twisted tusk hurled itself at Kierion. A blinding flash of green light zipped between the trees. The beast twitched on the ground, engulfed in emerald wizard flame. A cloaked, hooded figure ran through the snow, flinging a second fireball at another tharuk. Its face caught fire. The beast shrieked with pain.

A few ran off, but two stubborn tharuks remained—a beast with only one ear and another with missing fingers.

The mage threw Kierion his sword. "You dropped this."

"Thanks." Kierion snatched it out of the air and lunged, parrying One Ear's claws. He hit its arm.

The mage shot more flame at Fingerless. Then he aimed his fire at Kierion's sword. Green flames ran along his blade until it blazed red-hot.

With one look at the glowing sword, One Ear snarled, "Retreat."

As the beasts ran off, the wizard shot two last fireballs at their backs, felling them to the snow. Mage flame consumed the writhing beasts until they were burned carcasses.

The forest was suddenly quiet, except for crackling fire and Kierion and the mage's harsh breathing. The stench of tharuk and mage fire hung in the air.

"Kierion?"

This strange mage knew him?

The mage pushed his hood off his face to reveal blond hair and startling green eyes. "Is that you, Kierion?"

It couldn't be. Not here, in the middle of nowhere, so far north. "Fenni?"

His friend clapped him on the back. "Hey, long time, no see."

"By the Egg, am I glad to see you."

Fenni grinned. "My turn to save your sorry carcass."

Kierion kicked at the snow. "Did your ma ever forgive me for stringing up her chickens?"

Fenni laughed, shaking his head. "You had to have the last word before we left, didn't you?"

"I am so glad that wizard was here to help you," Riona mind-melded. *"How do you know him?"*

"I helped him out of a few scrapes in Montanara."

"No doubt, after you helped him into them first." Riona, circling above them, snorted. *"Follow me, I'll take you to Adelina."* She flew over the treetops.

"My friend, Adelina, is back there. We have to help her."

Kierion and Fenni followed Riona, jogging through the dirty snow. Acrid smoke from mage flame hung in wisps among the trees.

Fenni gazed up at Riona wistfully. "Must be amazing, riding a dragon."

"It is, but it's the bond that's the best. Mind-melding. Nothing quite like it. What are you doing all the way up here? I thought you were staying in Master Giddi's cabin."

"We're up at Mage Gate for the wizard trials."

A long way to come. "How'd you go?"

Fenni grinned. "I thought I was a goner, but I passed my trials. Seems they'd pitted me against some Naobian master mage." Fenni blew his breath out. "Jael's about our age, so I didn't know he was a master. Even though I lost most of our duels, I still passed."

Naobian? "What does he look like?"

"Our age, dark hair to his shoulders, dark eyes and skin." Fenni shrugged. "You know, Naobian, I guess."

Sounded like Roberto. Maybe that was the man Septimor had seen.

"There are a whole lot of Naobian mages here, and more from Spanglewood. Never knew there were so many wizards around. I thought most of them went through the world gate years ago. What about you? How long have you been a dragon rider?"

"Just a few days."

"And they let you—Ssh, what's that?" Suddenly alert, Fenni held a hand up, sparks flitting from his fingertips.

Kierion's hand flew to his sword. A fox broke out of the underbrush and ran off. "Thank the Egg that wasn't a tharuk. Come on, I don't know what's up with Adelina, but we'd better hurry. Things are way too quiet."

"I prefer the quiet to those stinking beasts snarling," Fenni said as they picked up their pace.

"Adelina's just through those trees," Riona melded.

"Any tharuks around?" Kierion asked.

"Just dead ones." Riona's tone was full of grim satisfaction—and worry.

Kierion and Fenni rounded a strongwood trunk. A huge tharuk was sprawled in the snow among a tangle of branches. It was dead, its neck bent. Beyond it lay Adelina. Face pale and lips tinged blue, she was unconscious. "Dragon's teeth." Kierion leaped over the beast and ran to her.

He held his fingers under her nose. Still breathing. Felt her pulse. Heart beating. Covered in scratches and bruises, she had gashes on her legs. He picked her up, cradling her against his chest.

"Wait." Fenni took off his cloak and tucked it around her. "Hang on for a moment. She's half frozen. You don't want her to die on the way to Dragons' Hold." Fenni ran his hands over her limbs and face. Adelina's skin lost that blue tinge. Her icy body grew warmer against Kierion's chest.

Kierion raised an eyebrow. Useful skill. They had to get her home before more tharuks came.

They traipsed through the trees until they found somewhere the dragons could land. *"Why didn't you tell me earlier that Adelina was hurt?"* Kierion demanded of Riona.

"Quite frankly, you were in no position to help. You had tharuks breathing down your neck."

Adelina's head lolled against his shoulder. What if she didn't survive? Anger surged in Kierion's chest. *"Don't withhold information from me again,"* he snapped at Riona. *"Ever. If we're partners, we can't have secrets."*

"I realize now that I should have told you."

Linaia nuzzled Adelina's face, her breath gusting over Kierion's neck.

"She's worried about her rider," said Riona.

"So am I," Kierion admitted. Something fierce stirred in his chest. He wanted to protect Adelina, make sure she was never hurt again.

"Linaia wants to help," Riona said.

The sapphire dragon sat on her haunches, holding out her front limbs. She wanted to hold Adelina. That made sense. He couldn't climb into the saddle with Adelina in his arms. He passed her to Linaia and climbed on Riona's back.

Fenni steadied Adelina as Linaia passed her back to Kierion. "Hang onto my cloak," he said. "It might come in handy. It's magicked to make you invisible."

"I'll get it back to you."

"Nah, keep it. I have a spare." Fenni hesitated.

"What is it?"

Fenni's brow crinkled. "You know, we fought well together, back there. I think we should practice together. This dumb prejudice about wizards and riders stops us from being our best."

Kierion tilted his head. "You're right. I would've been dead without you. Besides, you need a ride on a dragon. I'll meet you at dawn here, the day after tomorrow. Unless Adelina …" What if she didn't recover?

An icy hole yawned in Kierion's belly. She had to get better.

"She'll be fine," said Fenni. "See you then."

Wings flapping, Riona lifted off. Linaia flew beside them, crooning. Kierion gazed down at Adelina's tiny form, cradled against his chest. By the dragon gods, hopefully she'd be all right.

A chill wind sliced through his damp clothes, and he shivered.

Recovery

By the time they landed on the broad infirmary ledge, Kierion's backside was numb and Adelina's face was as pale as when he and Fenni had found her. The wizard cloak had protected her from the worst of the chill, but it hadn't been enough.

"I've melded with Liesar, so Marlies is prepared," Riona said.

Kierion sighed in relief. The master healer was the best in the realm. If she couldn't heal Adelina, no one could. He swallowed. Gods, it had better not come to that.

The infirmary door opened and Marlies rushed onto the ledge. Riona landed and Linaia dropped to the snow beside them and held her forelegs out for Adelina. Kierion handed her over carefully, then slid to the ground.

Marlies frowned, her turquoise eyes flitting from Adelina to Kierion. "Let's get her inside."

Kierion lifted Adelina out of Linaia's limbs and strode after Marlies into the infirmary. Warmth from a blazing fire hit him.

"Over here." Marlies indicated a bed near the fire.

Kierion lay Adelina on it.

Whipping off the mage cloak, Marlies rolled it into a tight bundle and handed it to Kierion. "You'd better put this somewhere before someone sees it," she said in a low voice, glancing at a patient in a nearby bed.

Possessing a mage cloak would get him into trouble? He'd known riders didn't like mages, but things were worse than he'd thought. Kierion stowed it under the bed, and eased his aching body into a nearby chair.

Marlies examined Adelina's eyes and ears and felt her head for injuries. "She's taken a blow here, at the back. That's probably what's knocked her out. Would you mind lighting this candle?" She passed him a stub.

When Kierion returned, Marlies held the flame near Adelina's face, lifting her eyelids and examining her pupils. "They're still dilating, so she should be fine. It'll just take time until she wakes, but we'll need to monitor her and keep her warm."

Seeing the wounds marring Adelina's legs roused fierce protectiveness in Kierion again, like a burning in his chest. Strange. He'd never noticed that when anyone else had been hurt. He shrugged. Actually, it wasn't weird at all. He'd been trying to hide how he'd felt about Adelina ever since he'd met her. Her cute smile was part of the reason he'd agreed to go with her this morning. Maybe he shouldn't have. Maybe she wouldn't have gone then. Or she could've gone on her own. That could've ended much worse.

Anyway, him liking her could never lead anywhere. She was way too young. Kierion sighed.

Marlies treated and bound Adelina's legs. "Now, let's look at you," she said, fists on hips. "Into that bed."

"But I—"

"Go on. No protesting. First, get that wet gear off."

His injuries were throbbing so badly, Marlies had to help Kierion strip off his shirt.

"Those are some nasty gashes there. Tharuk claws by the looks of things. You're lucky they weren't limplocked."

"Limplock's the stuff Lovina was poisoned with when she came to Dragons' Hold, isn't it?"

Marlies nodded. "It paralyzes you slowly over days, starting with your limbs and working its way inward until your heart gives out. Terrible stuff. Luckily, we developed an antidote years ago. Although I need to make more because our supplies are low." She gave a grim smile, rubbing healing salve on his ribs, the ache easing. Tilting her head, she looked at his throat. "How does it feel when you breathe?'

"A bit rough."

"Hmm." She rubbed salve into his throat around his neck. "Any better?"

"Still feels odd when I breathe."

"The tissue must be swollen." She held up a vial of green juice.

"Piaua?"

She nodded, rubbing it into his neck. His throat grew hot and the discomfort eased.

"I'm going to have to use piaua juice on these gashes." Marlies tipped a drop in one of the wounds 1777 had made.

"Shards." It stung, like wildfire racing through the wound. Before his eyes, the flesh knitted over. She worked on the next gouge. "A shame tharuks have claws," Kierion joked lamely.

Marlies didn't laugh. "A shame they exist at all."

That's right. Marlies had returned from Death Valley only two moons ago. It was doubtful she'd ever joke about tharuks.

"These should keep you warm until I get you some more clothes. I'm not having you put sodden ones back on." She covered Kierion's naked torso with blankets. "Right, that's better."

"Um. There's one thing."

"Yes?"

"Do you mind not telling Lars that I was out fighting tharuks?" he whispered.

"Kierion, I think—"

"Please," he wheedled, "I'll find whatever herbs you need for limplock remedy."

Marlies shook her head, chuckling.

"And please don't mention I was with a wizard. Riders really should fight with mages. It's much more efficient."

"I agree." She nodded.

"You do? We should do something about it," Kierion said.

"Can you keep an eye on Adelina while I help a patient back to his quarters? I'll be back soon."

"Sure," Kierion replied, but as Marlies turned her back, his eyes were already drifting shut.

§

Adelina opened her eyes. She had a pounding headache. Gods, where was she? In a bed. With rows of more beds along the walls—the infirmary. So, she'd made it back to Dragons' Hold. The last thing she'd known, she'd been fighting that tharuk in a tree. Shards, her head hurt, especially at the back. She ran her fingers over her skull. There was a huge tender egg. No wonder her head throbbed.

She flexed her leg. All good. Marlies must've healed her with piaua.

Kierion was sleeping in the neighboring bed, breathing softly, looking peaceful without his usual mischievous grin. His blankets had slipped, revealing his wide shoulders and a broad chest that tapered to a narrow waist. Shards, she hadn't realized he had so many muscles.

"Hi, sleepyhead," Kierion said softly.

He'd woken. Her eyes flew to his and her face grew hot. Claws, she'd been caught gawking at him.

"How are you feeling?" He threw his blankets back, swinging his legs over the side of the bed. A shaft of pale sunlight caught the fine blond hair on his tanned chest, making it glint. He was watching her, an odd expression on his face.

Adelina slid her eyes away.

His brow creased. "Hey, Adelina, are you all right?" He knelt by the side of her bed, his chest and shoulders even with her face.

"Um, I'm fine." Mouth dry, she swallowed.

"You must be thirsty. Here, have this." Kierion helped her to sit, and passed her a cup from her bedside table, those sharding muscles flexing right in front of her.

"Um, thanks." The cool water helped.

He grabbed a clean shirt from the foot of his bed and tugged it on, then put on a clean jerkin.

"Are you going already?"

He settled in a chair by her bed, patting her hand. "No, Adelina, I'm not going anywhere until you're well." For once he wasn't smiling.

Rumble Weed

"Flame it, Kierion." Lars stomped over to the fire and turned to face him. "I called you a fool last time, but at least you showed promise. Now you've *proved* you're nothing but a sharding fool. Please explain how Adelina got hurt so badly by tharuks?"

Behind Lars, the fire crackled in the grate, devouring the kindling.

"It was my idea, sir." She'd been feeling unwell for a day now, so there was no way Kierion was going to lay the blame at Adelina's feet. "I thought we could use a little combat practice." Kierion was surprised the lies fell so glibly from his tongue, but the alternative was unthinkable. Adelina's brother was missing. In the infirmary earlier that day, she'd told him that the council hadn't done anything about it. Not retrieving one of their own masters? That rankled. He couldn't land her in the dung. She was miserable enough already.

"So, you endangered a fellow rider, a young one at that, and two dragons—just to have fun?"

"It wasn't really fun, sir." Even though Marlies had healed them, Kierion's ribs still ached.

"No, fighting tharuks isn't," thundered Lars. "Why are you such an irresponsible whelp?" His boots stomped on stone, like a battle drum.

"I'm sorry, sir."

Flames leaped up, licking at a log. The wood issued a high-pitched squeak as the tortured air inside it tried to escape.

"I don't want you to be sorry. I want you to stop being so impulsive. Think before you act." Lars exhaled forcefully. "You missed kitchen duty as well."

"They hardly need me there, sir," Kierion muttered.

Lars shook his head. "You were given kitchen duty to remind you to think about the consequences of your actions. From now on, it's your top priority. Organize kitchen duty before anything else. Got that?"

"Yes, sir."

"And Kierion, although you might be willing to risk your own neck, don't ever risk your dragon or another rider again."

As if he'd ever risk Riona.

Lars glared. "Have I made myself clear?"

"Yes, sir, crystal clear."

"You're dismissed," Lars barked, eyes still fierce.

Kierion left Lars' cavern, the heavy wooden door thudding shut. Thank the Egg, Lars didn't know he'd been with a mage. He'd put him on kitchen duty for the rest of his life.

"Kierion, I have an idea," melded Riona. *"We'll lay a trap to catch some tharuks, then I'll flame them."* Riona showed him an image of her, bleeding out on the snow. When tharuks approached, she snarled, and flapped her wings helplessly, but when they got closer, she burned them.

Shards, it was brilliant, although he'd have to find some fake blood and a waterskin to put it in. Hang on. What was he thinking? He'd just promised Lars he wouldn't risk his dragon. *"No, Riona. You heard Lars. I'm not to put you in danger."*

"You? Put me in danger? Who do you think you are? It's my decision. Nothing to do with you or Lars. Besides, we're meeting your mage friend, and he's a fair shot with a fireball."

Kierion laughed. *"Well, Lars did tell me to organize kitchen duty. He never said I have to do it myself."*

Riona chuckled. *"Before dawn again?"*

"Too right," Kierion replied. *"That's when Fenni agreed to meet us."*

§

"Quick, they'll be here any minute." Leah squeezed into the cupboard beside Mara, wrinkling her nose. "Oh, this is tight. Here, let's move these pails." She nested the wooden pails inside one another, shoving them against the back wall.

Mara moved a soggy mop to one side. "Turn those pails upside down and I'll sit on them."

Mara got the comfortable seat, while Leah sat on the cold stone, hugging her knees. "Hurry, they're coming," hissed Mara. She grabbed the door, pulling it shut, nearly slamming her fingers. A tiny slit of light came through a crack in the door, giving them a narrow view of the cavern.

Girls laughed as they entered the dorm. "Of course he knows you like him. You turned as red as a blood-beet when he looked at you," one said.

"I couldn't help it. He's just so … I don't know."

Beds creaked as girls sat down. The cavern door thudded shut.

"Right, girls. You all know why we're here." Snake-tongue.

Mara nudged Leah. Leah automatically put her finger to her lips. If they were caught, they'd be beaten and made social outcasts, but they had to find out what Snake-tongue was planning.

"Enough gossip. It's time for action," said Snake-tongue. "We need someone from Anakisha's bloodline to fulfill the prophecy. Her heir should be Queen's Rider, ruling at Dragons' Hold alongside Queen Zaarusha. Are you all in?"

A drip from the mop hit Leah's hair, making her flinch. Shards, she had to stay still and not make a sound. The stone was chilling her backside, but it was too late to move now. If she bumped something, Snake-tongue would hear.

Mara squeezed her hand in the dark, and Leah squeezed back.

A timid voice spoke up, answering Snake-tongue. "W-what sort of action?"

Snake-tongue's voice was smooth, almost friendly. "Anyone else with questions?"

A shiver ran down Leah's neck, like fingertips walking across a grave, as two more girls expressed their concerns.

"Thank you for asking," Snake-tongue said in her oiliest tone. "Are you scared of hurting someone?"

"Y-yes, the thought m-makes me nauseous," one of them said.

Fingers snapped, and Snake-tongue's voice took on a hard edge. "I have the prefect cure for nausea. Bring her here."

The sounds of a scuffle ensued. The girl's muffled protests were cut off with the smack of an open hand meeting flesh.

Leah bit her lip. This was worse than she'd thought. Adelina had warned them not to get involved, only to gather information and not give themselves away. She pressed her nails into her palms, fighting the urge to burst out of the cupboard and scream, "Stop."

"Pass me the rumble weed tonic," Snake-tongue barked.

The girl gagged and spluttered as she was forced to drink the vile stuff.

"That should fix her." Snake-tongue laughed. "Now, get a pail before she vomits all over the floor."

Boots stomped across the stone toward the cupboard. Leah's heart froze. In the dark, Mara clutched her arm, making her start. The cupboard handle squeaked.

Leah grabbed Mara's hand and tensed, ready to run. The door opened a finger's breadth.

"Don't bother," Nadira—one of Sofia's closest friends—called. "I have a pail here."

The footfalls receded. Leah exhaled in relief. Soon, retching echoed around the cavern.

Leah peeped through the crack.

Nadira was standing over a young girl who was vomiting, her face gray and beaded with sweat. The girl clutched her belly, moaning. She vomited again and again, until she was dry retching. The acrid stench of stomach bile wafted through the air. Next to Leah, Mara heaved.

Shards, hopefully Mara could control herself. Fumbling in the dark, Leah clapped a hand over her friend's mouth and guided Mara's hand to her nose, so she could pinch it.

"By the Egg, that stinks," Snake-tongue said, cleaning her fingernails with her dagger. "The poor girl must've eaten something that disagreed with her." Striding to the girl, she held the dagger to her throat. "You'll be more careful of what you eat now, won't you?"

Pale, the girl nodded, eyes flitting to two other girls cowering in a corner.

"Take her to the infirmary. If any of you rat me out, there'll be worse," Snake-tongue threatened, waving her dagger.

One of Nadira and Sofia's friends marched the girl out.

"Meeting dismissed," Snake-tongue snapped. "Nadira, a moment."

The other girls left.

"That went well, Sofia. What are you planning next?" Nadira asked.

Snake-tongue's voice was filled with loathing. "I'm going straight for the Queen's Rider."

§

The spymaster cocked his head, frowning. Tonio had always had something against Roberto, so Adelina had been worried about coming to him with her concerns, but right now, he was listening. Adelina fiddled with a pebble in her pocket, turning it over and over.

"So, you're telling me this has gone on for some time?" Tonio said, his eyes flitting from her to Leah and Mara. "That Sofia has been slandering the Queen's Rider, and has abused a younger girl?"

"Yes," said Leah, "we heard it all, hidden in a cupboard."

He arched a slim eyebrow. "And may I ask *why* you were hiding in a cupboard?"

"To hear her plans," Adelina answered for them.

"Aha, very resourceful, but also dangerous if you were found. What would your strategy have been then?"

Next to Adelina, Leah gulped. "To run."

He nodded. "I train my dragon corps spies in a similar manner: to be discreet, but to flee should the situation get dangerous."

Leah beamed. Mara sat up straighter.

Good. Adelina was glad the girls were being recognized for their work.

Tonio continued. "I don't mind you keeping your ears open and reporting any more gossip or violence directly to me, however, I do not, under any circumstances, want you to play at being spies. Observe as you go about your daily duties. No more hiding in cupboards. I don't want you to get hurt. Is that clear?"

Leah and Mara nodded.

"You may also tell Adelina what you've heard, but only after you report to me," Tonio said. "Now, go about your day. Well done, girls."

Leah and Mara went to the door, waiting for Adelina.

"I'll be a moment," she said. "Please tell Master Jerrick I'll be late for archery."

"Will do," Mara called.

Alone with the spymaster, Adelina's palms grew damp. She rubbed them on her breeches.

Tonio's face was grave. "Be careful, Adelina, it's a dangerous game you're playing."

Well, that was unexpected. "What game?"

"Playing spymaster with these young girls. If something happens to them, you'll never get it off your conscience." Lines deepened in his face.

Familiarity knifed through Adelina's belly. They were grief lines. He was speaking from experience. Someone he loved had been hurt or died while spying for him.

"Now, what did you want to talk to me about?" His manner suddenly became brusque, as if she was a fly he wanted to brush off. This was the Tonio she knew.

Adelina straightened her spine. She couldn't back down now. This was the real reason she'd come. "Master Tonio, I know my brother is captive in Death Valley. What is the council doing about it?"

"Nothing," Tonio snapped, stalking to the door and opening it. He gestured for her to leave.

"Nothing?" She'd expected excuses, reasons, not just *nothing*. A dark pit yawned in her belly—ready to swallow her.

"What I meant was nothing at present," he said smoothly. "We have plans to rescue your brother straight after race day."

Adelina nodded. "Thank you." She didn't believe a word Tonio had just said. She'd bet a dragon's weight in gold that the spymaster would change his plans.

Archery practice could wait. It was time to visit Erob.

Riona's Trap

It was still dark when Kierion swung into Riona's saddle with a bladder of blood-beet dye and his quiver on his back, covered by Fenni's cloak. Once his feet were in the stirrups, he tucked the invisibility cloak tightly around him. It hung right over his boots. Brilliant—if anyone saw Riona, they'd think she was hunting. It wasn't unusual to see dragons flying solo. He pulled the cloak's hood down over his face.

Riona's feet crunched on the snow as she headed to the front of the ledge and took off. Clouds scudded over the moon, blanketing the basin in darkness. The muted flapping of her wings was the only sound. No one else was about. He'd planned this trip well, popping by the infirmary last night to collect the wizard cloak still tucked beneath Adelina's bed.

A chill breeze ruffled his cloak. By the Egg, it was cold, but soon enough it would be dawn and he'd be in Spanglewood Forest.

They were at the edge of Dragon's Teeth when a lone blue guard flew toward them. Heart pounding, Kierion yanked the hood lower and hunched over Riona's back. "*Who is it?*" He asked Riona, unable to see past the hood.

"*Septimor and Seppi. Stay still.*"

Kierion held his breath, in case he let out a cloud of fog in the cool air. Septimor's wingbeats sounded dangerously close. Could the blue dragon sense his heart thudding against his ribs? He willed himself to stay calm, his grip growing sweaty.

"*They're gone,*" Riona melded. "*Septimor wanted to know why I was out at night. I told him I'd heard there were fat bucks over the ridge and fancied a snack.*"

"*What were they doing out this early?*"

"*They went for a flight after the late patrol ended. Septimor had also heard about the bucks and gone to hunt.*"

"*With Seppi?*"

"*Seppi's been riding for years. It doesn't bother him to witness his dragon killing or eating. By the way, you know this means I'll have to catch a buck on the way home, or they'll wonder why I'll need to go hunting again so soon.*" Riona's belly rumbled.

Life was simpler as a dragon. Eating, killing tharuks, flying. Had Seppi really been fooled? Or would he mention Riona when he gave his patrol report? Kierion shrugged and threw back his hood.

Riona dived down the far side of Dragon's Teeth and swooped over the forest. Exhilaration rushed through Kierion. He felt like yelling at the top of his voice—but he wasn't that foolhardy. Anyone could be hidden in the dark sky. They headed toward Spanglewood Forest.

Fingers of light crept across the treetops, casting the forest in predawn gray. Moments later, a golden glow filtered across the land, setting the snow alight. Dragons' Realm was breathtaking. As a dragon rider, he was tasked to protect it. He'd heard stories of entire villages being killed or enslaved when tharuks had first come through the world gate. Maybe he and Fenni could develop new methods for fighting the beasts and get riders and mages to fight together. There had to be a better way to save his people.

Riona swooped down to the clearing where they'd arranged to meet Fenni.

His friend greeted him. "Good morning, Kierion. Ready for a little wizard flame?"

"I'm always ready. Seen any tharuks lately?"

Fenni's brow wrinkled. "A few. Could we do a sweep of the forest? I haven't seen Master Giddi for two days since he stalked off."

That was strange. "Why?"

"He won a wizard duel, but was angry at Master Starrus, the head of the Wizard Council, because Starrus' mage flame got out of control."

"Makes sense." Mage flame gone wild would be problematic. "I've been thinking about how we can fight best together. Climb up behind me and we'll try a few things out."

An hour later, they were at the clearing Riona had seen the last time they were here. *"Tharuks are close by,"* Riona said. *"We'll need to be quick."* She ripped a branch off a tree and landed in the snow.

Kierion pulled the waterskin off his back and tucked it in the skin fold between Riona's hind leg and her belly. He forced the branch into the waterskin, piercing it. Riona squeezed the branch between her thigh and belly to hold it in place. Blood-beet juice flowed down her stomach and leg onto the snow.

"That doesn't hurt, does it?" Kierion asked.

"Not a bit."

"Almost looks real, like she's impaled herself," Fenni said.

"Hopefully real enough to fool those brutes," Kierion replied. "Quick, let's get into the trees."

They climbed up strongwoods at the edge of the clearing, Fenni near Riona's tail, and Kierion closer to her head. Kierion nocked an arrow. A tiny shower of sparks flitted from Fenni's tree. *"Riona, we're ready."*

The purple dragon swished her tail in the snow, obliterating their tracks, and churned up more snow with her forelegs. She half-unfurled a wing, as if it was damaged.

"Great," said Kierion. *"Looks like you've been struggling."*

Riona bellowed.

It sounded like she was in pain—she was a better actor than he'd expected. *"Convincing, keep it up."*

She bellowed again and thrashed in the snow, careful not to dislodge the branch still gripped between her leg and belly. *"Be alert, I smell tharuk on the breeze,"* she snarled in Kierion's mind. Her visceral pleasure shot through him, making his heart race.

Gods, if she was hurt …

A lone tharuk broke into the clearing, lifting its snout to the wind and sniffing.

Oh shards, in his eagerness he'd forgotten to take freshweed. What a fool.

"Don't worry, you're downwind. That pathetic beast doesn't stand a chance." Riona whimpered and flapped her half-extended wing pathetically.

Behind the tharuk tracker, dark shapes moved among the trees. *"Wait, Riona. There are more."*

"Bring them on," Riona rumbled between sad moans. *"The more, the better."*

The tracker advanced, still sniffing, getting closer to Riona with every pace. It was halfway across the clearing when the wind changed. The tracker spun, nostrils twitching.

"If it scents us, our trap's blown," Kierion melded.

"If you shoot early, we'll scare off the others. I want to catch the lot, so hold tight."

As much as it galled Kierion, Riona was right.

The tracker narrowed its eyes. "Who's there?" it snarled.

A tharuk grunt with darker fur entered the clearing behind it. "We wants dragon meat," it bellowed. "Stop mucking around."

"I smell something," the tracker snapped. "Quiet."

The wind changed back, and Kierion sighed in relief.

"Trackers always smell something," Dark Fur said. "I only smell you."

Another tharuk emerged from the trees. "I hungry too."

"Careful," the tracker said, giving up sniffing. "Dragon still alive."

More beasts prowled into the clearing. Forming a line, they advanced on Riona. She cowered, whimpering. Shrinking in on herself, she let out the smallest burst of flame, as if her fire power was failing. She looked tiny, not like a ferocious fire-breathing dragon.

The tharuks grew bolder. "Stinking scale heap. Got hurt, did you?" Dark Fur sneered. "Hurt more soon."

Six tharuk archers stole out of the strongwood trees, their green-tipped arrows aimed at Riona.

Dragon gods and flames. Kierion's mouth dried out. They had limplocked arrows. A few of those, and Riona would be dead. Lars' words came back to him, *"Don't ever risk your dragon."* He was a sharding fool, all right, always thinking he knew best. *"Riona, fly away. You can't get hurt."*

"I risk injury every time I battle tharuks."

"But they have limplock," Kierion said.

"Then we'll have to kill the archers first."

"We could let the other tharuks get closer, so the archers are in range. But it's too dangerous."

"Kierion, we've come this far, let's go for it."

That sounded suspiciously like something he'd say.

Riona gave a pathetic snarl. A puff of smoke issued from her nostrils.

"Flame's broken," yelled Dark Fur, waving the troop forward. "Attack."

Tharuks rushed Riona.

Before the first archer could shoot, a green fire bolt sizzled through the air, hitting a furry chest and exploding. Dropping its bow, the tharuk archer writhed in the snow.

The other archers faltered until Dark Fur roared again, "Attack. Dragon meat."

Snarling, tharuks ran at Riona, claws extended.

As one, the tharuk archers raised their bows, but Kierion fired first. His arrow sailed through the air, hitting an archer in the eye. The beast howled, grasping its face. Kierion's next arrow hit another tharuk's arm. It dropped its bow. Fenni's fireball struck a fourth archer in the head, and it ran off, fur in flames.

The remaining two archers loosed their arrows at Riona, and re-nocked their bows.

"Riona, look out. Incoming arrows."

A plume of mage flame shot past Riona and one arrow combusted. The second arrow hit a tharuk's back.

"Thank the Egg," Kierion yelled aloud, then fired again.

Riona swatted two tharuks with her tail, sending them crashing into tree trunks. She opened her jaws and blasted a swathe of fire at three more monsters. The stench of burned flesh and scorched hair filled the clearing. Riona howled, this time for real, as tharuks swarmed onto her back, raking her hide with their vicious claws.

Kierion bellowed, unheard above the racket, and nocked an arrow. But he couldn't shoot. The risk of hitting Riona was too high. So, he focused on the remaining archers. Both had crept around the sides of the clearing toward him and Fenni. Oh shards, one was aiming right at him. He fired, but his arrow went wide. The beast ran toward him, kneeling to get a better shot. Kierion scrambled further up the tree to where the foliage was denser. A tharuk arrow thwacked into a branch near his boot. Swinging onto a higher branch, he yanked his legs up and readied his bow. His hand itched for his sword, but it'd be useless up here. He fired at the archer. It ducked. His arrow whistled over its head.

Fenni's fireballs were zipping around the clearing, targeting tharuks, but none near Riona—it was too dangerous. One sailed through the air, incinerating the archer.

Riona shook herself like a dog. The tharuks swarming over her went flying, except Dark Fur, who clung like a burr to one of her spinal ridges. She blasted more monsters with fire. *"That stubborn tharuk is worse than the most annoying tic,"* she said, leaping into the air. Riona tilted her body, trying to shake Dark Fur off. Feet swinging, the tenacious tharuk hung on. Pain ripped through her spinal ridge, ricocheting through Kierion's mind, as the tharuk twisted, gouging her with its claws.

"These monsters must pay for harming our people." Riona landed, the tharuk still clinging to her. She shredded another beast with her talons, flinging its carcass into the trees.

That was enough. Kierion scrambled down the tree and drew his sword.

"Kierion. You were supposed to stay hidden," Riona melded.

"Hold still." Kierion leaped onto the wide part of her tail. Running up her spinal ridges, he swarmed up her back and swung his sword at Dark Fur. The troop leader's head flew off. A spray of dark blood rained over his beautiful dragon's purple scales, covering their golden glimmer with a sticky slick. The tharuk's body twitched, its claws still impaled in Riona. Kierion yanked on the body, and it came free. He tossed it to the snow. Fenni incinerated it with wizard flame.

"*That mage is handy to have around, isn't he?*" Riona said. "*Get in the saddle. Let's finish these tharuks off.*"

Kierion was settling in the saddle when Fenni yelled, "Duck."

Riona sank to the ground and Kierion flung himself against her hide. An arrow dripping with limplock zipped past, ruffling his hair. Kierion gulped.

Riona bunched her haunches and took off, swooping over the clearing to flame the remaining handful of tharuk grunts.

When all of the beasts were dead, Fenni climbed out of his strongwood tree and sat in the snow, leaning against the trunk.

Riona landed and Kierion slid onto the snow. He grabbed a waterskin from her saddlebags and went over to Fenni while she snatched up tharuk bodies, tossing them into a pile.

"Hey, are you all right?" Kierion asked.

Fenni's face was pale and beaded with sweat. He was breathing heavily. "So that's what Jael meant about building up stamina before I got into battle," he gasped.

Kierion offered him a drink and he slugged it back. Riona set the tharuks alight and paced over. Kierion scratched her eye ridges. "*Are you in pain?*" He needn't have asked—he could feel it.

"*A little,*" Riona answered.

If only he had some piaua juice.

"I think I need to eat," Fenni said, wiping his mouth with the back of his hand. "Could you take me to Mage Gate?"

"Sure," said Kierion. "Riona will need healing, too. Oh, will the mages be all right, seeing a dragon?"

"They'll have to be," said Fenni.

"They will if I'm with you." A man, older than Kierion's father, with thick bushy eyebrows, came into the clearing, his wizard cloak swishing around his tall, gangly frame.

"Master Giddi," Fenni cried. "Ah, um, good to see you. This is my friend, Kierion."

"Your friend?" Master Giddi asked, raising an eyebrow.

"From Montanara." Kierion shook the wizard's hand, a tingle of magic stinging his palm.

Branches cracked behind them. Fenni and Master Giddi whirled, their hands dripping with sparks.

A Naobian ran into the clearing. "I'm glad everything's under control," he said, gesturing at the dark pall created by the burning tharuk pyre. "What a beautiful dragon. Such glorious scales. It's very rare to see a rolling gold."

"A what?" Kierion asked.

"Rolling gold, also known as golden flash. It's what the gold shimmer in her scales is called."

"I'm rare, did you hear that?" Riona melded. *"You'd better take care of me."*

Speaking of taking care of her … "Do you happen to have any piaua juice?" Kierion asked. "She's wounded."

"A little." Master Giddi nodded. "But piaua juice is the least of your troubles. I'd be more worried about finding an excuse for Master Lars when you return to Dragons' Hold."

Jael

By the time Kierion landed outside his new dragon rider's cavern, it was dusk and his kitchen duties had been long fulfilled by the people he'd organized. Keeping to little-used tunnels, he managed to sneak to the infirmary. "Ah, Master Marlies, do you have a moment?" He held Jael's sack of healing supplies against his side, with his jerkin thrown over it—a clumsy disguise, but better than walking around with a sack emblazoned with a Naobian brand.

"Are you here to see Adelina?" she asked. "Sorry, she's back in her cavern."

He winced. In his excitement about the skirmish, he'd missed visiting her. "Um, I've been busy."

Her eyes darted to his poorly-disguised bundle. "Ah, Kierion, I need a hand moving some remedies in my alcove. Would you mind helping me?"

"Sure." Good, she'd found an excuse for them to talk alone.

Marlies took him to the alcove at the back of the infirmary, away from the patients, and pulled the curtain shut behind them. The shelves were half empty because Fleur—the last master healer and as corrupt as a den of thieves—had destroyed so many healing herbs.

The last time Kierion had been in here was when Zaarusha had been poisoned and he'd helped Adelina and Lars search for remedies. That had been a tough night. He'd accidentally bumped Ezaara and half a bottle of tonic had shot down Zaarusha's throat. For a moment he'd thought he'd killed Queen Zaarusha. Luckily, everything had worked out.

"These are too high for my trainee to reach easily," Marlies said in a voice that carried. "Could you help me move them lower?" She gestured at the sack.

Kierion tossed his jerkin on a shelf and opened the mouth of the sack. "I've got your wizard cloak too," he whispered, pulling out pouches of herbs, vials and jars and placing them on the shelf. Marlies was clever. The clinks and thumps really did sound like they were re-sorting her supplies. He also passed her the wizard cloak from the bottom of the sack. "Oh, here's another one."

"Here, hold this," Marlies said loudly. She narrowed her eyes, whispering, "Where did you get these?"

Under her penetrating turquoise gaze, Kierion had to be honest. "From Master Giddi," he whispered back, rushing on to distract her. "Jael couldn't find the last sackful of herbs when you visited them."

"Thank you, Kierion," she said, stowing the empty sack and wizard cloaks under the shelves, out of sight. She leaned close. "Don't get caught consorting with wizards or the council will have your hide. For the Egg's sake, make sure you bathe before someone notices that you reek of mage flame." She passed him a small pouch of aromatic herbs. "These might help."

"Marlies?" a man called from the infirmary.

She peeked through the curtain and drew back in alarm, holding a finger to her lips. She slipped out. "Hello, Tonio, how can I help you?" Her voice got further away as she moved along the infirmary.

"Cut my finger helping a young dragon corps' member to slit his seams so he could hide his clear-mind berries. Sharding nuisance, because it's my bow finger."

"Let's have a look where the light is better," Marlies replied. "I remember slitting my seams for the first time. I nearly ruined my jerkin."

"You were one of my best in dragon corps," Tonio said. "A shame you had to …"

Kierion hadn't known that Marlies had been one of Tonio's spies, years before. He slipped out while their backs were turned and hurried along the tunnels to his cavern. He'd visit Adelina straight after he'd bathed.

When he got to his cavern, the door was ajar. Had he left it that way? He didn't think so. Hand on his sword pommel, he entered the room.

Adelina was sitting, red-eyed, on a chair next his bed.

"Adelina? What's wrong?"

"What isn't?" She ran to him, flinging her arms around him and burying her head in his chest. Her shoulders shook. "My brother's been captured, I got hurt by tharuks, and you were missing. Thank the Egg, you're all right."

Awkwardly he patted her back, but didn't know quite where to put his arms, so he gave her a quick hug. She was so small her head only came up to his chest. So cute, so full of life and energy—and so young. Oh, gods, what was he doing? His face warm, he pulled away.

"You smell odd," she said, "like …" Her mouth made an 'oh' shape and her eyes flew wide. Her eyes fell to the small herb pouch he was carrying. "You're not sick, are you?"

"No, I'm fine."

He placed the pouch by his bathtub in the corner of his room. "Ah, my cavern's not usually this messy." Kierion busied himself, tidying up his discarded boots, breeches and a shirt. Shards, why couldn't he stop blushing. This was silly. She was only fourteen summers and he was seventeen. There was no way—

"You've been with Fenni again, haven't you?"

"Yes." He sighed.

"I know I can't stop you, so be careful," Adelina said. "I don't want to lose someone else I care about." She gave one of her brave smiles, mock-punched him on the arm—the lightest punch he'd ever received—and marched out the door.

Kierion rubbed his arm where she'd just touched him. *Someone else she cared about?* A glow warmed his chest as he prepared to take a bath.

"She likes you," Riona melded. *"I told her you were all right, but she was very worried."*

"It must be hard, having her brother captured."

"Harder than you'll ever know. Have you forgotten that I can meld with other dragons? I've seen Erob's memories. I know what she and Roberto have been through, and it's far from pretty."

§

When Kierion woke, he sprang out of bed. Shards, he'd been dreaming of holding Adelina and slept in. He yanked on his clothes and flung his cloak around him. His stomach rumbled, but he didn't dare go past the mess cavern or the kitchens. Striding out to the snowy ledge, he melded with Riona. *"Did you hunt last night?"*

"Yes, but Septimor might be suspicious because he was at the hunting grounds too."

Not good news. "Oh well, nothing we can do now. Except get going, so no one sees us."

Once again, Kierion hid under his invisibility cloak, and they took to the sky, winging out toward Dragon's Teeth.

"Bad news, again."

"What?" It was hard to see with his hood pulled so low.

"Antonika is on the far ridge behind us. I'm sure she's spotted me."

Just his luck to be noticed by the spymaster's dragon. "Well, she can't see me," said Kierion. "So we should be fine."

A chill wind gusted from the north. His cape billowed, rising up to his knees. Shards, shards and double shards. He'd spoken too soon. *"My cloak. Do you think Antonika saw me?"*

"Hard to say, but Master Giddi is right, we'd better think of some mighty fine excuses before we get back, or you'll be banned from riding me."

"Banned?"

"The punishment for fraternizing with wizards."

Kierion swallowed. It had only been four days since he'd imprinted with Riona, but the thought of being without her left a gaping cold hole in his stomach.

"Don't worry, I feel the same."

"Then why are we doing this?"

"Because we're riders of fire. It's our job to wipe out those infernal tharuks and send Commander Zens back to where he came from. We can't do that without wizards."

Riona's words sent fire burning through his belly and limbs, blasting away the cold ache he'd felt. Kierion's veins thrummed as if they were molten. Riona sped over the peaks of Dragon's Teeth in a blur, leaving the hold-bound prejudice of the Council of the Twelve Dragon Masters behind.

"This is incredible. What's happening?"

"That's what it means to be a rider of fire. When a bond between dragon and rider is strong, the rider can harness the dragon's energy."

It was incredible. Kierion felt as if he could let go and soar through the sky on his own.

Riona chuckled. *"Don't get too carried away. I still want a rider tomorrow."* She popped an image into Kierion's mind.

Flinging back his hood, he sucked his breath in. *"Can we?"*

"I don't see why not," Riona replied, *"as long as we're careful. The queen and the Queen's Rider do this all the time."*

Kierion undid his harness and pulled his legs up, standing on the saddle. Far below, the treacherous slopes of Dragon's Teeth descended into the Great Spanglewood Forest. Shards, imagine being impaled on one of those pine tips below. Kierion pushed the thought away. Every new adventure had risks. *"Ready?"* he asked. Of course she was.

He jumped.

Kierion plunged through the air, his stomach rushing up into his throat and nearly strangling him. The wind ripped tears from his eyes. His cloak flapped around him as he plummeted toward the trees.

"You're a rider of fire," Riona said. "Let go of your fear, and relax."

Relax? Was she mad?

But then Kierion felt it—that fire burning through his muscles and surging through his heart. He let his body go floppy. Riona dived past him, her purple scales flashing as the sun peeked over the distant peaks to the West. Gods, she was glorious. His heart expanded until it was big enough to swallow the entire Spanglewood Forest.

She swooped beneath him and flicked her tail against his rump, slowing his descent. Again she swatted him with her tail, bouncing him in the air. He landed in her saddle with an "Ooff!"

Kierion couldn't help it—he whooped, his voice ringing off the mountains and echoing over the forest.

Riona joined him, roaring in triumph. His blood sang. This was what it meant to be a dragon rider.

§

Tonio raised his far-seers—two joined tubes containing magic glass that enabled him to see things at a distance. Years ago, Zens had brought a few through the world gate as gifts—before they'd known he was evil. Tonio and Marlies had often used them while spying. What had Zens called them? Binolars?

"Yes, that's Kierion all right." He patted Antonika's back. "Thank you for waking me." The fool's jubilant cry bounced off the mountainside below. What was the point in having a mage cloak if you made enough noise to wake the dragon gods? And why had he been sneaking out in the first place?

Tonio shook his head. Kierion was up to something.

"*I recognize their mood,*" said Antonika, landing in a depression between two boulders, high on Dragon's Teeth—one of Tonio's favorite places to lurk on the edge of Spanglewood Forest. "*He's just felt the fire burning in his veins for the first real time.*"

That made Tonio chuckle. "Remember, that very first time?"

"*I do.*"

Warmth flooded Tonio as Antonika's memory cascaded through him. Gods, those had been sweet times—full of hope and anticipation. He'd been in love, too, and the whole world had been bright and rosy.

Before Amato.

That was how he saw life now: before and after Amato. There was nothing else. Amato's actions had taken his life from happiness into bitter ashes of desolation. His former life had disintegrated, dispersed on chill winds. Fleeing Naobia, he'd come to Dragons' Hold and buried himself in work, soon rising to become spymaster. But even that had done nothing to ease the anger burning inside him. Nothing could bring his beloved Rosita back.

He hunkered down in the saddle, resting his arms on Antonika's ruby neck scales, and raised the far-seers again. There Kierion was, dancing along the treetops on Riona, as if he hadn't a care in the world. The lad probably hadn't. Lars had talked about Kierion so glowingly, Tonio had hoped to induct him into the ranks of dragon corps. Someone that stealthy would make a good spy. But now he wasn't so sure. Shrieking above the forest while out for a joyride … What was that damned fool doing? Kierion and Riona had disappeared among the trees.

"Where have they gone?"

"Mage Gate," Antonika mind-melded, adjusting her feet in the snow.

Tonio dropped the far-seers, letting them swing from the string around his neck, while he counted the days on his fingers. Yes, it was the week of winter solstice. *"That flaming fool. He's sillier than I thought."*

His eyes and ears across the realm had told him that Naobian mages had traveled north to Spanglewood. Wizards from all over Dragons' Realm would be dueling at Mage Gate. Not wanting to wait for Spring Equinox, they'd moved their wizard trials forward to Winter Solstice. For eighteen years, ever since Master Giddi had closed the gate there, mages held duels at Mage Gate to hone their powers—a sad tribute to the wizards who'd been lost in Zens' world. That fool, Mazyka, had opened the gate that had let Zens in, and taken many of the wizards through. After the slaughter of Anakisha's last battle, the councils had forced Master Giddi to shut the world gate. It had nearly killed Giddi, locking most of the mage population out of Dragons' Realm, but he'd had no choice. And now they were left, still battling to exterminate Zens and his monsters.

Thrusting the far-seers in his saddlebag, Tonio melded with Antonika. *"Whatever Kierion's up to, I hope he doesn't break his neck."*

"That would be a shame," she said.

"It would," he agreed, *"because he'd deny me the pleasure of breaking it for him."*

"So, you're going to report him to Lars?"

Tonio snorted. *"Lars will want evidence."*

"We could follow them."

"No, I'll bide my time and pounce when the opportunity is right."

§

Fenni clambered into the saddle behind Kierion, and Jael hopped on behind Fenni.

"*Are you sure you can carry three?*" Kierion asked Riona.

"*Why do you think these saddles are so large?*" Riona tensed her haunches and sprang. In moments, they were high above the trees. The extra weight hadn't slowed her at all.

"*Of course it didn't. You're all lightweights.*"

Kierion chuckled.

"Over there," said Jael, pointing to the west. A thin spiral of smoke rose through the trees. "That's where we saw tharuks camping, late last night, near a hut they'd destroyed. Remember, we're not playing heroes today. I want to get in and rescue any people taken as slaves."

They really needed another dragon to carry captives.

"*There's not a great likelihood of survivors,*" melded Riona. "*We're too far from Death Valley for them to be collecting slaves. We're practically at Dragons' Hold.*"

"Jael, tharuks aren't usually this close to Dragons' Hold," Kierion said. "Do you think they're up to something?"

"I don't know," Jael said. "I'm not from around here. You'd be the expert on that."

Fenni nudged Kierion. "Expert, huh? That's a promotion."

"Come on, we're nearly there," Jael said. "Weapons at the ready."

That was easy for him to say. Mages only had to hold their hands out. Kierion grabbed his bow from a saddlebag and leaned forward so he could snatch an arrow from his quiver without knocking Fenni's eye out. At the same time, Fenni leaned back. It was a squeeze, riding with two other passengers.

"I should sneak into their camp," Kierion said. "I can meld with Riona and, if you two place your hands on her hide, she'll relay what I'm seeing."

"No," Jael insisted. "I'm the most senior here. I'll take the risks."

"But neither of us will know what's happening."

"Which is absolutely normal in battle," Jael said. "Now, quiet."

Riona descended between the trees to a river, landing two furlongs from the tharuk camp.

Jael slid to the ground. "Give me a short head start. When you hear yelling or snarling, come and find me." He ran into the trees.

"I still don't like this," Kierion muttered.

"He's good," said Fenni. "He can beat me hands down, just by raising his eyebrow."

Kierion turned in the saddle to see his friend's face. "You're joking."

"No, when we were dueling, the twitch of his eyebrow created an ice wall as high as Riona between us."

"As high as Riona?"

"Mighty high," huffed his dragon.

"I thought he said you'd beaten him."

"Once, and only just."

"But he's only a bit older than us."

"And been training as a mage since he could walk."

"Lucky guy."

Distant snarls ripped through the forest. Fenni grabbed Kierion's waist as Riona leapt into the air.

"Not too tight. Got to reach my quiver," was all Kierion had a chance to say before they were over the tharuk campsite.

Mage fire crackled between the trees. Lances of brilliant green hit tharuks, as Jael fought them single-handedly. Roars and bellows rang out.

A beast with enormous tusks was sneaking through the trees behind Jael.

"Closer," Kierion urged, trying to get a clear shot.

Riona tilted, her wingtip nearly grazing foliage.

Mage fire blazed from Fenni's hands as he felled a beast. Kierion leaned out and fired. Green flames arced from behind him, hitting his arrow and setting it aflame. It flew between the trees and hit the startled tharuk in the chest. It batted at its fur, too late. The scent of charred fur and flesh rose through the trees.

Riona corrected her angle so they were level again.

A rock hit Kierion's head, thudding off Riona's back into the foliage. His temple throbbed. Tiny lights danced before Kierion's eyes. He shook his head, trying to clear his vision. Blood ran down his face, the coppery tang hitting his lips. Kierion slumped forward onto Riona's spinal ridge and his vision went black.

§

"Kierion." Fenni shook his friend, but he wouldn't wake up. Leaning over Kierion's prone form, Fenni placed his hands on the purple dragon's hide. *"Riona, can you hear me?"*

"Yes, Fenni, I hear you." Her voice was gentle, tickling his mind. In that moment, he felt her *sathir*, like a river flowing between them. Kierion must feel this power every day. No wonder he enjoyed being a dragon rider. *"Kierion's unconscious. We must get him back to Dragons' Hold."*

"Master Giddi's closer. He has piaua juice," Riona replied.

"He used the last of it healing you yesterday."

An angry rumble issued from the dragon's belly. *"I'll kill the beast that did this."*

As she banked, Kierion's head started to slip off her ridge. Fenni grabbed him. "Riona, watch out, Kierion's falling," he yelled aloud—forgetting he could mind-meld while touching her.

She righted herself. *"Tighten his harness. Use the rope from my saddlebag to secure him."*

He could do better than a rope, and faster. Fenni held out his hand. A vine flew from a tree beneath them, whipping around the dragon's middle and over Kierion, tying him fast.

"That works," said Riona. *"Now, where's that tharuk?"*

"To your left, behind us in the strongwood with the jagged branch sticking up."

As Riona flew over the evergreen treetops, Fenni pulled the *sathir* from the air, blasting the tharuk off its perch with a fierce gust of wind. It crashed through the trees, snarling, then hit the ground—silent.

The wind blew through Fenni's clothes, making him shiver. The roaring had stopped below and there were no glints of green flame. But there was a strange glimmer in the trees. What was it? Something was sparkling.

"Fenni," Jael yelled.

Fenni spun. Jael was on a small knoll near a smoldering cabin—or what was left of it.

Riona landed on the hillock.

Jael shook his head, his face soot-smudged and eyes brimming as he gazed at the ruins. "We're too late. They're dead: three littlings and their parents—every one of them. Those monsters must've killed them last night." He kicked at a lump of snow, then faced Fenni. "What's wrong with Kierion?"

"A rock to the head. We need to hurry."

Jael's dark eyes met Fenni's. "Take him back to the new master healer at Dragons' Hold. I'll stay and bury the remains of that family." He shook his head. "I'm not leaving them here, like that, charred bones in their beds."

"But—"

"Don't worry about me. It's not a long walk to Mage Gate. And I'll need the solitude, believe me, after cleaning up this lot." He gestured at the tharuk carcasses strewn among the trees.

Fenni twisted his cape in his hands. Shards, he should stay and help Jael. More tharuks could attack. But Kierion needed him too.

Riona rumbled. Fenni placed his hand on her hide. *"Jael is right. He'll cope, Fenni. Let's take Kierion home to Dragons' Hold."*

"She wants me to go to Dragons' Hold," he told Jael.

"It'll be a nice trip." Jael grimaced. "Just like entering the flaming jaws of a dragon."

Dragon's Jaws

It was mid-morning when Riona flew over a steep mountain and swooped into a basin ringed by mountains. So, this was Dragons' Hold. Fenni sucked his breath in. Dragons of all colors flew between caverns in the southern end of the basin, their wings catching the chill winter sun.

As they neared, a blue dragon roared and charged out to meet them, its rider calling, "You have a wounded rider? Follow me."

"As if I couldn't find the way myself," Riona mind-melded, Fenni's hand on her.

The blue dragon and its rider wheeled away when they reached a cavern in the southern mountainside. How they could tell which cavern was which, Fenni had no idea.

Riona thudded onto the enormous ledge. Liesar, the silver dragon he'd met at Mage Gate, padded over and nuzzled her. The next moment, a door flew open and Marlies, the master healer, rushed out. "Oh." Alarm crossed her face. She gave Fenni a quick glance. "Please, untie the vines."

Fenni waved a hand, and the vines fell to the snowy ledge. He passed Kierion down to Marlies and she carried him inside. Fenni slid off Riona, pausing to lay his hand on her side. *"Do you need anything?"*

"Just my rider to be healthy," she answered. *"Please."*

Fenni hesitated. Jael had said he was going into the flaming jaws of a dragon. He removed his wizard cloak, so he wasn't an instant target.

Fenni walked in the door. Beds lined the walls of a long cavern. A fire flickered in a grate at the far end, smoke funneling up a natural chimney. A few people were in beds or sitting near them, tending the sick and wounded. Everyone stared—everyone—their eyes roving over his clothing and lingering on his face. They were all dressed in riders' garb—jerkins, shirts and breeches of tough fabric, suitable for flying—although the hues varied.

He stood out like a blazing pyre of dead tharuks in the snow. He wished he was wrapped in his cloak's invisible embrace.

"Come in, Fenni," Marlies called from Kierion's bedside. "Everyone, this is Fenni, who saved Kierion and helped him get home. I expect you to welcome him." She lifted Kierion's eyelids and checked his pulse.

As Fenni pulled the heavy door closed, a blonde girl of about twelve summers approached.

"Are you a wizard?" she whispered, loudly enough for everyone in the silent infirmary to hear.

He hesitated. *The flaming jaws of a dragon* ... Flames, what should he say? He'd be thrown out in an instant if the Council of the Twelve Dragon Masters heard about him.

Hang on, he was proud of being a mage. He'd just passed his last trials. He'd been killing tharuks on dragonback with a rider. Who cared what a bunch of prejudiced dragon riders thought? "Yes, I am." Fenni held his hand out. Letting sparks flit from his fingers, he turned them into tiny green blossoms that disappeared in a volley of pops.

Eyes wide, she clapped and laughed. "I'm Leah, you're so lucky to be a wi—" She clamped her mouth shut.

The tension in the chamber spiked.

Fenni winked at her. "Yes, I am." He forced himself to chuckle. "And you're lucky to live at Dragons' Hold. It's beautiful here, even in winter. Now, if you'll excuse me, I have to check on my best friend."

"Kierion's your best friend? He's fun."

He could be—if he ever woke up again.

Marlies was looking concerned. "Leah," she said, gesturing at the girl. "Get me some blankets. He's freezing."

Shards, how silly of him. "I can help," said Fenni.

His friend was pale and his lips were tinged blue. The veins in his hands were a mottled purple. He'd been so concerned about getting him home, he hadn't thought about keeping him warm. If Kierion died, he'd be partly to blame …

Fenni held Kierion's feet. Jael had explained that if you warmed the peripheries first—the limbs, hands and feet—then it wasn't such a shock to the body when its temperature rose. Fenni focused on his friend. He channeled *sathir* through his hands, warming Fenni's extremities, then limbs and torso.

Slowly, his friend's hands lost their mottled purple appearance, and grew pink again. The pallor on his face faded and his cheeks took on a healthy hue.

"That's enough, Fenni," Marlies said. "Overheating can be as dangerous as under-cooling."

Fenni's breath gushed out of him. He rolled his shoulders. How long had he been working on Kierion? Moments or hours? In the underground warren it was hard to tell how much time had passed. How did these people live year round without daylight? He gazed around. There were regular holes in the outside wall, each stoppered with a large rock. They must be windows of sorts in summer. He shrugged. Who needed windows when you could jump on a dragon at a moment's notice? That was fresh air enough.

Marlies frowned, keeping her voice low. "I'm a little concerned. It's a bad gash. He's not showing signs of getting worse, but none of getting better." She took a slim vial of green juice from a pouch at her waist. "So, we'll try piaua juice."

Kierion twitched as she applied it to the gash in his head, but there was no other change.

"We'll need to sit with him."

Fenni shrugged. "I'm not going anywhere."

Leah brought more blankets and a bowl of steaming stew for Fenni. "You must be famished," she said, handing him some crunchy bread rolls. The food was good, better than Giddi's infamous wizard's porridge, day in, day out.

Marlies handed Fenni a set of riders' garb. "You might want to change into these while you're here. There's no point in stirring up antagonism." She shook her head, lips compressed in a thin line. "If only the fools would see reason."

"Fools?" Fenni wasn't sure how honest he should be. "You mean the Wizard Council? Or the Council of the Twelve Dragon Masters?"

"Both. And I'm a member of one of them."

Of course she was, as master healer. He ducked into an alcove crammed with shelves of healing supplies. Among them, he recognized some of Jael's jars and pouches. His new garb was much warmer than his wizard gear. He bundled his clothes in his cloak and knotted the ends.

Kierion's breathing was soft and easy, like a lamb. It was uncanny. Kierion was a restless sleeper, thrashing and even laughing in his sleep.

Fenni's own eyes grew heavy and soon his lids shut.

Hours later, Fenni woke to Kierion's chuckle. It was strained, but his friend was awake. The torches had burned low. Judging by the number of patients sleeping, it must be late at night. "Thank the Egg, you're all right," Fenni whispered. "You gave me a right fright."

"Not as much of a fright as that rock gave me," Kierion replied.

"Or as much of a fright as that tharuk got when Riona and I got it," Fenni said.

"Good," said Kierion, trying to sit up.

Marlies appeared at his bedside. "Leah, fetch a bedpan," she called, and the blonde girl dashed off.

"No way," Kierion muttered when Leah returned. "Give a man some dignity. Fenni, will you help me to the latrines?"

"Sure," Fenni said. He needed to go too, but he hadn't been keen to go on his own, here, in the midst of enemies.

Fenni helped Kierion out of bed. He leaned on him as they negotiated a maze of torch-lit tunnels. Around the first corner, they ran into a slim woman about their age, with long blond hair and jade eyes. Quite pretty.

"Kierion, are you all right?" she said, taking in Fenni supporting him.

"I'm fine. A small bump on the head. That's all. This is my best friend from Montanara, Fenni."

"Welcome to Dragons' Hold. I'm Ezaara."

"The Queen's Rider," Kierion said, nudging Fenni.

"Oh?" Fenni held out his hand. He'd never expected the head of Dragons' Hold to be their age, but then again, he'd never expected Jael to be a master either. "Nice to meet you, um, your royal rider."

She laughed. "Ezaara will do. I'm new at this game. Welcome to Dragons' Hold. It's not often we have mages here."

But he was wearing riders' garb. "How could you tell?" Fenni asked.

She smiled. "You have a smudge of mage smoke on your cheek." Her eyes flitted over their shoulders and her face tightened. "Excuse me, I have business with Master Lars. Enjoy your stay." Abruptly, she turned back the way she'd come.

Kierion glanced behind them. "Now, here's someone I wish you'd use your mage power on," he whispered. "Sofia's been spreading lies about Ezaara, saying she's not the Queen's Rider. That her bloodline's wrong. Apparently, some dumb prophecy is broken. Yesterday she even told someone Ezaara had murdered the real Queen's Rider so she could ride Zaarusha."

"But Ezaara seems nice." What he'd seen of her, anyway.

"She is." Kierion's vehemence startled Fenni. He drew himself up. "I'll walk on my own while that guttersnipe is around," Kierion muttered. "No point in showing weakness to your enemy."

That was it. Riders and wizards didn't have to be enemies if they worked together. It wasn't your vocation that made you enemies. It was whether your goals aligned.

Within a few paces, the girl passed them, her blond curls bouncing.

"Hello, Sofia," Kierion called. "Got a moment?"

The girl wheeled. "What? So you can play a prank on me?"

Fenni grinned. Troublemaker or not, Sofia knew Kierion.

"Of course not." Kierion put a hand on the wall to support himself. "I just wanted to introduce you to a friend."

Fenni moved closer to Kierion in case he toppled over.

Sofia cocked her head at Fenni. "I haven't seen you around. Have we met?"

"Not yet," said Fenni. "Nice to meet you." He extended his hand, letting a little wizard power trickle through his fingertips.

She grasped his hand then dropped it. "You have hot hands," she said, shaking her hand—as if that would ease the wizard sting.

"I'd like to remind you to support the Queen's Rider." Fenni gave Sofia a smile that was all teeth.

Sofia's face twisted. "What? That murdering usurper?"

"Ezaara is Queen's Rider," Kierion said, "and you should respect her. Her bond has been tested and proven."

"By an ex-traitor," she snapped.

"He's proven himself thrice over here at Dragons' Hold, helping save Ajeuria and assisting when the queen was poisoned by Fleur."

Sofia spat at Kierion's feet.

Fenni twitched his hands, but Kierion touched his arm briefly, warning him not to interfere. Fenni fumed. No one spat at his friends and got away with it. This girl was a nasty piece of work.

"Well," she said, "won't you be pleased to hear what's happened to Roberto?"

Who was Roberto?

Next to Fenni, Kierion's body tensed. "Oh? What now?" He yawned, as if he didn't care.

Fenni knew that artificially casual tone. Roberto must be a good friend of Kierion's. This woman was on dangerous ground.

She grinned. "Master Roberto is being held captive by Zens," she sneered. "I'll bet you didn't know that."

"Is that all?" Kierion acted disinterested, but Fenni could feel the change in Kierion's *sathir*, the anger simmering beneath the surface.

Sofia stalked past Kierion—and found her way blocked by a wall of green mage flame. She spun, face suddenly pale in the torchlight. "You're a—"

"Yes, I am," said Fenni.

She dashed in the other direction. Fenni waved a hand and another wall of flame sprung up.

"Sofia," he said, holding out his hand and examining his nails. Sparks dripped off his fingertips, bouncing on the stone at her feet.

She hopped from foot to foot, avoiding them.

Fenni sped up the sparks. Now she was literally dancing. "It's not nice to demean your Queen's Rider."

"It's not nice to trap people with wizard flame," she snapped, eyes burning with hatred.

"Of course not, but then again, I'm a wizard. Wizards aren't nice." A fireball shot from his fingers, flying at her head.

She ducked. "You sharding beast," she said through gritted teeth.

"Do you promise to be loyal, now?" Fenni asked softly. The fireball circled Sofia, getting closer, until she stood stock still, her arms pressed against her sides, not daring to move. "Or do I have to visit you again?"

"You, you …" she faltered. "Yes. I'll be loyal. I promise." Her eyes slid away.

There was nothing more he could do. He'd get in enough trouble for threatening her. Fenni snapped his fingers and the fireball flew into his palm. He closed his hands, extinguishing it. "Thank you, Sofia."

Sofia bolted, flinging words at them. "And I look forward to seeing Kierion before Lars and Tonio, explaining what this jumped-up mage trainee is doing here."

"That was fun," said Kierion, once she was gone.

"Come on, let's get you to the latrines and back to the infirmary."

When they returned, Marlies was concerned. "You'd better leave, Fenni. Riona will take you back to Mage Gate immediately. Alban's been in here, asking about you. We don't want a fight on our hands." She shoved Fenni's clothes at him. "Keep the riders' garb. You may need it in the future."

"Thank you." Fenni fastened his cloak about him. Did she want him to keep the garb to fight with Kierion again? He'd thought all riders hated mages. He strode outside, mounted Riona and they were soon swallowed by the inky-black night.

§

As Fenni and Riona descended to Mage Gate, a volley of mage flame shot at them, no doubt one of Master Starrus' defensive tactics. Conjuring an ice shield, Fenni stopped the fire. Riona landed with a thump in the soft snow, staying barely long enough for him to slide off her back.

He didn't blame her; no one wanted to be attacked. Although, he'd just threatened Sofia. Did that make him just as bad? No, the hostile snipe had needed to be stopped—he trusted Kierion's instincts. He held a hand high, sparks flitting from it to guide him across the dark clearing, the snow still pocked with gouges from their duels.

Within moments, he was surrounded by members of the Wizard Council—Masters Starrus, Reina and Hemlon. "Just one moment, young trainee," Starrus said.

Fenni was tired of Starrus' power trips. Everyone knew Master Giddi was more powerful than Starrus, so why wasn't he head of the Wizard Council? "Apologies, Master Starrus," Fenni said, "but I'm no longer a trainee. I'm a qualified mage. You said so yourself."

"Yes, yes, as that may be, however, that doesn't give you the right to come in at all hours of the night riding a dragon. They're dangerous beasts and you shouldn't bring them near here."

"Dangerous?" Fenni raised his eyebrows, sure they weren't as effective as Master Giddi's. "Not as dangerous as the twenty tharuks I've just killed while on dragonback."

Master Giddi was striding over the snow.

Master Starrus said, "We can't tolerate this. You've overstepped your bounds."

"Consorting with riders is despicable," interjected Master Reina. "They insisted we banish our friends and loved ones, then shunned us for years."

Master Hemlon gazed down his pudgy nose at Fenni. "Dragons can turn on you."

Behind Starrus, Master Giddi raised an eyebrow. A sudden chilly wind wove its way between the three council masters. The masters clutched their cloaks around them to ward off the chill.

"I have a question, if I may?" Fenni asked. "What's more dangerous? A dragon or a tharuk troop?"

Starrus snorted. "A tharuk troop, of course."

"Zens' blasted beasts," replied Master Hemlon.

Fenni nodded. "I thought so. Well, the dragon and I have just killed troops of those beasts, so that leads me to my next question. What is more dangerous, a dragon or a bunch of prejudiced fools who would let their own hatred get in the way of killing a common enemy?"

Master Giddi stifled a snort.

"Which master authorized this activity?" Starrus snapped. "You'll be raked across live coals if you've engaged in this manner without approval."

Fenni glanced at Master Giddi, who shook his head.

So Master Giddi wasn't going to get involved? Shards, he was about to have his new mage crystal stripped from him.

"I did." A voice rang out of the forest. Jael walked into the clearing. "And I've just returned from burying the family we were trying to defend." Ignoring the council masters, he came over, shaking Fenni's hand. "Well done, Fenni. You fought admirably, as did the dragon rider who was hurt. Did you get him to safety?"

"Yes."

"Well done. A successful skirmish." Jael clapped his arm over Fenni's shoulder and turned to the council masters. "Any more questions? If not, Fenwick and I are a little battle weary." Without waiting for an answer, he steered Fenni toward the cabins.

Master Giddi's voice drifted across the clearing. "I didn't give up my wife just to let you fools ruin the Wizard Council. Those young ones have mettle, and from now on, I'll be fighting with them for the good of Dragons' Realm. Even if it means fighting you."

Give up his wife? What was he talking about? Master Giddi had never been married, had he?

§

Kierion was used to waking up at dawn, so he was alert when Master Lars and Master Tonio marched into the infirmary. They chatted with Marlies, but by the way Lars' gaze kept flitting to him, Kierion knew he was in trouble. *"Riona, can't I flee on dragonback?"*

"Nonsense. Tell those men you were killing tharuks. Does it really matter who you fight with?"

"Good point. You're sharper than my sword."

Riona chuckled.

"Good morning, Kierion." Lars loomed over him. "How are you feeling? Marlies tells me you banged your head."

Had she said how? Could he get away with a lie?

At the foot of his bed, Tonio watched impassively, his eyes crawling over Kierion's face. Some people said the spymaster could smell a lie. Others said he could read faces. Whatever the case was, Riona was right. He might as well take the dragon by the talons. "Morning." Although the gash was healed, his head still throbbed. "Actually, a tharuk threw a rock at me, when I was fighting a group of them with two wizards, so it wasn't technically banging my head."

Marlies was at a nearby table, pounding herbs. She winked at Kierion.

"And you're aware that consorting with wizards is forbidden?"

"I'm aware that tharuks are overrunning the realm. Does it really matter who I fight with?"

Riona interrupted. *Good choice of words. You're quoting the wisest of dragons.*

"Kierion, I told you if you missed kitchen duty again, you'd be in deep trouble. I've spoken to Benji and you haven't helped in days."

"With all due respect, Master Lars, you told me I had to organize kitchen duty, which I did, impeccably, via my new roster."

Lars huffed his breath out. "Start from the beginning and tell us everything. I want to know who you were with, how many tharuks you killed and how you did it."

"And I want to know exactly how many times you've been out." Tonio folded his arms.

Gods, that man was so austere.

"And who got hurt in each fight," Master Lars added.

I might as well be honest, Kierion told Riona. *I've got nothing to lose.*

Except the privilege of riding me, she said.

Well, there was that.

Master Lars took a seat, beard in hand. Kierion told him about fighting with Fenni, his best friend. Although Kierion felt as guilty as a dragonet stealing tidbits, he glossed over Adelina's injuries, left Riona's out, and downplayed his own.

When he was finished, Master Lars said, "Despite your kitchen *duties,* you seem to have spare time on your hands. So, tomorrow morning, bright and early before our dragon races, you must catch the entire quota of fish for the race day feast." Master Lars looked at Tonio, and sighed. "The wizard was his best friend from Montanara. At his age, we might've done the same." His blue eyes pierced Kierion. "Although the wizard was your friend, mages are dangerous. If you consort with them again, we'll have no choice but to ban you from riding Riona." He stalked from the room.

Kierion melded with Riona, *"He has no right to prevent me riding you."*

"The council is the council. If Queen Zaarusha agrees to their ban, we dragons are bound to follow her edict."

Tonio hung back. "I see from your expression that you feel this is unfair. After all, you were only with your best friend, whom you trust. Is that right?"

Kierion shrugged. What was the spymaster up to?

Tonio sat, steepling his fingers. "I have a delicate compromise," he said quietly. "You may consort with mages if you agree to do me a favor."

"And what's that?" Kierion asked.

Tonio smiled, the type of smile a geezer in the Montanarian marketplace had given Kierion right before he'd nicked his purse full of coin. "You'll see," said Tonio. "Just the odd errand. All perfectly harmless."

Dragon Stunts

It was dawn, once again, as Riona and Kierion headed out over the basin, but this time their saddlebags were bulging with Roberto's fishing nets. He pulled his cloak tighter against the cold wind, and hunkered down on Riona's neck. It was good to be outside again after being cooped up in the infirmary yesterday.

"This breeze should blow the last of the cobwebs from your mind," Riona said as they flew toward the lake's dark surface.

"I'm afraid the fish will still be asleep."

"Do fish sleep?" Riona's curiosity stirred in his mind.

Kierion laughed. *"Who knows?"*

They landed on the shore, and Kierion laid the nets out on the snow, then clambered back up into the saddle. Riona grasped the ends of a net and trailed it through the water.

"You know," said Kierion, shaking his head, "using his nets makes me wonder how Roberto is." A dark shiver snaked down his spine. It seemed so wrong to be preparing for a feast when their master of mental faculties was Zens' captive.

§

Ezaara woke, gasping, her forehead beaded in sweat. She clutched her head, trying to clear the awful scenes from her mind. In this latest nightmare, Zens had held up his hands, squeezing them. A crushing pressure had tightened, like metal bands, around Roberto's head. He'd collapsed, writhing on the stone, screaming. The band increased until his nose bled.

Zens towered over a gasping Roberto. "You know you're mine. I made you what you are. Everything you have, everything you've done, everything you will do, is because of me."

000 had stalked in, claws dripping with green gunge. "Now, boss?" After a cursory nod from Zens, 000 raked Roberto's chest. The green slime entered the wounds, dissolving in Roberto's blood—limplock. He'd been poisoned and had a few days to live.

Ezaara's heart was still rattling like a quiver of arrows. With such frightening dreams, no wonder she was afraid to sleep.

What if this was really happening to Roberto? Some kind of premonition, like her father, Taliesin and Lovina sometimes had?

She shook her head. Ridiculous. Although she had some talents, prophecy wasn't one of them. Her hand flew to the comforting crystal at her neck. Oh, the teardrop was hot—not hot enough to burn, but hot enough to be uncomfortable. She touched it again. Yes, definitely warm. Strange. It shouldn't be. She'd had it on the outside of her nightgown all night.

Ezaara got out of bed and dressed quickly. She touched the teardrop again. It was cooling already. Today was race day. Tomorrow, the council would rescue Roberto. In the seven days since she'd visited Death Valley, she'd rushed from flight training high on rocky crags, to strategy lessons in the main cavern, then to the target range—time and time again—training new dragon riders. Derek, master of instruction, had been observing her lessons. Shards, she'd been so distracted with Roberto being tortured, she was sure she'd done a lousy job, but yesterday, he'd given her the nod. After three moons here, she was now able to train new riders without supervision. The last task before she was inducted as Queen's Rider was today's race.

Zaarusha snorted. *"Typical riders. I chose you back at the clearing in Lush Valley three moons ago. I knew you were right. But no, they had to perform mental tests and train you further … Ridiculous. They should trust their queen."*

"Roberto does trust you, Zaarusha. But dragons can be turned by swayweed. What if I was feeding it to you? Then the whole realm would be in danger."

"At least you'll be full Queen's Rider with all the power to rule the realm after the race tomorrow."

"What's the race like?"

"Challenging but fun. They'll test stunts and speed." Zaarusha appeared at the archway between her den and Ezaara's cavern. The queen huffed her breath out, warming the air. Ezaara scratched Zaarusha's eye ridges. *"Ah, that feels good, my favorite spot,"* Zaarusha purred. *"Your fingers are cold. You need a warm brew. Fetch your cup."*

She scalded the water. Ezaara added soppleberries to it, then sat back on her bed, drinking tea.

Feet sounded outside her door and someone knocked.

So early? Ezaara opened it to Tomaaz and Lovina. "Come in. Want some tea?"

"That would be great," said Tomaaz, taking cups to Zaarusha.

Lovina drummed her fingers against a flat bundle wrapped in cloth, tucked under her other arm.

"What's going on?" Ezaara asked.

Lovina chewed her lip. "I don't know if Zaarusha will be safe at the race today. This morning I saw a vision and was overcome with a strong compulsion to paint. This came out." She tugged the cloth away, exposing a painting of Zaarusha being swallowed by flame. The queen's scales were blistered. Her wings charred and ragged.

Dread coiled in Ezaara's stomach.

"I kept seeing it until I'd painted it."

"It's a shame you can't see the dragon creating the flames. Then we'd know who it is." Tomaaz brought the tea over. "We should go and see Pa. As master of prophecy, he'll know how to interpret this."

"I'm asking Zaarusha if she wants to cancel the race." Ezaara melded with the queen.

"I'm racing, no matter what," Zaarusha said. *"You must lead the realm and the council. I've had enough politics."*

"I don't want you hurt." Gods, no.

"I'll get Tonio and Lars to make a defensive plan."

When they reached Ma and Pa's chambers, Pa was just getting up.

"Lovina's had a recurring vision that a dragon will flame Zaarusha during the race," Ezaara said.

"You too?" Pa examined Lovina's painting, shaking his head. "That's an uncanny talent, Lovina. I've just woken from a similar dream."

Lovina nodded, Tomaaz's arm around her.

Ezaara felt a pang of jealousy. They got to express their love so freely, while she and Roberto had to hide theirs. Soon, when she was no longer his student, they wouldn't hide any more.

Pa replied, "Taliesin and I have both had a similar dream. Handel tried to see who the dragon was, with no luck."

"Zaarusha insists on racing," Ezaara said.

"As she should," said Pa. "There are enough rumors running wild in this place to unsaddle a dragon. So, race, Ezaara, and claim your rightful place. Hopefully we'll be able to smoke out the rogue dragon without Zaarusha being hurt. I'll sort something out with Tonio and Lars." Pa's eyes narrowed, fixing on the crystal teardrop at her neck. "Who did you say gave you that?"

Ezaara kept her voice offhand. "Oh, a friend." A friend who was in danger, right now. Nothing must happen to Zaarusha the day before Roberto's rescue.

§

Adelina bustled into Ezaara's cavern. "I've decided what you should wear for the race today."

Ezaara rolled her eyes.

"Come on," Adelina cajoled, giving Ezaara an overly-bright smile. "It's a public event and rumors are running rife about you. We need to do something that reminds people of who you are and what you can achieve." Her eyes were circled with rings as dark as Death Valley.

Ezaara put a hand on her arm. "We're rescuing Roberto tomorrow, Adelina."

Her dark eyes lit up. "You are?"

"The council will be meeting first thing in the morning to discuss how."

"More hot air." Adelina sighed, her shoulders slumping. "I'm not holding my breath."

"Adelina, they promised," Ezaara said. "I'm hoping we'll leave tomorrow." She couldn't stand waiting any longer.

Adelina's answering smile wasn't as perky as before. "I thought you could wear the same blue tunic you wore when you flew the loop. That'd remind people of how much they loved you. And your green ribbons."

The green ribbons that had made Roberto her protector when she'd unknowingly given him one.

"You'd need to wear a few layers underneath to stay warm. What do you think?"

"Yes to the ribbons, but not that tunic. They need to see me as I am today." Ezaara picked up her hairbrush. "Why don't you have faith in the council?"

Adelina started plaiting Ezaara's hair. "Apart from the fact that they recently banished my brother? It's Tonio. Ever since Roberto and I arrived here, Tonio's hated him, and I have no idea why."

Surely, they wouldn't leave Roberto, a valued master, languishing with Zens. Doubt prickled across her skin.

§

Zaarusha landed in the clearing below her cavern, the snow creaking with the weight of hundreds of dragons as they jostled to make space for more to land. Harnesses snapped against hides. Riders called out, wishing each other luck. More dragons were perched on outcrops above. Others dotted the ridge line. A crowd of onlookers stamped to keep warm, while two blue guards melted a line in the snow with their fiery breath.

Butterflies skittered through Ezaara's belly—actually, it was more like a murder of crows flapping. Lars and Tonio had better keep Zaarusha safe. If either of them were hurt, they couldn't rescue Roberto.

"Stop worrying. Antonika tells me it's all under control. Besides, I'm large and fierce, you know." Zaarusha snorted a tiny gust of flame.

Several dragons sidestepped.

"Zaarusha, this is your life we're talking about."

"Then let's live it, now, and show these riders why you're Queen's Rider and I'm the queen. If anyone harms us, I'll deal with them. The other dragons will back us up."

A horn blew. Lars, on Singlar's back, held his hand high for attention. When everyone had quietened, he addressed them. "Welcome. Today's dragon races are held in honor of our new and honored Queen's Rider, Ezaara." He inclined his head toward Ezaara. "After nearly three moons with us, she has proven herself many times over, even saving Queen Zaarusha's life. We are indebted to her and pledge to serve her. Every Queen's Rider in training must demonstrate their ability in the dragon races—both in stunts and speed racing."

People cheered. Lars held up his hand, cutting them off. "A matter of grave concern has come before the council. We are aware of rumormongers, setting themselves against Ezaara and Queen Zaarusha, quoting unfulfilled prophecy. But we warn you: prophecies often seem impossible until fulfilled. We advise you to be patient, and trust our Queen's Rider. Be warned: any dissension will be punished with imprisonment in the cage."

Ripples of concern radiated through the crowd. Zaarusha tensed.

"The cage?"

Zaarusha shot Ezaara an image of a dingy, cramped dungeon, next to a larger cell with strong chains for a dragon.

"We'll start with stunts. A well-performed stunt tests the courage of the rider and the bond with their dragon. Stunts are not compulsory due to their danger, however, any rider who'd like to display their skills is welcome. Ezaara will go last," Lars announced. "After stunts are over, all new riders, trainees and masters must meet here for speed racing. We welcome anyone who wishes to race."

"Great," said Ezaara sarcastically. *"Throwing the race open to anyone is a sure way to protect you."*

"Antonika says anything other than tradition would raise suspicion. I agree. There's less chance of me being hurt with so many dragons around."

Or more chance of being attacked.

Zaarusha roared and tensed her haunches, leaping into the air.

Wings flapped around them, sounding like Ma's bedsheets flapping on the washing line back in Lush Valley—only hundreds of them. Dragons grunted and riders whooped as they flew up to perch on the mountainside. Zaarusha and a few other dragons landed on an enormous plateau—the imprinting grounds. There was still a sizable crowd in the clearing below, some on dragons, but many on foot.

"You saved me here," Zaarusha melded, sending a wave of warmth.

"Shards, that was awful." Hopefully, she wouldn't have to do any saving today. Prickles of doubt ran down Ezaara's neck.

"Toni's going to ride our flank and Lars will ride our tail during the race, so we should be fine," Zaarusha said. *"Oh, and Maazini has just let me know that your parents, Tomaaz and Kierion will be nearby as well. Everyone's been briefed."*

Ezaara blew her breath out as Alyssa on Lysika, and Lars on Singlar, arrived. There were only four other trainees—Adelina, Kierion and Sofia's friends, Alban and Nadira. She sighed. If only she'd never injured Sofia.

"It was an accident," Zaarusha retorted. *"If Ajeuria hadn't launched a mental attack on you, none of that would've happened. I apologize for my daughter's actions."*

"We'll have Alban first. Show us what you've learned." Alyssa, master of flight, blew a horn.

Alban sneered at Ezaara as Banikan, his majestic dragon, stalked through the snow to the front of the ledge, green scales flashing in the sunlight. Banikan's wings rustled, breaking the silence as they shot up into the stark blue sky. Alban let out a whoop, then Banikan plunged, rolling his body around in a tight corkscrew, his wings pinned against his sides—a blur of green against the snowy backdrop of Dragon's Teeth.

Ezaara held her breath. *"Dragon's claws. That's fast."*

"It's not difficult, but impressive," came Zaarusha's offhand reply. *"Not many have attempted it since a dragon lost control five years ago. He and his rider plunged to their deaths in the lake."*

"It's that dangerous?"

"Only if the dragon loses its sense of direction. The key is to stop before your rider gets disoriented and confuses you. I bet we could do it."

With a roar, Banikan pulled out of his plunge and flipped his wings upward, rising into the air above the spectators. People cheered and dragons rumbled. Alban waved and stood on his saddle as Banikan circled past the assembled spectators.

"Banikan's worried that Alban's too dizzy." Zaarusha's urgent cry cut through Ezaara's thoughts. *"Liesar, quick."* Zaarusha leapt off the ledge, winging toward him.

Alban tottered upon the saddle, his arms flailing. He fell, plunging toward the trees.

Oh shards, they were too late.

In a flash of silver, Liesar was below Alban. She thwacked him with her tail, bouncing him in the air, and then caught him. He lay slumped across her saddle, his legs hanging down one side, arms barely clinging on. *"I'm taking him to the infirmary,"* Liesar melded with Ezaara and Zaarusha, and sped off.

Master Alyssa said to the assembled trainees, "Please don't hurt yourselves by trying to prove something. We want to assess your abilities, not injure you. Is that clear?"

Somber-faced, the trainees nodded.

"Who's next?"

Nadira and Diran prowled to the ledge's edge, and flew toward the mountainside where Zaarusha and Ezaara had performed their loop.

"Shards, they're not going to try a loop, are they?"

"I warned him not to, but Diran won't listen."

A bronze blur whipped below Nadira and Diran—Handel was monitoring them.

Silence blanketed the basin as Diran started his vertical climb, then looped upside down. Nadira's arms slipped out of her holds. Arms flailing, she tried to reach them again. Gasps rippled through the crowd. Handel zipped up to catch her, but before he could get there, Diran rolled, flipping right side up again.

The crowd cheered.

"That'll teach her and Alban to try and show you up. You're not Queen's Rider for nothing." Zaarusha growled. *"We'll show them we can't be outdone."*

Alyssa's horn blew again. Adelina rose into the sky on Linaia, standing in the saddle. She jumped, hugging her knees and Linaia swooped below, bouncing Adelina with her tail. Adelina flew into the air and landed, sitting, in the saddle. She raised her arms high as they swooped past the mountain face. The crowd cheered.

"One of our old moves," melded Ezaara.

"Appropriate for stunt races. She's showing off her skill without going too far. Good show."

Kierion and Riona paced to the front of the ledge. Still in the saddle, Kierion gave a bow. "My Queen and honored Queen's Rider, I pledge to serve you."

"Thank you, Kierion," Ezaara replied.

"He'll show everyone up. He has no fear," Zaarusha said.

"No fear?"

"He's a strategist. He believes in his ability to get himself out of any scrape." Zaarusha chuckled.

The horn blew again. Riona and Kierion were off, darting at the mountain faces. The downdraught of Riona's wings whipped spectators' hair into their eyes. Riona veered toward Ezaara and Zaarusha, Ezaara's ribbons flew around her face in a rush of wind. Grinning, Kierion hunkered down on Riona's back and they spiraled down in a tight coil, Riona's nose nearly touching her tail as they whirled down to the basin. Kierion's whoops and hollers broke the silence.

How was he doing that without feeling sick?

They touched down and Kierion leapt out of the saddle. Alyssa raised the horn to her lips, but Kierion called out, "Not yet." In a flash, Riona was aloft with Kierion in her talons, ascending. She threw Kierion into the air and plunged down, snatching him up. His laughter rang out above the shocked spectators. Riona tossed him again, and swooped underneath him, catching him on her saddle.

Suddenly he slipped, hurtling toward the ground. Riona dived after Kierion.

Ezaara's breath caught in her throat. Zaarusha's haunches tensed and they were airborne. Handel shot toward Riona.

Kierion hollered, "Fooled you all," as Riona snatched him in her talons again.

Shards, he was a trickster.

"That brat. We'll show him." Zaarusha's relief swept through Ezaara.

Heart still pounding, Ezaara relaxed as Zaarusha backwinged.

There was stunned silence. Then someone clapped. Others joined in. The stunt pair spiraled lazily toward the clearing and Riona let Kierion down to the ground. He pumped his fists in the air. Raucous applause and cheering broke out.

Ezaara's grip eased. *"He always has the last laugh, doesn't he?"*

"Not today. It's our turn. Hang on." Zaarusha beat her wings.

The chill wind flung Ezaara's ribbons into her face. She pulled up her hood, stuffing them inside. The basin was stunning, covered in its cool winter coat, stark against the blue sky. The icy forest and gray lake had been transformed from when she'd trained with Roberto on the sunny shore. Dragon's claws, she missed him. Worried about him. Thank the Egg, they were going tomorrow.

"Focus." Zaarusha broke into her thoughts.

Ezaara breathed deeply. *"I'm ready."*

"We'll start slowly," thrummed Zaarusha. The queen flashed images at Ezaara, preparing her for their stunts.

She sucked in her breath. *"That'll be challenging."* She swallowed, trying to ease the knot in her throat. Ezaara relinquished her thoughts, letting Zaarusha take over. Fire slipped into her veins, warmth rushing through her chest and limbs.

"First, we'll face our loyal and not-so-loyal subjects." Zaarusha flew low over the crowd.

Ezaara scanned their upturned faces, taking in friendly smiles, sneers and suspicion—a far cry from when everyone had cheered her when she'd first come to Dragons' Hold. Sofia had laid her poison well. Now, they had to undo it.

Zaarusha flew along the mountainside, past every dragon rider. *"We can't be divided when Zens attacks, or he'll slaughter us. Today we must unite our people in their loyalty to you."*

Countless eyes stared at Ezaara. She slipped her arms into the leather armholds on Zaarusha's saddle, anchored her feet in the stirrups, and pressed her knees against the queen's sides. Her stomach plummeted as Zaarusha flipped upside-down, looping over and over.

Everything tumbled. Snatches of mountainside. Snowy trees. Wan sky. Blurred faces of dragons and riders. Zaarusha's wingbeats whooshed in her ears. Her senses reeled, but through it all, fire danced in her, welcoming the challenge. She had Zaarusha. The queen would not let her down.

"I've stopped looping."

"I can't tell." Everything was still spinning, images whirling in her confused brain. Her ears were roaring. Ezaara closed her eyes and breathed.

She opened them. That wasn't her ears roaring, it was the crowd. She grinned, waving to them. "What's next?"

"That will put Nadira in her place." Zaarusha lazily circled the clearing. *"Their applause is a bit premature, don't you think? Wait until they see this."* Zaarusha shot up, zigzagging in and out of the peaks of Dragon's Teeth.

Exhilaration rushed through Ezaara, making her chest expand until she thought it would burst. This was living. This was what their bond had been forged for. The queen hurtled down the slope at breakneck speed, swooping up just short of the trees. Ezaara's laugh rang over the basin as they flew above the watching riders.

"*Ready, Ezaara?*"

"*Give me the signal.*" Ezaara stood on the saddle, waiting for Zaarusha's tail flick. *Sathir* swirled around them like a vibrant river of colors.

Zaarusha's tail twitched.

Ezaara dived, plunging head first, arms extended. Counting to four, she curled into a ball and somersaulted three times. Zaarusha flicked her tail against her back, bouncing her in the air. Ezaara readied herself for the second and third bounces, each one lighter than the last, then righted herself and fell into Zaarusha's saddle, straddling it. She fastened her harness, and prepared to corkscrew.

Up they shot, higher than Zaarusha had ever taken her. Everyone receded from sight. Bitter wind tugged at her jerkin. Shivering, Ezaara shoved her arms through the arm-holds as the peaks of Dragon's Teeth were dwarfed.

They dived, corkscrewing down. Zaarusha spun around her axis, wings tight against her sides. Ezaara's eyes stung from wind, running with tears. Peaks flashed past in a dizzying whirl. The mountain faces blurred in a whirlpool of light, snow and rock. Down they spiraled in a dizzy coil. Nausea hit Ezaara. She closed her eyes and tuned into Zaarusha, sensing her *sathir*. Her stomach calmed.

With a lurch, Zaarusha unfurled her wings and righted herself, shooting up level with the riders on the ledges. "*Sorry about pushing your limits, but they have to see that you aren't just another rider.*" Zaarusha's fire blazed through them both. "*They can't touch us with their gossip, politics or personal attacks. You are Queen's Rider, here at Dragons' Hold to stay.*"

Ezaara rubbed Zaarusha's hide. "*So, should we try some talon acrobatics?*" They hadn't practiced much, but why not?

"*Absolutely. We still have height if I drop you.*"

"*You won't.*"

"*You're as cocky as Kierion.*"

Ezaara laughed. "*Maybe I'll use some of his showy tactics.*" Heart pounding, she slid off Zaarusha, the wind clawing at her jerkin. "Yahooo." Just like Kierion.

Zaarusha dived, grasping Ezaara's arms, twisting her talons around her hands.

Shoulders burning, she hung on. *"I'm ready."*

Zaarusha's grip slackened. Hand by hand, Ezaara adjusted her grip down until she was holding a talon in each hand. *"I can't hold on for long,"* she melded. *"It's now or never."*

"Go," barked Zaarusha.

Taking a deep breath, Ezaara tucked her knees against her chest, tipped her head and spun over.

The crowd below, *oohed*.

Breath rasping, Ezaara uncurled her body and transferred her hands to a talon. Lifting her legs, she swung back and forth, holding Zaarusha's talon. Then Ezaara flipped upside down, hooking her legs around Zaarusha's limb and releasing her hands.

This was amazing. The world was upside down and she was high above the ground, wind tossing her hair as Zaarusha flew along the cliff faces, Ezaara upside-down, holding on with her legs. Faces flashed past, painted with shock and astonishment.

They cheered. Dragons rumbled, flames flicking from their maws. Applause rang off the mountain faces.

"My legs are tired, Zaarusha."

"Ready? I'm letting you go." Zaarusha flung Ezaara upward with her powerful legs and caught her in the saddle. The queen pirouetted mid-air before the screaming crowd.

"Was that enough?" asked Ezaara.

"Nearly," replied Zaarusha. *"Take the ribbons from your hair, like the day you presented them to Roberto. We need to remind them of that day too, and the loyalty they felt for you, back then."*

Ezaara unfastened her ribbons, holding them high, and Zaarusha leap-frogged through the air.

"E-zaa-ra! Zaa-ru-sha! E-zaa-ra! Zaa-ru-sha!" the crowd chanted, the way they had on her flight test.

In a whirl of faces and sound, Ezaara felt completely happy—well, not completely. Roberto was still captive.

"Don't worry, we'll get him tomorrow."

What if tomorrow was too late?

Dragon Race

Dragons flew to the starting line melted in the snow, their riders dismounting, boots crunching as they gathered to await instructions. Adelina came over to Ezaara. "That was impressive." She hugged her.

"Thank you," Ezaara replied. "Wasn't Kierion brilliant?"

The smile Adelina gave was genuine. "Sure was, the scoundrel."

A bunch of lads were clapping Kierion on the back.

"Well done, Ezaara," a woman said. "That was impressive."

Across the sea of people, Ma and Pa waved at her, smiling proudly.

Alyssa blew the horn for silence. "We acknowledge our Honored Queen's Rider, Ezaara, as the champion stunt rider of Dragons' Realm. We also honor Kierion's bravery, although he may have had more competition if our senior riders had participated."

"Not fair," called Kierion among good-natured laughter.

"Congratulations to our stunt riders. Good luck to all of you with future stunts. These are valuable in learning agility and trust, but be careful," Alyssa said. "We don't want to lose you. You'll all be needed in the war against Zens and his tharuks. I'll turn the time to Master Lars."

Lars' icy-blue eyes swept the assembled riders and spectators. "I'd like to remind you that Ezaara is Queen's Rider, has been since she imprinted, and will remain so. Any questions regarding her eligibility will be handled by the council. Just now, you've seen that she is fearless and has a deep bond with the dragon queen. Not one of you could do what she just did. Much will be required of her when we go to war against Commander Zens and his armies of tharuks. Do not envy the responsibility she's shouldered."

Someone jabbed Ezaara's back. When she turned, everyone was looking at their council leader.

"You've seen the trust she has in Zaarusha," Lars said. "Ezaara has earned the same trust from us. I ask that you give it willingly, freely. Let's put an end to these vicious rumors and have peace among us as we face war with our enemy." He stepped back.

"Ready?" Master Alyssa cried, holding her horn high. Everyone cheered. "You'll race to the clearing at the far side of the lake, swoop down to the dead conifer and pluck a cone from its branches. The winner is the first to drop their cone in this basket." She gestured to one of the huge baskets used for gathering fruit from the orchards. "Singlar has marked all of the cones in that tree, so there's no cheating."

"Got that, Kierion?" someone called.

"You're just jealous," he crowed, amid laughter.

"All trainees, including newly-imprinted riders, must participate," Alyssa continued. "You'll be racing against the Queen's Rider and your masters, except for Master Derek and I. We'll be judging the race. Any other riders can join in. The more who fly, the merrier. Now, go to your dragons, get to the start line, and await the horn. Good luck."

"You're a murderer, not a Queen's Rider," someone hissed, voice dripping venom.

Ezaara spun. The crowd was dispersing, so it was impossible to see who had spoken. "Did you hear that?" she asked Adelina.

"What?" Adelina asked.

"More insults."

"Ignore them. Zaarusha chose you. No one else has that right." Adelina said, dodging around a beefy rider.

"But Anakisha's prophecy …" Ezaara pushed her way through the throng.

"Handel says it will be fulfilled."

"How?"

Adelina shrugged. "Good luck." They knocked fists and Adelina headed to Linaia.

"Trust me, it will work out," Zaarusha melded.

"I do trust you. Others should too." She was nearly at Zaarusha when someone shoved her. She spun to see Sofia, Alban and Nadira smirking. She glared at them. "Feeling well enough to bully people again, are you, Alban?"

Zaarusha roared, sending them scurrying. People turned and stared. *"Climb up. Let's race."*

Ezaara scrambled into the harness, strapping it tight. Zaarusha took off and roared again, sending a warning flame above Sofia, Alban and Nadira's heads. *"We'll triumph over these gossipmongers, you'll see."*

"Who's the fastest dragon here?" asked Ezaara.

"I am, now that Syan is gone." A wave of sorrow swept across Ezaara—Zaarusha's, for her dead mate. "The next fastest are Erob, Ajeurina and Maazini, due to their royal blood."

"Has Erob recovered fully?"

"He and Maazini are both fit again."

In her worry over Roberto, she'd neglected Erob and Maazini. She must visit Erob when the race was over. He'd be pining for Roberto too. Dragons were landing, stamping, impatient to get going. They jostled into place, side by side, along the starting line, leaving at least two wing breadths between them.

Alyssa waved her horn. "Remember, healthy competition and strategy are allowed, but no violence. Save that for tharuks. Enjoy the race."

"Let's whip their tails." Zaarusha's body thrummed with suppressed excitement.

Cheers rose as dragons and riders were poised, coiled tight with tension, waiting for their signal. There was a short blast on the horn accompanied by Lysika's roar.

A sea of dragons rose like a giant tidal wave, cresting upward. The air was thick with rustling wings as everyone battled to get free of the throng. Roars filled Ezaara's ears. Tiny gusts of flame shot around them.

Zaarusha pulled above the thrashing wings. Only a few experienced masters were flying high above the crowd, until Ezaara heard a holler and Kierion shot above them, a few new trainees trailing him.

"'Atta girl, Riona," he called out. "Come on, you lot, let's show them." Riona streamlined her body and they shot forward.

Zaarusha's jaws flared with flame and she broke free of the other dragons, zipping ahead toward the forest. Smoke trailed from her jaws, enveloping Kierion.

Kierion spluttered and coughed. "Not fair."

A bitter winter wind rushed through Ezaara's hair. Tightening her hood, she glanced behind. Dragons were gaining on them.

"A purple one, coming in fast. It's Aria," said Zaarusha, *"and she's bent on catching us. Let's show her and Sofia a trick or two."*

Ezaara melded fully with Zaarusha, letting their *sathir* merge in a stream of color. Fire licked through her. The snowy fields whipped by beneath them. Soon they were over the forest, heading toward the lake, the dark fir branches dusted with snow.

Behind, the sky was teeming with dragons. Zaarusha was right: Maazini's orange scales stood out close behind, followed by Singlar, Ajeurina and Erob. There was a dark-haired rider upon Erob. Her breath caught. Shards, he looked like Roberto. He couldn't be back, could he? Heart pounding, she asked, *"Who's flying Erob?"*

"Tonio. He's here for security. Erob offered to take him, because he's fast."

That explained it. They were both Naobian. Disappointment knifed through her. *"Erob, the council have agreed to fetch Roberto tomorrow."*

"Good, because if they don't go, I'll go myself," he sniped.

Erob was usually good-natured, often humorous. *"I get it, Erob, I really do. The council have given their word."* If they kept it. Adelina's doubts niggled at her.

A snort was his only reply. Erob plunged below Zaarusha and swooped up to come alongside them. Ajeurina mirrored his actions on the other side, then they were off, with Singlar and Maazini on their tails, Tomaaz yahooing.

A sudden flash of purple above them told her that Kierion had joined them. *"We caught those sluggish old snails,"* quipped Riona so Ezaara could hear.

Beyond the forest, the lake was edged with icy lace. Wings thrashed as they flew across the deep blue toward the snowy clearing. Zaarusha forged her way ahead of the others, aiming for the massive conifer. Denuded of needles, its branches were heavy with unshed cones.

Zaarusha wheeled dangerously close, snatching a cone in her outstretched talon, then veered up into the sky. Flapping wings and dragon snorts sounded against the muted snowscape as Erob, Riona and Ajeurina darted in to grab cones.

With a crack, a dragon knocked a branch off the tree, sending it thudding to the snow. More dragons snapped branches off in their haste to get cones.

"Lars is clever," Ezaara melded. *"They're clearing the dead wood for him."*

Zaarusha rumbled, *"Never underestimate Lars. Here, catch."* Zaarusha stretched her foreleg out, flinging the cone to Ezaara.

Nearby, Sofia caught a cone from Aria. Ezaara grinned at her, trying, yet again, to be friendly.

Without warning, Aria wheeled toward Zaarusha and roared, flames exploding from her jaws. Aria's thoughts ripped through Ezaara's mind. *"Traitors. Anakisha's heir has a right to rule."*

Fierce heat engulfed them. Ezaara hunkered down behind Zaarusha's neck.

Zaarusha shrieked in pain, blasting Aria with fire. The queen's shock slammed through Ezaara as they twisted out of Aria's reach. Talons flailing, the purple dragon flew at them again, Sofia laughing on her back. With a glint of metal, Sofia threw her throwing knife.

"Zaarusha, duck," Ezaara screamed.

The knife embedded itself in Zaarusha's thigh. Her pain spiked through Ezaara.

Sofia threw another. Zaarusha batted that knife sideways, and it spun down to the snow.

"Oops, I slipped," Sofia crowed. "Terribly sorry—it was an accident. That's what you said when you gouged me."

Aria slashed at Zaarusha's tail. Wings bashing Aria's, Zaarusha darted in, ripping a gouge in her foreleg. She flipped her tail around and whipped Aria across the snout.

Aria screeched and reeled back for a reprieve. But there was no reprieve. Riona dived and Kierion threw Roberto's fishing net. It sailed through the air, landing over Aria. Maazini snatched a flailing rope at the end of the net and plunged under Aria and up the other side near Erob.

Suddenly, Kierion was near Aria, balancing upon the base of Riona's outstretched tail. He thrust a rope through the top of the net and scrambled up Riona's tail, back into his saddle, so Riona could fly around the net, tugging the rope tight. Liesar's silver scales, Handel's bronze and Erob's midnight-blue flashed past as they darted in to grab ropes and pull the net taut. Handel, Liesar, Maazini and Erob held ropes in their jaws, the net suspended between them. Aria struggled, her talons tangled. She fought to slash her way free, only making the ropes tighter. Her roars drowned out the yelling riders.

"To the cage," Lars yelled, charging past on Singlar.

Sofia screamed, "Let me out this instant."

Erob melded, *"Back to the race, Ezaara. Now, you* have *to win."*

Zaarusha wheeled, heading across the lake. Ezaara gripped the cone so tightly, it cut into her palms. White-coated trees blurred beneath them as Zaarusha and Ezaara raced toward the basket, Lars following on Singlar. Basket at their feet, Alyssa and Derek had their bows nocked, ready to protect them.

Ezaara melded with Lysika and Reko, showing them what had happened. *"Aria and Sofia attacked us."*

Now, there were only two dragons blocking the direct route to the basket. The others must have lagged behind, confused by Aria's attack. A cry sounded behind her. A blur of purple was coming up fast—Kierion on Riona.

She urged Zaarusha on.

When Zaarusha was flush with other two dragons, Ezaara realized who they were. "*Watch out, Zaarusha. That's Alban astride Banikan and Nadira on Diran.*" Ezaara's heart sank as the riders smirked. Sofia's cronies weren't done causing trouble.

When they were only a handful of dragon lengths away from the basket, Banikan and Diran closed in, hemming in Zaarusha's wings. She roared, flames licking at Banikan. Diran flamed her back, a blast of heat passing over Ezaara. They dived, then swooped, blocking Ezaara from aiming her cone.

Kierion and Riona passed them. They were about to win the race. Then Riona turned above the basket. Kierion gestured.

What? Oh. Ezaara threw her cone as far as she could. It sailed through the air, hitting Riona's hide, then clattered into the basket. Kierion's cone thudded in after it. A cheer rose from the crowd.

Zaarusha roared, whirling upon Banikan and Diran. The two riders innocently tossed their cones, and the dragons sped away.

Wings flapped and riders flung their cones, then took their places at the finish line in the snow.

By the time Tonio and Erob and their team arrived, carrying Aria and Sofia in the net, Lars was glowering. He bowed to Zaarusha, his voice carrying, "Honored Queen Zaarusha, what shall we do with Sofia and Aria?"

Zaarusha's snarl made the minds of every dragon at the hold flinch. "*Toss them in the cage.*" She roared, showing her fangs as the net-bearers approached.

"And Alban, Banikan, Nadira and Diran?"

"*The cage as well.*"

"The cage," announced Lars for the benefit of those without dragons to meld with. Blue guards pursued Alban and Nadira. The folk were silent as Aria and Sofia were flown away.

Feasting

The main cavern was swarming with people. Dragons flitted above the crowd, landing on ledges to observe the proceedings. Zaarusha thudded down on the natural rock stage that ran along one end of the cavern. The council masters and their dragons were waiting, arrayed in similar formation to the first night Ezaara had arrived here to have her imprinting bond tested by Roberto.

"You've come far since then, Ezaara. Remember how terrified you were?" Zaarusha rumbled.

"Of course I was scared. I wasn't sure if dragons existed before I met you—and the masters looked so tough."

"The toughest of all was Roberto, I'll bet."

"Too right. He was awful." Her stomach churned uneasily. Anything could be happening to him.

"Tomorrow the council will decide the best way to rescue him. Hopefully, he's discovered what these new creatures of Zens are." Zaarusha furled her wings.

Or was he discovering how cruel Zens' torture methods were? Oh shards, she was so cynical. Her nightmares were so realistic after glimpsing Death Valley, they were impairing her judgment. Ezaara slid out of the saddle.

Lars approached, shaking Ezaara's hand. "Well done, Ezaara. That was a fantastic display of talent."

"It was a measure of the queen's skill," Ezaara deferred.

"And yours." Lars turned to the crowd.

Derek, the training master, blew the horn, and Lars waved him to the front of the stage.

"After three moons with us, we finally declare the Queen's Rider, Ezaara of Lush Valley, fully trained," said Derek. "It's been years since Zaarusha's last rider, Anakisha, fell in battle—may her soul soar with departed dragons. You've seen Ezaara's skill, her trust in the queen, both today and throughout her time with us. They have bonded exceptionally well, and she has worked hard to reach the standard expected of a Queen's Rider. We thank her for saving Zaarusha from dragon's bane and the traitors who tried to kill our queen." Derek swallowed. "We owe Ezaara our allegiance." He thumped his hand over his heart, then gestured to her. "Ezaara, please take a victory lap. Then let the feast begin. Tomorrow, all duties are canceled—except patrol."

Zaarusha roared. *"Climb up on my neck."*

Ezaara clambered over Zaarusha's neck spines and straddled her neck, just below her head. Zaarusha leaped off the stage, her wings ruffling the crowd's hair. Below, the sea of upturned faces went wild, screaming, hollering and whistling. Zaarusha spiraled up to the vaulted stone ceiling. For a moment, they hung in the air as Ezaara observed the people, as tiny as berries, below. Then the queen dived, plunging toward them. Torches guttered in their sconces when she pulled up short and landed on the stage, wings spread wide.

Cheers and roars swept through the cavern as Ezaara dropped to the stage and gestured to Zaarusha with a flourish.

The masters behind them clapped. It was so hollow without Roberto here. He'd trained her. He'd fostered her talent, goaded her and driven her to be better. He loved her. Ezaara clutched the teardrop, rubbing her fingers over the smooth crystal. Roberto was in such danger while they were here having a good time. Except she wasn't. She was miserable without him.

A gong boomed. The crowd parted to allow Benji and his kitchen staff to enter. Kierion was behind Benji, leading a team carrying a table laden with fine food. They set their table against the wall, buffet style. More teams marched in. Trust Kierion to be everywhere. Ezaara's stomach grumbled as scents reached her—roast duck, succulent fish, spiced sweet potato. This would be a feast to remember.

"As it should be, in your honor," Zaarusha said.

"Actually, it's in your honor," Ezaara said. *"Without a queen, there'd be no Queens' Rider."*

Pa and Ma approached and both hugged her. "We're so proud of you," said Ma, eyes shining. "I know this hasn't been easy."

"Well done, darling." Pa's gaze fastened on her necklace. "This looks so much like Anakisha's dream catcher. A remarkable imitation. When Yanir was far away, the original enabled Anakisha to see what was happening to him in her dreams." He turned to Ma. "That would've been helpful when you were in Death Valley, honey."

"No." Ma shuddered. "I wouldn't have wanted you to know what I went through."

Ezaara felt the color drain from her face. Anakisha's dream catcher. Seeing through another's eyes. It all made sense.

"I'm glad you're safe here." Pa kissed Ma. "Let's eat. Ezaara, are you coming?"

Ezaara's smile froze. "Um, soon."

As her parents descended the steps to the cavern floor, her thoughts sped like racing dragons. She'd seen Roberto being tortured in Death Valley, right before her eyes. Then she'd seen it again in her dreams. She'd assumed her nightmares had been brought on by her brief trip to Death Valley. But what if the teardrop was Anakisha's dream catcher? What if Roberto really had been slashed by tharuk claws coated with limplock? Limplock took three days to act. Gods, in two days, he'd be dead.

"Ezaara." Kierion waved at her from the floor below.

People were milling around the tables, piling their plates with food. In a corner, musicians on the gittern, flute and drums started playing. At a nearby table, Tonio was downing wine like he was dying of thirst, slamming back a glass and reaching for another.

Roberto could be dying. Ezaara rubbed the teardrop. Or dead already. She had to go now. *"Zaarusha—"*

"It's dangerous on our own. The council are meeting first thing in the morning."

"I could speak to Tonio and Lars now."

"Good idea."

Ezaara made her way down the steps and pushed through the throng. People clapped her on the back and congratulated her.

Kierion popped up out of nowhere, beaming. "I've saved you a spot with your favorite food."

"My favorite food?"

"Fish and sweet potato." Kierion blushed as red as a blood-beet.

Oh. At her very first feast here, to honor her arrival, she'd tripped and spilled food over her clothes—fish and sweet potato. "Ah, I'm not hungry."

"After all those stunts? I'm starving."

"They turned my stomach," Ezaara lied.

He laughed. "You're still welcome to sit with us."

"I've some council business. I should sit with Lars."

The spymaster was now in a corner, embroiled in a discussion with Ma, waving his hands around and slugging back more wine. Emotions chased across his face—joy, bitterness and anger. He folded an arm across his chest and shook his head stubbornly, then suddenly stalked away from Ma to refill his glass.

She didn't exactly want to approach Tonio with him in such a mood. At another table, Lars was regaling people with a tale, while they listened, spellbound. She couldn't interrupt him either. Inside her, frustration warred with social nicety.

"Come on, Ezaara, have some dinner. You'll feel better," Kierion insisted.

"Just let me talk to my mother, and I'll be with you in a few moments."

She approached Ma as she left the buffet. "Ah, Ma, do you have a moment?"

Ma's eyes flitted to either side of them. "Sure, I need to talk to you, too." She placed her plate on the table next to Pa's, and led Ezaara into a quiet corner.

"Ma, I saw you talking to Tonio. Why was he so angry?"

"He's changed, Ezaara. When I first came here and trained as one of his dragon corps members, he was fiery, but not bitter. The years have done him a disservice. His heart has grown hard."

What was that about? "Ah …"

"Tonio has canceled tomorrow morning's council meeting."

"What?" That louse. "But we—"

"So, I broached him about the rescue plan for Master Roberto. I've been to Death Valley. Every day there is a living nightmare. Tomaaz got out, but our master of mental faculties is still there …" Ma gripped Ezaara's shoulders, her turquoise eyes burning. "I think the wine was talking, but Tonio admitted why he hasn't acted. Roberto's father killed Tonio's wife."

Ezaara's head reeled. "But Roberto's not his father. His father was a mean-spirited bully who beat his littlings and broke his wife's back. It eventually killed her."

"Oh gods. Amato?" Ma's face grew pale. She clutched Ezaara's arm. "Amato did that?"

Ezaara nodded. Ma had known Amato? She'd had no idea.

"And I thought I loved him …" Ma whispered to herself, a faraway look in her eyes.

Ma had loved Amato, that awful man who'd beaten his family?

Ma focused on Ezaara again. "So, what Tonio said is true. Do you love Roberto?"

The clamor of the feast died away. The seconds stretched out like sand on a never-ending shore. Ezaara swallowed. "Yes," she whispered. "Yes, I do."

Ma reached into her jerkin pocket and pressed something small and hard into Ezaara's hand. A ring. "Then go," she said. "Go and save the man you love." She enveloped Ezaara in her embrace. "Use Kisha's ring again, but be careful. I don't want to lose you."

§

Adelina picked at her food. It wasn't fair to have delicious food when her brother could be lying dead in Death Valley. Ezaara had insisted the council was going to rescue him tomorrow, but what if it was too late? And why had they waited so long? She pushed back her chair.

"Hey, are you off so soon?" Kierion asked.

Shards, his eyes were so sweet—that gorgeous blue that made her want to melt inside. "Just getting a drink." Adelina made her way over to the beverage table. She was filling her cup with grape juice when she heard her father's name. Casually, she turned her head. At the other end of the table, Tonio was gesticulating at Marlies, his voice slurred. Adelina turned away, sipping her drink and listening. Tonio mentioned her mother—and then Ezaara and Roberto.

She'd long suspected that her brother was in love with the Queen's Rider. No, she'd known it, but never dared discuss it with Roberto—not when the punishment for loving a trainee was banishment. Now Tonio was refusing to rescue him because Amato, her cursed shrotty father, had let tharuks capture Tonio's new wife years ago. She didn't blame him. She hated Amato too. But to visit that hate upon the very children Amato had beaten? And abandon her brother in Death Valley after sending him there? That was a whole new level of hatred.

Rage burned through Adelina.

Eyes stinging, she stalked from the table, just as Kierion reached her.

He took her cup, depositing it nearby, and flashed her a grin. "Want to dance?" His grin faltered. "Oh, are you all right?"

Adelina hesitated. Roberto's love for Ezaara was not her secret to spill. "Just a little tired."

"The music's good. It'll get your feet tapping."

Dancing was the last thing she felt like, but Adelina let Kierion lead her past the tables to the dance area.

"You were amazing today," he beamed. "I was so proud of you during stunts." Holding her hand in his, and placing his other on her waist, he whisked her around the floor in time to the music.

He smelled of leather and candle wax, a nice combination. "Your stunts were way better than mine."

Kierion quirked an eyebrow. "I was showing off, but yours showed precision and restraint in the face of Nadira and Alban's silly tactics."

"So, you got that?"

"I did." His eyes played across her face as the music changed tempo. "That's the introduction to the farlauf. We danced this in Montanara when I was a kid, but I always got in trouble for playing pranks during dances."

"That's hard to believe, Kierion." She had to laugh.

He grinned. "The key is to never play the same trick twice. That's what keeps it interesting."

"Never the same one twice?"

He leaned close. "Once I dropped my drink on the floor, and as I mopped it up, I tied my friend's bootlaces together. When the music changed, he stood up to dance and fell flat on his face." His eyes shone. "I've tried salt in the punch, sugar in the vegetables. Tuned the band's instruments to be off key. I even nailed someone's shoes to the floor, once. Another time, I put a few fish in pockets."

"You're shocking. Where do you come up with all these ideas?" He was incorrigible, but, gods, so adorable.

"Don't let Lars see us grinning, he'll think I'm up to something again. I haven't played a decent prank since I hid those arrows. What with seeing Fenni and Jael, I haven't had time."

Kierion's grin was as broad as his shoulders. Adelina found herself admiring both. He swept her into the throng, his arm around her as they waltzed down the center of two lines of people.

"Surely the other morning's effort counts?" she asked as they moved in time.

"Nah, that was nothing."

Swapping Sofia's butter for cheese really was nothing compared to what Kierion usually got up to, but Sofia had been as mad as a dragon with an ingrown talon. "How's tharuk hunting going?" Ezaara was talking to her mother, looking very serious, over in a corner. Was Marlies telling her what Tonio had said?

"Good, we're going out tomorrow and taking Tomaaz with us," Kierion said. "Do you want to come?"

Ezaara and Marlies left the cavern. What was the Queen's Rider up to? Adelina had to know. Once, Ezaara had gone to the Wastelands to get her brother. Maybe this time they could go together. "Ah, I think I'll rest tomorrow, like Master Derek suggested."

He cocked his head. "Are you sure? You're usually so full of energy."

How did he do that? Make her feel special with such a simple statement. "Since I've knocked my head, I tire easily," Adelina lied. Guilt flashed across his face. Oh shards, now her lie had made him feel bad.

The music slowed. "Another dance?" Kierion asked, eyes hopeful.

"Too much racing," said Adelina stifling a fake yawn. "I'm done in. I'll get a drink and go to bed."

"Let me walk you." Kierion took her elbow and steered her through the crowd to the drinks table. He grinned as he passed her a glass of juice. "None of this is salted."

"Thanks, Kierion." She'd love to spend time with him, but she had to see Ezaara—alone.

He swiped a plate of pastries from the desert table and they went into the corridor.

"Linaia, is Zaarusha about?"

"On the infirmary ledge."

"Is someone hurt?"

"No. Ezaara and Marlies are talking, and Ezaara's packing saddlebags."

Shards, Ezaara was leaving now—without her.

"Linaia," melded Adelina, *"meet me at my cavern. Kierion is proving hard to shake."*

"The only time you haven't enjoyed his company," teased her cheeky dragon.

It was true, especially since Roberto had left with Tomaaz two moons ago, for Death Valley. Two moons. Shards, he'd be a wreck by now. Or dead.

Kierion chatted, but Adelina barely heard him. *"Linaia, if we're going to Death Valley with Ezaara, I'll need warm clothes, healing supplies, food and water. Anything else?"*

"Not that I can think of. I've hunted, so I'll be fine. I'm waiting in my den."

"Can you meld with Zaarusha and tell her to wait for us?"

"I've tried, but I can't connect with her."

"What about Erob?"

"You didn't hear what I said, did you, Adelina?" Kierion asked.

His question jolted Adelina out of her thoughts. They'd reached her door. Adelina opened it. "Sorry, it's been a long day."

Kierion walked inside and deposited the plate of pastries on her bedside table. "There," he said with a flourish. "Now you can rest the whole day tomorrow and not even get out of bed."

He was so thoughtful. She'd lied to him and was brushing him off, yet he was still taking care of her. Adelina's eyes pricked.

"You are tired." Kierion looked down at her with his blue eyes and stroked a strand of hair behind her ear. "Good night," he said softly and walked out the door.

He was her best friend and she'd lied to him, but she had no time to lose. Adelina threw on a cloak and ran to Linaia's den with the pastries and a full waterskin. She didn't have adequate supplies, but she couldn't afford to miss Ezaara.

§

Linaia flapped her wings and they soared above the basin, a bitter wind rushing at Adelina. Ezaara was on Zaarusha, ascending to land on Heaven's Peak, the highest mountain in the southern end of Dragon's Teeth. Adelina melded with Linaia. "Let's make sure we aren't seen."

A throaty chuckle emanated from her dragon. *"That shouldn't be too hard."* Linaia could control her scales, changing them to match the sky, a talent that could prove useful tonight. Within moments, Linaia's scales were the darkest inky blue.

Zaarusha headed westward.

Even though she'd been expecting it, Adelina's heart leapt. *"Death Valley. Ezaara is heading off to get Roberto. Linaia, we have to catch them."*

Zaarusha was soon below them, a dark splotch above the snow laden forest.

"We've nearly caught up. I'll meld with Zaarusha in a moment," Linaia said.

With a pop, Ezaara and Zaarusha disappeared.

"We've lost them. Do you want me to go lower and search?"

"Yes." Adelina's gut tightened. She wished she could deny the pop she'd heard. Linaia skimmed the treetops of the tangled wilderness between Dragon's Teeth and Great Spanglewood Forest. Snow lay thick on the branches and shadows lurked among the snarled plants between the trees. *"Linaia, it's no use. Ezaara must have used Anakisha's ring. She's gone to Death Valley."* The chill nipped at her skin. Disappointment crushed her chest.

"Then we'll follow. It's only a few days' flight."

"Alone? Against all of those tharuks? I don't know where to look." Adelina bit her lip. "Should we ask Kierion for help?"

"With his help, what could possibly go wrong?" answered Linaia.

Adelina sighed. "You're right. Things do get out of hand when Kierion's involved. We'll go alone."

Broken

The skin on Ezaara's neck crawled, as if she was being followed, but whenever she looked around, there were no dragons in sight. "Something's not right, Zaarusha, we'd better get to Death Valley." She rubbed Kisha's ring, murmuring, "Kisha." With a pop, the eerie wilderness outside the rim of Dragon's Teeth disappeared, and they were in a tunnel of gold clouds, with Anakisha floating toward them. Between the golden clouds was a dark rift, weeping tendrils of black, cloying fog.

"Anakisha," Ezaara called, "there's fog leaking into your realm gate. It feels evil."

"Frequent use leads to rifts in the gate, which Zens could discover and exploit."

That would be awful. Imagine him appearing with troops of tharuks wherever and whenever he wanted. Ma had mentioned the risks—and they'd ignored them. Now, the gates were damaged. *"Anakisha, Master Roberto is Zens' captive in Death Valley."*

Anakisha pointed at Ezaara's chest. *"You're wearing my dream catcher."*

Pa was right—it was Anakisha's. Ezaara nodded.

"Have you dreamed of Roberto? Seen his pain and suffering?"

Ezaara stared at Anakisha in shock, nodding mutely.

Anakisha pulled the fine silver chain that rested at Ezaara's throat, bringing the tear-shaped crystal into view. *"This crystal amplifies Roberto's thoughts while you both sleep, enabling you to meld over long distances with him, feel his pain, and relive your memories together. The crystal only functions between the Queen's Rider and her true mate."*

Tomaaz's message from Roberto had quoted Roberto's mother, saying *teardrops amplify thoughts*. And she'd thought Roberto had given her a simple keepsake between lovers. Had he understood the message? "He's been limplocked. He could be dying."

"The future of Dragons' Realm depends upon you both, but be cautious, Zens is formidable."

"Anakisha," Ezaara asked, *"what of your prophecy? They're saying I can't be Queen's Rider."*

"My prophecy stands, and you are Queen's Rider. Now, go, and save your loved one."

With a flip of Zaarusha's wings and a crack, they appeared in the dark, landing just below a Terramite peak.

Ezaara shouldered the small rucksack of supplies Ma had given her, then slid off Zaarusha. She pressed her cheek against her dragon's muzzle. "*Thank you for bringing me.*"

"*The same applies as last time: find Roberto, but if it gets too dangerous, get out.*"

Ezaara flung her arms around Zaarusha's neck, then made her way up the hill and scurried behind some icy boulders. Zaarusha ascended into the night sky, swallowed by darkness. Ezaara was alone. No one was here to help. Only Ma knew she'd come. She tugged her camouflage cloak around her and skirted around the rocks, and headed down toward her enemy's lair, avoiding the tharuks on watch.

§

Ezaara woke in the passage outside the cavern where Roberto was captive. She'd been here for a day, mind submerged, waiting in the dark until Roberto was alone. Now, the torches in Roberto's cavern were extinguished. She could hear him breathing and the occasional grunt of pain or clank of chains, so he was still alive. Her stomach growled, gnawing a hungry hole inside her. She took a sip of water. Tore off some flatbread and chewed it.

She must've been missed at Dragons' Hold by now. What excuses was Ma making for her absence?

Ezaara stiffened as 000 entered Roberto's cavern again, carrying a torch. She pressed her face to the rock so she could see.

Roberto was facing her, slumped against the stone wall on the far side of the cavern, mouth slack, eyes shut, his hands curled in. One arm was shackled to the wall and his leg to the floor. As the enormous tharuk kicked him, he flinched. His eyes opened, then drooped again, and his head slumped on his chest. There was no doubt—he was limplocked. If she didn't help him soon, he'd be dead.

§

"To your feet," 000 barked. The tharuk's tusks ran slick with dark saliva.

Roberto staggered, chains clanking, an arm on the wall for support. His breath was short and his mind foggy. Shards, he'd forgotten to take clear-mind berries. The stench of 000's fetid breath took Roberto's own breath away, making his chest tight. The gray fog over his eyes was worse. If only he could think straight.

"Ready?" 000 uncoiled a short whip and cracked it on the floor.

Roberto's ears rang with the sharp retort.

"Time to dance." 000 flicked the whip near Roberto's feet, making him hop, the chain biting his ankle.

The monster cracked the whip again, then swept it in an arc along the floor. Roberto jumped. The whip hit the wall with a snap and flicked along the floor toward him again. Roberto leaped, pulling his legs up, but the chain yanked him down to the stone, bruising his backside. That sharding limplock. If only he could control his limbs. Scrambling to his feet, he jumped again, but his legs were clumsy and slow. The whip snared his chain. 000 yanked hard. Roberto smashed into the floor. Sharp pain pierced his side. He breathed in. Winced. Yep, cracked ribs.

Through the blurry gray, 000 loomed over him, a sadistic grin splitting the tharuk's ugly face. "Not learned to dance yet? Need more lessons."

The whip sang, coiling around Roberto's arm. 000 yanked him to stand, then forward, until the chains on his arm and ankle were gnawing his flesh, stretched taut behind him. 000 tugged again. His shoulder socket burned.

And again.

Roberto's hip seared. Dragon gods, would the monster yank his leg from his body?

000 released the whip.

Roberto crashed to the floor, shackles clanking, smacking face-first onto the granite. The tang of blood filled his mouth, flowing from his throbbing nose. His tongue was swelling. One of his front teeth was loose. He gazed through a swollen eye at 000, focusing on his pain, blocking any other thoughts from his mind.

"That'll keep you busy." 000 chuckled. "See you tomorrow." It slammed the door, its chortles echoing down the tunnel.

Roberto crawled to the wall, his sharding chains graunching against his bones as he got tangled in them. After waiting to ensure 000 wasn't returning, Roberto fumbled with the sleeve of his jerkin, trying to get his clear-mind berries. His stiffened fingers couldn't grasp the string. After 000 had first poisoned him with limplock, Roberto had taken some of the remedy hidden inside his jerkin. It had slowed the effect of the paralyzing poison, but he hadn't been able to access it since. Now, his fingers were definitely stiffer and his feet clumsy.

He'd wait until Zens' attentiveness slackened. The commander slept for a few hours each night—the only time Roberto could risk thinking clearly, without having to block Zens. Face throbbing and body aching all over, Roberto closed his eyes.

§

Ezaara gripped a rocky outcrop so tight, her fingers ached. Blood flooded her mouth from biting her lip to stop herself from screaming. Her stomach roiled with nausea. 000 left the cavern, slamming the door. Roberto was crawling agonizingly slowly back to the wall he was chained to. Those few short paces took him forever. When he got there, he slumped, his face a bloody mess. His jerkin was slashed, encrusted with dried blood and limplock. Gritting his teeth, he fumbled at his sleeve with awkward fingers. His eyelids drooped and he fell into a fitful doze.

She'd been a fool. Why had she listened to the council? Tonio's old grudge had broken the man she loved. Ezaara longed to mind-meld with Roberto, but Zens might sense her, so she kept her mind submerged, waiting for Roberto to wake.

Hours later, Roberto stirred and looked around the cavern. Ezaara started, dropping her flatbread. He seemed more alert than earlier, flexing his fingers, rotating his ankles and hands. Shards, no. He no longer had complete control over them. His fingers were stiff, curled like claws. Limplock was slowly paralyzing him.

Her nightmare had been two nights ago. He'd be dead in a day. Maybe less—he'd had a lot of limplock. Ezaara's throat tightened. She had to do something. Ezaara chewed more freshweed, and waited impatiently for it to take effect. Tharuk troops regularly tromped along the main tunnel, so she couldn't use that. She'd have to risk going deeper into the mountain. Would this maze of tunnels lead her to Roberto? There was only one way to find out.

She cast her mind out cautiously, but found nothing. Not a trace of a tharuk mind bender, nor Zens. She shook a vial of dragon's breath, covered it with a rag to dim its light, and set off. The tunnel twisted, angling toward Roberto's cell. She crawled on. Every scrape of her hands and knees on rock was nothing compared to how Roberto was suffering. After a while, a breeze wafted across her cheek. Stopping, she shone the dragon's breath around the tunnel. In the stone roof was a narrow opening. Ezaara hoisted herself up and squeezed into the gap. Gods, she could barely fit. On her stomach and elbows, with the vial of light between her lips, she dragged herself along this new shaft. Her rucksack caught on rock. She tugged. Something gave—with a crack. Ezaara wriggled off her straps and shone her light. The blade of her hacksaw had been sticking out of her rucksack and snapped off. Of all the cursed luck. She stuffed the broken blade back in and kept going.

Similar-sized tunnels branched off this one, but Ezaara stayed her course, elbows scraped raw. The passage plunged down to an opening. Ezaara pocketed her light, heart thudding, and peeked out.

A flickering torch illuminated a heavy wooden door—like Roberto's—barred with a wooden beam. No one was in sight. Had she found his holding cavern? Or was Zens behind that door? Her heart raced. Gods, not Zens.

Ezaara dropped to the ground with a soft thud, rolling to her feet. She lifted the bar from the door, staggering under the load, and stowed it in the shadows.

Further down the tunnel, a tharuk snarled.

Her heart whacking against her ribs, she opened the door and slipped inside, closing it behind her.

"You came back." Roberto, slumped against the wall, smiled. His teeth were stained with blood. He lifted a cramped finger to his lips. *"Please don't speak. We don't want to wake 000. Keep your thoughts calm. Zens is asleep, but not for long."*

Ezaara sped across the floor and knelt beside him. She kissed his blood-stained lips, pulling back when he winced. *"I'm sorry, I should have come earlier. He's hurt you so badly …"*

"Do you have a hacksaw? Something to cut my chains?"

"Yes, but I broke it …" She sawed his chains, barely scratching them with the broken, blunted blade. She yanked them, but they were firmly anchored into the stone. *"I can't free you."* Ezaara opened her healer's pouch. *"But I can heal you. What's worst?"*

"Leave the blood. Do it surreptitiously so he doesn't notice."

"I'll start with limplock remedy."

"And clear-mind, so I can see your face."

Roberto was a mess. Ezaara fought to keep her despair under control. If Zens woke, he'd sense her. Her hands trembled as she shook the yellow granules onto Roberto's tongue.

He swallowed them and slumped back against the wall. *"So tired."*

"You need food. Zens has been starving you." She popped a small piece of flatbread and two clear-mind berries into Roberto's mouth.

He chewed, his bent fingers scrabbling at her wrist. "You know I love you?"

"And I love you too." She fed him some more and he wolfed it down. The gray film over his eyes was fading, so Ezaara gave him powdered dragon's scale. "What's next?"

"I can see again. You're beautiful." He smiled, then winced. "My ribs ache and the wounds on my back may be festering." Roberto pointed at his front tooth. "This one's loose."

Ezaara unstopped a vial of piaua, put a drop on her finger, and rubbed it into his gum. She lifted his jerkin and applied more to the bruising on his ribs. Two of the wounds on his back were inflamed, oozing pus. There was no time for clean herb, so she dribbled piaua on them, hoping his body could fight the infection once the wounds had closed.

"My nose aches."

The bridge of his nose was swollen. She pressed it and he winced. "I think it's broken. Here, let me see what I can do." She rubbed piaua on it and the bone straightened. "I'm leaving the blood. With that swollen eye, I doubt Zens and 000 will notice anything's been healed."

"Good idea. Um ... I know another healing remedy ..." He grinned.

"I thought you'd never ask."

"We'll have to be careful so Zens doesn't sense us."

"Just a small kiss, then?"

The spark in Roberto's ebony eyes was his only answer. Their lips brushed. With the tang of Roberto's blood on her lips, Ezaara kissed him. His dark blue *sathir* mixed with hers, swirling around them. Like a bird basking in the sun, love unfurled inside her, in a warm glow.

Roberto stopped, holding her face in his hands. He gasped. "We can't. Zens will sense us."

"I'm watching through that wall. I see every time they beat you." Ezaara lips trembled. "We have to get you out of here."

"Are you alone?"

She nodded.

"I thought as much. Tonio said they wouldn't come after me if I got caught." Roberto got to his feet and stretched, his shackles clinking. "That's much better. Thank you."

"*You look good.*" Well, that was an exaggeration. Still battered, he was a mess. "*Too good.*"

"*And now?*" He slumped, drooping his head, his mouth lolling open and fingers curling inward.

"*Like before,*" Ezaara said, smiling, trying to encourage him.

Footfalls thudded out in the corridor.

"*Quick, up there,*" Roberto pointed to a narrow hole above his head, shrouded in shadow. "*Use this ventilation shaft.*"

"But I unbarred the door. They'll see." A bolt of panic shot through her. She stuffed the hacksaw blade into her rucksack.

"What's this? Bar gone?" a tharuk grunted outside the door. Wood clattered to the floor. "Hidden? Why?"

Another tharuk yowled. Scuffling echoed in the tunnel.

"*Hurry, on my shoulders. Now.*"

She scrambled onto Roberto's injured back and hoisted herself inside the shaft. Her cloak caught on the edge. She yanked, ripping the corner, leaving a tiny scrap hanging on the lip of the shaft. The door thudded open and tharuks bowled inside. Hopefully no one would notice it. She scrambled along the tunnel, Roberto's fresh screams slicing through the air.

Spangles

Tomaaz awoke to someone shaking him in the dark. He fumbled for his healer's pouch next to the bed and shook a vial of dragon's breath, illuminating a face. "Kierion? How did you get in here?"

Grinning, Kierion shrugged. "Ready to go?" He strode to Taliesin's bed and woke him.

"Should we really bring Taliesin? He's just a boy." He'd been so traumatized in Death Valley, how would he react to tharuks? "What about food? I—"

"Maaz, I want to come," Taliesin said, hopping out of bed.

"It'll do him good. Come on, Tomaaz, you're being an old woman. Let's go before someone sees us."

Tomaaz yanked on his boots, helped Taliesin dress and scribbled a note on parchment for his parents. They extinguished the dragon's breath and sneaked out to the den.

Riona was waiting next to Maazini with full saddlebags. *"Morning, Tomaaz,"* Maazini melded. *"I'm looking forward to killing some tharuks today."*

"Maazini and Kierion, I'm worried about Taliesin." He spoke aloud so they could both hear him.

"Here, try this." Kierion threw something to Tomaaz. It clinked as he caught it. "That's heavy." He shook it out. It was a tiny chain mail vest, the right size for Taliesin. "Maazini, could you give me some light?" Tomaaz asked, helping the lad into it.

Taliesin stroked the chain mail, eyes bright in a flame from Maazini's jaws.

They climbed upon their dragons, Taliesin in front of Tomaaz. Hopefully, he wouldn't regret bringing him.

"Here, breakfast to eat on the way." Kierion threw them two small packages, then Riona bunched her legs and took off.

Maazini and Riona flew up the mountain face to the top of Dragon's Teeth, then plunged down the southern drop under Heaven's Peak. Tomaaz's stomach dropped. Wind flicked Taliesin's hair into Tomaaz's face. The early rays of dawn tinged the snow gold as Maazini and Riona followed the ring of Dragon's Teeth west. Soon, they were above the northern tip of Great Spanglewood Forest, which spread like a haphazardly-thrown rug all the way to the foot of the Terramites. Tomaaz pulled Taliesin firmly against him, relieved when the boy's tense body relaxed.

Riona and Maazini landed in a snowy clearing among towering strongwood trees. They walked toward three cabins nestled at the edge of the trees. Taliesin's eyes were enormous as he gazed around at the forest—very different to the barren hills of Death Valley.

"Welcome to Mage Gate," Kierion said.

"Hope you've got some food here," said Tomaaz. "It's been ages since that paltry breakfast."

"There's nothing quite like wizard porridge," Kierion chuckled.

"The trees are so green, even in winter," Taliesin piped up, voice still croaky from years of disuse.

"It's the spangles. They keep the trees evergreen, even when they're not," said Kierion.

"Spangles?" Taliesin frowned. "When I was a littling, Ma told me a bedtime story about spangles."

This was new. Taliesin seldom spoke of his childhood.

"She said that Anakisha's littlings sat at her feet while the spangles perched on her knees, telling her littling stories. Ma said she always slept better after a spangle's tale."

Taliesin's mother was Anakisha's child? That meant Taliesin was her grandson. No wonder he had the gift of prophecy. Kierion shot Tomaaz a glance. He'd noticed too. "So, spangles are like magical story tellers?" asked Tomaaz.

Kierion laughed. "Magical, yes. Story tellers, no. But I've never seen one."

A door opened and a tall gangly man, with the bushiest eyebrows Tomaaz had ever seen, strode across the snow to greet them, his mage cloak creating eddies of snow. A Naobian wizard, about Tomaaz's age, kept pace with him, while Kierion's friend, Fenni, jogged after him.

"I'm Master Giddi," said the mage. "Are you Marlies' boy?"

The wizard's grip was firm with more than a trickle of magic zapping across Tomaaz's hand. "Yes, I am."

"Why's the lad so round-eyed?" Fenni asked Kierion and Tomaaz.

Tomaaz shrugged. "He's been in Death Valley for so long, he hasn't seen a forest in ages."

A deep belly laugh broke out from Master Giddi. "He's a seer, that one." He gestured at Taliesin.

"Yes, we've discovered his gift," answered Tomaaz. How did the master mage know?

Giddi knelt before Taliesin and looked him in the eye, wriggling his eyebrows like large hairy caterpillars. "They're spangles, lad. Aren't they fascinating?"

"Where?" Fenni glanced around. Tomaaz and Kierion craned their necks, searching too.

Jael laughed now. "You mean, none of you have ever seen them?"

"What's going on?" asked Tomaaz.

Master Giddi smiled. "All around you. Those shimmering beings in the trees."

Fenni's face lit up. "Kierion, I saw them that time you got knocked out by tharuks."

Tomaaz had no idea what they were looking at—he couldn't see a thing.

"What?" thundered Giddi, glaring at Fenni. "You told me Kierion was hurt, but not that he was knocked out!"

§

It was pitch black when Tomaaz and Taliesin returned home. They'd ended up staying overnight at Mage Gate and fighting tharuks the next day, after sending a message home to Ma and Pa via a passing blue guard. Now they were dog-tired, although Taliesin was the bubbliest Tomaaz had ever seen—almost like he'd never been enslaved. Kierion had been right, the trip had done him good, despite them battling tharuks. Tomaaz dropped Taliesin on the infirmary ledge and Ma took him inside.

"Let's go and find Ezaara. The council doesn't approve of us fighting with mages, but maybe as Queen's Rider she can influence them." They flew across the basin. Tomaaz patted Maazini's neck as they touched down on the ledge outside Zaarusha's empty den. *Great job today, Maazini. You've recovered well. Twenty tharuks was a good hunt.* His dragon furled his wings and he slid from the saddle, thunking to the ground. *And my hip's good again too.*

Twenty-two tharuks actually, while you only killed ten.

Hey, great swathes of fire are much more efficient than arrows, so you have an unfair advantage.

"And the mages?"

"They have an unfair advantage too," said Tomaaz, digging strips of dried beef out of Maazini's saddlebags and feeding them to him. Tomaaz ate one, too. "Wizard fire is pretty potent, so, all in all, I think every kill of mine should equate to three or four of yours and theirs."

"Four to one?" Maazini blinked a large golden eye. "Two to one is the best you'll get."

"All right, so my ten to your twenty-two, still means I'm only one down."

"I'm not a numbers dragon," Maazini snorted. "I'll take your word for it."

Tomaaz laughed. "I'll see if Ezaara agrees with us about fighting with mages. If she's keen, we'll go straight to Lars."

"I've tried to meld with Zaarusha, but I can't sense her."

"That's odd, it's so late." Not that it being dark would ever stop Ezaara going out. He'd seen her out with Zaarusha when she couldn't sleep, while he'd been roaming the mountainside feeling bad about leaving Roberto in Death Valley. "I'll just be a moment."

Ezaara's cavern was empty. A few of her clothes were tossed across the bed. Her healer's pouch was gone. So were her boots, weapons and cloak.

Maazini melded with him. "I've checked with the blue guards and other dragons. No one's seen Ezaara or Zaarusha since the feast. They'd assumed they were resting"

"That was two days ago. Where could she be?" As Tomaaz ran to the ledge, he knew the answer—sick of the council's inaction, Ezaara had taken matters into her own hands and gone to Death Valley. By the dragon gods, he'd told her he'd rescue Roberto if the council didn't, but he'd forgotten all about it.

§

Kierion banged on Lars' door. He shuffled from foot to foot until Lars opened it, and then burst into the living area. "Adelina's disappeared." He clenched and unclenched his fists, wanting to punch something. Why had he delayed coming back to Dragons' Hold a day, to hunt a few more tharuks? Sure, he'd been saving lives, but it was meaningless if he lost Adelina.

Lars' gaze was sharp. "When did you last see her?"

"At the race celebration, but something wasn't right. I've, um, been away since. She's not here. No one's seen her since the feast." Lars raised his eyebrows and opened his mouth, but Kierion interrupted, "And I mean no one! You know me, Lars, no stone unturned."

"Yes." Lars' voice was wry. "You are thorough."

Kierion nodded, waiting.

"Did she say anything about Roberto?" Lars asked.

"Only that it was hard with him gone, him being her only family and all."

Lars scratched his beard. "She could have gone after her brother."

"Why haven't you gone after him?"

"There are bigger things at stake." Lars was hedging. "We believe Roberto could still be gathering information vital to the realm, despite the circumstances."

"We can't let Adelina go to Death Valley on her own."

"I'll have to talk with Tonio and Aidan, master of battle, before we decide what action to take."

From Lars' tone, it wasn't likely he'd take action. Kierion thrust his clenched fists behind his back.

"Now, Kierion," Lars said. "You mentioned you've been away since the feast. You didn't happen to visit two particular young wizards at Mage Gate against my orders, did you?"

"I—" Kierion was saved by a sharp rap at the door.

When Lars opened it, Tomaaz strode in. "Master Lars, Ezaara and Zaarusha are gone."

Lars' brow furrowed. "Kierion, Tomaaz, please, take a seat."

Tomaaz's body was taut as he perched on the front of his chair. "Ezaara was at the opening of the feast, but then she left and no one's seen her since."

"And Zaarusha?"

"Gone too."

"What? No queen and no Queen's Rider!" Lars paced back and forth. "That'll give the gossips a feast."

Last time Ezaara had disappeared, she'd gone to the Wastelands to save Master Roberto. There were already rumors that they cared about each other, the way Kierion cared for Adelina. When she'd returned, the queen had been poisoned. No doubt, Zaarusha would never let her go into danger alone again. No, they were a truer partnership than ever. His strong bond with Riona was a pale shade of what the queen and Queen's Rider had. If Ezaara loved Roberto, Zaarusha would go too. Kierion piped up, "Tomaaz, Adelina's gone too, with Linaia."

Tomaaz's eyes widened. "So, they could've gone to rescue Roberto together?"

Kierion had offered Ezaara food, but she'd brushed him off. Then he'd danced with Adelina and didn't remember seeing Ezaara again. "Maybe ..."

"Dragon's claws, we'd best head after them. It's a four-or-five-day flight."

"Not so quick," Lars barked. "This is a matter for the council, not for two young hot-headed new riders. There are circumstances you're both unaware of. Wait here. I'll summon the war council." Lars left for Singlar's den, slamming the door behind him.

"We'll go now, with Fenni and Jael," said Kierion to Tomaaz, his jaw clenched. "What Lars doesn't know won't harm him." At Tomaaz's look of surprise, he added, "Lars hasn't expressly forbidden us to go, so we should go before he does. I'm not leaving Adelina or Roberto there a moment longer."

Tomaaz shrugged. "What are we waiting for?"

§

Lovina frowned. "Where were you? I looked for you today."

Tomaaz shrugged, shoving a few things in his bags—healing supplies and food mainly, and another warm set of clothes, and some clothes for Roberto. "On an assignment with Kierion."

"In Great Spanglewood Forest fighting tharuks with wizards. Taliesin told me all about it. He was happy to see spangles, and liked the way wizards killed tharuks." Lovina pursed her lips. "Now, you're leaving again, aren't you? But this time it's not to Spanglewood."

"Ah, no, it's not." Gods, the last thing he wanted was to keep secrets from Lovina, but he didn't want her getting into trouble for knowing.

"If you don't go, Roberto will die." Her eyes filled with tears. "Get them out, Tomaaz. Bring them all home. I never want anyone to go through what I did in Death Valley. If these mages are as good as Taliesin says, they may be our only chance."

He hugged her, burying his lips in her hair, kissing its soft silkiness, then her fine cheeks and finally, her lips—the sweetest thing he'd ever tasted. Her arms tightened around his back, pulling him closer. Gods, how could he leave her? His breath caught. What if he never saw her again?

"I, I—" She broke down, sobbing.

He smoothed the hair back from her face. "Lovina, what is it?"

"I'm just not brave enough." Tears trailed down her cheeks. He wiped them away. "Not brave enough to come with you. I can't. I just can't go back."

"Shards, no, Lovina." Horror engulfed him. "I'd never send you back there. No, not after what you've been through." He'd witnessed Old Bill, her slave master, deliberately break her arm. Her back was still a mess of scars, like a tangle of vines writhing across her flesh. He pulled her close again, resting his chin on her hair. She buried her face in his chest, her breath shuddering out of her. "You stay right here, safe. Please take care of Taliesin."

Lovina looked up at him with her soft cornflower blues. "You always understand. I'm so lucky I met you, Tomaaz."

His heart swelled until he thought he'd burst.

"There's something else, Tomaaz. Something terrible is going to happen to the mages in Spanglewood Forest." Lovina shook her head. "I can't shake the feeling."

Lovina's bad feelings often turned out to be prophetic. A shiver crept down Tomaaz's spine.

§

The craving in Alban's belly was driving him mad. His mouth flooded with the familiar taste of the fine herb tea that Sofia had made whenever he'd visited her in the girl's dorm—on the quiet, of course. Males weren't allowed there at night. He stumbled into the corner of the dungeon, his legs trembling. Yesterday he'd hankered after that tea, but today he had the shivers and shakes and would claw someone's eyes out for another cup. He leaned over a pail, vomiting in the corner, then huddled under the scratchy blanket on his pallet, trying to get warm.

His mouth watered, driving him mad. He moaned. Just another cup. Gods, he'd kill for one. He shook his head. This was crazy. He'd never been a great tea drinker. Why was he so raving mad over a stupid beverage?

A flickering light shone through the barred door. "Hey, you all right?" It was a guard, holding up a torch.

Alban rolled over and opened his mouth to answer, but dry retched instead.

"Fetch the healer," hollered the guard. "Prisoner's got a belly gripe."

It felt like forever until the quick steps of the healer entered the room.

"Watch him. He's dangerous," the guard warned.

"I'm armed," the healer said. "You can leave us." She was tall, with dark hair—Marlies, the master healer. She took the torch from the guard's hand, setting it in a sconce. "And don't lock the door." Marlies' voice had authority. "I can't get him to the infirmary through a locked door. Go on, be off with you."

She strode to the pail and examined the contents. "Yes, Alban, it's me. I didn't appreciate you attacking my daughter, but as a healer, I must treat you if you're ill. Now, tell me, how long have you been taking swayweed tea?"

Swayweed? That sharding Sofia had been drugging him. No wonder he'd been so angry lately. How long? "Sofia's been giving me tea since the Queen's Rider knifed her."

The Cage

Lars descended the uneven stone steps down the winding corridor. Torches burned along the walls at intervals, but not regularly enough to light the entire tunnel, so he'd brought his own. He gripped the torch shaft hard, harder than necessary for a council leader about to question a girl.

Sofia had come from a good family, a long line of dragon folk. It was understandable that she wanted Anakisha's prophecy to be fulfilled. They all did. But what was driving her to this hatred? He greeted the two guards and dragons on duty at the junction as he swept past. When he reached the guardian of the cage, he stopped, holding his hand out.

"Master Lars, I should accompany you," said the guardian.

Lars huffed. "The key will do. If I can't question a girl on my own, I'm not fit to be council leader." He waved his hand impatiently as the guard unfastened the key from his belt and reluctantly handed it over.

"I'll come and wait by the—"

"Stay here. I'll be back soon enough."

"Yes, sir." Pressing his mouth into a grim line, the guard nodded.

Lars didn't want an audience. Not for this conversation. He proceeded down the passage and came to a metal grill covering the end of the tunnel. Setting his torch into a sconce, he jangled the key in the lock and opened the door.

Sofia was hunched in a corner with her arms around her knees. Her head shot up as Lars entered. "Ooh, aren't I lucky to have a visit from the leader of the council?"

Lars' jaw tightened at the venom in her voice. "Sofia," he barked sharply, "cut the antagonism."

The caustic sting in her voice increased along with her volume. "Antagonism? What about my cousin's chance to be Queen's Rider?"

So that was it. Lars was glad he hadn't brought the guard—he didn't want anyone hearing this. "Sofia, your cousin may be dead. Tharuks took him so long ago. There's no certainty …"

"There's no certainty that the Queen's Rider has imprinted correctly."

"Master Roberto tested her and said she was the true rider. You were there when he declared it in front of all the folk at Dragons' Hold."

"Anyone could have pressured him to say that." Even you, her scathing gaze said. "Roberto has now conveniently disappeared. I know he's at Death Valley, sent there so he could be silenced. He's good at ousting traitors. Maybe he was looking to oust the head of the council next."

"You vicious snipe," thundered Lars. "What has gotten into you?"

Sofia sneered, "You're not perfect, Lars. I know your biggest secret."

Marlies. It had to be. How could she possibly know? He'd never told anyone how he'd felt about Marlies. Lars had been deeply in love with her, but too shy to say so. Then she'd met Hans. Actually, he'd admitted his feelings to one person, his cousin—Sofia's mother. Inside, Lars blanched, but he kept his face impassive. "What are you talking about?"

"How do you think Lydia would feel if she knew?"

Lydia didn't know that he'd still had strong feelings for Marlies, as he'd fallen for her. But Sofia's mother did. Thank gods, those feelings had vanished when Marlies had fled Dragons' Hold. "We're here to discuss you attacking the Queen's Rider."

"And your reasons for pretending she's the rightful rider, even in the face of Anakisha's prophecy. A prophecy which states one of the former Queen's Rider's male heirs will rule at Dragons' Hold.

"One of our progeny will reign in our stead
Filling our enemies' foul hearts with dread
Purging all evil will be his desire
Vengeance he'll wage with arrows of fire."

Sofia's harsh voice echoed off the cage's stone walls.

"*Him* doesn't necessarily mean a male, just as *master* applies to both females and males," countered Lars.

"Oh? So, we shouldn't take prophecies literally anymore?" Sofia arched an eyebrow, her forehead beaded with sweat. "Have you fallen for the daughter as you once fell for the mother? Really, Lars, I expected more."

"You gutter snake," Lars snapped. "You're worthy of the title they bestow on you, Snake-tongue. Enough. I'm finished here."

"But I'm not finished with you. If you were a half-decent leader, you'd summon all of Anakisha's progeny to be tested." She slumped back against the wall, her face a sickly shade of gray.

Grabbing his torch, Lars strode out the door, her barbs sticking in his gut as he swept past the guard who must've heard him bellowing at his cousin's daughter.

§

Lars slammed the door to his cavern and stamped inside.

Lydia gave him a sharp look. "What's the matter?"

"Sofia," muttered Lars. "I don't know what's gotten into her. She's as bad as Bruno and Fleur were. Attacking the Queen's Rider, dividing the hold. Argh." He yanked a boot off, hurling it against the granite wall.

"And Master Roberto's not here to test her," Lydia said. "Aren't you worried about him?"

"Of course, I'm worried sick about him." Lars sat on the couch, removing his other boot. Lydia sat next to him and rubbed his neck and shoulders. "Oh, that feels good."

"Why haven't you sent a team to rescue Roberto?" Lydia asked.

"It's Tonio."

"He has evidence against him?" Lydia raised her eyebrows, shaking her head as Lars nodded. "That poor lad, what does he have to go through next? Hasn't he suffered enough at Zens' hands? Can't you do something? Say something to convince Tonio?"

Lars' mouth took a grim set. "Tonio has evidence, Lydia. Evidence that would land Roberto in dire straits if he returned." He sighed. "Sofia accused me of not being fair to Anakisha's descendants. It's been eating at me. I guess I have to call a meeting."

Lydia kissed him and stood up. "The sooner, the better."

Not if he could help it.

Torture

Roberto let his jaw hang slack and kept his fingers curled against his palms. He focused on the gray walls flecked with silica, watching the way the torchlight flickered on the stone.

A wave of violence ripped through his thoughts, scattering them like driftwood on a tide. *"Still blocking me, are you?"* Zens' silky-smooth voice slipped into his head. *"Amato was right. You're useless."*

The granite walls wavered. Roberto forced them to the forefront of his mind again.

Zens flicked a finger.

Shackles rattling, Roberto's body flew through the air. His head smacked stone and he slid down the wall. Stumbling to his feet, he gritted his teeth against the pain.

Zens' yellow orbs loomed before Roberto. Roberto's granite wall faded, replaced with childhood memories: his father murdering his beloved dog, Razo, spraying Roberto with blood as he wept; Pa arguing with Ma, splintering wooden walls in his fury; Pa beating Adelina; and Roberto jumping in, to be beaten in her stead. Agony ripped through him, as if Amato was inflicting every punch anew: his father punched his head and pain sparked across his skull; he kicked Roberto's gut and his belly stabbed. Then Pa's dragon, Matotoi, dropped his mother onto the rocks. She lay broken. Grief tightened Roberto's throat, making it hard to breathe.

Zens' voice slithered between the violent images. "Tell me everything about the new Queen's Rider, and your memories will stop. You've tested her. You know her weaknesses, her strengths. Just tell me."

Ma was dying. Chest twisting with grief, Roberto rushed across the rocks to help her.

No, it was Zens, making him relive his worst moments. The wall. Granite. Gray. Flecks. Straining, Roberto forced the image back into his head. Gray, gray stone. Hard, impenetrable.

His childhood faded to dust. There, he'd blocked Zens out. Skull aching, Roberto breathed heavily, sweat running down his forehead. Gray stone. Gray stone.

"Triple," Zens called.

000 entered, stinking of the fetid carcasses it fed on.

"You thought you could leave me, did you? After everything I taught you? You'd only be half the man you are if it wasn't for me." Zens spat on Roberto's face.

The masters had accepted Roberto to the council because of the talents he'd learned from Zens. The commander was right.

No, he was wrong, oh, so wrong.

"So close, but you slipped away." Zens velvet voice turned to a snarl as he barked at 000. "If he wants to talk, or agrees to be my spy at Dragons' Hold, we'll give him the remedy to limplock. If not, he'll die soon, so you may as well beat him to a pulp."

§

After 000's first slash across Roberto's back and a vicious boot in his gut, Ezaara submerged, terrified. She couldn't give her presence away. She was his only hope.

Roberto's screams ricocheted off the stone walls. Curling into a ball, she held her hands over her ears and kept her mind submerged as tears tracked her cheeks.

The thud of boots against his body went on forever.

The thump of him hitting the floor.

Her mind fried with fear, but she had to keep her emotions hidden. Undetectable.

Abruptly, Roberto's screams cut off.

000's heavy boots kept thwacking Roberto's soft flesh, making Ezaara's skin crawl. Then 000 slammed the door, and the bar slid into place.

Ezaara sneaked to the crack. Roberto was sprawled on stone, covered in blood, all pretense of numlock and limplock gone. Silent, except for his rasping breaths.

She didn't dare move. Gradually, Ezaara eased her mind open, tentatively searching for a sign of Zens. Nothing. He'd abandoned watching Roberto's mental state while he was unconscious. It was too dangerous to approach Roberto while Zens was awake, but if Ezaara didn't help him, he'd soon be dead.

A Crow's News

Someone rapped on the door. "Come in," Lars called, putting down his spoon.

The door opened to admit Seppi, leader of the blue guards, carrying a dead crow. "Lars, we've found something you may want to see."

Lars frowned. After a late, taxing night, Seppi had interrupted his breakfast to show him a dead bird? "Go ahead." Seppi brought the crow closer. Lars shoved his breakfast to one side and gestured that Seppi should sit. "What is it?"

"Sorry to disturb your breakfast, Lars, but this is one of the birds Zens has been communicating with."

Lars raised his eyebrows. What was he on about?

"Look at this." Seppi lay the bird on the table and flipped it on its back, extending the wing. Underneath, flush against its body, was a bald spot where its plumage had been plucked and an incision made in its flesh. Seppi pulled the sides of the incision apart to show a fat yellow crystal slicked with blood.

Lars shrugged. "And …?"

Seppi's eyes drilled into Lars. "These crystals are how Zens and his tharuks mind-meld with animals. How he controls them."

That's right; during Bruno's trial, a guard had found a bag of similar crystals from Zens. Lars scratched his beard. "Roberto said Bruno's crystals were dangerous and should be destroyed."

"I'd believe that," said Seppi. "But were they? Or are some of Bruno's crystals being used at Dragons' Hold?"

§

The torches in the infirmary were burning low. Marlies held a bowl out. Sofia groaned, doubling over with her arms clutching her gut. A sheen of sweat beaded her face. A gush of gray vomit hit the bowl, splattering up the sides. Marlies frowned. Gray vomit? The acrid stench of stomach acid hit her nostrils, making her own stomach turn. Rumble weed—it must be. It colored the victim's vomit gray.

"What did you eat?" asked Marlies.

Sofia moaned, shaking her head.

"Or drink?"

"Water," Sofia replied weakly.

"Who gave it to you?"

"Why? Have I been poisoned?" Sofia groaned.

Yes, but she wasn't going to tell Sofia that. "Of course not. I'm checking if our water sources at the hold are tainted." Marlies passed Leah the bowl of vomit. "Could you dispose of that, please?" She gave Sofia a glass. "Here, drink this to settle your stomach."

She felt guilty giving Sofia double-strength woozy weed tea, but this was the snipe who'd attacked Ezaara. Lars had been in earlier, mentioning crystals that could control animals. Could a crystal have driven Sofia's behavior?

Marlies yawned and settled her tired bones into a chair. Waiting until Sofia was dozing soundly, she lifted the young woman's clothing up over her stomach to inspect her skin. Nothing. No irregularities. She ran her hands over Sofia's arms. All fine. Checked her legs through her breeches. Her fingers traced an irregular bump on Sofia's right thigh.

Marlies fetched a torch and mounted it on the sconce above Sofia's pallet. She slit the side of Sofia's breeches. A puckered scar marred Sofia's thigh, badly stitched, with a distinct bump under the scar tissue. She ran her fingers gently over the bump several times, nodding grimly. "Leah," she murmured, "fetch me the knife I use for lancing blisters."

Wide-eyed, Leah fetched the blade. "Does she have a crow crystal?"

"Let's see." Marlies made an incision along the scar tissue. Pressing firmly with the flat of her blade, Marlies pushed the lump under Sofia's skin toward the incision. Blood oozed out of the cut, then something yellow glinted. She squeezed the flesh. A crystal the size of Marlies' thumb slid out of Sofia's thigh in a trickle of blood. Using a cloth, Marlies deposited the crystal into a jar and corked it. How sharding awful. Zens was controlling innocent people around them. Her stomach roiled. Who else was affected?

She melded with Liesar. *Give this to Singlar. Lars ought to see this.*

Leah took the jar out to Liesar while Marlies stitched Sofia's wound shut.

Soon, Lars bustled into the infirmary, holding up the jar. "Master Roberto mentioned that these were dangerous. I thought we'd destroyed them all."

"Zens has been controlling Sofia," Marlies replied. "He's infiltrated Dragons' Hold by having Fleur plant them inside people as she healed them."

"That makes sense. Ezaara accidentally knifed Sofia, but her attitude only went downhill after Fleur healed her." Lars drummed his fingers against the jar.

"We'll have to check everyone. We can't let this get out. We can't have people turning against each other, seeking implanted crystals."

"Bill, a tharuk spy, has a similar bump on his arm. Zens must be controlling him too." Marlies bit her lip. "Let's start with the people most recently healed by Fleur." So much work ahead of her, when her bones already ached with exhaustion.

"The dragon gods forbid," said Lars, his hand hovering over his sword. "The hold could be crawling with spies—people we love and trust."

§

Lars outlined the danger of the crystal implants, reported Ezaara and Adelina's disappearances, then smacked his gavel to end the meeting. Hans caught Lars' eye. He glanced at the door, then left the council chambers. Lars followed, striding to meet him on the ledge outside.

"Thank you, Lars. I wanted to talk alone."

"What is it? Has Marlies found more riders with implanted crystals?"

Hans shook his head. "Not yet, and she's worked herself to the bone, checking twenty people already." And she'd been tired before she'd started. "No, it's something else, but just as grave. Tomaaz and Kierion left yesterday for Death Valley."

"Dragon's bleeding talons," Lars thundered. "Now they're gone too." He shot Hans an astute look. "Who else?"

"Lovina said they've taken two wizards with them."

"Great." He snorted. "Two young wizards to mess up their chances."

The visions that had been plaguing Hans for many nights roiled in his mind. Mages on dragonback amid whistling arrows. And tharuks sizzling with green mage flame. Hans put his hand on Lars' arm. "Lars, as master of prophecy, I'm telling you we must work with mages, not shun them. This team is our best chance of rescuing Roberto, Adelina, and Ezaara."

His only daughter, deep in Zens' territory. Thank the Egg, Tomaaz had gone, but he'd be in danger too. He'd barely made it home last time.

Would the twins return? Hans' visions had been silent on that front.

RIDERS OF FIRE

Devil's Choice

For an agonizing two days, Zens sent black-eyed tharuk mind-benders into Roberto's chamber, trying to break him. Unable to stand watching Roberto gripping his head and writhing on the floor, Ezaara searched the passages for an escape route.

The warren of tunnels led to cave-ins or back to the main tunnel, constantly swarming with tharuks. Useless—there was no way out.

When she returned to her vigil at the chink in the wall, Roberto was moaning, conscious again. He raised his head from the floor, stared straight at the fissure and mouthed, "Help."

It was all Ezaara needed. She'd already taken freshweed and owl's wort. She crawled along the tunnel, making her way toward the ventilation shaft to Roberto. Halfway there, snuffling slunk along the tunnel behind her. Tharuks. She scrambled to the ventilation shaft. Hoisted herself inside the narrow opening.

She stopped around the first bend, wrapping her camouflage cloak around her. Hopefully, the shaft entrance was too small for the beast. Quietening her breath, she strained, listening.

Tharuk stench wafted along the shaft. Her taste buds writhed.

Did it know she was here? With freshweed and her camouflage cloak, she should be undetectable. Was this a random coincidence? The beast's boots scraped on the tunnel walls. Its harsh breathing rasped along the shaft. Ezaara's blood ran cold. She drew her knife from her boot.

The tharuk grunted and wheezed. Thrashing and thumps echoed along the shaft. The beast wasn't getting any closer. Knife at the ready, Ezaara cocked her head. She peeked around the bend. Even with owl wort, it was too dark. Knife between her teeth, she shook her vial of dragon's breath, holding it up. The bright light revealed a tharuk wedged tight in the shaft's mouth. It snarled, its arms shooting up to cover its eyes—her light was blinding it.

"Smelled your bread, I did," it grunted.

Oh, shards, she'd dropped a scrap of bread in the tunnel.

As it lowered its arms, Ezaara rushed forward, plunging her knife into its eye, ramming hard. The knife sunk through the soft gelatinous tissue into the beast's skull. The monster's arms flailed, claws swiping her forearm.

Its head and arms slumped to the stone. Dark blood gushed over the rock.

Gritting her teeth against her stinging arm, Ezaara scrambled back and leaned against the wall. Taking a rag from her pouch, she bound her arm. Although the gash was searing, she didn't dare use piaua. She had to save it for Roberto. The shaft entrance was now blocked from pursuers—but so was her escape. Ezaara doused her light and crawled on through the dark. The ventilation shaft twisted then angled downward, growing lighter. Just around the bend and she'd be there.

Cautiously, she reached out for Roberto. *"Are you still alone?"*

The crash of his door against stone answered that question.

Ezaara tugged her cloak around her and crouched, motionless.

"There it is, again." 000's foul voice drifted up the shaft. "That same scent as from the small tunnel. What did 1352 find?"

"Bread? 1352 still searching," a grunt answered.

"That runt has a keen nose," said 000. Boots tromped toward the shaft. "What's this?"

"A scrap of cloth, sir."

Oh gods, the fragment of her cloak.

"I know that, 1554." There was a thump.

The tharuk grunt whimpered. "I can fit in shaft. I is small."

"Good idea." Feet neared. Scrapes sounded on the wall.

Ezaara had heard enough—she fled through the shaft in the dark, bashing her knees and scraping her hands. Soon, her hand hit a furry mass—the dead tharuks' arm. She shoved it aside and braced her feet against the shaft wall. Leaning her back into the corpse's head, Ezaara shoved. It didn't budge. She pushed again, but the corpse was stuck.

Ominous shuffling reached Ezaara's ears. 1554 was heading toward her. Frantically, Ezaara thrust her shoulder at the jammed corpse. She slid her knife between the beast and the stone, trying to jimmy the monster out of the way.

Harsh breathing came around the corner. 1554's fetid breath filled the tunnel. Ezaara lunged, thrusting her knife. The tharuk grunt slashed. Her knife clattered to the stone. She groped for it. 1554 punched her temple. Her head smacked the wall, and pain ricocheted through her skull. Dizzy. She was so dizzy.

Shuffling backward, 1554 dragged her along the shaft by the throat and hair.

Ezaara's scalp burned. She curled up, trying to kick the tharuk, but it yanked her hair harder. She screamed.

"Quiet." It tightened its grip on her throat until her breath rasped.

So much for rescuing Roberto.

§

000 held Ezaara by the scruff of her neck, her legs dangling above the floor. Her jerkin cut into her throat, making it hard to breathe. Not that she'd want to in this stench.

Commander Zens smiled, his bulbous yellow eyes cold. His calculating gaze skittered across her skin. He stretched out his hand. *"So, breathing distasteful, is it?"* His voice wended through her mind. *"Perhaps you'd prefer not to breathe?"* He slowly clenched his fist.

Ezaara's throat tightened. She let out a gurgle, fingers clutching at her neck. Her lungs burned. Gods, no air.

"Drop her, Triple." Zens laughed, flinging his hand open.

Ezaara smacked stone. Her chest heaved as breath rushed back into her lungs. She'd panicked and forgotten her mental defenses. Zens was a monster—a power-hungry sick being, playing with people's lives. She scrambled to her feet. While Zens was focused on her, he wasn't torturing Roberto.

"Stand still." Zens barked. *"Why are you here?"*

Ezaara remembered her favorite tree in Lush Valley; the bark against her cheek; a breeze rustling through the bright green leaves. She held the image fast in her mind, stilling Zens' voice.

Zens growled, flipping his hand.

Ezaara flew into a wall, slamming her shoulder against the granite. She had to tell him something or he'd destroy her. Climbing to her feet, Ezaara answered, "I'm here to rescue Roberto."

Zens guffawed. "He doesn't need rescuing. He's here of his own accord." Zens flicked his finger. Roberto's body twitched. "Roberto's here to do my bidding." Flashing his teeth in a manic grin, Zens flung Roberto into the air, holding him there, then slowly lowered him to the ground. "I can slam him so hard, I'll break every bone in his body. So, tell me, who are you?"

Zens was lying. Roberto hadn't come here willingly. She'd mistrusted him at his banishment, and he'd nearly died. She'd never make that mistake again.

Zens' mind shuddered into hers, but she blocked him.

"Talented, are you?" Zens sneered. "We'll see just how little talent you have."

Searing heat rippled across Ezaara's skin. A wave of nausea roiled over her. She clamped down, forcing it out. The tree. Breeze. Leaves rustling.

He hammered at her head, booming like a battle drum. Pounding her skull.

The tree slipped away. She needed something more tangible, immediate. Ezaara fixed on Roberto, bloodied, on the floor.

"So, he's important to you? Why?"

It was useless to deny it. She had to give Zens something, or he'd never let up. But not the whole truth. "I'm his trainee dragon rider. I wanted to save him." She sighed, making her lower lip tremble. "I've obviously failed." Hopefully, he'd buy it, not realize her strength.

Zens just laughed. "You have a sense of humor, too."

He'd seen right through her little act.

Zens sat in a chair, crossed his legs, and pounded her mind like a battering ram.

§

Ezaara woke as fists hammered on the door. Gods, not another day in this forsaken place. Her mouth was parched and she was weak from hunger.

Zens had left last night, but he was back in his chair. Roberto was clasping his head, sweat rolling down his forehead. No doubt, Zens doing. "Open that please, Triple," Zens said.

000 strode over and opened the door. Two tharuks entered, holding a grubby, battered Adelina.

Ezaara instantly blocked her mind, fixating on the flickering torch. If Zens realized they knew Adelina, he'd torture her to get them to talk.

Zens' sadistic smile was sickening. Pointing a finger at Adelina, he twitched it.

Eyes wide, her chin shot up.

"I recognize you from Amato's memories," he said. "You're Roberto's little sister."

"Am not." Adelina thrust her shoulders back, defiant.

A thin man entered the cavern, closing the door—Old Bill, Lovina's former slave master.

Ezaara turned her face away so he wouldn't recognize her.

"Beloved Commander Zens." Bill rubbed his hands together. "Twice this week, I saw a flash in the night sky. Stinking winged lizards, I thought. I summoned

743 and 567 to help me catch this Naobian girl." He licked his lips. "She'd make me a good slave. I lost my last one." Bill paced around Adelina, looking her over.

Then he saw Ezaara. "My highly-esteemed commander, I must congratulate you for capturing the new Queen's Rider."

"Queen's Rider?" Zens lifted an eyebrow. "Explain how you know her." His disdain for Bill was barely veiled.

Bill gave a fawning, sickening smile. "Beloved Commander, I was traveling through Lush Valley, spying for you and 458, when she left with the stinking queen of lizards. Her parents were riders, hiding in Lush Valley."

"000, reward him. Dismissed." Zens waved Bill and the grunts away. With ice in his voice, he commanded, "Roberto, stand."

Roberto hobbled to his feet. Ezaara's chest squeezed. Gods, he looked so weak, favoring his shackled leg, and cradling an arm against his side.

"Since you're proving so hard to break, we'll have some fun," Zens said. "Who would you prefer that I torture? The Queen's Rider? Or your little sister?"

Weakness

By the dragon gods, what a choice: his lover or his sister? There was no guarantee Zens wouldn't torture both. Or kill them, just to make him suffer. A chill spread through Roberto as Zens prowled toward his sister. Adelina's body jerked and went rigid. Her face contorted in a silent scream. Her hands clutched at her throat, nails drawing blood. Suddenly, she crumpled in a heap on the stone, gasping.

Roberto's gut tied itself in knots. No, not his sister. He'd spent his life protecting her.

Zens' gaze flicked to Ezaara, his lips twisting in a sneer. "So, Roberto, let's examine the Queen's Rider." The commander caressed her cheek with a fingertip. Roberto's skin crawled, but Ezaara didn't even flinch.

Roberto clamped down the rage seething inside him. If Zens suspected he loved Ezaara, he'd hurt her more to get to him. Zens wanted to break him, to prove to himself that he could master the only person who'd escaped his power.

If only Zens had a weakness he could exploit. He had to laugh at himself, looking for a weakness when he was chained, drugged and weak from torture.

Hang on, Zens' nightmare had shown Roberto his biggest weakness. His eyes flitted around the room. Now, if only he could use it.

Adelina was lying there, as if she was asleep, the blood on her neck glistening in the torchlight.

"A pretty one, this time," murmured Zens, eyes roving over Ezaara.

Shards, no. The hairs on Roberto's neck prickled.

"No one told me how attractive you were," Zens purred.

A keen mental energy hovered near Roberto's mind. Zens was gauging him, sensing his reactions as he walked around Ezaara, assessing her like a prime head of beef at the market.

Roberto wanted to rip Zens' head off, but he forced himself to breathe calmly and think of summer days, fishing off the coast of Naobia.

"Oh, Commander." Ezaara laughed. "No one ever told me how handsome you are. How utterly devastating. They'd painted you as a monster, but now I see your true colors—your consummate use of power for the good of Dragons'

Realm. I'm sure Zaarusha will agree to your suggestion of returning to Dragons' Hold with us, to rule at my side."

Sharding talons, Ezaara looked as if she meant it.

Zens paused mid-stride, cocking his head.

Roberto held his breath. What was going on?

Baring his teeth, Zens snarled, "You despise me." His voice turned as hard as flint. "You profess your love verbally, while secretly thinking I'm despicable." Without warning, he flicked his hand and Ezaara slammed into the granite wall head first with a nauseating crunch. She landed with her neck at an odd angle.

Gods, was she dead? A black hole ripped through Roberto's chest. As he struggled to contain his horror, his barricade against Zens disintegrated.

Zens loomed in his mind, stripping away his defenses, laying his emotions bare. *"So, you love her? Let's torture her some more."*

"No," Roberto yelled, the chains gnawing his flesh as he strained to get free. Not the two people he loved most. The only family he had.

Zens flung his hand out. Roberto flew into the air. His chains strained, threatening to snap their fixtures out of the wall.

"Love the Queen's Rider, do you?" Zens sneered. *"And I thought I'd cured you of weak emotions."*

"Cured me?"

"Surely, having your father beat you prevented you from trusting people, Roberto?" Zens spun him a half turn in the air, his voice worming its way through the caverns of self-doubt the commander had carved through his soul years before. *"Amato was clever, he hid Adelina's existence from me, but, in a weak moment, he revealed he had another whelp. So, I forced him to beat her."* Zens laughed. *"No one—not even his own flesh and blood—came between us. I mastered him, making him murder his own wife."*

Amato had tried to stand up to Zens and failed. He'd always assumed his father had been an eager accomplice. A chill skittered down Roberto's spine. Zens was a monster.

"Your father loved you, until I cured him of it."

He did remember his father loving him. But what good had it done him? Under Zens' power, Amato had killed the woman he loved, and driven his littlings to hate him.

What hope did Roberto have against Zens? At a young age, the commander had infiltrated his mind, training him to torture others mentally, to kill slaves, turning him into a powerful pawn. Gods, would he never be free of Zens' legacy? One day, would he, too, destroy the people he loved?

Zens' eyes gleamed fanatically. He flicked his wrist and Roberto spun around in mid-air, flat on his back, the chains twisting around each other as he whirled, making a thick umbilical cord to the wall. As he spun, the chains tightened, yanking him lower.

The commander laughed. "000, look at him. Hung in my web like a fly."

He kept Roberto spinning. The cave and its occupants became a blur. Zens' laugh reverberated off the walls, sounding like a thousand madmen. Roberto's gut heaved. He retched its meager contents over the floor. The chains tightened excruciatingly, getting thicker and shorter, as Zens reeled him in.

He had to pretend he was subservient. It was his only chance. Spinning faster and faster, Roberto shut his eyes, trying to feign defeat. *"Zens, please forgive me for leaving you. I'll do anything you want."*

"Forgiveness is not in my nature. Ask my parents." Zens twirled Roberto until the chain was a bundle of twisted metal.

Roberto's body slammed into the wall, the chains biting into his back. He buried his thoughts. It'd be dangerous if Zens knew he'd understood the quip about his parents—that he'd seen Zens' memory of murdering them.

Zens turned to Ezaara—still prone on the granite floor. Beyond her, Adelina lay, scratches on her throat still gleaming red.

Not Ezaara, not again. Zens stretched out his hand, lifting it. Her body didn't budge.

Was she dead? She couldn't be, or Zens would've tossed her like a sack of flour.

What was going on? Roberto didn't dare mind-meld with her. To keep his thoughts shielded from Zens, he examined his chains. His wrist and ankle were bloody and torn where the shackles had burrowed into his flesh. The chain was bunched in a tangled mess behind him, but the fixtures attaching the chains to the wall were now loose.

While Zens was occupied with Ezaara, Roberto stood. Body aching, he slowly turned until the chains were untangled. Then he hobbled back and forward, straining at the loose fixtures on the wall, playing the part of an agitated lover.

§

Zens radiated sickly yellow *sathir*, infected with an energy Ezaara had never seen. It felt wrong, unclean. Was this what gave him his formidable mental powers?

Her neck ached. She'd landed that way, but deliberately kept it at an odd angle, so Zens would think she was incapacitated. The cool stone chilled her back. She drilled down with her mind, focusing on the heaviness of the granite—its gray sluggish *sathir,* barely detectable, but there. She sucked the heaviness into her, desperately trying to become one with the massive immovable force.

Zens approached, boots scraping the granite. He flicked his hand again.

Heavy. Heavy as rock. Sweat broke out on Ezaara's brow. Her flesh was stone. She was granite. Immovable. Zens battered at her. Her mind was a wall of rock. Her body, married to the granite.

Regular footfalls and clanking sounded behind her. Roberto, pacing. Out of the corner of her eye, Adelina stirred—her eyes flitted around the cavern, then drooped again—pretending.

Zens tugged.

Ezaara resisted. Something had changed: Roberto was pacing further than before. An extra step at the end of his route. He was up to something. She had to keep Zens distracted.

"Triple, support me," Zens snapped.

000 lumbered over, grabbing Zens' hand. Eyes drilling into her, they stared, jaws tight, dark saliva running down 000's tusks.

A tidal wave slammed into Ezaara, shredding her mind. Yellow bathed her vision. Her head throbbed. Her bones rattled in her skull. She gritted her teeth, resisting. Her flesh tugged as if it would peel from her bones. By the flaming dragon gods, they'd kill her.

She let go.

Zens crowed as she flew into the air, stopping just beneath the rock ceiling. He laughed, rubbing his hands together. Beside him, 000 guffawed.

In a sudden clatter of chains, Roberto was behind 000, a chain around the beast's neck, garroting it. "Free the women, Zens. Or I'll kill Triple."

Zens turned, eyes radiating malice. "Go ahead. It's just a tharuk, Roberto, I kill them all the time."

"Really?" Roberto raised an eyebrow, as cool as a winter's morning. He tightened the chains.

000 gurgled, red eyes bulging.

Zens' face contorted with rage. "Harm 000 and the Queen's Rider's skull will be smashed on the stone, scattering her brains." Zens waved a hand.

Ezaara plummeted toward the floor. She'd never see Zaarusha again.

He flicked his hand, arresting her fall, a body's breadth from the granite. Ezaara sucked in a gulp of air.

"Just another tharuk?" Roberto said, tightening the chain a notch.

Ezaara shot back up, hovering below the ceiling.

Zens said, "Take your pathetic sister and go, but I warn you, Roberto, harm 000, and you'll hear your darling Queen's Rider scream."

"Adelina, open the door." Roberto yanked on 000's chain.

Zens snarled as Roberto manhandled 000 out the door, Adelina on his heels.

Ezaara tried to swallow, but couldn't. Oh gods, he was abandoning her.

Mage Fire

Zens twitched his fingers. Ezaara landed gently on the floor.

"And you thought he loved you? He's incapable of love. He's saving his own skin and leaving you to rot."

Ezaara barricaded her mind, shutting Zens out. Roberto had left to save Adelina. He'd had no choice. But as the door thudded shut, Ezaara's heart shattered into a thousand pieces, the shards plummeting to the floor.

§

Roberto stumbled out the door, keeping the pressure on the chains around 000's neck. Shards, he was weak. Physically, but also emotionally for leaving Ezaara behind. His chest was a ragged hole of desolation.

Adelina barred the door. The wooden beam rattled in its fitting—Zens, no doubt. Gods, what would he do to Ezaara? Adelina gathered up the loose end of the chain around Roberto's leg, swinging it. She hit the tharuk on the head. 000 dropped to the floor.

"Adelina, the key to my shackles is around its neck." Roberto disentangled his arm chain from around 000's throat.

His sister unlocked Roberto's burning arm and leg. That was much better, now he could move.

Thumping sounded in the tunnel. Adelina's eyes flew wide. "What's that?"

Someone was running toward them—a lot of someones. "Tharuks. Quick." Roberto hoisted Adelina up into a ventilation shaft near the door—must have been the one Ezaara had used when she'd first come through his door. Gods, Ezaara. He'd left her with that monster. Hot tears pricked his eyes.

"Hurry," Adelina hissed.

Roberto tried to jump up to the shaft but failed. Adelina held her arms down. "Grab hold."

He was too weak. Roberto rolled 000's body over against the wall, grunting and stopping to catch his breath. Then he propped the tharuk up against the wall and climbed up his body, grasping Adelina's hands and walking his feet up the wall. She hoisted him into the shaft.

Roberto crawled on battered limbs, his head throbbing and gashes bleeding. But it was nothing compared to the ache in his chest at leaving Ezaara behind.

§

Zens burned with anger, his mind searing hot. When had Roberto figured out that 000 meant so much to him? That his first creation was his only true friend? 000 was the only intelligent, formidable tharuk. Zens had deliberately engineered the grunts to be dumb, so he could keep them in submission. He'd sacrifice every other tharuk to save 000's hide.

He melded with 000. Darkness. Not dead, but unconscious. If Amato's whelp had damaged Triple …

Revenge would come later. Roberto would not get away with this. No one threatened 000.

Zens melded with the nearest troop, sending them into the tunnels after Roberto and his sister. He would own Roberto. Break him and mold him to his will.

Although weak, Amato's whelp had been walking properly. So, Roberto wasn't limplocked anymore. Someone had given him antidote. Now that he wasn't going to die, Zens could still use him.

His eyes slid over the pretty Queen's Rider lying on the floor. Roberto had found love, despite all Zens had done to him. The best way to break Roberto would be to make him destroy this girl himself.

Zens licked his lips. Now, that was the perfect plan.

§

The tunnels echoed with thumping and snorts. The stench of tharuk crept along the shaft toward Roberto and Adelina. He crawled on, every strike of his palms and knees ricocheting through his battered body. One arm gave out. His face hit stone. He couldn't go on.

"Come, on, you can do it," Adelina whispered, voice trembling.

He had to. For Adelina. For Ezaara. Gods, Zens had ruined him.

Adelina hoisted him to his elbows, half dragging him along the shaft.

A low snarl made the hair on Roberto's neck rise. He forced his clumsy, broken body on. The snarls grew louder. Closer. "Flee," Roberto whispered. "Leave me and flee."

Adelina shook her head, yanking him forward. They crept around a corner.

Tusks gleamed among a mass of dark fur.

Adelina screamed. She kicked and fought, but the wall of tusks and fur dragged her off.

Pain seared through Roberto's leg. "Got you," the tharuk behind him snarled, digging its sharp claws in, and hauling him backward, away from his sister.

§

The door opened. Ezaara glanced up. Was Zens returning? No, it was 000 with tharuk grunts. They dragged someone inside. The shrotty beasts had recaptured Adelina. The grunts manhandled Roberto inside too, and left, slamming the heavy door.

Roberto swayed, then crumpled to the floor. Ezaara scooted over, cradling his head in her lap. She didn't care what Zens thought anymore—or anyone else. "I love you, Roberto." She was sick of denying it. Strange that she could show her love for him here, in Death Valley, but not at Dragons' Hold. When they returned, that would change.

If they returned.

The odds weren't great, but she refused to give up. She was Queen's Rider. Roberto was a master. They had to get back and lead their people. "Adelina, are you all right?" she whispered.

"No," Adelina whimpered. Neck still covered in scratches, Adelina crawled over, and leaned against Ezaara's side, shaking. "Reminds me of Pa … beating us."

Ezaara put her arm around Adelina's shoulders. With the other hand, she stroked Roberto's hair. Eyelids fluttering, he looked up, then drifted to sleep. "Adelina," she whispered, "I've always wanted a sister. I found one in you."

"Me too," said Adelina, tears tracking down her face as she gazed at her broken brother. "Is there anything we can do for him?"

"Yes, I still have a little piaua, but we'll have to heal him discreetly, so Zens doesn't notice."

Ezaara peeked in her pouch. All of her vials were smashed. Useless. "We'll let him sleep a little, first," she lied. Ezaara felt awful, but the flash of hope on Adelina's face was worth it—even if they never got out of here alive.

§

The door to the holding cell thudded open. Roberto roused himself, sitting up. 000 and a bunch of tharuk grunts entered. He squeezed Ezaara's warm hand.

"You two," 000 said, indicating the women. "Zens has changed his mind. You both go free. Tharuks will escort you."

"No," said Ezaara. "We're not going without Roberto."

"Please," Roberto managed weakly. "Go." Gods, they'd come to save him. And failed. Was Zens really setting them free? Or sending them to the slave camps? Either way, they had more chance of escaping if they weren't with him. His life was forfeit anyway. Zens had marked him from a young age. He'd been lucky—with what he'd been through, he should've died already, many times over.

"Roberto, no." Tharuks dragged Adelina away, her screams bouncing off the walls, hammering through Roberto's skull.

"Better to go quietly," Roberto called. Better for her to give in to tharuks? Gods, this place had driven him mad.

Ezaara squeezed his hands. "I love you, Roberto. We'll be back," she whispered, then tharuks ripped her from his weak grasp.

"No, don't risk your life for me. It's not worth it," he replied. Zens was probing at the edge of his mind, evaluating him.

A grunt shoved Ezaara. She walked, head high, eyes on him.

He'd learned to love and he was losing it all. And he'd led the new Queen's Rider, with all her unique talents, right into Zens' lair. His sister too. He was worse than useless, he was dangerous. When people loved him, they got hurt.

What was Zens going to do with them? Would he break them too? Torture them? Make them senseless pawns, shells of themselves, hurting others on Zens' behalf?

As they pushed Ezaara to the doorway, Roberto was desperate to mind-meld with her, one last time, to tell her he loved her. Tell her he was sorry. But he couldn't. He'd risk Zens breaking through her mental defenses. He'd failed in everything he'd dreamed of, and once again become a pawn in Zens' hands. Hot tears slid down his cheeks, washing salt, grime and blood over his lips.

Then the door slammed, locking out the only people he loved.

He curled on the floor, sobs wracking his body.

§

Oh, Gods, no. Ezaara's chest ached. Zens had succeeded. Roberto's body and spirit were broken. He'd wept unashamedly, despair etched in every bloody, battered pore, as tharuks had hustled her out the door. Zens had been pummeling her mind, so she hadn't dared meld with Roberto, but, inside, she was screaming his name. Throat tight, she vowed she'd get revenge on that shrotty rat, Zens, for hurting those she loved.

For enslaving her people. For destroying all they loved. Anger seared through her. Zens must die and all his tharuks with him.

But right now, she was only one dragonless rider against a monster and his troops. Bitterness flooded her mouth. She'd been a fool to think she could've rescued Roberto. Just as much a fool for thinking she could have revenge.

A tharuk troop surrounded her and Adelina, rushing them out of the tunnels. Ezaara winced, bright sunlight hitting her eyes. Adelina clutched her hand as they trekked along the valley floor, dust stirring underfoot. The barren hills were riddled with caves, like gaping maws, with lines of slaves trooping into the hillside's underbelly. More tharuks tromped past, cracking whips at herds of slaves. A young girl, as thin as a slip of parchment, stumbled. A tharuk whipped her, but she didn't even flinch as her tattered rags and skin split under the bite of the lash.

Ezaara tensed, about to protest, but Adelina gripped her hand, and whispered, "No, Ezaara, they'll kill us if we interfere. We must escape and get help."

Ezaara bit back her retort. Escape? Help? Who was Adelina fooling? This was *Death* Valley.

The tharuk booted the fallen girl. "Dead," it called. "To the flesh pile. You, there."

A male slave shambled forward, eyes vacant and jaw hanging open. He hefted the girl onto his shoulder, then stumbled off down the valley.

Adelina's grip bit into Ezaara's hand. Thank the Egg. The pain was stopping her from screaming.

Their tharuk escorts crowded around them, herding them along the valley past groups of half-starved slaves—many with fingers, hands or ears missing. All staring at the ground, mindless. Gods, Tomaaz had been here—Roberto, Lovina, Ma and Taliesin, too. No wonder the boy hadn't spoken for so long.

"Faster," the lead tharuk bellowed, glancing nervously at the sky.

Ezaara snapped her head up. Was that a flash of orange? Maazini?

Adelina glanced up too, hope flickering across her face.

Their tharuk troop drew their bows and fired. Thank the First Egg, their arrows fell short. "Get higher. To the hills," the troop leader barked.

Keeping Ezaara and Adelina in their midst, the tharuks swarmed up a steep trail. Adelina stumbled, and Ezaara pulled her upright. These beasts were fast. If they didn't keep up, they'd be trampled. Was Maazini alone?

Ezaara melded, *"Maazini, can you see us? Adelina and I are in the middle of a tharuk troop, heading up a hill."* She squinted at the sky. *Was that another dragon up there?"*

"Ezaara? I see the troop. We'll have you out in no time."

If only it were that simple—there were hundreds of tharuks to get through. *"Thank the Egg, you're here. Is Zaarusha with you?"*

"No, just Riona."

Kierion? Thank the dragon gods that reckless fool and Tomaaz were daring enough to come to Death Valley.

The tharuks stopped halfway up the hill. Shoving Ezaara and Adelina behind a rocky outcrop, they fired arrows at Maazini. He swerved, dancing out of reach, then swooped, drawing more fire. *"Are you behind that rock?"* Maazini asked.

"Just me and Adelina. Roberto's still captive."

Maazini's answering snarl seared Ezaara's mind. *"When I give the order, drop to your bellies."*

Nerves tight, Ezaara waited for Maazini's signal. More tharuks swarmed up the hillside, eager to kill the dragons with their limplocked arrows. How could Tomaaz and Kierion ever get them out of this mess?

"Now. Duck!"

She thrust Adelina to the ground, saying, "Cover your head."

Ezaara peeked around the rock. A bolt of purple shot through the sky—Riona! Green fireballs zipped from her back, hitting screaming tharuks. Maazini's scales flashed as he flamed tharuks. Arrows hit beasts. Tharuks fell, blasted by wizard flame.

"Ezaara, stay down," Maazini called. *"Riona, now."*

"Gladly," Riona answered.

The dragons opened their maws. Ezaara yanked her head behind the rock as a wave of heat hit the outcrop. Tharuks crackled with flame, the stink of their burned fur crawling up Ezaara's nostrils. Shrieks and bellows rang out. Dragon roars filled the air. Flashes of yellow and green light glanced off the hillside.

Then there was silence.

Ezaara risked peeking out. Dead tharuks were scattered across the hill, green and yellow flames licking at their fur. A pall of black and green smoke hung in the air. She scrambled to her feet, hoisting Adelina up.

"Wizard fire." Adelina's voice cracked. "Kierion and Fenni are here."

Roars echoed from the valley and more tharuks surged up the hill.

"Quick, Maazini."

"Stand far apart. We're coming to collect you."

Ezaara dragged Adelina past smoking bodies, coughing on the foul smoke-laden air. "Adelina, brace yourself."

With a sickening lurch, Maazini grabbed Ezaara in his talons and they were sky-bound. Riona snatched up Adelina.

An aching, empty hole gaped in Ezaara's chest as they ascended, fleeing tharuk arrows. Leaving Roberto behind.

Retaliation

The air reeked of mage fire. The godforsaken stuff clung in Zens' nostrils. Green smoke wafted across the hillside above the carnage of Zens' dead troops, carrying the stench of burned flesh. A pair of dragons were fleeing over the Terramites—one of them was the orange specimen he'd captured. It didn't matter that the dragon had escaped months ago. Zens had harvested its DNA long before. But it was worrying that mages and dragons were working together again. Years ago, he'd driven a bitter wedge of mistrust between dragon riders and mages, deep enough for them to hate each other forever.

When tharuks had reported dragons overhead, he'd deliberately brought the girls into the open. By rescuing them, the fools had played into his hands.

His slow smile turned to a grimace. A hundred stinking corpses littered the mountainside. He'd been prepared to sacrifice a few tharuks in a pathetic skirmish. But this? Fury roiled inside him at his wasted troops. Someone would pay.

Zens faced his assembled tharuks. "A hundred tharuks have died defending Death Valley. Those stinking dragon riders and mages did this. Will we let them get away with this carnage?"

His troops roared.

"We will avenge them," Zens bellowed, rousing their bloodlust. "000 will take a troop to execute a hundred slaves."

"Yes, sir." 000 and his troop marched down the valley, their feet stirring up dust that mingled with mage smoke.

"Tharuk 766, take a raiding party and scour Spanglewood Forest for a hundred more slaves to replace them."

"My pleasure, sir," tracker 766 answered, tusks salivating.

766's troop raced up the rocky mountainside, stomping over dead tharuks in their eagerness to hunt humans. Zens smiled. He'd trained them well.

"967, come here. The rest of you, clean up those corpses. Throw them onto the tharuk flesh pile. When you're done, I want everyone on lockdown. Sleep in the slaves' huts tonight. No one is allowed out in the valley. And post no lookout."

"Yes, Commander," the tharuks said as one, pounding their fists on their chests. They traipsed up the hill to gather the dead.

967, a wiry tharuk with an affinity for crows, approached. "Commander, how I help?" It wrung its hands.

His grunts' lack of language skills was irritating at times. "Send crows to the tharuk troop leaders, telling them to kill all the wizards in Spanglewood Forest. Raze their homes and destroy their young, but bring me back two captives."

"Kill all wizards. Bring two back."

He mind-melded, showing a face to 967. "And 967, tell them I want Master Giddi alive."

§

Hours after tharuks had taken Ezaara and Adelina, 000 returned to the holding cell, waking Roberto from a broken, hollow sleep.

"Commander Zens wants to see you." 000 grabbed Roberto in a headlock.

As if he could put up a fight. He was a shadow of himself.

000 dragged Roberto along tunnels, his head wedged under the tharuk's stinking armpit. When they reached the tunnel mouth, it was dark outside and the air was tinged with bitter smoke. The tharuk adjusted its grip, slipping its arm over Roberto's shoulders so he could walk upright. Roberto wasn't fooled. 000's sharp claws could shred him in an instant.

They crossed the deserted, barren valley. Moonlight bathed a blackened mountainside. It had been burned. His throat tightened. They hadn't incinerated Ezaara and Adelina, had they? That made no sense, but then again, Zens' actions seldom did.

Mist crept out of mining pits in the barren hillsides, writhing around his ankles. Zens had destroyed all the vegetation in this valley while mining yellow crystals. Before being caught, Roberto had infiltrated a mining crew so he could snoop, and he'd frequently seen Zens entering a large cavern with a door of stone. Is that where Zens was making his new creatures? Were they heading there now?

Sure enough, 000 took him underground. Dim torches lit the walls as the track sloped down, narrowing as they went. The acrid stench of the mines hit Roberto's nostrils, making his eyes water. He blinked, trying to clear them as 000 marched him deeper into the network of mines. Every footstep jarred his head.

"The commander has something special in store for you," 000 said.

The vapor rising to greet him made his head throb. Where were Adelina and Ezaara? He doubted Zens had let them go. He trudged on, keeping his thoughts submerged.

000 took a shadowy turnoff that spiraled down until they came to a large stone that blocked the tunnel. This was where Roberto had seen Zens go. 000 pressed on the stone, and it rolled sideways, revealing a large chamber lit with a yellow glow.

Workbenches and tools similar to Zens' parents' workshop littered the room. Dark furry blobs were floating in glass tanks lining the far wall, illuminated by large yellow crystals. Beyond the tanks, bright light poured from another chamber.

000 shoved Roberto forward. "We're here," he said. "Enjoy your stay."

A familiar voice spoke behind him. "Welcome, my protégé."

He spun. Zens was leaning against a recessed counter, the yellow light tinging his sallow face. "000, please bind him to worktop four."

000 flung Roberto onto a bench. Roberto thrashed, but 000 bound his chest, hands and ankles to the bench with metallic bands. Zens forced a clear flexible tube between Roberto's lips while 000 lifted his head.

Roberto clenched his teeth, blocking the tube from entering his mouth.

"Suck," commanded Zens.

Roberto refused. 000 pinched his nose with its stinking furry hands. His lungs burned.

"*Suck*, I said." Zens bulging eyes drilled into him. A dull band of pressure tightened around Roberto's head. He fought to block Zens out. The pressure spread across his skull, unclenching his jaw. Zens rammed the tube into his mouth, smiling, his yellow orbs drilling into Roberto.

Roberto sucked in bitter air and blacked out.

§

Roberto groaned as he awoke, face down. Mustard light reflected off the cool metal beneath him. His back was sore. What had Zens done to him? He moved his legs. Wait, his restraining bands were gone. He rolled over and sat up.

No one was in the room. Zens wasn't pounding at his head either. He cautiously reached out with his mind, searching for Zens and found nothing. What was going on? Roberto swung his legs over the bench and slid to the floor. He wouldn't be alone forever—Zens or 000 could return any moment. He should escape, but first …

His queen had sent him here to find out what creatures Zens was developing—he may never get another chance. Heart pounding, Roberto crept toward the entrance to the inner chamber and peeked inside.

The room dwarfed this one, easily five times larger. Zens stood at a counter, his back to Roberto, working with strange metal implements. Hundreds of tanks, large enough to fit a man in, stood in rows, with workbenches between them. Tharuks were mixing things in bowls and sprinkling some sort of dust into the water in the tanks. What was inside? More furry blobs, some with legs. Roberto squinted. That was a tusk. There were some claws …

By the dragon gods' First Egg, they were tharuks. Sweat pebbled his skin. Zens grew them in these tanks.

Commander Zens and his tharuks were dwarfed by more tanks—as large as houses—along the back wall. Weird black creatures were suspended in fluid, curled up, with ragged bits of cloth hanging from them. These must be Zens' secret weapon—the creatures Zaarusha had sent him to find out about.

Although they were illuminated by glowing crystals at the bottom of their tanks, it was hard to see what they were. Roberto lingered, trying to get a better look. One of the creatures moved, and something white flashed. A tusk or a horn? Was that a tail or a limb? The cloth around the beast swirled, preventing him from seeing more.

Shards, he'd better get out of here before someone turned around.

Roberto retreated across the cavern to the rock blocking the door. What had looked like a rock from the outside was only as thick as his upper arm and mounted on a metal rail. He pushed the rock, like 000 had, trying to open it. No luck. He leaned his full weight on it and shoved. It still didn't budge.

Zens' voice drifted from the inner cavern.

Flames, he had to get out of here. Cold sweat beaded his neck. He couldn't get caught now. Scanning the wall, he found a lever and pulled. With a soft hum, the layer of rock slid open and cool air rushed in.

Would Zens notice the change in air current? Roberto slipped out of the chamber as the door clicked shut behind him. He had to hurry before his absence was detected. Legs aching, head throbbing and his back on fire, he plodded up. Exhausted, he often stopped to lean on the wall. Finally, the tunnel intersected with the main trail through the underbelly of the mountain. He waited in the shadows, but no one was around. His shoulder blades prickling, he pushed himself, hurrying up the tunnel to the valley.

He didn't encounter a single tharuk or slave. It was nearly dawn. Tharuks should've been patrolling the valley. About now, slaves would normally be woken for a meager breakfast. This was too easy. What was going on? Was Zens letting him escape?

He half-ran, half-stumbled across the valley, his raw ankle throbbing, his torso a mass of bruises and gashes from Zens' games. Each step was agony. But he had to get out.

Shards, Ezaara and Adelina. Where were they?

As he picked his way up the burned slope, Roberto recognized the tang of mage fire and the sulphuric stench of dragon flame. What had gone on here? Had dragons saved Ezaara and his sister? He hoped so.

Darkness flickered across his eyes and a wave of inexplicable anger roiled within him.

Where had that come from? He shrugged, stumbling up the hill, covering himself in soot from the charred ground. He'd have to trek halfway across Dragons' Realm to find someone to take him to Dragons' Hold. Years ago, Erob had helped him escape, but there'd be no one here to help him now. He hadn't even asked Ezaara if Erob was still alive.

Oh gods, what if Erob *was* dead and Ezaara and Adelina too? A hollow ache gnawed inside Roberto as he climbed up the blackened mountainside.

Dragons' Hold

The main cavern rippled with rumor, people arguing, pointing and whispering. Lars could taste the tension. Septimor landed on the stage in front of the council masters and their dragons, furling his wings. Seppi helped Sofia dismount amid boos, jeers and discordant cheering.

"Creating quite a stir, isn't she?" Lars muttered to Tonio.

"To be expected under the circumstances," Tonio replied, keen eyes flitting around the cavern. "I'm interested to see how this plays out." He gave a subtle flick of his fingers, and several blue guards and dragon corps members moved among the crowd to stand near the most vocal objectors.

Seppi blew a horn for silence, then brought Sofia before Lars.

Lars smiled encouragingly at Sofia. He'd been pleased with her progress since Marlies had extracted the crystal. The council was keeping the crystals quiet until everyone had been checked for the *silent pox*—Marlies' fabricated excuse for examining their skin. Over the past four days, the master healer had checked more than a hundred people, but there were many more. Horrified at the effect Zens' crystal had worked on her, Sofia had been helping—under close supervision.

This was going to be a tough session. "Good evening," Lars addressed the restless crowd. "We're here to discuss how Anakisha's prophecy relates—"

"We want justice," someone called. "Sofia attacked the Queen's Rider."

"Ezaara's not the right Queen's Rider," someone else called.

Angry yelling broke out.

Lars raised his hand. Seppi had to blow the horn three times before the shouts died down.

"Zens would be laughing at your bickering factions," boomed Lars, thunder in his chest. "He'd love to see us ripping each other's heads off. With discord in our ranks, we could never face him in unity in war. And war is coming. Zens is moving against us."

That shut them all up, Singlar melded.

"Sofia will be tried, but not tonight. Today, our master of prophecy, Hans, will put these malicious claims that Ezaara is not our rightful Queen's Rider to rest. Sofia will explain her views of Anakisha's prophecy. I ask for respectful silence as each speaks. Anyone disobeying will overnight in the cage." Lars jabbed a finger at the audience. "And I don't care whether I have to stack you to the ceiling. The more the merrier. I will not have disunity in this meeting."

There were a few grumbles and a lot of nodding heads—better than he'd expected. "First Sofia, then Hans." Lars motioned Sofia forward.

"Thank you for the opportunity to speak," Sofia nodded at Lars. "I apologize for my actions. I will pay for my crimes."

Surprised murmurs broke out.

"Lars has asked me to recite Anakisha's prophecy and explain why I feel it hasn't been fulfilled.

"One of our progeny will reign in our stead
Filling our enemies' foul hearts with dread
Purging all evil will be his desire
Vengeance he'll wage with arrows of fire.

"This prophecy indicates that the Queen's Rider should not only be Anakisha's heir, but also male. Ezaara is neither. I must confess, I've had a vested interest. My cousin is Anakisha's heir. He was taken to Death Valley two years ago. I'd hoped he'd become Queen's Rider, but ..." Eyes bright with tears, Sofia swallowed. "He may not have survived. Tonight, I would like to pay tribute to Rhun of Waykeep, son of Rhun senior and Maria-Anakisha, Anakisha's daughter. Rhun senior is my uncle by blood."

Near the middle of the crowd, people moved as a group made their way to the front. Who were they? Murmurs grew.

Gret, Lovina and the young slave boy walked up to the stage.

"Permission to speak, Lars," Gret asked, clutching the boy and Lovina's hands.

Lars nodded. "Permission granted."

Gret addressed Sofia. "Taliesin says he's your cousin."

Of all the sharding things. Lars' felt his eyebrows shoot up in amazement. The lad was Sofia's cousin? Then they were related, too, by marriage.

Sofia flung her arms around the thin boy, tears falling on his shoulders as she hugged him. "Rhun, is that you? You're so thin."

Gret spoke to the crowd. "We know him as Taliesin, but his full name is Rhun Taliesin of Waykeep."

People cheered.

"Wait, there's more," Gret called. The cheering stilled, and silent expectation surged through the cavern.

Lovina cleared her throat, and Gret gently nudged her toward Lars.

"Yes, Lovina?" Lars asked the shy girl.

"Ah, Lars, no one has ever asked me before, but Anakisha was my grandmother too. My father was Argus, Anakisha's son. My family died in Death Valley. I survived as a slave to a tharuk spy." She smiled sadly. "Tomaaz rescued me."

Taliesin piped up, "Tomaaz rescued me too."

Sofia bowed. "Then I owe Tomaaz's family a debt. My apologies for besmirching Ezaara's name."

"Would the rest of Anakisha's grandchildren come to the stage?" Lars called.

Soon eleven more people, ranging in age from teens to littlings, stood on the stage.

"Please tell us of your connection to Anakisha." He waved his hand at Lofty, who had a gaggle of littlings with him.

"My ma is Ana, after her mother, Anakisha. We come from Lush Valley, and these four are my brothers and sisters."

"And you?" Lars questioned a blond lad.

"The blue guards flew us here yesterday after a long journey from Western Settlement to Montanara. I'm Urs, eldest son of Anakisha's daughter Esmeralda. My father's Nick, the innkeeper." Urs rattled off the names of the five littlings with him.

Marlies spoke up from the back of the stage, "There's another grandchild in Last Stop, too."

"How many more of Anakisha's descendants are here?" muttered Tonio. "I know of two that currently aren't here."

Lars scratched his beard. He must ask Tonio who those two were.

"Great family reunion," a man called, voice laced with sarcasm. "But Ezaara is still not Anakisha's progeny, or male. Why is she Queen's Rider?"

"Who has seen Ezaara fly Zaarusha?" Lars boomed.

Across the cavern, a sea of hands rose like high tide.

"And who has seen her stunts?" Down the front, Lofty whistled. Others joined in, cheering.

"And who can do as well?"

The cavern remained silent.

Master Hans stepped forward. "As Ezaara's father, I've been loathe to speak, but Handel insists that my daughter can remain Queen's Rider while the prophecy is fulfilled."

"How do we know you're not lying?" someone jeered.

Handel leaped, landing on the edge of the stage, bronze scales gleaming. His roar made the air quiver. Flame shot from his jaws, scorching the vaulted ceiling. A backwash of heat licked over the crowd.

"I guess that answers that question," said Tonio dryly. "Any others?"

Perhaps it was Tonio's grim frown, or perhaps it was Handel's rage, but there were no more responses.

§

"Wake up, Lars!" Lars jerked awake as Singlar mind-melded again. *"Linaia's back."*

Lars thrust on his breeches and boots and rushed out to Singlar's den. He tugged his jerkin around him. Shards, it was cold. A bitter wind drove flurries of snow in from the ledge, whipping his hair across his forehead.

Linaia was huddled near the rock face under Singlar's wing.

Lars placed his hand on her head to mind-meld. *"Linaia, I'm glad you're home, but where is Adelina?"*

"She's been caught," the dragon whimpered, her blue scales fading to an icy hue. *"I don't know where Ezaara or Roberto are. The Queen's Rider may be captive too."*

Adelina had been foolish, going off like that, but still, worry gnawed at Lars' mind. So young, so full of life … *"Tomaaz, Kierion and two wizards are on their way to Death Valley on Riona and Maazini. Did you see them or Zaarusha?"*

"No." Linaia's head sank to the floor.

"The Master of Prophecy told me they're the best team to rescue the others. Hopefully, we'll have them all back soon." He removed his hand and melded with Singlar. *"Take care of her. For now, there's nothing else we can do. Their fate lies in Kierion and Tomaaz's hands."*

Homeward Bound

A blur of green trees rushed at Ezaara as Maazini lowered her toward the ground. *"Now, Ezaara."* He opened his talons, and she dropped, rolling as she hit the snow. Ezaara lay, staring at the drab desolate sky.

Maazini landed, then Tomaaz rushed over. "Ezaara, are you all right?" He helped her up and hugged her, not letting her go for a long while. At last, he pulled back, asking gently, "Did you find Roberto? Is he alive?"

She grimaced. "Alive. Hurt." Her chest ached. She hadn't saved him. Might have made things worse. She had no idea where Zaarusha was. And now Adelina was hurt, too. Her throat tightening with grief, hot tears slid down her cheeks.

"We'll come back for him, I promise," Tomaaz said with a ferocity that surprised her. "Gods, Ezaara, I thought we'd lost you."

"Roberto was limplocked. I gave him the remedy, but what if Zens gives him more?"

"We're taking you and Adelina home first. That's our priority." Tomaaz's voice was firm. "I'll come back with a ring and get him out."

Riona deposited Adelina on the grass. Kierion came over, with his arm around Adelina's shoulders, two men trailing him. "My honored Queen's Rider, you've already met Fenni. This is Jael." He gestured at the blond wizard and a Naobian—who looked so much like Roberto that her eyes pricked all over again.

They nodded at her as Kierion continued. "Tharuks are everywhere. With three of us riding each dragon, we can't risk them finding us. We're only stopping here for a bite to eat, then we'll press on to get some distance between us and Death Valley."

And Roberto.

The Naobian, Jael, passed them strips of dried beef and dried apples. "As soon as the dragons have fed, we'll be leaving." He motioned to the bushes. "I'd recommend a quick privy stop, but stay close to avoid tharuks."

The snow-tipped Terramites loomed above them, their shadows reaching deep into the forest. Ezaara shivered. It was no use mentioning Anakisha's ring. It worked for the rider wearing it and everyone their dragon was carrying, not for another dragon nearby. She couldn't disappear to Dragons' Hold, leaving three people on one dragon in the wilderness alone. The risk of being captured or hurt was too high. But it was four days' flight to the hold. Even with a ring on the return trip, that was at least four days until they returned.

Would Roberto still be alive?

§

When Roberto crested the peak, no one was manning the lookout towers. He couldn't figure it out—not a single tharuk was around. Something was up, but he was too exhausted and sore to care. He slid and tumbled down the slushy hillside, leaving streaks of soot and blood in the snow. Anyone could track him.

He pressed on. They'd be after him soon enough.

Emptiness gnawed in his gut. Was he walking away from Ezaara or toward her? He cast his mind out, trying to meld with her or Erob. Nothing. But he wouldn't give up.

Late in the morning, he entered Great Spanglewood Forest. Weaving between the trees, he came to a stream, scooping up a drink. His limbs throbbed, his back ached and his body was screaming, but if he rested, he'd never get up again. So he staggered on, the day wearing into afternoon.

One step. Another. And another …

Shards, he had to get to … where was he going? Why was his head throbbing and his back searing?

Left, right. Keep going. Another step. Through that puddle … over that log …

Roberto tripped, landing in a snow drift. He groaned and tried to push himself up, but his hands sunk into the snow. He tried to roll, but his stubborn body wouldn't budge. With one last desperate attempt, he sent out a mental cry for help before he collapsed.

§

Marlies poured Tonio a cup of tea. This would be tricky, but she had to try.

"Thank you, Marlies." Tonio eyed the brew warily.

"It's just soppleberry, nothing sinister." Marlies chuckled. "Come on, Tonio, I'm not about to poison my old spymaster."

He sniffed it, then took a sip. "Tasty, thank you." He flashed a wan smile—a tatty remnant of their former friendship—and had another sip. "What did you want to see me about?"

Marlies took a deep breath. "I don't think anyone else has the courage to tell you, so I will. You've changed, Tonio, and it's not for the better."

He bristled. "It's my job to be mistrustful. Whoever heard of a trusting, gullible spymaster?" Tonio snorted. "Huh!"

"That's always been your job, Tonio," she said gently. "Even when I knew you before. Remember how we checked every fact and rumor, and hunted down treachery? There wasn't a truth we didn't examine. Or a lie. Remember that Naobian merchant?"

"The one we caught smuggling dragonets?"

Marlies smiled. "That was a tricky situation, but we handled it impeccably."

Now, Tonio's grin was genuine. "You were brilliant. I never even knew you could play the gittern until that moment."

"And I didn't know you could juggle. Although I still think we should've left the merchant his gold."

"He wasn't much the poorer for losing that purse. Besides, that was justice for him trading in dragons."

"Yes," said Marlies. "You always were one for justice, weren't you?"

Tonio's brow drew into a thunderous scowl. "So that's what this is about," he snapped. "You want me to be lenient on Roberto for your daughter's sake." He stood, shoving his chair back.

"No, Tonio, that's not it." Marlies sipped, locking her eyes on his.

"Then what?" Tonio perched on the edge of his chair. "Don't fool with me, Marlies. I'm too shrewd for that."

He was. "No, this is about you, Tonio. You've become a bitter man, chasing vendettas. When I knew you, you were tough, ruthless when getting a job done, but you were fair."

"When my wife, Rosita died—"

"She was already dead for years when I met you again, so that's no excuse." Marlies cradled her tea in both hands, leaning over the table. "What happened, Tonio?" she asked softly.

His face crumpled. "You did," he whispered hoarsely.

She gasped, gut-smacked. "Me?"

"Yes, you." He tapped his nails on the table in woodpecker staccato. "Murdering that dragonet and forsaking us all. My best spy, my closest friend, gone."

Was that moisture glinting in his eyes? She'd missed them all, of course, but she'd had no choice. "I couldn't really come back to say hello."

"Why did you kill that dragonet?"

"I didn't," Marlies whispered—once again, seeing the fragile purple dragonet writhing in its translucent golden shell. "He gave his life to bless me with fertility. That's how I had the twins. For years, I felt guilty, until Maazini told me that the dragonet had seen a vision that I would give birth to an heir who would be Queen's Rider. He sensed I wasn't fertile and wanted to help."

Tonio's eyes flew wide, shock rippling over his face. "So, you didn't murder one of the last royal dragonets?"

"I thought I had, so I fled."

"I searched for you for years, attending every incident further afield than Montanara." Elbows on the table, Tonio put his head in his hands. "I trusted you. My only friend. And you betrayed me, sabotaging the realm and slaughtering the Queen's royal progeny. And I trusted Amato, too, and he…"

Marlies gripped his hand—harder than she'd intended. "I'm sorry, Tonio," she murmured. They'd been close, the best of friends—as spies had to be, to work well together. Her leaving had destroyed his trust in people—the last thing she'd wanted.

"These crystals, Marlies. I've been thinking …" His gaze was frank. "Is it possible that Zens used one on Amato?"

"Yes, it's possible." Marlies nodded. "So, Zens could've been driving Amato's behavior all along."

Tonio's shoulders slumped. "Oh gods, what have I done to Roberto?"

Marlies' heart tugged, as she'd known it would when he finally saw sense, but she had to drive the lesson home. "If we're going to win this war, we should be fighting with mages. We need to heal rifts, not create them."

A mask snapped over his face. "Lucky we have healers, then, isn't it?" He stood without a smile and walked to the door.

That stubborn fool. She'd hoped to win him over, had been so close, but Tonio's ugly pride had reared its head. Never mind, she had other nukils in this game. If she couldn't get Tonio to heal the rift, she'd bring the rift to him.

Marlies melded, *"Liesar, it's time to pay a visit to Mage Gate."*

The Rift

Marlies turned to Master Giddi and Giant John, behind her in the saddle. "You know Hans says this is our only chance?"

"That's why we're coming," said Giddi gruffly. "Now, get on with it."

"Ready, Liesar? Back to Dragons' Hold." Marlies rubbed Hans' ring. Mage Gate disappeared with a pop.

Behind Anakisha, there were dark rifts in the golden clouds. *"I'm pleased to see wizards, warriors and riders working together again,"* Anakisha said.

"Don't get too excited yet," Master Giddi muttered in Marlies' ear. Behind him, Giant John chuckled.

"Greetings, Anakisha." Marlies' throat tightened, remembering Anakisha's fall in battle. *"If possible, we'd like to appear in the den outside the infirmary, please."* No one must see her bringing the dragon mage into Dragons' Hold or there'd be an uproar—the only reason she'd risked using the ring.

Before they could utter *thank you*, Liesar was landing on the infirmary ledge. Marlies, Giddi and Giant John dismounted and rushed through the infirmary into Marlies and Hans' sleeping quarters.

"It's been so long." Hans embraced Giddi. "I'm sorry, you've lost so muc—"

"You've made sacrifices for the Realm yourselves," replied Giddi gruffly, cutting him off.

That short exchange made Marlies' throat tight again. So many losses. So much pain. So many years since they'd all worked together.

"Marlies," Hans said, "war council has started. I don't know how we're going to convince the council to work with mages again, but my visions have shown me that it's our only chance of success."

"Believe me, said Giddi, "if we pull this off, I'm going to have the same battle with the Wizard Council."

"Right, Hans," she replied. "I'll mind-meld when we're ready for you."

Once she was in the council chambers, Marlies took her seat, belly fluttering. "Master Lars, Hans is a little late, because he's meeting with visitors who could help shape our battle strategy." That should pique Aidan's interest, but would Lars buy into it?

"Excellent," said Lars. "They can speak after the master craftsman outlines his weapon-making plans."

"Thank you, that would be good."

"You hope," quipped Liesar.

"Hope's about all we've got," Marlies replied grimly, keeping her smile intact. Tonio's curious gaze burrowed into her.

When the discussion about the allocation of resources for weapons was winding down, she melded, *"Hans, now's about right."*

"Good, we'll be there soon." A short while later, there was the thump of Handel landing, and a knock at the chamber doors.

"Let them in," Tonio called.

A blue guard opened the double doors. Hans and Giant John walked in. Master Giddi swept through between them, cloak swirling and sparks dripping from his fingers.

Lars' face froze.

Tonio's face blackened. He leapt to his feet, pointing to the door with a trembling finger. "Get out!"

Giddi's gaze grew hard. "I told you it was no use, Marlies," he said bitterly.

"I've invited Master Giddi to speak to us." Marlies inhaled deeply. "If you won't listen, Dragons' Hold can get another master healer." She stalked from her seat to stand with Master Giddi. Giant John and Hans closed ranks on either side of them. Talons scraped on stone behind her. The huff of Handel's breath warmed her neck. Judging from the expressions around the table, they looked formidable. The doors thudded shut.

"You've made a grave error in judgment, Marlies," Lars snapped, glaring at her with icy eyes.

"I say we vote on it," said Hendrick, master craftsman.

"Vote?" Tonio spat.

"A vote will be binding," Lars pointed out. "Are we voting on dismissing Marlies as master healer? Or about casting this traitor out of our midst?"

"Traitor?" Giddi muttered, bristling.

Marlies straightened her shoulders. "Without Giddi and the Wizard Council, we won't win this war. We'll all be slaughtered, so there'll be no point in having healers."

"Or a Master of Prophecy," Hans said. "I've seen a vision of the slaughter. This is our only chance."

"You're bluffing. You've pledged to serve Zaarusha."

"We don't want our riders to fight a losing battle," said Marlies. "We must work together to oust Zens."

"Wizards admitted Zens in the first place," Tonio snarled. "Now you want us to trust them? Next you'll be asking us to work with spangles."

"If we must, Tonio." Marlies stared him straight in the eye.

"No one's seen sight of them for years," Lars burst out.

"If I may—" started Giddi.

"No, you may not," snapped Lars, face flushed. "You definitely may not. We'll put it to a vote. Raise your hand if you're prepared to listen to the wizard. Hans and Marlies may not vote, because their tenure is on the line. Marlies, Hans, if you don't like our decision, you'll have to step down."

Nodding curtly, Marlies pursed her lips. Her threat would be worth it, if it swayed them. But would it?

Hans melded with her, *"Shards, Marlies, we've only been back a moon or two and you're risking everything."*

"I had no other nukils to throw on the table." He'd stand beside her, no matter what.

Lars' eyes were fierce. "This vote is binding. Raise your hand if you want to hear Marlies' proposal."

With Ezaara, Roberto and Master Shari's replacement absent, two masters dead, and Hans and Marlies excluded, not all could vote.

The battle master's hand shot up. "Think of the strategic advantage," Aidan muttered, "if they don't betray us."

Derek, master of instruction, raised his arm, mumbling, "I've always liked magically-enhanced weapons."

Alyssa, master of flight, spoke directly to Marlies. "I don't like it, but I don't want to lose our healer."

"I ignored the evidence against Bruno and Fleur. I won't be closed-minded again." Hendrik put his hand up too.

"I will side with Lars and Tonio." Master Archer Jerrick left his hands on the table. "Even though one of my dear friends is on the Wizard Council, my loyalty lies here."

Tonio sat with his arms crossed in front of him, jaw clenched.

"I said the vote was binding. I hope I won't regret this," Lars said. "Mages got us into this. Without Mazyka's headlong quest for power, we wouldn't have Zens or those bloodthirsty tharuks destroying our realm. Our people would not be enslaved, dying by the hundreds, tortured and without hope, in the dreary hell he's created. Such was the blessing bestowed by an errant wizard and her foolhardy master."

A buzz of power emanated from Giddi.

Lars came around to the front of the table, face to face with Giddi. "You were our friends and we fought together, but I'm not at liberty to put the past behind me on a whim at the Wizard Council's request. The damage has been too great."

Head high, Giddi's eyes flashed. "The Wizard Council do not wish to treat with you. They're bigger fools than you are. I'm here because my friend Marlies, and Kierion, a young dragon rider, thought the realm could be saved. They're right—the only way we'll triumph is to fight together—but I'm not begging for your allegiance." Giddi's cloak swished as he strode to the door. Halfway, he spun, jabbing his finger at Tonio. "Never belittle the spangles again. You may have need of them yet."

Raised voices sounded outside the doors, and Lovina burst inside, face flushed. "Excuse me, Masters, but I've seen a vision. Tharuks will kill all the wizards in the Spanglewood by nightfall, unless we stop them." She held up a painting, showing a bloody massacre.

A shiver rippled down Marlies' spine.

Giddi barked at Hans, "You're still Master of Prophecy. How reliable is she?"

"She's always been right, so far."

Shards, if they didn't accept the wizards, it would be all-out slaughter. "Council masters, I implore you. We have a duty to protect every citizen of Dragons' Realm, no matter their vocation," Marlies pleaded. "Please, we can't let this threat go unchecked. What if tharuks were killing your family?"

A pointed gaze passed between Lars and Tonio. The spymaster nodded.

"We've all taken vows to protect the citizens of Dragons' Realm, whether we like them or not." Lars was all action. "Masters, meld with your dragons, and mobilize all dragons and riders," he commanded. "Giddi, meld with Singlar and tell him where the wizards are. We'll bring them to the hold."

Thunder flashed across Giddi's face, sending a jolt through Marlies. No one ordered the dragon mage about.

"Hurry," said Lars. "We may not like you, but we don't want Zens to kill the last handful of your kind."

"The last handful?" said Giddi dryly. "There may be more of us than you think."

Home

Torches flickered in the downdraft of their dragons' wingbeats as Singlar and Antonika landed on the stage near the few members of the council that remained at the hold. Lars slid from Singlar's back and held his hand high. The main cavern was packed, but gradually, the crowd settled into silence.

"The rumors are true," Lars said. "Tharuks have been hunting wizards in Spanglewood, so we're taking in refugees. We're expecting guests at any moment."

Angry mutters rippled through the crowd.

Lars raised his voice, overriding them. "Yes, years ago, wizards brought peril into our realm. Because of them, we're battling tharuks today. But we cannot stand aside and let Zens slaughter our people—mages or not, we've sworn to protect everyone."

An older rider hollered, "It's a mage trick. They'll slaughter us in our sleep."

Now, that was just ridiculous. Lars shook his head. "Wizards don't kill riders, only tharuks."

The man yelled back, "No, but they let in Zens, who slaughtered my parents. I say we make 'em pay."

"Zens killed my sister's whole family before my eyes."

"I don't want wizards at my hearth."

He understood it, he really did. But despite his feelings, he had to abide by his vows and the council's vote. Lars motioned to Tonio, who blew his horn. The deep note reverberated off the cavern walls.

Tonio stepped forward. "I understand. I, too, have lost family to Zens. But it's Zens we want to fight, not wizards. They let him in, but they haven't stopped fighting him since. We can't allow them to be slaughtered right on our doorstep out of spite. And they won't be here forever."

An uneasy silence before a hand shot up. "How long will they stay?"

"Only as long as necessary, believe me," Lars said, eliciting a few chuckles.

A lad called out, "Long enough for me to learn magic?"

A ripple of laughter broke out. Good, this battle was half won.

"Lars," melded Singlar, "*Seppi will be here any moment with half the blue guard.*"

By the Egg! "*Half the blue guard? How many mages is he bringing?*"

"*Some of them are still fighting. Others will be here on the morrow.*"

Lars turned to Tonio. "Call the council together."

Tonio motioned them into a huddle and Lars broke the news. "It sounds if we'll have nearly a hundred mages turning up. The main cavern is the only place big enough to sleep them all, although they'll need to warm it with mage flame."

"We don't want them getting too cozy, or they may decide to stay," said Tonio.

"And supplies?" asked Lars. "How's our food looking with additional mouths to feed?"

"We have plenty," Hendrik said. "As long as they're not here too long."

Lars nodded. "That's not our intention. This is temporary. Any extra bedding in the infirmary, Marlies?"

"Some. We'll ask families to bring spare blankets and quilts."

"Right." Lars turned to the crowd.

People were staring at the entrances high in the cavern walls. The blue guards were arriving. Seppi led them, spiraling down. In tight formation, the ring of dragons created a powerful downdraft. Many were carrying a rider and two mages. More mage-bearing dragons followed, joining the spiral.

"Where have they all come from?" Lars asked Marlies.

"Naobia, Spanglewood and the Flatlands. We're lucky most of them were gathered at Mage Gate for their wizard trials. Now, we can train our riders to work with them more easily."

"Marlies." Tonio nodded tersely. "I misjudged the situation. With these numbers, as long as there are no rogue mages, they could be an asset."

Despite himself, Lars had to agree. Imagine all that firepower.

Talons scratched stone as dragons landed and their passengers disembarked. Most of the blue guards carried four full saddlebags, and the rearmost wizards had bedding strapped to their backs.

"I thought they'd left in a hurry," said Lars. "How did they have time to pack?"

Marlies smiled. "I expect they used magic."

"Well," said Tonio, grinning, his hand drifting to his sword, "if they think they can move in permanently, I know some magic that would send them packing."

§

It'd been ten days since Marlies had sent Ezaara to Death Valley. Ten days of her waiting up at night, worrying whether she'd sent her daughter to her death by encouraging her to chase after the young Naobian master.

Marlies had known Mazyka, and fought beside her. Understood the pain Master Giddi had gone through and why he loved her so much. She'd been brilliant. Impulsive. And loyal. Mazyka had taken a large contingent of mages through the world gate to Zens' world to find a means of destroying Zens. She'd been trying to fix her mistake. But both councils had misunderstood and assumed she was seeking more power.

And they'd insisted Giddi lock her out forever.

She shook her head. In her eyes, that gave this council no reason to ban her daughter from loving who she wanted. But had her encouragement—and her wrath at Tonio's hatred for Roberto—sealed Ezaara's fate?

Liesar mind-melded, *"Riona and Maazini are approaching, bringing Ezaara."*

Thank the flaming First Egg and dragon gods. "And Adelina?"

"They have her too. They're injured, but all alive."

She sighed in relief. They'd made it. Injuries she could heal, but she couldn't bring anyone back from the dead.

"And Roberto?"

"Still captive."

That poor man. How much could one person withstand? She whirled. "Hans, Leah, Tomaaz is bringing Ezaara and Adelina home. Ready the clean herb, bandages, clear-mind berries and limplock remedy."

"I'll make sure we have piaua on hand too. Is Ezaara all right?" Hans melded as she organized supplies with Leah.

Marlies strode to the ledge. *"She's alive. In this game, that's what counts."*

§

Ezaara had stayed the night in the infirmary, being mollycoddled and healed by Ma, lectured by Lars and Tonio about losing the dragon queen, and soothed by Pa. Tomaaz got it. He knew there wasn't much to celebrate—they'd left Roberto and Zaarusha behind. Jael and Fenni, the two mages, got it too. All of them were determined to return. But the council had expressly forbidden her to leave the hold. And without Zaarusha she couldn't go anywhere.

She reached her cavern, entered and closed the door. Leaning her back against the sturdy wood, the aching hole in her chest caved in. She slid to the floor and buried her head in her hands. Was this what it meant to love? To feel the heart-wrenching agony of leaving Roberto alone in a filthy, stinking hole with a vicious enemy? What if he never came back?

Gods, what use was being Queen's Rider without Roberto? And what was a Queen's Rider without a queen? Where was Zaarusha? Ezaara had assumed she was back at the hold, but no one had seen her since the feast. Eleven days ago. What if Zaarusha were dead? Her chest grew tight. It was hard to breathe.

Her few days in Death Valley felt like years. Roberto had been there for weeks. And she'd thought she could rescue him. If only she'd rallied the council, done a better job of convincing—

"Ezaara," a dragon melded, breaking into her thoughts.

A familiar voice. One she hadn't heard for a while. *"Erob? Shards, I'm so sorry, I tried, but …"* Tears ran down her cheeks, salt sliding over her lips.

"Ezaara, you should bathe. You'll want to smell sweet for Roberto."

"Very funny." The thought made her cry harder.

"No, Ezaara, I'm serious. Zaarusha melded and she's bringing him home."

Zaarusha? And Roberto? Something light and sweet unfurled in her chest. *"They're safe?"*

"Yes, she's bringing him here. I've already told Maazini not to go back to Death Valley. Did you want me to ask Liesar to send Marlies here?"

"No, not yet." Scrambling to her feet, Ezaara dashed to her bedside drawer and pulled out some healing supplies, spreading them on her bed. It might be greedy, but she wanted her first moments with Roberto alone.

A thud sounded on the ledge. A few heartbeats later, Erob's head poked through the archway from Zaarusha's den. He breathed over her bathtub, heating the water. *"They're going to be a while yet. You'll feel better greeting him without the stench of tharuk in your hair."*

Ezaara threw her arms around Erob's warm scaly neck. "Thank you." This time, her tears were tears of gratitude.

"I'll warn you when they reach Dragon's Teeth." Erob retreated to the ledge, his wingbeats sending flurries of snow through the den as he took to the sky to meet his mother and his rider.

Ezaara shut the door, abandoned her filthy riders' garb, and sank into the warm water.

A short while later, she was combing her hair, when Zaarusha melded. *"Ezaara, he's home."* A wave of the queen's exhaustion washed over Ezaara, making her knees falter.

"Hang on, Zaarusha, I'm coming." She rushed outside to the ledge.

Zaarusha was descending, holding Roberto's limp body in her talons.

A chill breeze slid along Ezaara's damp scalp, making her shiver. *"Is he dead?"*

"Not quite." Zaarusha descended, lowering Roberto toward the ledge.

Ezaara rushed over, arms out, to receive him. The queen delicately lowered him into her embrace.

Zaarusha nuzzled her neck. *"Must hunt."* She flew with ragged wingbeats toward the hunting grounds.

Roberto was bloody, gaunt and bitterly cold. So unlike himself, her eyes pricked. Ezaara carried him inside and laid him on her bed. Moments later, Erob's bulk filled the archway as he squeezed his head and a shoulder through the door. *"How is he?"*

The shackle marks on his wrist and ankle were raw and weepy. Ezaara cut open the sides of his ratty breeches and shirt to check his body for injuries. The old wounds she'd healed in Death Valley were overlaid with fresh gashes and bruises. An angry welt had raised a lump on his back.

"Erob, please warm this water for clean herb infusion."

"Gladly." Solemn-eyed, the dragon huffed his breath over the cup.

Ezaara began the painstaking process of cleansing and tending his wounds. She used healing salve, stitched the worst of his slashes shut, and applied piaua juice. This morning, in the infirmary, she'd overheard Ma telling Leah they didn't have much piaua left. Guilt flashed through her. Zens had smashed Ezaara's precious vials of the restorative juice when he'd battered her. Maybe she shouldn't have taken so many with her. She'd thought she could heal some slaves, but she'd barely escaped with her life.

"Ezaara, my son is blocking the archway. How's Roberto?" Zaarusha asked.

"I'm healing him now, but he's still unconscious."

"I'm sorry I wasn't there when you escaped. Tharuks were attacking Monte Vista, so I had to defend our people. It's been a long flight. I'm going to rest."

"Thank you for bringing him home. I'm glad you're back. Sleep well."

Erob shifted, adjusting his weight. *"He's tough, you know."*

"No one should have to withstand this." Anger burned through Ezaara. *"I have an arrow with Zens' name on it. One day I'll fire it."*

"I hate what Zens has done to him, but do you know what's special about Roberto?" Erob asked.

Everything. "What?"

"Zens taught him how to manipulate human minds—a terrible power to wield. Yet he only uses his talents for good."

True. Even though Roberto had been through hell, he'd risen above it.

Ezaara looked at her unconscious lover. His face was sunken, making his cheekbones stand out like mountain ridges. Dark shadows lay under his eyes. She'd healed his broken nose, cleansed the blood from his face, yet under the wear and tear of his captivity he was still beautiful.

But what had Zens done to his mind? Had he broken him? Would he rise above this too?

§

Adelina cautiously opened Ezaara's door. Ezaara, sitting at Roberto's bedside, glanced up. "Come in," she said softly.

Adelina approached the bed. Roberto was home. He was here. Breath rushed into her lungs. She hadn't even realized she'd been holding it. "He's thin, isn't he?" And as pale as death.

"He has a lot of new scars, even with piaua."

And those were only the physical ones. What mental torture had Zens inflicted upon her brother? Would he scream in the deep of the night, the way he had for two years after last escaping Zens? Adelina sat and stroked his hand. It didn't matter. No matter how badly damaged he was, he was her family.

§

"You're joking? All the mages are here?" Fenni asked.

Master Giddi's infamous eyebrows wiggled an affirmative. Fenni had never thought he'd be so happy to see those sharding eyebrows again.

"How are the riders reacting?" Jael asked, getting up off the pallet they'd given him in Tomaaz's cavern.

Giddi shrugged. "Time will tell."

Giant John leaned back against the wall. "Fighting tharuks together helped form some bonds between riders and mages. You missed a ferocious battle."

What exactly had gone down at Mage Gate? "There's only one thing I want to know," Fenni said. "Did anyone shoot fireballs from underwater?"

Jael chuckled.

Master Giddi only lifted his eyebrow again. *"I told you the main purpose of that exercise was to help your control,"* he mind-melded.

"Will you get out of my head?" Fenni thought back. All that training and he'd missed the best fight.

"*Sure,*" Giddi melded.

What? He'd just mind-melded back. Fenni gaped at Giddi, but his master just laughed.

"Don't worry, Fenni," Master Giddi said. "It won't be the last battle. Spanglewood is teeming with tharuks."

"Good," said Fenni. "Kierion, Jael and I have ideas for training mages and riders together. Can we try them?"

"Try whatever you want," Giddi chuckled. "Just don't get flamed by an irate dragon."

Giddi didn't think he was serious. Just wait until he saw what they'd planned.

There was a bang at the door, and Hans entered. "Giddi, there's been bad news. The Wizard Council have done a head count. Two young mages have been taken by tharuks—Velrama and Sorcha," Hans said. "Apparently the tharuks boasted Zens is hunting for you, as well."

Master Giddi was on his feet in a heartbeat, striding to the door.

Jael nudged Fenni. "Those were the two mages who were dueling when Sorcha was disqualified. The girl who made the doorway in the ice wall."

"Shards, they're so young. Only our age." Kierion was suddenly glad he'd missed the battle.

Shadows

Roberto had been cold, cold, cold for so long. Now he was warm. Bleary peace stole through him. He could sleep like this forever. Never wake up. A face flashed to mind. Deep green eyes that he could lose himself in, blonde hair, and a smile to die for. Ezaara. That's right, he'd been searching for her, but now he was too tired, so he'd just stay asleep, roaming the halls of his lost mind.

Wait—he couldn't sleep in this snow drift forever. He'd die. But why was he warm? Snow burn? Or numb nerves? He had to keep moving.

Roberto stirred, his limbs heavy. Most of his pain was gone. He dragged his eyelids open.

He was no longer in the forest. There was still a blanket of white, but it wasn't snow; it was Ezaara's quilt—white, edged with golden dragons. He was home. The gods knew how, but he'd made it. If he wasn't so tired, he'd be joyful. He sighed, his eyelids fluttering closed again.

He forced them open. There she was: looking every bit as lovely as his dream, bending over a table, sorting herbs into pouches. The torchlight played across her blonde hair like sun on liquid honey.

Writhing shadows flickered at the edge of his vision. His knife, resting on the bedside table, called to him, the shine of its blade alluring. His fingers fastened around the handle. Its grip felt good, so natural. He had to use it.

His gaze fastened on the beautiful girl at the table. Shadows writhed around her, beckoning him forward.

Roberto slid his feet noiselessly to the floor, holding the knife at his side where it wouldn't be seen.

§

Ezaara put clean herb into a pouch and tied it, then poured some soppleberries into another. It was better than wearing a hole in the stone with her boots. Hopefully Roberto would wake without some gods-awful head injury or permanent damage. The dull ache in her chest hadn't eased completely. It wouldn't until she knew he was well.

"*Liesar, when's Ma coming to check on him?*"

"She knows he's here, Ezaara, please be patient. She has injured wizards in the infirmary."

And a helper. Couldn't Leah take care of them? This was Roberto, for the Egg's sake. A master on the council.

How would it be, loving him, now that she was no longer his trainee? Glorious, no doubt. She hardly dared hope he'd recover.

A scrape sounded on the floor. She glanced up. Roberto was standing by the bed, wan and thin. Seeing him awake was like the sun breaking through storm clouds. Everything was going to be all right. "Roberto. You're up. Welcome home."

"Hello, Ezaara."

His voice was strained, poor thing. "How do your legs feel?" She stood, her chair scraping stone.

He shuddered at the noise. The tiny moon-shaped scar below his eye twitched as he prowled across the cavern. "My legs are fine. Thank you for healing them." His voice was stilted, not like Roberto.

Something was wrong. Even in Death Valley he hadn't stared at her like that. As if she were prey. "Roberto, I've missed you." She tried for bright and cheery, but her voice squeaked.

Roberto's face twisted into an ugly grimace. He lunged, slamming her against the wall. A blade flashed. In a heartbeat, his knife was at her throat.

Oh gods, Handel's prophecy had come true: Roberto was attacking her. She'd tried multiple times to deny it, but her father's bronze dragon had shown her a vision of Roberto lunging at her. And then, they'd seen it again. They'd seen *now*.

"Now we can talk, Queen's Rider," Roberto sneered.

"Zaaru—" An iron wall slammed across her mind, blocking her attempt to meld with the queen.

"Your mental talents are puny compared to mine." His thoughts were dark, evil, like a choking fog.

Ezaara snapped meld and blocked his probing mind. Her throat grew tight. This man was not Roberto. His eyes glinted with malice, the whites tinged yellow—Zens had gotten to him.

"You, an ignorant little farm girl from Lush Valley thought you could waltz in here and become Queen's Rider? Thought you could take me for your lover— the man with the best mental skills in Dragons' Realm? I, who have learned from the master of the mind."

Dragon's flaming claws and teeth. He was gone. The man she loved was gone. This was Roberto's shell, controlled by Zens. Ezaara's hope crumbled. Zens had broken Roberto physically and mentally. He'd found a way to steal her lover's mind, chaining it to his will.

Her thoughts raced. She couldn't let Zens win.

Roberto would be weak. She could probably fight him and break free. But she'd be pitting him against her, not winning him over.

She'd better play this cool, downplay his aggression.

"Oh, Roberto, you're testing my skills." She faked a laugh, but it came out strangled. The knife pricked her skin, stinging. Warm blood trickled down her neck, under her collar. "It's been a while since we've had a training session. You've been through quite a rough time. You know, maybe it would be better to have a cup of tea and train later?" His eyes narrowed and he licked his lips as she mentioned tea. He was bound to be hungry and thirsty. "Look, I have fresh soppleberries, right here."

He glanced down at the table, the pressure of his knife easing.

What else? If Zens had turned him, perhaps she needed to remind him of who he was and whom he loved. "Have you missed Erob?"

"Erob?" Wistfulness flashed across Roberto's face. "Yes, I've missed him." The tension on the blade loosened. Then his face contorted with hate. "Sharding dragons." The blade bit into her flesh again.

"Yes, they're so fickle, terrible creatures, aren't they? Remember the time Erob met you in Death Valley and saved you from Zens? I'll just pop the tea on, shall I?"

He frowned. "I like soppleberry tea, don't I?"

Gods, Roberto's mind was truly gone. Her eyes stung. "Yes, you love it," Ezaara said. "I'll make a cup now. Please, take a seat, Master Roberto."

He shook his head, as if to clear it. The knife clattered to the floor, his arms hanging limp at his sides.

Ezaara pulled out a seat. "Please, sit down." Whatever it was that was driving him, he was battling it. He wasn't completely under its control—yet.

Roberto picked up the knife and jammed it into his belt, taking a seat. "Thank you, my Queen's Rider."

Shards, she'd hoped to grab the weapon while he was distracted. Ezaara threw some soppleberries into two cups. "I'll only be a moment." She rushed out to the ledge, getting Zaarusha to heat the tea. Thank the Egg, Erob wasn't around. It would break his heart to see Roberto like this—just as it was breaking hers. She blinked away tears. Not now.

Ezaara crumbled a double dose of woozy weed into his cup and bustled back inside.

Roberto was cleaning his fingernails with his knife. "How did you know I wouldn't kill you?" he asked, his voice as chill as the ice on Dragons' Hold's lake.

She forced a brittle laugh. "Here you go, tea for two. Drink up. Would you like some food? You must be hungry." Ezaara took a huge sip and smiled, her heart splintering into thousands of tiny icy shards.

Who was this man? Roberto hadn't come home at all.

§

Ezaara was so beautiful, so sweet, giving him tea. The tart berries soothed his raw throat, the warmth stealing through him.

Dark fog crept along the edge of Roberto's vision. Murky blackness writhed across Ezaara's face and curled its fingers around her throat. *"Kill her,"* it whispered. *"No, she isn't beautiful. She's a usurper. Zens is the rightful leader of the realm. This girl is puny, breakable. Zens will reward you finely if you're brave enough to spill her blood."*

Of course he was brave. He'd stood up to Amato hundreds of times, taking Adelina's beatings. He'd killed tharuks and slaves for Zens before. He had courage enough to kill this wench.

He saw himself slitting Ezaara's throat, her beautiful blood spraying high, dribbling red down the cavern walls.

Smiling, Roberto sipped his tea. He'd bide his time and strike when Ezaara trusted him.

§

Roberto's head slumped to the tabletop. He snored softly.

Ezaara removed the knife from his grip and turned it over in her hands. He'd wanted to kill her. She'd seen it in his eyes. She turned the knife again. He might have, had she not knocked him out. The irony hit her. She'd been sitting here, desperate for him to wake, and now he was out cold again.

She spun the knife in her fingers, then spun it again.

There was a whump on the ledge outside, and Erob melded, *"How's Roberto?"*

Ezaara blocked her thoughts, staring into space as her fingers flicked the knife again. And again.

"Ezaara." Erob's tone was frantic. *"What aren't you telling me? Is Roberto dead?"*

He might as well be. The man she'd loved was gone.

§

RIDERS OF FIRE

Marlies hurried along the tunnel, a bag of healing supplies slung over her shoulder. Liesar said Ezaara had requested her hours ago, but there'd been one injured mage after another in the infirmary. Finally, she'd left Leah and Lovina in charge, so she could visit her daughter.

She cricked her neck. Tiredness dogged her steps every day since she'd returned from Death Valley. She'd been trying to hide it, but her bones knew—and Hans knew—just how exhausted she was.

Marlies opened Ezaara's door. "By the dragon gods," she murmured.

The torches had burned down, sputtering in their sconces, casting a pale glow over a tableau: Master Roberto was hunched over a table, sleeping, and Ezaara was sitting opposite him, twirling a knife in her hands. Light glanced off the blade as it slid across her skin. Then again.

It was Ezaara's face that made Marlies suck her breath in. Blood at her throat, eyes vacant and dried streaks on her cheeks, she stared into nothing. Marlies had seen people in severe shock—usually after an accident or the death of a loved one. But Master Roberto's breathing was even—he was alive.

She moved slowly into the cavern, keeping her voice low and even. "Ezaara."

Ezaara jolted. The knife clattered on stone.

Roberto grunted in his sleep.

Ezaara's hand flew to her mouth, panic on her face. "Don't wake him," she hissed.

Marlies placed a hand on her daughter's shoulder and crouched to look in her eyes. "Why not?" She whispered.

"Roberto's home, Ma, but he's dead inside. Zens is controlling him."

§

Ma picked up a cup and sniffed it. "How much woozy weed did you give him? How long has he been out?"

"A double dose." Shards, how long had it been? It felt like forever. "I don't know … um … four hundred and two knife turns?"

"We've no time to lose. Help me lift him."

They carried Roberto over to her bed. He was so light, so thin. "Ma, this isn't something a simple remedy or surgery can fix."

"Actually, it might be. Let me see. Do you have any rope?"

"Yes, in Zaarusha's saddlebags." She melded, *Zaarusha?*

On my way. How can I help?

Ezaara rushed out to the den as Zaarusha landed.

A worried Erob butted her with his snout. *"Is Roberto all right?"*

Ezaara shared her memory of Roberto's attack with both of them as she fished in Zaarusha's saddlebags for rope. When she went back inside, Ma was examining Roberto's chest and arms.

"You've done a good job of healing him, Ezaara. Did you see any unusual bumps or swelling? Anything that wouldn't heal properly?"

"Yes, under his right shoulder blade." She turned him over and lifted his shirt. "Here." The angry red bump glared at them.

"Zens may have implanted a crystal inside Roberto that controls his thoughts and actions. Sofia had one, too. Let's tie him down."

Ezaara tied Roberto's wrists to the bed, while Ma tied his legs. So cruel. He'd only just escaped shackles and now she was the one tying him. The irony made the icy shards of her heart twist deeper into her chest.

Ma lit a new torch so they could see, then sliced along the apex of the lump in his flesh. Ezaara staunched the blood seeping over his back. Inside the wound, something yellow glinted. Ma squeezed the edges of the wound. Red and yellow rivulets ran out of the wound, leaving trails over his back. Ma edged the crystal out of Roberto's body.

"Help me," she grunted.

Ezaara applied pressure to the sides of his wound. A blood-smeared yellow stone—as long as Ezaara's finger and twice as thick—slithered out onto Roberto's back.

Roberto's body tensed, then went limp.

"This stone is how Zens controls people?"

Ma nodded. "Fleur did the same to Sofia. We found that Unocco—the dragon that the traitor Bruno used to ride—had a crystal embedded under his wing." Bitterness flashed across Ma's face. "It's strange, because Fleur only used swayweed with Ajeuria, yet they implanted Sofia and Unocco. I can't figure out why."

Why had Ma looked so bitter? Fleur and Bruno had been from Montanara, and Ma had grown up there. On a hunch, Ezaara asked, "Did you know Bruno?"

Ma gave her an odd look. "I just found out yesterday that Master Bruno was the same man who had run the Nightshader crew in Montanara—a terrible street gang who stole from littlings and beat people up. I'm glad he's been banished. Now take that crystal to Zaarusha so she can destroy it."

The crystal emanated an angry hum, like a swarm of bees, against her fingertips. Ezaara rushed outside.

"*Drop it,*" commanded Zaarusha. She blasted the stone with dragon flame until it was a bubbling mass, giving off a nasty stink. "*Don't breathe in the fumes,*" Zaarusha warned. "*Who knows what they'll do.*"

Erob sidestepped the bubbling mess, lowering his head to gaze at Ezaara with golden eyes. Ezaara rubbed his eye ridge. "*What is it?*"

"*Zens nearly broke Roberto,*" Erob said, the wave of his sorrow socking Ezaara's stomach. "*If Roberto had succeeded in killing you, he would've been filled with self-loathing. We would've lost our Queen's Rider and one of our most valuable masters.*"

Ezaara nodded, swallowing. They'd been lucky.

Prophecy

Roberto woke face down in bed, his back on fire. The swirling dark mist that had teased the edges of his mind was gone. So were the whispering voices, thank the Egg. His head was clear for the first time since leaving Death Valley. He stretched and winced. His right shoulder blade burned with pain.

He rolled onto his left side.

Ezaara was asleep in an armchair by the bed. A pale shaft of sunlight filtered through a crack in a stone shutter, falling across her cheek, highlighting the freckles on her nose. He'd first seen them when she'd flown her first loop on Zaarusha—the day he'd sworn to be her protector.

Strange, he hadn't noticed her freckles in all these moons. He lay there, watching her breathe. He was so lucky.

Shards. Lucky she was alive. Memories of him holding a knife to her throat rushed through his head. Shame and remorse flooded him. He wasn't her protector—he'd been a heartbeat away from murdering her. He was a worthless piece of shrot. His stomach tied itself in painful knots. Zens had been right. He'd made him his beast, no better than a stinking tharuk. He'd nearly killed the woman he loved—the Queen's Rider, for the dragons gods' sake.

Ezaara opened her eyes.

Skewered by his memories, Roberto froze, a dark pit gaping inside him.

He opened his mouth. No words came out. No excuse for making her bleed.

Her green eyes regarded him.

He saw the blade, him holding it. Lunging, slamming her against the wall. And using that sharding knife. Always the knife—again and again—glinting red with the promise of death. Her death, the woman he loved. The memory burned through his mind, worse than Zens' torture.

Ezaara slipped into his mind. *"Show me."*

He tried to hide the memories, the shame, but she wrapped her warm presence around his thoughts, and watched with him, her love shining through the darkness, like a beacon fire welcoming him home.

Tears wet on his cheeks, he stared at her unmoving.

Her eyes bright with tears, she whispered, "Welcome home. I've missed you."

§

When she'd left Death Valley, Roberto had been a broken man, weeping on the stone floor. Now, he was home, but still broken, weeping beside her. His ebony eyes were filled with the horror of what he'd done. Anguish painted his features. His chest heaved with sobs.

As he'd been sleeping, Ezaara had wondered how she could ever trust him. And here was her answer.

This is what Zens had wanted. To destroy the man she loved.

And so Ezaara reached down within herself, dragging up courage she didn't know she had, and stroked his cheek. "Roberto, do you remember what you promised me?"

He stopped sobbing, eyes wide. Tentatively, he reached up and cupped her hand where it lay against his face. His touch was warm, gentle. "I remember," he whispered, soft as a moth's wing, husky with love and grief.

This was the Roberto she loved. The man who'd spent all night carving a cane for her when she'd first arrived here. The man who'd helped hone her skills, offered his life to protect her. *Bled* for her.

He was not the man who'd held a knife at her throat. No—that was Zens.

And so she said what she'd been wanting to say ever since he'd left. What she'd been saving up for when he returned. And what she wanted with all her heart.

"Are you ready to ask my parents?" She leaned in, brushing her lips across his.

He nodded and kissed her back, his lips as welcoming as a soft spring rain.

§

Roberto ran a hand through his hair, then tugged his jerkin. He paced outside the door, then scratched his chin. This was stupid. He'd faced the horrors of Death Valley, but couldn't face Ezaara's parents. He knocked on the door, then immediately wished he hadn't.

Ezaara's mother knew what he'd done. Would she forgive him? Or banish him like a rogue dragon?

Hans opened the door. "Come in, Roberto."

He wiped his palm on his breeches and shook Hans' hand. "Morning."

Hans ushered him inside. The entrance tunnel swallowed him and the door thudded shut. Hans showed him into the family's living area.

Marlies looked up. "Morning, Roberto, how are you feeling?"

"Fine, um, thanks." How did you thank someone for saving you from murdering their daughter? He was mired in dragon dung.

"Hey, Roberto, good to see you on your feet." Tomaaz gave him a bear hug.

Roberto hadn't expected that. He hugged him back. "Thanks for getting Erob home."

Tomaaz shook his head, green eyes blazing—so similar to his twin sister. "I'm sorry I couldn't get you out."

Roberto shrugged, then cleared his throat.

Tomaaz winked. "Come on, Taliesin, let's go and look at Lovina's latest painting."

"Sure," the slave boy grinned, trailing Tomaaz out the door.

"So, he's talking now?"

Hans chuckled. "And so are you. Please sit down, Roberto." He gestured to a sofa.

Roberto sat. He may as well get straight to it. "I, ah, would like permission to, um, be hand-fasted to your daughter, Ezaara."

"I assume you've asked her if she's keen?" Hans asked, emerald eyes gauging him.

He nodded.

Marlies leaned forward. "Roberto, I gave Ezaara my blessing to go to Death Valley and find you."

He sucked in his breath. "You did? Why?"

She counted her reasons off on her fingers. "Firstly, I wanted to prevent your needless death. Secondly, she loves you, so why would I hold her back? Thirdly, Tonio had made it clear the council weren't going to rescue you because he had a vendetta against Amato. That wasn't fair. No one should pay with their life for their parents' mistakes."

It always came back to his father. Every foul rotten thing came down to his father. No. His father had been turned by Zens, maybe even with one of those yellow crystals.

Zens was the one to blame for every disaster in his life.

"Son," said Hans, grasping his hand across the low table. "As long as the council is happy with you being hand-fasted to the Queen's Rider, we welcome you and Adelina to our family."

A family? Roberto swallowed. It had been so long.

§

That afternoon, Tonio cornered Ezaara in the tunnels. "My Queen's Rider, Marlies told me about the crystal. I suspected Roberto may have been turned."

Anger burned in Ezaara's belly. "We've extracted the crystal, and he's in perfect control of himself." She glared at Tonio. "Don't ever accuse him of being a traitor again. Having his gut slit in the Robandi desert and being held in Death Valley was punishment enough for his father's crimes."

"Roberto doesn't need to be punished for his father's crimes. Zens is to blame. I see that now." Tonio shook his head. "I've been talking to Master Giddi, your parents and Kierion. We must work with mages to wipe Zens and his armies out."

Gods, where had that come from?

Tonio grasped her hand, shaking it. "And I've heard the news, Ezaara. Congratulations. I'm glad for you both."

Ezaara stood open-mouthed as he walked away.

Dire News

Not all of the masters were gathered at this private meeting, only those who knew what was going on: Ezaara, Lars, Tonio, Marlies and Hans. And, of course, Roberto had to be present—there was no one to accuse without him. Erob, Zaarusha and Antonika were sitting near the back wall—the only dragons allowed.

Roberto stretched his legs under the table, circling his ankles. *"Ah, Erob, it's good to move without a shackle dragging on my leg."*

"Next time chose a lighter piece of jewelry, perhaps an earring?" Erob teased.

Lars rapped his gavel. "Today we have a few issues to address: Sofia's punishment; Master Roberto loving Ezaara, his trainee, before she was qualified; the nature of these yellow crystals; and Zens' new creatures. First, we will deal with Sofia, then Roberto."

A blue guard opened the door and led Sofia in. Roberto was shocked at her appearance. She'd lost weight and her eyes had the look of a creature being hunted. Is that what those crystals did to people? His gut roiled. Shards, he'd been lucky.

Sofia slumped into a chair, staring at the floor.

Lars read out the charges against her. "Inciting rebellion against the rightful Queen's Rider. Attacking the Queen's Rider. Abusing girls at Dragons' Hold. Subverting public opinion. Sedition against Dragons' Realm."

Sofia looked up, shame smeared across her face.

She'd spurned the Queen's Rider and made Ezaara's life difficult. She needed to be cast out from Dragons' Hold.

"These crimes were, in large, against me," Ezaara said. "May I conduct the proceedings?" She got up, her boots creating soft echoes as she moved around the granite table to face Sofia.

"What are you doing?" Roberto mind-melded.

"Trust me."

"Sofia." Ezaara waited until Sofia met her gaze before she continued. "I forgive you. You were under Zens' influence. I'm guessing you'd do anything to right this wrong."

Sofia nodded. "I feel awful. Horrible black shadows kept whispering at me, goading me to be mean and making me violent. Now they're gone, I feel so rotten about what I've done."

Anger burned, slow and deep in Roberto's belly. *"How could you forgive her? They said she tried to kill you."*

"Roberto." Only one word, full of love and kindness.

Roberto's chest grew tight. He'd done the same. With that knife at her throat.

Lars' voice was low. "Ezaara, this is not in your hands."

"I know, it's Zaarusha's decision."

She'd put Lars right in his place. It was Ezaara and Zaarusha who led the council now.

The queen nudged Lars with her snout. His expression softened as he listened to her, a hand on her head. "Sofia, Zaarusha is giving you a chance."

Sofia's eyes grew round. "Anything. I'll do it. Please."

"She's ordering you to muck out dragonet dens for a month."

Roberto melded with Ezaara. *"Did you put Zaarusha up to that?"*

Ezaara clasped Sofia's hand. "I never had a chance to apologize for injuring you. It was an accident, but even so, I've regretted it ever since."

Sofia stood and hugged Ezaara, sobbing. "Th-thank you."

"It's going to be all right," Ezaara murmured.

A blue guard entered with Alban swaggering in behind him, Nadira on his heels. Jaw clenched, Alban stared at Sofia with a face hewn of granite. "You gave us sway weed. Me and Banikan. How could you?"

"And you had me doing your dirty work with the girls," snarled Nadira. "I believed in you, trusted you, and you made me nasty." She looked as if she was about to spit on Sofia. Even without sway weed.

"I've forgiven her and you," Ezaara said quietly, stepping up next to Sofia. "And I'm the one she tried to burn and knife. This just shows us how powerful Zens is. He not only bends minds, he infiltrates Dragons' Hold, trying to ruin friendships and create hate between us. We'll never succeed if we let his tools of war drive us apart."

Roberto wasn't sure what Alban was expecting, but it wasn't that.

Alban blustered for a moment, then nodded. "Very well." He turned for the door.

"Alban," Ezaara called, "Sofia's going to need some help mucking out the dragonet dens. Might be a good way to get to know one another on new terms."

He nodded tersely and left. Nadira hung back, "You know, Ezaara, I think you're right." She slipped an arm through Sofia's elbow and wandered outside with her.

"All's well that ends well," said Lars. "And now, Master Roberto." He turned to him. "We understand you kissed Ezaara while she was still your trainee. Ever since the world gate was shut, loving your trainee has been a grievous offense, punishable by banishment."

All eyes turned to him. Funny, having everyone acknowledge he loved Ezaara. He could lose everything, but he wouldn't live a lie. "I loved her from the moment I tested her imprinting bond."

"I thought you were pretty awful back then." Ezaara kept her face deadpan. *"Perhaps we shouldn't tell them everything."*

"I won't hide our love anymore."

Tonio nodded to himself. "You've been mind-melding with Ezaara for moons, haven't you?"

"Yes." *"And I am right now—and there's nothing he can do about it."*

Ezaara snorted, putting her hand over her mouth to pretend she was stifling a cough.

Lars cut in. "Yet you say the first time you kissed her was in the orchard, when Antonika flew over and saw you?"

"After Fleur, Bruno and Simeon's banishment," Tonio added.

"Yes," Roberto said. This was ridiculous. He'd kissed Ezaara, but the masters' crimes were worse. "I'd been wrongly banished by you, captured in the Robandi desert, had my gut slit and came home to save Zaarusha from Ajeuria's attack. So, yes, after all that, I did kiss my trainee, the woman I love, who'd saved me from desert assassins." And had saved him from himself. He hadn't wanted to return at all, but she'd convinced him.

"Our apologies for banishing you unfairly," Lars said. "I'm sorry."

"Apologies accepted," Roberto said tersely. "Are you going to repeat the same mistake now?"

"It's not your position to question council procedure," Lars blustered.

"It is when that procedure nearly kills me, isolates me from the woman I love and stops me doing my duty to the queen."

"Tread carefully, Roberto," Ezaara pleaded.

"They need us." Gods, he hoped he was right. He couldn't really run away with the Queen's Rider if they did attempt to banish him. Dragons' Realm needed Ezaara and Zaarusha just as much as he did.

Lars gestured to Ezaara. "Apart from that kiss, is it true that you weren't physically involved throughout your training?"

"*They could just ask me,*" said Erob, scratching the stone with his talons. "*I knew what you were up to.*"

"Naturally, I kissed him goodbye before he went to Death Valley." Ezaara arched an eyebrow, looking bemused. "But apart from that, Master Lars, Roberto wouldn't kiss me, despite me once begging him."

A ripple of laughter ran around the cavern. "Hardly grounds for banishment," commented Hans dryly.

Lars turned to Ezaara's parents. "You two have been mind-melding for years. How probable is it that they've loved each other, but only kissed once or twice?"

Lars wasn't going to let this drop, was he?

But thank the Egg, Tonio was unusually quiet, staring at his nails as if they held valuable secrets.

Marlies met Lars' frank gaze. "It's a strong bonding experience. It would have been difficult not to have a physical relationship after sharing emotions by mind-meld. Under the circumstances, I think they've shown remarkable restraint."

"Lars," said Hans, "this rule was established to prevent a relationship that could endanger the realm. These two have done nothing but good. And besides, before Ezaara even arrived, Handel says he'd received a prophecy that they should be together."

Tonio shot Lars a meaningful look. "Anakisha's prophecy has yet to be fulfilled."

Something passed between them, then Lars turned in his chair. "My honored Queen Zaarusha, Roberto has pledged fidelity to you and to the realm, even though he has loved your rider while training her. What is your verdict?"

The queen lowered her head and Lars and Tonio placed their hands on her forehead. "She thanks Roberto for his service and apologizes for his suffering in Death Valley," Lars said.

Tonio grinned. "She also wants to know when the hand-fasting celebration will be and says, the sooner the better, because war is coming."

Roberto knocked his chair over as he leaped to his feet and hugged Ezaara, kissing her. Her joy rushed through him and his chest felt as if it would burst wide open.

"Wait until later," she melded, *"then I'll really kiss you."*

Tonio cleared his throat. "When you're done, we'll move on to discussing Zens."

Ezaara blushed, right to the tips of her ears.

"Pink suits you." Roberto laughed as they sat down, holding hands.

She rolled her eyes at him. *"Be serious. This is war."*

"No, this is love. War will come later."

"Focus, you two," Erob said.

"Marlies," said Tonio, "tell us more about these crystals."

"We've found only three so far," the master healer said. "Sofia had a crystal, which Fleur implanted after the knife accident." Ezaara mentally flinched. Roberto squeezed her hand as Marlies continued. "Unocco had one under his wing. And Roberto, could you please explain the effect yours had?"

His face heated. Now it was his turn to blush—but in shame. "Shadows wreathed my mind, driving me to seek Ezaara's life." He swallowed, remembering. "I had coherent thoughts, moments where I admired her. And surges of anger against dragons, even Erob. I could move and talk, but darkness stalked me. I … I …" He shrugged, overwhelmed by his memory of Ezaara bravely trying to distract him as his blade pricked her soft skin, blood dribbling down her throat. He closed his eyes, breathing deeply.

An image shot into his head: him and Ezaara feasting on fish by the lake in summer. *"That's what I want you to remember every time that other horrible memory pops to mind,"* Ezaara said.

Hope surged inside him. With her, he could face down his darkest demons. *"Thank you."*

He addressed Tonio. "Zens wanted to break me. He knew if I killed Ezaara, I'd be filled with self-hatred and be useless to the realm. It would've only been a matter of time until he coerced me into abusing people with my mental talents." He shuddered.

Tonio scratched his head, looking awkward. "I personally apologize for leaving you in Death Valley, Roberto, and for the grudge I've held against your father. If these crystals had such an awful effect, maybe your father had a similar crystal. Zens could've driven him to do what he did."

The spymaster looked disconcertingly humble. "I agree." That was odd, too, understanding his father, instead of hating him. Gods, he had to tell Adelina about Pa.

"What about Zens' creatures?" Tonio asked.

"I saw his workroom. He grows tharuks in tanks, hundreds of them. And he's growing something else too. Large black creatures the size of a haystack with strange dark cloth draped around them."

"Cloth? Like a cloak?" Tonio frowned. "Do they have tusks, like tharuks? Any horns or claws? What are their jaws like? We need to know how they can harm us."

Gods, it was hopeless. He'd spent weeks in Death Valley and hardly discovered anything. No, he knew they were big. He knew where they were, and how to get into that cavern.

"No. You're not going back again," Ezaara melded.

"They were suspended in liquid in glass tanks, all curled up, so they were hard to see. I saw a flash of a horn or tusk, something that was a limb or a tail, and that strange cloth that hung around their bodies. I couldn't risk lingering, because Zens and a whole lot of tharuks were in that cavern."

Elbows on the table, Tonio steepled his fingers. "As big as a haystack? Something the size of Erob, then? Or Zaarusha?"

Oh, gods. "The cloth—it could be wings. A horn, a tail. Zens might be creating an army of dragons."

"The dragon gods help us," Lars whispered.

No one spoke, torches crackling in their sconces as they all stared at each other.

Hand-fasting

Ezaara lay in her bathtub, steam rising around her in the chill air. She huffed out her breath, the fog swirling among tendrils of steam. *"I could almost pass for a smoke-breathing dragon."*

Zaarusha's head appeared at her door. *"Not by a long shot. You'd need horns and a tail."*

"And wings."

The queen set the wood in the grate alight. Soon a blaze was crackling. *"You'd better get out. Linaia's warned me that Adelina will be here soon."*

Ezaara stepped out of the bath, dried herself, and pulled on her undergarments and a thick robe. She sat by the blazing fire, drying her hair.

The door opened and Adelina appeared with armfuls of luxurious multi-hued fabric.

"What's all that for?"

"You." Adelina smiled. "Don't look so surprised, I've been working on your outfit since Roberto asked if you two could be hand-fasted. Although today's come around so quickly, I can hardly believe it." She popped the pile on Ezaara's bed.

"The cloth's so beautiful. Those colors look like Zaarusha's scales. Where did you get it?"

"There are advantages to having mages in this place. Master Giddi magicked the fabric so it shimmers. He said it's your hand-fasting gift. Now, come here and try it on. These shiny ribbons fasten the dress. See? And here …" She held up riders' garb made of the same material. "These go underneath. The whole idea is to echo your first public flight. A similar robe and breeches, a dress over the top that you can undo when it's time to fly, and a similar hairstyle. But better, oh, so much better."

When she touched the silky fabric—the colors flitting through it in the torchlight—Ezaara had to agree.

Hours later, her hair in braids and coils threaded with thin shimmering ribbons, Ezaara was dressed in her elegant garb, flowing gown and matching slippers. She sat in Zaarusha's saddle, on the ledge, her stomach a stampede of butterflies. "Do you think he'll like it?"

"Roberto wouldn't care if you turned up in dragonet dung." Adelina winked, already in her own finery. "He'll love it, trust me."

Ezaara grinned. "Remember the first time we surprised him?"

"At your flight? It was fun to see my brother flummoxed—he's usually so in control."

Ezaara squeezed Adelina's hand. "Thank you for being my friend. You mean the world to me, Adelina."

Adelina's eyes were bright with moisture, but Ezaara didn't care because hers were too.

Linaia landed on the ledge, and Adelina flew off, calling, "Give me a few minutes to check Roberto's ready."

Dusk had come early. The moon glinted on the snowy basin, the lake a carpet of shimmering silver. A gentle breeze drifted over Dragons' Hold, ruffling the skirts of her gown. A few moons ago, Ezaara had left her home in Lush Valley, where she'd not even known whether dragons existed.

So much had changed. And now, with the possibility of Zens bringing war to the skies, even more would change. Life would be uncertain. She'd nearly lost Roberto already—several times—but they'd been lucky enough to have another chance. Today they'd be joined, but she'd live every day not knowing if the next battle could steal him from her. So, she'd make sure they *lived*. Loved. And laughed, so when he was gone, she'd have a treasure trove of precious memories.

"Rather morbid thoughts for one about to be hand-fasted." The glowing colors of Zaarusha's *sathir* swirled in the torchlight. *"Time for a happier tune, perhaps?"*

"You're right. Let's go."

Zaarusha whipped through the chill air, entering a passage high in the main cavern. They perched inside the tunnel mouth to wait until they were summoned. Hundreds of glowing wizard lights hung below the ceiling. Torches burned brightly in sconces. The cavern was packed with mages and riders, folk young and old, their hubbub rising up the passage.

"Ready?" Zaarusha asked.

"Yes, I'm ready." Ezaara's heart thrummed. Roberto was waiting for her.

A haunting note pealed from a horn, echoing off the cavern walls and reverberating through the tunnel.

Zaarusha melded, *"Hold on."*

Ezaara tensed, ready for action. The dragon queen bunched her legs, flapped her wings and sailed into the main cavern, circling high above the folk. Ezaara's ribbons fluttered, her dress shimmering in the light from green mage flame.

Standing on the stage with the horn in his hand and Erob behind him, was Roberto, dressed from tip to toe in black. At his waist was a sash from the same fabric as her dress—Adelina's doing, no doubt. He glanced up, smiling. *"You look radiant."*

Ezaara's breath caught in her throat—with his broad shoulders, lean muscular frame and love painted across his face, he was stunning. *"Thank you. You look rather fine, too."* She could hardly believe he was hers. *"Better than fine. Kissable."*

"Trust him to see you before anyone else did," Erob quipped.

Roberto gave a mental chuckle.

"There she is," a boy cried, pointing. "It's Ezaara." Everyone gazed up.

"Now." Zaarusha swooped toward the crowd, wings gusting their hair, then shot up to the mage lights, flipping upside down. Exhilaration rushed through Ezaara, fire burning through her veins as she melded with her lover and both of their dragons. The *sathir* of hundreds of people eddied through the air, but none was as strong as Roberto's flowing river of blue and silver that danced with her own multicolored light. Zaarusha righted again and corkscrewed toward Roberto on the stage.

The crowd cheered and applause broke out. Sparks flitted from mages' fingers, and dragons roared. Within two tail-lengths of Roberto, Zaarusha swerved and ascended, beating her wings.

Roberto tucked the horn in his belt, leaping upon Erob. *"Let's show them what we can do, Ezaara. Let's show them we belong together."*

Erob and Roberto flew alongside Zaarusha and Ezaara, mirroring every move. People ducked as they swooped over their heads and oo-ed and ah-ed as they whirled through the cavern.

Something loosened in Ezaara's chest. *"Finally, I can love you without hiding."*

"Nothing can stop us now." Roberto's smile flashed as Erob zipped past them to land on one end of the stage.

Zaarusha landed at the other end. Lars strummed his harp, and a soaring melody filled the cavern.

Roberto dismounted and walked toward Ezaara, still pale from his time in Death Valley, but just as attractive as he'd always been. Better.

"*Stay in the saddle,*" Zaarusha warned.

She took him in, in dark garb, from his boots to his shoulders. "*Adelina's done a fine job kitting you out.*"

He moved toward her with the grace and strength of a mountain cat, and smiled, his dark eyes sparkling with warmth, his love flowing through her. "*Gods, your love is glorious,*" he melded. "*It fills me, makes me want to soar.*"

Her whole being sang. Was he really all hers?

"*I sure am.*" His joy washed over her, making her heart swell with sweetness. If she felt any better, she'd burst.

Roberto scratched Zaarusha's snout, then reached up to take Ezaara's hand, his warm fingers enclosing hers.

Her heart raced. "*Remember that moment when I first really saw you, at the river?*"

"*During the race? How could I forget? At night in Death Valley, when Zens was asleep, I took that memory out, turning it over and over in my mind. It kept me strong. You make me stronger, a better man.*" He kissed her fingertips, sending a jolt of fire spiraling to her core. Then he reached up and placed his hands at her waist, lifting her down from Zaarusha.

Sandalwood and mint wafted from him. They were so close, his body warmth radiated through her thin garments. He inhaled deeply, his dark eyes reflecting mage light, and his blue *sathir* swirling around her, wrapping her in its soft embrace. It felt like coming home.

§

Gods, she was gorgeous. It blew his mind. How did he—the useless, abused son of a traitor— deserve someone this loving and beautiful?

"*With good taste in dragons,*" said Erob.

"*The best,*" Roberto agreed.

Ezaara shimmered with colors. The threads and braids in her hair reminded him of her first flight, when he'd already suspected she was someone special. A riot of color flitted through his mind. Her *sathir* was like a vibrant multifaceted jewel. Her emerald eyes were bright with excitement and her cheeks flushed. His fingers itched to trace her skin. Dragon's claws, her smile was so sharding alluring.

§

Amid applause and cheering, Roberto took Ezaara's hand and led her to the center of the stage to stand before Lars. Dragons roared as he held her hand high and they faced the crowd. Mage lights zipped through the air, leaving fiery trails.

Ezaara was filled with wonder. How had she gone from being an ignorant girl from Lush Valley, to this?

"*By being yourself, having courage and working hard,*" Zaarusha said. "Well done."

Lars blew a horn until the crowd quieted, then cleared his throat. "Master Roberto has requested the hand of Ezaara, honored Rider of Queen Zaarusha, to be his lifelong mate and lover, the mother of his littlings and his companion forever. Are there any objections to this marriage?"

A catcall broke out from the folk, "She's far too pretty for him."

"Thank you, Kierion," said Lars dryly. "Anyone else?" Silence. "Then I request Ezaara and Roberto's families upon the stage."

Marlies, Hans, and Tomaaz came upstairs to Ezaara's side. Adelina joined Roberto.

Ezaara had rehearsed this with Lars and her parents, but now it was actually happening. She stepped forward with her hand upon her heart. It was thrumming so wildly, she could feel it against her palm. She faced Adelina, raising her voice. "I pledge to love and cherish your brother Roberto to the end of my days and beyond, sacrificing my life for his, if necessary."

Adelina inclined her head, lip trembling. "May your love soar upon dragon wings."

They embraced, Adelina's body shaking as Ezaara held her tight. Ezaara whispered, "It's all right, Adelina, you're not losing your brother, you're gaining a sister."

§

Roberto placed his fist upon his heart and faced Hans and Marlies. "I pledge to love and cherish your beautiful daughter Ezaara, to the end of my days and beyond, sacrificing my life for hers, if necessary. I also pledge to be a good and loving father, always tender and compassionate to our littlings."

Hans raised an eyebrow at Roberto's added words about fatherhood. "May your love soar upon dragon wings."

Marlies squeezed his hand, saying, "I know your love will soar upon dragon wings. I believe it already does."

"*You'll make a fantastic father,*" Ezaara melded.

He hoped so. The only decent role model he'd had was his mother.

Hans gave Roberto a bear hug, holding on to him. "Welcome to our family."

Family—he and Adelina had been alone for so long.

§

Roberto held Ezaara's hand in his, his thumb tracing tiny circles on the back of her hand, making her skin tingle.

Adelina took two green ribbons from her pocket, passing one to Hans and Marlies. She smiled at Ezaara. "These are the ribbons from your first flight."

"Fitting," Roberto said. *"Those ribbons bound us together."*

He'd offered his life for her, bleeding on the orange Robandi sands.

Her parents and Adelina tied the ribbons around their joined hands. The crowd waited with bated breath.

Heart soaring like a dragon taking flight, Ezaara gazed at Roberto. "I vow to love you, cherish you, and help you to grow and become the best you can be. I will support you and Erob and our littlings in this life and forever once we pass beyond, into the land of departed dragons. I vow to be one with you."

Fire seared in Roberto's eyes. "I will always love you, protect you and hold you precious above everything else in the world. I pledge my life to you, our family, Erob and Zaarusha, and promise to serve you and love you for the rest of my days and beyond. I hope my best will be good enough. I, too, vow to be one with you."

"You're good enough. Perfect for me."

He tilted his head and grinned. *"You don't mind me kissing you in front of all these people?"*

"I'd mind if you didn't." Gods, please.

He tilted his head and, with his free hand, cupped her cheek, stroking her skin with his thumb. *"I love you, Ezaara."*

"And I love you." She placed her hand at the back of his neck, and gently pulled his mouth to hers.

Roberto's lips were warm, soft, and, gods, so delicious.

The roar of the crowd was deafening, but Ezaara didn't care. She kissed the man she loved, wrapped in the warm shimmering strands of their joint *sathir*.

Nearby, Lars blew a horn. The clapping subsided.

"We'll finish this later," Roberto melded.

"I hope so."

He laughed, his face open and carefree. *"I know so."*

Lars' voice boomed through the cavern. "We, the Council of the Twelve Dragon Masters, stand today as witnesses to the hand-fasting vows of Roberto of Naobia, son of Amato and Lucia, and Ezaara of Lush Valley, daughter of Hans and Marlies. We hope that dragon fire may keep their love glowing through the years." Lars grinned. "And I personally thank them for their service to Dragons' Realm."

"Master Lars." A sweet voice floated to the stage. At the front of the crowd, a littling girl with red curls stretched her hand up.

"Do you have a question?" Lars asked her.

"I have three," the littling said.

"Don't worry, Master Lars," the girl's mother said, blushing. "It's really all right."

Lars crouched down at the edge of the stage, addressing the girl. "Please ask."

"Can I have a pretty dress like Ezaara's?"

There was a smattering of laughter as Lars responded. "Yes, you may. Master Hendrik will get one of his tailors to make you one." Behind him, Master Hendrik nodded. "What's your next question?"

"Will I be as pretty as Ezaara one day?"

Lars smiled. "I believe you already are. What's your last question?"

"Me, pretty? Thank you, Master Lars. Ma, did you hear that?" she squealed.

Lars smiled. "Your last question?"

"It's about Anakisha's prophecy. Someone said it wasn't filled. What does that mean?"

Ezaara groaned. *"Oh, not this. Will it never go away?"*

"No, it won't," Zaarusha melded.

"Ah, a good question. One Master Roberto was going to address tonight," Master Lars said, gesturing Roberto forward.

With their hands bound, Ezaara had no choice but to go with him. Turning to her, he took the fine silver chain holding Anakisha's teardrop and tried to lift it over her head.

"Um, I'm having problems taking this off with one hand," Roberto confessed.

"Here, let me hold the clasp," Ezaara said, helping him.

Roberto held Anakisha's teardrop high. It twirled on the end of the chain, flashing. "Ezaara wears this crystal, which was bequeathed to me by my mother, Lucia. It once belonged to my grandmother, Anakisha, the last Queen's Rider and my mothers' mother. I didn't know who my grandmother was, until Master Tonio told me this morning. Some of you may not know that Anakisha's children were scattered throughout Dragons' Realm, in hiding, to prevent them from becoming targets. Apparently, Ma kept it a secret, not even telling us or my father, Amato."

A shocked silence met his statement.

Then Sofia called out, "They're hand-fasted. Bonded as one. Roberto's Anakisha's progeny, so the prophecy's fulfilled."

Roberto grinned, holding their tied hands high.

Lars blew his horn once more. "Yes, Anakisha's prophecy is fulfilled." Handel roared, shaking the stage. "Now, Roberto and Ezaara will have the first dance as a hand-fasted couple," Lars said. "Let's celebrate, dance, and enjoy this fine feast."

Musicians struck up the lively hand-fasting tune.

Sathir rippled around them as Roberto placed his hand at Ezaara's waist and swept her around the stage in time to the music. Enfolded in his strong arms, his eyes caressing her face, and his mind melded with hers, her joy was complete.

"This feels so right," he melded. *"I never thought I'd amount to anything after Amato and Zens' abuse. Never thought I'd be able to give my heart to anyone. I was broken, nothing."*

"You're everything to me." Ezaara rested her head against Roberto's shoulder, and he pulled her tight as they danced. *"Everything."*

§

Lars was fetching another carafe from the drinks table as Tonio approached him. "Evening, Tonio. You happy with how things have turned out?"

"Very. That was a close thing. Roberto could've been killed by Zens and Anakisha's prophecy never would have been fulfilled."

Lars took a sip of grape juice. "She could have married Urs or Lofty. They're both Anakisha's descendants."

Tonio shook his head. "Neither of them are right for her. Roberto is. I shouldn't have insisted on leaving him in Death Valley. I apologize for my terrible lapse of judgment. With his talents, he's an asset to the council, but could have been a terrible weapon in Zens' hands."

"He'd rather be broken or dead than harm our people," Lars replied.

"I think you're right." Tonio selected a bottle of wine and headed back to his table.

Lars stared after him, muttering, "That's a good change. What in the Egg's name has gotten into him?"

§

Leah tugged Mara over to a group of mages, all dressed in their fancy cloaks. "You've got to see this, it's incredible."

"I haven't met any wizards before," Mara said. "I'm not sure if they're safe."

Leah smiled. "They're nothing to be scared of. Kierion fights tharuks with mages all the time. One of them is my friend."

"Really?" Mara asked, round-eyed. "Your friend?"

"Yes, he even gave me flowers once." Leah's chest swelled with pride. "You might get some too, if you're lucky."

Mara just bit her lip.

A Naobian mage twitched his fingers, sending a line of mage lights spiraling down toward the dancers. He spread his fingers and the lights spun off in different directions, casting their green glow over people's faces. The man stepped back, nearly bumping into Leah. "Oh, I'm sorry." He smiled. "I'm Jael. Nice to meet you."

Mara shrunk back, but Leah held herself tall. "Hi, Jael, I'm Leah and this is my friend Mara. Have you seen Fenni?"

"Sure, he's over there." Jael pointed to a row of wizards sitting in chairs along the back wall. Fenni was watching the dancers, his long legs crossed at the ankles.

"Thanks." She dragged Mara over. "Hi, Fenni."

"Lovely to see you, Leah." He smiled. Flourishing his hands, he created a beautiful bouquet of flaming flowers. "Just for you." The flowers exploded into tiny green stars and disappeared.

Leah grinned. "Thanks, Fenni. Could Mara have some too?"

His green eyes twinkled. "You were my first friend at Dragons' Hold, Leah, so my flowers are just for you." Fenni's gaze drifted over Leah's shoulder.

She turned. Gret was walking by, her long blonde plaits swinging.

"Ah, excuse me." Fenni made a beeline for Gret.

"He's nice," said Mara. "You're so lucky." Her gaze followed Fenni. "Do you think he likes Gret?"

As Fenni whisked Gret into his arms, leading her around the dance floor, Leah nodded. "Definitely."

§

In the corner, sitting on an overstuffed sofa, Giant John nudged Giddi. "See those two?" He waved his goat's haunch toward Fenni, who was dancing with a tall girl, holding her as if she was fragile. "Maybe there's hope for riders and wizards after all."

John had always had an appetite to suit his frame, so Giddi ignored the meat waving about under his nose, and followed John's gesture. Young Fenni was beaming at his dance partner—an athletic-looking dragon rider with long blonde plaits. She ducked her head shyly then glanced up at him, blushing. Fenni beamed.

"Hope?" Giddi snorted. "So, a rider falling in love with a wizard will make Zens go away?" he said, laying on his sarcasm, especially for John. "And Lars is going to welcome Mazyka back, is he? And the moon has turned a violent shade of pink? Hope, indeed. The only hope we have is in combating Zens' new threat."

"Or finding your two young mages." Giant John speared a potato with his knife and ate it in one bite.

"Zens must've taken Sorcha and Velrama for a reason." Giddi scratched his head. What, though?

Lofty danced by with a short girl in his arms. "Got a great reach, that one," said Giant John.

"You mean with a sword or with that girl? She's half his size."

Giant John sighed in mock exasperation and rolled his eyes.

Truth was, the Queen's Rider's hand-fasting reminded Giddi of his own, when he'd been head of the Wizard Council and Mazyka had been his trainee. Although it had been years since Mazyka had been lost through the world gate, his fierce, aching heart had never stopped loving her.

§

Kierion raised his arm so Adelina could twirl under it. As well as being pretty and vivacious, she was as graceful as a swan. He could hardly believe his luck. He'd been sitting there, trying not to stare, because, wow, she looked gorgeous— with her hair up in a knot and a scarlet dress that swirled as she danced, showing off her dark, dark eyes. And tan skin. He cleared his throat, glancing away as she smiled up at him. She'd asked him to dance. He could hardly say no, could he? Not that he'd wanted to say no …

He looked down and met her sparkling eyes. She looked much better than when he'd rescued her in Death Valley. Too good. Kierion sighed. She was still so young.

Adelina twirled again. Kierion pulled her back into his arms. She was so tiny, so compact, yet full of energy. She snuggled her head against his chest.

Shards, Kierion's bones were *melting*.

Adelina murmured. He bent his head down to hear her better. "It's my name day next week and I'll be sixteen summers," she said. "Would you spend the day with me?"

Kierion felt a jolt in his gut. Sixteen? He'd thought she was turning fifteen. He swallowed, lost for words.

She laughed at his nervousness, eyes dancing.

"Sure, I'd love to." Maybe she wasn't too young for him after all.

§

Tomaaz tightened his grip around Lovina's waist, pulling her toward him to kiss her as they danced. As their kiss deepened, she pulled away, cheeks warm. She just couldn't. "Not in front of—"

"Not in front of who?" he grinned, winking.

"Everyone." Lovina's cheeks grew hotter.

"Don't worry," he said, kissing her again. "They're all too busy watching Ezaara and Roberto."

So Lovina kissed him back, enjoying every moment.

§

A horn blew, startling Lars from the story he was telling. Who in the Egg's name—

He should've known. Kierion was on stage—with two mages—Riona behind them. Now that Kierion had everyone's attention, what was he going to say? Despite his cynicism, Lars waited with bated breath. That lad was always full of surprises.

"I know many of you have welcomed our mages with open arms, like sons and daughters returning from battle," Kierion said, eliciting a ripple of laughter. "Yes, we've been pining to have them here at the hold for years ..." More laughter. "So now we should take advantage of this opportunity." His voice dropped. The cavern was silent as people strained to hear. Even the musicians stopped playing.

"That's why I'm letting you in on a secret." He leaned forward conspiratorially, using an exaggerated stage whisper. "Mages can kill tharuks."

Kierion, Fenni and Jael whooped and raced to Riona. Kierion leaped up first, the two mages behind him. Riona sprang into the air, flexing her wings. Fenni and Jael leaned out on either side of Kierion as he mimed shooting an arrow from a bow. The wizards weren't miming, though. Real mage flame shot from their fingers, striking stone high on the cavern walls.

Amid cheers and hollers, Kierion slowed down. "Anyone who wants to kill tharuks with mages, meet us for training before breakfast. With a hundred mages here, we'll take as many riders as we can get."

Both blade thrusters and arrow flingers were among those cheering, pushing their way forward as they clambered to talk with Kierion and the two young mages.

"Another new training regime." Master Jerrick leaned over the table. "We did say he was sharding amazing, didn't we, Lars?"

§

The music swelled, filling the cavern. Guided by wizards, mage lights zipped between the dancers, in time to the music. Ezaara smiled at Roberto as he whirled her around the cavern. "Your eyes reflect the mage light."

"Mage light is nothing compared to the magic we'll have together." Roberto's whisper was like the brush of a feather against her ear.

A thrill ran through her, making goosebumps break out on her skin. "I look forward to it."

Roberto kissed her hair, laughing.

Adelina, dancing with Kierion, sidled alongside them. "Your dress, Ezaara, and the ribbons," she hissed.

Oh, right. Ezaara had nearly forgotten. She winked at Adelina. "Got it."

Roberto frowned as they danced away. *"Kierion? I mean, really?"*

"They suit each other—he's cute and funny, and she's so bubbly."

"Cute? So, that's cute?" Roberto melded, making Ezaara giggle.

The music wound down, and Lars made an announcement. "Roberto and Ezaara will be leaving us for a week for their hand-fasting holiday. They'll be traveling tonight, so I suggest we all join them in their last dance. But first, Queen Zaarusha, will you do the honors?"

Zaarusha flew down from a ledge and landed on the cavern floor in front of the stage, near Roberto and Ezaara. She stretched out a talon and cut the ribbons binding their hands. Roberto caught the pieces, tucking them in his pocket.

The gittern player strummed an upbeat piece, and they danced, wheeling, Ezaara's dress spinning in a colorful whirlwind about her legs. She tugged on her ribbons, loosening them.

"I knew you had matching slippers, but your legs are covered too," said Roberto. "What are you wearing?"

"This," she replied, pulling the ribbons, slipping her dress off and flinging it at Roberto.

He caught it, slinging it over his shoulder.

Dressed in her colorful riders' garb, Ezaara ran up onto the stage and vaulted onto Zaarusha's back, laughing. Roberto leaped up behind her and waved to the crowd, who cheered, stomped and whistled as Zaarusha flew out of the cavern with Erob following. Ezaara leaned back against Roberto, his warm arms around her waist and his lips trailing kisses in her hair as they broke out into a midnight sky studded with thousands of stars.

§

Thank the flaming dragon gods Ezaara had come into his life. He'd been so bitter, so mistrusting, so broken—and her love had healed him. She was snug and warm in his arms, but the winter wind would soon chill her. Roberto reached into one of Zaarusha's saddlebags and pulled out some furs, wrapping them around her. *"You looked so beautiful tonight. Absolutely radiant. Are you ready to come to Naobia with me and discover the land of my littlings years?"* He kissed her hair again.

"So that's where we're going? I'd love to."

"Then I'd better hop back on Erob."

"Have you got Pa's ring?" she asked.

"Yes. Have you got your ma's? They're both from my grandmother. Funny how our families are intertwined, isn't it?"

Ezaara leaned forward and Roberto shuffled back, swinging his leg over Zaarusha's side, instantly missing Ezaara's warmth. *"Erob, ready?"*

Erob flew below Zaarusha and Roberto slipped off the queen's back, landing neatly in Erob's saddle.

"Ana," he cried.

"Kisha," called Ezaara.

With a pop, they were surrounded in golden clouds riddled with deep cracks of dark mist. Anakisha floated toward them.

"We're hand-fasted," said Ezaara. *"Me and your grandson, Roberto."*

"That's wonderful." Anakisha addressed Roberto, *"I'm sorry Zens found you all those years ago, despite your mother being in hiding. Lucia was a fine daughter, and her blood runs in your veins. I'm proud of you for withstanding Zens and the temptation to use your extraordinary talents for evil. Stay strong and remain true to the realm and the Queen's Rider."*

Roberto bowed his head and pounded his fist on his heart. *"I will, Grandmother."*

"Now let me guess. You want to go back to the cottage in Naobia."

"Back?" said Ezaara.

"I went there this morning to prepare," melded Roberto.

With a crack, Zaarusha and Erob were in the warm night air above the black Naobian Sea, tipped with white crests. Roberto breathed in the familiar briny air, the warm breeze rustling the ribbons in Ezaara's braids.

"Oh, I'd forgotten how good this air tastes," she said, inhaling deeply. She took off her furs, stowing them in a saddlebag.

They flew along a strip of beach, pale in the moonlight, and Erob alighted behind a small cottage. Zaarusha landed. Roberto lifted Ezaara down into his arms. Gods, he couldn't wait. He had to kiss her now. He leaned in and she did too. Their noses bumped and she gave a little laugh.

So, he swept her off her feet, carrying her to the door and over the threshold.

§

Ezaara nestled against Roberto as he carried her into a shaft of moonlight drizzling through a window, and lowered her onto a couch.

"Just wait here," he said, brushing his lips against hers before disappearing out the door.

Just that single brush sent fire through her veins.

A hearth was laid in the corner with a huge rug sprawled before it. Through an archway, there was an enormous bed, draped with canopies of white net. She swallowed. She and Roberto had loved each other for moons, but neither of them had ever …

Roberto entered the cottage with the saddlebags and Ezaara leapt up to help him.

Zaarusha poked her head inside the door. *"Enjoy yourselves. Erob and I are going hunting."* She shot a jet of fire at the hearth. The wood ignited, bursting into flame. *"Meld if you need anything, but I imagine you'll be too busy."* She winked, and left them alone.

Ezaara knelt before the blaze. Roberto sat behind her and gathered her hair in his hand, tracing his lips down her neck.

She turned, Roberto's dark eyes burning into hers, the familiar heat of dragon fire coursing through her veins. As he took her in his arms and kissed her, they created a magic of their own. Sathir swirled around them, dancing with the fire, and the flames crackling on the hearth burned brighter.

Promise

High on a bluff above the beach, Bruno lowered the far-seers and wriggled back on his belly to join his son, Simeon. "I was right," he said. "The Queen's Rider and Roberto are down there, dancing on the sand without a care in the world."

"So that sharding arrogant shrot-heap got the girl," Simeon snarled. "I should've taken her when I had the chance."

Bruno sniggered. "A fine thing that would be, your seed in the belly of the Queen's Rider." He scratched the scraggly beard that had grown since he'd been banished to the Wastelands. "Good idea, Son. Let's arrange that. We'll bide our time—strike when their dragons are gone. When you've taken your fill of the girl, she'll make good shark fodder."

Simeon grinned, eyes glinting with lust.

Good, that had put a bit of color into his son's cheeks. Gods knew, they both needed something after that awful orange hell, the tragic raft trip and burying poor Fleur in a shallow grave. Someone had to pay for his wife's death. Why not Roberto and that snivelly girl?

Riders of Fire continues in
Dragon Strike

Commander Zens unleashes an army of evil dragons. Dragons with terrible powers. Dragons that will tear Dragons' Realm apart…

Don't miss out! Sign up for your next adventure at EileenMuellerAuthor.com

Riders of Fire
Complete Series Available Now

Ezaara—Book 1

Dragon Hero—Book 2

Dragon Rift—Book 3

Dragon Strike—Book 4

Dragon War—Book 5

Sea Dragon—Book 6

Riders of Fire
Dragon Masters

Coming Soon

Anakisha's Dragon—Book 1

Dragon Mage—Book 2

Dragon Spy—Book 3

Dragon Healer—Book 4

Prequel

Ruby Dragon

To find out how Tonio, the spymaster who saved Marlies' life, met Antonika, his dragon, read Ruby Dragon, a Riders of Fire short prequel.

Herbal Lore in Dragons' Realm

Arnica—Small yellow flower with hairy leaves. Reduces pain, swelling and inflammation. The flower and root are used in Marlies' healing salve.

Bear's bane—Pungent oniony numbing salve with bear leek as the primary ingredient.

Bergamot—Citrus fruit with a refreshing scent.

Clean herb—Tangy, pale green leaves with antibacterial properties.

Clear-mind—Orange berries, used to combat numlock. Stronger when dried, but effective when fresh.

Dragon's bane—Clear poison that, when it enters the blood, makes wounds bleed excessively, and then slowly shuts down circulation and breathing.

Dragon's breath—A rare mountain flower that, when shaken, produces a soft glow.

Dragon scale—A gray powder that when swallowed gives the appearance of being numlocked, i.e. gray eyes and fingernails.

Freshweed—A weed that is chewed to mask the user's scent.

Healing salve—A healing paste that contains arnica, piaua juice, peppermint, and clean herb, and promotes healing.

Jasmine—Highly-scented white tubular flowers. Promotes relaxation.

Koromiko—Thin green leaves that, when brewed as a tea, prevent belly gripe.

Lavender—Highly-scented lilac whorled flowers. Relaxant, refreshing.

Limplock—Green sticky paste with an acrid scent used to coat tharuk weapons. Acts on the victim's nervous system, causing slow paralysis, starting with peripheries and making its way to the vital organs.

Limplock remedy—Fine yellow granules that reverse the effect of limplock. Dose: one vial for an adult; three vials for a dragon.

Numlock—Thin gray leaves, ground into a tangy powder. Saps victim's will, determination and coherent thought. Used by Zens and tharuks to keep slaves in submission. Creates a gray sheen over the eyes and fingernails.

Owl-wort—Small leaves that enable sight in the dark.

Peppermint—Dark green leaves with aromatic scent. Good for circulation, headaches and as a relaxant.

Piaua juice—Pale green juice from succulent piaua leaves. Heals wounds and knits flesh back together in moments.

Rubaka—Crushed leaves produce a pale green powder used as a remedy against dragon's bane.

Skarkrak—Bitter gray leaves. A Robandi poison. In mild doses causes sleepiness and vomiting; in strong doses, death.

Swayweed—Fine green tea. Reverses loyalties and allegiances.

Woozy weed—Leaves that causes sleepiness and forgetfulness.

About Eileen

Eileen Mueller is a multiple-award-winning author of heart-pounding fantasy novels that will keep you turning the page. Dive into her worlds, full of magic, love, adventure and dragons! Eileen lives in New Zealand, in a cave, with four dragonets and a shape shifter. She writes action-packed tales for young adults, children and everyone who loves adventure.

Visit her website at www.EileenMuellerAuthor.com for Eileen's FREE books and new releases or to become a Rider of Fire!

Please place a review

I absolutely love reviews! Hear the dragons roar and me squeal with enthusiasm when you post one. Readers are my lifeblood, so I'd love you to pop a line or two on Amazon or Goodreads. Thank you.

Printed in Great Britain
by Amazon